Dear Kate

Dear Kate

Gerard Thomas Straub

A NOVEL

Prometheus Books • Buffalo, New York

Published 1992 by Prometheus Books

96 95 94 93 92   5 4 3 2 1

Library of Congress Cataloging-in-Publication Data

Straub, Gerard Thomas.
  Dear Kate / by Gerard Thomas Straub.
  ISBN 0-87975-793-0
  I. Title.
PS3569.T69138D4   1992
813'.54—dc20   92-35433
                                                                                CIP

Printed in the United States on acid-free paper.

This book
was written for
Adrienne Frances Straub

And is
dedicated to
Kathy,
my best friend,
who believes in me
even when I don't,
and without whose
loving support
this book
would never have
been completed.

With special
thanks to
John Sikos
and to
Edmund D. Cohen

The human species alone is engaged in an adventure whose end is not death but self-realization.

—Raymond Aron

Every increase in consciousness is an increase in suffering.

—Delmore Schwartz

There is but one truly philosophical problem, and that is suicide. To judge whether life is not worth the trouble of being lived is to answer philosophy's fundamental question.

—Albert Camus

PROLOGUE

The letters you are about to read were written by my father. His name was Christopher Ryan. He was a writer, though he never fully believed he was. (He claimed, "Anyone can say they are a writer; but, in truth, hardly anybody can write . . . least of all, me!") He wrote the letters to me during a nine-month period between July 1990 and April 1991. I was just a child then, but these letters were not intended for a child's eyes. In fact, I was not supposed to receive the letters until the year 2000, when I will turn twenty-one. They came last month, ahead of his schedule, but I think I was ready to read them.

Since their arrival, I've read the letters at least a dozen times. I see different things with each reading. The letters reveal my dad's many faces and moods. I can't say I understand all of them. At times, he sounds a little loony, ranting and raving about religion or politics; at other times he's witty, poking fun at himself and society. Then he becomes a philosopher, his voice ponderous and deep, or a historian, searching antiquity for insight into today. Frequently, my dad sounds angry, cursing the darkness of humanity. But through it all, he remains a man "at odds with himself"—as he put it. I'd say he was a man at odds with God, although what he really wanted was only to be one with God. In a way, his was a tragic love story.

The letters pretty much speak for themselves and need no elaborate introduction. Still, I think a few words about Christopher Ryan would be helpful.

My dad was a dreamer, his mind restless, his thoughts, far traveled. In the world of commerce and business, he was like a fish out of water. He disliked car salesmen, loathed insurance salesmen, and disdained lawyers. He had a low tolerance for corporate executives. He wasn't fond of Republicans in general and had a downright hatred of Conservatives. He had no interest in science and was totally befuddled by anything mechanical or electrical. He feared computers and believed that most machines, especially Xerox and answering machines, sensed that he was an idiot when it came to their correct operation. I don't think he ever saw the engine of his car. He mourned the loss of the days of full-service gas stations, because he hated pumping his own gas. Not that he was lazy, he just couldn't do it without, as he put it, "filling up my shoes at the same time." Dad was a klutz, an accident waiting to happen. I guess dreamers have little use for the realities of science, mechanics, corporations, insurance, law, business, or politics. He built his castles in the clouds.

Dad was not macho. He respected women. He loved baseball. (I mean he really loved baseball. There was a time when a New York Yankee loss upset him so much that he wouldn't buy the paper the next day in order to avoid reading about it.) He knew virtually nothing about basketball or hockey. He enjoyed watching football, but he was bothered by the violence of the game. He hated golf and couldn't understand why otherwise sane people would spend their time walking around in ugly clothes trying to get a ball into a hole. He played tennis and enjoyed skiing, though he wasn't especially proficient in either sport. He hated losing, even at miniature golf or Monopoly.

Dad was obsessed about his weight; in his eyes he looked heavier than he did to others. He never tired of making up puns, even though they were frequently greeted by groans of disapproval. His favorite outfit consisted of faded jeans topped off with an elegant sport jacket. He enjoyed jazz and classical music, and his record collection had very few recordings that featured lyrics. He claimed that words get in the way of music, that music should speak for itself; he thought of lyrics as musical propaganda. He hated country-and-western music. He loved animals, especially cats. Animals seemed to know he was a soft touch. He preferred the company of kids to adults. "Grownups are boring," he once told me. He also claimed, "All my real friends are under twelve." He exaggerated sometimes.

I sense that he was a proud man but not an ambitious one, a man more inspired by love than by money.

As a teenager, he wanted to be a priest. As an adult he worked as a television producer. My dad never went to college. He was bitten by the show-biz bug during a summer job at a TV station when he was seventeen. That was in 1964, when television was still mostly black and white. Television was all he really knew, all he really cared about.

Until God once again tapped him on the shoulder. He'll explain that in the letter.

While my dad may have been a bit offbeat, perhaps even downright unusual, I believe the things he struggled with aren't. No, I think his struggles were very universal and will strike a harmonious chord in anyone who dares to look at human life, who dares to try to understand the meaning of our existence.

I've divided the letters into three parts, for reasons which will become obvious later. The name I gave to each part is taken from The Apostles' Creed, a creed my father memorized as a child, believed as an adolescent, and repudiated as an adult. That creed created him and destroyed him.

Kate Ryan
May 27, 1993
Montclair, New Jersey

PART ONE

He descended into hell. . . .

Los Angeles, California

Wednesday, July 11, 1990—8:30 P.M.

Dear Kate,

It is dark. I am alone. The summer evening air is still, with just a welcomed hint of a chill. I have been sitting in absolute silence at my desk for most of the evening, deep in thought. My mind has been racing through a series of scenes from my life. It is as if the highlights of my existence had been recorded on videotape, which I have been watching in the fast-forward mode. No sound, just streaking images of a life hurling headlong toward a tragic demise. It is as if I have been in a trance, coolly and without emotion watching bits and pieces of me zoom by.

I saw a funny kid with a crew cut chasing a white duck across a lawn near a pond. A smiling kid holding a toy gun while sitting on the fender of his dad's black 1942 Ford. A serious-looking boy dressed in a white suit clutching a small, black prayer book on the day he received his First Communion. I saw a child taught to deny his feelings. A sore loser desperately trying to win at Monopoly. A sensitive young boy being teased by a drunken father. A shy, cherubic altar boy with aspirations of becoming a priest. I saw a chubby kid unsuccessfully trying to play touch football on the streets of New York City. An excited kid thrilled by his first visit to Yankee Stadium in 1959 with his best friend, Dennis Gaffney, despite a disappointing 5-4 Yankee loss to Baltimore. I saw a young teenager ashamed of his body and his budding sexual urges. A teenager distraught by the threat of nuclear war and the injustice of racial bigotry. A teenager staring out the classroom window, oblivious to his teacher and his classmates. I saw a dreamer who was told not to dream; a youngster who loved the new-found magic of television and spent his days waiting to watch Sid Caesar, Red Skelton,

17

Jackie Gleason, or Steve Allen; a fifteen-year-old crying after a nun had announced to the students that the President of the United States had been shot and killed in Dallas, Texas. I saw a confused, lonely teenager turning to the pages of pornographic magazines for consolation and deliverance. I saw a young man horrified by the madness and carnage of Vietnam. I saw a young man get married, become a father, and get divorced. I saw a man pretending he was a hotshot television director. I saw a man falling in love with all the wrong women. I saw a man suffering from the pain of not being able to see his daughter growing up. I saw a middle-aged man who firmly believed that God did not exist, but fervently wished God did exist. I saw a man overwhelmed by life, exhausted by thinking about the meaning of life. I saw an out-of-work man caught in a vice grip of depression.

I saw a life I hated—my life, which I will soon end.

"My life" . . . when I look at my life, I feel as if I am observing the life of some person I do not know.

Who am I? I hide behind the person I claim to be, too scared to reveal the real me, who, out of fear of rejection, lives alone concealed from all . . . including me. It is as if, at the core of my being, there is something so ugly it must be hidden, something so unlovable, it lives in a darkened prison of loneliness so no one can see my true repulsiveness for fear they would not love me.

Who am I? I do not know. I only know who I pretend to be. I live in the prison I have built, and I am the mask I have donned. The prison is real; but the mask is a delusion, and behind the mask, an illusion.

As I looked back over my life, I saw a landscape of regrets. My life is a pointless collection of mistakes, a silly song sung out of tune. A short while ago, I broke the deafening silence of the evening by playing a compact disc of Ennio Morricone's soundtrack from the movie *The Mission*. The haunting, somber flute music that gives way to a dramatic orchestral crescendo on the album's second cut—a short piece titled "Falls"—manages to express my mood. I've been slowly drifting down river for many months, and, like the missionary priest strapped to the wooden cross in the movie, I'm about to plunge over the falls.

Yes Kate, it is dark. Very dark. It is an ebony evening with no North Star to guide me through the darkness of despair. I am alone. Very alone. And very lost. The game is nearly over.

I sat down at my desk some hours ago to write you a letter. The beginnings of ten different opening sentences—all of them now crumpled up in the bottom of my wastepaper basket—were unable to express what's in my heart and on my mind. The "Dear Kate" of this letter sat staring at me for more than a quarter of an hour. As I sit here alone and isolated from the world, I feel as if I'm slowly drifting into an unmarked grave in a godforsaken graveyard . . . and there is nothing I can do about it. Nor is there anything I want to do about it.

Of course, you already know *what* happened; I just want to tell you *why* it happened.

I have reached the conclusion that the world is one huge insane asylum, an asylum run by the holy carpenters of religion. The inmates who ran the ecclesiastical cuckoo's nest of my childhood convinced me that I was born a sinner. They raised me to obey and to never question authority, and they taught me that my only hope for happiness lies in death. No wonder I'm such a mess. Nothing makes any sense. My plan is to escape—soon.

Kate, there is so much I want to say to you that I hardly know where to begin. Or even how to say it. Sadly, I barely know you and that makes it even tougher.

As I write this, you, my precious daughter, are far away. We've lived apart for nearly half of your life. I know everything about your first six years of existence, but of your last five I know very little. I suppose you don't realize that I carry you always within my heart; no, of course not, all you know is the great distance between us and the infrequency of my visits. I have not made your life easy—I'm not even sure if that is what a father is supposed to do.

Still, I'm not writing to the you I do know: the sweet, funny, pretty, eleven-year-old girl. No, I'm writing to a Kate neither of us knows—the Kate you will grow into during the next ten years. You see, what I have to say can't be said to a kid—even a bright one like yourself. That's why I'm leaving instructions to delay the delivery of this letter until shortly after your twenty-first birthday.

Kate, I desperately need to tell you all about me.

Inside me there is a ticking time bomb—I'm liable to explode at any second. I feel like Christ, who, when he was hanging on the cross, cried out in agony and pain to his Father in heaven: "Why hast thou forsaken me?"

God has turned his back on me. I have turned my back on Him. Between us there is an unseen tension and coldness that chills me to my very bone. God and I are about to have an Old-West-style shootout. We are slowly and deliberately walking in opposite directions down a dusty, silent street. God's the guy with the white hat; I'm the bearded bad guy about to be blown away.

But before that happens, and with some sense of urgency, I want you to know who I was. I want you to know all that was inside of me—my pains, my fears, my confusions, my regrets, even my secret thoughts. I want you to know me. I want you to know why I left you for a second time.

I guess this is both an introduction and a farewell.

Somehow, even though I have decided to end my life, I'll live on in you—so, you need to know me; I am a part of you, a part I hope you haven't hated.

I'm not exactly sure what I'm going to say to you. Maybe this missive is just a feeble attempt to give my life meaning and order, a little late perhaps, but nonetheless feeble because I have come to see that the last word on truth is that there are no truths. There are hunches and theories, guesses and hypotheses, but truth escapes our grasp. Even at its best, life is sordid, sodden, and soiled. And pointless.

I once accepted the values of our society: McDonalds, Coca-Cola, and a brand-new Chevy. I once enjoyed all the toys and candies of this life. But never fully. The Church made me nervous, dull, and dim by fear, by guilt, and by foolish prohibition. For a long time, jobs and family helped me conceal from myself my desperation and despair, my imprisoned and condemned hopes, my hanged hopes. After years of solitude and unemployment, life has become mostly friction and contradiction. I found some relief in the therapy of food and drink and the therapy of ordinary tasks. But no longer.

I've come to a dead end, and I'm too exhausted to turn around and start over. I've run out of energy. And hope. The bright promise of yesterday has yielded to the dark gloom of today. Tomorrow I'd rather not face. My unmercifully meager life has woven among the mysteries of the universe a wholly meaningless course—if you can even call it a course. The "course" followed directions I got from equally lost strangers. In all I have done, in all I have seen, I've seen no meaning at all. None. Nada. Zero. Zippo. Zilch. There is no meaning, never was, never will be. I'm leaving as I came, dazed and bewildered. In God I find no succor, no relief, no way out.

Faced with nothingness, I only see absurdity and feel superfluous and even unwanted. I find myself at odds with the world. I have looked for rationality, but found none. There is no clarity, only confusion. Happiness is fleeting and always just beyond my reach. Oh, where is God? I can remember my childhood, those halcyon days when there was an order to life—but order, along with meaning, is now only a distant memory.

Nothing makes sense. I can no longer assume that life is worth living; in fact, I can't see how anyone ever reached such a ludicrous conclusion. My mind has turned heaven into hell, life into a haphazard string of pains. And such unbearable pain—it's there to see in the eyes of any person you meet, everyone, that is, except religious fanatics, in whose eyes you see only emptiness. It has taken me over forty years to understand nothing, and most of that time was spent searching for understanding.

I've studied philosophy and theology, searching for answers. I found only more questions. I've read all the self-help books that promote the gospel of positive thinking to the talk-show generation looking for simple answers, but their blueprints for happiness didn't work. Life hurts, and the pain is very real to me tonight. I think I've always had the sensitivity to get a gun and point it at my head, but, up until now, not enough guts to pull the trigger.

I question whether I possess the honesty to set down on paper a true self-portrait. Will I resort to deception and exhibit the me I want you to see, the me I wanted to be? I honestly have no interest in penning a long-winded excuse for how I came to be the me I am, but I fear I might. Don't get me wrong, daughter. I intend to tell you the truth, but can I tell the whole truth? Will what I leave out say more than what I put in? Besides, I never say what I think, and I doubt I could ever write what I feel.

I guess what I'm asking myself, dear daughter, is whether any self-portrait can be sincere, can capture the true colors of its subject. For openers, vast portions of any person's past, including their dreams, thoughts, and conversations, are unrecoverable—buried beneath the ever-constant onslaught of the now. Additionally, memory is an artist who transforms the ugly realities of the past into an impressionistic thing of beauty. We cannot help but vary and misrepresent our past according to our interests in the present, an artistic trick that requires no deception, only recognition.

I suppose that total sincerity would demand that I could observe myself as dispassionately as I could the chair I'm sitting on—which, of course, I could not do because my chair is made of materials I clearly can see, while the story of my life will be constructed from memories hidden behind a veil of time. Besides, there are bound to be immense lacunas—gaps as wide and deep as the Grand Canyon—in one's own memory. The eighteenth-century English novelist Laurence Sterne believed that the human personality consisted, at best, of a "bundle or collection of different perceptions, which succeed each other with an inconceivable rapidity, and are in a perpetual flux and movement." Who can recall that state of flux with any degree of accuracy? Certainly not me. I can remember most vividly only the peaks and valleys of my life, mere minutes among the thousands upon thousands of hours spent in the boring, mundane meadows of daily existence. Try, daughter, to recall everything you did, everything you felt, during every minute of yesterday. It's impossible. Life blooms and withers each moment of every day. Life and death breathe and expire in seconds, not years.

On a number of occasions during my life, I've attempted to keep a diary. But I found the task a real struggle because I realized that what takes place in our brain in the space of a minute would take pages upon pages to describe. To follow and describe the thread of thought during successive moments would be impossible. At the end of any given day, it would be equally impossible to recover and discern more than a small fraction of the deluge of ideas that flooded through our mind. So, how much truth could a diary contain? When I reread pages of my diary, I can't help but think that I was better or worse than I had implied, even though as the pages were written I thought I was being truthful. Truthfulness should not be confused with accuracy. All I can say about this letter is that I do not plan to bear false witness. But, I probably will.

If in between the time this letter is written and you read it you become interested in learning about me, I suppose you will seek to hear the story of my life from my friends and relatives. But none of them really knows me, knows the inner workings of my mind. Those who know me know only fragments of me, and they can only speak in generalizations—"He was funny," or "He was sensitive." My family and friends could not know how one day I exalted in life, and how the next day life would drive me to despair. They could not know that personal fulfillment always eluded me. They could not know how I frequently tumbled—without a hint of transition—from ecstasy to utter wretchedness, from heavenly hope to the bowels of hell. In his book, *The Real Life of Sabastian Knight,* the Russian-born novelist Vladimir Nabokov wrote, "Remember that what you are told is really threefold; shaped by the teller, reshaped by the listener, concealed from both by the dead man of the tale."

No, my dear Kate, my friends and family do not know me. The dead man of this tale concealed much of his life.

Worse than not knowing me, if I ever had the courage to tell them how I feel about things, they wouldn't even like me. No, nobody knows me.

My life is known only to me. Still, the words I'll use to describe my life may not even introduce you to the real me, because the real me, ever the deceiver, will be able to hide itself behind my own words. I suppose Anatole France, a French novelist who died in 1924 and whose writings ridiculed all theological, metaphysical, or scientific attempts to arrive at absolute truth, summed it up best when he wrote: "It is in the ability to deceive oneself that one shows the greatest talent."

Kate, the simple fact is that no confession is true, no confession tells all. In my diary I tried to write an accurate depiction of the day's events and my feelings about them. But in reading them this past week, I was struck by the fact that my instant replay and analysis of those daily events had no resemblance to the reality retained by my memory. My past is really what it has become in my present. My memory is a montage of reality and impressions. For instance, I'm not sure whether what I remember about my grandfather is based on things I experienced, or merely on stories my mother told me about him. I'm not sure whether memory itself is an illusion or a delusion; but either way, it's weak history—incomplete and misinterpreted. I do not know whether memory is something we have or something we've lost. Memory can never free itself from the constraints of time, so the past can never be fully recalled in the present. Anyway, the man you are about to meet is the man I *believe* myself to have been. I can not say that what you are about to read is a true record. It is—as they say in law—"to the best of my knowledge and belief."

This letter will introduce you to a me based on "facts" that conform as closely to historic truth as my memory permits, but the "feelings" I fear will more closely resemble a piece of fiction constructed by my imagination. So, kiddo, here it comes: the truth, the whole truth, and nothing but the truth about your dad, by your dad—that is, the truth as far as your dad's human weakness makes such telling possible.

I just had a weird thought—you'll be reading this in the next century, the year 2000. Geez, for all I know, you might be living on the Moon or on the planet Pluto. Actually, if living in outer space becomes a reality in the next century, I hope it's reserved only for preachers and politicians, because the further away from earth those parasites go, the better.

Imagine, the year 2000. I would have been fifty-three years old.

Even though I am forty-three, up until a few years ago I felt like a kid, a kid filled with the magic of childlike wonder and innocence. Now, I feel worn out, at the end of my road, with little reason or desire to live.

For as long as I can remember, I've been on a wild roller-coaster ride of ups and downs. I've felt the exhilaration of being at the peak, having reached the top of my profession, earning $8,000 a week. As you may remember, I once lived in Beverly Hills and drove a Jaguar. I had it all. I've also felt the despair of being at rock bottom, enduring long stretches of unemployment and poverty, to the point of even taking handouts from monks. Imagine, taking money from a bunch of guys who took a vow of poverty. Yet I had less than they. They had each other; they had God. I had me. Still, when I was rich I felt poor, and when I was poor I felt rich.

Extremes. I've been at both ends of the religious, professional, philosophical, social, and financial spectrums. The middle ground is unknown territory for me. All or nothing, that's been my life. No middle-of-the-road "Golden-mean" Aristotle for me.

Tonight it's nothing.

But it's a different kind of nothing. Darker, bleaker than ever before. Hope and happiness can't penetrate this void. This is no crisis of faith; this is a crisis of living. I've reached a point in my life beyond which I cannot go, because I can no longer understand things.

I can't stop crying, even though I have no real reason to cry. My problem, the unseen cause of my uncontrollable tears, is despair, the death of hope.

I'm tired, too damn tired to make sense of anything. Oh God, the struggle to understand and the search for some meaning to this absurd thing we call life has left me so completely exhausted and so thoroughly confused that I see little point in continuing. Why bother. I'm sick of going around in circles—circles of doubt. The heavy burden of unanswerable questions can no longer be carried. Hell is home for the questioners of heaven.

My life has been a continual exodus—wandering through a desert of bewildering ideas and daydreams—in search of a place to feel at home. I've shouldered this feeling of impermanence and perplexity as to where I really belong for far too long. The honest truth (as opposed to the dishonest truth) is that I have nothing in common with anything going on in the world today. Why stay? I'm tired of the past, trapped by the present, and tormented by the future. I'm too weak to continue to wrestle with the insanely terrifying chaos of life.

In a letter to his brother, Vincent van Gogh wrote, "Dying is hard, but living is harder still. . . . " Vincent was right.

Don't get me wrong Kate, I'm not afraid of life; I just long to escape the endless cogitation that torments me. You see, somehow my intelligence is just bright enough to lure me down blind alleys of thought and speculation, yet I'm not able to think my way out. My brain at times seems all thumbs. Still, I want to understand immortality, to understand God. No, in fact wanting to know about immortality and God does not adequately express the pull these twin topics have on my thoughts; in truth, they form the leitmotif of my thinking. But I'm powerless to know more than I can know—a fact that, I suppose, makes me an agnostic. But is agnosticism a sound intellectual position or just a bad case of indecision? I feel I am stuck between belief and unbelief, in a gooey muck of nonbelief. I have equal dislike for arrogant atheism, which asserts the nonexistence of something not yet defined, and for the presumptuous "belief" in anything equally undefined—but I much prefer the company of atheists over believers. It amazes me how irrelevant abstractions can give birth to sweeping statements, careless generalizations, and undefined terms.

Still, I carry around a ragbag of schoolboy philosophies. I believe in humanity's natural depravity and its native goodness. I want to reform the world and at the same time just sit back and watch it turn; to do both is impossible, so I swing back and forth between dreams and delusions. Sadly, the song I have come to sing, I have not sung—worse, I have not yet heard it. And I'm running out of time as fast as sugar spilled from a torn bag.

For the past year I have been torn between the horror of living and the horror of dying. That tug of war is now nearly over. My soul, unguarded against an invasion of melancholy, has slowly succumbed to defeat.

It's time, my dear Kate, to pink slip my life. My life has become a prison, and the wide horizon of my existence has become a narrow cell. I long for the liberty of death. Fear of the unknown world after death and the judgment seat of God no longer forces me to cling to life. Death is a comfort, a dreamless sleep, and not so terrible as a joyless life. Even Jesus, who had the power to escape his enemies, consented to his own death. (Of course, it can be argued his consent was a function of obedience not escape; still, I bet death was a comfort even for Jesus.) Only the phantoms of superstition prevent more people who are crippled by pain and want from opting for a quick self-determined end. The bottom line is simple, dear Kate: I have lost my love of life. I feel as if the most tenebrous forces of my unconscious have emerged, creating total despair. My life no longer has any value to me, and I can be of no real assistance to others—so why stay? In the calmness of thought and choice, I see serenity in death, peace in the grave.

For years, my prayer echoed that of St. Anselm's, an Italian medieval philosopher who went from Benedictine monk to the Archbishop of Canterbury; he prayed, "Lord, I am not trying to invade and pry into Your Majesty, for I do not liken my knowledge to It in the least. But I long for a glimpse of the truth that is believed and loved in my heart."

For years, the response has been the same: silence.

I don't know what St. Anselm heard before his death in 1109, but he wrote that God is that which cannot be conceived not to exist, and he believed faith paved the way to reason. His essay "A Model for Meditation on the Reason of Faith" carries as a motto the phrase that summarizes the meaning of all his philosophy: "Fides quaerens intellectum"—"Faith seeking understanding." That's all I was looking for—just a little understanding. None was found. St. Anselm wrote, "For I do not wish to understand in order to believe; rather, I believe in order to understand."

Stupid me—I had that backwards, I guess that was my mistake.

St. Anselm is credited with developing the "ontological argument" for the existence of God, which moves from the definition of God's nature as a perfect being to the conclusion that He exists. I don't get it. There is nothing more ignorant than an air of false knowingness. The main contention of St. Anselm's argument is that from merely understanding the concept of God, we can prove there is a God. Like I said, I don't get it. More theological mumbo jumbo that can't be believed and loved in my heart. God, have I tried. I've cried out in the darkness, "Lord, Lord help me to believe."

The reply, as always: silence—silence punctuated by contradictions.

If St. Anselm were here tonight, sitting with me in this hour of despair, I know what he would tell me; it's something he wrote: "The Christian should approach understanding through faith; he should not approach faith through understanding, or withdraw from faith if he cannot understand. When he can reach intelligence, he will be contented; and if he cannot understand, he should worship."

I can't understand, and I can't worship. If I could only do one or the other, I could live.

Sweet daughter, in thinking about this letter, my mind has floated back across the vista of my years. I feel as if I'm in a hot air balloon, soaring high over the terrain of my past. I see mountains of anger, fields of fear, valleys of doubts. I see meadows of love and forest fires of desire and pain. I see a river of rage and canyons of despair. I see a vast desert of loneliness and small gardens of happiness. I look and I look and I look, yet I can't make any sense out of the images below me. High above it all, there is a feeling of calmness to all I survey, yet I know the air below is turbulently swirling in all directions, blowing me this way and that way.

Kate, what I see are stories—stories I want to leave with you.

Stories. Boy, have I got stories! For most of my adult life I've been handsomely paid, perhaps even obscenely paid, for creating stories. As a television producer and writer, I've plotted murders, destroyed marriages, abused children, raped women, assassinated political leaders, robbed banks and graves, sold cocaine, hijacked planes, embezzled huge sums of money, run prostitution rings, fixed elections, made porno films, bilked old people out of their life savings, injected poison into Halloween candy, and burned down an orphanage—all in the name of entertaining America. Ain't TV grand! Television loves to put vice and passion on display, loves to wallow in human depravity. Some critic once correctly called television chewing gum for the mind.

Television mindlessly breeds dozens of clonelike shows serving the same morphinic end. Most television shows have become formula-ridden and indistinguishable from advertising. Television worships at the altar of ratings upon which ideas are sacrificed to the God of mediocrity. Television is addicted to personality, to the breathless embrace of celebrity, insuring a tyranny of the televised over the great mass of the untelevised. After twenty years of toiling in the television field, I've grown to hate its crop.

A network executive at NBC once told me, "Forget about art. All we want from you is filler, just something to keep the commercials from bumping into each other. Keep your aim low, just give the viewers what they want—you know, babes, beasts, and blood—and you'll do fine." The simple truth is that television feasts upon the depravity of humanity. It offers a mental junk-food diet of cheap sensations and disposable ideas. But even worse, it has helped create a culture that is inundated with visual images. Take it from one who knows, the triviality of television and movies is breeding an actual triviality into society; they are manufacturing boundless illusions in a materialistic world that stimulates an economy based on waste—but that's another story, one nobody wants to hear, and I'm not about to tell.

No, I have just one last story to tell—mine. Part tragic and part comic, my life has produced its own melodrama that is stranger than all the fiction I've created. I want to leave behind my story in the hope it may do you some good—even though it has no lessons to teach, no truths to reveal, no morals to convey; my story merely portrays my invisible inner struggles, my fruitless search for transcendence and some kind of spiritual intuition and reality. Maybe these words—my last story—will give some meaning to my life.

If "my" story has a theme, I guess it's this: "unlearning" is frequently more essential than learning—especially in the realm of religion. Religion is nothing more than an egotistical hope for immortality, to live forever. It's funny, but most people don't know what to do with a free weekend, yet they long for eternity. Do Christians truly think that when death comes that it will not really be death, but some kind of transition into another life, a better life? Are they really sure? I don't see anyone living as if they are convinced of it.

No one is indifferent to the riches, pleasures, and material things of this world. Even monks dedicated to simplicity are concerned about some minimum level of comfort and security. Is anyone—other than Mother Teresa—as happy in poverty as in wealth? Is there anyone who does not care about social status and esteem? Is anyone completely dedicated to the very highest and most unselfish ideals of life? The percentage of Christians who actually believe in their hearts what they profess with their tongues must be miniscule, because if they truly did believe they could not continue to live the lives they do.

Hypocrisy and deceit abound in every arena of life—especially in the arenas of politics and religion. Religious faith was conceived in the fretting, fearful brain of man, and there is not an ounce of divinity in it. The annals of Christianity are stained with crime, violence, innocent blood, racism, and discrimination against women.

I'm sorry. I didn't mean to get so worked up. But I'm angry. Angry at religion—and yes, angry at God.

Anyway, if "my" story has a central character, it is God. I wasn't always mad at God. No, not by a long shot. There was a time I loved Him dearly, and wanted only to serve Him all the days of my life. For the first dozen or so years of my life, my love of God was intoxicating. But my first carnal sins and a growing knowledge of myself quickly helped sober me up. As my heavenly dream faded, my soul began to feel sadness for the first time. I had loved God and wanted only to live for Him. But the Devil, in the form of my humanity, thwarted my desires and cooled my love. "I have not lost faith," says someone in George Bernanos's *Diary of a Country Priest,* "because God has pleased to preserve me from impurity." I was not so spared. St. John of the Cross claimed that human nature yearns for God but this divine aspiration is inevitably accompanied by a rising flood of carnal cravings. The mystic saint believed the greater our impulses toward God are, the more powerful the temptations offered up by the Devil will be. Of course, St. John of the Cross believed the Devil was real. And so did I, and I was ashamed that I had succumbed to his temptations. My soul was no longer in love and I was no longer happy.

I suppose that if I were Geraldo Rivera and writing about the Devil, I could make some boffo bucks on the story, but I'm not and I won't. God is a bad business risk, unless you are a television evangelist other than Jim Bakker or Jimmy Swaggart. (By the way, I think Bakker is the lesser of those two "weevils.")

Geez, this is strange. I just realized in ten years the names I have just mentioned—Geraldo Rivera, Jim Bakker, Jimmy Swaggart—may have faded from the public square and will have no meaning to you. I hope so. Geraldo claimed to be a journalist, but was really a huckster of hype and the patron saint of sensationalism. The two Jimmy's used the power of television to sell salvation at discount prices—just say "yes" to Jesus, send them twenty bucks, and in return they'll send you the keys to heaven. They claimed to know God personally, but were on more intimate terms with women other than their wives. Piety does not always equal goodness. Hardly. In fact, piety is most often merely a pious fraud. These two clerical con artists shamelessly picked the pockets of the gullible. Bakker got caught with his hands in the cookie jar and also frolicking around naked with a couple of guys in a steam bath, and is now serving time and God in prison for his sins. Forgetting Christ's warning to the rich, Bakker and Swaggart thought they could go to heaven in a limo. Geraldo and the two Jimmys were television circus performers of different stripes.

My story is really a story of faith. You see, my dear daughter, I once had faith—I was born with it. But I lost it. Years later, I regained it. Then, I lost it again. Finally, I threw it away . . . gladly, I think. All the bends in the river of my life were directed by the hurricane force of faith. Sadly, faith turned out to be nothing more than willful belief in the absence of evidence. Belief begins where knowledge and proof ends. I can't know anything that lies beyond the realm of my experience.

I don't think God exists; yet, I feel He does. Some days my thoughts are in control; other days, my feelings. I inherited a substratum of sensibility, formed by my force-fed belief in the supernatural, which denied the nonexistense of a Supreme Being which my intellect accepted. In my mind, there is no God; yet, in my heart, there is. You see Kate, I'm at odds with myself; yet until recently I pressed on searching and questioning, looking and listening. My doubts never before pushed me to the brink of total despair and over the edge into the dark abyss of complete emptiness. After spending years of being battered by a fundamentalist Christian faith that taught me to see myself as evil, I had recently learned to see my doubts as a shield that protected me from error disguised as the truth. But not tonight. Tonight I have no protection—I am completely vulnerable.

Basically I've always been at odds with myself—and not just over this God issue, although that unresolved matter has a way of permeating every other aspect of my life. I seem to see things with equal clarity from opposite points of view. If I were a country, I'd be Switzerland—neutral. But neutrality doesn't create peacefulness; if anything, it creates stagnation. Take for example the simple subject of friendship. I bought the old proverbial adage that no man is rich enough to throw away a friend. Then someone comes along and hits me with the idea that no friendship should outlast its usefulness, that friendships do not have to last forever unless they are meaningful. Unfortunately, both premises seem to have validity. The result: I struggle to hang onto friendships that are destructive, or torment over discarding a friendship that might have hidden riches. What a bitch . . . either choice leaves me feeling guilty.

Without a clear point of view, I've ended up with no point of view. The problem is magnified when I address the explosive issues of the day: abortion, women's rights, pornography, homosexuality, divorce, patriotism, the arms race, the legalization of drugs, and freedom of speech. A litany of divisive issues divides me. Even simple issues are problematic: should I buy an American-made car or a foreign car? Knowing beyond any doubt the "correct" position on all these issues seems preferable to struggling with the shades of gray one discovers just beneath the surface of these seemingly black-and-white matters. Nothing is black and white, save early television shows.

Does an open mind lead to lunacy or freedom—or neither? Does a closed mind lead to death or safety—or both? Is doubt good or bad, helpful or harmful? Does certainty create peace within us or convert us into idiots? Should I follow my head or my heart? Should I respond to passion or rationality? Should I favor faith over reason? Must I choose between spirit and intellect, between heaven and earth? Why is it that I am able to entertain a contrary opinion, understand it, respect it, even envy it? Is it simply a respect for open dialogue, not wishing to silence the voice of an adversary? Is it a simple respect for the ideas of the opposition? Is it nothing more than terminal indecision?

Questions, questions, questions; the questions seem to be without end—and every answer gives birth to new and more complex questions. The human mind is a wonder. Its complexity is beyond comprehension . . . it can create canned whitefish and tuna for cats and atomic bombs for people. Is there any hope we can understand the human mind?

Is it possible to appreciate both Merton the Monk and Mencken the Skeptic at the same time? I do. Is it necessary to choose between the truths both men represent? I can't. (Both Thomas Merton and H. L. Mencken were writers. One based his life on faith, the other, reason. Both men were honest.) Was Jesus God? Did Mohammed hear God's voice? Does it matter? Perhaps the best blessing in life is to be blessed with absolute certainty. I doubt it, though I wish I didn't. Knowing where you are going is the best way to get somewhere. I'm tired of chasing my own tail.

Talk about tension, even shopping is a problem because every purchase is reduced—or, rather enlarged—into a debate on the nature of man and the existence of a Supreme Being, who, despite His or Her majesty and power, is keenly interested in the minutest details of my meager, impotent life. Either God is crazy or I am.

Fill in the blank: "Life is _____." A bitch. A cabaret. A puzzle. A bowl of cherries. An adventure. Absurd. Wonderful. Or perhaps, a poker game where you can win with a pair of jacks but lose with a flush. The choices are endless; yet for me the one word that most satisfactorily completes that sentence is—*paradoxical.* It seems the more I know, the less I know. Every thought, word, or action that I think, say, or do can justifiably raise its contradiction. I suspect that I'm not alone in this—even the life of Jesus was filled with contradictions: the self-proclaimed Prince of Peace proclaimed that he came "not to bring peace but a sword."

It's late, dark, and I'm alone. Very alone. It's unusually quiet. The noise of the rowdy teenagers armed with their ghetto blasters and skateboards who normally roam up and down the alley behind the townhouses where I live are strangely absent. Even the crying infant next door is still. Maybe the rotten teenagers kidnapped her. Good. The only sound I hear is the constant dripping of water coming from the bathroom. The shower has been leaking for a year. I pretty much stopped hearing it about six months ago, long after my one and only attempt at fixing it ended in frustration and near drowning. I could never have worked for former president Richard Nixon—a plumber, I'm not. Drip, drip, drip. Tonight each drop of water punctuates the silence with a loud thud.

I'm sitting at the large oak desk in my study. Wait a second—having a "study" makes me sound a bit too uptown, which I'm not. In fact, I hate people who have studies; people don't study anything, they merely seek to reinforce whatever they already believe. My study is just a small second bedroom posing as an office. Not that I do any real work in here, I mostly daydream about making movies with Woody Allen, singing songs with Paul Simon, or playing second base for the New York Yankees—all of which I could do, given the opportunity. When my daydreaming kicks into overdrive, I imagine myself conducting the New York Philharmonic Orchestra—which I could never do because I don't understand music, I only enjoy it. My Leonard Bernstein fantasy has nothing to do with music, it's the drama of conducting that appeals to me: the baton tapping, the arms waving wildly, the shaking head that sends the hair flying in all directions, the intense stares at the musicians, the big finishes, and the bow. Oh, what drama, what flair!

When I'm not daydreaming, I pretend that I'm a "serious" writer. This room—my study—has become a "black hole"; I enter it and disappear for hours. I don't write to sell books. I have no grand illusion of becoming a best-selling author—OK, few illusions. I write to examine myself, to shed a little light on my own life and give shape to my experience. Writing has become a means of thinking, a way of saving my soul. It forces me to scrutinize myself, to discover what I really believe. The artist finds in himself the subject of his work. While writing, I become a surgeon operating on my own brain—without anesthesia.

Tonight, I have put down the pen-turned-scalpel.

A bit of cheap wine has made me fuzzy around the edges; I've never had much of a capacity for liquor. Anyway, my study has become my personal Walden Pond. Within these four walls, I spent endless hours in Thoreauvian solitude, during which time my thoughts transform this study into heaven and hell—mostly hell. As my eyes aimlessly roam around the room, I suddenly realize that this simple room, turned refuge from reality, reflects the unseen war raging within me. Books on television, movies, and Hollywood line one wall; books on spirituality, theology, and philosophy line the opposite wall. Literally every inch of available wall space is covered with framed photos from my life in show biz.

It's funny how I treasure and proudly display pictures of myself with some well-known celebrity—even celebrities who I think are jerks. I guess those shots of me with "special" people make me special—at least, in the eyes of the starstruck visitors to my home.

As I stare into the nearly empty tumbler once filled with wine that sold for only $2.49 a quart, I'm trying to make some sense out of my life. A life that has taken me around the world and introduced me to some very famous people—megastars from the galaxies of movies, rock & roll, and religion. There has also been a wide assortment of unknown wackos who have crossed my path—like the doorman at my old New York apartment who believed that Jesus arrived on earth in a space ship. Holy cosmic Christ! Sometimes I feel as if there's a bright neon sign flashing across my forehead that reads: "If you're a religious lunatic, please feel free to talk to me—I'll listen without laughing." And I'm sitting here hoping to make sense out of my life. The odds are better that I will win the lottery, and they're about one in a zillion.

If only life was like a videocassette we could play back and view our lives as they actually happened—that would be very helpful in objectively studying our life. Unfortunately, memory is selective, it carefully saves some things and discards others and generally acts as a censor to our minds. Yeah, I know a lot of stuff is stored in some musty file in the basement of our subconscious, but that isn't very helpful when you need it . . . besides, you can never find anything because the boxes are poorly marked or, worse, incorrectly labeled.

During the past few weeks, it has become very clear to me that life is devoid of any meaning whatsoever. It's not a matter of hopelessness, although I feel the game of life is pointless and irredeemable at best; it's more a matter of "who cares, why bother?" I want to put an end to the madness, and suicide seems the best method—the ultimate solution. Perhaps, more accurate than the ultimate solution, suicide is the final separation.

Like all modern men and women (don't you hate sentences that start this way), my life has been marked by separation. Separation is the curse of the age in which we live. But you know all about that. People talk of unity—the one world philosophy musically expressed in the song of the eighties, "We Are the World"—yet, what we experience is separation, detachment from beliefs, values, family, and loves. Every marriage, every relationship contains the seeds of its own destruction. Every "Hello" echoes "Goodbye." Even if you live in the most crowded of cities, isolation is the lot of most of our lives; I know that I am lonely, though seldom alone. We are anchorless, drifting in a sea of contradictions, tossed about by waves of opinion masked as truth. I am a solitary drop of water in that sea, surrounded yet alone and struggling to be me. It is easy to float, and, easy to drown. Tonight, my choice is the latter.

Unlike Hemingway and so many countless others, I haven't had a lifelong fascination with death. The act of suicide has held no magical enchantment for me. It has seemed shameful at best and a tragic waste at worst. I've had occasional impulses to end my life, but usually for no discernable reason. One day, for example, I was out jogging. The sun was shining, and all was well with my world.

The route I was running took me across a highway overpass. As I was huffing and puffing my way over the six lanes of traffic, I suddenly had a strong urge to leap over the rail. I saw myself plunging head-long toward the pavement, hearing as I fell the screeching of car brakes and knowing that if the fall didn't kill me a car would finish me off. The idea and the image haunted me. Years later I had a despondent character in a soap opera I was producing choose to end his life that very same way—only to be saved at the last possible second. On a few other occasions, while driving down a highway, I've been hit with the impulse to aim the car at a bridge embankment, or turn into the path of a speeding truck. Again, these were just isolated incidents, seemingly coming from out of the blue and not triggered by any depressing or hopeless problems. I just filed them away in a category of my mind labeled "Weird Thoughts."

Tonight is different. It is deliberate. It is motivated. And, with all the urgency of a crook ransacking a house, I feel I must do it soon before I'm caught in the act at the last second—as if I were some kind of a soap opera character.

Suicide always comes as a shock to the friends and relatives of the ones who end their lives that way. Snuffed out with the life are the reasons for ending it. Left only are the questions why. Abbie Hoffman was an icon of sixties activism who almost single-handedly turned the country inside out with his protests against the Vietnam War. Abbie had a world of friends and admirers, yet, no one was with him on the lonely night of April 12, 1989, when he ingested a lethal amount of barbiturates and booze in order to escape the depression holding him prisoner and robbing him of his freedom. All he left behind were questions. Did he find life in the 1980s to be irrelevant? Was his suicide one final act of protest against a system that places profits before people? One can only wonder what was going through his tormented mind as he swallowed 150 phenobarbital pills and washed them down with liquor. Without hope, the outspoken conscience of a generation closed his eyes, and quietly ended his life—alone in a sparsely furnished apartment in the small town of New Hope, Pennsylvania. Imagine the irony, that in the town of New Hope, death was Abbie Hoffman's only hope.

I find no fault in what he did. Hope is the first line of defense against suicide— and it has broken down for me, as I'm sure it did for Abbie. Hope, dear Kate, is the music of life, and when the music has faded it is hard to keep dancing.

Essentially, life is resisting death, which I no longer can do. The instinct for self-preservation is no longer stronger than the lure of death.

I wish I could turn the clock back on my life. Not to undo the mistakes I've made. I've come to grips with them, even learned from them, though perhaps not enough to stop repeating them. No, I wish I could go back—just a few years— and turn off the impulse I felt to probe, to probe not only the meaning of my own life, but life itself. I felt that the world was insane, yet I wanted to make some sense out of life, to find some order in the chaos. Why? Why couldn't I just have lived it, enjoyed life, and let it go at that? My life became sidetracked by a wrong signal: I believed in the existence of an ultimate answer, and I wanted to find it.

At first, the questions were few and unconnected, and I considered them to be little more than idle curiosities. But the questions mounted, and I became obsessed by the fear that all I had believed to be true was in fact false, and that life was meaningless. That didn't make getting up each morning easy. Was the struggle to survive all there was? Was Earth little more than a stage on which to enact the drama of salvation, a place of trial and testing, of pain and suffering? Did real life only begin after the death of the body? Was the point of life nothing more than the avoidance of eternal torture? Was the idea of a personal, white-bearded God simply a human invention, and God really nothing more than the impersonal energy of the universe? Does not the wide diversity of religious belief prove the weakness of each? Why do so many people think the late mythologist Joseph Campbell had all the answers?

What good is a God who does not abolish the absurd, but only intensifies it? What good is a God who is not a source of comfort, but only a source of despair? What good is a God who promises immortality, but only delivers death? What good is a God who allows such cockroach-messiahs as Pat Robertson and Jerry Falwell not only to speak for Him, but also lets them prosper and get rich while doing it? A farmer in William Faulkner's novel *As I Lay Dying* asks, "If there is a God what the hell is he for?" The farmer resented God's tolerance of evil, and saw God chiefly as an expletive. What good is God?

If God is good, why did He not confine the world within the bounds of that eternal dwelling place known as heaven? If God is all-powerful, why did he not, in creating the world, keep it free from suffering? Why would a perfectly wise Being create a world filled with imperfections? Why would God the all-loving Father allow his innocent children to die of starvation and an assortment of horrible diseases? Why would an intelligent and merciful God create a system of life that required living creatures to devour other living creatures, for life to feed on life, for survival? If God's mercy is unbounded, how could he permit the horrors of the Holocaust? Why should all of mankind, billions upon billions of people, be doomed to disease and death because one woman ate an apple? If God is all-good and all-powerful, why would He allow evil to have a home in the world He made? And, worst of all, why would God make cake fattening and health food taste like styrofoam?

Why, why, why? Then I had the bright idea that if I could just take a few years off and dedicate myself to studying and thinking, I could figure it all out, figure out why.

What a stupid jerk! Anyway, I'm getting ahead of myself.

After years of probing, asking questions that have no answers, I'm left in the predicament of feeling that the things I can do to earn a living in television, I no longer want to do. But what do I want to do? I can't continue to want money—or, better put, need money—and continue to deplore the almighty buck. I once had myself convinced that purity of intention could include making money, that I could grow rich without losing respectability. But that conviction didn't last long, and I soon slipped back to an attitude that was best summed up by Aristotle: "All paid employments absorb and degrade the mind."

Last week, a friend's son told me he was going to Harvard Business School, and I thought, "Great. The kid is going to learn how to cut throats." Still, searching for meaning doesn't pay, doesn't put food on the table, and is no road to riches. Maybe the young man is not so dumb after all—business may not be the point of life, but it is definitely a part of it. Unfortunately for me and my exchequer, I hate business. Life in America often leaves me with the sensation that I'm living in a vast industrial complex devoted to the manufacture of tweezers and electric can openers. I manufacture questions.

Questions, questions, questions. I'm drowning in a sea of unanswerable questions. The mind, all dressed up in its finest wardrobe of reason and understanding, can't help but ask questions, but, alas, it doesn't have the power to answer them. Does God exist? Reason seeks proof, without which it is rendered powerless to decide. How can we know? And even if we could know, how could we even begin to talk about it? How can a limited mind grasp and discuss an unlimited being? What did God do before He/She created the world? (I hate referring to God as He/She—it makes Him/Her sound Japanese—but, if I refer to God as He, then I would sound like a sexist. Better God sounds Japanese.) Was He/She bored before He/She created the world? Did He/She take long naps? Does He/She like sushi?

Questions, questions—an ever-changing, ever-flowing river of questions—but never any answers, answers that last. At best, God is a hunch, and confusion is the lot of men and women. We come from nowhere, and we are going nowhere; and, in between our coming and going, we do nothing. Everyone wants reason and order, some ultimate purpose; yet, what we get is random chaos and Vice President Dan Quayle.

There is nothing and nothing matters. Our life is a bottomless empty vessel, into which we can pour as much of whatever we like. I wonder what my life would have been like if I hadn't poured into it so much religion, which is nothing more than the industrial waste of spiritual life.

From birth, the Christian faith of my parents was breathed into me. Just as Santa Claus and the Easter Bunny were very real to my uncritical mind, I accepted my parents' religious myths and beliefs as real, as truth. Time and reality destroyed my false notions about the existence of the gift-giving, bearded fat man from the North Pole and the egg-bearing rabbit. But time alone couldn't throw cold water on their religious myths; it took reason. Still, even though reason gave birth to questions and doubt, I nonetheless hung onto the myths for a very long time with the determination of Linus clutching his blanket.

I suppose that if I had my security blanket of myths tonight, I wouldn't be thinking about snuffing out the candle of my life. If. If's are a damn waste of time.

I found it as impossible to renounce Christ as to renounce myself. I wanted very much to find God—a real God who could comfort and guide—yet all I found in church was a God who ruled and judged. No one seemed interested in going beyond the letter of the catechism. No one seemed to have a real knowledge or experience of God. It was all ritual and formulas, all plastic piety and degrading platitudes. Even in my attempts at denying Christ, I felt closer to him than many

Christians are. They deny, yet do not deny.

It is clear to me that human life is at the mercy of chance and the most arbitrary circumstances. How I wish it were otherwise, that somewhere out there beyond the stars, someone cared about me, about all of us. But I see no evidence of the existence of a cosmic parent, and I can't know anything that lies beyond my realm of experience.

The reality of my situation is simple: I cannot seem to orchestrate the dissident voices within me, and I can no longer live with my contradictory multiplicity of views. I live in discord, torn by conflict, reduced to a silent debate between Man and God. At times, Man speaks, but then he relinquishes the stage of my soul to God. I am divided within myself. I want to believe, I just wish God would give me a little more evidence. I don't need to hear His voice—to hear Him clear His throat would do just fine.

My dear Kate, I'm bursting with things to tell you, but seeing as my thoughts are so scattered and unfocused and the wine is pressing my eyes closed I must end this letter for tonight and continue it in the morning. Final thought: wine alone is almost proof of the existence of God—it's the vino argument, and it's far sweeter than St. Anselm's ontological argument. Good night, my sweet.

Thursday, July 12—9:45 A.M.

Good morning, my love. It's going to be a helluva day here in L.A.—the morning is hardly awake and the heat is already in midday form. Temperature is expected to hit 108 degrees. I'm sure there will be another "smog alert," warning the citizens of this sprawling metropolis that the air is too unhealthy to breathe. Of course, no alternative to breathing air is offered. Suicide might be as easy as inhaling.

Just as I was falling asleep last night, I started thinking about St. Anselm and all the stuff I wrote to you about him. As I lay there in that wonderful, dreamlike spot found halfway between going to bed and going to sleep, my mind began to entertain the fantasy that St. Anselm and I were back in my study. He seemed short, even though he was wearing his miter, which is a tall, ornamented headdress that features twin peaks in the front and back. They are worn by popes and bishops as a sign of their high office and rank. I had on a Yankee baseball cap, which symbolized my wish to be a kid again, catching fly balls in Smokey Park, rather than sitting there discussing theology with a long-dead Doctor of the Church. He had just told me that understanding comes through faith, and that if I couldn't understand, then I must worship.

"Wait a minute Anselm . . . do you mind if I call you that, I've got a problem with the Saint part. People make poor saints, because Sainthood is a weight far too heavy for anybody to carry."

"Anselm will do fine."

"Great. Well, listen to this, Anselm. About 500 years after you checked out, there was an English philosopher named John Locke. This guy was very highly respected, and his philosophical influence is still felt today. Anyway, he wrote a very famous essay that examined the uncertainties about the limits of human understanding, titled "Essay Concerning Human Understanding." Not a very snappy title, but nonetheless, in it he wrote: 'He that believes without having any reason for believing may be in love with his own fancies, but neither seeks truth as he ought, nor pays the obedience due to his Maker, who would have him use those discerning faculties he has been given him to keep out of mistakes or errors.' Anselm, the point is simple: I've got a brain, and I must use it. My problem is the Bible, which is the foundation for all this stuff about God and Jesus. The simple truth is that it is loaded with contradictions and hearsay evidence in support of God. Why should I believe it? Let me quote Locke again: 'There can be no evidence that any traditional revelation is of divine origin, in the words we receive it, and in the sense we understand it, so clear and so certain as that of the principles of reason; and therefore nothing that is contrary to, and inconsistent with, the clear and self-evident dictates of reason has a right to be urged or assented to as a matter of faith, wherein reason hath nothing to do.' "

"Chris . . . do you mind if I call you that, I've got a problem with Christopher, as it means Christ-bearer, and you certainly are not that."

"Chris is fine."

"Great. I've got just one question for you Chris."

"Shoot."

"Shoot?"

"Yeah . . . just, just ask the question."

"Fine. Do you believe in God?"

There is a pause, St. Anselm presses the issue.

"Or, more specifically, do you believe that God exists?"

"That's a tough one," I said.

"Tough one? What's tough about it? Do you believe in God—yes or no?"

"It's tough, Anselm, because for a long time I claimed that I didn't know. I mean, I couldn't prove it one way or the other. The Bible isn't proof, because not all the statements in it are true. If you tell me God has communicated with you, or that you have experienced God in some mystical way, or He appeared to you in a vision, I can only assume that you are hallucinating. I just didn't know, so I guess I was an agnostic. But, recently, I've moved into the NO camp; but, at times my heart isn't in it. I guess, I'm a halfhearted atheist."

"Oh please, spare me all the waxing and waning. You moderns are so indecisive, so wishy-washy. You claim to be enlightened and free, yet you can't go more than a week without visiting your psychiatrist. Just give me a yes or no, not a weak yes or maybe."

"Wait just a second—I've never visited a shrink, nor do I ever plan to."

"Chris, you don't have to visit one—their ideas are part of the fabric of modern life."

"Listen, I'm telling you that I'm not influenced by every passing fad of pop-psychology."

"Are you sure? Let's face it, with more than one in four people trying some form of therapy with a psychologist or a psychiatrist during their lifetime, the stuff they hear is bound to become a part of the culture."

"So what? Even glib, reckless, off-the-rack psychology can't do any more harm than religion has."

"So you don't care that people are spending ridiculous amounts of money on their shameless self-indulgence. You don't care that they'll try overcoming their angst with psychoanalysis or transactional analysis or primal scream therapy or rolfing or client-centered humanistic psychology or bioenergetics or neurolinguistic programming or behavorism or any other manmade form of personal salvation."

"Hey, it's a free country. People can spend their money on anything they want and for any reason. Listen, Anselm, trust me—I don't worship at the Altar of Freud, or Jung, or Rodgers, or Skinner, or Morita. They aren't my gods."

"Who is your God? You?"

"I'm not God."

"I'm glad to hear it. Come on Chris, let's get back to my question: Do you believe in God? Just a yes or a no, please."

"No."

"So, you are an atheist."

"Yes, dammit."

"You've got that right, my friend."

"Funny."

"Not really. Let me quote your friend Locke, who I might add developed the philsophical method know as 'empiricism,' which claims that all knowledge comes from experience, that there are no innate ideas stored in our brains at birth. Man begins as a tabula rasa."

"A what?"

"A blank slate. So much for your Latin. Back to Locke. Chris, this counselor, physician, and teacher didn't throw away his reason in order to discover God. No, he used his brain; through inquiry and experience, he came to the true knowledge that God does exist. Here is what John Locke wrote: 'Although we have no innate idea of God, beginning with our intuitive knowledge of our own existence, it is possible to demonstrate with certainty that God exists. How would that demonstration proceed? I am an actual thinking being. The "being" of my nature could not have come from nothing, for certainly those ideas are repugnant to each other; to prevent saying that it has come from nothing, I must finally say that it came from an eternal being; and the power of my being from eternal power.' "

"I'm sorry, Anselm—I just don't get it. That drivel doesn't prove anything. The 'big bang' theory makes more sense. Furthermore, even if I accept Locke's rationale, there still needs to be proof that this 'eternal being' really is as described in the Bible. This is all very frustrating. I'm not going to be able to convince you of anything, and so far you aren't convincing me. You know, when I was in high school, the parish priest, old Father McDermott, told me that I did not have to reject reason, what I needed was to go beyond reason. What's beyond reason? Nothing! Let me throw another Locke quote at you, OK?"

"Shoot."

"You're quick. Locke wrote, 'One unerring mark of the love of truth is not entertaining any proposition with greater assurance than the proofs it is built upon will warrant.' I'm sorry, Anselm, but I'm interested in truth, not clever speculation. Your proof about the existence of God does not rest on terra firma."

"So you do remember a little Latin."

"Very little."

"Listen, Chris, we don't seem to be getting anywhere with this discussion. Don't you see, the key is faith. Just trust in God, and your feelings and emotions will come along in short time. You'll soon see just how reasonable belief in God is, and how utterly foolish atheism is. Let me just quote John Locke one more time."

"Do you have to? It's getting very late."

"You started this, it's your dream."

"Go ahead, but I hope it's a short quote."

"It is. Listen. 'Religion should turn from arid theological speculation to the simplicity of the Gospels whose central point was the practical ackowledgment of Jesus as Messiah. Persecution must not be permitted. Toleration of religious differences is essential and to be extended to all save atheists.' "

"I guess it's true."

"What's true?"

"Even the Devil can quote scripture for his own purposes."

"Since when is John Locke's writing 'scripture?' "

"Hearsay is hearsay, and I hear say it is."

"Salvation is not a laughing matter."

"I'll be serious. Was it not typical in your day to accept the validity of Church authority without question and to view the natural world as if it were saturated with sin?"

"Generalizations are dangerous."

"Including that one. My point is that men like Peter Damian, the theologian and Church reformer who died in 1072, were advocates of ascetic piety and claimed that fleeing this world was the way to salvation. He went so far as to conclude one sermon with an exhortation to 'scorn all that is visible.' "

"Damian was responding to a movement headed by a teacher named Berenger who taught at the Cathedral school of Tours and who asserted that reason was superior to Church doctrine."

"Sounds reasonable."

"To you."

"Listen Anselm, we both know that Berenger's sin was questioning the nature of the Eucharist. He was dangerous because he viewed philosophy as separate and equal to theology. Damian condemned philosophy that was independent from theology, saw it as the sinful work of man. Damian believed that philosophy is only justified when it functions as the handmaid of theology."

"Damian's views were very conservative."

"Conservative? That's an understatement if I ever heard one! Damian viewed the layman as essentially a concupiscent creature and believed the only worthwhile occupation for humans was contemplation, that we need to get far from 'worldly vanities' and 'secular concerns.' Geez, this guy was even suspicious of priests who didn't live in monastic seclusion, but chose instead to stay 'close to laymen, and fraternize with them in daily life.' He wrote, 'The majority of priests do not even manage to distinguish themselves from the disorderly morals and lifestyles of their flock.' He thought of human sexuality as sordid and hideous, and sexual communion, even between husband and wife for the sake of procreation, as a form of servitude and slavery. How grotesque: our senses are pimps of sin, and the only way to save ourselves is to, according to Damian, 'spit on the rot of the world.' No wonder the world is so fucked up."

"Hold it a second Chris. You're scrambling together too many different issues. Please try to understand that Peter Damian was a hermit who had the responsibility of a diocese thrust upon him. Out from the sanctuary of the monastery, he couldn't help but notice that people were forgetting the miserable condition of humanity as a result of original sin, and therefore they were becoming lax in viewing earth as a place of exile, as a vale of tears; they were forgetting that all hope lies only in the rewards of heaven."

"Great. So his task was to remind everybody they were miserable sinners, so that they would learn to view themselves as St. Francis de Sales viewed himself a few centuries later: 'I am but an excrescence of the world, a sewer of ingratitude and iniquity.' That's a real healthy attitude."

"And a correct one. Chris, no one can love both earthly and eternal things at the same time: Say with the blessed apostle Paul, 'The world is crucified for me and I am crucified for the world,' and like the same apostle look at all transitory things as if they were dung."

"Are you dung . . . er, I mean . . . done?"

Anselm sat sternly for a few seconds, his eyes staring coldly at me.

"Chris, it is important to remember that when Peter Damian and I were here on earth, it was a time of great struggle. People wanted to understand the relationship between reason and revelation, between individual reason and Church authority. I accepted the basic truth of authority, and my task was to trace the foundation of faith, to uncover the rationale of faith."

"You tried to understand the truth you believed and loved."

"Yes."

"Faith, in your mind, was an absolute precondition for understanding."

"Was and is."

"That boggles my mind, that kind of faith, to me, is unreasonable."

"I know it is. I sense your frustration. You think of me as closed-minded, don't you?"

"Yes."

"I'm really not. I'm thankful for what I can understand about God, and what I don't understand I must humbly bow down before in adoration. Theologians before me busied themselves with supporting Church authority. I strove to go beyond all the dogmas and writings of the Church Fathers. I wanted to achieve a rational insight into the content of faith; I desperately wanted to solve the difficulties arising from the speculative preoccupation with the truth of faith."

"An impossible dream, I would say."

"For you perhaps. I believe I discovered a thoroughly rational understanding of the mysteries of faith. For me, prayer, meditation, and theology formed one whole, a threefold course of action that will deliver a foretaste of heavenly glory."

"For a split second you sounded like a televangelist offering his adoring audience the 'Secret Keys to the Kingdom,' which God had just revealed to him and he was now offering to his viewers for a mere twenty bucks a tape. But I know a few televangelists and you're no televangelist."

"Thanks."

"No, I really appreciate your sincerity, and admire your dedication. But— don't you hate the word 'but'—but, your spiritual insights must be questioned. I mean a fellow saint and Doctor of the Church, who lived in your day and age, Bernard of Clairvaux . . ."

"Bernard was born in 1090; I was fifty-seven at the time of his birth."

"Gee, you're quick with the dates. Anyway, Bernard of Clairvaux thought that knowledge for the sake of knowledge was an empty curiosity and he therefore had little time for philosophy. He had misgivings about your methods of pursuing theology and questioned whether the insight into the nature of God you sought could be found on earth."

"Bernard trusted intuition more than intellect. He feared that speculative and intellectual curiosity deflects man from his true relation to God—that is, to love God and to do His will. Bernard believed that truth is received through faith, and that reason should function only as a method of unwrapping the gift of faith."

"Bernard talks a lot about love, yet his main preoccupation seemed to have focused on protecting tradition and persecuting heretics. His hatred of heresy gave birth to a hatred of reason. His wrath against those who opposed his view of God's will knew no limits."

"You love to generalize."

"Did he not organize the Second Crusade in 1146?"

"Yes."

"Did not his ascetic austerity in food and his zeal for strict monastic discipline eventually lead to the destruction of his health?"

"He did become so prostrated that he had to relinquish his leadership of the monastery for a year in order to save his life. But you're missing the point."

"I'll bite. What is the point?"

"Chris, we are born in the image of God . . ."

"God's balding and fat?"

Anselm shoots a pissed-off look my way.

"I'm sorry Anselm. Please go on with the point."

"We are born in the image of God, but through sin, we have lost that image. Since the Fall, man has become bound to his physical needs and is now motivated by his desire. Life has been turned upside down; man is now on top. Bernard understood that man lost his true likeness to God, lost his ability to choose between good and evil, and lost his strength to do what he was chosen to do. Man finds pleasure in himself instead of God. This idolatrous revolt is the origin of evil according to Bernard. He strove to restore man's likeness to God."

"His path was asceticism, right?"

"Humility is more accurate."

"He condemned his own wretchedness and punished himself by mortifying his flesh, right?"

"Bernard knew that mortification alone was fruitless; he combined mortification and meditation."

"Which is why he vehemently objected to all intellectual activity, believing it distracted man from loving God."

"Chris, the point that seems to elude you is that Bernard was a Cistercian monk who saw monks from other orders, especially the Benedictines, becoming soft—monks were living in luxury and developing artistic interests that had nothing do with monasticism. He wanted the monks to seek the ecstatic experience, to seek 'the bridegroom's kiss,' by progressing through stages of humility, contemplation, and purification. He was mystic. His aim was monastic reform."

"And yours was scholastic theology."

"So?"

"So, Bernard didn't trust reason, or, at best, kept it on a short leash. Like Bernard, you believed revealed truth must be first accepted, but you went further in claiming that in light of that certainty, one can use reason to interpret all else."

"So what's the problem? Bernard's conception of the Christian life is not the only conceivable one."

"One saint distrusts reason, another uses it."

"Chris, you're getting hung up on shadings. Bernard of Clairvaux and I both know that reason and knowledge are of little value in achieving salvation. We are saved by faith . . . end of story."

"I can't believe what I can't understand. Belief must follow understanding, not the other way around."

"There was a man who Bernard and I both opposed. He said, 'For by doubting we come to inquiry, by inquiry we discover the truth.' "

"Peter Abelard."

"Yes. Figures you would know about him. Notice which one of the three of us—Peter, Bernard, and me—is not called 'saint.' "

"What does that prove, except the Church's ignorance? Bernard was relentless in his condemnation of Abelard and eventually managed to convince Pope Innocent

II to declare Abelard a heretic, excommunicate him, and order all his books burned. Abelard's conception of Christianity was inconceivable to St. Bernard of Clairvaux. Abelard had his balls cut off for loving a woman—a young student of his named Heloise. Worse, Peter Abelard claimed sin implies both knowledge and intent to do evil, without which there is no sin. He seemed ethical to me."

"And heretical to me. Abelard was a regenerator of old heresies and the inventor of new ones. He had to be punished."

"This is going nowhere."

"I agree."

"Maybe I'm wrong."

"You are."

"I mean about this going nowhere."

"It isn't."

"It can't. Abelard may have been silenced, but his questioning of authority hasn't been. Say good night, Anselm."

"Good night Anselm."

I smile in the darkness, and fall asleep.

As is my habit, I arose shortly after six this morning and ventured out into the early morning stillness to get the papers and a cup of coffee. It's the same routine every morning: pick up the *Los Angeles Times,* the *New York Times, USA Today,* and a cup of java to go. It seems as if we are nothing more than a collection of habits, yet if that is all we are then we are really nothing at all. Through our habits, we cling to the familiar, to the person we think we know. Habit is a creature tortured by the fear of the unknown. I think that youth is a time of spontaneity and freedom because it has not yet been drugged or crippled by habit. Reading three papers each morning is what Christopher Ryan does. Habit allows me to live, and helps me avoid Life.

"Habit and routine," wrote Henri de Lubac, "have the power to waste and destroy." Amen.

The habit of reading three—and sometimes more—newspapers a day, in addition to reading a wide assortment of weekly and monthly magazines, reveals yet another of life's paradoxes: reading can help you grow, and it can also stifle your growth. Let me explain. I began my reading mania in my early thirties. It was not the kind of reading one does for pleasure—finding adventure in novels, or beauty in poetry, or discoveries in philosophy, or knowledge from history; no, this was little more than an information binge where I devoured an endless procession of words. I spent at least an hour a day informing myself about a plethora of far-flung problems, everything from ecological disasters to mindless wars fought in every corner of the globe. I thought I was becoming a well-informed citizen. But I was powerless to confront or do anything about these concerns— all I could do was speak superficially at a cocktail party about the big issues of the day. (Not much of a benefit, considering I rarely go to cocktail parties.) And what price did I pay for this collection of facts, if indeed they can be called "facts": a very high one—my time, time I could have better used learning about myself.

My daily reading was passive and hollow, and it left me without any time for my own thoughts. I wanted to write, so I thought I needed to be knowledgeable about the world. What I needed was to forget the world around me and concentrate upon my own ideas and images. Besides, the reading yielded plenty of information, but hardly any knowledge. I knew everything but what was important; had all the information but the truth. I have retained very little of what I read during those thousands of early morning hours, the information has faded away like the darkness at dawn. If I had only spent that valuable time each morning at my desk writing instead of reading—if. I studied the world around me and ignored the world within me. Of course, only looking within without ever looking around is foolish also. Balance, it all comes down to balance.

This morning, my life is out of balance.

Kate, I've mixed up and matched so many different types of spirituality and philosophy that I've become thoroughly mixed up. I used to be confused, and it's only recently that I graduated to thoroughly mixed up. I'm certain only of uncertainty. If only for a day I could take refuge in the comfort of certainty. It's funny, everybody I know seems to be absolutely certain about everything. I mean they know who they are. They know what they want to do. They know what foods are good for you. They know where they're going—both in this life and the alleged afterlife. God, some of them even know where they've been and who they were in a past life. Oh . . . this reincarnation crap bores me to tears; but creating magical rumors from the remote past is a favorite present-day pastime. This past-life rubbish is really silly. The funny thing about that kind of cosmic hindsight knowledge is that it is very self-serving.

I lived for a short while with a bright lady who believed that in a former life she had been Chopin. She happened to be a very nice person, but—like most of us—hardly exceptional. Her beliefs had the same effect on her outlook as a can of Lemon Pledge had on the look of an old wooden desk. Somehow, being extra special in a previous incarnation added a little luster to her present dull life. I found it odd, assuming her Chopin connection to be true, that she had virtually no interest in the piano this time around.

Why do people always, or at least for the most part, think they were someone famous in some previous incarnation? You don't hear of many people claiming to be slaves or murderers in a life lived long ago. Some people like to explain away a string of bad luck and disasters as an indication that they are burning off some "bad karma" from the sins of a past life, but they never know exactly what those "sins" were. More crap. Karma is just an easy way to explain the unfairness of life by claiming that there is cosmic justice whose mercy or retribution is not restricted by time.

There seems to be an epidemic of what I call "theoidiocy" sweeping across America these days. "Theoidiocy" is a word I just invented; it comes from the Greek word *theos*, which means God, and the English word *idiocy*, which means the state of being an idiot, or exhibiting behavior like that of an idiot, and can also mean great foolishness or stupidity. My little word-invention is a play on a word coined by the German philospher Gottfried Wilhelm Leibniz in 1710: "Theodicy." The roots of that word are the two Greek words *theo* and *dike,* God and justice. Leibniz's word describes a system of natural theology aimed at seeking to vindicate divine justice in allowing evil to exist. Old Gottfried was a thoughtful soul, and his thought led him to the problem of how to reconcile his belief in God's infinite goodness and justice with the obvious existence of evil and with human freedom, both of which God allows. The result of all his cogitation was a long treatise titled *Theodicy: Essays on the Goodness of God, the Freedom of Man and the Origin of Evil,* which solves the problem of how to justify God's rather odd ways. I suppose theoidiocy, great foolishness in the name of God, has been going on for centuries, and modern-day America is no exception.

A few years ago I was having lunch with a very bright actor. He had a Master's degree in drama from Marquette University, a Catholic school run by the Jesuits. The actor's claim to fame was not his brain nor his acting skill. He looked great with his shirt off—which is all that is needed to make it big in the shallow world of television. This hunk, whose animal charisma made him one of the hottest soap opera stars, was a strict vegetarian. I asked him why. His response: "When you eat the flesh of an animal that was killed in an act of violence, you absorb that karma." Sure. I could understand his being a vegetarian if he cited health reasons or if he simply stated that he deplored the killing of animals, but to base his diet on the unprovable theory of karma made no sense to me.

Private karma seems too simplistic; however, global karma, which is the collective karma of all who have lived and are living, is more realistic. As a society, we are no better than the worst individual. And in this so-called "enlightened age" in which we live, there are a lot of lousy people among us.

I once overheard another actor telling a crew member about his three-week-old son. It was a case of New Age parental boasting. "I think he's an older soul, I really do. There's something about him that's very aware for someone his age." Right. That or the kid has a problem they don't know about—like a diaper pin stuck up his ass, that would make him look very aware.

I recently heard a soap opera writer say that when her cat dies, she is not going to get another one. The reason: she had burned off her "cat karma." What the hell is "cat karma?" Tell me that you don't want another pet because you realize how they restrict your freedom, or that you no longer need the unquestioned affection of an animal, and I'll buy that; but not to get another cat because of some kind of karma having been burned off is utterly ridiculous. Even politicians are playing the karma game. Ed Koch, the Jewish ex-Mayor of New York City, claimed that, "Graffiti on the walls of trains or subway stations creates bad karma." Rational people seem to have little difficulty in embracing some rather irrational notions. The mind is easy to trick.

L.A. is a mecca for gurus and prophets promising to unlock the secrets of the metaphysical world. Some new-time religious leaders get messages channeled from nonphysical entities, and the mantra-loving Hollywood stars crave these transformational communications from outer space. Spiritual psychotherapy seminars are packed, and bookstores catering to the town's metaphysical hunger are doing a booming business.

Hang around the sound stages of any Hollywood studio and you'll hear people talking about "communicating telepathically," as if it were as easy as getting hooked up to AT&T. People visit "channelers" who help them—for a fat fee—chat with the spirits of their dead loved ones. Out here in Lalaland, "out of body" experiences are as common as a cold; and astral travel, ESP, and clairvoyance are as real as Hellman's mayonnaise.

I actually heard an older actress, a woman who has been a soap star for more than twenty-five years, tell how she communicated with her dead husband. I'm not making this up; nor did I read it in the *National Enquirer*. After he died, she believed his "spirit" would actually be "hanging out around his grave plot" for a short period of time. So, after his burial, she wasted no time in taking a potted plant out to the cemetery, where she left it overnight. She believed that the plant would "absorb his aura and spiritual intelligence." The next day she returned to the grave, retrieved the plant, and brought it home, where it now serves as a consultant to her on a wide range of issues.

How, you may ask, does the plant "communicate" with her? Well, in the morning, before she left the house, she would ask the plant a question or leave a decision she was facing with the plant, and when she came home, if the plant's leaves were open, the answer was "yes," and, if they were closed, the answer was "no." This highly regarded actress, who has millions of loyal fans, actually believed she had her husband back in the form of a potted plant. She referred to the plant as "him." And the flesh became tulips and dwelt among us.

I've known some actresses with the intelligence of a potted plant, but this is the first one I've ever met who actually communicated with one. All jokes aside, the woman was very sincere; she really believed she was close to God. Like I said, the mind is very easy to trick—in fact, I think it enjoys being tricked.

Me, I have a hunch that I invented the wheel, but unfortunately I didn't think to make it round, a fact that destined me to eternal obscurity—perhaps for a time in a remote corner of India because I have an unexplainable lust for Indian food that is totally out of character for my otherwise bland culinary taste that shuns all forms of spicy foods. It all sounds like easy and explainable answers to the tough questions of life. A belief in reincarnation means there is no need for you to rush to perfection. Your life doesn't end at the gates of heaven or hell. Screw up, and you get another chance in another life to get it right. In fact, you get as many times around as you need to reach a state of "oneness" with the Almighty, after which you are freed from the tortuous cycle of living. I suppose Eastern philosophy offers a kinder, gentler approach to eternity than the one-shot deal offered by Christianity, because in its view ignorance and error only postpone an eternal victory, and nobody ultimately loses.

I'm not surprised by the fact that so many Americans are trading in their belief in a Day of Judgment for the doctrine of Reincarnation. I recently read a poll that reported 23 percent of Americans have jettisoned their Christian belief in the biblical resurrection, and replaced it with the Hindu doctrine of reincarnation. Yet, like the Christian faith, the religions of the Orient affirm that this life is not all there is and satisfy mankind's craving for ontological justice. But the Christian God is more personal, less compassionate, and far less patient than the Divine Ground of the Eastern religions; worse, He employs pitch-forked con artists who specialize in tricking you into straying from the straight and narrow path to heaven, and, once you wander off a bit, He jumps out from behind a burning bush and carts you off to jail, where you will serve an eternal sentence for your transgression. In one view God comes across uninterested; in the other, unfair. If God does exist, he/she is more than likely both unfair and uninterested. Reincarnation, like any other concept of immortality, has been invented by humans to satisfy human longings. I think. Why I like Indian food remains a mystery.

Oh, Kate, if I could just go to the beach and find a magic lamp inhabited by a genie willing to grant me one wish, I'm convinced I'd ask for certainty—that is to know what I know sans any doubts or nagging suspicions. Doubt seems to be my closest companion, but, damn, she can be a royal pain in the ass. Every word that issues forth from my mouth seems to trigger a diametrically opposing yet equally valid thought in my mind. On second thought, maybe I wouldn't ask for certainty—after all, the people who are the most certain are usually the biggest jerks around. I've both praised and damned the day I began to doubt. In the Lewis Carroll tale *Through the Looking Glass,* there is a story called *The Walrus and the Carpenter,* and it contains this line: " 'I doubt it,' said the carpenter, and shed a bitter tear." My doubt has caused me many a bitter tear.

Like I said, I'm mixed up, and it ain't fun. I suppose a few years of analysis would reveal that all my problems of dealing with reality can be traced back to my parents indoctrinating me with their warped ideas of life. Bullshit—the real reason, more than likely, stems from a childhood overdose of the Three Stooges, the real Trinity of my childhood.

Realizing that I might be running the risk of sounding like a scholar paid to examine life while avoiding living it, people who are my age were the first generation to be raised with television as a baby sitter . . . it was cheaper than the pigtailed teenager down the street, but in the long run what was the cost?

During my impressionable teenage years and subsequent awkward passage into early adulthood, I witnessed the following events through the probing eye of TV: the election of a president who ignited a spirit of Camelot and was snuffed out by a man who would in turn be shot to death live on television; race riots that exposed deep hatred in the hearts of man; warfare in far away rice fields that would claim the life of the kid next door and divide the nation into doves and hawks; a man jumping around on the moon; another assassin's bullet striking down another Kennedy headed for the White House; and, the most amazing of all, the New York Mets, the Three Stooges of baseball, winning the World Series. I watched it all on the boob tube, an invention that made reading passe. The cool medium delivered to my living room a hotbed of conflicting images and ideas that made the world both larger and smaller. As I passively watched, the infant industry grew quickly into a force that would elevate triviality to truth and turn superficiality into reality.

Television has changed us. People now seem to prefer to batter their minds with the flickering images of TV rather than beguile them with words from a book. Images are the new mode of communication—words are out, pictures are in. With the invention of the radio, the written word's supremacy in the mass communication of ideas was challenged by the spoken word. Families gathered around the radio to hear the news of the world and to be entertained. Before television, writers provided the words, and people's imaginations created the pictures.

TV babies perceive visual messages better than all the previous generations; they can "read" a picture and understand body language at a glance. Because of television, I received and processed information and formed ideas in a vastly different way than my parents did. In the sixties, I remember watching television's coverage of the Vietnam War with my parents. I watched the pictures, while my parents, who grew up with radio, listened to the commentary. I saw carnage and craziness; they heard how the war was honorable and winnable. The video image conflicted with the narrative, and that gave birth to another conflict: my parents supported the government's efforts in those faraway rice fields and I didn't.

Like it or not, language is now multidimensional. This is nowhere more evident than in political campaigns. In the past, politicians relied on ideas that were expressed in well-crafted speeches. John F. Kennedy's inaugural address springs to mind: "Ask not what your country can do for you, ask what you can do for your country." Still, I'd bet Kennedy's victory over Nixon in 1960 had more to do with his ability to perform on television (which magnified his good looks, warmth, and humor—all surface attributes) rather than to his ideas. Nonetheless, in contrast, Ronald W. Reagan summed up his 1984 Presidential campaign with an eighteen-minute music video that said nothing. In his 1988 successful run for the White House, George Bush communicated an attitude, not issues, through powerful images—his grandchildren, the flag, sludge in Boston Bay, and the release of black, convicted felons from jail. Even newspapers, long the home of words, are now relying on larger-than-ever pictures, graphs, and charts to tell the big story at a glance, because they must appeal to the MTV rock-video generation that thrives on being bombarded with fast-paced snippets of information. Kids today do their homework, watch TV, talk on the phone, and listen to their stereos all at the same time.

Oh, Dear Kate, the sad truth is today we want everything, and we want it all at once. It wasn't always that way. Just a short generation ago people took things one at a time. My dad took the time to read lengthy articles in the *New York Times* or the *Wall Street Journal* from beginning to end. When it was time to eat, we ate. The radio and television were turned off and we all gathered around the table. We fed ourselves and met each other. It's much different today. We get little more than headlines from *USA Today,* a newspaper created and written by and for the TV generation. We eat when we can, and, thanks to individually pre-packaged frozen dinners, what we want, and with one or more TVs flickering in the background. (I know one couple who eats together every night, but the man has his dinner with Peter Jennings, while the woman has hers with Larry King.) On the table sits our cordless telephone equipped with a feature that lets us know that somebody else is calling while we are talking. How odd that with all the time-saving electronic gizmos at our disposal, we actually enjoy less leisure time than our parents did. Still, on the average, seven years of our lives are spent plopped down before a television set. What a colossal waste of time.

There is no denying it—television shaped my life and became my life—but more about that later. It's too early in the morning to write about television or philosophy, so let's turn to history—my early history. Make that my ancient history.

Christopher Ryan. It's a strange name, the Christopher part, that is; it means, as St. Anselm reminded me, Christ-bearer, in reference to the legend of St. Christopher, in which he supposedly carried a young boy across a turbulent river and later found out that the child was an apparition of Christ. It also suggests someone who bears or carries Christ within him. Quite an image to give a kid to live up to. But your grandparents were Catholic, very Catholic. So Catholic, in fact, that they went way beyond the once-a-week minimum of church attendance demanded by church law, a law written by men but whose violation was punishable by eternal damnation in accordance with divine justice. Mom and Pop went to Mass almost very day. Rosaries, novena devotions, Stations of the Cross, The Legion of Decency, holy water, votive candles, meatless Fridays, Lenten fasts, indulgences, incense, Latin, and confession form as vivid a memory of my childhood as a towering home run by Mickey Mantle or a circus catch by Willie Mays. The Saints were my heroes, the ballplayers a mere diversion. Religion was a part of my life before I took my first breath, and I suppose it will be on my mind during my last—of course, if I'm hit by a truck I might just be thinking about something else . . . like women.

My parents didn't live long enough to see what havoc their Catholicism created in my life. They thought their faith would be my ticket to heaven. Didn't really work out that way; it turned out to be an express ride to hell—hell on earth, which, I think, is where hell is.

Heaven and hell—that's what it's all about. Life I mean. If Helen and Ralph hadn't checked out early, I'm sure their hearing me say, "Listen, I don't believe in heaven or hell," on a television talk show last year would have been a life-threatening experience for them. Their dream of my becoming a missionary priest that they nurtured in my tender and impressionable spirit not only withered in the hardened soil of life, but worse, I ended up writing a rather antireligious book—a scathing attack primarily aimed at TV preachers called *Profits of Heaven*. I compounded my crime of throwing stones at the glass church of religion by talking about it on television.

My pious mother died about a dozen years ago, when I was in my late twenties and you were not yet a year old. My father was laid to rest next to her a few years later. At least she beat him at something. Their deaths were my first adult experience of separation. True, I wasn't alone, but they were gone, the roots of my life were severed, and I felt incomplete, less whole.

But I'm getting ahead of myself—I usually do! I can't help it, I'm hyper. I talk too fast. I eat too fast. I crave action and excitement. I'm impatient and hate waiting—which is why I don't have time for baked potatoes anymore, I nuke them in the microwave for seven and a half minutes on high. (Even at that speed, I get annoyed because it's not fast enough.) We are surrounded by time-saving devices, still we don't have time for anything—least of all, thinking.

As a true child of a fast-paced generation fed on fast foods, there is for me only one sin—boredom. Maybe that's my problem. What is boredom? Is it the inability to live in the present moment? If so, then perhaps boredom doesn't need to be overcome; perhaps it needs to be confronted. My mind has always been restless, my thoughts, scattered. Nothing holds my interest for very long; much is started, little finished. I have longed for stillness, yet filled my days with frivolous activities. My life seems little more than a series of crises—real ones and ones I created out of boredom. I wish I had taken more time to think, really think—think for myself, and not have been so influenced by the thoughts of others. At worst, boredom is a venial sin; however, avoiding boredom is a mortal sin. OK, before I bore you, let's rewind the tape and go back to my beginning.

In the beginning was the word—oops, wrong book! My beginning began somewhat later, the year was 1947, the month was March, and the weather was as stormy as my life would be. If I could remember being a fetus, I imagine that I would recall not wanting to come out. It must have been nice in there. I was warm, safe, fed. I grew and was comforted by the steady beat of my mother's heart. Today, as my mind pulls into focus a picture of my mother, I can see the worry on her face. Would the mounting snowstorm jeopardize her trip to the hospital? Would I be a healthy baby? As I saw her do so many times during my life, I'm sure that she turned to her faith for strength, endurance, and comfort during the final days of her pregnancy.

Your grandmother knew nothing of theology; she knew only prayer. This gentle, caring, compassionate woman didn't seem to harbor any unasked questions; quiet acceptance (of both Church doctrine and her husband's unquestioned authority) was her strong suit. Her faith in the Catholic Church, its Popes, and priests was implicit. She fully accepted the notion that as a woman and wife she must submit to the divinely appointed headship of her husband. (The superstition of male superiority led Thomas Aquinas to believe men were more rational than women, and it turned marriage into a relationship of master and slave instead of a partnership between equals. As Bertrand Russell pointed out, the belief in the superiority of males created a situation where the only interesting and adventurous women were social outcasts because all the respectable women were dull and boring. I find it interesting that in the New Testament, Mary Magdalene is discredited as a prostitute, as a woman who violated the most fundamental androcratic law that she should be the sexual chattel of her husband or master, and that in John 8:3–11, women are still regularly stoned to death for violating their husband's sexual property rights by committing adultery.)

My mother accepted literally the Immaculate Conception, the forgiveness of sins, and the transubstantiation on the altar. She even believed that all priests and nuns were chaste and as pure as mountain spring water, and she was untroubled by the fact that the Church established its priestly system upon the suppression of one of the deepest instincts of human nature. You needed only to be around her for a short time to learn that to her God was a blazing reality. Your grandmother was sweet and dreamy, but she didn't have a clue how life was organized. Yet she was quick to forget the pain of the past and contemplate the joys of the present, or, those wanting, the possibilities of the future. She knew nothing of the humming world of commerce; she was a housewife and mother by choice— even though she probably had no choice.

I waited, the storm ended, and, after offering prayers to St. Christopher asking him to grant us safe passage over the snow-covered streets, your grandmother and I made it to the hospital for my birth. I'm sure God got the credit. I got circumcised. I can't remember being born. If I could, I should imagine that it would have been horrible beyond belief. Leaving the safety of my nine-month home, squeezing my way through a bloody canal, being handled by a masked stranger, having my lifeline cut, and being wrapped in cloth and left alone in a bassinet—talk about a lousy day. Still, I bet everyone else was very pleased.

In a pious act of gratitude for answering her prayers for a safe trip to the hospital, my mother named me after St. Christopher. St. Christopher was the patron saint of travelers, and a plastic statue of the saint, which had a magnet attached to its base, always stood guard on the dashboard of our car. I remember once sitting in the front seat of the car staring at the statue, which always faced the passengers, and suddenly saying, "Hey, if St. Christopher is supposed to protect us, don't you think he should be facing the road so he can see where we are going?" My father smiled at me and said, "You got a good point Chris." With that, I turned the plastic saint around so that he faced the windshield, and from that day on we saw only St. Christopher's back. And we never had an accident.

Home from the hospital only a week, my first outing into the world was a trip to Church. For my parents, this Church excursion was not a matter of ritual, nor was it merely a social occasion. It was serious, it was urgent. You see, I was born a sinner. I had a black mark on my soul. I was in need of a spiritual cleansing. About seventeen centuries ago, St Augustine, who went from a sinner and heretic to bishop and saint, wrote, "Do not believe, do not say, do not teach that infants who died before being baptized can attain to forgiveness of original sins—not if you wish to be Catholic." Like I said, your grandparents were Catholic, very Catholic.

St. Augustine, who connected the transmission of original sin with the sexual pleasure of intercourse, was obsessed with the cruel notion that unbaptized infants would be damned to an eternity in hell. Bishop Julian of Eclanum, a contemporary of St. Augustine's, called Augustine's God "a persecutor of infants, who throws infant babies into the eternal fire." Bishop Julian wrote, "Augustine, you are far removed from religious feelings, from civilized thinking, indeed from healthy common sense, if you think that your God is capable of committing crimes against justice that are scarcely imaginable even for the barbarians."

The clear-thinking Julian of Eclanum was considered a great heretic, and the inhuman St. Augustine became the determining spiritual force of the Church. Augustine's twisted logic eventually led to a practice that denied dead pregnant women from being laid out in church because her unborn child was not baptized. During the twelfth century in France, before a dead pregnant woman could be buried in a consecrated cemetery, her unborn child had to be cut out of her body and buried outside the cemetery.

Over time, the Church softened its doctrine on the damnation of unbaptized infants, who are now sent to limbo, where they experience natural happiness though being denied union with God in heaven. Still, parents sin mortally if they neglect to have their children baptized as soon as possible. I'm sure my parents never heard of Julian of Eclanum, and I'm equally sure they had no problem with St. Augustine's equating pleasure with perdition. Good Catholics don't question Church teachings, no matter how ghastly they are.

As good Catholics, my father and mother fully believed that if I should die before a priest had sprinkled water on me and said a few magical words, I would be destined to spend all of eternity in a cold, sad place called limbo, a state that floated between heaven and hell and was populated by the unforgiven souls of babies whose parents failed to have them baptized. So they wasted little time before bundling me up and carrying me off to Church. I suppose that I had not yet opened my eyes for the first time or had a chance to see the world around me. No matter, I was safe, and on the road to heaven—or at least not doomed to limbo.

My parents believed there was refuge in religion; worse, they were convinced that the least neglect or infraction of such forms and ceremonies as baptism that were ordered by the Holy Roman Church was all it took to evoke the disfavor and wrath of the one true God. They believed St. Augustine's claim that salvation could not be found outside of the Catholic Church. They bought, lock, stock, and barrel, the pitch of the black-robed, white-collared sacrament and indulgence salesmen, who were peddlers of little more than unverifiable dogma and just plain lies. I'm sure they never questioned the harshness of the creed that sent innocent, unbaptized babies to the dungeon of limbo because some guy named Adam got hoodwinked into eating an apple centuries ago. Is this divine justice?

My parents never realized that it was sheer folly for them to throw away their reason in order to save their souls. They never saw Church dogma as inflexible and unforgiving, never saw it as opinion presented in the guise of absolute truth; they never felt the Church's teachings were cold and severe. No doubts, no questions—just passive acceptance, blind faith in Papal authority. (I suppose their submissiveness can be attributed to a genuine fear of hell—after all, without fear, submissiveness of any kind could not exist.) Yet for me, the son they hoped to see become an emissary of Christ on earth, the notion that faith in Christ will be rewarded by an eternity of bliss, while a reliance on reason, observation, and experience will merit everlasting pain is insane.

I was taught to view the world in black and white. But the world is full of color, full of shadings. The Church fully understood that doubt leaves room for interpretation. And for the Church to remain universal, interpretation must be left to one man, the Pope. Individual interpretation of the gospels and faith would lead to chaos. Neither the Church nor my parents could handle chaos.

It seemed to me that the Church, under alleged divine guidance, legislated rules that weren't any better than the man-made rules of the government, which frequently displayed more compassion and understanding than the Church. The God of the Old Testament was alive and well and living in the Vatican. The Old Testament presents a capricious God who endorsed the punishment of the innocent for the sins of the guilty, as when Saul's two sons and five grandsons were killed because Saul slaughtered the Gibonites. God violated two central principles of justice, namely, that only the guilty should be punished, and the punishment should fit the crime. In the Old Testament, God frequently assigned the death penalty for fairly harmless actions. God administered excessive and misplaced punishment on numerous occasions, for such crimes as adultery, violating the Sabbath, not properly worshipping Him, and not believing in Him. (The Church said that failure to go to confession at least once during a year was a mortal sin, which, if unrepented, could land me in hell for all eternity.) God even condoned excessively harsh treatment of children, who were put to death for laughing at a bald man, being overly rebellious, and cursing their parents. God encouraged the slaughter of countless Gentiles, including women and children. God led us to believe that animal sacrifice could purge people of their sins. God had no problem using deceptive tactics and a variety of famines and plagues to destroy those who stood in the way of His chosen people. The God of the Old Testament is a cruel and vengeful god. Like the pagan gods, the unpredictable, swift-to-anger God of the Bible has to be feared and appeased by sacrifices, constant worship, and petitioning.

I had little interest in the legalities of the Church. I was fascinated by mysticism, the "terra incognita" of the psychic phenomena. I tried to develop a rich meditative inner life, but my attempts left me with an incapacity to act, and I was turning into a religious vegetable. Catholicism was little more than a psychological safety net for the guilt-atonement mentality, both relieving it and reinforcing it. All religions offer basically the same thing: guilt with different holy days.

The religious quest for the ineffable within yourself or in the transcendent must end in failure, for it is not to be found in the profane life of the modern, desacralized inner life. I doubt even St. Teresa of Avila, the great mystic from the Middle Ages, could have maintained her form of spirituality if she had been exposed to the diversity of the late twentieth-century America. The fixity of tradition, of custom, of language insured her a life untroubled by spiritual unrest and doubt. The variety of modern life confuses the poet and the saint and drives the philosopher into the cold arms of reason.

The Church and my parents spoke of morality, of knowledge, and of hope. I saw none. Must the desperately paradoxical situation I confront project a nihilistic acquiescence to meaninglessness? "Whatever we dream, we can achieve" is the motto of the day. Artistically, perhaps; existentially, by no means. We dream of the absolute, but we cannot achieve it; we speak of God, but we cannot believe in him. In his play *The Potting Shed,* Graham Greene, the great English writer who was Catholic, wrote, "When you aren't sure, you are alive." I'm not sure and barely alive.

My parents were in bondage to the traditional precepts of the Church. I suppose we are all in bondage to something, whether we are bound in the chains of logic, reason, religion, family, work, or a relationship. Everyone is in bondage. Eventually, I rejected the Catholic tradition my parents so cherished, because I came to view tradition as a poor substitute for reason.

I don't know what I did after baptism. Those early days are fuzzy and hard to pull into focus; they had an airy translucency to them. I can't recall any difficulties or traumatic events, no trials or tribulations come to mind. Sickness and death had no meaning to me. The little house that was home was as warm and as nourishing as the womb from which I had emerged. All was peaceful, all was calm; those first few years were the silent night of my life. I knew nothing of sin or hate; my body had not yet become a prison cell for my soul. I heard from sources more reliable than my memory that I neither talked nor cried very much. I don't remember learning how to walk or how to use the toilet. I guess I just hung out for four or five years and played with Lincoln Logs and other nonelectronic toys until I got old enough to be handed over to the nuns who ran the Catholic school.

Why, with money in short supply, would my parents elect to send us to a costly Catholic school instead of the free public school? Certainly not because they thought we would receive a better education. After all, the public school dispensed a fairly liberal and honest dose of information concerning life and the world in which we live. In contrast, the Catholic school, concerned more with preparing us for the next life, placed religion above science and faith above logic. And no wonder, because in the realms of science and logic, a young mind might encounter strange facts and paradoxes that might endanger their belief in God and the Pope and also might threaten the survival of a stultifying medievalism that they represent.

History also posed a threat to faith, because even the slightest familiarity with history would have destroyed our image of the Church as timeless and unchanging. Of course, the Church of other ages would have been unrecognizable to most Catholics. Celibate priests, regular confession, and Latin weren't always part of the faith. We were kept in the dark about the history of our own religion and taught nothing about the essentials of other faiths. The nuns were not educators, they were painters. On the canvas of Church history that accurately portrayed the Church's vile record of brutality and slaughter, the nuns painted a much different portrait, a portrait that was rich in sanctity and holiness. In their revisionist painting, there was no hint of carnality or corruption; their only focus was mysticism and saintliness. Under the layers of their freshly painted lies was the historical truth, now hidden from our young eyes.

I never heard about Pope Innocent III, a man who was anything but innocent. He was guilty of launching a savage persecution in 1209 in which heretics were massacred wholesale for espousing the heresy that this world was created by Satan, and that peace and happiness are to be found only in the next world, the creation of God. Innocent III found that piece of theological speculation (known as Albigensism) a bit too pessimistic for his tastes—though it is far less pessimistic than St. Augustine's earlier doctrine that most of the human race are damned irrevocably. It took awhile, nearly a hundred years, for the Church to exterminate this anticlerical heresy, but, thanks to holy persistence, it was eliminated, along with all the heretics who followed it.

There is one very haunting line spoken by the French priest Amalric Arnaud, the Abbot of Citeaux, that reveals just how brutal these crusades to eliminate heresy were. During the sack of Beziers in 1209, a soldier asked Arnaud, a leader in the crusades against the Albigensians, how they were to distinguish between Catholics and heretics. His answer: "Tuez-les tous, Dieu reconnaitra les siens"— "Kill them all, God will know his own." Horrifying words spoken by a servant of God.

In 1252, another not-so-innocent pope, Pope Innocent IV, authorized the use of torture in the process of interrogating suspected infidels. Popes Clement VII and Paul V declared that the faithful should inform the Inquisitor of the Faith of anybody who spread the "lie" that kissing, touching, and embracing for the sake of sexual pleasure was not a grievous sin.

Salvation was not as clear-cut as I was taught. There never was a universally agreed upon path to heaven within Christianity. In A.D. 324, Constantine, the first Christian emperor, gathered the Church leaders together in order to put an end to the confusion caused by the existence of so many different "theories" growing in the garden of Christianity. The meeting produced the "Apostles' Creed" and decreed that those who did not support the document were to be banished to the darkest and remotest regions of the earth. In the name of unity, existing Christian documents that conflicted with the newly emerged truth of the "Apostles' Creed" were destroyed. Pagan cults were no longer tolerated, and those who subscribed to non-Christian beliefs were executed. Even Christians who had different ideas about Jesus and what he taught were eventually eliminated.

Roman Christianity became powerful and universal. Still, rival documents were hidden and survived, only recently surfacing. These documents cast serious doubts about the historical facts about Jesus that were decreed to be true by the Nicean Council chaired by Constantine. The time between Jesus' putative crucifixion at the hands of the Roman Empire and his confirmation as cocreator and coruler of the universe by a Roman emperor, a period of nearly three hundred years, has been a dark, mysterious fog in history.

In A.D. 1095, Pope Urban II launched the first crusade to "recover" Jerusalem, which had fallen into the hands of those heathens from hell, the Turks. On November 26 of that year, Pope Urban II gave a rousing speech before the Council of Clermont, in which he said, "Wherefore, I pray and exhort, nay not I, but the Lord prays and exhorts you, as heralds of Christ, by frequent exhortation, to urge men of all ranks, knights, and foot soldiers, rich and poor, to hasten to exterminate this vile race from the lands of our brethren, and to bear timely aid to the worshippers of Christ." He also proclaimed that those who lost their lives on this holy rescue mission would automatically have their sins remitted in the hour of their death, thereby gaining quick entrance into heaven.

I wonder if Urban's top assistant was known as "Suburban." It's funny— not that line—but nearly a thousand years later, the "pope" of the Muslim world, the Ayatollah Khomeini, led his followers into a holy war with the same promise of instant entrance into heaven as a reward for fighting and dying for Allah. Spiritual bigotry is still alive and well; but, hatred, whether wrapped in white sheets or scriptures, is still hatred.

Down through the ages, religion has spoken the language of condemnation. Why, why, in the name of God, why?

How many people were tortured and killed by the Church because of differing spiritual points of view is impossible to tell. During the course of the Inquisition, it is estimated that in Spain alone more than 31,000 persons were burned for their non-Catholic beliefs, and more than 290,000 were condemned to harsh punishments less severe than death. (At its outset, the Inquisition operated mainly in France, Germany, and Italy. It was not extended to Spain until the fifteenth century, but the first Spanish Inquisitor-General, a guy named Torquemada, became so notorious for his atrocities that the Inquisition in general came to be referred to as the Spanish Inquisition.) Why is there no moral outrage over this? Why has the world forgotten, when these crimes seem more outrageous than those committed just this century during the Nazi holocaust? The Germans exterminated the Jews in secret. But the sadistic tortures of the Inquisition were carried out in public and watched by gloating crowds as a form of entertainment. St. Thomas Aquinas, who the nuns called the "angelic doctor," claimed that the happiness of the blessed in heaven would be enhanced by their unrestricted view of the agonies of the damned in hell. What a sadistic bastard.

Oh daughter, can you see how the obscene doctrine of hell gave the Holy Roman Catholic Church a rational defense for the worst cruelties of the Inquisition? They were inflicting a few hours or days of torture in order to induce a heretic to recant and save him or her from everlasting torture in the life to come. They were doing the heretics a favor! Jesus, quick get the matches! Hey, and if the poor misguided soul should die in his or her error, the suffering endured before his or her death became simply a very brief preview of the torments they would endure for all eternity. Non-Catholics today are surprised to hear that the Catholic Church still teaches a literal belief in the fires of hell. In September of 1971, Pope Paul VI said, "Hell is a grim reality even though man seems to be losing sight of the frightful danger of eternal doom. . . ."

As a kid, I was taught that hell is a place where devils and such human beings who die in enmity with God suffer torments forever. If an inquisitive child should ask, "If God knew that certain souls would be damned to hell, why did He create them?" the answer would be something along these lines: "We have already proved that hell is a fact. It is part of the plan of an infinitely wise, good, and powerful God. Therefore, it must be the best for His purposes. Who are we to dictate to Him? If we find it hard to reconcile certain facts, we must blame our limited knowledge, not God's infinite wisdom." And it wasn't even possible to pray for those poor souls who were suffering in hell, because St. Thomas Aquinas wrote: "The damned in hell are outside the bond of charity. . . ." I wonder now how Christianity ever became known as the religion of love. Only through its own propaganda, I guess.

When I close my eyes and think back to my Catholic school days and try to recapture the flavor of the spirituality, I see an image of Jesus at the Last Supper. The Son of God has just broken in half a loaf of bread. He holds a piece in each hand, which he extends toward the apostles. He says, "Take, eat . . . this is my Body." I see myself reverently kneeling in Church, my entire attention focused on the priest, as he bends over the small host he is holding in his hands and whispers the words, *"Hoc est Corpus Meum"*—Latin for the very words Jesus spoke centuries ago. Words that have traveled down nearly two thousand years in an unbroken chain (known as the Apostolic Succession) to the Church where I was kneeling, the One True Church of Jesus Christ.

The priest, after saying those powerful words, would genuflect in front of the bread that was transformed in substance, if not appearance, into the body of our Savior. He stood and reverently lifted the consecrated Host heavenward, pausing as his arms reached full extention. The altar boy vigorously rang his bell, announcing to all that Christ once again was being offered up for the forgiveness of our sins and the redemption of our souls.

What magic! What power! What a hold this sacred moment had on my mind and imagination. All I ever wanted to do was to say those words. Little did I know how the doctrine of the real presence, which claimed the bread was no longer bread but the very substance of Christ, split England and Ireland in half, just as Christ did to the bread, and caused centuries of division and hatred within the hearts of English and Irish Protestants and Catholics. For Protestants, communion (another name for the Eucharistic Feast) was a commemoration of the Last Supper; for Catholics, it was an actual recreation. To this day precious blood is being spilled in the streets of Ireland over an issue that is ludicrous beyond belief.

Now, with my eyes open, I no longer see a raised Host, the Prince of Peace, being offered for me. No, I see violence and hatred. And what unspeakable violence. I laugh when I hear people, mostly Christians, decry violence on television and in the movies. Listen, I firmly believe the skyrocketing body count on both the big and small screen is getting out of hand. This summer's big money makers are a funeral director's dream come true: *Die Hard 2*—264 people killed; *Robocop 2*—81 people killed; *Total Recall*—74 people killed; *Another 48 Hours*—20 people killed. Still, all this mayhem is child's play compared to the violence perpetrated in the name of religion from the thirteenth to the eighteenth century. As late as 1766, just six years before the Inquisition was abolished in France, a young man, the Chevalier de la Barre, had his tongue ripped out of his mouth and his ears cut off, and he was then hanged. His crime: singing blasphemous songs.

A favorite pastime in the good old medieval days was attending an *auto-da-fe*. That literally means an "act of faith," a cynically euphemistic term for mass burnings at the stake. In Spain, these little miniholocausts were presented as special added attractions at state celebrations such as royal weddings or the birth of an heir to the thone. When young King Charles II of Spain married the French Princess Marie Louise of Orleans in 1680 in Madrid, a spectacular auto-da-fe was arranged in honor of the newlyweds. Eighty-six Jews were burned as the King, his bride and court, and the clergy of Madrid looked on in glee. Those who failed to attend the holocaust incurred the risk of being tainted as heretics. In fact, if an onlooker failed to express enthusiasm for burnings they ran a similiar risk for appearing to be sympathtic to the roasting Jews.

Dear Kate, I hope you don't mind this short, nonpersonal historical sidetrack. It's just that it is part of my inner turmoil and anger . . . more evidence for the pointlessness of life. Anyway, it seems to me that most people today have little understanding of religion's negative impact on humanity. The activities of the Catholic Church during the Inquisition could be compared with the extermination policies of the Nazis; in fact, they could even be considered more brazenly barbaric. The Nazis, behind barbed wire fences, secretly and quickly gassed their victims, then burned their bodies. The Christians took their victims to the public square, and openly and slowly tortured them, and then burned them alive—in front of cheering audiences of kings and clerics. The papacy has never renounced the Church's sins of the past. The Catholic Church, even to this day, believing as it does that it is the One True Church, divinely guaranteed against error, is inevitably and basically intolerant. Pope Leo XIII, in 1885, said, "The equal toleration of all religions . . . is the same as atheism."

I was taught to see the Church as a mother, as my spiritual mother. We referred to Her as The Holy Mother Church. We believed St. Augustine's postulation, "He cannot have God for his father who refuses to have the Church for his mother." Dear daughter, can you begin to understand the pain I experienced as my love for my mother the Church slowly turned to hatred? Hating your mother is hard and the most painful thing a person can do. The sad thing is that somewhere deep in my subconscious, I still want to be a priest, still want to save people, still want to say Mass. Yet, here I am alone, confused, rejected, hurting—throwing rocks at the stained glass windows of my childhood.

You see, dear Kate, I had lost the object of my belief, but not the habit of belief. I needed something new to believe in, but, sadly, I never found anything.

Listen, kiddo, I need to take a little break from this, I've really managed to upset myself.

Thursday, July 12—11:05 A.M.

OK, back to my early history and Catholic education. But first, this brief warning from Marcel Proust: "What intellect restores to us under the name of the past, is not the past."

My childhood was governed by a fixed canonical code administered by my father, the priests, and the nuns. This code was developed during an age I could not know or understand; it was rooted in the Old World, and in an even older religion. The code knew what to expect of a young man from a good family and proper upbringing. It expected conformity and faithfulness.

I confounded those expectations. God, did I ever!

I did not plan a rebellion against the code. It just happened. I would not have deliberately chosen to rebel. I was far too passive for rebellion. In truth, I miss those tender days of unquestioning faith and unsoiled motives. The illusion of safety offered by the code gave birth to a warmth of heart and an unconscious generosity. Like the Latin Mass, the days had order and precision; they were lived beyond logic and above reason.

No, I didn't plan to rebel. It just happened. Paradise was not lost; it was outgrown. Actually, I'm sure those days were hardly set in paradise, because the code demanded abnegation of important human needs and desires. Paradise could not be paradise if it included such deadly, orthodox dogmas as original sin, the existence of a personal God, the purposiveness of human life, and the need for regarding your life on earth as preparation for a refined spiritual life after death. There is no room in paradise for such trash. Paradise is not lost, it is not outgrown; it is just a myth. The goal of my parents, the priests, and the nuns was to perpetuate the myth through the propagation of the faith.

All that was expected of me was conformity and faithfulness. Thanks to a little devil named Doubt, it turned out to be more than I could deliver. Much more. The Church fully understood that doubt leaves room for interpretation. And for the Church to remain universal, interpretation must be left to one man, the Pope. Individual interpretation of the gospels and faith would lead to chaos.

Anything, including logic and history, that could wake the sleeping devil of doubt was considered dangerous. The Roman Catholic Church demanded total acceptance (no picking and choosing allowed) of its creed and dogma, and discouraged us from investigating matters of faith diligently in our own lives through meditation, study, and service. Intellectual curiosity became a near occasion of sin, and doubt became an impure thought—together they were stepping stones to sin that must be ignored, avoided, or destroyed. There was a French Jurist and Philosopher named Baron Montesquien, who died in 1755, and I think he summed up best the Church's attitude toward education: "Churchmen are interested in keeping the people ignorant. I call piety a malady of the heart. The false notion of miracles comes of our vanity, which makes us believe we are important enough for the Supreme Being to upset Nature on our behalf."

Kate, what the Church knew, and I didn't, was that we inquire only when we doubt. If my religious beliefs are a comfort to me—no matter how ludicrous they may be—then my mind will be at rest regarding the matter involved in those beliefs, and it will cease to inquire about them. What I've discovered is that even if you begin to have doubts and slowly commence an inquiry into the area of those doubts, that inquiry will be held back by an emotional drag holding onto the very belief and faith in question. Desire to want to believe causes an inaccurate weighing of evidence. Most of us want to justify and strengthen the beliefs we grew up with, and rarely do we seek to find out whether those beliefs are the most reasonable ones for us to hold. But I'm getting way ahead of myself again.

In Catholic school, I would learn that the Holy Ghost (more recently referred to as the Holy Spirit), the third in the Trinity of persons who make one God, inspired men to write the Bible. Yet the Holy Ghost, it seems, never heard of the Western Hemisphere, and didn't know that the earth was round, which is odd considering that he helped make it himself. It took the telescope, a creation of man, to destroy the biblical firmament, a vault in the sky that houses heaven, and render the Ascension of Christ and the Assumption of Mary an absurdity.

But science isn't necessary to refute the Church's claim that the Bible was the inspired word of God; plain old common sense will do fine. The Bible is a miasma of myths. It is merely a collection of words, and words, like the telescope, are the creation of man. It took more than twenty thousand years—give or take a few months—for evolution to develop writing as we know it. The first crude phonetic alphabet is less than five thousand years old. Writing's entire development is the handiwork of man. God did not invent the alphabet, but he should have, because we now have fifty or more alphabets instead of one. Why would a smart God allow his message of salvation to be disseminated through such a multiplicity of differing languages and cultures, greatly increasing the odds of error and misinterpretation?

Apparently God dictated sacred words to the Jews, the Christians, and the Muslims—each of them cranking out inspired Bibles. Each of them with a different message. If there is only one inspired Bible, then all the others must be frauds. Why should we have all this confusion? Why doesn't God straighten this biblical mess out so we can make sense of what He is trying to tell us? The answer seems simple: either there is no One out there, or there is some One out there, but He has nothing to say. Either way, we should be free and not enslaved by religion.

"How do we know the Bible is true?" some kids asked the nuns. "Because the Bible says it is" was the response. But I didn't really ask any tough questions back then, my doubts were few and minor. I was caught up in the mysticism of the faith. I wanted to believe. I did believe.

After twelve years of Catholic schooling, I had not a glimmer of true history or logic; I heard virtually nothing of Galileo, Charles Darwin, T. H. Huxley, Robert Ingersoll, Giordano Bruno, Baruch Spinoza, Voltaire, Denis Diderot, Thomas Paine, Friedrich von Humboldt, Immanuel Kant, Baron d'Holbach, Johannes Kepler, René Descartes, and an entire army of distinguished students of life who fought and meditated on behalf of reality. A dozen years of grade and high school had not awakened me to the importance of facts. I was left poorly equipped to offer my best to the times in which I lived. My education was draped in dogmatic trumpery. But hey, what the hell—I did know Latin. No, a better education was not what motivated my parents to spend their hard-earned money so we could go to a Catholic school. We were turned over to the nuns, so they could turn us into good Catholics—beyond that, nothing else really mattered. The Catholic grammar school I attended was really a stultification center.

The nuns! More than my parents, more than my brothers and sisters, more than society, more than even television, more than anything else—the nuns molded me, shaped me, and formed me. The nuns colored my thoughts and made me religious. The good sisters introduced me to the wacky world of the supernatural.

Actually, I had my first brush with the supernatural a few years before I started school, and the event forms my first conscious memory. The occasion was the death of my grandfather. I really don't remember much about him, and I suppose the only reason I can recall his death is because it was my introduction to mortality, the realization that life ends. Or so it seemed. The fact that Gramps looked dead—was dead—was just an illusion. Or so I was told. "Don't be sad Chris. You'll see Grandpa again. He is still living, only now he is living in heaven; and, someday you will see him there." He took a trip and didn't bother to take his body—that was the basic message that my parents wanted me to swallow. And I did.

Gramps's death was a curiosity in another way also. I knew that people died, even though no one I personally knew ever had; but I thought of death as accidental. People were killed in car accidents, or got shot by bad guys, or died in wars—things like that. That's why we had to be careful crossing the street—you didn't want to get killed by accident. But gramps didn't have an accident, and nobody shot him either—he just wore out, he just stopped living. He died, they said, of "old age." Death, it seemed, was a natural end to life. Accidents weren't natural; they were accidents—mistakes. Gramps's death was natural, no mistakes involved. That was scary. Someday, Mom and Dad will wear out too. Someday, I'll wear out.

The "nevermores" are the most insufferable and terrible part of the loss of someone you love. Nevermore to see their face and smile, to hear their voice and laughter, to feel their warmth and comfort. Nevermore. The "nevermores" of the survivors in the death of a loved one are not really "nevermores" for the believers in an afterlife, they are merely "until later." I believed I would see my grandfather again, that I'd once again sit on his lap, and he'd once again give me a little sip of his wine.

Still, I had this secret little doubt, which I hid from everyone, everyone but Herbie that is. Herbie was a skinny little kid who lived down the block. I wasn't real close friends with him, but he was important when my real friends and I needed one more kid in order to choose up sides for a game of slapball. My parents said his parents were strange—they didn't go to church. In fact, Herbie's father didn't believe in God—that made him more than strange; it made him an absolute rarity. Still, I liked Herbie's dad. He was a butcher, a burly man with a broad smile. (Now that I think of it, he didn't seem to suffer any ill-effects from the bad karma involved with cutting up cows and chickens. Unless, you count the time he chopped off the top of his index finger on his left hand in a meat grinder.) He had an infectious sense of humor and never ran out of fresh jokes to tell.

But more than make me laugh, Herbie's dad made me think. He was always throwing puzzling points of view my way. Like the day he walked up to me and said, "Chris, I hear you're praying for a new baseball glove." I felt embarrassed and sheepishly nodded yes. He flashed a gentle, knowing smile and said, "I think you're taking the wrong approach. Why not steal a glove and pray for forgiveness." I laughed, but later I realized that God had to answer a plea for forgiveness, but a request for a baseball glove sounded like something He could easily ignore—especially considering the billions of requests He gets for real important stuff. I didn't steal a glove, but I stopped praying for one.

Herbie's dad may not have believed in God, but he understood theology. He knew that religion was a system invented for the purpose of reconciling contradictions by the aid of mysteries. He knew all religious principles were imaginary and that religion was not necessary because it was unitelligible.

One day while I was sitting in his backyard waiting for Herbie to come out, an annoying fly began circling my head. As I took wild swats at it, Herbie's dad asked a strange question. "Did an intelligent life form invent the fly? If so, why?" Why indeed. In an offhanded way he made me think about things, to probe the unnoticed goings-on right before my eyes. He was real in a way I didn't fully understand back then. Today, I'd call him genuine, without a phony bone in his body, and intellectually honest. Anyway, Herbie said that his dad told him that when a person was alive he wasn't dead, and when he was dead he wasn't alive. That made sense to Herbie. And to me.

Yet the message I was getting at home was that Gramps was both dead and alive. My first puzzle. How ironic that my first real memory was a question. If Grandpa was happy and in a better place, why was every one sad, crying? It didn't seem to add up, but in time the nuns would teach me the spiritual mathematics involved. Now, as I think back on those days and my early doubts, my mind flashes these words written by Thomas Paine, one of the intellectual heroes of our nation and the master mind behind the Declaration of Independence: "Any system of religion that shocks the mind of a child cannot be a true system." Christianity is more shocking than sacred—but not to the nuns.

The nuns taught me everything I needed to know to get through this life and gain entrance into an eternal life spent in the splendor of heaven, where I would undoubtedly meet my grandfather—unless he had screwed up down here and landed in hell for being too human. The nuns offered a womb-to-tomb plan with an eternal lifetime guarantee. Nuns might look gentle, devout, prayerful, and pure, but—they really were tough, very tough. The nuns could out "hell, fire and brimstone" even Jerry Falwell; in fact, Falwell is a moderate, a religious pussycat, compared to the nuns of my youth. The nuns were always quick to flash an angelic smile, but funny they were not. Life—and the afterlife—for them was serious business.

But not as serious as it was back in the year 1418, when the Pope gathered together all the Cardinals from around the world for the Second Council of Constance. One of the ordinances that this august assemblage of holy men had written into church law stated that: "If any cleric or monk speaks jocular words, such as provoke laughter, let him be anathema." Fun guys, regular party animals. When we use the word "anathema," we apply it to a thing or person who is greatly detested. But back in the 1400s, the word carried an even harsher meaning; it implied a formal curse or condemnation excommunicating a person from the Church. Imagine, being cursed and damned for causing someone to laugh. The nuns 540 years later in Queens, New York, could never be accused of provoking laughter.

A current-day Prince of the Church, His Eminence John Cardinal O'Connor of New York, once lashed out at comic Robin Williams after the funnyman claimed that members of the Pro Life Movement had "a fetal attraction"—a harmless, yet accurate play on the words of the title of the popular movie *Fatal Attraction.* Yet, the pugnacious prelate publicly assailed the comic as if he was a dissident monk. What I find funny is that this Cardinal, who decries the aborting of an unborn fetus and has publicly stated that Catholic politicans who support abortion are in danger of going to hell, once wrote a book about the morality of United States involvement in Vietnam. In *A Chaplain Looks At Vietnam,* O'Connor concluded the United States not only had a right to be there, but had a moral obligation to send troops. I'm sure God finds O'Connor and Williams equally funny, with the edge going to Robin for originality. I hope.

But then again, according to Christianity, God doesn't have a sense of humor. Early Christianity condemned laughter. John Chrysostom, a Church Father and archbishop of Constantinople from 398 to 404, declared that jest and laughter are not from God but from the devil. The Church demanded solemnity and attempted to control laughter. Why? Because satire pokes fun at prohibitions and power, something the Church did not (and does not) want—and something Robin Williams does very well. The Church was in the mood-control business because laughter liberates us from fear of the sacred and from the past.

OK, back to my past and the nun story.

The nuns loved to dish out corporal punishment to those misguided kids who broke the rules. It was a form of Christian nun-violence. (Sorry Mahatma. Hey, speaking of Mahatma Gandhi, when you were only eight years old, I forced you to watch the movie *Gandhi,* and during the intermission of the lengthy film about the life of a man who used fasting as a weapon to overthrow the British Empire we stuffed ourselves with pizza. Life is most delicious when it is served with irony.) The recalcitrant students were quick to get their knuckles cracked with a ruler wielded by a nun. I remember one tall nun—Sr. John Capistron—who favored an even more painful method of punishment: she would pull you up out of your seat by the hair of your sideburns. The wincing young boy being disciplined would try his best to out-stretch her reach, but once he got up on the tip of his toes he was still no match for her towering size. Sr. John Capistron—known behind her back as "Jack the Knife"—never adopted the gentle glide of the other nuns; no, her gate resembled that of a storm trooper.

Sr. Mary Helen's cure for uttering a "dirty" word was an instant visit to the janitor's room where you were forced to wash your mouth out with soap.

I made that distasteful trip once for uttering the word "shit." Another nun, whose name eludes me, preferred to sprinkle pepper on the tongue that uttered a foul word. Sr. Alice Lorretta never failed to remind those kids she was disciplining of the biblical foundation for her stern actions: "Whom God loveth, He chasteneth." Why God spoke Elizabethan English, I never understood; but, according to Sr. Alice Lorretta's logic, He did seem to "love," more than all the others, the kids who needed to be straightened out on a regular basis. During my eight years in parochial school, I had my knuckles wrapped and my sideburns yanked more times than I can count. The physical abuse could easily be outgrown. The mental abuse they inflicted by filling my mind with the absolute "truth" was another story. The nuns instilled in us a cowardly and inordinate fear of God. They followed the plan.

For the nuns, the master plan for salvation devised by the Church was simple. Do it, and you would have no problems. The problem was doing it. And this is all you need to know: Obey the Ten Commandments. The Commandments are not the problem; the problem was the punishment dished out for failure to live up to the standards the Commandments mandated. Transgression could be divided into two categories: mortal and venial. A mortal sin was a grievous offense against the law of God—such as murder and masturbation. Jerk off after killing somebody and you would place yourself in double jeopardy—without Alex Trebek and parting gifts. A venial sin was a minor infraction—such as a little lie or stealing a small amount of money.

An unconfessed mortal sin at death meant eternal damnation in hell; an unconfessed venial sin, meant time in purgatory—which was a kind of waiting room for heaven, a not-so-pleasant place to do time, but at least, you knew that eventually you would get into heaven—even if it took a billion years. As I mentioned earlier, unbaptized babies went to limbo—forever. So that was it, all you really needed to know: ten Commandments, two classes of sins, and four possible post-death destinations.

The Catholicism dished out by the nuns was primarily concerned with perpetuating the myth that there was eternal punishment for even trivial offenses. Some nuns even made poor bladder control and nosepicking sins that God not only saw but dutifully noted so He wouldn't forget them on Judgment Day. The nuns lived in a structured, enclosed world where values were constant and safe, but where sanctity was constantly threatened by sin. For the saintly nuns, the world and life after life were very ordered and all prayers were answered—though at times the answer was "no." The nuns' belief in a rational world controlled by cause and effect was a fantasy contradicted by the facts.

I encountered a world far from ordered—it was a world of chaos into which I graduated. Randomness and madness were the order of the day. There was war, violence, disease, famine, nuclear bombs, rape, alcoholism, unethical business deals, corrupt politicians, tax fraud, racial bigotry, drugs, cancer, and appalling catastrophes. It was a world fraught with more criminal delights than with saintliness. It was a world where everybody talked about peace and prepared for more and worse wars. I quickly saw that the mayhem of armies, inquisitions, murders, robberies, and rapes is present in all places, at all times. Man is a very vicious animal. Prayers weren't answered; God didn't cure my mother's cancer—even though there was no real reason for Him/Her not to heal her. "No" is no answer. Out from under the long, dark shadow of the nuns, my life became a struggle between accepting a life that's tainted with realistic imperfections and pursuing a life to be lived in an unrealistic paradise beyond the grave. The paradisiacal fantasy won out.

No matter what the nuns had taught me, I came to see that I lived in a world without a design, a world without preconceived order. I wondered why there was so much evil, so much hatred. I had no answer, but no answer was better than the wrong answer the nuns shoved down my throat and indelibly stamped onto my mind by memorization. Sr. Saint Dorothy told me that wisdom was seeing things the way God saw them. Baloney. Life has taught me that wisdom amounts to nothing more than knowing what you don't know. The nuns either pretended or presumed to know what they did not know and could not know; they turned ancient speculation into gospel truth.

Don't get me wrong, Kate, I don't hate nuns. All through grammar school, I had a love for the nuns. An innocent, pure love. I had forgotten how much I respected the nuns back then, until a recent discovery jarred my memory. I was going through an old box of memorabilia that had been stored for years in my brother's attic when I came across a little blue autograph book with the school name emblazoned across the cover in gold letters—Saint Michael the Archangel School. The book was filled with colorful, blank pages. During the last week of our last year of school, we went around seeking autographs from our classmates. We wrote clever stuff like "Let me say forget-me-not, for surely you are never forgot," and "When you get married and live in a tree, send me a coconut C.O.D." Those were simple times, happy times.

As I browsed through this artifact from my distant past, I was struck by the fact that I had very few of my classmates' signatures, but I did have the autographs of thirteen nuns. There was Sr. Alice Lorretta, Sr. John Edmound, Sr. Saint Dorothy, Sr. Anne Philip (whose private mission was praying for the conversion of Russia, while our country prepared for the worst by building nuclear fallout shelters), Sr. Margaret Helena, Sr. Christina Maria, Sr. Anne Kathleen (who loved reading to us about the lives of the saints and who never tired of saying, "It's such a joy to know we have friends in heaven eager to help us join them."), Sr. Irene Francis, Sr. Alma Therese (who bore a striking resemblance to W. C. Fields, only she had no sense of humor), Sr. Joseph Alphonse, Sr. Mary Borromeo (who claimed Jesus wanted us to mortify our flesh), Sr. Rene Marie, Sr. Mary Bertille. What wonderful names! I still love the nuns; I love their dedication, their spirit, their willingness to turn their backs on a more conventional life. (The black habits they wore symbolized that they were dead to the world and its ways.) I admire their faith and convictions.

Still, they helped mess me up, but I can't imagine what my life would have been like had I never attended Saint Michael's School, never met a nun. No, I don't hate the nuns. I just feel sad that they wholeheartedly embraced the virtues prescribed by a nineteenth-century, male-dominated Church: humility, self-abnegation, and childlike dependence on the will of their superiors. They believed they were consecrated virgins, brides of Christ. They where stripped of their sexual identity, their habits carefully concealing their breasts, hips, and hair. The nuns were neutered, set apart, and untouched; they were allowed only the most guarded gestures of human affection or need. The piety the nuns instilled in us was deferential and unquestioning—like them. The nuns of St. Michael's put a sweet smile on the face of harsh religious indoctrination.

St. Michael the Archangel's parish consisted of four buildings spread over three-quarters of a city block. There was the church, the school, the rectory, and the convent. All were made of brick. The church was the centerpiece of the property. To its right stood the rectory, to its left, the convent, and behind it, the school. The school was the largest building, but the church was the most important, the soul of the parish: it was the house of God, the place where we received the Body of Christ. The rectory was the mind of the parish, the convent its heart, and the school its womb. This was the holy ground and the sacred heart of my young life.

In less than thirty years, the safe refuge of the familiar world of my youth would collapse, not able to withstand the pressure from the pace of change that confronts the world today. It seems to me that throughout the course of human history, that during the span of a person's life, not much changed; today, during our lifetime, not much remains the same. A kid today can't imagine a world without space travel, a world without television, a world without computers, a world without "rock & roll" and music video's, a world without bikinis. The world of my parent's youth knew none of these. Their life and their faith were simple.

A picture of my Aunt Mabel just popped into my mind. She died around 1970, at the ripe old age of 96, in full possession of all her marbles. I remember visiting her as a teenager. She seemed ancient then, with deep creases of time crisscrossing her face. She always looked frail and slightly bent over. But her mind and spirit were sprite and spunky. She was an avid baseball fan. Old Aunt Mabel knew stats and facts about all the players and checked the box scores of all the games every day. She chain-smoked unfilterd Lucky Strike cigarettes, and her language was salty. I distinctly remember her cursing the day her "Bums"— the Brooklyn Dodgers—headed for the coast and to become the Los Angeles Dodgers . . . and that was years after the fact!

But as tough and as "with it" as this old lady was, there was one advancement mankind made during her lifetime that she could not accept: space travel. She refused to read or watch on TV anything about astronauts or America's space program. The concept of human beings leaving earth, traveling into outer space, and perhaps even landing on other planets was simply beyond her comprehension, so she just tuned the whole notion of it out. During her lifetime, she saw transportation evolve from horse and buggy to jet planes—and that was more than enough for her, transportation to the moon was unthinkable.

"Christianity put the end of man beyond the limits of this earthly existence."

That sentiment was expressed by a French philosopher named Etienne Gilson. Born in Paris in 1884, Gilson buttered his philosophical bread with the thoughts of the medieval theologian and Benedictine monk Thomas Aquinas. You remember him, the "angelic doctor." Aquinas set the Catholic Church on an Aristotelian foundation and believed that the existence of God could be proved on rational grounds. In time, Aquinas's thoughts became the Catholic doctrine, which I was taught in high school. I remember learning that God was the fount of all existence, and in Him alone is there no objective difference between essence and existence. As I said, I learned that—of course, I had no idea what it meant. Still, I believed all that stuff (it's funny how certain we can be about things we don't understand), though I eventually forgot it; yet, in some unknown way, it's still a part of who I am, buried deep in my own personal archives.

You're probably wondering what Etienne Gilson and St. Thomas Aquinas have to do with my Aunt Mabel. Well, nothing really. Except that I put a little twist on Gilson observation, and it goes like this: Science put the days of man beyond the limits of earthly existence. Maybe Aunt Mable thought a space ship could penetrate heaven . . . or worse, not find it.

The Dodgers are still in Los Angeles, but since my Aunt's death nearly twenty years ago, not much else has remained the same. Especially in the realm of television where twenty years ago sex was hardly mentioned and rarely shown. Back then, even married couples had to sleep in twin beds. Yesterday, I happened to catch a nationally syndicated talk show, just as the host was about to introduce the next guests—a husband and wife in their late twenties who performed sex together —along with a female third participant—before a video camera and sold the tape to an adult-video distributor who specializes in selling triple X-rated videos featuring amatuer performers. Welcome to the world of nooky video! The host's introduction was spoken over a clip from the tape, which showed the couple sitting naked beside a pool as they began to fondle each other. Of course strategic body parts were electronically blurred. Still, there was no doubt what the film was about or where it was going—no need to look for plot or character development in this home-made movie. As I watched I thought of Andre Malraux's interesting observation that eroticism appears in full force only in countries where the notion of sin exists.

Believe me, Kate, your father is no prude; however, what struck me as odd about the show was not the couple or the topic, but the host's matter-of-fact introduction and the audience's response. The host spoke as if the couple were as normal as TV commercials, as if taking your clothes off and screwing before a video camera was as commonplace as having your photo taken in front of the Lincoln Memorial. When the introduction was completed and the barely censored clip ended, the couple proudly walked onto the set. The camera cut to the studio audience, made up of your average, run-of-the-mill Americans— they were young, old, male, female, black, white—and they all were greeting the couple with a very warm round of applause. If there was any doubt that anything goes on TV these days, this erased it. To me, the interview itself, though very explicit, was anticlimatic compared to the reception the couple received. There were no looks of disgust, no looks of disbelief, no looks of outrage, no looks of shock—my parents probably would have dropped dead if they were in the audience.

The couple spoke freely about having sex before the camera operator, about having another woman join them in the sex act, about how much they got paid ($500). They explained how they each had sexual fantasies, and rather than fulfill them behind each other's back, they explored them openly, together. The message was simple: their's was a much healthier relationship, a much better marriage because they had absolutely no sexual hang-ups.

In addition to all this, a vice president (no pun intended) of the company that sells the tape was also a guest. He was greeted and spoke as if he sold Hallmark Cards. Again, not a hint of disapproval from the audience of a man who distributed pornography for a living. I couldn't help but think how just a few years ago I was loudly and resoundingly hissed and booed by a television studio audience when, as a guest on a talk show, I said that I didn't believe that heaven or hell existed.

The point of this little story, Kate, is not that I object to the couple's philosophy of open and free sex in marriage—hey, they may be 100 percent right—or the making and buying of pornography; the point is—oh, I don't know what the damn point is. No, the point is that this type of discussion would have been beyond the realm of imagination just two short decades ago. Today, network television is bold and daring. The language and situations are provocative. Who can outshock whom is the name of the game. Cable television brings movies into our homes that couldn't have been made when I was a kid. I remember being forbidden to see Alfred Hitchcock's classic *Psycho* because of the shower scene where a woman was seen in a bra and panties. (I sneaked in anyway.) You see more than that in commercials today. No, the point I'm getting at is change, very rapid change. Change that is so fast that many people can't cope with it.

My imagination is not powerful enough to imagine my parents reaction if they could just for a moment be sitting in my living room tonight as I turn on the TV and happen to catch a video of Madonna, the slut-queen of rock & roll, strutting about in little more than a bra and garter belt, and, with crosses dangling around her neck, singing "Like a Virgin." They'd like die.

During my lifetime, patterns of living that had existed for thousands of years were destroyed. Scientists and philosophers probed the mystery of life and discovered the vast but smoothly running machinery of the universe, of which Man, so long as he knew and obeyed the rules, was master. God died and any pretense of society having a religious foundation and framework began to vanish. Commerce was elevated to divine status, and industry began creating a new urban "mass" people, outside the old social structure. Change, which up until this century had taken tiny, baby steps forward, was now making quantum leaps into the future, and the religion of my parents and my youthful understanding could not cope with the new world of tomorrow that had become today.

If you played a word association game with any person who attended a Catholic grammar school in the fifties and mentioned the word "Baltimore," the chances are their response would not be "Orioles" or "Maryland," but "catechism." The dreaded *Baltimore Catechism* was a virtual *Baedeker's Guide to Heaven*—it was the nuns' Bible. The catechism asked 3,500 questions. Comprised of six volumes arranged in a progressive plan of study, the answers were intended to furnish a complete course in the Catholic faith. We had to memorize a seemingly endless list of almost incomprehensible questions. It was pure torture. I'm not sure we necessarily understood the answers, but we knew them. We were religious parrots— "Polly want salvation!"

In the beginning, the questions were easy: (*Q*) Who made us? (*A*) God made us. With each passing year of school, the questions became tougher and more obtuse. Holiness, it seemed, required a good memory. A few years ago, I was wandering through a used bookstore when I spotted a tattered old copy of Volume Three of the *Baltimore Catechism,* its cover worn down from the sweating young, nervous hands that once held it. (Incidentally, next to the catechism was a book titled *How to Reach the Jew for Christ.*) As I stood among the cluttered shelves of books, a warm wave of nostalgia washed over me. I could hear Sr. Saint Dorothy asking question number 797: "Christopher, why is it foolish to conceal sins in confession?"

I saw myself nervously standing in front of my classmates and rattling off the answer: "It is foolish to conceal sins in confession because we thereby make our spiritual condition worse; we must tell the sin sometime if we ever hope to be saved; it will be made known on the day of judgment, before the world, whether we conceal it now or confess it."

God, I got it right; but, Sr. Saint Dorothy is about to ask a follow-up question— damn, she is worse than Sam Donaldson. "What must he do who has willfully concealed a mortal sin in confession?"

How did she know I didn't tell Fr. Swarbrick about looking at *Playboy?* After a long pause, I answer, "He who has willfully concealed a mortal sin in confession must not only confess it, but must also repeat all the sins he has committed since his last worthy confession."

God, two for two—this is my lucky day. I hope she doesn't ask question number 799. She does. "Very good Christopher. Just one more question. Must one who has willfully concealed a mortal sin in confession do more than repeat the sins committed since his last worthy confession?"

Don't choke, don't let her see that you are guilty. "Yes Sister. One who has willfully concealed a mortal sin in confession must, besides repeating all the sins he has committed since his last worthy confession, tell also how often he has unworthily received absolution and Holy Communion during the same time."

I wonder how God kept track of all these offenses before the computer was invented. "Thank you Christopher, you may sit down."

I closed the book, took a deep breath, and felt the nostalgia turn to anger. Suddenly, I had this flash of insight into how I became so screwed up, so guilt ridden, so susceptible to the salvific sorcery of fundamentalism.

Who are you Christopher Ryan? That is the question, my dear Kate, that haunts me. I suppose that who I am is all I have been. I am the sum total of everything that has happened to me and everything I have done. No matter where I go, my past comes along with me. I can no more free myself from my past than I can from my body. I thought that for me to understand who I am, I needed to understand the things that shaped me, the things that influenced me. On the day I found that copy of the *Baltimore Catechism,* I realized that I had discovered a hidden key to my past. The *Baltimore Catechism* had given me my worldview, it taught me how to look at things. It was time for me to look at it.

Like another Christopher, the one who sailed the ocean blue in 1492, I needed to set sail—not for some new world, but for the old world of my past in order to discover myself. I'm going to take a break from the blue screen of my computer and get a bite of lunch; later, I'll tell you what I discovered.

Thursday, July 12—4:20 P.M.

Hello again, Kate. I guess this isn't going to be an epistolary splinter. In fact, if I continue at this pace I might still be writing this letter in the year 2000. Not really. My time is short and I have many tasks to perform before my final curtain.

Kate, I'm glad I'm writing this letter to you. I took a long walk after this morning's letter-writing session. I thought of you the whole time. In a lifetime of struggles, troubles, tears, and sorrows, my separation from you has grieved me the most, made me the saddest. My times with you, on the other hand, have been the happiest of times, the source of my greatest joys. Before this letter is another word longer, this needs to be said: I love you very much.

I really like kids. I like being around kids, playing with them, watching them. They are free, open, honest. I have a dozen nieces and nephews, and each one of them is special to me. Not being with the most important kid in the world— you—has hurt me more than I can express. Sometimes I feel like I just push you out of my mind, so that I don't have to think about how much I miss you, how much I want to be with you. Every child I see reminds me of you. Seeing a father walking down the street holding his young daughter's hand is a sight that makes me crazy with jealousy. I become angry with myself: how did this happen, why did this happen? I feel so guilty. I know that we talk a lot on the phone, and that we send each other stuff in the mail—but it is not the same as seeing you fall asleep, seeing you laugh, holding your hand, watching you grow.

Long-distance love is the saddest love there is.

This morning I was going through a stack of letters and cards you have sent me over the past four years. The early mail, sent to me when you were only six, consisted mostly of crayon drawings—lots of hearts and flowers. You liked to trace copies of "Snoopy" and "Garfield," which you then colored and inscribed the finished product: "To Daddy, Love Kate." Each drawing or cartoon also carried the message: I love you. Once I received a small piece of tissue paper on which you had traced a rabbit and a duck, each neatly colored. Then you put these words in the rabbit's mouth, by means of writing them in a circle with an arrow pointing to the rabbit: "Hi daddy! I love you very much. Happy New Year!" I suppose you thought I might not understand, so you included this explanatory note printed on a second piece of paper: "I am the rabbit, you are the duck. P.S. Did you like the present I sent you? Call or write. Love, Kate."

Gradually, the drawings evolved into short notes. You would tell me that your cat said "Hi" to me. You always drew a heart on each letter. Here is a line from a letter you sent to me when you were about seven: "Picture of me with my hair cut will be coming soon or whenever Mommy takes the picture." In time the short, one-sentence notes developed into letters. Here is one you sent when you were eight: "Hi Dad, Thanks for the clothes and the letter. I am getting a hamster but I have to get rid of my rabbit. We found a hamster, but we have not found a home for the rabbit. A cage cost $35.00, so I guess the hamster will have to live in my old fish tank. Be sure to drop me a line. OK? I love you. Kate."

Between the two of us, we ensured that Hallmark Cards didn't go out of business. But cards are not flesh, letters are not hugs, long-distance calls are not goodnight kisses. In my collection of your drawings, notes, letters, and cards was one short, undated note that made me cry when I read it this morning. You were young, perhaps seven, you had just advanced from printing to writing in script. "To Pop, Thank you for the lolly pops. I love you very much. I wish you would come back. Notice my writing Pop. Write me back. Love, Kate." In between the thank you and the news about the advance in your penmanship came the honest sentiment that you missed me. I knew when I first received this note, and I know now, that my leaving hurt you. Hurt you more than I fully can understand. For this, my dear, sweet Kate, I am more sorry than . . .

Before I get the damn keyboard wet with tears, I better return to the story of my search for my past.

I went to church a few months ago. I didn't go looking for answers or divine comfort. I went looking for memories, memories of me. I wanted to find the me of my past, a stranger I barely remember. After all these years, I'm still not on intimate terms with my own self; I remain elusive from me. Illusion and self-deception are brothers-in-arms ready to fight any honest and fearless look at my own life. Especially, the spiritual aspects of my life, which have been complicated by the fact that I have continually struggled between hypocrisy and sincerity when it comes to my religious faith.

I think that we are either formed by experience, which we then try to justify to ourselves, or we are formed by dogma, and then we try to develop ourselves in terms of that dogma. For me, it was the latter. At times I believed the dogma, but couldn't live up to its demands; at other times, I rejected the dogma, but couldn't justify the rejection. The result: I've been both sincerely religious and a religious hypocrite. So, Kate, as I tried to say last night, my mind may be guilty of infidelities—both minor and major—which this letter may reflect. But

I do not—consciously, at least—bear false witness. Still, is what I remember really what happened, or is it just my impression of what happened? Booga, booga!

Before this visit, the last time I had been in a church was two years ago. That visit made me angry. An aunt was visiting from the east coast, and as Sunday approached I was sure she would want to go to Mass. Should I go with her or just drop her off? I didn't want to be a hypocrite, besides she knew I had "fallen away" from the Church, had—as my oldest brother was fond of saying—"lost my faith." Yet, I thought that the polite thing to do was to go with her—it wouldn't hurt. As we entered the church, I felt that the last pew would do fine, but I followed her to one near the front. She genuflected, I gave a reverent but reluctant bow, and we quietly slipped into the pew. As she knelt to pray before the Mass started, I sat down. I felt very uncomfortable, and started wondering whether or not I should stand or kneel at the prescribed times during the Mass, pretending to be an active participant in the liturgy, or just sit, clearly indicating that I was not a believer. I went along with the crowd, deciding it was best to just blend in.

I didn't last too long. As soon as the priest began his sermon, my hostility began to surface. The priest was old, and his sermon echoed his traditional training. His topic was every sinner's favorite of the seven capital sins (those deadly offenses of pride, lust, anger, covetousness, gluttony, envy, and sloth that quickly cut you off from God): lust. I couldn't take it. I whispered to my aunt that I needed to excuse myself and I got up and walked out.

I think the Church's hang-up about sex is easy to explain. The Church is selling transcendence, promising a nonmaterial future of eternal bliss. Sexuality promises the pleasures of its reward here and now; it reduces eternity to one climactic moment, whose postponement can't be tolerated.

The church I visited last month was one of the string of nine Spanish mission churches founded by Fr. Junipero Serra between 1767 and 1784, the year of his death. There is a groundswell of activity and support within the Catholic Church to declare the Franciscan priest, who was born on the island of Majorca in 1713, a saint. However, many people consider this architect of the California mission system as a symbol of eighteenth-century feudal forced labor and abuse to Indians, a symbol of successful foreign domination over the established society. As I entered the church that day, the image I held in my mind of Fr. Serra was the same image that most Californians had of him—he was an authentic hero and noble man. I had bought the myth without ever examining the facts.

The little mission church was nothing like St. Michael's. The mission church was primitive, while St. Michael's was majestic; it was like a seed housing a dream, while St. Michael's was the flowered dream. The first thing I noticed about the exterior of the mission church was the twin bell towers that framed the building. In front of the church was a large courtyard and garden. Standing tall among the gladiolus and pelargonium, the roses and calla lilies, and the pepper and olive trees were two statues of Franciscan friars. One was a young, angelic-looking friar wearing sandals and the simple sacklike habit of the followers of St. Francis of Assisi, distinguished by the knotted cord pulled tight around the waist. He was holding an infant child, the baby Jesus. The child had one arm raised up, as if blessing those who looked. The index and middle finger on the hand of the extended arm were pressed together, pointing heavenward, while the thumb and the two end fingers touched. I recalled the symbology. The two fingers represented the two natures of man, both divine and human; the three fingers recalled the Trinity, three Gods in one. In the child's other hand was a round ball, the world, which the child came to save. Theology in art. The concepts of theology are arduous and abstract, but the statues of saints and the spires of cathedrals raise heavenward the thoughts of even the most doubting of souls. Art illuminates the concept.

Close by, the other statue was of an older, bearded friar. He was gently cradling in his arms a rustic crucifix made of tree branches. The tortured body of Jesus was nailed to the cross beneath the sign INRI—Jesus of Nazarath, King of the Jews. The monk's face reflected sadness and affection. Sticking out from under his habit, next to his sandaled feet, was a skull. As I contemplated the meaning of the skull, three old, hunched over, pious women, each with their heads devoutly covered with crocheted veils, slowly walked by. All three women were clutching rosary beads. I heard one say, "This is holy ground."

As I walked across this "holy ground" towards the church, I had a fleeting flash of envy of the old women's piety. Their faith made things very simple for them. They had no doubt, no torment.

But does faith really simplify things, or does it foster a closed mind that breeds confusion, a confusion that expresses itself in a warm, "feel good" sentiment that is enlarged to cosmic proportions. This was "holy ground" for those women; it momentarily freed their imprisoned spirits from the chains of evil earth in order to savor a tiny taste of the purity of heaven. For them, earth and this life were a prison, and Jesus a "get out of jail free" card.

I wondered if it was possible for a "believer" to love life, to fully experience the human joys and sorrows that are rooted in this physical world, to be able to respect other mere mortal human beings. It seems that the "believer's" hopes and dreams are hitched to the wagon of the next life, leaving little reason for them to want to create a paradise on earth, to make the entire planet "holy ground." This garden, with its beautiful flowers and peaceful tranquility, was no holier than Hollywood Boulevard—God is either everywhere or nowhere. The old ladies wanted simplification; I wanted clarification. Their's was an easier goal.

It is odd that women have become the most faithful supporters of the Church in light of the fact that the Church has institutionalized a hatred for women. Jesus, to the shock of his own disciples, treated women with openness and respect; however, the male leaders of the Church have viewed women with a mixture of repressed fear, mistrust, and arrogance. St. John Chrysostom, who was known as "Golden Mouth" because of his outstanding preaching abilities, believed that the Garden of Eden was an asexual paradise that was not subject to sensual lustfulness, and that the first humans were not corrupted by a desire for sexual intercourse. The idyl of virginity was lost, according to Chrysostom, when Eve led Adam into sin, and as a result we exchanged paradise for the "slavish garment of marriage," the pains of life, and the destruction of death. Chrysostom, who described Jews as "carnal," "lascivious," and "accursed," viewed marriage as a curse for disobedience and saw women as a dangerous personification of the snares of the devil. Speaking of women during his Ninth Homily on 1 Timothy 2:15, the saint said, "The whole sex is weak and flighty." I wonder what he would have thought of Maggie Thatcher or Golda Meir.

In his "On Priesthood," St. John Chrysostom wrote:

> There are in the world a great many situations that weaken the conscientiousness of the soul. First and foremost of these is dealings with women. In his concern for the male sex, the superior may not forget the females, who need greater care precisely because of their ready inclination to sin. In this situation the evil enemy can find many ways to creep in secretly. For the eye of woman touches and disturbs our soul, and not only the eye of the unbridled women, but that of the decent one as well.

Early in the third century, Clement of Alexander wrote, "Women should be completely veiled, except when they are in the house. Veiling faces assures that they will lure no man into sin." Nearly two hundred years later, St. Ambrose, who wanted priests to cease having sexual intercourse with their wives and who considered marriage as a burden to be avoided, also insisted that women wear veils when they are in public, least they tempt a man.

The three old women I had seen probably never thought that the veils they wore on their heads symbolically reflected the sexual neurosis of men who lived nearly two thousand years ago. The early Church leaders' abhorrence of pleasure led to an abhorrence of marriage, which in turn led to priestly celibacy and the creation of the doctrine of the Virgin Birth.

Before entering the church, I paused at a small shrine in honor of the Blessed Virgin Mary. Mary played no small part in the lives of Catholics, she was the mother of our faith, our last hope in times of trouble. Knowing that no son could refuse his mother, our most desperate prayers where directed Mary's way, in hopes she would hear our pleas and intercede for us by asking her son to grant us our wishes. As a kid, I threw a lot of late fourth quarter spiritual "Hail Mary" passes to the Mother of Jesus, though I can't recall scoring any touchdowns.

The statue of Mary in the shrine had the infant Jesus sitting erectly upon the palm of her right hand, with his right arm reaching up as if to bless those who came to pray to his mother. The statue distorts biblical history, for it clearly conveys the feeling this infant knew he was God, was divine. But then again, the statue's aim was to inspire, not inform.

As I stood before the statue, I began to recall how little statues of Mary dotted the landscape of my youth. There was one in almost every room of the house. Many Catholic families had shrines to Mary in their gardens (we didn't— why, I don't know). At St. Michael's School, every classroom had a statue or a picture of Mary. Our day began by saying the rosary, a ritual that included saying fifty, yes fifty, "Hail Mary's" and a few other prayers. I remember there was a formulaic prayer before we said the rosary that included praying "for the conversion of sinners and Russia." In those cold war days, commies and sinners were synonymous. On many occasions, especially if a priest or a nun visited our home, we gathered together as a family at night to say the rosary. At funeral parlors, everyone in attendance always knelt in front of the open casket and said the rosary together.

On the base of the shrine upon which Mary's feet rested, two pennies had been left behind as an offering by some poor pilgrim in search of an answer to prayers. Who, if they had the power, would not answer those prayers, prayers tendered by someone with far more than two cents' worth of faith.

No, I hadn't lost my faith; I just could no longer hold onto it. I would have preferred to have come to this shrine with faith rather than questions.

The two pennies brought a tear to my eyes and a prayer to my lips: "Hail Mary full of grace, the Lord is with thee. Blessed art thou amongst women, and blessed is the fruit of thy womb, Jesus. Holy Mary, Mother of God, pray for us sinners, now and at the hour of our death. Amen." At the word Jesus, my head bowed—just as the nuns taught me to do out of reverence for the Son of God. I felt a chill run down my spine—I wanted to believe, but I had no faith, no pennies.

In my satchel, I was carrying my copy of the *Baltimore Catechism;* I reached in and pulled it out, because I wanted to read what I was taught about Mary. Questions 27 through 48 dealt with Mary and the prayer I had just uttered— the "Hail Mary." I had forgotten that the official name of the formulated prayer known as the "Hail Mary" was "The Angelic Salutation." The official name stems from the fact that the opening of the prayer uses the words the Archangel Gabriel used to greet Mary when he appeared to her in order to deliver the news that she was pregnant. (Make that the angel's alleged appearance to the alleged virgin.)

Question 36 asks: Why do we address Mary as "full of grace"? The answer: We address Mary as "full of grace" because she was never guilty of the slightest sin, was endowed with every virtue, and was blessed with a constant increase of grace in her soul. (Note: the Church wasn't concerned with the fact that this answer is unbiblical.) Question 37 asks: Why do we say "the Lord is with thee"? The answer: We say "the Lord is with thee," for besides being with her as He is with all His creatures on account of His presence everywhere and as He is with the good on account of their virtue, He is with Mary in a special manner on account of her dignity as Mother of His Son. Question 38 asks: Why is Mary called "blessed amongst women"? The answer: Mary is called "blessed amongst women" on account of her personal holiness, her great dignity as Mother of God, and her freedom from original sin. Question 39 asks: Why is Mary called "holy"? The answer: Mary is called "holy" because one full of grace and endowed with every virtue must be holy. Question 40 asks: Why do we need Mary's prayer at the hour of death? The answer: We need Mary's prayer at the hour of death because at that time, our salvation is in greatest danger, and our spiritual enemies most anxious to overcome us.

Wow! My head felt like it was in the spin cycle of a washing machine, dizzily spinning in circles of doubt. I closed the catechism and placed it back in my satchel. I stood motionless for a few minutes gazing at the face of the Madonna, while pondering what I had just read. The answers to those five simple questions managed to incorporate a wide range of questionable theological premises. I found myself talking to the statue.

"Mary . . . I just can't believe that you were a virgin."

The eyes of the statue appeared to be looking right at me, piercing my very body as if it were looking into my soul. It was not a look of pity or disgust. It was a look of love, a mother's pure love. I felt compassion, warmth.

Mary spoke: "Why can't you believe?"

Geez, a statue is talking to me. Oh, God, the men in white coats will be here any second.

"The whole story is a myth, I just can't buy it. Besides, the evidence tells a different story, a much more believable story."

"The evidence, my son. What evidence?"

"Come on, you know. The evidence unearthed by biblical scholars."

"Tell me about it."

"I just can't tell you about it. I mean there is a lot of stuff . . . stuff I've read over the years, no specifics come to mind."

"Forget about specifics. Tell me your impression of this 'stuff' you've read."

"OK. To begin with, the notion that you were a virgin before and after conceiving Jesus seems to be an idea that was created long after Jesus had died. Listen, I feel like a lawyer, and that's a feeling I hate. Just tell me, did you sleep with Joseph?"

"Does it matter? What I want to know is what you think."

"I guess I want to believe it—that you didn't, I mean, but I would really like some proof."

"Faith doesn't require proof."

"I hate that answer. I'm being serious—as serious as I can be considering I'm talking to a statue. Listen, the point is there seems to be a considerable amount of proof you weren't a virgin."

"That's what you keep saying, but I haven't heard any of this proof yet."

"OK, I'll try again. Stories of divine conception are found among the traditions, legends, and beliefs of many pagan peoples before and after the birth of Christ. In addition, ancient Greek and Roman mythology, along with nearly all the Eastern religions from India and China, in existence long before Jesus, contain tales of divine sons and prophets being born of young women without the aid of a husband. There was Yesoda, mother of Krishna; Celestine, mother of Zulis; Chemalma, mother of Quezalcotl; and Semele, mother of Bacchus—to name just a few."

"Is that your proof?"

"There's more. The early Christians didn't claim Jesus was born of a virgin. Textural analysis of the scriptures makes it clear this belief was injected into the teachings about a hundred years after the death of Christ. Some speculate it was added as the infant religion spread into pagan lands where the story of a virgin birth had great appeal. I guess you can say the virgin birth story was born out of evangelistic zeal. The fact is the New Testament barely mentions the idea. Only two of the gospel writers—Luke and Matthew, I think—even mention it. And, many biblical scholars believe the Gospel according to Matthew wasn't even written by the apostle, but was penned by a disciple of his during the later part of the first century. The educated hunch is that this disciple "fit in" the legend of the virgin birth that was being spread by converted pagans. One other major point is that Paul, who had something to say about everything, is utterly silent on the topic. Should I go on?"

"Please do."

"Well, there is one bit of cultural information that tends to repudiate the virgin birth story. The Jews found the idea of a virgin birth to be obnoxious, because it denigrated the sanctity of marital sex, and, more important, it weakened the concept of the family, which they held in very high regard. You were Jewish, and Jesus was the Jewish Messiah—why would God choose to enter the world in a fashion that His chosen people would not understand or appreciate? Listen, it's the same story today: for many people, the idea of a Jesus conceived and born of human parents without the direct intervention of God somehow seems less divine, less special. And for you to have conceived a child in your womb without having sex, makes you more pure, as if sex were dirty or at least not holy. I'm rambling on, so I'll stop; besides, I can't think of anything else to say."

"Well I'd say you did a pretty good job recalling the 'stuff' you read. Why is the virgin birth issue so important to you?"

"I don't think it's that terribly important to me. I don't think it really matters. In fact, many of the great Christian writers of the first four centuries—guys like Irenaeus, Clement of Alexander, Origen, Athanasius, Cyril, and Basil—didn't seem to consider it a very important issue, and each of them explained it in a slightly different way. But it does show how facts get distorted, how myths get started."

"Did you really read all those guys. They wrote some pretty boring stuff—a lot of it was Greek to me."

"Hey, you're a funny lady. That's nice to know. I've always thought that God had to have one hell of a sense of humor—don't tell me, I know. . . . He gets it from his mother."

"You're pretty funny yourself. I think this virgin birth question is important to you because if you can prove it's a fraud, then you'd feel comfortable ignoring or even throwing out all the teachings of Jesus."

"I'm not looking to throw out all the teachings of Jesus. Some of what he preached is excellent, not all his teachings were original—some can be traced back to Lao-Tzu and Buddha, and some of what he said was just plain crap—like his belief his second coming would happen during his follower's lifetime. But that's another story. Let's not change the subject."

"You seem angry."

"I'm not angry. This religion stuff is very emotional. People get hot under the collar; they hate having their beliefs challenged, probably because they fear being wrong. No, I'm not angry. But it seems impossible to express reasonable doubt without infuriating people. Reasonable doubt, do you hear me—reasonable doubt. There are some people—honest and sincere people—who doubt Jesus ever existed. I'm not talking about commies or atheists, I'm talking about concerned scholars who have major, major—I'm talking almost unreasonable—doubts about whether or not Jesus ever existed. Forget about whether or not he was born of a virgin, they think, and have evidence, Jesus never existed, and that Christianity can be explained without a historical Jesus."

"This religion stuff is a crazy business. But you didn't come to this church today looking for religion. I think you came to find spirituality. You didn't stop at this grotto that honors me because you where concerned about my biological virginity. No, what intrigues you is my virginal consciousness, my complete openness to God. Am I right?"

"You're pretty smart for a statue."

"And you're smart enough to know it doesn't really matter whether the virgin birth is fact or fiction. What matters is the symbol, because the symbol itself can awaken in you a new awareness of the inner meaning of life. I am what you want to be. You hunger to surround, enfold, possess, hold, embrace, as a mother does her child in her womb, God. Virginally by total surrender in faith, hope, and love, you can conceive God within you."

I stood there speechless.

I wanted to believe, but couldn't. Within me I felt the familiar tension between submission and revolt that I've struggled with most of my life. Suddenly, the statue turned wooden, lifeless. Sadly, I turned and headed for the church.

Highlighting the timeworn, sandstone facade of the church was a large star-shaped window just above the main entrance. As I entered the church, my hand—without taking any direct orders from my brain—dipped into the font of holy water. With my moistened fingers, I blessed myself—that is, I made the sign of the cross by touching my forehead, my stomach, my left shoulder, and then my right shoulder while silently saying: "In the name of the Father, and of the Son, and of the Holy Spirit. Amen."

The reflexes were there, the emotions weren't. Faith creates excitement, doubt, frustration. In my youth, the Trinity was a vibrant reality; today, it's a lifeless concept. My adult brain, looking for evidence, cannot understand the arithmetical conundrum which claims three times one is one, once one is three. Yet the Church demands that I must believe, that my salvation, my escape from eternal damnation, depends upon belief. As a child, I bowed my head before the Lamb of God dwelling in the wheat and wine; as an adult, the doctrine of Transubstantiation (which claims that during the Eucharistic Liturgy the substance of bread and wine is actually changed into the substance of the Body and Blood of Christ, while retaining the appearance and taste of bread and wine) strikes me as absurd and little more than theological hokus-pokus. Santa Claus in the North Pole makes more sense than the Trinity in a wafer. Still, through the magic of the priest, the faithful believe they can devour the Creator of the universe by eating a piece of bread and swallowing a little wine.

As I stood motionless in the back of the church, I felt as if my soul was being torn asunder, split in half—and it hurt. My nonreligious friends scorn faith in God as if it were some kind of a childish game. But the benefits of faith are far from childish. The man or woman of faith, fully equipped with an essential certitude and stability of belief, has a rallying point he or she can gravitate to in times of crisis and trouble. His or her faith gives birth to some very positive emotional qualities: hope, trust, a sense of meaning and wholeness. In addition, faith is an antidote to the painful existential conditions of life: it offers a source of nurturance, a sense of transcendence to counteract the corrosive quality of daily life, and it helps overcome the sense of ultimate nothingness each of us eventually face. Faith is a reality even if its object is an illusion, just as hope without reason is still hope.

Yet for me, the promises of faith were never realized. I found the beliefs of my childhood to be cramping and inhibiting as an adult. I started viewing faith not as a healthful tonic, but as a harmful drug. My lack of faith, however, was no bargain: it brought me deep despair and a chronic, nagging sense of futility. I never really said "no" to my beliefs; it's just that I couldn't live by them and my best efforts to live with them failed.

Still, I anguished over the existence of God—as if it were a life or death question. My doubt does not mean denial, it merely means that I swing back and forth between yes and no—like a kid playing "Monkey in the Middle." There was a period, during my mid-twenties, when I rejected all the dogma of my faith, but did not stop believing in some dark corner of my soul that God was real, and watching me. In truth, dear Kate, the subject of God is beyond the scope of my intellect, and the mystery of the beginning of all things is a puzzle beyond my ability to solve—I guess, in that respect, I am like all men, but not all men will admit it.

I paused to look at a memorial plaque in the floor. It was dated 1793 and dedicated to the memory of a corporal of the Mission Guard. The church was dedicated in 1771, some twenty-two years before the plaque was set in place. For over two hundred years, people had faithfully come to this place to worship God—that's a long time, though a mere wink in the eye of eternity. I came as a heretic. I would imagine that for most of the people who came to this church during its two-century-long life, their faith was a matter of fate: their parents belief gave birth to their belief. I could not accept my fate; I wanted choice.

The Greek word from which "heresy" is derived means "to choose," and it carried no religious connotation. Today, the word "heretic" sounds more like a disease, a truth-denying virus—thanks to the New Testament, which presupposed the authority of one religious tradition. The church was built on the rock of external authority, I craved an internal experience. I wanted to hear God's voice, not church dogma. For the corporal, this simple mission church was bastion of religious certainty, a place where heresy was only a remote possibility—unless you were an Indian. Today, there is far more heresy—far more choosing—than certainty.

The corporal of the Mission Guard lived in a world of fate, I live in a world of choice; he was at home in a world of myths, I was incapable of mythological thought. Still, I wanted some kind of divine intervention. If the corporal wanted to hear God's voice, the Church was the only place he would have come—he knew nothing of plurality; he had no choices. I am constantly confronted with choices.

The modern era gave man more than technology, it gave humanity plurality, it gave humanity options. I'm no more intelligent than the corporal, but the society in which I live demands that I think more than the corporal had to think. I had educational choices, career choices, marriage "style" choices, and political choices that the corporal never had to face. Beyond more choices, I am confronted with far more information to wade through than the corporal. According to a recent Bell Labs report, in one day's edition of the *New York Times* there is more information than a single man or woman had to process in the whole of his or her life in the sixteenth century. I can't afford the luxury of the unreflective spontaneity that must have marked his life—I must plan my life.

Yes, I came as a heretic—I had no choice; still, I hated the label and wished I could believe. But if I am honest, and I believe I am, how can I surrender an honest doubt? I took comfort in something I once read that claimed, "Heretics are the only (bitter) remedy against the entropy of human thought."

I slowly walked down the aisle, heading for one of the empty pews where I would silently sit for awhile—hoping that perhaps God would speak to me.

As I walked down the aisle, I turned my head from side to side, looking at each of the Stations of the Cross. I suppose an explanation of exactly what the Stations of the Cross are would be helpful. For starters, they fall under the general heading of "sacramentals." What is a sacramental? Funny you should ask, that just happens to be question #1052 in the *Baltimore Catechism*. The answer: "A sacramental is anything set aside or blessed by the Church to excite good thoughts and to increase devotion, and through these movements of the heart to remit venial sin." Oh.

If memory serves me correctly, sacramentals included things like medals and relics that had been blessed. And older Catholics are sure to remember scapulars. A scapular was a tiny piece of cloth, usually blue, red, white, or brown, that had a picture—a sacred image of a saint or Mary—sewn on them; attached to the upper corners of the cloth—I think it was actually a piece of felt—was a long strand of string that did the job of a chain necklace. Red scapulars honored the passion of Christ, blue ones, the Immaculate Conception of Mary, and the white ones, the Holy Trinity. The scapular was worn under your clothing, and was never to be taken off—except, I guess, to bathe. Never is a long time, however, and the string usually rotted away from sweat and wear and tear in a rather short period of time.

Wearing a scapular entitles the wearer to indulgences. An indulgence was like time off for good behavior. Basically it was a concession from God in exchange for doing something good; the concession, or favor, the sinner received was getting a reduction in the temporal punishment he or she had coming to him or her in the next life for sins committed in this life. Even though his or her sins were forgiven and he or she was absolved from the guilt of his or her sin, the sinner still had to suffer the pain of some form of temporal punishment attached to the sin in purgatory. Certain acts and certain objects, however, had the power to bring about the remission of all or part of the punishment due.

Indulgences were issued in increments of time; that is, some were worth forty days, some a year, which meant your time of punishment in purgatory was reduced by that amount. You could also apply these pain-relief credits to somebody already doing time in purgatory, thereby quickening the deliverance of their soul from the suffering of this penance penitentiary and into the celestial joy of paradise. They must have clocks and calendars in afterlife. The theory behind the Church's practice of granting indulgences worked along the lines of a family inheritance securely placed in a bank for future generations. I'll let the catechism explain.

Question #853: How does the Church by means of indulgences remit temporal punishment due to sin? The answer: "The Church, by means of Indulgences, remits the temporal punishment due to sin by applying to us the merits of Jesus Christ, and the superabundant satisfactions of the Blessed Virgin Mary and of the saints; which merits and satisfactions are its spiritual treasury."

Question #854: What do you mean by the "superabundant satisfaction" of the Blessed Virgin and the Saints? The answer: "By the superabundant satisfaction of the Blessed Virgin and the saints, we mean all the satisfaction over and above what was necessary to satisfy for their own sins. As their works were many and their sins few—the Blessed Virgin being sinless—the satisfaction not needed for themselves is kept by the Church in a spiritual treasury to be used for our benefit."

God, that treasury by now must be in worse shape than the government's— the church must have been into deficit spending centuries ago. Of course, during periods of financial difficulty in the past, the Catholic Church resorted to selling these indulgences, and, worse, it granted them to those who performed the pious work of killing and confiscating the property of wealthy Jews and Mohammedans in Spain during the Middle Ages. For example, the construction of St. Peter's Basilica in Rome was largely financed from funds raised by Pope Leo X, who was pope from 1513 to 1521, through the sale of indulgences. (This same Pope once raised a ton of money by creating thirty-one new cardinals on a single day, June 26, 1517. Each new Cardinal paid a small fortune for the honor.) In Wittenberg, Germany, there was a large collection of relics. For a fee, a Catholic could view these relics and earn 1,443 years' indulgence. The printing press made the reception of indulgences even easier. You no longer had to journey to a sacred shrine; you could simply make a donation at your door and in return you would receive an indulgence slip. Well, you get the idea and I need not spend any more time on this can of indulgence worms.

The abuses aside, the idea of indulgences are downright ridiculous. A Dominican monk named Johann Tetzel, who traveled from town to town displaying relics and selling indulgences, summed up the whole nutty business with this satirical couplet:

> As soon as the coin in the coffer rings,
> The soul from out of the fire springs.

Tetzel was considered the most accomplished indulgence pitch artist in the Church. He received a handsome salary and an unlimited expense account. He traveled in a carriage drawn by three horses, and he was accompanied by a retinue of servants and assistants. Tetzel and his fellow indulgence salesmen usually hit town with all the hoopla of a traveling circus. An advance man would ride ahead, loudly announcing the message, "The grace of God and of the Holy Father is at your gates." Church bells would ring, and the priests and nuns led a welcoming procession with lighted candles. The preachers carried with them the pope's coat of arms, which was suspended on a large cross set up near the pulpit from which they would deliver their pitch. Indulgences varied in price according to the economic class (princes paid more than barons), and specific sin (the price for polygamy was three times that of the sin of practicing magic).

Tetzel had several illegitimate children and spent much of his spare time raising hell in taverns. Perhaps his love of taverns foreshadowed two lines written by the poet William Blake nearly three hundred years later in his poem "The Little Vagabond":

> Dear mother, dear mother, the Church is cold.
> But the Ale-house is healthy and pleasant and warm.

The cherubic Dominican's response to those who questioned his efforts in raising money to rebuild the Basilica was blunt: "All those who criticize my sermons and indulgences will have their heads ripped off and be kicked bleeding into hell; heretics I will have burned until the smoke billows over the walls."

If you want to read about sex scandals, insatiable hunger for power, grotesque savageries, avarice, greed, debauchery, and corruption, read about the popes who reigned from 926 through 1534. Now that I think about it, that span of Church history has all the ingredients for a great TV miniseries.

The act of blessing yourself, that is making the sign of the cross was also considered a sacramental, though its benefits may be negated if you do it in a sloppy fashion—neatness counts in religion. The *Baltimore Catechism* states: "A common fault with many in blessing themselves is to make a hurried motion with the hand which is in no way a sign of the cross. They perform this act of devotion without thought or intention, forgetting that the Church grants an indulgence to all those who bless themselves properly while they have sorrow for their sins."

OK, back to the Stations of the Cross and the question: What are the Stations of the Cross?—which happens to be question #1057 in the *Baltimore Catechism*. The answer furnished: "The Stations of the Cross is a devotion instituted by the Church to aid us in meditating on Christ's passion and death. Fourteen crosses or stations, each with a picture of some scene in the passion, are arranged at distances apart. By passing from one station to another and praying before each while we meditate upon the scene it represents, we make the Way of the Cross in memory of Christ's painful journey during His passion, and we gain the indulgence granted for this pious exercise."

As I made my way down the aisle, my mind flashed back to a montage of scenes from my childhood school days at St. Michael's. With my tattered scapular honoring Mary hidden beneath my shirt, I made the Stations with as much piety as a child could muster. The images depicting the fourteen stops along the way of Christ's passion were mounted along the side walls of the church—seven on each side. Each station had a name, such as, "The Scourging at the Pillar" and "Christ Falls for the Third Time." Some kids performed this devotional as if it were a race, pausing for just a few scant seconds at each station. For me, piety meant time. I stood devoutly before each image for two or three minutes. I looked "holy," but I realized my "holiness" was just a show. After all, what should I think about standing before the depiction of Christ being stripped, whipped, and crowned with thorns? My young mind wasn't capable of much deep meditation, and it wasn't capable of drawing any lessons that I could apply to my life in Queens, New York.

I paused briefly before the eleventh station: "Jesus Is Nailed to the Cross." The first thought that popped into my mind was: how cruel, how barbaric. I realized that this image of a man being nailed to two pieces of wood was emblazoned into my mind at a very young, impressionable age. Imagine taking a child to a holy place and showing him representations of torture and images of a dying man. As I stood there, I felt myself floating back across the decades to St. Michael's Church. I heard Sr. Saint Dorothy's gentle voice saying, "Hear the sound of the heavy hammer as the soldiers pound the nails into Our Lord's feet and hands. But You are silent, Jesus. You were very brave. Good Jesus, You are suffering for me. I love you." Her voice fades into the silence of the mission church. Geez, the guided meditations of the New Age that are so in vogue today were nothing new to me—the nuns successfully employed the technique thirty-five years ago.

I'm sorry Sr. Saint Dorothy, but I don't hear the sound of the heavy hammer. But I now see something I never saw before. What I see is not merely cruelty but injustice. The foundation of Christianity is built upon the sacrifice of the innocent and the acceptance of that sacrifice by God. Jesus of Nazareth was an innocent man unjustly killed. How—dear Sr. Saint Dorothy—can I dismiss the injustice of the crucifixion? You told me that this sacrifice was right and necessary. But how can that be when it denies the one undeniable truth that it is horrible and unjust that an innocent man should be killed?

Oh, how clever and paradoxical is Christianity! In this metamorphosis of injustice, Christianity found an attitude which transcends and minimizes the abiding reality of human suffering. About five years ago, a friend of mine and his wife were awakened in the middle of the night by the cries of their three-month-old daughter. They hurried to her crib and found the child burning with fever. They rushed her to the hospital. Within hours the infant was dead. At the funeral, the death was described as "God's will."

People found comfort in that explanation; I found it unsettling. As I stood before the eleventh station of the cross, I suddenly knew why. If this is a world in which innocents must be tortured, and if there is a God who rules, guides, and sanctifies this world, then God must be unjust. How is it possible that so many people can stand before the infinite gulf between the sufferings of humanity and the designs of God and not become angry? If there indeed is a God waiting in judgment in the next world, He has much to answer for in the boundless suffering that is so much a part of this one.

A few years ago, a cousin of mine died. It was very sudden and unexpected. He was only thirty-nine, trim, fit, and the picture of good health. He had a wife and four young kids. He was a great guy—kind, caring, considerate, generous, and a host of other laudable adjectives. He had a good job, paid his taxes, and went to church. Why did he die so young? At the funeral my brother said, "There are some things we are just not meant to understand. That is where acceptance comes in. . . . We must accept God's will, not question it. If some events in life seem incomprehensible—like deadly fires and plane crashes or the sudden death of a good man—it is because God makes these decisions behind closed doors. . . . It is none of our business, everything is in His hands." I wanted to say, "Even the outcome of the state lottery," but didn't—a pointless argument in the presence of a corpse had little appeal. My sister said, "I think God takes the good ones early. The rest of us he leaves here on earth to suffer the pains of living." One good question; two shitty answers. Funerals are the most vacuous rituals that exist, filled with meaningless cliches. I overheard one relative say my cousin looked good. Looked good? He fucking looked dead!

As I continued my walk down the aisle, I gazed at the remaining Stations of the Cross and thought how art helps make errors appear attractive and can make the mythical look like reality. If the core of my religious beliefs, which regulated the way I responded to everything I encountered in life, was based on myths and not facts, and therefore was not true, I couldn't help wonder what the impact of being trained from infancy to believe in errors was. Damn, for a long time I believed what I read in papers, I believed what politicians said. I'm embarrassed by my gullibility. The Church hadn't taught me anything that was clear, certain, or of any use in my life. I was mad, but yet in the quiet of that mission church I began to think that true wisdom should be positive and not made up of what we don't know. Wisdom, I thought, must be grounded on the fullness of what we do know. But where do I go for such knowledge?

Always the questions. I thirst for answers.

Halfway down the aisle, there was a break in the rows of pews in order to form an aisle leading to a small, side chapel adjacent to the main church. The chapel contained a kneeler in front of a small altar. Above the altar was a shrine dedicated to Our Lady of Bethlehem. A richly gowned statue of Mary holding rosary beads in one hand and Jesus in the other was enclosed in a glass case. In the early days of the mission, the chapel had been used as a mortuary. On the day of my visit, two women, each in their mid-thirties, knelt alone in the candlelit room. In deep prayer, they were motionless, their eyes tightly closed, their thoughts focused on the Mother of God. Perhaps, Mary would conquer their problems for them.

I stared for a few seconds at the burning candles, each reflecting a stranger's prayer, and wished that somehow a little glimmer of light could be shed on all the mysteries of my former faith. I took one last look at the statue and the women kneeling before it, and then returned to the main church and continued walking down the center aisle. I paused next to a pew and genuflected. It was another reflex action, albeit a wobbly one. As my right knee touched the hard, stone floor and I began to get up, I could feel the strain in the muscles of my left thigh—muscles not used in this reverent fashion in years, and they protested. The nuns hated sloppy genuflecting—like knees not really touching the ground, or backs bent over. Sr. Saint Dorothy was the best of the nuns at genuflecting; she looked holy doing it. Her back was always straight and erect, her right knee gently touched the floor, where it took a noticeable pause before beginning its ascent, and her hands remained joined in a prayerful manner throughout and were never used to maintain her balance or to push down on her left thigh to help lift herself up. Sr. Saint Dorothy would have frowned at me for the way I had genuflected.

I sidestepped my way into the pew and sat down. The visit to the church had drained me, left me mentally exhausted. I felt as if I was in a museum, a museum housing artifacts not from an ancient, long-dead culture, but from my dormant past. Disturbing those memories was in itself a disturbance. I closed my eyes. My mind was restless, my thoughts scattered. I tried to block out all rationalizations and attempted to be still. Somewhere in the Bible it says, "Be still and know that I am God." In effect, God was saying: "Sit down, shut up, and listen to Me." I tried.

But thoughts of the corporal of the Mission Guard, my parents, and the notion of my being a heretic kept interrupting my endeavors at being mentally settled and hushed. The invisible cross my parents bore, along with all Catholics of their generation, was the agony of watching the erosion of the shorelines of their faith. Theirs was an age of massive changes, and change hurts. Their parents knew nothing of doubt; their children knew little of faith. They had to step from a world of Papal authority into a world of religious plurality. My parents didn't understand me, and I held that against them. As I sat before the gold tabernacle with winged angels atop it, I started to understand how difficult it would have been for my parents to have understood me. I was a curious child in a religious environment that not only didn't appreciate curiosity, but also tried to crush it. I questioned the unquestionable, and it baffled them, it hurt them. I wished we could talk about it.

I reached into my satchel and pulled out my *Baltimore Catechism*. I opened it at random, and my eyes fell upon question #1380: "Will the damned suffer in both mind and body?" Knowing exactly how it would be answered, I closed the book—slammed it closed.

I felt hatred for the book. But I knew I had to read it, because it contained important clues to my understanding the role religion played in my creating the me I have become—the me I wish I wasn't.

I think that part of my problem as an adult has been my exaggerated concern over doing what is right. I felt there had to be one right way, one right choice, one right answer. I hated ambiguity, yet the older I got the more ambiguous

I became, and I hated myself for it. In every situation I encountered, whether it was a simple matter of buying a new television, or a more complex issue of deciding to take a new job or move to a new city, I not only wanted to do the right thing, I was obsessed with doing the right thing. Worse, I feared doing the wrong thing. But the "right thing" more often than not turned out to be a coin toss between two or more equally valid choices. Something could be right today and wrong tomorrow. Where did this over-blown concern for the "right answer" originate? I think it can be traced back to the *Baltimore Catechism*. Each of the thousands of questions—none of which I would ever have asked— had one answer. Slowly over time, the notion that every question had just one "right answer" became engraved upon my mind. Once I had memorized the "right answer" to the questions, I had little reason to look for a different answer.

I fear, dear Kate, you might consider these reflections as little more than psychobabble. But they aren't. I think that the method used by the Catholic Church to teach religion was doubly disastrous. First, on the spiritual level I was encouraged to accept the truth handed to me and not to search for the truth myself. Also, it promoted the false idea that there was only one truth—their's. Second, on a psychological level it produced inflexible people. Also, it stymied creative thinking because I became so accustomed to a one "right answer" approach that whenever I encountered a problem I opted for the first solution I found. The side effects of having drunk of this polluted water of faith still lingers in my subconsciousness. Out of sight perhaps, but not out of mind.

As an adult, my gullible Catholic mind looking for new answers found it easy to accept unbelievable solutions to the mysteries of life. One of the early Fathers of the Church, I think it was Tertullian, said, "I believe because it is unbelievable." And Tertullian, a holy man who exaulted in the thought that he would be able to look out from heaven at the suffering of the damned, wasn't raised on the *Baltimore Catechism*—in fact, he didn't even know Baltimore existed. That's OK, for most of my life I didn't know that Tertullian existed, even though this man from a different time, a far different culture, helped to father my beliefs.

But today, those beliefs seem unbelievable, and because they are, unlike Tertullian, I can't believe them.

But, I can't let go of them either. They are a part of me, woven into the very fabric of my being. I pull on its loose thread, and I start to unravel. I can no longer believe, but I can't divorce myself from the emotions and the effects of that belief. My spirit still looks "for the hand of God" on my life. At times, I wish I had the faith to believe that Virgin Mary story the nuns so piously told me, so I could just get on with my life.

I wonder how I would have turned out if I had been raised on Thomas Paine's book *The Age of Reason,* instead of the insidious *Baltimore Catechism*. Humor me a bit more, my dear Kate, and allow me to share just a small piece of that magnificent book:

> Every national church or religion has established itself by pretending some special mission from God, communicated to certain individuals. The Jews have their

Moses; the Christians their Jesus Christ, their apostles and saints; and the Turks their Mahomet, as if the way to God was not open to every man alike.

Each of those churches show certain books, which they call "revelation," or the Word of God. The Jews say their Word of God was given by God to Moses, face to face; the Christians say their Word of God came by divine inspiration; and the Turks say their Word of God (the Koran) was brought by an angel from heaven. Each of those churches accuses the other of unbelief; and for my own part, I disbelieve them all.

But admitting, for the sake of a case, that something has been revealed to a certain person, and not revealed to any other person, it is revelation to that one person only. When he tells it a second person, a second person to a third, a third to a fourth, and so on, it ceases to be revelation to all those persons. It is revelation to the first person only, and *hearsay* to every other, and consequently they are not obliged to believe it.

It is a contradiction in terms and ideas, to call anything a revelation that comes to us at second-hand, either verbally or in writing. Revelation is necessarily limited to the first communication—after this it is only an account of something which that person *says* was a revelation made to him; and though he may find himself obliged to believe it, it cannot be incumbent on me to believe it . . . for it was not a revelation made to *me* and I have only his word for it that it was made to him.

When Moses told the children of Israel that he received the two tablets of the commandments from the hand of God, they were not obliged to believe him, because they had no other authority for it than his telling them so. The commandments carrying no internal evidence of divinity within them. . . .

When I am told that the Koran was written in heaven and brought to Mahomet by an angel, the account comes too near the same kind of hearsay evidence and second-hand authority as the former. I did not see the angel myself, and therefore, I have a right not to believe it.

When I am told that a woman called the Virgin Mary, said or gave out, that she was with child without any cohabitation with a man, and that her betrothed husband, Joseph, said that an angel told him so, I have a right to believe them or not; such a circumstance required a much stronger evidence than their bare word for it; but we have not even this—for neither Joseph nor Mary wrote any such matter themselves; it is only reported by others that they said so— it is hearsay upon hearsay, and I do not choose to rest my belief upon such infirm evidence.

Well, I wasn't raised on Paine. Perhaps if I were, I wouldn't now be living in pain.

How come I never heard about this book when it really mattered, when it could have made a difference? My Catholic education protected me from Paine's influence. In his own time Paine was accused of being an atheist, which he wasn't. Paine was a Deist, a person who holds that God must have existed to create the universe with all its laws, but beyond that, God has no concern for man or justice and has none of the anthropmorhic attributes for which we worship him. It is said that a Deist is an atheist without nerve. The Deist considers the Bible to be full of baloney.

"Full of baloney" is too kind a description for a book that presents a God who floods the world and drowns all its inhabitants in a violent fit of anger and then, in an act of remorse, repopulates the planet with the same kind of faulty people; a book that presents a God who enjoys the smell of animals burned as a sacrifice to him; a book that presents a God who haggles with Abraham over how many righteous men it will take to spare Sodom the agony of total destruction; a book that presents a God who sent a plague that killed seventy thousand people because King David took a census; a book that presents a God who sanctions slavery, polygamy, and religious persecution; a book that presents a God who denies civil rights to women; a book that presents a God who poopoos science and logic; a book that presents a God who was the first in a long line of tyrants to forbid his subjects access to knowledge; a book that presents a God who was primarily concerned with ritual purity laws involving food and bathing; a book that presents a God who prohibited shaving certain areas of the face with a razor; a book that presents a God whose idea of justice includes the death penalty for such "crimes" as working on the Sabbath, homosexuality, and not being a virgin on one's wedding night; a book that presents a God whose actions say that violence is an acceptable way to deal with problems; a book that presents a God who acts like a pokenose who enjoys sniffing into the minutest affairs and trifles of each individual and making entries of all their shortcomings in his blacklist; a book that presents a God who enjoys having his human creations prefer illusion over evidence and encourages his subjects to evade, deny, or gloss over life's bitter truths by blurring reality; a book that presents a God who inculcates guilt in connection with pleasure; a book that presents a God who is a cruel, ruthless mass-murderer and a military strategist as violent as any human tyrant known to history—I'd say such a book is full of shit.

Thomas Paine displayed none of the inflamatory rhetoric of the *Baltimore Catechism;* his writings reflect his cool rationale. I think he hit the nail on the head when he wrote, "Of all the tyrannies that affect mankind, tyranny in religion is the worst; every other species of tyranny is limited to the world we live; but this attempts to stride beyond the grave, and seeks to pursue us in eternity."

This towering man of reason and uncommon common sense, who played such a vital role in the founding of this country, would be rolling over in his grave if he could have heard then Vice President George Bush say in August 1987 while campaigning for the presidency, "I don't know that atheists should be considered citizens, nor should they be considered patriots. This is one nation under God." Even Thomas Paine, a Deist, wouldn't be a citizen according to Mr. Bush. We haven't come a long way, baby.

I can't believe how hungry I am. I'm going out for a bite to eat, and when I return, I'll resume this epistle.

Thursday, July 12—9:10 P.M.

Had the old standby—pizza, with extra cheese. Kate, my sweet, the Spanish Inquisition is still weighing heavily on my heart from this morning, and I just have a little more I want to tell you.

A few days after my visit to the mission church, curiosity about the early days of the California missions drove me to the library. I spent a whole day trying to put the missions into some kind of historical perspective. What I found shocked me.

Educated during the waning years of the Spanish Inquisition, young Father Junipero Serra was a professor at a college under the Inquisition's control. The Inquisition was formally established by Papal decree in 1478, with the objective of examining the genuineness of Jewish converts to Catholicism. Most of the Jewish conversions had little to do with faith—the Jews were merely saving their skins by accepting baptism. Centuries before, the Crusaders planned to purge Europe of its "Christ killers." Although the papacy opposed violence, it did nonetheless resort to conciliar provisions for their humiliation, social sequestration, and relegation to occupational misery by leaving them no other outlet for earning a living than to resort to usury, a practice the Jews found hateful. Church and state, with a little help from Christian mobs, drove the Jews to the periphery of medieval society. They were excluded from trade, handicrafts, and the professions and were deprived of the right to bear arms.

In the beginning of the thirteenth century, The Fourth Lateran Council, a special meeting of the Church hierarchy convened by the Pope, forced temporal rulers to compel Jews and Muslims to wear a badge distinguishing them from Christians. The intensification of popular piety and growing resentment against Jewish usury led to a series of expulsions: Jews were kicked out of England in 1290, Normandy in 1296, France in 1306. For awhile, the Jews found a safe haven in Spain, but by the end of the fourteenth century Christian fanaticism managed to cross the Pyrenees. Sparked by a fanatical archdeacon of Seville, deadly riots erupted in 1391. Thousands of Jews were killed, but most escaped persecution by converting to Catholicism.

Since Christians believed that baptism, even forced baptism, was binding, open "relapse" to Judaism was persecuted as heresy. Some Jews were forced to flee the country, but most chose to formally remain Christians, while privately adhering to the faith of their fathers. These Jewish "Christians" were called "Marranos," a derogatory term meaning "swine." As the ranks of these converts swelled, the hostility against them by the lower classes of "authentic" Christians intensified. Anti-Marrano pogroms and social ostracism soon became the order of the day. The unconverted Jews and less-than-genuine Jewish converts were blamed for causing the sincere Jewish converts to "backslide"—to not completely let go of their former faith. The powerful and highly placed members of society demanded an official inquisition that would weed out all Jews who were considered not to be genuine Christians. The Spanish Inquisition unleashed a wave of terror that shook Spain to its foundations. By 1492, Catholic monarchs issued a decree of expulsion, thereby purging the country of open Jewish adherence.

The Inquisition had and freely used the power to bring before its Holy Tribunals any person who was deemed a danger to Catholicism. It lasted well into the nineteenth century. The priests of the Holy Tribunal of the Inquisition were brought to the New World following the Spanish occupation of Mexico. A Jesuit missionary priest, Bartalome de las Casas (1474–1566), faced a New World Tribunal because his crusade on behalf of the Indian people was considered a threat to Catholicism. Las Casas wrote a book titled *The Tears of the Indians,* which tells the story of the holocaust endured by the native peoples of the West Indies, Mexico, Guatemala, Cuba, and Peru. Las Casas paints a harrowing and gruesome picture of the massacres and wanton killing of women and children by the Spaniards. The Tribunal issued a decree banning the las Casas book exposing the Spanish atrocities, on pain of punishment.

The theology, structure, and the power of the Spanish Inquisition held sway in the New World. In 1767, at the urging of the Tribunal, the Spanish monarch banished the Jesuit priests from the lower California missions because they protested the racial genocide that was taking place, and named Junipero Serra as the Father-President of the California mission system. Prior to his elevation, Serra had spent nearly twenty years as a missionary in Mexico.

Fr. Serra's diaries include notations of soldiers on horses firing at Indians who demonstrated against the missionaries' presence. Letters and diaries of other friars reveal that rape of Indian women by the soldiers was widespread, and that the priests did little to stop it. The economics of the mission system was built on forced labor. Women were forced to transport bricks and tiles; children combed wool and assisted weavers. Serra worked hand-in-hand with the Spanish authorities, who viewed the Indians as a source of profit. Of course, forced conversion was part of the mission picture. Padre Antonio de la Conception Horra wrote in 1779, "The treatment shown to the Indians is the most cruel I have ever read in history. For the slightest things they receive heavy floggings, are shackled, and put in stocks, and treated with so much cruelty that they are kept whole days without a drink of water." For his criticism, Horra was declared insane and escorted out of California.

The native Californians were viewed as savages in need of salvation. Various letters from missionary priests described the Indians as "wild and dirty," "disheveled," "ugly," "small," and "only because they have the human form is it possible to believe that they belong to mankind." The missionaries needed a heathen people to bestow the blessings of the Christian church upon. The Spanish Crown needed to secure, colonize, and protect their California land. The spiritual and secular need of each went well together. The missionaries would Christianize the natives, who in turn would be used to colonize the territory, provide a labor force, and supply the resources the Crown sought. Making the American Indians good Spanish Catholics made sense to Serra and the Crown. Wittingly or not, Fr. Serra was more than just a priest, he played an important secular political role. His "work" in California was performed at the discretion of the Spanish government—to put it bluntly, Serra was an agent of Imperial Spain.

Now the Church wants to make Father Junipero Serra a saint. In spite of the bloodthirsty actions of this priest, the Vatican under Pope John Paul II has decided that this draconic demagogue is worthy of veneration. But in promoting sainthood for this relic of the Spanish Inquisition, the Church must close its eyes to cultural chauvinism and racial bigotry that was at the heart of the destructive church-military colonization of California, and continue to promote a myth created by Catholic propagandists proclaiming that the Franciscans created a civilization from a wilderness—the Church must continue to rewrite history. Sainthood for Serra will only further distort the reality of his life. In truth, dear daughter, people make poor saints and worse icons.

During my fourteen years of Catholic schooling, I never learned of the atrocities connected with the Inquisition or the early mission days of California. Sure, I heard of the Inquisition, but I really didn't understand what it was all about. In the fall of 1989, the Chinese Communists rewrote the history of the student revolt right before our eyes, but I had no idea the Church pulled the same crap on me when I was in school. I didn't hear about the bad Popes, or the Popes who had an insatiable hunger for temporal power, or the Popes who had mistresses, or the Popes who had kids, or the genocide committed against entire races of people in the name of Jesus. I never knew that Popes led armies, assassinated enemies, and made love and war.

After my day at the library, I felt stupid for not knowing the real history of the Inquisition and the early days of the Spanish colonization of America. A Paul Simon song claims: "My lack of education didn't hurt me none." I can't say the same. Cicero, a philosopher who died forty-three years before the birth of Christ, came a lot closer to reality than Paul Simon when he wrote, "Not to know what happened before one was born is to remain a child." I am still a child.

I was mad at having been misled by the Church I loved so as a child, a Church I still have a hard time not loving. The Church would have us believe that Jesus really wanted to start a new religion, that He was the first Catholic, and that He said Mass with altar boys ringing bells and His noble faith had traveled untarnished down through the ages. The world is much different today, much smaller, and the Church couldn't get away with distorting the truth, with covering up the evil, on the grand scale it once did. For openers, they are no longer in bed with the government, they don't control the arts, and they don't own the press.

But they still try, they still lie. Old habits don't easily die. For example, last March, a draft of a new catechism prepared by the Catholic Church was circulated among bishops, who were asked to read the document and send their comments to the Vatican. It was the first time in more than four hundred years that the Church issued a comprehensive summary of its belief. The hefty, 434-page volume was titled *A Catechism for the Universal Church*. It was sent out to the bishops with the stamp "sub secreto," which means under secrecy. Critics of the document claimed that it ignored recent developments in theology, used the Bible inaccurately, confused central Catholic beliefs with less important ones (it gave equally detailed attention to the Trinity and to angels), and elevated theological positions that are still open for discussion to the level of established dogma. Some priests charged that the draft cites biblical passages out of context, without regard to what modern scholarship has found to be their original meaning—in other words the Vatican devils have narrowed scripture to prove preconceived dogmatic points. The sacraments are presented as if they were always celebrated in the manner they are today, when in truth, they evolved over centuries. The draft also ignored the fact that the New Testament writers held a diversity of views of Jesus, and it quotes Paul or Mark as if they held not only identical views but also highly refined philosophical concepts that the Church developed after centuries of theological controversies. Of course, the language used in the catechism remains sexist, referring to humans in general as "man" and using masculine pronouns throughout.

I'm sure all criticism will be ignored, because the Pope fears the Church is swerving toward the left and becoming too liberal. Since his election in 1978, Pope John Paul II has determined not only to put a curb on the sweeping changes set in motion by Vatican II (a 1960s gathering of the Church hierarchy that boldly decided to open the windows of the stuffy Church in order to let in some fresh air), but also to turn the hands of the clock back to a time before Vatican II when bishops, priests, and the laity were uncritically loyal to the Pope and his curial associates, back to a time when no Catholic ever dared question a Vatican teaching or Papal document.

When bishops and cardinals retired or died, Pope John Paul II has systematically replaced them with clerics who were more hard-line than his predecessor and who have unquestioning institutional loyalty and whose theological views are simplistic and reliably safe because their understanding of the faith is untouched by, if not hostile to, the most significant developments in theology and biblical studies since the 1950s. Across the globe—in Austria, Brazil, Canada, the Netherlands, Peru, West Germany—and across America—in New York, Detroit, Los Angeles, and Denver—Pope John Paul II has chosen religious neanderthals who don't cotton to debate or free thought or plurality of views to lead the faithful. And the faithful respectfully kiss their rings and asses. The average Catholic need not fear heretics like me. The Church will die from a cancerous disease from within itself.

The press rarely pokes its journalistic nose into the shady internal affairs of the Vatican, but the sexcapades of today's Protestant electronic missionaries—like televangelists Bakker and Swaggart—have garnered much media attention. Frustrated old virgin farts playing back room power games will always lose out in a battle for headlines to a juicy sex and money scandal involving the rich and famous. (The divorce of zillionaire tycoon Donald Trump gets more coverage than the collapse of communism in Eastern Europe.) The religious clowns who peddle salvation on television are creampuffs compared to the religious misfits of the past.

Can you imagine Ted Koppel doing *Nightline* during Serra's day? "Tonight from Baja, California, we'll be talking to Father Horra, a priest the Church has declared insane. Also joining us will be exiled priest Father las Casas, who claims the Spanish government is guilty of heinous crimes against the Indians of the New World. Later in the broadcast we will talk to members of The Holy Tribunal in Mexico City, and, from Spain, with a representative of the Crown. First these words."

During the interview "El Ted the Terrible," which is the way members of the Tribunal might have referred to Koppel, had a couple of loaded questions to throw the clerics' way. "Isn't fanaticism little more than a tool to squash doubt?" And the real killer question: "If Jesus was God, he therefore was omnipotent. If so, could he create a rock he could not lift?"

If only.

For more than a thousand years, our culture has been smothered in religion. And what good has it done? Religious zeal initiated the Crusades, the Holy Inquisition, the Puritan Revolution, the Thirty Years War, and countless other vulgarities. The disease of religion was responsible for the subjugation and cultural destruction of India, Africa, China, and the native civilizations of North and South America. The business of religion is primarily involved in the repression of all ecstasies and the exaltation of righteous indignation and violence.

Enough.

I'm tired. I wish I could let go of all this stuff. I'm overwhelmed by how much I don't know. I'm not just talking about history. My mind has been malnourished in so many essential mental foods: science, philosophy, literature —to name just three. I shared this little snippet of history—a mere microscopic grain of sand on the beachfront of humanity's past—because it excited me to learn about it. But at the same time it depresses me to realize how little I know about life.

On numerous occasions during the past few years, I would spend my spare time at UCLA's library. My hobby was self-education, my goal to learn as much as I could about spirituality. I can't say I went looking for God. No. I went looking for ways to understand the concept of God. I went as a detective looking for clues—looking for truth. I think I went with an open mind; at least it was ajar to the idea of God. I read books with both pro and con viewpoints; although works critical of religion were heavily outnumbered by those sympathic to the Almighty. Most of the time, the hours spent among all those books were exhilarating. I managed to find scores of books that looked at the Bible through skeptical eyes, exposing lies, myths, errors, and contradictions. It was a comfort to discover that many people down through the centuries had the same doubts as I had. I took delight in discovering such writers and thinkers as Bertrand Russell, Miguel de Unamuno, Sidney Hook, and Thomas Hobbes to name just a few. I read countless overviews and introductions to philosophy.

But there were an alarming number of times when I would walk up and down the seemingly endless aisles of philosophy, theology, and religion books and become so overwhelmed with a feeling of futility that my eyes began to tear up. I'd cry out to myself, "Look at all this. Look at all this. What fucking good has it done? What can I possibly learn? So much propaganda! So much bullshit! There can't possibly be any answers here!"

Most philosophers do not confront the tough problems of good and evil, of fate and freedom, of life and death, and instead retreat into the safe obscurities of logic and linguistic analysis. Philososphers seem to favor prolixity over clarity, and publication over truth. Sadly most philosophical dyspepsia cannot be savored. Philosophers offer no answers to the riddles of the universe.

Dear Kate, I don't think it's possible for you to understand my level of frustration. I hope you don't understand it. I hope you are happy and enjoying life. I hope you are only interested in humanity. I hope you are not obsessed with God the way I am.

You probably have no idea how much printed material there is on that simple little word . . . God. Simple word. No way. It is the most complex word known to man. At UCLA's library, there must have been two or three dozen books by and about the German philosopher Gottfried Wilhelm Leibniz (1646–1716) alone. Leibniz offered to the world cosmological proof for the existence of God and declared that God had created the best of all possible worlds, but it is not a perfect world. Not a perfect world—talk about insight! I remember pulling one of his books off the shelf one day, and in it Leibniz is babbling on and on about distinguishing between truths of reason and truths of fact, as well as the distinction between analytic and synthetic truth. I found the stuff unreadable. Theoidiocy, as I called it this morning. This guy wrote over a dozen books, and without the aid of a computer. I really don't know how all the intellectuals of the Middle Ages did it. Leibniz is just one of the titans of thought who take up a lot of space in the library. There are scores of books by and about such great minds as René Descartes, Denis Diderot, Peter Abelard, Blaise Pascal, George Santayana, Georg Wilhelm Hegel, Immanuel Kant, Soren Kierkegaard, Martin Heidegger, Ludwig Feuerbach, David Hume, and countless others. Where do you begin? How can you take it all in?

And this is just the philosophy section, which is small in comparison to the religion section, where there are innumerable books on the history and theology of every religion you can imagine, and then some. There are books on Jainism, Judaism, Zoroastrianism, Shintoism, Taoism, Lamaism, Bahai, Buddhism, Hinduism, Islam, and every other religion under the sun. There are books on polyism, pantheism, deism, dualism, fatalism, epicureanism, empiricism, existentialism, modalism, mithraism, maoism, monothelitism, monotheism, monophysitism, montanism, sabellianism, parseism, gnosticism, and god knows how many other isms. I even found a book on eutychianism, which claimed that at incarnation Christ's human nature was absorbed into the divine nature. This doctrine denied that Christ had two natures and implied that God was tempted, suffered, and died. Of course, the monk who dreamed up this doctrine sometime around A.D. 450 in a monastery in Constantinople, a guy named Eutychus, was excommunicated.

All these isms split hairs. For example, monothelitism, which flourished in the seventh century, claimed that while Christ had two natures, he had but a single will. (No mention of who was in it.) And speaking of Christ, let's not forget the myriad different denominations within Christianity, far too numerous to mention. Every single book of the Bible—thirty-nine in the Old Testament and twenty-seven in the New Testament—has scores of books offering exegesis, commentary, and interpretations. There are books on the Vedas, the Hindu scriptures. There are also many books on and about the Koran, the sacred scriptures of Islam, which, by the way, were lessons revealed by God to Mohammed who in turn dictated them to a disciple. The Muslims believe the original text of the Koran is in heaven. Isn't that special?

I really don't mean to be flippant. The point is that on some days my visit to the library sent me into a downward spiral of depression. So much stuff. So little time. Worse, who cares? What good has it done?

I have an unquenchable thirst to learn, but unfortunately my well is empty—drained by time, opportunity, and money. How does a broke, forty-three-year-old television producer whose only skill is his ability to put skin on baloney transform himself into a student of life? The futility of my life makes the choice to continue to exist seem irrational.

Kate, my sweet, take the time to look around, to learn about everything human. Never think that you know it all. I remember flunking Ancient History in high school. But I had a great excuse. I convinced myself that Nebuchadnezzar (he was the king of Babylonia around 550 B.C.) had nothing to say to me, it was more important that I listened to what Mr. Ed (he was a talking horse who had his own network sitcom) had to say. Cursed be the arrogance of youth. Cursed also be the arrogance of the Church in telling me not to concern myself with this life, but to worry instead about the eternal life that follows death.

Well, daughter, this Inquisition crap has worn me out and fired me up. I better call it quits for tonight and try to get some sleep. Good night, my love.

Friday, July 13—8:50 A.M.

Hi. Had a fitful, restless night. I suppose I took the anger I felt about religious injustice to bed with me. Try hard, dear daughter, never to go to bed angry—it's a waste of sleep.

I just thought of a humorous postscript to my visit to the library. In order to escape the oppression I felt from spending so much time among the racks of philosophy and religion books, I took a stroll through the fiction section. I wasn't looking for anything in particular, I was just walking and daydreaming. As I made my way along a row of books written by authors whose last name began with the letter "S," my attention was arrested by a book written by Jean-Paul Sartre (a pipe-smoking, French writer who turned a bad mood into a philosophical outlook known as Existentialism, and whose first book announced that life made him puke, and who once said man "is alone, abandoned on earth in the midst of his infinite responsibilities, without help, with no other aim than the one he sets for himself") titled *The Age of Reason*. I pulled it off the shelf.

The book was published in July of 1947, the copy I held in my hand was part of the book's seventh printing, in June of 1952. It had a plain, faded gray cover. The spine simply listed the title and the author's last name. There wasn't even a dust jacket. The card in the back of the book indicated that between October 4, 1989, and March 22, 1990, the book had been checked out nine times. That seemed like a lot to me. But somewhere along the line, a fundamentalist, self-righteous Christian borrowed the book and decided to add some penciled commentary in the margins. The first notation came on page 20. The text read:

> "Take off your slip." She obeyed; he tipped her backwards on the bed and began to caress her breasts. He loved their taut, leathery nipples, each in its ring of raised red flesh. Marcelle sighed, with eyes closed, passionate and eager.

You get the idea. Anyway, in the margin, the crusading Christian wrote: LUST. THIS IS FORNICATION.

A few pages later, we discover that Marcelle is pregnant. Mathieu, her lover from the above quoted scene, responds to the news by telling another character:

> A baby. I meant to give her pleasure, and I've given her a baby. I didn't understand what I was doing.

The Christian understood: FORNICATING was neatly printed in perfectly formed bold letters in the margin. When the topic of abortion comes up, the Christian informs us that this is a sin, a very big sin.

Another character mentions that Mathieu stays with Marcelle because "he must sleep with someone." That line received this editorial comment in the margin: DEFINITELY FORNICATION.

Another character mentions he is going to "blow my brains out." Next to that line was written: MORTAL SIN.

Next to the line "He was now about to be engulfed into an enveloping and strong-savored sensuality" came this clarification: i.e., LUST.

Throughout the book, the words "lust" and "fornication" are written in the margins about a dozen or more times. One character says, "One can't change." That drew this observation: NONSENSE. All off-color language, even the word "bitch" is labeled as: PROFANITY. A character says, "I don't care a damn for morality," which according to our self-appointed censor means: THEN YOU ARE A SINNER.

Sartre concludes his book, which paints a powerful picture of moral and social decay and which many people consider to be a masterpiece (despite the fact that the Roman Catholic Church placed it on its "Index of Forbidden Books" in October of 1948), with: "Various tried and proved rules of conduct had already discreetly offered him their services: disillusioned epicureanism, smiling tolerance, resignation, flat seriousness, stoicism—all the aids whereby a man may savor, minute by minute, like a connoisseur, the failure of a life. He took off his jacket and began to undo his necktie. He yawned again as he repeated himself: 'It's true, it's really true: I have attained the age of reason.' "

Our Christian reviewer then supplied his or her own ending: GOD MAKES

A SPECIALTY TO REDEEM FAILURES. THE MOST HOLY CHRISTIAN RELIGION IS
FOUNDED ON FAITH RATHER THAN REASON.

I closed the book. I had never read it before, but I knew of it, knew about
its existentialist theme. I had no real interest in reading it now. But after skimming
it and reading all the penciled comments in the margin, I couldn't help but wonder
why this person would bother to read the book and, without regard to public
property, deface it with their twisted views.

As I started to walk away, I spotted another book, *The Last Puritan,* by
George Santayana. Like *The Age of Reason,* this also was an old book, published
in 1936, and it too had a dull, wordless cover—only drab green instead of gray.
The first page I opened to carried the following penciled note in the margin:
OLIVER HAD GOOD WORKS BUT WITHOUT FAITH IN CHRIST. THUS HIS WORKS
ARE UNACCEPTABLE BEFORE GOD ALMIGHTY.

You guessed it. The same Christian got to this book. His or her—I get the
feeling it's a her—distinctive printing style let's me know this person has carved
out a little career to counteract the evil effects of books offered by the City of
Angels. Her notes have a heavier editorial tone in this book. For example: WEALTH
CAN BE AN OBSTACLE TO CONVERSION; ONLY SALVATION BRINGS VIRTUE; JIM WAS
NEVER SAVED; WE WILL BET THE VICAR NEVER PRAYED FOR THE SALVATION OF
HIS SON JIM; THE KINGDOM OF HEAVEN IS SPIRITUAL AND NOT THE STARRY SKY.

You get the point. In *The Last Puritan,* Santayana writes that the character
"Oliver" was a good puritan. The self-appointed reviewer and defender of the
One True Faith took exception to that claim and offered this definition of a
puritan: A GOOD PURITAN IS VERY STRICT IN MORALS AND RELIGION. OLIVER
DOES NOT PRAY OR GO TO CHURCH AS YET. HE IS ONLY ABOUT EIGHTEEN YEARS
OLD AND STILL UNSAVED.

Another character was described as "methodically making love," which the
Christian made clear was: SENSUAL, BUT NOT GODLY.

Someone, either a librarian or reader, took the time to try to erase the comments;
but, the task most have been far too time-consuming and they only managed
to erase about half of them.

Oh, dear Kate, there may be freedom "of" religion in America, but not freedom
"from" religion. Religion is everywhere, from bumper stickers to the dollar bill.
Two presidential contenders in the 1988 race for the White House were ordained
ministers. This society is so saturated with religion that there is no escaping "God"—
even the author of the daily newspaper column "Dear Abby" serves as a divine
mouthpiece. In a recent column, a twenty-three-year-old male who loved sports
and Jesus told Abby he wanted to be a woman and run on the U.S. Olympic
women's track team. This desire was destroying him, and he questioned why
God would give him a man's body but a woman's feelings. Abby informed him
that, although the Lord created him, somehow "nature" made a biological blunder.
Furthermore, she stated that the doctors who developed and performed sex change
operations did so with God's guidance in order to rectify such blunders of nature!

The only blunder I see is newspapers printing such nonsense. Yes, Kate, "God"
is everywhere, and almost everyone seems free to speak for the Almighty or use

"God" to justify whatever they want to justify. Polls indicate that over 97 percent of Americans believe in God, and 60 percent claim they attend church on a regular basis. Maybe I should just move to Europe, where I understand that 40 percent of the population do not believe in God, and only 10 percent attend regular church services.

I know this is going to sound strange, but this morning I was wondering if one should bother shaving for suicide. As I look at the pictures of myself on the walls of my study, I can't help but notice that in half of them I have a full beard, and in the other half I'm clean shaven. There is one photo where I'm sporting a goatee—evidently taken at a time when I was torn between the two looks.

The other thing I notice in the pictures of myself is that there appears to be two of me: the fat me and the not-so-fat me. During my lifetime, I've lost at least three hundred pounds. And found almost every single pound again. I shed ninety pounds on one diet, sixty on another. Losing a mere twenty pounds was a snap—I've done it at least a half dozen times. I don't think a year of my adult life has passed without seeing me lose and/or gain ten pounds or more. I've gone on more fasts than Gandhi, without toppling any empires, only gaining a little discipline and wisdom. I have an extensive wardrobe of "fat clothes"—shirts and jackets that could easily provide shelter for a family of six. They hang in my closet as a testament to my fat past and as an option for my fat future.

Cookies are to me what the apple was to Eve—my downfall, the forbidden delight of the bakery of my life. I can't walk past a Mrs. Field's cookie shop. It is as if there was some strange and powerful magnetic force pulling me in. The taste of "Debra's Special"—your basic oatmeal raisin cookie with extras—fills my mouth and mind. This mysterious force not only pulls me in, but also turns me into a zombielike creature—I'm stripped of all my will power and I march like an unthinking robot to the counter. I order one more cookie than is humanly possible for one person to consume. Once my stomach is full, the guilt sets in.

This morning, as I stared into my bathroom mirror, I saw a man who hasn't shaved in four days and who is about twenty pounds overweight. OK, thirty. I like the stubble; I hate the flab. As I stared at my reflection, quizzically rubbing my beard, I couldn't help wonder, "Who the hell are you? What's your story?"

Am I the flesh and bones I see? Is there more to me than meets the eye? How did I get here, get to be whoever I am? I feel like a spectator watching a play I don't understand. Would it matter if my existence came to an end tonight? Has the play gone on too long, like some kind of Greek tragedy? Is it time for my final curtain?

Kate, I'm so very tired of being a spectator. I want to be a performer. But would that make my life nothing more than play-acting? Who writes the script of a life, is it God or man? My life seems to have been written by neither God nor me; the author has been circumstances. But to hell with circumstances, soon I am going to write the ending. Still, I wonder if the ending I am about to script has been predetermined. If so, why? What did I do to wind up so alone, so empty, so dead?

The seasons come and go; is it simply my time to go? More important, will I survive the death of my body?

Questions, questions. More damn questions. I feel like punching that damn mirror, shattering into a thousand small pieces the glass that reflects my outer image. My mind suddenly leaps back in time to my days as a TV producer. This morning, those days seem like the ancient history of a person I can hardly recall.

I was producing the most popular daytime soap opera in America—"Harvest of Life." The show's leading male—a guy every woman went to bed with in her dreams (despite the fact the actor was gay)—was doing a scene where he was alone in the bathroom, staring into a mirror, just like I am doing. Only he saw a hunk; I see a chunk. He was wondering why his girlfriend had left him; I am wondering why my exuberance for life has left me. The actor was drunk or high on something. For many of the actors, the set doubled as a drug store. During the scene, the actor, known for his penchant for ad libbing, followed his inner emotional instincts, and suddenly punched the mirror. It was a brilliant piece of acting, you could feel the character's frustration and rage. Unfortunately, the actor punctuated the action, with a loud scream of, "Fuck!" Obviously, we couldn't use it, and I ordered the scene to be shot over, hopefully with the expletive deleted. The actor went nuts, demanding to know why. While the studio nurse worked on his hand, which he cut while punching the mirror, and the stage crew replaced the shattered mirror, I had to calm him down and coax him into doing the scene again. The offscreen soap behind the soap is far more interesting than anything the viewers get to see on the screen.

I guess I won't punch the mirror. This isn't a scene from a soap opera—it's the harvest of my life. It's funny, I can see the opening of the show running through my mind. The pictures convey warmth, romance, and love: couples embracing, kids playing, panoramic vistas, all underscored by the lush sounds of classical music. After about twenty-five seconds, a deep, richly textured, male voice intones, "A little stardust caught, a piece of a rainbow clutched . . . this is the true HARVEST OF LIFE." Pure soap. I wrote that years ago, reworking a line from Thoreau, but today, there is no stardust to catch, no rainbow to clutch.

I hate soap operas; yet, in a strange way, life is like a soap opera, only without the melodramatic music and the high occurrence of amnesia. My mother was hooked on them before we even owned our first television. In the late fifties, owning a TV was a sign of affluence, a sign we could not display. But that didn't stop my mom from getting her daily fix of "Guiding Light." Each day, we would walk six long city blocks, past Mr. Beerman's grocery store, Mr. Elsworth's candy store, Mr. Gill's bakery, Jimmy's butcher shop, and Johnny's barber shop with its candy-striped pole outside, to a local, family-owned department store named Frankel's. We lived in a quiet little slice of the Big Apple, in the borough of Queens, far from the screaming haste of Manhattan. As we entered the store, my mom clutched my hand and quickly pulled me past racks of clothes that never tempted her. She only wore drab housedresses. She made a beeline for the steep flight of stairs that rose to the second floor: housewares and appliances. We hurried past the shiny new refrigerators, which we still called ice boxes, past the pots and pans and dishes. Finally, we made it to our destination, the far corner of the store where the televisions were displayed. For the next fifteen minutes she visited her TV friends—the Bauer's.

Thirty years later, Mom is gone, I'm about to go, but "Guiding Light" is still on the air. Sure, the show has changed over the years—in fact, it bears no resemblance to it's early days; it has changed with the times.

"Guiding Light" began its broadcasting life in 1937 as a radio show. The central character was a minister—the Reverend Dr. John Rutledge—who kept a reading lamp in his window to serve as a beacon for his troubled parishioners. Reverend Rutledge was the "guiding light" of the community. The nonsectarian minister delivered sermon after sermon, whose themes denounced the futility of war, espoused the brotherhood of man, and the sentiment that love given to others will enrich our own lives. Every Good Friday he spoke of how the faith of one man, the crucified Christ, was still the hope of mankind, the "guiding light" to all peoples at all times. The show was created by a young Jewish woman who was raised without any formal religious training, but who turned to Christianity because she felt that her life was missing something, and she wanted something to believe in, something to comfort her.

I had—stealing a term from the *Baltimore Catechism*—a "superabundant" amount of religious training. Yet, oddly enough, today I feel something is missing in my life, and I desperately want something to believe in, something to comfort me. But once you are confronted with the emptiness of life and see nature as hostile and knowledge as illusory, where do you go for comfort? (It's no wonder drug use is rampant.) In some corners of Hollywood turning from worship of God to the worship of nature is now in vogue. I am enchanted by nature, but I find the ingenious ways it creates calamities—floods, tornados, hurricanes, earthquakes—more than reason enough not to worship nature. As playwrite Tennessee Williams wrote in *Suddenly Last Summer*, "Nature is not made in the image of man's compassion."

I wish I could simply believe in myself. But, how do I make the transition from belief in the supernatural, to belief in the natural? I seem unable to turn the clock back. I'm stuck here in the worst of times.

"Guiding Light" made the transition from radio to television in 1952, a change that meant my day then included walks to Frankel's Department Store with my mother. Those were the simplest of times, the best of times. I had no beliefs and no doubts.

Things are no longer simple. I imagine it's going to be nearly impossible for you to understand just what's going on in my head. I had hoped this letter would explain some of it, but I'm not so sure I'm succeeding. Part of what I'm trying to say is that kicking the religion habit is harder than quitting drugs or alcohol. I feel as if I'm trapped in some kind of cruel detox ward—just a prayer away from being hooked on religion again. The transcendental temptation is great. The ex-alcoholic must always see himself as a drunk who doesn't drink, but how should the ex-religious see himself? I'm viewed as a heretic, a person who has lost his faith, while a person who has kicked a drug habit is praised for his or her heroism.

My religious training taught me to see the universe as a battleground of dualisms engaged in constant conflict. This world that I was born into was pitted against the next world where I would wind up. This world of time and space was pitted against a coming world of eternity. A world of faith battled a world of reason. The spiritual world fought the material world. Things were either sacred or secular. People were either Catholic or non-Catholic, saved or unsaved. Where is the evidence for such religious segregationism? These unreal opposites had been partitioned into pairs of false dichotomies. The nuns claimed that the things of heaven were holy and that the things of the world were profane. This imagined separatism is a shame—and a sham. The Hebrew word for "holiness" implied service to others and a detachment from the profane. The Latin word for "profane" meant "outside the temple" and therefore separated from the sacred. In other words, "holy" and "profane" weren't warring opposites, they were merely different concepts. Something secular could be sacred, and something sacred could be secular. Do things and people "outside of the temple" still not share in God's nature?

The nuns fed us "facts" about creation, the Trinity, incarnation, redemption, salvation, the resurrection and the ascension of Christ, heaven, hell, Satan, and God. But these were empty, lifeless words representing concepts and theories. If the "facts" made no sense in the minds God gave us, we were told to think of them as mysteries—sacred mysteries that eternally lie beyond the reach of human comprehension. That tidy explanation was handy for the nuns—it put an end to our questioning and probing, and in their place offered only blind acceptance. We were lead into a willing suspension of disbelief. But labeling speculation as truth and theory as fact was both presumptuous and intellectually dishonest.

Man being man, he must think, must question, must probe, and must seek greater understanding. If something looks irrational, sounds irrational, then it's hard to continue to pretend that it is rational. I think many people who pledge their allegiance to God and church pretend that their loyalty is rational, but pretense is neither virtue nor knowledge. Why is it that people so easily accept propositions that defy natural reason? I really don't know, but we do get on planes without the foggiest notion of how they fly, so I guess mankind has little difficulty accepting something they find incomprehensible—a "fact" which keeps churches in business. In fact, here is the one universal law behind all religions: The more ridiculous a belief system, the higher the probability of its success.

But believing something doesn't make it true.

Yes, daughter, I lost my faith; no, I'm not going to shave.

Damn, these last few pages have been heavier than I am, which reminds me: it's time for lunch.

Friday, July 13—2:30 P.M.

Hello again. While eating, a Woody Allen line popped into my head: "The chief problem about death, incidentally, is the fear that there may be no afterlife— a depressing thought, particularly for those who bothered to shave." It managed to bring a slight smile to my stern face. I envy his ability to remain humorous while probing the more solemn aspects of life.

During a short walk after lunch, I realized that today was Friday the Thirteenth. Luckily, I didn't walk under any ladders, and no black cats crossed my path. Superstitions are obviously too foolish to believe, yet we treat them as if we do believe them. I guess nothing is too degrading to affirm once it has become imbedded in common belief. People seem to enjoy superstitions so much that they are not readily inclined to give them up. When I was about ten years old, I was walking to school on a Friday the Thirteenth and a black cat crossed my path. I smiled to myself because I gave no credence to the myth that such an occurrence on such a day would bring bad luck. Later that day I broke my arm playing football.

It's easy for a young mind to allow superstition to triumph over coincidence, which is exactly what I did. Not that I actually ever really believed the superstitions associated with black cats and Fridays that fall on the thirteenth day of the month; it's just that I figured why take chances, why tempt fate? The human mind seems more attracted to magical thinking than to thoughtful reasoning: 95 percent of the country believes in God. Just a casual look at the movie guide in any newspaper, or a quick review of the network television schedule will clearly reveal that the public prefers falsehoods to reality. If they didn't, they wouldn't go to the movies or watch television.

Yesterday morning, I started to tell you about my early history, but in less time than it takes a black cat to cross your path, I wandered off into a lengthy digression on faith, church history, and soap operas—an unlikely but fitting trio of topics. I can see how this letter is taking on a life all its own, going into all sorts of unplanned directions—a lot like my life did. This afternoon, dear daughter, I want to return to my early days.

My childhood differed very much from yours in one major way—I was part of a functioning family. I feel badly that you were robbed of that experience. All I can do now is tell you about it, and maybe help you see its importance.

When I was growing up, I saw family life in two conflicting ways. On one hand, it was boring drudgery, something to escape as quickly as possible. On the other hand, it was a safety zone cushioned by a deep sense of communion. It is both.

Outside of the home, people love you for a reason. It could be your wit, or your charm, or your looks, or your money. Inside the home, your family's love needs no reason. It comes with your birth, you are its flesh and blood.

In my teenage years, I felt that I could not be me at home, that I had to escape in order to develop. They didn't understand me, and I didn't understand them. I didn't like the way my father did things; his values were not my values.

Years later, when I was out on my own, surrounded by strangers and fighting for survival in the world of commerce, my mind often drifted back to the days when I would come home from school upset about something, and there was my grandmother with the sure-fire antidote of cookies and milk. I frequently thought about the days when I was sick, and my mother patiently catered to my every wish, and my father would come home from work bearing some little gift to lift my spirits.

Family life can be like a tether that binds you up in order to keep you hostage, and it can also be like a lifeline that pulls you up from a sea of disasters.

I was lucky. My mother's love for me was complete and unselfish. Her love showed me that the world was not altogether hostile and that people can be trusted. Despite the fact that I would eventually come to see the world as mad and cruel, to see that the earth trembles and men declare war, to see that everything is bad, I nonetheless believed everything could be bettered. My basic optimism was nurtured in a hot house of maternal love, which gently whispered that kindness and affection can always be found, that there are people who will give everything without asking anything in return. My life experiences never confirmed that kind of blind faith in humanity, yet I never stopped believing it—until recently that is.

Stories of child abuse appear with alarming frequency in the news these days. I can't imagine the impact on a child who is born into a home where his or her mother substitutes cruelty for love. What a tragic influence—a perfect environment to breed pessimists and neurotics. The home should be a schoolhouse of love. Family life is where we learn about love, learn to love. For many children, however, it is a prison of hate.

I'm sure you have already realized that much of life is consumed by role playing. We have professional responsibilities to fulfill. Social life demands certain behavior. There is public protocol to follow. The simple fact is we can't be ourselves wherever we please. When I was a network television executive, I had to wear a jacket and tie to work, though my personal preference leaned more toward jeans and a sweatshirt. But in the company of our family, in the world of our home, we are free to be ourselves. No need for makeup, no need for false fronts, no need for formalities—we are home, we are free.

Still, the home doesn't guarantee peace and harmony, only tolerance. My sister never cared for my brother's taste in music, and everyone thought he played it too loud—this, of course, was long before the days of headsets. My monopolizing the TV when a Yankee game was being broadcast irritated my sister—yes, this too was long before the days of each family member having their own personal "entertainment centers." My father's falling asleep in his favorite living room chair annoyed my mother, primarily because she had the unenviable task of waking him up so he could go to sleep. Everybody did something that got under somebody's skin. But these feelings didn't need to be concealed; only politeness was required. Each of the family members can view the others as insufferable fools not worth enduring, but he bears with them and knows that he may expect a similar grumbling tolerance from them.

But tolerance and the freedom to be yourself are not the only benefits of family life. The family also shares one another's burdens. My brother and I may have grown far apart, separated by distance and divergent interests, but, deep down, I know that if I really needed him, he'd be there. In a world of strangers, family members are our only real friends. Sadly, however, family members frequently argue and shut themselves off from one another. In these modern times, the tight-knit family units of days gone by are hard to maintain. Families are spread out, with many members answering the call of distant opportunities, making frequent contact a near impossibility. Being a family takes work, it takes commitment, yet all too often we are not up to the task. We can't find the time for a simple phone call, because we are completely absorbed in our own private worlds. Days quickly turn into months, which in turn easily become years, and before we know what happened, we've become strangers to the very people we call family. It saddens me greatly, that my family, which could have been a port in the storms of your life, are strangers to you, and my ending my life might insure they remain so. I know that if I called my brother and told him what I was planning to do, he'd be on the next plane to L.A., even though he would know he was powerless to change the course I have set for myself—which is why I don't call. I've let too many years of silence slip by. It's too late now for us to talk about my state of mind.

I guess I'm rambling on about families because I hope you don't repeat my mistakes. I had a friend once I thought I could always count on. I thought our friendship was stronger than that of any blood relation. I was wrong. Friendship can end, but you are always a part of your family, even if they hate you. I hope when I'm gone, that you reach out to my family. They will always love you, even though they hardly know you.

Friday, July 13—7:20 P.M.

I can't imagine how it was that I came to accumulate so many books. It is taking me forever to sort them out and dispose of them. Actually, I suppose the reason I have so many books is that I was constantly searching for concrete proof for something I had already believed or wanted to believe. As a Christian, I read only Christian books; books that strengthened my faith. When I sidestepped my way into Zen Buddhism, I devoured books on Eastern spirituality. I was especially drawn to the writings of Catholic priests who found genuine comfort in the Buddhist approach to God. When my interest shifted from theology to philosophy, used book stores featuring more scholarly tomes attracted my new curiosity. When the notion that God might not exist seriously entered my mind, books on atheism and humanism started piling up on my desk. In retrospect, I accepted or rejected the hypothesis of God on purely emotional grounds and then proceeded to hunt for reasons to justify my faith or my atheism. The hunt pretty much excluded people—people, for the most part, do not like talking about their beliefs, preferring to let sleeping dogs lie—and so I was forced to stalk in the field of books for my reasons to believe or not to believe.

Of course, beyond theology and philosophy, I had a large collection of books that dealt with my only other real interest in life: television and films. The funny thing is that all these books were purchased during the past dozen or so years. Before the ripe old age of thirty, I hardly did any reading at all.

I really thought I would find answers to my questions in the books I bought. But books have no answers. At best, they stimulate thought. But for the most part, they offer only propaganda masquerading as art or intellectual exploration. As I mentioned this morning, there are times when I visit a library and I leave with an overwhelming sense of hopelessness. Think about all the stuff that has been written and printed during the last century alone. I mean good stuff, written by talented, thoughtful, sensitive, creative people—works of great literature and profound philosophy. Try to imagine a collection of all the important books penned—the number and size of the collection would be staggering, and the building needed to store them would require the floorspace of a half dozen or more football fields strung together.

Yet with all the thinking and creativity left behind by those books, where are we? What have we learned? How have we improved? The world is still filled with hatred, war, corruption, violence, bigotry, superstition, and stupidity. People are starving and living in the streets. The educated can't make sense out of their lives. Pollution and waste are rampant. Teenage suicide is on the rise. There is no escaping crime. Drug abuse and alcoholism are rampant. Divorce is almost as common as marriage. The world's economy is beyond understanding. High-school students in America can't locate Japan on a map or name the Vice President of their own country; yet, baseball players make three million bucks a year, actors pull down a cool five million per picture, and teachers earn about $25,000 a year to shape the minds that will shape our nation's destiny.

People get worked up over the termination of a pregnancy, calling it the murder of a fetus, and yet they are unconcerned about large corporations causing nearly 400,000 deaths a year through the manufacturing and sale of cigarettes, or the destruction of the environment with careless oil spills. Religion blithely continues to explain the unexplainable, while ministers are put in jail for tax fraud and priests stand trial for molesting young boys. Inner cities across the nation are decaying and roads can no longer support the number of cars using them. Jails are overcrowded, and there is inadequate housing for the working poor. Inflation is out of control, yet billions of tax dollars are going down the drain to bail out failed Savings and Loan institutions forced out of business by widespread corruption. Islamic fundamentalists hold hostages for years upon years, and threaten to assassinate a writer whose opinions they find sacrilegious, and the powerful nations of the world can do nothing about it.

No one seems interested in creating an integral, just, and redeemed world. The buck—the Almighty Dollar—is the bottom line. While the world rejoices in the fall of Communism around the globe—and rightly so—the fact that to live as free men and women does not of itself produce qualitative or generous existence goes unnoticed. Soon, countries like East Germany will be producing their own sixteen-year-old blonde mall rats with squeaky voices and eyes aflame with consumer fever—girls, in tight jeans and T-shirts, who just wanna have fun, just wanna grow up to be like Madonna.

But none of this is anything new. The past echoes with forceful, articulate jeremiads that cursed the darkness of each age. Not long ago, I came across a book of essays by Thomas Carlyle, a Scottish writer and university rector. In an 1829 essay, he decried how commercial life was no longer governed by the old honest intention of making good merchandise for a reasonable price but by a new zeal for collecting as much as the market would bear for a shoddy product. And I thought that practice started with the manufacturing of American automobles. Everywhere he looked, Carlyle detected what he called "the signs of the times": hypocrisy, complacency, pretension, dependence on slogans and legislative contrivance, and expediency. Gee whiz, Jesse Helms and George Bush hadn't even been born yet. Carlyle found the contemporary English world to be a hubbub of talk without substance, action without wholesome results. I see the same "social gangrene" here and now. Everything changes, yet everything remains the same. There remains a dark underside to modern civilization, a darkness that seems to increase in the human psyche in inverse proportion to what we call "progress." Progress, my foot. Barbarism is alive and well in a world of mechanical efficiency.

The faith I once had in the notion that life was real and worth living has been uprooted by the conviction that it is a cosmic joke with no point but its pointlessness. The hope that mankind may be worth saving has been dashed by the evidence that we are, to use Swift's phrase, "the most pernicious race of little odious vermin that nature ever suffered to crawl upon the surface of the earth." Reality provided me with a shattering test to the endurance of my human identity as a child of God. Every human being is a flawed and impotent creature, floundering among petty frustrations. Life is a series of unhappy interruptions.

What a curmudgeon! And all I started to do this evening was tell you about all the books I had.

Books. Each one of them stirs up a chapter of personal history for me. One of the books I packed this morning stirred up more than mere memories. It also clearly demonstrated how we live in an age of mixed signals. It was a very popular book on running, written by an exercise guru named Jim Fixx, who wrote many books promoting the healthful benefits of daily jogging. Unfortunately, Jim died of a heart attack while jogging alone on a country road. A lot of us chunkos, who bought the book but failed the road test, got the last laugh on the exercise crowd and felt less guilty about skipping the daily jog.

Oh, Kate, I hope you take notice of all the mixed signals we receive—how society frequently says one thing and does another. The past few years have provided countless examples.

During the 1988 Presidential campaign it was revealed that Gary Hart, an intelligent, handsome politician, who had the Democratic presidential nomination in the bag, had an affair with a young blonde. Moral America, who turns a blind eye to the homeless, looks at Senator Hart and points a judgmental finger at him saying, "You don't have the morals to guide this nation. You're outta here," and he withdrew from the race.

Around the same time, Oliver North goes on trial for obstructing justice in the trading-of-arms-for-hostages scandal that tarnished Ronald Reagan's second term in the Oval Office, and it is revealed that the former Marine Lieutenant Colonel lied to half of Washington and Congress in order to protect Reagan. This same moral America, who supported a second-rate actor as he presided over the largest military buildup in human history while letting the infrastructure of his country collapse and the nation's budget deficit skyrocket to new heights, responds by making Oliver North a national hero and suggesting that he run for political office.

A short while later, President-elect Bush, whose unelectable "wimp" image was transformed into a winning "macho" persona through clever TV advertising, nominates Texas Senator John Tower for Secretary of Defense. During the congressional confirmation hearings, it is revealed that Tower, a short, rotund man with greased-down hair, had a drinking problem and was a womanizer as well. (I just love the word "womanizer." It describes a sexually promiscuous man who loves to chase after women. Of course, a woman with the same proclivity toward men is not a "manizer," but a slut. Language is wonderfully entertaining and revealing.) OK, back to John Tower, the womanizer. Moral America expresses its outrage, and the tainted Tower is denied the position, despite his strong professional qualifications. Yet, another womanizer, the more famous and more handsome Teddy Kennedy, drives his car off a bridge on Martha's Vineyard following a party, swims to shore as a young, single woman drowns while trapped in his car, and gets re-elected over and over again.

Just a short time before the Tower hearings, Michael Dukakis ran against George Bush for the presidency. The mild-mannered, intellectual Governor of Massachusetts embodies the American dream: the son of immigrant parents, squeaky clean, Harvard graduate, professor, public servant with years of experience. Moral America takes notice and declares that he is "boring" and "dull" and instead chooses as its leader a former director of the CIA and "yes man" Vice President who promises a kinder gentler nation, then fights for the rights of citizens to own guns.

Go figure. Like I said kiddo, mixed signals, they are all around us.

I suppose I send out my own mixed signals. I'm always trying to be funny, playing the clown, telling jokes; it's a charade, a ruse to conceal my sadness, my hopelessness. I say that I love you, yet I don't spend much time with you. I claim not to be materialistic, yet I drive a car that cost far more than I needed to spend. I have a fancy compact disc player and a wide assortment of electronic gadgetry that would be found in any yuppie's home. I play the part of a television producer and spend my time creating television shows, yet, inside me, I harbor deep resentment of the industry. Like all television producers, I can switch my opinion in mid-sentence without losing my convictions.

No doubt about it, I send out my share of mixed signals. Honesty is very, very hard. Who amongst us is honest, true to themselves and others in all situations and at all times? We are all liars, counterfeiters and impostors—and the religious zealots are the biggest liars, counterfeiters, and impostors of us all.

Books. Each one tells a story. And my collection of books in a way tells my story. My quest for understanding can be traced in their titles. So far, I've only managed to throw away the overtly religious ones, that is, the ones that are pure propaganda. It's easy to throw the religious books away; it's not so easy to throw religion away.

Well, Kate, it's nearly eight o'clock on a Friday night in Hollywood, the glitz and glamour capital of the world. There should be something I could be doing instead of sitting here writing about life being nothing but a series of unhappy interruptions. Maybe it's time to interrupt this and venture out into the night. I think I'll take a drive to Venice Beach. I like the ocean, and hopefully there will be a cool breeze to enjoy. Besides, I want to see it one last time.

Bye for now, my love.

Saturday, July 14—8:10 A.M.

As I drove through Hollywood on my way to the ocean last night, I watched the crowds lining up for a night of fun. Friday nights have become a mini-Mardi Gras in reverse, in which every one puts on a party costume and celebrates the end of the dreary work week and the beginning of the frolicsome weekend. There were lines to get into all the trendy little Thai restaurants that dot L.A.'s landscape, and outside the movie theaters, dance clubs, comedy clubs, jazz bars, and Sushi bars. There was even a line in front of "Tail O' the Pup"—a little hot dog stand that operates out of a building shaped like a giant hot dog on a bun. The tables at a sidewalk cafe that features Szechuane dumplings and chili dogs were all taken. Even Chatteron's Bookshop on Vermont Avenue, a hangout of poet-carpenters, philosophy teachers, and gay hairdressers, looked crowded. In the shadow of Hollywood High, a sleazy joint featuring LIVE NUDE DANCERS was doing a brisk business—I'm sure of the patrons wondered why the word "live" was necessary. The hookers were displaying their goods along Sunset Boulevard, and the male prostitutes were offering their wares along Santa Monica Boulevard; it looked like it was going to be a busy night on both streets. Hollywood Boulevard was jammed with cars stuffed with teenagers out for a night of cruising. The punkers and bikers were mingling peacefully with tourists and panhandlers in front of Mann's Chinese Theatre. The city-wide party was in full swing.

I drove past one of the old mission churches. I thought how ironic it was that the Spanish missionaries' plan to Christianize and civilize the Indians culminated in the virtual extinction of the Indians and that the missionary City of Angels was transformed into a city were anything goes, any dream can be bought. L.A. has become a city of extremes, a city of super-haves and super-havenots. It's a city that is home to Beverly Hills and to Watts. I hate it. I pushed those thoughts out of my mind, and before long I made it to the ocean.

(I bet when you just read the words "mission church" you thought I'd launch into another harangue about the Inquisition. Fooled ya. But maybe I'll just slip in a little nugget I failed to mention the other day: frequently, when heretics were burned at the stake, the Chrisitians would first baste their feet with lard before lighting the fire, in order to magnify the pain the heretics were about to endure. This Inquisition crap really makes me sick.)

Venice Beach was equally bustling with party animals, only in this part of L.A. many of them are wearing roller skates. Under the moon light, a woman from some Hindu-inspired cult, wearing a long flowing white dress and a large white turban, was giving acupressure treatments to clients seeking relief from the stresses of the week. I've always liked Venice and its louche boardwalk, featuring mini swimsuits, sword swallowers, acrobatic skaters, elderly residents from a Jewish nursing home, mime artists, painters, psychics, hustlers, street vendors, singers, jugglers, clowns, tarot card readers, soapbox politicians, wild clothes on straight people, wilder clothes on gay people, and the roar of the sea. The incongruity of buildings, people, and lifestyles is a constant surprise. The hyper-hedonistic yuppies share the sands with the homeless and the drug addicts.

While the city and the seaside were alive with life, death was on my mind. Not actual dying, but what happens after death. As I drove and walked around a city of dreams and illusions, my mind stumbled through the puzzle of immortality, wondering if it was just another dream, just another illusion. Life so batters and bruises us that it is only natural that we crave some assurance of a compensatory afterlife, that we seek some ultimate redemption for the pain.

After renouncing my Christianity, along with my faith in God, death still had a terrible sting. Death makes life ugly. Knowing we are going to die diminishes our life. Man is the only animal that knows he or she will die. My cat knew about death—she even killed—but she didn't have a clue of the inevitability of her own death. One morning, a few years ago, I found her dismembered body in front of my house; she was the victim of a pack of wild dogs.

Unlike us, animals have no fear of death. "It is with death and the fear of death," wrote the philosopher Franz Rosenzweig, "that all perception of the universe begins. To cast off earthly fear, to take from death its sting and from Hades his pestilential breath—that is what philosophy presumes to do."

Which is why I read philosophy. But all the philosophy books ever written have done little to dull the sting of death. In his book *The Conscience of Words,* Elias Canetti, the Italian writer who won the Nobel Prize for Literature in 1981, wrote, "So long as death exists, any utterance is an utterance against it. So long as death exists, any light is a will-of-the-wisp, for it leads to it. So long as death exists, no beauty is beautiful, no goodness is good."

Friday night in Los Angeles is a loud scream against death.

It's odd how at times, without any warning, there flashes across my mind a fragment of something I have read. As I walked along the ocean front, I recalled a line written by the poet Alfred Lord Tennyson: "If there is no immortality, I shall hurl myself into the sea." That triggered the remembrance of something an English historian, whose name escapes me, wrote sometime during the nineteenth century; it went something along the lines of, "If immortality is not true, then it doesn't matter whether anything else is true or not."

Nobody I had seen last night seemed in the least bit concerned with immortality, yet I'm sure most people believed they would experience it. Me—I was concerned with it, very concerned, yet I doubted I'd ever experience it. But that isn't why I wanted to throw myself into the sea.

My doubts about what I was taught to believe caused me to ask myself some very basic questions. The answers that I arrived at caused my original doubts to be transformed into despair. Are the grandiose claims of religion the result of an unbridled use of speculation? Yes. Is it possible to know anything about God and immortality? No. Are God and immortality nothing more than vague, meaningless concepts created by the mind? Yes. Is it possible for me to know what I cannot experience? No. How can I know God if I can't experience him? I can't. Can I hope to know any "higher truths" about ultimate reality? No. Do you need a ladder to find "higher truths"? No reply.

I believe that the ideas of God and immortality overreach the human capacity for knowledge. But, sadly, my heart cannot accept that conclusion . . . it wants to love God, because it still craves a higher sentiment over a flat statement. My mind strives for clear-thinking skepticism; my heart beats with religious romanticism. The dualism within me is why last night I wanted so very much to throw myself into the sea.

Kate, my sweet, I thought I could find peace in knowledge; I found only disillusionment. I tried finding understanding in writing; I found only exhaustion.

The disillusionment and the exhaustion will come to an end within a few days . . . I do not see any way to overcome them, except through death. Despair has robbed me of my will to go on.

Saturday, July 14—2:45 P.M.

While cleaning out my desk this afternoon, I came across some notes I had written for a book I was once planning to write. The book was going to be called *Exit Stage Left*. The main character was a guy named "Keith Hettenbach." "Keith" worked as a stage manager at CBS in Hollywood. Even though he was successful, he was fed up with his life and career in show biz. He thought about killing himself but rejected the idea and instead decided he would simply disappear by getting on a plane and starting life over again in another country. "Keith" felt his days were empty and without meaning. But change was not enough. He wanted to start over, he wanted to be erased, relocated, renamed, and resurrected—to be born again in his own image and likeness!

I never wrote the book. I guess I quickly realized I didn't really want to write about disappearing; what I really wanted was to actually disappear. "Keith Hettenbach" was fed up with the shallowness of show biz; I was fed up the shallowness of Christopher Ryan.

I suppose the idea for the book traces back to a January night in 1987. I had been in bed for about an hour, unable to sleep. In the dark silence of the night, thoughts of suicide tiptoed into my bedroom. It was not an overwhelming presence; it was more a passing thought carried on a gentle breeze. But it wasn't a passing thought—it moved in and set up shop in my mind, and I was unable to evict it. The thought of actually killing myself bothered me, and I never seriously thought I would actually do it. Then one day, a compromise to ending my life popped into my head: I could run away from all that I hated.

Quickly, the notion of getting on a plane and starting life over in a foreign country became an obsession. Even though I have always been impulsive and spontaneous, I was unable to actually live out my fantasy. So, I decided to write about it rather than actually doing it. I was very excited about writing the book and thought it had tremendous potential. As the process of planning for "Keith Hettenbach" what I really wanted for myself, I logically arrived at the point where "Keith" saw that his problem had nothing to do with his surroundings but had everything to do with himself and he realized he couldn't actually run away from himself. Having seen the ending, I no longer wanted to embark on the trip of writing the story.

Disappearing or running away was not a viable option to suicide for either "Keith Hettenbach" or Christopher Ryan. I knew I was unable to transform "Keith's" odyssey into a voyage of personal salvation, so the book was doomed.

And so was I.

I don't remember what pushed the notion of suicide to a back burner in my mind, but something did. I thought about it, on and off for a couple of years, but never really came close to performing the actual deed. It was like an undetected terrorist bomb in the cargo belly of a jumbo jet . . . ticking, ticking, ticking. Suddenly, about a year or so ago it exploded, and I knew I had to do it. I've lived the past year with a dogged sense of determination to end the flight of my life.

The flight is about to terminate.

Saturday, July 14—7:50 P.M.

As I near the end of my life, I cannot help but feel very insignificant. I am not talking about an insignificance that is based on a feeling of worthlessness or that springs from a sense of exaggerated humility. I, as an individual living creature, feel insignificant in relationship to the vastness of the cosmos. Forget about the cosmos, in a city the size of Los Angeles, it is difficult to view myself as anything more than a mere speck.

I was taught as a child that God considered me to be very important in His overall scheme of things, that He wanted me to be saved and to live for all eternity with Him. But Jesus taught neither the resurrection of the dead, nor the immortality of the soul. Both these ideas were introduced by the Church Fathers to overcome the apparent meaninglessness of a finite life. Jesus taught that the meaninglessness of life caused by death can be overcome through the denial of this life by means of a radical transformation and voluntary sacrifice of it for the sake of others. The doctrine of immortality of the individual soul only extends the selfish life into eternity. Life after death is an egotistic existence that is meaningless and beyond comprehension.

This notion of immortality was formulated back in the old days long before the invention of the telescope and the rise of modern science. It was a time when the earth was thought to be the center of the universe and the dimensions of time and space were worked out on a very diminutive scale. In the early days of Christianity, when the Fathers of the Church were setting down the orthodox ideas of God and immortality, they thought the end of the world was looming in the not too distant future. They thought the world was only a few thousand years old, and that it wouldn't last much longer. It didn't seem unreasonable to think that man, as the highest of earth's creatures and the crown of all creation who was made in the image and likeness of God, was created by God simply to face extinction at death. When God created man, He had perfection and eternal life in mind for each individual, or so thought the early fathers of the Church.

The primitive picture of the universe that encouraged the religious view of immortality was shattered by modern science. We know that living forms of some kind have probably been in existence on earth for as long as two or three billion years, and the human species has been around for over 500,000 years. We know now that our little home planet earth revolves around a majestic sun more than a million times its size. Furthermore, the distance between the mighty sun and the tiny earth is nearly 93,000,000 miles. And that's just a hop, skip, and a jump compared to the distance between our solar system and the nearest star, which is a dazzling 25,000,000,000,000 miles, or 4.27 light-years. (A light-year is about six trillion miles, and is the distance that light, speeding at the rate of 186,300 miles per second, travels in a year.) The Milky Way, the great star cluster to which the sun and its planets belong, contains some 100 billion stars. The galactic system of which earth is just a mere dot, is just one out of millions of similar galaxies scattered throughout the cosmos. Think of the sun as something less than a single speck of dust in a vast city, of earth as less than a millionth part of such a speck of dust, and we have perhaps as vivid a picture as the mind can really grasp of the relationship of our home in space to the rest of the universe.

Yes . . . I feel insignificant, very insignificant.

It seems well within the realm of possibility that God (assuming there is a God), whose activities are not confined to earth, has far greater interests than troubling Himself with the immortalization of an admittedly very imperfect and sinful race of humans, who have only recently (in terms of cosmic times) gained a foothold in one tiny corner of His immense universe. God has every right to give a big, cosmic belly laugh at our outrageous lack of humility in thinking we are important and deserving enough to go on living forever, in violation of the natural laws He has established, and, for all we know, may not even be capable of suspending on our behalf.

The Spanish philosopher Miguel de Unamuno, in his book *The Tragic Sense of Life,* states that "faith in immortality is irrational" and that "all the labored arguments in support of our hunger for immortality, which pretend to be grounded on reason or logic, are merely advocacy and sophistry." Then he declares, "To believe in the immortality of the soul is to wish that the soul may be immortal, but to wish it with such force that this volition shall trample reason under foot and pass beyond it."

My dear Kate, God and immortality have little to do with reason and logic; people believe in them because of the comfort they provide. The Prussian philosopher Immanuel Kant (1724–1804), considered by many to be the greatest philosopher of modern times, understood the need in most humans to believe in God and immortality. In his nearly unreadable book *The Critique of Pure Reason,* the methodical bachelor showed why all proofs of God's existence must fail, because all attempts involve illegitimately applying notions of space, time, and causality to the noumenal world, when in fact these concepts can only be applied to the observable world. Kant knew that we humans must despair at ever knowing of God or immortality. But just as it looked as if Kant had kicked God out the front door, he let the Almighty slip back in through the back door. Kant said that there was no logical necessity to conceive of the world in terms of God and immortality; but, without such inspirational concepts, many humans would lose their enthusiasm for life. Therefore—philosophers love the word "therefore"—people have the right to believe (without claiming to know) that God, the soul, and immortality exist not as metaphysical necessities, but as practical or moral necessities. Kant, who tried to restrict reason to make room for faith, distinguished knowledge from belief, but grounded belief in moral necessity. Kant was an idealist who presented a picture of both the world and religion in which science and religion are no longer at odds with each other.

Immanuel Kant may have been skeptical in intellectual matters, but in moral matters he fully believed the maxims he had been taught as a child by his mother. Psychoanalysts always emphasize the immensely stronger hold upon us that our very early associations have than those of later times in our lives. All the reason and logic that I have applied to the problem of God during the past ten years has done little to convince my heart.

Still, my disbelief in God and immortality is not responsible for bringing me to the brink of the end of my life. I don't believe people would really consider life not worth living without God or the promise of immortality. Nobody really worries very much about what is going to happen a million years down the road. They are too busy worrying about such mundane matters as indigestion and income tax. I'm not really worried about what I will encounter when I end my life. I don't think I'll encounter anything; but, if I do, I'm sure God will understand what drove me over the edge, and if He/She doesn't, then I don't want any part of Him/Her anyway.

The meaning of life seems to be reduced to a choice between self-denying love or self-affirmation. Is it case of "either/or" or a little of each? I don't know. After years of searching for the truth, I've uncovered countless lies masquerading as truth, but I still have not found truth. I'm tired of looking. I want out because I want out. I'm sick and tired of the lies and lunacy that surround every aspect of life. I simply have no reason for living, no hope for happiness.

Peace is in the grave.

Sunday, July 15—9:40 A.M.

There is a peaceful tranquility to the early morning hours of Sunday. The streets are still, the roads are not clogged with cars carrying their passengers to work. Without the commercial hustle and bustle of the other days of the week, you can hear the birds chirping. Sundays seem to dawn in slow motion. You can notice squirrels beginning their hunt for food, you can feel the day starting. The rest of the week awakens to a shout, Sunday, to a whisper.

For Christians, Sunday is the Sabbath, a day reserved for rest and worship. The Church bells gently penetrate the stillness, beckoning their parishioners to come before the altar of the Almighty and to lift up their hearts and minds to God.

I lift up the heavy Sunday edition of the *New York Times*—today for the last time.

Monday, July 16—8:20 A.M.

Good morning, my sweet daughter. Another day, another "smog alert."

It's time. Time to go. I began this letter nearly a week ago. It's gone in directions I could not have imagined, and it's taken longer to write than I would have guessed.

I'm sadder today than I can ever recall being before. I guess it's this letter. Oh, I'm glad I'm writing it. I'm pleased that I'm leaving a little piece of myself behind for you. I wish things could have been different. I wish this letter could have been a face-to-face conversation.

I wish I could hold you.

I've tried to imagine what it will be like for you to receive this letter. A letter from the grave, as it were. I'm sure it will be a shock. I was shocked to get a birthday card from my mother, a card which arrived nearly a month after her death. Let me explain. My father was organized to the point of overkill. As soon as a bill would arrive in the mail, he would sit down and write out a check, place it in the return envelope, seal it, and in the upper right hand corner of the envelope he would pencil in the date on which the payment should be mailed. When the date arrived, he would cover the date he had penciled in with the postage stamp. A month's worth of bills sat in the correct dated order on top of his bedroom dresser.

Sandwiched in between the bills were birthday cards addressed to family members whose birthday's fell during that month. The routine seemed a bit too mechanical for my tastes, but then again I guess it beats my custom of usually sending belated birthday greetings to those I love.

Anyway, my mother died on March 3. Just three days prior to her death, my father had her sign my birthday card. After she signed it, I'm sure he penciled in the date of March 25 on the envelope in order to insure that it arrived on March 29, my birthday. I can vividly recall how saddened I became upon opening it and seeing her handwriting. It gave me an eerie feeling.

I know that the reception of this letter is going to be a shock to you. I suppose it can't help but cause you some sadness. I'm sorry. But my hope is that in time it will be a comfort to you. That at the very least, you'll know your father better than you have.

This is the day. The time has come when enough is enough. I feel it. The time is right, the time is now. But there are still a few odds and ends I must take care of.

I know I've written a lot, and I don't think I have much more to say, but I haven't a clue how to end this letter. Perhaps something will come to me.

Monday, July 16—4:05 P.M.

Well, things are pretty much in order. I've prepared my will. I've disposed of those things that wouldn't be of any use or interest to anyone but me. I have numerous boxes marked Good Will—stuff that I can't see throwing out because some poor person will be glad to have them. Everything is ready. It took me more time than I thought to reach this point.

It's amazing how much crap a person accumulates in a lifetime. The process of getting rid of my things was slowed down by daydreaming. Everything had a memory attached to it, and I found myself constantly stopping to reflect on those memories. The reflections produced tears, smiles, sadness, anger, and regret. No object was too insignificant not to have memories clinging to it. I remembered where I bought my favorite lamp and who I was with when I bought it. I was in love that day. Love? The word sounds too weak, too overused to describe what I felt. I was intoxicated by her—by the way she walked, by the way she talked, by the way she smiled. Her simplicity, her beauty, her purity, and her innocence captured my imagination and soul. I worshiped her like I have no other woman before or since. Where is she now? What went wrong? I have no idea.

We lived together for two years. I saw no problem; for me it was paradise. She loved me too. She was a dozen years younger than me. I was her first love. Shyness had kept her for me. As I stared at the lamp, somehow my mind selected from an almost endless choice of moments of ecstasy, tenderness, unbridled happiness, madcap fun, or even exasperation and irritation a brief moment from what was otherwise a very ordinary day—so ordinary that I can't recall a single thing about that day, other than this tidbit my memory had safeguarded for all these years.

We were in a park. Actually, it may have been the arboretum near Pasadena. No, it could have been a state park in New Jersey. Doesn't matter. Wherever it was, we were walking along a peaceful pond under a brilliant blue sky. We loved taking long walks together. As we walked hand-in-hand, enjoying the ducks in the pond, suddenly on the other side, a group of teenage boys began hurling rocks at the ducks. Nicole was horrified. She screamed at the boys, who ignored her. I could see the rage in her eyes. Like a bat out of hell, this gentle, dainty woman started sprinting around the pond, quickly closing the gap between herself and the boys. I stood frozen for a second or two, and started running after her. By the time I reached the other side, she had already managed to scare the kids off and was standing alone trying to catch her breath. As I approached her she torpedoed me with, "How could anyone throw a rock at those wonderful creatures? I hate those fucking little bastards." I don't think I had ever heard her use the "f" word, nor had I ever witnessed such intense hostility. I did my best to calm her down.

Some people are perhaps just too gentle for this cruel world. As I wrapped the lamp up in old newspaper and placed it in a box I intended to donate to Good Will, I realized how much turmoil Nicole had hidden from me. Perhaps I was a bit overwhelming, not by temperament but by virtue of the fact that I had lived longer, traveled farther, seen more, and was so concerned about the alleged "big issues" of life. I thought that we talked a lot. We had. But she never really expressed what was inside of her. Did I not let her? I'll never know what really happened, or why she got on a plane one day to visit her parents in Duluth and never returned. She vanished without a call, without any explanation.

That lamp took a long time to pack. Then there was a large box that was taped closed and hadn't been opened in years. It was buried beneath a pile of crap out in the garage. On it I had written with a large black marker the words: Stuff From My Study—Old Odds and Ends. I had moved a number of times in recent years, and the box always came along, although its exact contents were by now unknown. "Just dump it. Don't even open it. Just toss it," I thought upon discovering it. But I did open it, discovering letters from friends and family, ticket stubs from movies and plane trips, an old passport, an assortment of photos taken on the sets of television shows I had worked on, political buttons, a take-out menu from a Chinese restaurant, newspaper clippings from Robert F. Kennedy's assassination, a photo of me and former Yankee shortstop Tony Kubek taken in 1959 at Yankee Stadium by my father, NYC subway tokens, an old CBS ID card, my high-school diploma, an assortment of old baseball trading cards, a July 1979 issue of *Playboy* magazine, an empty can that once contained "It's A Girl" cigars that I had passed out after your birth, and old Visa bills that helped me recall restaurants that I had eaten in ten years ago. I could trace the patterns of my life in the pieces of memorabilia I had saved. Four hours later I reached the bottom of the box, and had plumbed the depths of my memory. I saw in the box that much of my life had disappeared from my conscious memory— the old papers and photographs were all that remained of a shipwrecked life.

Marcel Proust said in the overture to his masterpiece *Remembrance of Things Past* that the individual's past lay hidden "beyond the reach of intellect" and could only be recalled by involuntary memory, set in motion by chance sensations. I had a day of chance sensations.

Memory is the process of isolating the essence of a prior experience. However, this essence has been torn from its prior context and the surviving image takes on the absoluteness and immediacy that it does not deserve. Everything from the past is exaggerated; nothing is as it was.

Kate, my little sweetheart, as I finished the task of putting my things in order, I thought about the time I spent in my father's apartment after his death. I had the sad task of disposing of his things and vacating the apartment. He didn't expect death to come when it did—who does? It is a very strange feeling going through someone else's stuff and having to decide what to do with those things that were still useful: dumb things—a vacuum cleaner, suitcases, a radio, stuff you just don't throw away. In fact, I still have his old suitcase. I spent many quiet hours sorting through papers and photos he had neatly stored in his closet. Stuff of interest only to him, but still tough to just throw into the garbage. These were leftovers of his life and they said something about him.

One box had a collection of memorial cards given away at the funerals of his friends and relatives. These small—I suppose two inch by three inch—cards had on the front a pious picture of Jesus, Mary, or some saint. On the back side was printed: In Loving Memory of ———. Just below the name of the deceased was printed the date of his or her death. Below that was a short prayer. He had a lot of cards from my mother's funeral. The prayer on the reverse side of her's said:

> Most merciful Father, we commend our departed into your hands. We are filled with the sure hope that our departed will rise again on the Last Day with all who have died in Christ. We thank you for all the good things you've given during our departed's earthly life.
>
> O Father, in your great mercy, accept our prayer that the Gates of Paradise may be opened for your servant. In our turn, may we too be comforted by the words of faith until we greet Christ in glory and are united with you and our departed.
>
> Through Christ our Lord, Amen.

Faith, I was taught, is the substance of things hoped for; faith, I learned, is not the substance of truth. Nothing is true simply because it is believed, or because you have faith in it. Truth warrants faith or belief; but faith or belief warrants no conclusion that the proposition believed is therefore true. There was a time humans believed fire to be a miracle, but we learned it is a chemical reaction. Each of us, at one time or another, puts faith in falsehoods. I think my father believed he would see all those "departed" people whose cards he had saved in a box in his closet again—in a place far sweeter than earth. It was his hope, the substance of his faith. I wish it were true.

I took some of the memorial cards my dad had saved, mostly those of my aunts and uncles. Now it's time to throw them away. It's funny, but I just didn't want somebody coming in here after my death and going through my things, poking around the artifacts of my life. During these past two weeks I have been meticulously going through my possessions and chucking them or giving them away. I suppose I still have the cowardly trait of being overly concerned about what people think of me. I am sorry I spent—make that wasted—so much time and energy trying to please everybody and becoming so uneasy if even a single person disapproved of something I did. I lived the life of a coward, afraid to be me.

I had a lot of Woody Allen movies on videocassettes. I watched one last night, a flick named *Sleeper*. The character played by Woody—a mild-mannered neurotic named Miles—wakes up to find himself surrounded by white-robed scientists. The awakened sleeper slowly realizes that he somehow has managed to wake up in the future. It seems the poor schlepp checked into a Greenwich Village hospital for a minor surgical procedure and died. But that wasn't the end of his life on earth. As part of an experiment, he was frozen with the hope of being thawed out at some future date when the technology would be available to cure him and restore him to life. Of course, this former health-food-store owner has no idea of what has transpired; he just wakes up cranky from a 200-year-long nap. But Miles gradually comes to grips with his situation. He finds that life in the future is pretty much the same as it was before his operation. The world still revolved around war and politics; the people still were either good, bad, or indifferent. There was one big change. Miles is stunned to learn that all the things we today believe are harmful, are, in fact, healthful. Red meat, tobacco, coffee, rich desserts—it turns out that these "goodies" are goodies and they really promote long life.

The movie reminded me of two real situations. First was the news that most apples are sprayed with alar, a chemcal that is hazardous if consumed in large quantities. Alar is sprayed on apples for one reason: cosmetics—it makes apples more attractive, more appealing. Alar doesn't make a better apple, it makes a better looking apple. Similarly, the chemicals used in the manufacture of milk cartons also proved to be hazardous to humans. Again, these chemicals have only one purpose: cosmetics—to make the cartons white instead of the brownish color they would normally be. Research tells the milk producers that people won't buy brownish milk cartons.

Kate, it all comes down to looks. We as a society are obsessed with physical appearances. That obsession has made fitness guru Jane Fonda and *Playboy* publisher Hugh Hefner millionaires because they both in their own way cater to our fantasies. *Cosmopolitan* magazine has turned women into anorexic slaves to beauty, fashion, and makeup by telling them they better look like the models that grace their pages if they hope to catch a man. We are to blame. We have bought into someone else's concept of the perfect body, the perfect woman, the perfect lifestyle, the perfect apple, and, yes, the perfect milk carton.

While reading the *Los Angeles Times* this morning, I couldn't help but notice that the first section of the paper, consisting of twenty-four pages, contained thirteen ads for fitness centers, diet centers, and clinics that specialize in plastic surgery. (Of course, the ads featured scantily dressed women who didn't look like they needed to visit a fitness center or a diet center or needed any part of their already perfect anatomy reshaped by a plastic surgeon.) This adult obsession has trickled down to young kids and is robbing them of many of the joys of childhood. It is not uncommon today for young teenage girls to show signs of depression because of their preoccupation with their appearance. They feel ugly and un-attractive when objectively that is not the case. Their self-worth is tied almost exclusively to their body image.

We, who so readily accept mediocrity in our inner lives, want physical perfection in ourselves, in others, and in things. We demand more from a car than mere transportation; we demand style, grace, power, comfort, luxury, and excitement. A car is not a car; it is a statement of who we are. In this town, not owning a $50,000 BMW makes you a loser. We have become prisoners of our own minds.

Tonight, I escape.

Is death the only way out? I guess this rambling review of my life was really a search for an alternative. Perhaps I could find out what went wrong, and fix it.

I didn't find anything. There are no alternatives. There is nothing to fix.

It's just time to go. It is that simple. There is nothing more to think about—except possibly how to end this letter.

I'm going to take a walk, clear my head, and try to come up with a way to say goodbye.

Monday, July 16—6:20 P.M.

I'm back. I did more than just walk. I thought about how I would end my life. Oddly enough, I hadn't considered the actual instrument of my destruction. How should I do it? Pills? Hang myself? Slit my wrists? Drive my car into a highway overpass? Shoot myself? Jesus Christ, what a crazy assortment of methods from which to choose. I started getting nervous, even nauseated at the thought of the physical violence I was about to commit. Suicide is a messy business. God, I'm suddenly scared, but I've got to do it, there is no turning back.

But how? Pills seemed far too passive for such a decisive act. Hanging is an interesting idea, but I was afraid I might somehow screw it up. Slitting my wrists means watching myself bleed to death, which is something I'm not sure I could do. Autocide leaves room for error, I could survive the crash. A gun, I thought, was the way to go, fast and efficient.

I'm here in my study, the gun in my hand. I've never held a gun before. It looks so easy in the movies. It's heavier than I imagined. The steel is cold and menacing. I wonder how much noise it will make. I wonder whether it will hurt. I don't want to feel any pain. I'm scared. Until this second, suicide has been an idea in my mind, a word on a piece of paper.

Now it's real.

Monday, July 16—8:05 P.M.

The gun is to my head.

My finger is on the trigger.

For the first time, I know fear.

My heart is pounding. I'm sweating. My body is quivering.

Only seconds separate me from mortality.

I know what I must do. I planned this. Every fiber of my existence is focused on squeezing the trigger.

The barrel of the gun presses against my temple, as if I am afraid I might otherwise miss.

Time has stopped.

My entire existence is reduced to this one act.

I'm terrified.

God, it's as if someone else is holding the gun, but there is only me.

I am both frightened and determined.

I can feel the barrel. I can feel my finger.

This is it. It will be easy. Just squeeze the trigger and it will be over. No more struggles. No more sadness. No more tormenting questions.

Just squeeze the trigger.

My finger is paralyzed.

The fear is turning to tears.

Tears are streaming down my face. This moment of release is being overtaken by remorse. Why this urge to cling to life? Why this sudden doubt?

Just squeeze it. Just end it.

A single thought flashes through my mind: Is death the only way out?

Just squeeze the trigger!

Is this the only way out?

Just squeeze the fucking trigger!

Is death the only way out?

Suddenly, the answer is clear.

Monday, July 16—10:30 P.M.

I never expected to be writing this.

I've been sitting here for several hours since lowering the gun from my head.

The gun is sitting on my desk, a silent reminder of that moment of shear terror when I decided not to squeeze the trigger. I'm not sure why I made that choice. Or even if it was right.

I've thought about this letter and how it evolved into a form of self-examination, which now makes me see that I am still a child—still aimless, bouncing from one idea to another, from one thinker to another.

Now it is beginning to make sense.

Socrates claimed that the unexamined life wasn't worth living. But Aristotle had a different take; he went beyond Socrates' view and declared that the unplanned life is not worth examining. Kate, what I never saw before now was that I never knew what I was trying to do with my life, or why I did anything.

How could I have been so stupid? Of course, I never knew where my life was going and so it never really went anywhere. No wonder this mess of a life is hardly worth the trouble of examining. I have lived thoughtlessly. A life without a plan is an unlived life. I had no plan, I just shuffled along with the crowd, window shopping for answers along the way. I had witlessly inverted René Descartes's dictum—"*Cogito, ergo sum,*" "I think, therefore I am."—into my own dictum for defeat—"*Non cogito, ergo non sum,*" "I don't think, therefore I am not." I didn't think about ends to be pursued and the means to achieve them. I had no vision for my own life, and, without a vision, I almost perished. Worse than adopting the wrong plan for my life, I adopted no plan. How paradoxical: by planning to end my life I may have discovered a way to live.

Tuesday, July 17—12:40 P.M.

What a day! I am alive and glad for the first time in years. Everything looks different. I really don't know what is ahead for me. All I know is that I must start thinking for myself. I'm excited about planning the rest of my life. All of a sudden I've got a lot of time on my hands. Hey, I'm not that old. In fact, I'm the same age as Nolan Ryan—no relation—who at the young age of forty-three pitched yet another no-hitter last month for the Texas Rangers.

Kate, I've got to be honest—I'm still kind of stunned that I am here, still around and writing to you. Suicide is drastic. And permanent. I'm not sure I know what happened last night when I pointed that gun at my head. I've been so tormented by questions during the past few years, unanswerable questions about God and life, that I shouldn't have been surprised that at that critical instant a question should cross my mind. But for the first time, I had an answer. I knew beyond knowing, beyond doubt, that death was not a solution. Of course, exactly how to go on living is not so clear. All I know for sure is it's time to seize the day, time to start life over.

But where do I start? How do I begin to shed the "Zelig" persona I have worn for so long? Will the burst of enthusiasm I feel quickly dissipate? Can I learn to act instead of react? God, more questions. Maybe I should forget about searching for truth and understanding, and settle for a good fantasy; if only I could. No. I'm going to start by throwing out all my philosophy books. All they have taught me is how to talk with some plausibility about some thorny theories of life after life, and they have done little to help me deal with the important questions of everyday living. Contemporary philosophy is a mist and mirage of logic and epistemology concerned with the theory of the origin, nature, methods, and limits of knowledge but of little real help in understanding the heart and soul of mankind. I'll create my own philosophy, my own point of view.

This is an age of confusion and revolution, where things once only thought are now freely spoken out loud, a time when each individual and society as a whole are faced with more choices and options than ever before—yet, the ability to make choices has not increased. The experts of philosophy, hiding behind their masks of scholastic purity, ignore the general public and are content to offer each other solutions to problems that only they can understand. No, the philosophers have nothing to tell me; they are too busy talking to themselves, writing things only other philosophers will—or can—read. Somerset Maugham said it best: "The philosopher who will not take the trouble to make himself clear shows only that he thinks his thoughts of no more than academic value."

I stumbled through my life because no one introduced me to Logic, no one nurtured in me an ability to Reason. I was fed fable as fact. I was told to follow the crowd, not to find my own way. What I need is not more learning, what I need is some unlearning. Truth is not found in religion, philosophy, or books; it is discovered in living. No one knows better than I what's best for me. I must learn to trust myself, to create my own outlook on life.

Anton Chekhov claimed, "A prudent life without a definite outlook on the world is not a life, but a burden." That was never clearer than it is today. My life has been a burden. Now the burden must be dropped, not ended.

I need a definite outlook, a new attitude, a new set of beatitudes. I can see a new beginning over the horizon. I can see myself creating a new storyline for my life. I can see myself preaching to an audience of just one: me. I can hear my own Sermon on the Mount for myself:

Blessed are those who by a fortuitous blend of genetics and circumstances are so sane and sensible that they are able to sail through life without the aid of any philosophical or theological lifeboat. I was not so blessed.

Blessed are those who think for themselves and never became dependent upon the "experts" of religion and philosophy in order to understand the alphabet of human wisdom. I was not so blessed.

Blessed are those who know how to best endure what they have to endure, and know how best to enjoy what they are able to enjoy. I was not so blessed.

Blessed are those who can see beauty, magic, wonder, mystery, and poetry without theological glasses. I was not so blessed.

Blessed are those who can accept their fate until they can escape from it. I was not so blessed.

Blessed are they who have absolute faith in nothing save the "self" or consciousness of self within them. I was not so blessed.

Blessed are those who have no mystical need to love and are able to simply be kind to both those they like and those they don't like. I was not so blessed.

Blessed are those who have no need to hate, no need to worship, no need to explain, no need to interpret and instead are simply able to enjoy. I was not so blessed.

Blessed are those who are not self-cursing or self-pitying. I was not so blessed.

Blessed are those who are able to embrace all of life, the good, the bad, the beautiful, and the ugly. I was not so blessed.

Blessed are those who find a purpose for their own life, instead of seeking a purpose for the universe or the purpose of life in general. I was not so blessed.

Blessed are those who hear their own voice and preach only to themselves. I was not so blessed.

Blessed are those whose thinking can embrace the past, the present, and the future at the same time. I was not so blessed.

Yes, yes, yes—I was not blessed. Big deal. I can bless myself now; I can be happy with myself now. I can go on in spite of my past and in spite of my future. I'm sure those rotten "what's the use" days will work themselves onto my calendar, but I realize now that the quality of life is measured over the long haul, not in any of its moments. Moments have ups and downs, time has balance. Time is everything. If it weren't for time, we wouldn't need God. God has no real purpose, except for his ability to give us immortality, to give us time without end. Fear of running out of time has made immortality our biggest wish.

The bottom line, dear Kate, is simple: in time, my life will run out of time. Until then, each moment is a miracle, a man-made miracle of struggle and triumph, of pain and gain. This is just such a miraculous moment. The complexion of my life changed in an instant last night, my pain has eased, and my resolve to live has returned. Today, I have the courage to refuse to die. Kate, every minute is important, every minute is meaningless: every minute is a minute, to do with as you wish. It is not time that is of value, it is yourself that is valuable. Time can be your master, or it can be your slave.

For a long time—far too long, I have been a character in search of a playwright. After a tedious, tiresome search, I have found him, and, much to my surprise, it is me. I am the author of my own life. In writing the rest of my life, I will no longer pencil in a hope for eternity; instead I will create tranquility in the present. Death, like love, must catch me by surprise. Life's value is life, not some questionable afterlife. The role I shall continue to play in life is unlike any other role played by all the other actors on earth. To pattern my performance on some preestablished rule or dogma would be a betrayal of myself. I shall play my part in my own voice, in my own temperament; my acting shall remain natural and true to the only author of my life's play—me.

Perhaps I've come full circle, gone back to the beginning and can start over. Four lines from the poetic pen of T. S. Eliot seem clearer to me than ever before:

> We shall not cease from exploration
> And the end of all our exploring
> Will be to arrive where we started
> And know the place for the first time.

While the world continues to turn, its inhabitants divided between total indifference and the need for "ultimate" answers, I must turn my attention to seeking ways for me to feel relatively safe without the aid of absolutism or the ease of indifference. More than ever before, tonight I am convinced that we need each other, and there is no longer any room on our dying planet for religious bigotry and hatred. We need a genuine concern for others, not merely indulgence ready to forgive, but respect for what the other is. We need to see the universe as one giant living organism that includes all things.

I have no God to guide me, no God to save me. My days of magical thinking are over. I'll put my trust in my brain, not the Bible; I'll put my faith in reason, not religion. But those who believe in God have no recourse but to feel sorry for me, to pity my godless life. I can't help feeling frustrated by their failure to see my point of view. We publicly can say that we respect each other's belief or unbelief, but privately we really don't, we really can't. We are at odds with each other. Life has taught us both that one of us must be right and the other wrong. We both want to be winners, to be seen as superior. When it comes to the question of God, there is no room for ambiguity. We demand a "final" answer. The great cosmic snow job is this: there are no ultimate answers—to think that there are is the Master Deception. The best we can hope for are practical answers to practical questions.

Life without ambiguity would be like Indian food without curry. Ambiguity is an essential ingredient of life, an ingredient my religious friends could not stomach. During my life, I moved from a fear of the unknown, to a fear of the unknowable, which is an even more profound fear. But fear is a mental habit, a habit I'm close to breaking. My need to know has been painful, but certainly not harmful. I still want the truth, I will still seek the truth, but I shall not demand answers. Nor shall I demand consistency in my beliefs—honesty and inconsistency live together in the same house. I'm not going to be afraid to contradict myself, and I will allow no "ism" to hold me rigid in its grip. I will reserve the right to differ with myself and to change my mind. My life, from this day forward, will be a living experiment. I shall cultivate my own garden, in the soil of reason, justice, and humanity. My tools will be art and history.

It's painful to think that I've lived so long so stupidly, and it's frightening to me to realize just how long I entertained the notion of killing myself. When I finally took off my religious glasses, I looked into the mirror and didn't know who I was. Before that time, my understanding of my self seemed solid; suddenly, it was fragile. It is as if, one day I was one person, the next, another; I felt lost, confused. I was mad at myself because I knew intellectually that I believed something stupid, but that alone didn't push me to the brink. No, it was the suffering I had to endure while coming to that realization that robbed me of my will to live. I resented being duped by religion. I resented falling for their deceptions. I resented the suffering both caused me. My remorse over the course my life took, thanks to the rotten directions given to me by religion, was so severe that I truly hated my life. In my anger and my pain, I lost the ability to laugh at life, to enjoy life, and chose instead to roll around in the muck of despair. The extremism of suicide appeals to people who feel they have no hope, no future.

But I was saved by love. My love for you inspired the writing of this letter. How paradoxical: what began as farewell to you ended in a greeting to me. The ambiguous gloom I had mistaken for my twilight turned out to be the dawn of the rest of my life. In writing to you, I found myself. I was born again—this time, the child became the parent of the father.

Thanks for being there.

Love,

Dad

PART TWO

He rose again. . . .

Wednesday, July 18, 1990—7:40 A.M.

Dear Kate,

Good morning, it's me again—your dear old Dad. Woke up with this weird problem: I had a long letter to you, and I suddenly didn't know what to do with it. But during my early morning cup of coffee I got an unexpected jolt of a solution: what began as a herald of death should now continue as a celebration of life.

Say what?

What I'm saying is: I'm going to continue writing to you. And why not? Writing to you taught me a lot about myself. And there's more for both of us to learn. Education is freedom.

Wait. Maybe "learn" is the wrong word; explore is better. What I want to do is share my exploration. What I don't want to do is offer you advice. Advice given by someone else is almost always useless, because the extraordinary singularity of each person makes his or her particular problem unique. The answers my search discovers may not have any value to you. You undoubtedly view the world from a different perspective than I do. Besides, the quest to understand ideas different from your own may be of no interest to you.

Marcel Proust asserted that there is not one universe, there are millions of them, "almost as many as there are human eyes and intellects awaking every morning." What he was saying is that each of us imagines the universe the way we see it. Unknowingly, we are constantly creating a world colored by our passions. This created world is a world of illusion, a world that does not exist in "reality."

I once toured Venice, Italy, with a woman I loved dearly. Long after the love I felt for her died, there still was buried in my heart a treasure of wondrous memories of a city beautiful beyond compare. Years later, I returned to Venice. But this time I was alone and lonely, and all I saw was a dirty city with reeking canals. Even the pigeons in the piazzas lost their appeal. Love's passion had distorted

127

reality, making the filthy beautiful.

Our illusions stem mostly from the fact that we project our thoughts, our prejudices and our passions upon nature. We say the weather is "foul," which it is not, and the sea "cruel," which it is not; nature neither feels nor thinks. The gods of old were the projections of man's desires and his dreads. We see what we think we see. People claim to see angels. In fact, recently I watched a TV talk show that featured a host of guests, each of whom claimed to have had angelic encounters. After the show, I did a little channel surfing, and hung ten on a TV preacher who claimed that record numbers of people are possessed by Satan, and his guest that day told her dramatic story of how she was freed from a cult of devil worshippers. Neither those visited by angels nor those possessed by devils offered any real proof that such rendezvous actually took place. It is not uncommon in our day for people to pray that a coming hurricane spares them; if it changes its course, the people then claim God was responsible. Preconceived ideas can make us see what does not exist, and they can stop us from seeing what does.

Yes, Proust was right, there are millions of universes; but, he knew that beyond the millions of inner impressions and illusions there is one real outer world common to all men and women which must be understood.

That is my quest. I confess, dear daughter, that I am at a loss as to how to reach such an understanding. Perhaps it is an unreachable goal. Each day, all I can do is place one foot in front of the other and take whatever steps I can toward reaching it. The only compass I can use is knowledge, which is gained by reason, not faith. We are bound by the laws of nature, of logic, of reason; we control our own destiny and life.

I think one of the reasons I wanted to end my life was because I consumed the poisonous notion the religious people had fed me: the notion that the rejection of God leaves us with the belief there is nothing left to live for without God. How absurd! What's left is people—people caring about people. The poet Thomas Hardy, in a lyric called, "A Plaint to Man," personified and gave a voice to the false God of Christianity, who then addresses mankind:

> When you slowly emerged from the den of Time,
> And gained percipience as you grew,
> And fleshed you fair out of shapeless slime,
>
> Wherefore, O Man, did there come to you
> The unhappy need of creating me—
> A form like your own—for praying to?

This false God, being told that we humans had need of some agency of hope and mercy, tells mankind that he, God, dwindles day by day "beneath the deicide eyes of seers . . . and tomorrow the whole of me disappears," so the "truth should be told, and the fact be faced"—the fact, Dear Kate, that if mankind is to have love, mercy, and justice, the human heart itself would have to provide it.

I truly believed that Christianity was based on love. It is not. Christianity is based on faith. Religion serves in many ways to impede the development of a flexible thinking process. This ultimately results in adult thinking that is rigid and confined. Love is a human emotion; faith is an error in judgment—an error resulting from the wilful belief in the absence of evidence. Faith demands belief; love demands nothing—it only promotes action. Faith is not so much peace as tragic hope. Human struggle can only end in provisional victories that will ceaselessly be questioned.

My task is clear: acceptance of an existence at best paradoxical and frustrating. How? I'm not sure, but my hunch is it will only come through humor, kindness, and compassion.

I see now how religion is merely a maze for the mind, a game so tortuous and tedious that once you enter its mysterious labyrinth it is virtually impossible to find your way out. We feel compelled to play the game, which is where the deception begins; the truth is that we do not have to enter the labyrinth, we do not have to play the game. But once you enter the maze, it is no longer a game—it's a deadly serious trial without end. A trial by "mire."

I'm lucky. The trial ended for me—thanks to you.

So, my dear Kate, I shall not throw away my week-long letter to you. Instead, I will continue it. From time to time, I will share the highlights of my quest for understanding. My hope is to give this suddenly perpetual letter to you as a present for your twenty-first birthday, which I now expect to see.

During the past few weeks, I was frightened of admitting that I was wrong about killing myself. I methodically and dispassionately went about the business of preparing for my death. I didn't fear death; I feared questioning my plan to die. What if it was wrong? What would I do? I didn't want to know.

But this morning I was able to at look myself in the mirror and admit I was wrong, admit I was weak. Am weak. As I stood there, with the early morning light flowing in through the window, I could feel the exhilaration of having received a full pardon. Suddenly, I have a new truth, a new reality: I am free. Free, to become whatever I am, whatever I want to be. I began my first day of freedom by shaving . . . and I didn't cut myself!

From this day forward, I say to hell with the straight and narrow. I'll take the crooked and wide! In Sanskrit, the classical Old Indic literary language dating back to the fourth century before Christ, the root of the verb "to be" is grow or make grow. I want to grow; I want to experience the fullness of life.

I can't believe how tidy this place is. I had done such a good job preparing for my death, that it will take a few days to reorganize things—to give the place that messy, lived-in look.

I'll talk to you again when this place is messy enough for me to think straight. Ciao.

Thursday, July 19—7:45 A.M.

I just read a very strange story in the papers. The story concerns six U.S. soldiers who were reported AWOL from their intelligence posts in West Germany on July 9. All six soldiers held top-secret security clearances and were intelligence analysts assigned to intercepting, identifying, and exploiting foreign communications. But it seems the men had intercepted a very foreign communication—a message from outer space! The six intelligence experts believed that they had been chosen by aliens to be on hand when they reclaimed the earth. These chosen few earthlings believed they were selected to greet alien spaceships and lead a group of people to a science fiction-style heaven.

According to friends, the men believed in the Christian doctrine of the "rapture," which proclaims that Jesus is going to return to earth and take believers to heaven before the world is destroyed. The soldiers had added a new twist to the rapture theory by suggesting that Jesus had been an alien and would return to earth in a spaceship in order to pick up the chosen faithful.

The soldiers, who ranged in age from twenty to twenty-six, abandoned their post in early July and split for Chattanooga, Tennessee, where they picked up a Volkswagen van and started driving to a place called Gulf Breeze, Florida, and an anticipated August 6 rendezvous with a spaceship commanded by Capt. Jesus. The men believed the spaceship's arrival would be heralded by a war in Lebanon and a shakeup of the U.S. military. But a funny thing happened on the way to the rapture. Gulf Breeze police stopped the van in a routine traffic check at 3 A.M. The police entered the driver's name into a national crime computer and found out the driver had been reported AWOL.

It's nice too know that America's intelligence operation is in such intelligent hands.

I mentioned earlier in this letter that a doorman of a New York City building I once lived in fully believed that Jesus was an alien who arrived on earth in a spaceship. We tend to think we live in a sophisticated, rational age, but evidence abounds that suggests such a view is merely an illusion. Even in a secular society, religious-based myths do not die easily.

Sunday, July 22—10:40 A.M.

Good morning, my sweet. It's been four days since I've written to you. I had hoped that the balance of this letter would have had a brighter, more upbeat tone. I wanted all my future scribblings to you to reflect my new sense of hope. Yet this morning, I am so overwhelmed with sadness, I needed someone to talk to about it, and you, my ever faithful, patient listener, were my first choice.

My sadness is rooted in the complexity of life and the barrage of images that assault my senses each day. Since my rebirth of almost a week ago, there have been a variety of stories from around the globe that have touched a nerve of discord deep within me. These weren't big, front-page stories. The stories involved six deaths, one in Japan, one in Italy, and four in Pennsylvania, but yet they stood out, even in a week where, at last count, 1,621 people died in an earthquake in the Philippines. I hadn't really linked these three stories together until this morning, when a series of photos appeared in the *New York Times*.

First, the photos. There were only five, spread over a full page. The commentary was limited to a few short sentences. Words were not needed; the photos said it all. The topic of the photo essay was the very visible trail of physical carnage left behind in Cambodia's hidden war.

The photo that said the most is difficult to describe. The photo is of child, a boy, perhaps eight or nine years old. He is lying on the floor, alone in a corner of a room in a hospital. The photo gives no hint it was taken in a hospital; there is no hospital bed, no medical equipment or personnel. It looks more like a darkened corner of a slum dwelling. The walls are bare, dotted with splotches where the paint has been chipped off, revealing years of neglect. The boy is laying on his back, behind a very thin veil of gauze, not meant to provide privacy, but I suppose used only to keep flies and other insects out. He is naked, except for a what looks like a rumpled, old shirt carefully drapped over his genital area, as if just placed there by some unseen passerby as a small gesture in the direction of modesty. The child is thin, the bones of his rib cage clearly visible. His left leg is missing from just below the knee. The stump is swaddled in a white, cotton cloth functioning as a make-shift bandage. The caption beneath the photo gives the details: the boy's leg was blown off when one of his cows stepped on a land mind as he was taking them to graze. He is marred for life by the sins of his elders.

As I look over my description of the photo, I see the inadequacy of the words I used to communicate the emotion that the photo does: the loneliness, the horror, the pain. One more nameless, innocent victim of hate. Who is this boy? Was he happy seconds before the blast, whistling, or singing as he herded the cows to pasture? Can he possibly understand what happened, or why it happened to him? He looks as if all life, all playfulness, all youthful vitality has been drained out of him. I can't imagine what his future holds.

Another photo perhaps foretells the boy's future. It is of a teenager, a boy, I think. He is sleeping in the street—on a coarse, cloth mat much smaller than his body, with his artificial leg temperarily being used as a pillow. One worn-out shoe, worn on his good leg, sits inches away from his crude prosthesis. But perhaps, by Cambodian standards, this teenager is lucky, because a third photo reveals a one-legged, shirtless man making his way through a dirty, dusty street in Phnom Penh with the aid of a stick doing the job of a cane. The entire leg is gone, and I can't help but wonder how he maintains his balance as he hops down the street. The picture clearly shows he is hopping: his right foot is off the ground, and his left arm is supporting all his weight as it leans on the stick. Was he a soldier, or just another innocent victim of terrorism? Where is he going? Where has he been? Why doesn't he at least have a prothesis to help make getting around a little easier?

I feel ashamed for letting my problems, all of them confined to the small space between my ears, overwhelm me to the point of self-annihilation. What wimps we Americans are—or at least this American is. We sit sipping our Perrier and listening to motivational cassette tapes, and as soon as trouble comes our way, we fall apart or rush off to our therapist.

There is one more thing about the last photo I just described that captures the absurdity of life. The photo was taken from behind the man as he struggled down the block, so we are able to see what was in front of him: two large billboards, one on either side of the street, advertising movies. While the titles and descriptions were written in Cambodian, the movies were obviously action/romance dramas featuring well-dressed sexy, young people. One of the male actors was sporting a pair of expensive sunglasses, the type you see by the thousands here in Hollywood. There, as if magically floating above the filth, pain, poverty, and squalor that are the spoils of war, was the key to escaping it all: steamy cinematic soap operas, that more than likely incorporate liberal dosages of greed, lust, violence, jealousy, and passion—and, of course, the obligatory car-chase scene. My quest for understanding is going to be harder than I imagined—and that's without trying to explain professional wrestling or the United States Congress.

Kate, I'm tempted not to bother describing the last two photos. The alacrity with which I began this letter has dwindled down to drudgery. But I had better press on—why I'm not sure.

The setting for the next-to-last photo is a hospital corridor. Obviously a poor hopsital; in fact, if it weren't for the gurney on which the photo's subject was laying, the setting could easily be mistaken for a hall in a factory. On the gurney was an adult male, perhaps no more than thirty years old. He is wearing only shorts. His body is covered with cuts and deep wounds of all sizes and shapes. No part of his body seems to have been spared; wounds are visible on his face, chest, stomach, both arms, and both legs. It looks as if he had been clawed by a tiger. He lays there, with an intravenous feeding needle taped to his arm, staring blankly at the ceiling. Standing next to him, looking confused and dazed, is a woman who must be his wife. She is holding in her arms a very young child, who is completely naked and is nursing at her right breast, which is poking out from under a simple shirt that looks as if it is covered with her husband's blood. According to the caption below the picture, the man is a peasant who struck a mine while plowing his rice field. His assailant was not a tiger, but shrapnel. Another victim in a war of guerilla tactics and terror that kills, cripples, and maims more than soldiers. In every city, in every countryside village, the aftermath of hate is visible: people with one leg missing, sometimes both; sometimes just the foot has been blown away, sometimes the hand. No one knows for sure just how many crippled there are in Cambodia, but their number is in the thousands.

Now, the last photograph. It is not as shocking as the others, perhaps because it was taken on the road to recovery, and the memory of the initial pain had receded. The photo is of two young men, perhaps nineteen or twenty years of age. They are sitting in wheelchairs, very old wheelchairs that look as if they are almost homemade—wooden chairs with bicycle wheels attached to them. Both young men have both their legs missing. One lost both his legs above the knee;

the other, both his legs from below the knee. They are both wearing shorts, neither has on a shirt. They are trim, but don't look malnourished. They appear to be in some type of lounge area of a hospital; rehabilitation probably means little more than a rest from the hardships they have seen, before they face the hardships they will see. In their eyes you can see anger and bitterness.

Evil abounds, its power unmatched, while beauty, gentleness, and goodness quiver in the shadows. Our lives are not lived out upon a stage, but on a battleground. We are all casualties.

As these haunting photos sit on breakfast tables across America, will anyone notice them? I mean really notice them, and take the time to think about them. Or will they take a bite of their croissant and a sip of their coffee, and skip to another section of the paper and read how Spandex is the latest fashion craze. Today's local paper devoted nearly two pages to the Spandex revolution. It had pictures also. But they were very different from the pictures from Cambodia. These were pictures of muscled men and shapely women enjoying the good life in their tight-fitting Spandex wardrobe. I learned that Spandex was the latest thing in fashion statements because they managed to conceal yet reveal. Three cheers for American ingenuity. One woman interviewed for the article said, "I like it because it shows everything that you've got. But you are still covered." A young man chipped in with, "If you've got a good body, it makes it look better."

I'm not sure that a pictorial on the violence in Cambodia can compete with pictures of the young and the beautiful modeling Spandex outfits, especially on Sunday morning, during breakfast.

We have been bombarded with so many images—images created by commerce, images manufactured by political propaganda, images delivered by photojournalists reflecting the cruelty of war and hate—that they've all become a blur. Life is being reduced to slogans, commercials, and photo opportunities. National politics has become a game where politicians jockey for position in order to get a few precious seconds of "face time" on the network news. Look around . . . there is no substance, no meat. Understanding takes a back seat to selling. I suppose it always has; I suppose it always will.

The world is shrinking, its size reduced by supersonic travel and satellite communications. News anchors broadcast live from China one night, and then live from Romania the next, giving instant anaylsis of revolutions and social upheavals. The network newscast takes us on a nightly adventure, skipping from earthquake disasters in Afghanistan or San Francisco, to the mayhem of drug-related violence and assassinations in Columbia, to the madness of race riots in South Africa, to the lunacy of terrorist bombings in London and in the air over Scotland, to religious genocide in the Middle East. Every night, another big story moves to center stage, only to be forgotten by breakfast.

Oh, Kate, how is it possible for any concerned person to keep track of all the global conflicts or possibly understand the political and social shadings of each of them? The struggles of earning a living, maintaining a relationship, and raising a family are more than enough to overwhelm most people.

They overwhelm me.

I better move on to the three stories I mentioned earlier. The first one comes from the Land of the Rising Sun, Japan. It's a tragic story of rules and discipline, of crime and punishment gone mad. It's a story of how a few seconds rocked a nation.

It was almost 8:30 in the morning. School was about to begin. Standing at the front gate of the school yard was a male teacher. He was ready to slide the heavy iron gate across its track and slam it closed. Hurrying toward the gate was a fifteen-year-old girl. She was racing to beat the clock and the gate. For the teacher, punctuality was a matter of discipline. For the young girl, tardiness was going to prove fatal.

At precisely 8:30 A.M., the teacher threw the full force of his strength into sliding the massive, weighty gate closed. The student rushed headlong toward the quickly narrowing space between the sliding gate and the wall that surrounded the school.

She didn't make it. She couldn't have missed by more than a fraction of a second. The gate slammed into her head and pinned her to the wall.

She died a little later of a concussion.

Why?

Why indeed. All of Japan wanted to know.

Some say the teacher saw the girl approaching the gate, but was determined to rigidly enforce the rule and send a clear message to the students that tardiness was unacceptable. Others claimed he was taunting the students, wanting to cut them off by just a few seconds. Some say the girl tripped on the track and the teacher didn't notice her amid the chaos of the dozen or so other children attempting to squeeze their way through the gateway. Who can say exactly what happened in such a short space of time? There is no videotape instant replay—this was not the NFL, it was real life. No matter where the fault comes to rest, the undeniable truth was that the little girl was just barely late, but very dead.

School discipline in Japan has not waned the way it has in America. Corporal punishment is routine. Shortly before this incident, seven teachers were suspended for their involvement in beating two students and then burying them in sand up to their necks on a beach as the waves crashed in on them. The Japanese believe strict rules in schools are necessary because it is a place of group responsibility. Japan's school system is generally admired for turning out high-caliber students. Children are pushed to their limits. But critics say schools rely too heavily on rote learning and on a multitude of rules on clothing, hair length, what movies or coffee shops students can go to, and even the number of pleats in girls' dresses. But all this is being examined now. Unfortunately, it comes a little late for the girl who paid for her lateness with her life.

And people tell me life isn't absurd.

For the second story, we go to Italy and another young girl. She was only about six or seven years old; I can't remember her exact age. She was driving with her father on a busy highway that led out of Rome. It was the beginning of a long weekend, and the road was jammed with cars heading out of town.

As the road approached a tunnel, which gnawed its way through a mountain, the girl's father grabbed his chest in pain. He managed not to lose control of the car, and he was able to bring it to a stop on the shoulder just outside the mouth of the tunnel. He lost consciousness and slumped down onto the seat. The young girl was stricken with panic but retained enough composure to get out of the car and try to flag down a motorist for help. She stood behind the car, jumping and waving for help for hours before a motorist stopped. The father died.

As in Japan, the question that tormented all of Italy was: Why?

Why didn't anyone stop? The girl was very young and obviously in need of help. Had the nation grown so callous, that nothing could interfere with their own desire to get a jump on the long weekend?

For the third story, we go to Philadelphia. The main player in this saga was a forty-nine-year-old physician who had emigrated to this country from Sri Lanka eighteen years ago. He had only two concerns in life: his work and his family. He was a highly regarded specialist in gastrointestinal cancer, who tirelessly preached the medicine of hope to patients. He was known for using the most aggressive new procedures for keeping patients alive. The doctor lived in a fashionable suburban neighborhood and was a dedicated family man with two children: a severely retarded seventeen-year-old daughter and a bright twelve-year-old son. He and his wife were both educated in England. She too was a doctor, specializing in pediatric psychiatry. Lately, she had been suffering from arthritis and depression.

His life was based on the philosophy of hope. He loved his wife, his kids, and his work.

There was no hint of what he was planning. At work, he had recently submitted his plans for research and patient treatment for the coming year. At home, his plan was to kill his wife, his two children, and himself.

One day last week, he went about his morning chores at home. He cared for his wife and daughter, and when all their needs were met, he rushed off to work where he spent a typical day of caring for his patients. He showed no signs of stress, gave no hint of the plans he was about to "execute" that night at home.

Around 4:00 P.M., he said he wasn't feeling well. Before leaving, he casually told the receptionist that he left a note in a manila envelope on his desk, which he wanted her to deliver to his assistant in the morning. In it were a suicide note and a substantial amount of money.

"We lived together, we loved together, we die together," the doctor wrote in the note. He stated that there was no alternative but death for his wife, and he had to end her suffering. His daughter's condition was helpless. He believed he could not spare his son because he feared that the boy would be placed in foster homes and become a social misfit.

The doctor swabbed the arms of his family and inserted intravenous tubes leading to a bottle containing the solution that would kill them. They all appeared to have died peacefully—together on beds and mattresses in the master bedroom.

His note claimed, "I have no regrets."

So there you have it: three stories, six senseless deaths. These unrelated stories and the distressing pictures from Cambodia came together in my mind this morning. Whirling around in my head were the tortured images of the survivors of a deadly war, thoughts of a schoolgirl's head crushed in a thoughtless act of stupidity, of a man dying alone in his car as his child's frantic pleas for help go unheaded by hundreds of not-so-good Samaritans, and of a doctor dedicated to healing others deciding it's best to kill himself and his family. The spinning images and thoughts created a numbing blur of pessimism. Life seemed so random, so pointless, so chaotic, so helpless, so cruel, so absurd. How can I overcome it? How can I ignore all that is going on in the world?

I don't know. But I know I must. I've got to find a way.

I started by writing to you.

Putting it all down on paper doesn't seem to have helped much. I have no clearer understanding. I have not discovered any explanation that makes sense. But, at least, the stuff is no longer bottled up inside me.

I wish I wasn't so sensitive. I wish I didn't feel things so deeply. Not really. Insensitivity is no bargain; it's nothing I aspire to achieve. Balance is what is needed. There isn't anything I can do for those six lives. Cambodia is half-a-world away, far beyond my reach. I can care. I must care. But I can't despair. I can't give up wanting to live.

In a letter to a troubled friend, novelist Henry James wrote, "Remember that every life is a special problem which is not yours but another's and content yourself with the terrible algebra of your own. . . . We all live together, and those of us who love and know, live so most." Maybe I need to think more about "the terrible algebra" of my own life.

Well my precious daughter, I guess for now I had best just take a deep breath, feel the life within me, and go on despite the madness around me.

I love you.

Monday, July 23—9:30 A.M.

I guess part of "going on" includes getting a job. Jesus, the thought is enough to make me puke. Not that I have a disdain for work, it's just that I loathe the work that I do, or better put, have done in the past. I haven't given much thought to a full-time job for quite a long time. It seemed silly to look for work when I was convinced that I wanted to end my life. Besides, before the notion of suicide had crystallized in my mind, I had abandoned full-time television production in order to devote all my energy and time to writing.

I haven't made much money over the past few years. I've been living primarily off the savings I stashed away when I was making the big bucks working full-time on soap operas. My only steady income has come from residual payments that I receive when soap operas I directed air in a foreign country. Fortunately, two shows I worked on are now popular in Italy and France. (So much for

European taste.) But residuals don't really amount to much money. Every once in a while I get a call to direct a show, usually only when the show's regular director gets sick and no other staff person is available. I sold one sitcom script, but the show was cancelled before my script was ever produced.

(Speaking of money, I think I bought into the notion that money was the root of all evil. But if you really think about it, that is really a rather naive cliche. After all, such evil men as Lenin, Stalin, and Hitler were contemptuous of money. Eric Hoffer, the working man's philosopher who went from being homeless to a best-selling author, pointed out that the horrors that this century has produced were more the result of attempts to realize ideals, dreams, and visions, rather than the result of the pursuit of money.)

Anyway, my transition from a producer/director to a writer has been a financial disaster. I suppose worse than trying to change jobs, I tried to change the medium in which I worked. I didn't want to write television shows, I wanted to write novels and screenplays. I know some writers who have made a very good living writing screenplays that have never been produced. You see, studios are always looking for new properties. They buy screenplays and then try to develop an interest in them by pitching them to big-name directors or stars. I know one guy who has managed to sell one screenplay a year—at about $100,000 a script—for the past four years, yet not one of them has made it to the silver screen. The guy's mother keeps asking, "When are we going to see something you wrote?" He claims she thinks that he really sells drugs for a living.

I should have the problem selling screenplays that don't get produced. I haven't come close to selling anything. I have been hired a few times to do some rewriting on a script that a studio has purchased. But those opportunities are few and far between, and, worse, don't pay that much.

I guess what I'm saying is that it might be time for me to try to get back into television production. I think I need a real job.

Ugh.

Sunday, August 5—8:50 A.M.

Good morning, my sweet. It has been nearly two weeks since I've set my thoughts down on paper for you. A tough two weeks. The melancholy I was experiencing has been hanging in the air like a stratus cloud formation for the entire time. The days have been long and grey.

Why?

I have no answer. I'm not personally depressed, yet my outlook is somber. While most people around me are happy to view the world through rose-colored glasses, I'm stuck wearing ashen-colored ones. The trouble is not internal, but external—not me but the world around me. My problem is hardly unique. In fact, it is so common there is a word describing it: Weltschmerz, excessive pessimism over the state of the world.

Just when it looked like peace was breaking out around the world, and the threat of communism has virtually disappeared, Iraq invaded Kuwait this week. Iraqi troops stormed into the tiny, desert sheikdom and seized control of its capital city and its rich oil fields, plunging the world financial markets into turmoil. Explosions and gunfire echoed around the steel-and-glass skyscrapers of Kuwait City as columns of tanks pushed their way to the Persian Gulf coast. Hundreds of people were killed in what George Bush called an act of "naked aggression."

The president of Iraq, Saddam Hussein, has been described as a megalo-maniacal, bloodthirsty leader who sees himself as destined to dominate the Arab world. It was reported that Saddam had one hundred army officers who refused to take part in the invasion of their Arab neighbor Kuwait executed. A radical revolutionary, the fifty-three-year-old Hussein attempted his first political assassination when he was twenty-two years old. Ten years ago, he presided over a firing squad that executed more than twenty officials, including one of his closest companions, for disloyalty during his successful struggle to become president. Saddam Hussein presided over a brutal eight-year war with Iran, a war whose casualties numbered in the millions. And recently, it was reported that he poison-gassed 8,000 nomadic Moslems known as Kurds who were living in northern Iraq. (Because this act of barbarism had no worldwide economic impact, there was no outpouring of condemnation from world leaders, not even George Bush. Barbarism was barbarism, but business is business.) Amnesty International, an organization dedicated to the protection of human rights, claims that Hussein's regime is the most brutal on earth and that Hussein's government has executed 35,000 people who oppposed the dictator's views. And it should come as no surprise that experts predict Hussein will have the capacity to produce nuclear bombs within four years—or less.

Behind all this is oil and money. Saddam was broke from the war with Iran, and he had a million-man army to pay, so he marched into Kuwait and helped himself to their oil and gold. But his heavy-handed robbery has worldwide impact. Despite the fact that the world is currently sitting on a near record stockpile of crude oil, the price on the spot oil markets surged to new highs on the heels of the news of the invasion. In less time than it takes a cat to catch a mouse, gas prices in America jumped nearly ten to fifteen cents per gallon—this is on gas the dealers purchased before the invasion—without any real justification. The stock market is expected to plummet tomorrow as fear that rising oil prices will trigger at least a recession, and possibly a depression. The real problem will come when Hussein turns off the Kuwait oil supply and forces the price of a barrel of oil to double. While large industrial countries that import 50 percent or more of their oil, such as Japan, Germany, and the United States, will suffer, it's the poor third world countries that will be hurt the most.

Oh, Kate, I can't pretend to know about all this global economic stuff— I can't even balance my own checkbook. Yet, no one can escape its impact. When one wacko with a strong army in some hell hole of a desert country halfway around the world is able to bring the family of man to its knees, you've got a pretty sorry state of affairs. This Hussein character is getting away with it. The world leaders have responded by slapping his wrist by imposing some trade sanctions, freezing Iraqi assets, and threatening a naval and economic blockade, but basically he appears to have walked into Kuwait and replaced the Emir (whose family has ruled the country for 243 years in the old-fashioned tribal way of benevolent paternalism) with a puppet government that he will control. I suppose the fighting could escalate—Bush has ordered a naval flotilla into the area, no one seems sure.

That's the point. No one is "sure" of anything. The world has become very fragile. I was just about to say that the world seems like its on the verge of exploding, when a smile gently crossed my face. Not that I find that a pleasant prospect. No, it's just that scene from a Woody Allen movie—I can't recall which one—flashed into my mind. In the scene, a kid portraying a young Woody is in a psychiatrist's office, where he has been dragged against his will by his concerned but dominating mother. The child has been experiencing extreme depression, to the point of not doing his homework or even going to school. The doctor asks him why and the kid responds along the lines of, "What's the use." He goes on to explain how the universe is expanding, and that eventually it will explode, so why bother going to school and doing homework. His mother, totally frustrated by his negative outlook, yells, "What business is it of yours if the universe is expanding!" The doctor patiently explains that while it is true that the universe is expanding it would take billions of years for this to pose any problem for mankind.

I can hear my mother saying, "What business is it of yours if Kuwait has been invaded? Worry about your own life."

After all, what can I do about Kuwait? Nothing. Should I just ignore it? The pragmatic American philosopher and psychologist William James claimed, "The art of being wise is the art of knowing what to overlook." Is it possible to overlook what's going on in the world? I seem to be in control of nothing, except my own thoughts. Now that those thoughts have turned from suicide, I'm left with the prospect of thinking about resuming my life . . . a life that must be lived in the world, even though the world is out of control.

Weltschmerz: is there a cure? I could try looking at the positive. Let's see: Bush is alive, which means Quayle isn't the president. No, this isn't working. How can I be anything but pessimistic about the condition the world is in? Buried on page six of today's paper is a headline that on any sane planet would have been front-page news: "Tamils kill 110 Muslims at Two Sri Lankan Mosques." I start to read the article, which describes how militant rebels sprayed machine-gun fire into mosques that were crowded with worshippers. I had to stop. I just couldn't absorb the information. This story ignited no outrage; in fact, it wasn't even reported on the television news—they've got only twenty-two minutes to cover the news of the world.

How can people read the papers without feeling a sense of total frustration? I guess with one eye closed, and the other fixed on the sports, comics, or horoscope sections. But I don't read the comics, the horoscope takes only a few seconds to read, and with the Yankees having their worst season ever, I no longer bother to read the sports section.

It's funny, but this all keeps coming back to religion. It is impossible to understand the Middle East today without a full knowledge of the historical context of the religious issues that have divided these people for centuries. That kind of knowledge seems to be in short supply, or at least inaccessible to most people. So we blindly blunder on in the dark about religions past.

My pessimistic view of the world is not traced back to war and religion alone. There are other stories in the news these days that contribute equally to my Weltschmerz. Perhaps these are even more unsettling . . . war, aggression, hatred, and religious bigotry, while intolerable, are at least understandable. But try understanding the dynamics behind this headline: "Caring for Children, Men Find New Assumptions and Rules." The gist of the story, is that at a time when there is pressure on men to be more caring and demonstrative to children, more and more men and organizations are worrying that casual physical contact with children may create the impression of sexual misconduct.

The sexual abuse of children has generated widespread alarm as reported cases have soared. One study estimated that there are 500,000 victims of serious child abuse each year in this country. Because of that, men who care for children, including teachers, social workers, day care workers, and scoutmasters, now toil under the presumption of perversion. Imagine, Boy Scout manuals now deal with molestation directly, using such words as "recognize, resist, and report." New Scout rules prohibit any scoutmaster from spending time alone with any scout if he is out of the view of another leader or parent.

And the men guilty of the heinous crime of sexually abusing a child are not limited to the stereotypical image of the "dirty old man in a rain coat." One man was a saint. Or so many people thought, including myself. His name is not important, but his story is.

He was a Franciscan priest who taught philosophy at a major Catholic university in New York City. His students confronted him on how his vows of poverty, chastity, and obedience were out of harmony with his relatively soft life. He had a car, an apartment, a stereo—all the normal yuppie things. He hardly seemed to be walking in the austere footsteps of the little flower of Assisi. The priest was shaken by his students' observations—he wasn't living what he preached and professed.

That was the beginning of the end of his career as a college professor and the beginning of his life as an advocate for the throwaway kids of our day, the homeless runaways who live in the dark shadows of every big city, scratching out a living by turning tricks. He had no plan, he simply responded to the needy kids he encountered. His apartment became a shelter for the first street kids he met.

His story reads like something out of Butler's *Lives of the Saints* and is filled with what looks like miraculous intervention, such as when he was literally handed the keys to a prime piece of midtown New York property. The building was owned by a Protestant denomination and had at one time been a retreat center for its missionaries, but recently it sat abandoned, except for a caretaker who patiently waited for the arrival of the person God wanted to have the building. The priest's notoriety grew and grew. He was the subject of numerous television documentaries. He became the nationwide spokesperson for teenage runaways and a highly successful fundraiser on their behalf. He was a genuine, modern-day American saint.

And an alledged child molester.

When the story of possible sexual misconduct, as well as financial hanky panky, first hit the news, it was met with complete disbelief. It was a "set-up" the priest claimed. Everybody believed him. I believed him. I wanted to believe him. I contributed to his organization and had complete faith in his integrity. But the story did not go away. It dragged on for over a year. The evidence against the priest kept mounting. Finally, he resigned, without admitting any guilt. He quit, he claimed, for the sake of the kids. Even in the midst of the growing scandal, many still viewed him as a persecuted saint, the victim of some perverted plot.

His sainthood ended this week, when a four-month-long investigation, which was headed by a former New York City police commissioner, concluded that the priest engaged in sex with young men living in his shelter. Witnesses saw the "saint" in bed with those he professed to be protecting and sheltering. The New York District Attorney also uncovered "some questionable financial transactions." The priest's only response, "Garbage."

I'll say. But none of this should be surprising. A study of over 1,500 priests conducted between 1965 and 1980 by a former priest revealed that 50 percent of the priests were not practicing celibacy. Moreover, 10 percent were involved in homosexual activity, and—this is the shocking part—6 percent were involved with minors. In recent years, it has become clear that many priests are pedophiles, even though their actual numbers may not be more than a fraction of the total number of priests. In 1988, it was discovered that a priest in New Orleans made videotapes of his sexual rendezvous in the rectory with teenage boys. In 1985, a priest from Lafayette, Louisiana, was convicted of molesting thirty-five children. During the last ten years, it is estimated that four hundred priests have faced criminal charges stemming from their illicit sexual activity.

The notion that little is what it appears to be is creeping into our consciousness. Earlier this week I was in line at the check-out counter of a supermarket. A young mother just ahead of me was busy emptying her shopping cart. It was overloaded with food. She had with her two small children. One stood next to her, tugging at her purse and trying to get her attention. The other child was young enough to be sitting in the cart. He was perhaps two years old. And very cute. But his face was severely bruised, especially around the eyes. The check-out lady commented on it. The woman explained how it happened and claimed that it looks worse than it is. The mother had a very natural beauty about her. She was thin, nicely dressed, and her short hair framed a very innocent but troubled face. She looked like your average American housewife, if there is such a thing. What I'm saying is, she looked like a frazzled but loving mother.

But was she, I wondered? Did she beat this child? The question was on my mind, as perhaps it was also on the mind of the check-out lady. The stories of severe physical punishment inflicted on children by their mothers have surfaced with such frequency that any thinking person upon seeing a badly bruised child cannot help but wonder whether the bruises were the result of an accident or abuse. Imagine, questioning motherhood, calling into doubt the natural child-nurturing instincts women are supposed to be endowed with.

Mistrust of everything is in the air. A month ago, the Catholic Archbishop of Atlanta resigned after only two years in office. The reason given was that he was exhausted by the demands of the job and needed a prolonged physical and spiritual retreat in order to rejuvenate himself. It was also hinted that the Archbishop would be receiving some psychological therapy. The real reason for his resignation was reluctantly disclosed by the Church last week: the Archbishop had an ongoing, intimate, two-year-long affair with a twenty-seven-year-old woman who was a lay minister—no pun intended!

But the scandal did not end with that bombshell. It was also revealed that two other priests had been intimately involved with the same woman prior to her fling with the Archbishop, and she had claimed one of the priests was the father of her child! The paternity charge was refuted following a blood test, but, nonetheless, the Church still paid her medical expenses.

There is still more to this story of clerical passion. It was also reported, and confirmed, that this same woman, when she was nineteen years old, had an affair with a nun! Maybe this is where sex became habit-forming for the young lady. Even the worst hack writer in Hollywood would not invent such a plot as a woman working her way up from a nun, through a pair of priests, to the holy of holies—an Archbishop.

The New York City priest and the Archbishop of Altanta help confirm my belief that the devout are as prone to hypocrisy as the rest of us.

This is America. These are the headlines. A power-hungry madman in Arabia threatens the economic stability of the world, and, at home, saints and prelates are knocked off their pedestals, and fear of sex-abuse charges may be stifling male efforts to be more nurturing.

How can anyone take a good look around them and not become pessimistic? But pessimism is un-American. ("Are you now, or have you ever been a member of the Pessimist Party?) We are a culture obsessed with success; yet, failure is what most of us experience. I look at society and see enthropy, anomie, breakdown, and ruin. It's hard to put a smile on that picture.

Weltschmerz. I've got it. I've got to shake it. I've got to think about me.

Or do I?

On that note, I'll end this for now. Next time I'll write before I read.

Wait a minute. Something just hit me.

Perhaps the loss of faith in the world people are experiencing is responsible for what some see as a rise in faith in God. Who can we trust? Surely, not the government. Surely, not individual men of the cloth. Surely, not humanity itself. In many cases, people don't even trust their own spouses. So who can we trust? The only "person" who is left—God, the Supreme Being. Maybe the turbulent world situation explains why people cling to the idea of God, while at the same time church attendance is on the decline.

So, whom can I trust . . . whom can I turn to . . . who can help me with my Weltschmerz?

Not God.

Not man.

There is no one to stand with me before the insoluble paradox of human existence. I am all alone, and it's turning into a very cold world.

Fortunately, the warmth of my love for you keeps me from freezing. The question is no longer: Do I want to live, but how do I endure in a world of chaos?

I know! I think I'll go live in Paris or Madrid for a few months—kinda get a new perspective on things. That may very well get me out of the rut I'm stuck in or, more correctly, get me out of the rut in which I'm stuck. (Isn't it odd how the proper verson sounds unnatural, while the improper version sounds natural? Maybe impropriety comes as natural to humanity as it does to grammar.) The American novelist and poet Edward Dahlberg claimed, "When one realizes that his life is worthless he either commits suicide or travels." Life still seems worthless, but now that I've ruled out suicide, perhaps I should travel.

OK, this is really the end for now, no more flash thoughts—I've got to ponder this Paris idea.

Au revoir.

Thursday, August 9—1:15 A.M.

Couldn't sleep tonight. Tossed and turned for a while, then got up and turned on the tube. It was a little after midnight. Thought maybe I'd catch a flick. Found the cable guide, buried beneath a pile of old newspapers. (Tomorrow I'm going to clean this dump!) Here were my options:

Bits & Pieces (1987) A young woman is stalked by a mutilator. Adult situations, profanity, nudity, violence.

The Witchmaker (1969) A professor of parapsychology and his group find the bayou coven of warlock Luther the Berserk. Adult situations, nudity, violence.

Satan's Cheerleader (1977) Young girls are lured to the altar of the Devil by a high-school janitor. Adult situations, nudity.

What delightful choices. Rather than watch any of these movies, I decided to read the cable guide . . . see what was on other nights of the week. Here are some more of the cinematic offerings being presented this week:

Blood Relations (1988) A guy brings his girlfriend to the family mansion to help him kill his father. Adult situations, profanity, nudity, violence.

New York's Finest (1988) Three 42nd Street hookers try to change their images. Adult situations, profanity, nudity.

Blazing Stewardesses (1974) Three stewardesses go to a western brothel and encounter wacky gunmen, naked women, and all-out zaniness. A six-shoootin', sexy romp. Adult situations, profanity, nudity.

Child's Play (1988) Gunned down in a kiddie shop, a homicidal psychotic casts his soul into a pudgy doll named Chuckle, becoming a toy for a six-year-old and a terror to the rest of Chicago. Adult situations, violence.

The Toxic Avenger (1985) A ninety-eight-pound nerd lands in a vat of toxic waste and becomes a monster. Adult situations, profanity, nudity, violence.

Reform School Girls (1986) It's every "women in prison" film you've ever seen . . . and then some! A young girl learns the hard facts of reformatory life when she finds herself up against sadistic matrons, lesbian gang leaders, and more. Adult situations, profanity, nudity, violence.

Motel Hell (1980) Just what could be the secet ingredient that makes farmer Vincent's sausages so tasty? Guests of his know the answer. In fact, they are the answer. Plenty of gore. Adult situations, profanity, nudity, violence.

Here are a handful of additional titles—I'll spare you the descriptive captions: *Virgin Machine, Deadly Dancer, I Spit on Your Grave, Satan's Princess, A Girl to Kill For, Demon Wind,* and *Ilsa, She-Wolf of the S.S.*

It boggles my mind that those movies actually were produced. And I can't sell a screenplay. Well, I'm going to sip a little more wine and go to bed . . . I think I'm ready to sleep now. If I can't sleep, I'll get up and write a screenplay titled: *Blood Relations of New York's Finest Meet the Blazing Stewardesses at Motel Hell, Now Run by Ilsa the She-Wolf of the S.S. With the Help of Satan's Cheerleaders and the Reform School Girls.*

Now that's a picture that will sell, because I'll make sure it has the four necessary ingredients: adult situations (What are adult situations? They don't mean paying bills, do they?), profanity, nudity, and violence.

Say goodnight, Kate.

Saturday, August 11—11:30 A.M.

Hi, my sweet. This is going to be short entry. I don't have much to say—although I just realized that this letter began only one month ago, on July 11. What a month!

For the past week, the world's attention has been focused on Iraq. American troops are now in Saudi Arabia, in a "defensive" position ready to thwart any further Iraqi aggression. The story dominates the news. I really have nothing much to say about it, and I only wanted to put down on paper one ironic observation.

Actually, it isn't even an observation; it's more a comparison. This morning, I was reading a statement released by Saddam Hussein yesterday, in which he declared a "jihad"—a holy war—against those who threaten the holy shrines of Mecca, and I couldn't help but be struck by how much it sounded like the rousing call-to-arms speech given by Pope Urban II when he initiated the crusades 995 years ago. So, after I read Hussein's harangue, I dug up Urban's tirade. I placed them side-by-side. Wow! The similiarity was shocking.

Because speeches and statements like these don't find their way into the "once over lightly" history books used in schools, I thought it would be worth the trouble to give you a sample from each.

Here is a brief portion of Pope Urban's speech, given on November 26, 1095:

> Wherefore, I pray and exhort, nay not I, but the Lord prays and exhorts you, as heralds of Christ, by frequent exhortation, to urge men of all ranks, knights and foot-soldiers, rich and poor, to hasten to exterminate this vile race from the lands of our brethern, and to bear timely aid to the worshipers of Christ. I speak to those who are present, I proclaim to those who are absent, but Christ commands. Moreover, the sins of those who set out thither, if they lose their lives on the journey, by land or sea, or in fighting against the heathen, shall be remitted in that hour; this I grant to all who go, through the power of God vested in me.
>
> Oh, what a disgrace is a race so despised, degenerate, and slave of the demons, should thus conquer a people fortified with faith in omnipotent God and resplendent with the name of Christ! Oh, how many reproaches will be heaped upon you by the Lord Himself if you do not aid those who like yourselves are counted of the Christian faith!

Here is a snippet from Saddam Hussein's statement, issued on August 10, 1990:

> O Arabs, O Muslims and believers everywhere. This is your day to rise and defend Mecca, which is captured by the spears of the Americans and Zionists. Revolt against oppression, corruption, treachery and back-stabbing. . . . Keep the foreigner away from your holy shrines and raise your voices and evoke the honor of your rulers so that we all stand as one to expel darkness and expose those rulers who know no sense of honor.
>
> Revolt against the oil emirs who accept to push the Arab women into whoredom.
>
> Tell the infidels that there is no place for them in the land of the Arabs after they squandered the people's rights and humiliated their dignity and honor.
>
> Burn the land under the feet of the aggressive invaders who have evil designs against your people in Iraq.
>
> Strike at their interests everywhere. Save Mecca and the Tomb of the Prophet Mohammed in Medina.

Urban's rhetoric was more sophisticated than Hussein's, but what Hussein lacked in polish he made up with bravado. While the time and the situations were different, the language and the theology were very similiar. For Urban, the Turks were a "vile race," "heathen's," and "slaves of the Demons." To Saddam Hussein, Americans are "infidels" and "imperialists." Both men fought to protect "holy" shrines from being plundered by infidels and barbarians. Urban raised the banner of Christ, while Hussein hoisted high the flag of Mohammed. Both men urged the people to put down their petty differences and their personal concerns and join together to fight a holy war against God's enemy.

Earlier in the week Hussein said, "As always, we depend on God." George Bush, in his televised speech to the nation in which he announced he was deploying troops to the Middle East, also called on God for help. He asked American's to go to church and pray for the protection of the soldiers. He ended his speech with, "God bless America."

Obviously, God is on our side. I'm sure the Almighty is very concerned about protecting our materialistic way of life and doesn't want some silly oil shortage to threaten our pampered existense. I'm sure he wants to keep our cars merrily rolling down our beautiful highways as the fumes being emitted from them clog our atmosphere and destroy our ozone layer. I'm sure.

And Kate, if you're not sure just which side God is on, here is a little sampler of the positions and sides God has allegedly taken in the past.

"The Divine Law is against communism." Or so claimed E. F. Landgebe.

"Facism is God's cause." Or so claimed Arthur Cardinal Hinsley.

"God did not mean for women to vote." Or so claimed Grover Cleveland.

"God ordained the separation of the races." Or so claimed Rev. Billy James Hargis.

"Who says I am not under the special protection of God?" So asked Adolf Hitler.

"God has marked the American people as His chosen nation." Or so claimed Senator Albert Beveridge.

"God had a divine purpose in placing this land [America] between two great oceans to be found by those who had a special love of freedom and courage." Or so declared President Ronald Reagan.

"None of us is here by accident. Behind the diligence of our staffs, supporters, and our own individual campaign efforts, behind the votes of the people, we recognize divine appointment." Or so claimed Rev. Richard Halverson opening the predominantly Republican United States Senate session in 1981.

So, as you can see, God is for fascism, against communism; for Hitler, against women; and for America, against integration.

I suppose God is up in heaven, saying, "Oh damn, I've got to choose again. Let's see should it be George or Saddam. Enny meanie miney moe . . ."

Only a month ago, back on July 12, I mentioned in this letter how as a kid I couldn't have cared less about learning about King Nebuchadnezzar II of Babylon. As I wrote those few lines the name Saddam Hussein carried no special meaning to me—or, for that matter, I would say to 90 percent of the world's population. Now, his name is known by all, his face dominates the news morning, noon, and night. In order to understand Saddam Hussein, you need to know about Nebuchadnezzar, whose reign of terror reached biblical proportions nearly 2,600 years ago when he besieged the Tyre seaport for thirteen years in an effort to gain trade dominance and bring his nation worldwide glory. In 597 B.C., Nebuchadnezzar marched into Jerusalem and carted off ten thousand of the cities inhabitants to Babylon. Today in Iraq, whose land mass makes up much of what was known as Babylon in Nebuchadnezzar's day, the citizens have erected billboards comparing Hussein with Nebuchadnezzar. More important to Hussein than the gold and oil he grabbed by invading and annexing Kuwait, is his ability to establish himself in the annals of Arab history and to place himself squarely among the pantheon of great leaders who have ruled the area.

Both the ancient King of Babylon, Nebuchadnezzar, and the current leader of Iraq learned hatred as children. Under the tutelage of his uncle, a government official in Baghdad, Hussein developed an intense hatred of foreigners. Hussein honored his uncle and his ideas by reprinting his uncle's book when he came to power in 1981. The book's title: *Three Whom God Should Not Have Created—Persians, Jews and Flies.* Flies I can understand. And so could Herbie's father. Nebuchadnezzar's father, a general who overthrew the King of Assyria and established himself as King of Babylon, cultivated in his son a hatred for all those who differed with his views.

Even though Iraq lies in ruin after his long war with Iran, not long ago, Hussein ordered a multi-million dollar restoration project of Babylon's Hanging Garden's, once considered to be one of the seven wonders of the world, and which still contain visible ancient inscriptions lying in the gardens hailing Nebuchadnezzar as "The King of Babylon from Far Sea to Far Sea." In addition to the garden face-lift, with its signs boasting "Rebuilt in the Era of Saddam Hussein," Hussein is building a billion-dollar palace for himself, a shrine he hopes will outlast even the famous gardens.

No doubt about it, in Saddam Hussein's mind, he is the successor to Nebuchadnezzar, the King of Babylon. Hussein is far more than a madman who is hungry for power and oil, he is the creator of a New Babylon. In order to succeed, Saddam needs an ally in heaven. Even though he heads a secular government, Saddam knows he must bow to Mecca, must call his military campaign a holy war against the evil powers of the West, and must wave the banner of religion to reach his secular goals. But the Koran and the Sharia (Islamic Holy Law) not only forbid aggression but also clearly articulate who is authorized to lead a jihad and outline tough requirements that must be met for a war to be called just. Many Muslims have pointed out that not only hasn't Saddam met those conditions, but he has neither the right nor the qualifications to lead a jihad.

History, dear Kate, is important. We can't forget about Nebuchadnezzar or Pope Urban II and hope to understand what's happening now. I've been reading a book that has helped me better understand the historical roots behind today's Middle East headlines. It is titled *Holy War.* The author is Karen Armstrong, a former Catholic nun who attended Oxford University. The book explores the origins of Judaism, Christianity, and Islam. As I read it, I was ashamed how weak and vague my understanding of Islam was. I thought of it as the religion of the sword, but that impression just reflected centuries-old cultural prejudices.

In the beginning, Islam was a just and kind religion. Before Mohammed began hearing God's voice, the Arabs, according to Karen Armstrong, felt a strong sense of religious inferiority. The Christians and Jews viewed them as pagan-worshipping barbarians. At the summit of the pagan pantheon of Gods, stood Allah, who was *the* god. But Allah didn't seem to have much power over the other gods. A pagan sect known as "hanifs," or infidels, claimed that Arabs should worship only Allah; moreover, they said Allah was really the same God that the Jews and Christians worshiped. This new belief brought the Arabs into God's original plan for the world and traced their roots back to Ishmael, the son fathered by Abraham and his Egyptian slave girl Hagar. In the beginning of the seventh century, a hanif named Mohammed, a merchant married to a wealthy woman, began hearing voices, which he came to believe were revelations from Allah. The messages he heard became the basis of a new religion, which Mohammed believed was the ultimate revelation of the Jewish-Christian tradition. He called the new religion "Islam," which means "submission" (to Allah), and his followers became known as "Muslims," which means "those who submit." Mohammed was concerned about the plight of the poor and wanted to relieve their suffering. He was kind, generous, and just, and he taught that Jews and Christians must be respected. He placed a high value on liberty of conscience and the freedom of thought.

Of course, this is not what we see when we look into the eyes of Islamic fundamentalist holy men in the Middle East. We see hate-filled, narrow-minded men eager to wage a jihad. Over the centuries, the humane religion of Mohammed became the religion of the sword. The same thing happened to Christianity. Jesus was a pacifist, who had nothing in common with Pope Urban II. Jesus was a Jewish humanist. It was Paul who infused Christ's humanitarian message with the imagery, mythology, and apocalyptic tradition of Judaism. The kinder, gentler Judaism of Jesus gradually gave way to the crusading, devil-chasing cult of Christianity. All three faiths have a violent history; none of them is innocent; all of them are guilty of fearsome savagery in the name of the one, true God.

When will the three blood-stained, spiritual monsters of Judaism, Christianity, and Islam finally be buried and their ancient myths be put to rest? I fear it will not be for a long time, and until then, the cycle of violence and conflict shall continue unabated.

Oh, just one more thing before I split. (OK, so this wasn't a short entry!) Last week, I mentioned to you about the Tamil rebels in Sri Lanka—here is a quick update. Last Tuesday, rebels boarded a bus in the Trincomalee district and gunned down twenty-seven Sinhalese civilians. About ten miles away, in the village of Bandaraduwa, another group of rebels hacked to death twenty-seven more people. These attacks netted virtually no media coverage. In fact, the seven-year war for Tamil independence has claimed an estimated 14,000 lives, many of them civilians, yet, I doubt that I could find a hundred people who have even heard of this deadly struggle.

Well, I'm outta here—taking a drive up Mt. Wilson to escape the noise and heat of Hollywood. I'm still thinking about Paris. I'll tell you more next time.

Monday, August 13—9:30 A.M.

I had a dream about my father last night. I really can't remember much about it. Actually, I can't remember anything about the dream. Except that I saw my father clearly. He looked the way he looked when I was a teenager. Healthy, robust. That was long before age turned him grey and cancer made him weak.

His hair was dark brown, but it looked almost black thanks to the greasy stuff men put in their hair back then. His hair was combed straight back, without a part. The greasy stuff kept it slicked down. He had on a suit and tie. The collar of his white shirt, he only wore white shirts, was heavily starched. I used to have to take those shirts to the Chinese hand laundry. "No ticky, no shirty." My father used to say, "Chris, did you remember to pick up my shirts from the Chinks?" The Chinese were Chinks.

I don't know why my father invaded my dreams last night. I rarely think about him. But I do know that his presence in the dream was disturbing. So much so, I woke up. I quickly fell back to sleep, which is why this morning I can't recall what he was doing in the dream.

But it has made me think about him this morning.

My father never really told me he loved me. Never said he was proud of me. He never acknowledged the fact that I did pretty damn good in a very tough and competitive business. The one person whose affirmation I needed the most, I didn't get. Even when I achieved what has to be considered a fairly decent degree of success, I still saw myself as a failure. Becoming a big-shot network television producer at a very young age, was, in my eyes, a matter of luck, not talent. I saw myself the way I thought my father saw me: a nothing. I didn't measure up to his standards, didn't do things the way he thought they should be done. Worse, I was a sinner, and he knew it and hated the fact that his son was not good enough to resist evil.

How did he know I was a sinner? One day he was in my bedroom. He had decided, with no input from me, the room's sole occupant, that the room needed new wallpaper. He was measuring the walls when he realized he didn't have a pen on him. He walked over to my desk, espied none, and so he opened my desk drawer. As he rummaged through the drawer looking for something with which to write, he dislodged some papers under which was buried a copy of *Playboy* magazine. Later that night, as I got up from the dinner table and started to walk out of the kitchen, he said, "Christopher, I threw out the garbage from your room." I turned and looked at him. I had no idea what he was talking about, but he refused to look at me after delivering that terse statement, so I felt it best not to press the issue and simply shrugged my shoulders and left the kitchen. On my way to my room, I realized what he meant. I quickened my pace and within seconds I was at my desk. My heart was pounding in anticipation. I pulled open the drawer. It was gone . . . he threw "the garbage" out.

I was sixteen at the time. And naturally curious about the opposite sex. Things were different back in 1963. A shy kid had a tough time finding stuff on sex and women. Guys got their older brothers to get them *Playboy* and the few other magazines that featured naked ladies. One of my classmates loaned me the copy of *Playboy* that his brother got for him and that my father threw out. He never said another word about the incident. The room eventually got new wallpaper. But I kept waiting for him to say something . . . anything. I thought from that day on, he looked at me in a different way. Colder, less loving. Maybe it was just my imagination, but I believed he no longer loved me.

About six months later, by which time the incident had slowly crept to the back of my mind, nervously sitting in a corner, but not out of sight, I was caught in another act of mortal sin. About twelve blocks from our house, there was a movie theater that played movies that were not suitable for family viewing. I'm not talking about the triple X porno films that are made today; these were harmless films that showed nothing more than an occasional topless girl. That week the theater was playing one of those British "nudist" movies that were popular back then. Short on story, and long on skin, the plot always featured three or four pretty secretaries out for some clean fun in the sun and one of them suggests a nudist camp. After a bit of hesitation and giggling, they go. The rest of the film is nothing more than naked volleyball and shuffleboard. Most of the creativity in these movies was spent on how to shoot the wide shots without exposing the pubic area, which was then a big no-no. That day, driven by boredom and curiosity, I sat in the darkness of the theater filled with old men with raincoats on their laps. It wasn't raining out. As I left the theater, I was nervous that someone I knew might spot me. Three blocks from the theater was the subway station that my father used. Ninety-nine percent of the time the route he took from the station to our house did not go past the theater. You guessed it, this was one of those rare occasions when he changed his route. He had to stop at a hardware store a few blocks past the theater.

My eyes were still squinting as they adjusted from the darkness of the theater to the setting sunlight of the street, but I still saw him clearly. And he saw me even more clearly. I stopped dead in my tracks. He never broke stride. He looked right into my eyes as he approached me, then turned his eyes away from me and walked right past me as if he didn't even know me. I turned and watched him walk away. I cried.

I wandered around for an hour or more. I knew I was missing dinner, and my mother would be worried but I couldn't go home. I wanted to just run away. When I entered the house, dinner was over, the dishes done, and my parents were sitting alone in the living room. Mom was knitting and watching television. Dad was sitting in his chair, reading the paper. She asked where I had been, I mumbled something, as if waiting for him to tell her, knowing all along he knew I was adding lying to lechery. He never said a word. He never even looked at me.

I was a senior in high school during the "Great Nudie Movie Scandal," as I called it. Was going to that movie so bad? Why couldn't he have talked to me about it? Didn't he realize that when a teenager is faced with having to choose between eternal life and naked women in movies or magazines, eternal life doesn't stand a chance?

We were never very close after those two episodes. Sure, we spoke. But I never lost the feeling that I had let him down, that I hurt him in some way that I couldn't fully understand. I always felt like he wanted to say to me, "Read any filthy magazines or see any dirty movies lately, you pervert?"

My parents thought sex was dirty. I don't think he should have been so upset that a teenager read a magazine or saw a movie he found objectionable. Adults acted in the movie, adults produced the movie, adults distributed the movie, adults owned the theater that displayed the movie, adults published the magazine, adults shipped the magazine, adults sold the magazine—because adults wanted to see the magazine and the movie. If all these adults acted in accordance with the Judeo/Christian ethic, which is supposed to guide this country, then this stuff would not be available for teenagers or anyone else to see it, nor would any adult want to see it.

But that's democracy. Freedom means having the right to choose. People have the right to make and buy what some people see as pornography. When home videos hit the marketplace a few years ago, "adult" titles were few and out of sight. Now, they take up 10 to 15 percent of the video store's stock and are openly displayed in a corner of the store. Most twelve-year-olds today see more sex and flesh on cable TV than I saw in the movie that day.

I have a great deal of anger against a church that would teach teenagers they could burn in hell—right alongside a Nazi sadist—for French kissing or reading *Playboy*.

Tuesday, August 14—2:10 P.M.

Good afternoon, my darling daughter. A bit of relief today from the summer heat; the temperature, for the first time in a long time, will not make it into the eighties.

My Weltschmerz of the past few weeks fades in and out, as if it were a radio station on the outer edge of its range. I feel it strongly, then, without warning it fades out.

When people are stuck in a blue funk, or overly worried about money, or confronted with some hardship that seems unbearble, somebody is always ready to point out how much worse things could be as a way of getting you to be happy. Everyone can look around and see people worse off than they. The homeless are visible in every city, in every town.

When I think of people like Stephen W. Hawking, I feel like shit. This brilliant scientist overcame a crippling disease that deprived him of his voice and left him sitting helpless in a wheelchair, and he still was able to propel himself across the vastness of space and time to unlock the secrets of the universe and make theoretical physics and quantum mechanics more understandable to the average person. And I allow myself to be paralyzed by Weltschmerz. How stupid.

Not too long ago, there was a "Be Happy" fad sweeping the country. There was a popular song that said little more than "don't worry, be happy." T-shirts featuring big, bright yellow smile faces and the words "be happy" were the rage.

But how?

Was it only a matter of positive thinking, of just not worrying?

I don't know. Obviously, it is important to develop a positive outlook, to work at creating the belief that you can accomplish what you want to accomplish.

Or is that just pushing reality aside?

But what does seem certain, is that there always will be somebody worse off than you. Maybe people just have different limits of endurance to pain.

God—I'm babbling. I hate my thoughts being so unfocused, but what triggered this latest bit of babbling was something I read that was written by a woman who survived the horrors of a Nazi concentration camp. Her name was Micheline Maurel, and she wrote, long before the aforementioned T-shirt craze, the following:

> Be happy, you who live in fine apartments, in ugly houses or in hovels. Be happy, you who have your loved ones, and you also who sit alone and dream and can weep. Be happy, you who torture yourselves over metaphysical problems, and who suffer because of money worries. Be happy, you the sick who are being cared for, and you who care for them, and be happy, oh how happy, you who die a death as normal as life, in hospital beds or in your homes. Be happy, all of you: millions of people envy you.

Be happy Christopher Ryan, you who torture yourself over metaphysical problems.

I'm going to try my sweet, little Kate. Damn, am I going to try. No, not try—I will succeed.

I woke up with an urge to renew my long dormant habit of taking a daily jog. I got out my running shorts, my oldest sweatshirt, and my sneakers and hit the streets fairly early. I think I spent more time finding and putting on my running clothes than I actually spent running. I ran about six and a half minutes and had to stop. I hate being so out of shape. It will probably take weeks of dedication to build myself up to the point where I can run for thirty minutes. I already know, however, that I lack the conviction needed to reach that goal.

I actually like running. It's a great way to let the mind wander and see where it goes. It went to Paris this morning—which is a lot farther than my body got. When I got home, I dug up some old notes and thoughts I had once scribbled down about my desire to travel. I'd like to share them with you.

But before I do, I want to tell you about the extremes of cruelty and compassion that I witnessed during the past two days that show humanity at its worst and its best. Actually, I read about one incident in the paper and watched the other on television. One of the stories involves a young father, the other, a pair of gifted surgeons.

Last weekend, in the borough of Queens in New York City, the place where I was born and raised, a nineteen-year-old father commited a beastly act of senseless violence that horrified and repelled the entire city—and New York is not a city that is easily horrified or repelled. The teenager's six-day-old infant woke up crying in the middle of the night. The young man got up and lifted the baby out of the bureau draw that doubled as a crib. While changing the baby's diaper, the baby urinated on him. In a fit of rage, he threw the baby to the floor, killing it. He then sliced up the dead baby with a razor blade and fed the dismembered parts to his recently purchased $3,500 German shepherd.

The young man's nineteen-year-old wife and eleven-month-old daughter slept through the slaughter. "He was friendly" was the way one neighbor described the young man who the police said committed the crime with depraved indifference. Another neighbor said the young couple "looked just like you and me." The photo of the father being taken into custody revealed him to be a good-looking young man: nicely cut blond hair, handsome face, trim body. Normal in every way. He had moved his family from Nebraska only two weeks ago, had already landed a job in a local convenience store, and was attending classes at the K-9 Behavioral Science Center in order to become a dog trainer.

What happened? What made him snap? We can only wonder. Obviously this kid wasn't ready to be a parent. Better the child should not have been born than to have met such a dreadful fate.

Sometimes I've got to just shake my head in disbelief at people who spend so much energy fighting to outlaw abortion. Somehow, I've managed to write 153 pages without really commenting on that explosive topic. It is the most divisive issue facing our nation today, and for a long time it divided me.

For a long time I was against abortion for any reason. I was a card-carrying member of the Mandatory Motherhood Movement. Now, I'm pro-life and pro-choice. That is, I am opposed to abortion, and I'm in favor of keeping it legal. How is it possible for me to be both for and against abortion?

Well, for openers, it seems insane to confer constitutional rights on a fertilized egg—two microscopic cells, the spermatozoon and the ovum, with the combined size of an amoeba. I can't identify with an embryo. Human potential? Sure. Human? Hardly. If it is morally acceptable to prevent the sperm and the ovum from joining, either by contraception or, as the Catholics would like, by the rhythm method, and thereby denying the potential for life, why is it morally unacceptable to end the early life created when a sperm and ovum have joined? More important, the idea of forcing a woman to have a baby against her will strikes me as the ultimate in self-righteousness.

Sure, if I were a pregnant woman, I would refuse the abortion. At least, I think I would, but who knows? If men could get pregnant, I'm sure the rules about terminating pregnancies would have been much different. Besides, I wouldn't want to sit down and have a cup of coffee with most of the people who are adamantly opposed to abortion. Many are godaholics who protest against any woman killing a cell inside her body for any reason, yet lobby for the state's right to kill human beings it finds guilty of murder.

Happily, I will now move from abortion and infanticide to something I saw the other night that vividly showed that while humans are capable of extreme acts of cruelty, we are also capable of extraordinary compassion.

It is the story of a fifteen-month-old infant girl. She suffered from a condition know as plagiocephaly, which results in severe facial deformity and which strikes one in five thousand newborn babies. As best I can, I'll try to describe plagiocephaly. The skull is made up of numerous bone plates fused together to form the cranium and the skeleton of the face. The brain lies well protected within the cranium. The spaces or joints between these bone plates are called sutures. In the adult skull, these sutures or spaces have joined together. But the infant skull needs flexibility to accommodate the growing brain, therefore the spaces between these plates are fairly wide. (Gee, I sound like Dr. Ryan, M.D.—"Take two aspirins and call me in the morning.") By the time a person is six or seven years old, he or she's got all the brains they'll have for life, so there is no need for the skull to be able to expand any longer and the bones then begin to fuse, to stick together and form the thick skull of the grown up. (Some skulls are thicker than others—my Uncle Harry, for instance, had a very thick skull!)

So, the point is Kate, during the first years of life, the skull has to have the ability to give. I remember very well your tiny little head. At the top there was this soft spot, and god did that make me nervous. I was told it was normal and that the skull hardens in time, which is not exactly what is happening— doctors just want to spare you the details, I guess. Meanwhile, I felt like you should be wearing a football helmet to protect your soft head. The soft spot is simply a junction where the three major plates meet. It is kind of a safety valve for the growing brain.

OK, with that little anatomy lesson behind us, what happens in the skull of a child who has plagiocephaly is one or more of these sutures closes to soon. This causes two problems: first, the brain will press against the bone plate, which has no flexibility or give; second, as the rest of the head expands one side will not and as a result it will pull part of the face out of alignment and result in a very unpleasant looking facial and skull deformity that the child will have to endure for life.

Now to the story of the little fifteen-month-old girl with plagiocephaly. Her name is Michelle. The premature closing of one of her skull sutures resulted in a subtle disfiguration of her face, which would eventually grow worse. In a bold and dramatic piece of television programming, a PBS station broadcast live the graphic reconstruction surgery performed by two doctors that would completely correct Michelle's condition and allow her to have a life not marred by an ugly deformity. It was mesmerizing television. It stayed in my mind for days.

At first, it was very difficult to look at, almost grotesque beyond description; but, slowly, I became in awe of the surgeon's skills, and I watched in utter fascination. Whatever I could say about the actual operation would be a gross oversimplification of the two-hour surgery. These guys used knives, hammers, chisels, drills, pliers, tweezers, scissors, and saws as if they were carpenters working on a piece of furniture. They explained in vivid detail everything they were doing, step by step, from the opening incision to the closing up of the scalp.

The operation began with the doctor explaining how the skull had been prepared for surgery by shaving the hair and sewing in two rows of parallel sutures, which will function as a tourniquet to minimize the flow of blood. As the doctor spoke the camera zoomed in on the angelic face of the child, whose eyes were closed and whose little, button nose peaked over a blue, cloth mask that covered her mouth. She looked so helpless, so fragile. The rows of sutures running across the top of her head from ear to ear were already enough to turn the squeamish away. Forewarning the television audience that what came next was very graphic, the doctor made the incision between the rows of sutures, cutting through the flesh of the scalp, right down to the bone of the skull.

My body cringed in aversion as the scalpel worked its way across the child's scalp. Then the doctor, using delicate hooklike knives, began to peel the scalp downward off the bone of the underlining skeletal structure. Gradually, moving toward the forehead, they pulled the scalp down. Within minutes, the surgeon had literally rolled up the flesh of the child's face, separating it from the bone. the flesh of the child's face was rolled back to a point below the eye sockets. It was as if her face was a mask that was removed, revealing a bloody skull.

I was horrified beyond words. Yet, I was spellbound by what I was watching. At times, there were four or five rubber-gloved hands in the picture working on the child, each holding some kind of surgical instrument. I kept wanting to avert my eyes, yet I really wanted to know what was going on.

My face hurt.

For the next ten minutes or so the doctor did all sorts of things that I couldn't begin to describe. They wired things, they scrapped, poked, and altered bone structure. Meanwhile, the neurosurgeon began to scrub up for his part of the operation—the frontal craniotomy, which would expose the brain—the really gory part of the operation.

The neurosurgeon explained that the right side of the head was in good shape, but that the curvature on the left side was deformed because the bone suture on that side was missing and the bones had fused together. He then pulled out an instrument that looked like a carpenter's drill, a Hudson Brace Drill, which was used to make holes in the skull. He proceeded to drill several openings which would allow him to lift out a section of the skull.

It was hard to comprehend the sight and the sound of a hand drill drilling a hole in an infant's head. The doctor was so blasé that you would think he was working on a chair.

Through the drilled holes you could see the membrane of the brain. The neurosurgeon then used an instrument that cut through bone. It was like a power saw that made a cut from one of the drilled holes to another. Three holes had been drilled in the form of a triangle, and when the surgeon made three cuts in the bone skull between the drilled holes, he was able to lift out a triangular piece of the skull. The brain was exposed; you could see it pulsating.

For the next hour or more, the two doctors worked at rearranging the various bones in the child's head. I'll spare you all the details, but there was plenty more drilling and sawing, as they rearranged the bone structure of the child's face.

Throughout the operation, nurses squirted water to wash away blood. There was a constant sucking sound as a tubelike vacuum sucked up excess blood. Sections of facial bones were removed, and, by using a bone-bending forceps, the bones were bent into a different shape. Gradually sections of bones were wired together. The eye socket was actually moved. The surgeons were like sculptors.

Finally, after a couple of nerve-wracking, tense hours, the mask of the face was rolled into place and sewn back together.

Amazing! I was overwhelmed by the creativity, compassion, courage, nerve, and energy of the two skilled surgeons helping that little girl. The operation reminded me of humanity's amazing potential. Yet, most of us chose very unexceptional lives.

When the program was over, I was emotionally drained. I switched channels, I guess in search of some light entertainment.

I didn't find any.

As the operation was airing, one of the networks was broadcasting a news magazine show that featured a report on the dreadful conditions that exist inside the orphanages of Romania. I went from watching a program that documented the overwhelming concern for the life of one child, to an expose of the brutal mistreatment of legions of children. The totalitarian policies of the Ceausescu regime has created a situation in which thousands of suffering Romanian children are being imprisoned in hidden asylums that bear more of a resemblance to Nazi concentration camps than orphanages.

The news documentary was already in progress. I quickly picked up on the fact that a visiting doctor had managed to use a home video camera to capture on tape the inhumanity of the treatment of children in Romanian orphanages.

Mere words cannot portray the horror and cruelty captured by the videotape within the padlocked gates of some of the more than fifty state-run asylums hidden in remote areas of Romania. Filthy, unattended children, many of them naked and near death from starvation, lay curled up on cots, many laying in their own waste. Flies buzzed around their malnourished bodies, but they are too weak to shoo them away. Many of the children are crippled by disease and years of confinement; others are sedated and bound. The video was difficult to watch; it was a brutal display of inhumanity and man-made misery.

And it got worse; it went from difficult to watch to nearly impossible, when a visiting doctor recorded the horrors of bath time at one institution with his home video camera. Naked boys and girls, ranging in age from six to sixteen, were being beaten to get them to enter a room of bath tubs. The children, with panic-stricken faces, entered the bathing area shrieking and crying. They were forced and shoved, two and three at a time, into tubs half-filled with dirty, blackened water. The children emerged from the "bath" as dirty as they entered. The doctor said the water is rarely changed, and an official of the asylum claimed they didn't have enough clean water to bathe the children.

The exterior of some of the buildings looked like medieval dungeons. Inside, the terrified children were packed into overcrowded rooms. The corridors were dark, dilapidated, and foreboding. Dazed toddlers, laying in their cribs, were tightly wrapped in sheets functioning as straight jackets. Many of the children had severe physical disabilities or were neurologically impaired; some had Downs Syndrome and Cerebral Palsy. One child had a very crooked leg, the result of a fracture that was never set. Many of the children appeared normal and had been either haphazardly misdiagnosed or abandoned. The truly hopeless cases were banished to spend the remaining few weeks of their lives in a basement that was in effect a death row. The children in the basement, many suffering from infectious diseases and curable cases of anemia, were virtually ignored by a staff lacking any substantial medical training.

The doctor and the camera crew also managed to trick their way into a guarded institution that was surrounded by a barbed-wire fence. It was literally a death camp. Many of the children were starving to death. The food budget was only thirty-eight cents a day per child. The children are fed a watery broth soup and scraps of bread. Some of the children could not even feed themselves. Meals were served in a cage that contained plastic potties.

I could go on, but I can't. It was far too repulsive to watch, and just writing about it is making me nauseated. Countless children are dying cruel deaths, deaths they face without any comfort, without anyone even holding their little hands.

The juxtaposition of the two television programs left me reeling. Still, I am grateful to PBS for showing me the compassion and ingenuity of the doctors who performed the skull surgery and to ABC News for graphically reminding me just how brutal humans can be. Within each of us, there is a potential for greatness, and an equal potential for depravity. The human race has come a long way, but we still have a long way to go before we can be proud of ourselves. Look around—you'll see a world populated by large numbers of crooks, cheats, rogues, rascals, charlatans, chiselers, swindlers, shysters, liars, deceivers, villains, and assassins; you'll also see a lot of angels, altruists, philanthropists, humanitarians, saints, and thoughtful, compassionate people. We are fragmented, but part of the same body.

Gee, I sat down a little while ago to tell you about my thoughts on travel, and why I feel I must go to Europe as soon as possible—even though I have virtually no money. Listen, I'm going to tell you all about that—right after I have a cold bottle of German dark beer. Be right back.

Tuesday, August 14—3:50 P.M.

Ah, that tasted good. I love dark beer from Germany and port wine from Portugal.

OK, I've got my notes on travel in front of me. There will be no more side tracks from the headlines.

Kate, I'm obsessed with the idea of living in Paris for a few months. From Paris, I would explore Spain and Portugal. I don't know why Paris has this magnetic pull on my thoughts. I have, of late, become interested in a number of French writers, all of whom are now dead. Maybe that's the reason. But I think it's more than that . . . but I just can't put my finger on it. The idea of traveling around Europe, of actually living there for a while, is not a novel one for me.

For the past ten years, I have been keeping—on an "off and on" basis, mostly off—a journal. Every few days, I try to scribble down my thoughts and emotions. I'm faithful to my journal duty for weeks at a time, then I might have a period of unfaithfulness that could last as long as a year. The other day I was reading over some things I wrote during the past few years. I couldn't help but notice how frequently random thoughts on travel found their way into my journal. For instance, December 16, 1988, there is a two-page entry. Among thoughts on a screenplay I was working on, came this sentence: "I want to travel . . . see London, Paris, Madrid, Athens, and Rome. Is it out of boredom? Is it out of the question?"

In September of 1987, there is one lengthy entry on travel, which I would like to share with you. This was not an "up" time for me. Just before the travel thoughts came this sentiment: "Every single thing in life, whether it is the pursuit of knowledge or pleasure, is a diversion from dealing with the pain of living." Your dad was a real fun guy back in those days.

Anyway, here is what I wrote about travel, a little over three years ago:

What would I do if money were no object—if I had enough dough to guarantee greeting the end of my life without having to endure the bottomless pit of problems that attach themselves to the lives of the chronically poor or those who are merely financially strapped and impoverished? I'm talking daydream time with this question, and the answer shouldn't include any philosophical digressions into the nature of money, or the ability to live a life without a great deal of it, or even the noble idea of sharing one's wealth with those in need, or fulfilling the dreams of your family. Money is a fact of life, but I don't want my response to have anything to do with facts—fantasy is the question's only concern. At issue is what really interests ME and how I'd like to spend my allotted time in the space and place that makes up planet earth.

In order to find bliss, I must know where it lies.

Notions of writing immediately spring to mind. Do I want to devote myself to cranking out a string of books, perhaps someday having one of them hit the *New York Times* best-seller list? Writing books only demands writing more books—to begin is to never stop. I guess everything we attempt to do with our time will eventually turn into a prison, a prison of demands and addiction. My nature seeks freedom, my spirit wants to soar; for me, feeling trapped is worse than feeling like I'm about to throw up. Still, if forced to do something, writing is what I'd prefer to do because it is probably the best way to get to know myself, if not the best way to make money. Writing is exploring, exploring the known or tangible world around us by traveling through the unknown or intangible world of ourselves. Inadvertently that last sentence contains the two words that best answer my question: exploring and traveling.

Exploring and traveling are not interchangeable words. Traveling can mean as little as going from one place to another, or seeing some sights. Touring holds no interest for me, and the picture that develops in my mind of an American tourist in Europe—a person bedecked in gaily colored shorts, a baseball cap, sunglasses, and an instamatic camera, who is oddly out of character with the environment, scurrying, map in hand, from monument here to museum there, and thumbing his nose at the local cuisine for a side order of familiar fast food from a franchise imported from America—is one I find laughable, perhaps because I have been a typical tourist and am capable of laughing at myself. I have no desire to be a tourist. My travel ardor is kindled by my burning need to explore.

For as long as I can remember, I've been imbued with the spirit of wanderlust. As a teenager, I was always ready to hop on a bus to explore other areas of Queens. No excuse was too small to take a subway ride to Manhattan and walk along the concrete canyons created by the towering buildings. Passing the driver's road test and getting my hands on an old used car was the highlight of my youth. With a driver's license in my wallet, a few bucks in my pocket, and some gas in the tank, I was free to explore the beauty and simplicity of New England. To this day, those virgin travels hold a special place in my heart. In the late sixties, I spent a couple of weeks in Europe. I may have been just another run-of-the-mill American tourist (If it's Tuesday, it must be Belgium!), but those few weeks introduced me to new cultures and photography.

Unfortunately, life—that is, family and career—put travel on the back burner. During the past five years, my desire to travel has intensified. But I primarily looked at it—or better, came to think of it—as an escape from reality. But is it an escape, or is it a gateway to understanding?

Damn it! How did a simple question lead to a complicated question? I don't know.

But, if money were no problem, this is what I would do: I would pack up some pads, pencils, and film and hit the road for one year. The itinerary: South America, New Zealand, Australia, Japan, China, Tibet, India, Czechoslovakia, Italy, Greece, Austria, France, Spain, Portugal, and England.

So Kate, as you can see, the notion of living abroad for awhile has been floating around my old noggin for a long time.

Listen, I'm meeting a lady friend for dinner tonight, so I've got to get ready. We're going to a Thai restaurant in North Hollywood. Do I see a question mark in your mind regarding the aforementioned "lady?" She is an old friend. Well, she's not really old, I've just known her for a long time. She shares my passion for Thai and Indian cuisine, plus she also has a taste for the same kind offbeat and obscure movies that I like. We don't actually date, we just do some fun things together. We're pals or, as she puts it: playmates.

More on my thoughts on travel later.

Saturday, September 8—11:30 A.M.

The past few days have been very difficult. Recovery is frustratingly slow, and my patience is growing faint-hearted. My efforts to get on with life seem to be floundering. Some days it is almost impossible to shake the feeling of worthlessness that clings to me like a frightened child. Oh, don't worry, I haven't lost my conviction that suicide is unacceptable. It's just that some days are joyless, some nights . . . I don't even want to talk about some of the nights. But this morning, my despair became open to negotiation by the light of day.

My spirits were lifted when I came across the following two sentences written by Jean-Paul Sartre: "Every truth, says Hegel, has become so. We forget this too often, we see the final destination, not the itinerary, we take the idea as a finished product, without realizing that it is only its slow maturation, a necessary sequence of errors correcting errors themselves, of partial views which are completed and enlarged."

Errors correcting themselves—that's the ticket, that's the story of my new life. I can't help smiling. No, not because of the insight I gleaned from Sartre this morning, but because of his mention of Hegel. I'm glad Sartre got something out of his reading of Hegel. Not too long ago, I spent nearly a half a day struggling through some 150 pages of Hegel's work, and, to be very frank, I didn't have an inkling of what he was after. I thought his main idea was to produce thick books. Professional philosophers love to wander into the mammoth caves of metaphysics, they like the labyrinths of logic, and they marvel in the mysteries of mathematics; however, they don't seem to concern themselves with the actual problems of life.

Georg Wilhelm Friedrich Hegel was a German philosopher. He was born in Stuttgart in 1770. He died in 1831 during a cholera epidemic that ravaged Berlin. The time he lived in was as eventful and unsettled as our own. No one knew what the next morning would bring. Yet, even though Hegel lived practically on the battlefield at Jena where the Prussians were routed by Napoleon in 1806, he managed to be totally absorbed in producing thousands of pages of obtuse philosophy. Hegel's philosophy defies summary restatements. Expert interpretations of his work often contradict each other. I would say that at its core, Hegel's work concerned itself with the justification of the ways of God. He thought he had cornered the truth and seemed drunk with words to express it. Hegel became famous for the book he finished during the battle of Jena: *Phenomenology of the Mind.* Great title, hey? Phenomenology—to save you a trip to the dictionary—is an approach to philosophy centering on analysis of the phenomena that flood man's awareness. Take a peek at the book someday. I promise you that you will wind up scratching your head and asking yourself, "What is this guy talking about?"

I shouldn't feel badly. Hegel himself, near his death, is reported to have said, "Only one man ever understood me . . . and he didn't understand me." Anyway, like I said, I'm glad that Sartre got something out of his reading of Hegel, because this morning I see more clearly that the truth that it is good for me to live has to become a reality. I must discover . . . no, create the itinerary I shall follow to reach the destination of that truth. The days ahead will be days "of slow maturation, a necessary sequence of errors correcting themselves."

Before I sign off this morning, I'd like to say a few words on the topic of my old bugaboo: the complexity of the conflicting images I see each day. Images that still manage to greatly distress me.

One of the tragedies of the "Gulf Crisis"—as the military build-up in the Middle East has come to be known—is the refugee situation in Jordan. Tens of thousands of Asian foreigners who comprised the lowest rung of the pre-invasion Kuwaiti economy fled into Jordan after the invasion. Long before the invasion, most of these people left India, Pakistan, Bangladesh, Sri Lanka, Thailand, and the Phillipines in order to build a better life in Kuwait. They were happy to do the menial jobs that the Kuwaitis didn't want to do themselves. They worked in dry cleaners, they were maids, cashiers, truck drivers, janitors. They washed dishes, swept the streets. But they were working, building their own future.

Now they are all huddled together in the blazing heat of the Jordanian desert in refugee camps. Their dreams have turned to desperation. They have no food, no water, no shelter, and no relief from the 120-degree temperatures. Besides hunger, thirst, and heatstroke, they must cope with the extreme psychological distress of having lost everything. Some of these people had worked for years in Kuwait, putting most of their money in the bank in order to save enough to buy a small house and to send their children to school—and now, all that is lost. For these people, there is no relief in sight. They are slowly dying. These are dispensable people, their lives are not worth squat in the eyes of Bush or Hussein.

Their native countries are too poor to cover the cost of repatriation. Jordan is overwhelmed by the sheer number of refugees streaming in over the border— some ten thousand a day. It is estimated that the desert camp population has reached 105,000 people, about half of them in two camps in the no-man's-land along the Jordan and Iraqi frontiers. Imagine that many people, in that heat, without toilet facilities. The stench from the open latrines is said to be unbearable. People are being bitten by scorpions. (Or do scorpions sting? Whatever.) It was also reported that four cases of cholera have been detected. International relief efforts are underway, but progress is slow, thanks to bureaucratic delays, bungling, and poor financing. Yesterday, four hundred tents from West Germany and fifty tons of rice from America arrived. Ironically, the refugees were not provided with any means to cook the rice. Earlier in the week, twenty tons of Dutch Army biscuits were delivered by truck to a camp, only to be rejected by the Jordanian officials, who mistook the manufacturing date of 1986 as the last-use date. After many telexes, the biscuits were released. The situation is as close to hopeless as it can get.

This morning's paper had pictures of their plight. Thousands upon thousands of people just standing in the desert. A few lucky ones had umbrellas. A more symbolic picture of despair would be hard to imagine. Then I popped on the television. And what by chance do you think I would happen to tune into?

A goddamn fashion show! The show featured the fall collection of some top designers. Gorgeous, tall, lean, high-fashion models strutted up and down a long runway decked out in clothes you will never see in K-mart. As the models paraded the goods, there were off-camera voice-overs featuring the designers describing their use of color and fabrics, and fashion critics commenting on the rising hem-lines. They spoke of "an important evening look," "the richness of the collection," and the use of embroidery, prints, brushed velvets, and transparent fabrics. Ruby red and emerald green are in this year. One designer described his line as "savy and sensible," and another claimed his collection was "fashion that balances opulence and simplicity." Isn't that special?

While the fashion world worries about opulence and simplicity, the refugee world worries about food and water. And tonight, while tens of thousands sleep on the stony desert floor, America—or at least a good-sized chunk of it—will be glued to the height of irrelevancy: The Miss America Pageant. What sexist bullshit!

Well as I said, this entry will be a quickie. What can I say about these clashing images? Nothing. Today is one of those days when my brain feels like a damp match that can't be lit.

Monday, September 10—10:35 A.M.

Had a bright idea this morning. I'm going to open an existentialist bookstore and espresso bar and call it "Beans and Nothingness."

Actually, I did have a bright idea this morning, but it had nothing to do with existentialism, books, or espresso.

I woke up very early, just before 5:00 A.M. I sat up, wide awake, ready to go. But where, at that ungodly hour? Bingo, it hit me: drive to Malibu and take a sunrise walk along the beach, then have a big breakfast at "Gladstones for Fish," a popular beach-front eatery overlooking the Pacific Ocean that serves omelets the size of Pittsburgh.

Jesus, it's been years since I did that. I don't think I could have gotten out of the house any faster if it had been on fire. The freeways were empty—it was worth the trip for that experience alone. As I drove, I was absent-mindedly listening to the news on the radio. One report caught my attention. It had to do with the marked increase in the popularity of prophecy books. The reason is twofold. First, during any periods of trouble or uncertainty, people have a heightened need to know what the future holds. With Congress unable to reach a budget agreement, with the economy heading for at least a recession if not a full-blown depression, with over 200,000 American troops in the Saudi desert, and mounting tensions in the Middle East, this is certainly a period of trouble and uncertainty. Second, the end of a century always brings anxiety and predictions of a universal utopia or global gloom and doom. The upcoming *fin de siecle* not only marks the end of a century, but also the end of a millennium. Fears of global decay and fantasies of renewal will multiply along with the doomsday predictions and New Age prophecies of politicians, pundits, poets, and high priests of religion.

Fin de siecle craziness has been in full swing for a few years now. Nancy Reagan consulted an astrologer before determining the President's schedule. A book by the sixteenth-century physician, cosmetician, and chef Michel Nostradamus, known as "The Man Who Saw Tomorrow," is selling like hotcakes as we approach the end of the twentieth century. I saw a bumper sticker on a car the other day that read: Honk If You Believe in Nostradamus. Lots of people are *Dancing in the Light* with actress Shirley MacLaine, who is *Out on a Limb* looking for new human beings to breakthrough the polarized mess we are in. The top-grossing movie of the year is *Ghost*. In it, a woman communicates through a medium with her dead lover. After 115 days in release, the film grossed just over one hundred eighty million dollars. The film's theme—that there is a possibility of things not ending when we think they end—has struck an emotional chord. Bookstores are giving more and more space to books on the occult, and police are increasingly pointing to satanism and devil worship as factors in violent crimes. Pollsters are asking, "Do you believe in reincarnation?" There has been an increased interest in UFOs, and I'm sure the tabloids will be featuring many headlines like: "Elephants Snatched by UFO. Eyewitnesses confirm: Pilfered pachyderms sucked into sky." Many of the big sellers in bookstores are written by fundamentalist Christians predicting that "End Times" are near, Armageddon is coming.

The radio report didn't go into any great detail, probably not realizing that there is a real story behind the increased book sales. They pretty much only said that people are worried about the future, so they are buying books that proclaim to know what the future holds. I thought about the booksellers. They really don't care that people are worried and fearful, they are more than happy to cash in on those fears and worries and have no problem selling them bullshit. That's free enterprise.

Anyway, the news droned on. Headlines, traffic, weather, and sports—all we need to know, all the time. My mind wandered off and I continued my absent-minded drive to the beach.

As I walked along the water's edge, I became absorbed in nature's beauty. I began to think how it all began—earth and life, I mean. Perhaps my mind was reacting to the "End Times" predictions I heard on the radio, only it went in the other direction. After walking and thinking for awhile, I sat down in the sand, took out my notebook, and scribbled:

> I do not think it is possible for us to understand either the beginning of things or the end of things. Sure, we can produce some rather resplendent metaphysical and theological musings. We can fill countless books with elaborate ontological and phenomenological nonsense; words are never a problem. But the wisest course is to say nothing about the Alpha and the Omega, and be modest enough to admit we shall never know how things began or how they will end. A fixation with the Beginning and the End are for those obsessed with ultimates. Such concerns are, to me, pointless. I live here in-between, somewhere in-between my own beginning and my own end. In reality, everything is a combination of being and nonbeing, or as Sartre put it, "Being and Nothingness."

I closed my pad, put my pen away, and sat staring at the crashing waves. The rhythmic pounding of the surf was thunderously loud, yet the beach felt quiet, peaceful. The ebb and flow of the tide prompted me to think of the flux of time and how in each moment I am different, changed. I am a far different Christopher Ryan than I was ten years ago; I am not even the same Christopher Ryan as I was last month. I am a lifetime of successive moments plus this one moment, which is already gone. The essence of my being is the gradual and ever-changing product of my existence in the flux of time. I am formed by my total past, to which I add every moment of my life.

My problems and the problems of the world seemed far removed from my spot by the seashore this morning. In the tranquility of the moment, I saw how the ever-changing individual is confronted by the ever-changing world. We are lonely and we are anxious. No wonder prophecy book sales are soaring. No wonder drug use is out of control. No wonder so many find solace in the bottom of a bottle. No wonder so many turn to God for guidance.

We each choose the size of our own cell. Let yours, dear Kate, be as large as the universe.

Tuesday, September 11—2:35 P.M.

I was driving down Wilshire Boulevard this morning, on my way to a breakfast meeting with a friend. In front of me was a car with a bumper sticker that blazoned in big, bold, red letters the word HELL. There was something over the word "hell," but I couldn't make out what it said. At the next traffic light, I managed to get close enough to read the small print: "What do you miss if you are a Christian?" I think you miss a hell of a lot more than hell, you miss life.

A few blocks later, I noticed a bumper sticker that suggested: "Burn Commies Not Old Glory." Imagine—preferring to see human flesh and blood burning to a piece of fabric. One symbolizes an idea, the other embodies a reality.

The friend with whom I had breakfast is a writer. He supports himself by working—on a free-lance basis—as a second A.D. (Assistant Director) on movies. I was hoping he could give me some job leads. No dice. But he did tell me a very funny story. In the middle of the filming of the movie he just finished working on, the "star" of the picture—a high-strung, temperamental actress known for throwing temper tantrums on the set—managed to shut down the entire production for three days because she had to go to Brazil to consult a psychic. Ain't show biz grand!

Wednesday, September 12—8:20 A.M.

Last night, George Bush addressed Congress in a nationally televised speech. He had just returned from a one-day Summit with Mikhail Gorbachev in Helsinki, Finland. His topic was twofold: Iraq and the budget deficit. Bush was tough. He was decisive. He was forceful. He was determined. The President was at the top of his game; he knew it, and he liked it. He was unquestionably "presidential," and the leader of the free world.

This will be my last comment on the subject of Iraq. I don't know what will happen. Nobody does. The embargo and other related economic efforts might achieve their objectives—eventually—but it is doubtful because the tactic of starving one's enemy into submission hasn't worked often in the past and there is little reason to think that it will now. Leaks in the blockade are bound to spring up, especially if Iran overcomes its animosity toward Iraq and joins its former enemy in a Holy War against the hated West. The long border between Iraq and Iran is virtually unpoliceable by the West. Diplomatic negotiations may result in a solution; that is, if Hussein wants to reach a diplomatic solution. We could get involved in a full-scale war, a war that will have staggering casualties. And it could be started by mistake. When you have two massive forces armed to the teeth staring at each other anything can happen. A few days ago in Kuwait an Iraqi soldier shot an American citizen who refused to stop for questioning. The American's wounds were minor, but many feared a small incident like that could lead to full-scale fighting.

The fact is that the crisis will end. Everything ends. Which of the three scenarios will lead to the eventual conclusion is unknowable. A room full of journalists and "experts" on the Middle East probably couldn't agree on what time it is, let alone how the crisis will play itself out.

As I sit here, watching all the reports on TV, and reading endless newspaper articles about the conflict, I'm left with one overriding feeling: I don't get it! I mean I understand what is going on; I just don't get the unilateral support for the President's massive military buildup. Nobody is even timidly raising their hand and asking, "Excuse me, Mr. President, could you possibly explain that again? Are you sure this is the right course of action?" Or, "Mr. President, back in early August you said we were in the Middle East for oil, to protect oil. Sir, why is it that we are so reliant on foreign oil? Why did the Reagan-Bush Administration contemptuously dismiss all kinds of special programs to improve energy efficiency and develop renewable energy and thus reduce our dependency on foreign oil?" Or, "Sir, if there is a war, what will it do to our economy? Afterall, the economy is very fragile, unemployment is rising, and the banks and real estate markets are already shakey."

I'm not saying there should be widespread dissent, but there should be at least a few questions, a little bit of doubt. But, there isn't; almost everyone supports Bush's policy. I even saw a kid the other day, perhaps seven or eight years old, wearing a T-shirt bearing this gung-ho message: STICK IT TO IRAQ. Isn't capitalism grand!

Soldiers in the desert are ready to die, willing to die for their country. They are toys in the hands of fate. But, if they are killed in combat, will it be for their country? One soldier interviewed by a TV reporter said, "I'm ready to do what my country asks me to do." But has the country asked him to go bake in the desert? Of course not. One guy asked him—George Bush. The country just chose not to question *his* request that the soldier pack his stuff and head for the Middle East. Before I would march off to war, I would listen to the reasons for sending troops that were offered by the leader of the nation, and then I would do the following: doubt, analyze, synthesize, and verify. In the case of the present conflict, I would follow that sequence of steps and decide to stay home.

Why would I stay home? Because it is a mistake to ignore principle for the sake of supposed practicality; it is a mistake to support those who share neither our values nor our goals. For years we closed our eyes to Hussein's brutality, never protested his gassing his own people. It was not in our best interest to do so. The oil-rich emirs don't share our values, our goals, yet we are quick to come to their aid, not out of principle, but mainly because it is in our best interest. What I'm saying, Kate, is that no country, not even a "God-fearing" one like America, should ever place national interest over principle. That is a lesson we have been taught repeatedly, and it is a lesson we repeatedly forget. And now we get to pay the price for not remembering, but hopefully we will not pay with the blood of unquestioning young American men and women. Our troops are poised for combat in the blazing heat of a foreign desert because during the past eight years our leaders have placed political practicality, albeit masquerading as national interest, ahead of principle, but you will not hear that from the guy who ordered over 150,000 troops into battle—he's into persuasion, not truth.

Since he seized the presidency of Iraq in 1979, Hussein has made no secret of his consuming desire to become the preeminent power in the Persian Gulf and the sword of the Arabs against the West. And his strategy to achieve those goals was equally clear: military strength and the will to use it. Iraq currently has an extraordinary arsenal bought with their oil revenues. Half of their conventional weapons were bought from the Soviet Union. But Russia was not alone in helping to arm this repressive tyrant. France, China, Egypt, Brazil, and South Africa all sold sophisticated weapons to Iraq, which by the late 1980s had become the biggest arms importer in the world.

In order to develop his arsenal of nonconventional biological weapons, Hussein turned to the West for help. Despite an "official" arms embargo against Iraq during most of the eighties, western companies in West Germany, Great Britain, and the United States sold Hussein the key technology he needed to develop the most dangerous weapons we now face. The bottom line was money. Companies and individuals would do anything asked of them because they were making huge sums of money.

Behind the headlines and the rhetoric, there is a complicated story of miscalculation, deceit, and greed, which leads inevitably to the conclusion that the most dangerous weapons that the western forces face today in the desert are in many ways our own creation. The entire situation is sheer madness.

Kate, this is a story of such complexity that I can't begin to fill in any of the details. I'm no journalist, no expert on anything. I can only leave you with a few general impressions. In reports that I've seen, I learned how Hussein needed very sophisticated machinery, such as computer-controlled lathes developed in England, to make metal parts for his missile weapons. To get them, Iraq set up dummy corporations in England that not only acquired the hardware but also obtained the know-how to produce them at home. This is high-stakes, real-life spy stuff. Most of the world goes about the tedious business of daily life without a clue as to all this dastardly industrial espionage hot on the trail of arms money.

How did this happen? It all can be traced back to the late seventies and the years that Iran held Americans hostage and managed to topple the presidency of Jimmy Carter.

Iraq was not our friend, but it was the enemy of our enemy. For America, the best possible outcome of the long war between Iran and Iraq was a stalemate. In fact, that was Reagan's policy: hope for a stalemate, and never publicly criticize Hussein, not even for his sheltering terrorists, not even for his using missiles against civilian targets in Iran, and not even for his repeated use of poison gas in the war. In 1987, in the name of freedom of navigation, the United States threw the weight of its navy behind Iraq's position in the Gulf. A large American armada protected tanker traffic and crippled the Iranian Navy. The war, which had been going against Iraq, was transformed into a stalemate. We put our interests ahead of our principles when we supported Hussein's fight against Iran. We danced with a dictator. We thought post-war Iraq would pose no threat; in fact, we thought it would provide America with valuable and immense markets for our business communities. Well, in 1988 we got our wish: the long war ended in a stalemate.

And now we've got Hussein, who we suddenly describe as a Hitler—and Iran's supreme religious leader, Ayatollah Ali Khomenei, urging all Muslims to join Hussein in a Holy War against American aggression and greed. Our worst fear could come true: Iran could join forces with Iraq and . . . and who knows?

This is being called the first crisis of the post–Cold War era, an era where the United States and the Soviet Union are friends. It's funny how everyone seems to have forgotten how not too long ago the United States launched an act of armed aggression against Panama and established a puppet regime—sounds a lot like the Kuwaiti invasion. Our actions were resoundly condemned by the United Nations. Still, our invasion was considered benign, and Hussein's invasion is considered nefarious, but at the level of principle and law, there is no difference between the two invasions. Like any other world power, the United States acts not on principle but in its interests. Our guiding principle seems to be the principle of expediency. In the case of our sending troops to Saudi Arabia, our interest happened to be in accord with a valid principle—forcible annexation of a country is unlawful.

(I might as well point out that our military activity in Panama was hardly benign. Shortly after the Panama invasion, the United States claimed that 202 civilians were killed during the assault, which was called "Operation Just Cause." That was a lie, the casualty number that is, and, I guess, the invasion title, too. Recently, at least a half-dozen mass graves dug by the United States after the invasion have been exumed, and it is believed anywhere from 1,000 to 4,000 innocent Panamanian citizens were killed during our efforts to dispose of Manuel Noriega. Fearing international outrage over the high civilian casualties, the United States tried to cover up the actual death toll. Imagine, our government digging mass graves and secretly burying innocent victims of our military aggression.)

It really is hard to see the big picture in this Middle East mess. Yet few are really questioning why so many young men and women are being asked to risk their lives in a desert far from home. I heard a soldier say on the news the other night, "If God calls me home [i.e. heaven] early, that's fine; if He lets me go home to my family, that's fine too." What madness, blood for oil.

Enough.

In a sense, life is all about temptations—temptations resisted, succumbed to, regretted. I've had more than my fair share of each, but the one temptation that has never haunted me is that of politics. Politics rarely excites me to intense emotion or troubled thoughts. I see politics as a human activity with little value in and of itself. I mention this because the Iraq crisis, which is all about politics and oil and not about defending a country that was annexed by force, has managed to occupy a great deal of my thoughts of late. It is very frustrating. I'm getting all worked up over something I really can't do anything about. I'm not about to become some kind of political activist. No. What I'm thinking, dear Kate, is that perhaps this would be a good time to cut down on my daily newspaper reading, and my recently acquired habit of religiously following the network news coverage of this story. Perhaps I'll confine myself to reading just the Sunday edition of the *New York Times* and the rest of the week devote myself exclusively to putting my life back together. I have much to do. I need to find a new direction for my life.

It has been almost a month since my "rebirth." During that time I've done little in the way of creating a new script for the rest of the play that is my life. In reading what I wrote to you back on July 17, I was delighted to read, "Life's value is life and not some questionable afterlife." And my life can't consist of becoming consumed by the desperate condition of world events. That's why I started this morning's entry by saying it would be the last time I wrote about Iraq. I fear getting mired in a downward spiral of "Weltschmerz."

I've got to lighten up. I've got to smell the roses, visit an art museum, get a job. Anything. Anything but read the papers.

Wednesday, September 12—10:45 P.M.

Tried running again this morning. Thought it would help relieve the frustration I felt after writing about that country I said I wouldn't mention again. About a month ago, I announced my plans to resume my long-dormant habit of taking early morning runs. My burst of enthusiasm lasted about ten days. My longest run was eleven minutes and forty-three seconds. Today I barely made it to the five-minute mark before I had to stop for fear I would collapse.

I'm going to tell you a secret: I once entertained a fantasy that I could run in the New York City Marathon. My training didn't get too far beyond buying an official marathon T-shirt. I think a marathon covers twenty-three miles. Maybe twenty-six. Whatever. I doubt I could walk twenty-something miles, let alone run it. It's funny how we manage to deceive ourselves into thinking we can do something beyond our abilities. I am not a runner. Never was, never will be. Yet, I imagine that I could be. No, I imagine that I "am" a runner. Sure, and Elvis is alive and well. Part of this new life I have must include learning to accept and like who I am and stop wasting my time trying to be who and what I am not.

After this morning's letter-writing and running escapes, most of the afternoon lay before me open and empty. Decided to pass the time at the library. It was a pleasant and relaxed time. It felt good to spend a perfectly useless afternoon in a perfectly useless manner. I think we have an unnatural fear of being frivolous. I know I do. It seems I'm always "serious." I wish I could just kick back and watch a perfectly stupid sitcom on TV without feeling that the show is an insult to my intelligence.

While browsing, I came across a stack of books someone had left on a table; they were all by or about Oscar Wilde. Wilde was born in Dublin, Ireland, in 1854. His work was a mixture of humor and pathos, superficiality and depth,

Christian piety and Bohemian decadence. He sounds like somebody with whom I could have been friends. In the spring of 1895, Oscar Wilde was put on trial for the crime of homosexuality. He was convicted and sentenced to two years of hard labor. So much for the good old days.

Kate, here are a few of Wilde's well-chosen words: "The only way to get rid of temptation is to yeild to it." And, "The way of paradoxes is the way of truth." And, "What a man really has, is what is in him. What is outside of him should be a matter of no importance." And, "None of us can stand people who have the same faults as ourselves." And, my favorite, "Truth, in matters of religion, is simply the opinion that has survived."

Oscar Wilde also had something to say about truth, deception, and American politics.

The President of the United States of America, the Honorable George Herbert Walker Bush does not tell the truth. Nor does he lie. This morning in my letter to you, I wrote that Mr. Bush was "into persuasion, not truth." Oscar, ever the insubordinate cad, wanted to correct me on that statement. He said Georgie Bush, like all politicians, practices the art of "misrepresentation."

In his essay, "The Decay of Lying: An Observation," Wilde rejects what passes for lying in mere politicians:

> They never rise beyond the level of misrepresentation, and actually condescend to prove, to discuss, to argue. How different from the temper of the true liar, with his frank, fearless statements, his superb irresponsibility, his healthy, natural disdain for proof of any kind! After all, what is a fine lie? Simply that which is its own evidence. If a man is sufficiently unimaginative to produce evidence in support of a lie, he might just as well speak the truth at once.

What Oscar Wilde is saying is that lying is opposed to misrepresentation, because lying is a mimicry of truth. George Bush has chosen to misrepresent the reality of the situation in the Middle East, which is why he can go from tolerating to hating Saddam Hussein without skipping a beat.

Good night, my sweet.

Saturday, September 15—4:20 P.M.

Dominus vobiscum. That's Latin. It means, "The Lord be with you."

I used to know a lot of Latin. I spoke it almost every day. Not at home, only in God's house. Other Americans may have worshiped God in English, but not us Catholics. We used the language God liked the best—Latin.

I hated Latin. But, seeing as I wanted to be a priest, I had to know it. I remember spending long torturous hours memorizing the responses the altar boy had to give during the Mass. The altar boy actually spoke for the people— in Latin. For example, frequently during the Mass, the priest would turn toward the congregation and loudly say, *Dominus vobiscum*—"The Lord be with you."

The altar boy would respond on behalf of the people, *Et cum spiritu tuo*, which means, "And with thy spirit."

The Mass is like a play, a very long-running play in a foreign language. I had lots of lines to memorize, even if I had forgotten what the words actually meant. The Mass was a very solemn event, the core of our faith. And I couldn't blow my lines. This was high drama and, as I think about it now, real theater. The script was written long ago, the executive producer lived in Rome, the pastor was the director, and the priest, the star performer. As an altar boy, I was an actor, a bit player, in the drama of the Eucharist. I arrived at the church early to put on my costume and set the props. After donning my black cassock, I would switch on the house lights. There was a long series of switches to flip: one for the flood light over the altar, one for the light over the tabernacle, one for each of the small side altars, one for the light over the pulpit, one for the light that illuminated the statue of the Blessed Virgin, and one, the Statue of our patron Saint, Michael the Archangel. Each flip of a switch sent a loud clicking sound reverberating through the silent, cavernous space engulfing the church. I put the key to the tabernacle on the altar, filled the cruets with water and wine, lit the candles. Besides learning about heaven and hell, Adam and Eve, sin and punishment, St. Michael's is where I learned about drama.

The Mass is divided into two separate acts; it had entrances and exits; it had complex staging and elaborate choreography; there were ornate costumes and numerous props; and, there was even a musical score and a full chorus. And, oh, what writing! It was subtle, rich, majestic, poetic, and powerful; it would build, and build, and build until it reached a crescendo: that magical moment when bread and wine were transformed into the body and blood of God. Damn, the Church really knew how to put on a show!

Just like in the theater, there were tryouts and auditions. Aspiring young actors seeking the role of altar boy were given pages of text to study and memorize. Once you proved you could deliver the lines with clarity, they gave you your "blocking"—when and where to move on the stage we called the sanctuary. The numerous steps involved in the complex liturgical dance of the Mass were often harder to learn than the Latin—not to mention easier to forget. I remember one horrifying moment from my days as an altar boy when just such a lapse occurred. I probably should preface the story by saying that the awesomeness of the sanctuary instilled in my young mind a real sense of fear. This was the Holy of Holies. Only the priest and his server—that's me, altar boys "served" Mass—were allowed to walk around the altar area. This was sacred territory, and you really had to watch your step.

Anyway, I was serving Mass early one Sunday morning. It was winter, and still dark by the time I reached the Church. The marble altar steps of St. Michael's on which I knelt were actually cold. Sane people, I thought, were still warmly tucked in bed; I'm kneeling here shivering. The first big "move" the server must execute during the production came after the priest read the epistle. The priest had been standing on the right side of the altar, his back to the congregation. He read aloud, in Latin, one of the New Testament letters, and when he concludes the reading, the server says, *Deo gratias.* "Thanks be to God." The priest then moves to the center of the altar, and standing before the tabernacle he says a prayer asking God to cleanse his heart and lips so that he may worthily proclaim the holy Gospel. While the priest is saying this short prayer, my job was to stand up, move to the center of the altar steps, genuflect, and ascend the stairs on a diagonal path to the far right side of the altar. I then had to lift the large missal from which the priest had just read the epistle, turn and descend the steps with it, pause at the bottom center of the steps, turn, genuflect, and once again ascend the steps, only this time on a diagonal line to the left side of the altar, where I would place the missal. Then the priest, his prayer now concluded, would turn and walk to the missal and read the Gospel.

The altar had an "epistle side" and a "Gospel side," and the moving of the missal from the one side to the other was complicated by the size and weight of the book. The book's dimensions must have been around eighteen inches by twelve inches, and it had to have had at least a thousand pages. Also, the missal rested on a wooden stand that allowed the book to sit open on a forty-five degree angle. The altar boy had to carry the stand and the open book together. It was a heavy sucker, especially for an eight-year-old to carry up and down stairs in a reverent and holy manner.

Well, on that cold winter morning, as Fr. Andrews finished reading the epistle, my mind must have still been tucked in bed. I never said, "Deo gratias." I never saw him move to the center of the altar, never heard him ask God to cleanse his heart and lips. As I knelt in a dreamlike state, Fr. Andrews began coughing louder and louder in order to get my attention. He finally resorted to rather undignified "Psst!" I snapped to attention and immediately panicked because I knew I had lost my place in the ritual. I knew something was wrong, that I was supposed to be doing something—but I didn't have a clue as to what! Fr. Andrews shook his head toward the missal, and suddenly I realized my goof. I got up, genuflected—it must have been a sloppy one—and raced up the steps. I lifted the book, and in my haste as I turned to descend the steps, my shoe caught on the hem of my cassock. I saw eternity before my eyes, I was about to fall straight into hell. Somehow, my guardian angel must have been on alert and he managed to help me regain my balance without falling. I genuflected at the base of the steps, feeling like every eye in the Church, not to mention God's, was on me. I made it to the gospel side without any further incident and placed the book on the altar. As Fr. Andrews, a grumpy man under the best of conditions, turned and walked toward the missal, he shot me a look that almost made me cry. I felt like an idiot, and my heart was pounding in fear. I had been caught napping in the Holy of Holies.

Afterward, when we were safely back in the vestibule, Father Andrews, a spare, tall man with sunken brown eyes under thick, bushy eyebrows, said in his refined voice, with its liturgical modulations, "Perhaps next time young man you can do your sleeping at home." "Yes Father." "Thank you. Have a nice day." "Yes Father." No idle chitchat with Father Andrews. The altar boys dubbed him Father L&M—he smoked L&Ms and he was lean and mean.

Latin. It was once an international language, but it has been steadily losing ground in that quarter during the past two centuries. It has disappeared from most university curricula. In the mid sixties it was dislodged from its last stronghold: the Roman Catholic Mass, which is now said in the vernacular of the people where it is celebrated. The sounds of my past have been hushed by indifference, silenced by neglect, its voice rendered *non compos mentis,* no longer able to care for itself.

I never learned another foreign language beside Latin. I wish I had. (Actually, I did study Spanish for a year, but I never learned how to speak it, with the exception of one short phrase: *No hablo Español.* Which means: I don't speak Spanish.) I didn't plan to tell you about Latin today. But I was browsing in a used bookstore earlier this afternoon, and I came across a book of Latin quotations. On one page, the text was in Latin, and on the facing page, the passage was translated into English. The tattered, old paperback was a bargain at fifty cents.

When I got home, I began reading it. While there was much timeless wisdom from the minds of such well-known men as Cato, Cicero, Horace, Livy, Lucretius, Seneca, Tacitus, Vergil, and Pliny the Elder, there were some observations about life and living written by a few obscure authors that really captured my imagination. I'd like to quote three short observations.

The first comes from the pen of Publius Terentius Afer, known to us moderns as Terence. He was born in 185 B.C. Terence wrote: "When you're late, your wife gets ideas: you've picked up some girl or a girl picked you up, you're drinking and having a good time, and while you're having a good time, she's miserable."

I can hear the comedian Billy Crystal delivering that line in a thick, exaggerated Jewish accent. I can hear my friend Peter saying the same thing to his drinking buddies at some trendy pub in Santa Monica. It just struck me odd, that some guy living in Rome nearly two hundred years before the birth of Christ could say that. I guess my sense of history is so weak and naive that I pictured a guy from that time just sitting around in a toga eating grapes. But they didn't sit around in togas eating grapes all day. They thought. They discovered. They debated. They wrote. They fought. They built. They explored. They created cities and civilizations. We watch television. Yet I found it hard to picture a dude in ancient Rome "picking up" some girl—where did he take her for a drink? Did they have bars back then? Is it just me, or do a lot of people today think of the people who inhabited the planet in ancient times as backward and not nearly as enlightened as we are? I don't think I'm alone in this regard. Sadly, the vast majority of the human race hasn't a clue as to where we have been, and even less as to where we are going.

The next guy from antiquity I want to quote is Quintus Ennius. Ennius was born in 239 B.C. Ennius wrote: "I have always said and will go on saying, there is a race of gods in heaven, but I do not believe that they concern themselves with what the human race is doing: for if they did, good men would fare well, and bad men ill, which is not the case now."

Nor now neither, Ennius. Who today, except televangelists preaching the coming end times, can look around at the world and see any evidence that there is a God who cares about us pissy, little humans? And if there is a God, and he/she doesn't care, which seems very obvious, why should we care about him/her?

The last observation comes from Appius Claudius Caecus. He was born around 355 B.C. He wrote: "Every man is the artisan of his own fortune."

I was nearly the artisan of my own death, now I must become the craftsman of my new life.

Monday, September 17—2:00 P.M.

I'm in shock. My agent called about an hour ago to inform me he had arranged an interview at NBC in New York for this coming Friday morning. I'm being considered for the job of executive producer of the soap opera "Friends and Lovers."

After we hung up, I tried to sift through a mixed bag of emotions. First, I was thrilled at being considered. My ego was jumping up and down with excitement over the possibility of landing such a powerful job. The executive producer of a soap is the top gun on the show. He or she sets the direction and tone of the show, hires the writers and directors, casts the actors, oversees everything from sets to costumes. In short, if I get this job, I will be installed as God in the world of "Friends and Lovers." God is not a bad job.

My spirit responded quite differently from my ego. It slunk into a darkened corner of my being and sat on the verge of tears. My spirit hates soap operas. It knew that if I got the job, it would be dragged every day into a world of excess and sleaze.

The rational side of my mind saw the job possibility as a way for me to reorganize my life. It knew that within a year of working at such a high-paying job—perhaps $10,000 per week—I would completely erase my mountain of debt, and sock away enough money to allow me to pursue the things that really interest me; two years on the job would provide me with a number of "money worry" free years. And the agent was talking about a three-year contract.

The creative side of my mind was ambivalent. Sure there are moments of creative intensity while producing a soap opera. I love helping an actor shape a performance. But, most of the time it is endless hours of administrative drudgery combined with an interminable series of conferences with writers and network executives. A writer of books sits alone with a blank piece of paper, answerable only to himself; producing a television series is a collaborative effort boxed in by time and financial constraints. Writing books allows me complete creative freedom, I write about what I like, in a way I like; producing a soap opera permits little room for fresh creative and artistic expression, because the soaps all follow rigid formulae. I remember encountering tremendous flack on one show I produced by suggesting that a nightmare sequence be shot in black and white; and I ran into even more trouble on another show when I attempted to set an entire episode in one location, using only two actors. These things were just not done, I was told. When asked why, I heard they just weren't. (My rational mind just tapped my creative mind on the shoulder and said, "Freedom schmeedom. Your book writing has earned a big fat zero. Let's talk about putting some bread on the table.")

My heart took an unexpected track. It saw the job interview as an all-expense-paid trip to New York, and a chance to spend a little time with you, Kate. That heart of mine is quite an organ. Let's not worry, it counsels about the pros and cons of the job; after all, you are not the sole candidate for the position, and the interview does not mean the job is in the bag. The only sure thing about all this is a visit with your daughter. For that my heart is very happy.

So, the plan is simple. I will fly to New York on Thursday afternoon, spend the night in a midtown Manhattan hotel, and meet with NBC on Friday morning. NBC booked me on a return flight to L.A. on Friday afternoon. I'll change the return trip to Sunday afternoon. That means we can spend all of Saturday together. I can't wait to call you tonight and tell you this news.

That's all for now my sweet.

Tuesday, September 18—11:30 A.M.

Had a breakfast meeting with my agent in Beverly Hills—that Oz of affluence where you might see a Rolls Royce with a licence plate that reads "2ND CAR." He wanted to give me the inside poop on the show and the people I will be meeting in New York. He wasn't that encouraging, not about my chances at getting the job, but the show's chances of avoiding the cancellation ax. According to him, the show is in the toilet, and the head of programming has her hand on the handle poised to flush. But, then again, agents love sounding like they know key bits of inside information unavailable to the rest of the industry. Of course they are, for the most part, full of shit.

You were very excited last night when I told you the news of my visit. You wanted to go to a mall, a movie, and bowling.

I'm very excited too. A little over a month ago, I was planning to end my life. Today, I'm planning to spend a day with you in Montclair, New Jersey.

I'm still very confused about life, but there is no confusion about my love for you. Our separation still hurts. I'm still uneasy about being "dad" in person. I'm never sure what to say to you. The problem I always have when I see you is leaving you. The happiness I experience when I'm with you is always diminished by the sadness I feel when we part.

Wednesday, September 19—4:00 P.M.

A couple of days after I chucked my plan to do away with myself, I bought a lined composition notebook. I thought that during this time of transition from doing myself in to figuring out what I was going to do, it would be useful to jot down things I was thinking about. I wasn't interested in keeping a diary or a journal of my activities and feelings. I thought of it as a storehouse for my ideas and insights. My hope was to integrate some of my musings into things that I write.

This afternoon I read through my month-long compilation for the first time. There was a lot of twaddle . . . or better put: I did scribble a considerable amount of drivel! Still, my sweet Kate, there was also some good stuff, which I thought I would share with you—unedited and without commentary.

So, without further ado, some odds and ends from the cuckoo's nest of my mind:

Life is full of delicate shadings, of contrasts, of sunlight and shadow; it is a constant play of opposites.

*

It is necessary for one experience to die, so that another experience can be born. Life is a series of deaths, the disappearance of values that no longer serve.

*

The mind needs no training in how to destroy through willful memory loss whatever in its past doesn't support its present point of view.

*

Religion is little more than a series of ineffective techniques designed to allay anxiety.

*

Religion explains the unexplainable.

*

Blasphemy is the tool totalitarian religions use to stop new ideas.

*

The only sin is to be unkind.

*

The most sure-footed way to discovering truth is to follow the path of science, logic, and common sense. Of course, for the Church, for whom truth is derived from revelation and not from observation, this is a path they ignore.

*

Do the lovers of religion seek truth or certainty? I'm certain truth is not on their mind.

*

What we believe to be true today, we should be ready to accept as false tomorrow.

*

I'm concerned with what I can see, the visible world around me. I'm interested in the here and now, and not in a testing ground for eternity. I want to know humanity, not divinity. Both malevolence and benevolence originate in the mind of mankind; good and evil are not mysterious forces outside of ourselves. The religion of the future must become a religion not of God, but of man, a religion of humanity.

*

The artist's job is to deal with the true and human world he or she knows.

*

The good of humanity on earth, not in some projected heavenly afterlife, should be the principle concern of humanity and ethics.

*

In a rational world we wouldn't park in a driveway and drive on a parkway.

*

I suspect others share the sensation I have of not belonging to a world that bombards me with such a bewildering assortment of philosophies, theories, and strategies for living; I suspect I'm not alone in feeling that all these views and ways have created a world that each day resembles more closely a Sisyphean mass of mumbo jumbo tumbling down a slippery slope from the hilltop of their lofty ideals; I suspect others are refusing to seek refuge in the supernatural and instead chose to gallantly stand before the horrors of life. But where the hell are they?

*

The longer you live, the more often you die. Yet at the end, no one is ever ready.

*

An uncertain certitude hangs over everything: the hour of death for every organism and every civilization.

*

Some people worship the mind, some the body, and some the soul. Wholeness and humanity are ignored. Some people seek fame, some fortune, and some power. Gentleness and service are orphans.

*

Power and fame are preferred above simplicity and purity. We strive to be more productive, more comfortable, more content; we ignore how to become more sensitive, more proportionate, more alive.

*

For most of my life I bowed before what I did not understand—I think most people do.

*

Life is wonderful and horrifying—and new each day.

*

Life is filled with ambiguity, failure, and false starts . . . and that's OK.

*   *   *

Well, kiddo, there you have it. Keep what you like, dump what you don't. Anyway, I'm going to keep scribbling down my thoughts in the notebook.

Tomorrow is the big day. I'll be landing at JFK Airport at 8:15 P.M. I'll go directly to the hotel, check in, relax, and hit the sack early, so that I am wide-eyed and bushy-tailed for my 10:00 A.M. meeting at NBC.

Well, I'd better start packing.

Thursday, September 20—10:45 P.M.

Greetings from the Big Apple. Flight was smooth and problem free. In fact, it landed five minutes early, but thanks to ground traffic it arrived at the gate twelve minutes late.

The taxi ride from the airport to the hotel was more frightening than any plane ride. I must have told the driver at least a half-dozen times, "Hey, I'm in no hurry." He didn't speak English. But it didn't matter; the fact was, he was in a hurry, a helluva hurry. It took the plane longer to taxi to the gate after landing, than it did for the taxi to get from the airport to Manhattan.

There was a message waiting for me at the hotel: the meeting at NBC has been postponed until 3:30 in the afternoon. Great. Everybody will be looking at their watches looking to get an early jump on the weekend. What me worry?

Suddenly, I have the morning free. I think I will spend it at the Metropolitan Museum of Art. Years ago, when I lived on the upper, west side of Manhattan, I frequently took a walk across Central Park in order to spend some quiet, reflective time in the presence of the great French Impressionist artists whose works adorn the walls of that prestigious museum. I can use a quick fix of inspiration.

Well, kiddo, this tired old body of mine doesn't care that I have picked up three hours crossing time zones coming east, and is telling me it's tired and it wants some sleep. It doesn't want to hear that it isn't even eight o'clock in California, so I guess I better just say good night, my love. See you in thirty-six hours. When did you start bowling?

Friday, September 21—9:40 P.M.

I was up and at 'em pretty early this morning. I took a walk to a Jewish delicatessen located on West 57th Street. There's nothing like good ol' New York City bagels for breakfast. It was a brisk, fall morning. Manhattan wakes up a lot earlier than Hollywood. This is a city of constant motion.

After breakfast, I headed for the Metropolitan Museum of Art, but instead of finding inspiration, I left with a feeling of outrage.

The museum had on display a special exhibition titled, "Mexico: The Splendors of Thirty Centuries." It was a comprehensive and extraordinary exhibition that brilliantly traced the complex history and diversity of Mexican art from the earliest times through the twentieth century. The exhibition was laid out in such a way that you could only walk in one direction, starting with pre-Columbian sculptures and pottery and working your way past thirty centuries of art that ended with the paintings of such modern Mexican artists as Diego Rivera and Frida Kahlo, the famous husband and wife whose paintings and murals reflected their Communist point of view.

So why the outrage? To begin with, it was very unexpected. I was enjoying the arts of ancient Mexico, marveling at the mosaic of styles represented in the beautiful work and carvings of such culturally rich native Indian civilizations as the Olmecs, the Aztecs, the Mayas, the Toltecs, and the Zapotecs; there were even meticulously detailed models of the ancient cities of Izapa, Teotihuacan, Palenque, Tenochtitlan, Monte Alban, and La Venta to go along with the diverse collection of decorative ceramic urns, alabaster and jade pendants, gold facial ornaments, elegantly carved wooden drums and stone altars, painted murals, and mythological masks and figures. I found this part of the exhibition to be not only vastly informative but highly inspirational as well.

Then suddenly, I turned a corner and entered the Viceregal Age, which began in the sixteenth century with the Spanish conquest of Mexico, and almost instantly I became outraged at the destruction of the native civilizations, which were crushed in order to make room for Spanish Catholicism. The Spanish Crown had no concern for the cultural heritage and artistic patrimony of the people already living on the land they coveted, they were simply heathens in need of salvation, as well as slaves who could perform manual labor. Bernal Diaz del Costillo, one of the original conquistadors, explained that the Spanish came "to serve God and His Majesty, to give light to those living in darkness, and also to gain riches." Evangelization was the theological justification for the Spanish presence in Mexico and for the subjugation of its people, and so converting the natives to Christianity became an essential aspect of the Conquest and subsequent colonization. Converting the Indians was a brutal and bloody enterprise.

The people who populated Mexico before the arrival of the Spanish were treated as less than human; in fact, it wasn't until 1537 that Pope Paul III officially decreed that they were humans, whose rights must be respected and who were capable of understanding the tenets of Christianity. The Indians had to endure not only a drastic change of religion, but also a profound transformation of social structures and behavior. Because the art, architecture, and objects of worship used by the Indian cultures could be utilized in the practice of Christianity, they had to be eradicated. The Indians had to make a transition to art forms that the Catholic world required: churches and images. The emerging new art form fused European sensitivities with the tastes of the local society.

While the exhibition focused on the art of New Spain, showing that it was not a second-rate derivative of that of the European capitals but as one with its own values and development, which had enormous creative and inventive power, I saw only the destruction of a vibrant culture. The sight of so many crosses, so many paintings of saints, martyrs, and the Virgin Mary, so many Bishop's miters and crosiers, and so many chalices, reliquaries, monstrances, candlesticks, altars, and priestly vestments made me sick, though each item was elegant in its own right. A cornstalk-paste sculpture of an oversized Christ, was excessively cruel and gory. No one seemed to share my outrage, and many people displayed a sense of reverence at the religious artifacts.

As I made my way downtown, my mind seemed fixated with the way Christianity ruptured the social and artistic life of the Indians in Mexico. It was difficult for me to shift my thoughts into a soap opera gear. As I was walking, I passed a newsstand and bought a copy of a soap opera fan magazine. I sat in a restaurant, ate a light lunch and read the magazine. Gradually, I made the transition from tirade to triviality. By the time I got to the interview, I was calm and ready to pour on some phoney charm.

The interview went well—at least I thought it did. I think I impressed them even though I did have one moment of sheer panic. The VP asked me, "Chris, tell me what your philosophy of soap opera is?"

"Philosophy of soap operas! Is this jerk kidding," was my initial, unspoken reaction to his question. I paused, as if formulating the correct words to articulate my philosophy of soap operas, but before I could even open my mouth, the VP began to tell me *his* philosophy of soap operas. He rambled on for about ten minutes. I kept smiling and nodding my head in affirmative agreement to his stream of bullshit. When he finished, I then told him my philosophy of soap opera, which amounted to nothing but a rephrasing of his philosophy. He then said, "I'm glad we think along the same lines."

And this idiot is deciding what America gets to watch on daytime television! I told him a few war stories from shows I had produced—insider stuff, mostly gossip about actors—and he seemed to thoroughly enjoy them. After the interview, I walked around midtown for an hour or so and came back to the hotel room. Now, all that's on my mind is seeing you tomorrow.

I can't wait to see you. When I spoke to you a little while ago, I could hear the excitement in your voice. It made me happy. I'll be catching a 9:00 A.M. bus. It should roll into Montclair about 9:35 A.M. You and your mom will meet me at the bus stop. We'll drive her back to the house, and you and I will hit the road for a day of fun and adventure. Tomorrow night, you and your mom will drive me to a hotel near Newark Airport, because my flight back to L.A. leaves at 8:00 A.M. Sunday morning.

Saturday, September 22—10:45 P.M.

How ironic that such a perfectly delightful day should draw to a close in the barren sterility of a second-class hotel room.

God, I feel so very alone. Just a short while ago, I was basking in the warmth of your smile. I was a dad. Now, I am just the faceless occupant of room 427. The room has all the warmth of a winter's day in Siberia. I've gone back into exile.

Seventy-two days ago, when I sat down to write a farewell letter to you, I was in a grip of depression that was darker than the darkest darkness. I think that I am a writer, yet when it comes to putting into words the desolation and despair that was within me, I am confronted with my true lack of ability. Words are not capable of conveying that kind of blackness. I cannot elucidate the darkness that engulfed me. I cannot describe what almost killed me. The poet Dante managed to compose a few lines that come close to capturing the essence of this darkness:

> In the middle of the journey of our life
> I found myself in a dark wood,
> For I had lost the right path.

Novelist William Styron describes his devastating decent into depression in his book, *Darkness Visible,* which concludes with this paragraph, which is then followed by a single line of hope from Dante's poem:

> For those who have dwelt in depression's dark wood, and known its inexplicable agony, their return from the abyss is not unlike the ascent of the poet, trudging upward and upward out of hell's black depths and at last emerging into what he saw as "the shining world." There, whoever has been restored to health has almost always been restored to the capacity for serenity and joy, and this may be indemnity enough for having endured the despair beyond despair.

> "And so we came forth, and once again beheld the stars."

Today Kate, when I saw you, I too "once again beheld the stars." Writing to you somehow managed to help me lift myself out of the black depths of despair. But I am not yet free.

There is still sadness, but there is also hope. Now that I am out in "the shining world," I need to find a direction; I need to get on the right path. The right path for me, not somebody else's right path. The struggle is far from over; in fact, I doubt the struggle ever ends. Life is a battleground that constantly provides us with excellent training in resistence to misery and pain. For so long, I thought the confusion that surrounded me would eventually fade away. Perhaps the truth is that confusion never goes away and that each day only presents us with a fresh confusion. Every time I think I spot the truth, the truth moves, leaving in its wake a new confusion.

I hate this room, but I'm glad I'm here. I'm thrilled to have had the chance to spend the day with you. Perhaps some day when you are much older and I give you this letter, you may very well read this section and not remember this Saturday in Monclair, this day you helped your father see the stars.

We did have fun. I really enjoyed watching you pick out clothes in that little boutique in the mall. You were so concerned with matching colors and patterns. I was surprised by your taste in clothes. They seemed rather preppy.

We really did cram a lot of fun activities into one day: bowling, a movie, miniature golf, eating out, and shopping. It was a very special day, and you are a very special little girl. We shared a lot of laughs and giggles; you seemed to enjoy even the worst of my puns, and there were a few really bad ones.

The day's only bad moment for me—and I could see in your eyes for you also—was saying goodbye. Oddly enough, despite the overall happy tone of our time together, for me, the day only intensified the pain of our separation.

I really do hope I get this job, simply because it is in New York City and would enable me to spend many more happy days like today with you.

Sunday, September 23—7:30 P.M.

I'm back in Hollywood, sitting alone in my study. All I can say is: I miss you very much.

I wish I were a sunflower, perhaps like one of those magnificent, giant yellow ones from the South of France made famous by van Gogh. Unlike man, sunflowers are not unhappy, are not burdened with mankind's tragic character and limitless longings for inaccessible things.

Sunflowers are fully unconscious.

Sunflowers know nothing of themselves and the world. Sunflowers do not know despair nor do they have the urge for self-realization. Because van Gogh had confronted despair, he was able to delight in the nature of the sunflower because a sunflower does not have to be anything else but a sunflower. Man wants to be more than a man. Man wants more from life than life. Man wants to live forever, to deny the natural cycle of birth, growth, decline, and death, to pretend that death is not a period at the end of the sentence we call life, but merely a comma. Man has ideas, aspirations, and dreams, and so we are not as free and natural as a sunflower that is happy just to be a sunflower.

Having seen the horror of life, Vincent was able to see the beauty of life. I'm still overwhelmed by the horror of life, by the madness and violence of the world around me; yet I am beginning to see the flowers and the birds and the beauty.

I came so very, very close to not seeing anything. Once in a while, I think about that moment when I pressed the barrel of the gun to my head. My torment desperately wanted me to pull the trigger. My fear fervently wanted me to put the gun down. Fear and torment became like two different people, the one trying not so much to convince but to motivate the other into action. Fear did not win a clear-cut victory; it merely wore down torment. Torment became emotionally exhausted and gave up.

And so the inner drama ended and I was still alive.

I was pushed to the edge of life by an intensity to understand life that was so great that I lost all sense of equilibrium and stumbled into an abysmal maelstrom of doubt and chaos. Two months ago, I felt I could not survive the whirlwinds of my thoughts. My life was a sorrowful procession of loneliness and despair. Everything became an occasion for death. I was a prisoner of my own madness and the world offered no relief, no escape from the consuming flames of hopelessness that scorched my every thought. At the edge of life, all moral, esthetic, social, and religious arguments for living and not succumbing to the nothingness of death were absurd. I became obsessed with dying. My salvation lay hidden in my confession to you. This letter transformed the torment and tears of my life into thoughts which helped me choose life.

Thanks for helping me see the beauty of a sunflower while still realizing that death is an immanent part of life and that everything is ultimately nothing.

Tuesday, September 25—11:00 A.M.

There's a lot stuff in the news these days about the sorry state of the education system in this country. Kids aren't motivated, can't read; teachers can't live on their paltry salaries. Blame for the situation can be spread wide and far. Solutions are few and far between. Part of the blame and some of the solution sits in every living room across the country: the television.

This season there are five new sitcoms that are either set in high schools or feature high-school teachers. In the hands of a Hollywood script writer searching for an easy joke, the principals are portrayed as grumbling misfits, the teachers as blithering incompetents. Students who show the slightest interest in their studies are depicted as wimps, while the students who relish the idea of frazzling the nerves of teachers and who enjoy the idea of fouling up the system are portrayed as super-cool, and for their silly schemes they are awarded the prize of the best-looking girl in the school. One insipid sitcom features a gorgeous young female teacher who comes to class in sexy, body-hugging dresses and then wonders why the students aren't learning their lessons—isn't that an innovative gimmick!

Television has the power to create healthy role models and suggest solid values. A few years ago I was at a birthday party for a well-known television director. During a conversation with a producer I met at the party, I mentioned TV's power to create positive role models. I made the mistake of thinking that I might have an intelligent chat with this guy, he seemed sharp and on the ball. But he cut the talk short when he said, "Hey, I'm out to make money. So I don't have the slightest interest in creating role models. That shit don't sell. The people want sizzle, and if you don't give it to 'em, you'll fizzle in this town." In Hollywood, using sizzle and fizzle in the same sentence is a sign of creativity, and the producer's Beverly Hills home and Maserati lets everybody know that he is very creative.

Jokes more often than not mask truth. Here's an old Hollywood joke in the form of a letter written to a newspaper advice columnist:

Dear Ann:

I have a problem. I have two brothers. One brother is in television, the other was put to death in the electric chair for murdering his wife. My mother was put in an insane asylum when I was only three years old; she died there six months later. My sister is a prostitute. My father sells drugs to high school students. Recently, I met a woman who was just released from prison where she served time for smothering her illegitimate child to death. I want to marry her. My problem is—if I marry this lady, should I tell her about my brother who is in television?

Television offers a mental junk-food diet of cheap sensations and disposable ideas. The truth, dear Kate, is that in Hollywood, money is God and beauty, the Goddess.

My money is running low. I've got to get a job. Television is all I really know. But I don't know if I can still work in television.

Wednesday, September 26—11:10 P.M.

If I was given ten minutes on prime-time network television to say whatever I wanted to the youth of America, I would tell them to turn off their televisions. What would I really tell them?

A tough question. I think I would say that the code of my youth claimed that I was a sinner, and that turned out to be nothing but a formula for failure. If I could give you—youth of America—a code to live by, it would be this:

- Practice prudence; trust your common sense.

- Study all of humanity; know yourself and others.

- Be leery of ambition; avoid selfishness.

- Do not engage in envy; avoid avarice.

- Nurture friendships; be charitable.

- Create peace in and around yourself; laugh often.

- Enjoy the joys of life while you can.

- Live each day to the fullest; be kind.

- Do not fear hell, nor hope for heaven.

- Accept death as the inevitable conclusion of life.

Well, Kate, no one is going to give me ten minutes on television, so my code is just for you.

Friday, September 28—6:40 P.M.

Kate, my sweet, my pledge not to mention the Middle East has been honored for more than two weeks now. But I gotta tell you something—it's nothing crazy or anything, just a healthy dose of irony.

I just happened to turn on the news and there standing next to President Bush on the front lawn of the White House was the Emir of Kuwait. Through a translator, he said something along the lines of looking forward to greeting President Bush in free and independent Kuwait in the near future. The Emir was clad in the traditional Arab garb including the long, flowing headdress. Back on August 2, when Saddam Hussein's troops marched into Kuwait, the Emir was forced to flee his palace, barely escaping the Iraqi invaders whose primary objective was to kill the Kuwaiti leader. He has been living in exile ever since the invasion.

So what do we know about this guy? Not much. The Emir's name is Sheik Jaber al-Ahmad al-Jaber al-Sabah—but you can call him Al. He is sixty-four years old and has little formal education. At regular intervals, sometimes weekly, Jaber marries a young virgin on Thursday night, the eve of the Islamic sabbath, only to divorce her on Friday. Sounds good, if you can afford the alimony, which Jaber can.

Kate, here's what I find ironic—and puzzling: That this mysterious, Muslim, billionaire oil baron, who has had as many as forty wives (but never more than four at one time), and who has fathered well over seventy children, is standing on the White House lawn next to the President of the United States, Mr. George Bush (aka Mr. Family Man, Mr. Straight-Arrow Republican, Mr. Christian), who is vowing to return this head of a powerful clan (which controls all aspects of the Kuwaiti government and recently has refused to allow a free, democratic parliament to be elected or to lift press censorship), and nobody is saying "Hey, what's wrong with this picture?"

Also, nobody mentions that Kuwait has voted against the United States in the United Nations more often than Russia. There is something going on here that we are not being told.

I fear Sheik and Bush will lead to shake-and-bake for our troops in the desert. I hope I'm wrong.

OK, that's it. I won't talk about this subject again.

Friday, October 5—8:22 A.M.

Back on July 16, following that radiant epiphanic moment when I instantly understood that suicide was an inappropriate response to my problems, I said I would, as part of my fresh start, throw out all my philosophy books.

I didn't.

I couldn't. I'm addicted to philosophy books.

I guess I still think I'll find something in them that will help me understand the human condition.

I never do. Probably never will.

Yet I read on, ever hopeful I will discover some hidden secret, some obscure formula that will solve the mysteries of life.

The odd thing about my preoccupation with philosophy is that most of the stuff is unreadable and difficult to comprehend. Some of it is pretentious nonsense. My attraction is not so much to the philosophical musings of the philosophers, but to the philosophers themselves. These deep thinkers from the past were the best and the brightest of human beings, or so we are led to believe. Living philosophers tend to act as if their specialty is one that is beyond the grasp of the average Joe Schmo, who needs help in deciphering the complex thoughts of the great philosophers. The message professional philosophers send out is clear: philosophy is for experts, and you poor slobs, who busy yourself with the daily grind of life, need us to help explain life to you. In the process of helping us understand the great thoughts of mankind, professional philosophy peddlers make us feel stupid and inferior.

I tried to read what the great philosophers wrote. I was afraid to admit that I didn't really get what they were talking about. The fault, I thought, was mine: my intellect wasn't up to the task. I struggled with the concepts of determinism, dualism, empiricism, epistemology, existentialism, idealism, inference, naturalism, nihilism, ontology, pragmatism, rationalism, relativism, semiology, skepticism, solipsism, structuralism, and subjectivism. I could define all these things, and even understand the meaning. But so what? I'm still left with an empty feeling.

After feasting on philosophy, I'm left unnourished.

Why?

Is my too brain inadequate to digest philosophy's food?

I hope not.

Then what is the problem?

Philosophers have a penchant for camouflaging their metaphysical speculations in quasi-scientific jargon. Philosophers use a lot of big, vague words to explain a few, small ideas. New and clear ideas do not need to be dressed up and made to look enticing; muddled ideas, on the other hand, require some make-up to cover-up the imperfections. It is amazing what a little rouge and eye-liner can do for a "plain Jane" idea. There's a lot of "Max Factor" philososphy out there. Additionally, it is reasonable to suggest that a faulty psychological outlook could produce bad philosophy.

As writers, most philosophers are showoffs, trying to impress their readers with their range and depth of knowledge. More than being understood, they want to be seen as authoritative. Simplicity, clarity, and euphony are avoided at all cost. More than being understood, they want to be seen as an authority in the realm of knowledge. It is important to them that they are perceived as experts, because experts get published and their opinions are sought. So they dazzle us with their mental gymnastics. Most of what I have read has obscured not clarified.

Kate, some time ago, I realized that in the past I had been guilty of muddled and incoherent thinking. I knew I lacked logic. I thought reading philosophy would help me cultivate a more rational way of looking at life. Oh, for sure, I think my philosophy studies assisted me in thinking a bit more logically, but this morning I was lamenting that those studies had not been more helpful. I wondered why—I mean I really applied myself to the task of studying philosopy. Then it hit me—why was it a task? I mean I liked reading about ideas, I wanted to study philosophy; yet, it was a drag.

Why?

The answer may be very simple: the writing.

Let me give you an example. One of the outstanding philosophers of this century, John Dewey, in his book *Logic* presents the very "plain Jane" idea that if a person gives some thought to an action he or she is about to take, they may avoid the consequences of a hasty act. Dewey got out his "Max Factor" make-up kit and applied it to that rather familiar idea, which he then presented thusly: "Organic biological activities end in overt actions, whose consequences are irretrievable. When an activity and its consequences can be rehearsed by representation in symbolic terms, there is no such final commitment. If representation of the final consequences is of an unwelcome quality, overt activity may be foregone, or the way of acting be replanned in such a way as to avoid the undesired outcome."

Jesus, talk about mental gymnastics. What Dewey was saying is that if an idea pops into your head and you jump on it, you can't escape the end result of your actions. But, if you think through the idea and visualize what is going to happen if you do act out the idea, you can either avoid taking any action on your idea or take a different action if the consequences of the idea appear not to be in your best interest. Hey, this Dewey dude could have said, "Look before you leap." But that would have sounded trite, and philosophers must sound authoritative.

One more short example, again from John Dewey, this time from a book on psychology. He writes, "The significant condition for play seems to be a metabolic state which is conducive to a high level of activity when there are no stimuli with which to contend leading to the serious business of living."

Say what? What Dewey said was people tend to play when they feel lively and have nothing better to do. Oh, yeah, that's right.

The German philosopher Arthur Schopenhauer (1788–1860) saw this problem in philosophical writing. He wrote, "German authors would, all of them, profit from realizing that, although one should, wherever possible, think like a great mind, one should on the other hand speak the same language as everyone else.

What is needed are ordinary words to say unusual things. But in fact authors do the opposite. We find them concerned to conceal trivial ideas with elegant words and to deck their very ordinary thoughts in the most unusual expressions."

They still do, Art.

Schopenhauer thought most philosophers were "windbags." But, in truth, Arthur Schopenhauer didn't like people in general. As a philosopher, Schopenhauer was the prince of pessimism. He thought the world and all of life had no value whatsoever, and the world was the worst of all possible worlds. This is the exact opposite of our friend Gottfried Leibniz's view that this was the best of all possible worlds. (The word *pessimism*, by the way, comes from the Latin word *pessimus*, which means worst.) Oddly enough, Schopenhauer strongly condemned suicide. He thought people who kill themselves are only serving their own interests, that they desire something better. In my case, I thought escape was better than continual struggle. Schopenhauer thought nothing existed except our blind will to live. For Arthur Schopenhauer, there was no happiness, no God, and the only salvation for humanity comes from compassion for each other and individual will. Schopenhauer looked long and hard at the world in which we live. This did not cause him to despair; it just made him very angry.

Me—I go straight to despair. Or used to.

Old Schopenhauer once said that if you can read Hegel without feeling that you are in the madhouse, then you ought to be in the madhouse. Amen. I wish I read that comment before I read Hegel.

This excessive verbiage problem that exists in philosophy applies also to theology—only magnified tenfold.

In his huge and cuckoo book *Summa Theologica*, St. Thomas Aquinas claims that man is predestined. He writes, "It is fitting that God should predestine men. For all things are subject to His Providence. . . . As men are ordained to eternal life through the Providence of God, it likewise is part of that Providence to permit probation. . . . As predestination includes the will to confer grace and glory, so also reprobation includes the will to permit a person to fall into sin, and so impose the punishment of damnation on account of that sin."

In the same book the sainted theologian claims man is free. He writes, "Man has free choice, or otherwise counsels, exhortations, commands, prohibitions, rewards and punishments would be in vain. If the will were deprived of freedom . . . no praise would be given to human virtue; since virtue would be of no account if man acted not freely; there would be no justice in rewarding or punishing, if man were not free in acting well or ill; and there would be no prudence in taking advice, which would be of no use if things occurred of necessity."

Gee . . . can we be both predestined and free? Aquinas handles that paradox this way: "The predestined must necessarily be saved, yet by a conditional necessity, which does not do away with the liberty of choice. . . . Man's turning to God is by free choice; and thus man is bidden to turn himself to God. But free choice can be turned to God only when God turns it. . . . It is the part of man to prepare his soul, since he does this by his free choice. And yet he does not do this without the help of God moving him. . . . And thus even the good movement of free choice, whereby anyone is prepared for receiving the gift of grace, is an act of free choice moved by God. . . . Man's preparation for grace is from God, as mover, and from free choice, as moved."

And I thought I had problems with logic! None of that makes any sense, but he certainly sounds like he knows what the hell he is taking about, which is the name of the game.

The American playwright Tennessee Williams, in his play *Suddenly Last Summer,* put all this theological bullshit into perspective when he wrote, "We are all children in a vast kindergarten trying to spell God's name with the wrong alphabet blocks."

As the philosopher Alain wrote, "All proofs are for me clearly discredited." Actually one can prove everything if the words one employs are not clear and precise. The history of philosophical doctrine shows that, in the course of the centuries, men and women have been able to prove almost everything. They have proven the truth of contradictory philosophies and their falsities.

Even the same "facts" can be twisted to serve different purposes.

Medieval Christians were convinced that the Jews were causing the plague and somehow mysteriously making the Christians sick. This conviction, which was not grounded in any factual evidence that the Jews were responsible for the plague, stemmed from a belief that "punishments from God" frequently in the form of pestilences and natural disasters, and this belief made it easy for them to gather "evidence" to "prove" their supposition. The Christians noticed that the Jews seemed immune from the peril of the plague and jumped to the irrational conclusion that because the Jews were not dying in numbers proportionate to the rest of the population that they must therefore have had something to do with causing the plague. However, the real reason Jews were spared is because the Jewish dietary and sanitary laws insured that the Jewish sections of the cities were kept free of garbage, thus free of rats, thus free of pests that live on rats and cause the plague by passing the viruses from rats to people. This explanation was ignored in favor of the faulty concept ("Jews cause plague"), which was readily demonstrated by the "facts."

You see, Kate, the same "fact" can be seen as evidence for many different things. Things that we consider to be "facts" today, may in the future be considered fallacious, just as in the past it was an accepted "fact" that the earth was the center of the universe.

Up until about two hundred years ago, insanity was believed to be caused by demonic possession. The insane were savagely beaten in accordance with the further belief that any pain suffered by the insane was also felt by the devils, and so the best way to cure insanity is to make the patient suffer so much that the devils would be unable to endure the pain and would decide to flee the patient's body.

Pious people objected to the use of anesthetics when they were discovered on the grounds that they considered them an effort to evade the will of God. When it was argued that God put Adam into a deep sleep prior to extracting his rib, the religious responded by acknowledging that anesthetics were acceptable for men only, and women must suffer because of the curse of Eve.

Bertrand Russell, an English philosopher who adopted the intellectual position of rational skepticism and who believed all religions were both untrue and harmful, in his 1943 essay, "An Outline of Intellectual Rubbish," wrote, "The superstitions about Friday and thirteen were once believed by those reputed wise; now such men regard them as harmless follies. But probably 2,000 years hence many beliefs of the wise of our day will have come to seem equally foolish. Man is a credulous animal, and must believe something; in the absence of good grounds for belief, he will be satisfied with bad ones."

Kate, my sweet, I'm surrounded by people telling me one thing, other people telling me other things, and they're calling each other liars. When I listen, all I really hear is a lot of noise. We are constantly being buffeted by slogan-mongers. People are always trying to get us to believe their way, trying to get us to support them. Everybody is in competition for your mind. And it is sad that philosophy doesn't really help us learn how to separate the truth from the falsehoods, and that so many of us wind up distrusting everybody. That sucks. It still upsets me to realize that I was so easily manipulated by the people who knew the right games.

I'm sure I'll keep reading philosophy, but in moderation. And if what I read makes no sense, I won't throw stones at my own mind.

Tuesday, October 9—4:40 P.M.

Everyone loves to talk—unless the subject is the meaning of life. That topic draws yawns or silence. People are never at a loss for words when it comes to sports, business, movies, the weather, the opposite sex, cars, clothes, diets, politics, family, music, pets, money, neighbors, and work. Bring up the meaning of life and suddenly most people become mute.

All the people that I would like to sit down and talk about the meaning of life with are dead. Almost all. Among the living, there is Bill Moyers, Woody Allen, Steve Allen, and Andy Rooney. The list of the dead that I would like to engage in a one-on-one conversation, perhaps while sipping coffee and smoking cigarettes at some little cafe, is a long one. There is: Andre Gidé, Oscar Wilde, Thomas Hardy, Robinson Jeffers, Henry David Thoreau, John Stuart Mill, Jean-Paul Sartre, Wolfgang Amadeus Mozart, Sidney Hook, Mahatma Gandhi, Bertrand Russell, Robert Ingersoll, Franz Kafka, Albert Einstein, Andre Maurois, Marcel Proust, Norman Cousins, Nikos Katzantzakis, Eric Hoffer, Albert Camus, and Kahlil Gibran.

Jesus, imagine having all those guys over for dinner! Wait a second, there are no women on that list—living or dead. No, I'm not gay. In fact, I much prefer the company of women to men. Men are animals. Come on Chris, there must be some women with whom you would like to talk about the meaning of life. Let's see . . . women, women . . . OK, let's start with living women. Good. There is . . . um . . . Diane Sawyer. Jesus, this is harder than it ought to be. OK, let's skip to dead women. Fine. Um . . . let's see . . . there is . . . Margaret

Mead . . . George Sand. Um. . . . Damn, this is crazy. Why can't I think of some women to talk to about life? I mean women probably know more about life than men. BINGO. Maybe that is our problem—men have been in charge for far too long. They have suppressed women. We—men that is—have really screwed things up. Maybe it is time women ran the world. As long as it is not England's man-in-a-dress, Maggie Thatcher.

Wednesday, October 24—11:00 A.M.

It's been a couple of weeks since I've written. I haven't been up to anything special. I'm just anxiously awaiting word from NBC about the soap job. I thought I'd hear something by now. The agent says, "No news is good news." Agents are clever. NBC has a few weeks before the current Executive Producer is set to retire, so I guess there is no real pressure to name a replacement yet. I just hope "no news" isn't "bad news."

I recently read that a Saudi official claimed that the Kuwaitis' woes were certainly "God's will," and a divine judgment on their excessive way of living. "Allah teaches that those who forget God too much will suffer this," the official said. I guess, my sweet, the trick is to learn to forget God just a little.

The simple truth is that the Saudis envy the Kuwaitis' wealth and view them as arrogant and undeservedly rich, simply because they happen to live atop an abundant oil reserve. Saudi Arabia is also rich, but Saudis make a great show of strict religious observation and a very conservative Muslim approach to alcohol, sex, and ostentatious displays of wealth. The Kuwaitis' plight helps the Saudis justify beliefs they really don't believe.

God, religion is stupid!

But the Saudis aren't unique. Don't we all pretend to believe what we say we believe? We are all cheats, taking from the world and from ourselves only what serves our ends and re-enforces our own prejudices. It is easy to see why the Saudis want to believe the Kuwaitis' suffering is God's will.

Sunday, October 28—8:40 A.M.

Good morning, daughter. Today being Sunday, I thought I'd give you a quick Catechism lesson. The lesson will demonstrate religious logic.

Ready?

Question: Why can there be only one true religion?

Answer (from my *Baltimore Catechism*): "There can be only one true religion, because a thing cannot be false and true at the same time, and, therefore, all religions that contradict the teaching of the true Church must teach falsehoods. If all religions in which men seek to serve God are equally good and true, why did Christ disturb the Jewish religion and the Apostles condemn heretics?"

Maybe they were wrong.

Thank you for your attention, Catechism class is now dismissed. Have a nice Sunday.

Thursday, November 1—7:40 P.M.

I survived Halloween. No ghosts or evil spirits got me. As usual, hoards of kids dressed up as mice, pirates, witches, cowboys, ballerinas, bums, and bandits scoured the neighborhoods in search of sweet-tasting treats. As usual, a few found deadly tricks in their bags, such as candy and apples laced with small pieces of glass. It's just another day I don't understand.

As with many modern-day secular celebrations, Halloween has its origins in the religiosity of antiquity. Today is All Saints' Day, which is a special Feast Day in the Liturgical Year of the Catholic Church on which the Church honors all Saints, those holy souls who during life loved Jesus and strove to imitate Him and to practice His virtues. All Saints' Day was originally called Allhallows Day, hallow meaning to regard as holy or sacred. The evening of October 31 was known as Allhallows's Eve, from which we get halloween. The prayers and piety of the past have turned into fun-making and masquerading.

Today in New York City, that old funster Cardinal O'Connor was doing a bit of grave-digging in a church cemetery in lower Manhattan. The small cemetery is behind Old St. Patrick's Cathedral, located on a quiet, tree-lined street in Little Italy, a part of the city where pasta and pizza joints far out-number tall buildings, and where the old has not given way to the new. His Eminence was taking a small, ceremonial shovelful of dirt from in front of a tombstone that had its incription erased by time and weather. The grave is thought to be that of a black refugee from Haiti who, more than a century ago, went from being a slave to a hairdresser catering to New York's wealthy society women. His name was Pierre Toussaint and he died in 1853 at the ripe old age of eighty-seven. Toussaint became famous not for his hair teasing technique, but for caring for the sick during the city's yellow fever and cholera plagues. He also founded an orphanage and spoke out against the religious and racial bias of his time. By all accounts he was a good man, generous and compassionate.

Lately, there has been a movement in the Church to have Toussaint, whose name means "All Saints," canonized as the first black American saint. It seems the Church feels black Americans need a role model they can pray to for special favors. So, the Cardinal was presiding over the removal of Toussaint's remains from it final resting place. An exhumation team, headed by a forensic anthropologist, will sift through the grave with their fingers, paintbrushes, tweezers, and pliers, carefully uncovering brittle bones, buttons, and slivers of wood from a casket. The bones are to be examined, and, if they are determined to be the hairdresser's remains, the bones will be transferred to St. Patrick's Cathedral where the faithful will be able to pray to them. Toussaint's remains will be placed alongside the remains of the Archdioce's highest ranking clergymen in a crypt beneath the main altar of the cathedral.

You see, my sweet, in order for somebody to be officially declared a saint by the Church, there must be proof that the person was responsible for a miracle. (Of course, a miracle is an action that apparently contradicts known scientific laws and is hence thought to be due to supernatural causes. A miracle is the transgression of the law of nature. Therefore, the election of Dan Quayle and the popularity of Roseanne Barr can be considered miraculous.) So the Church's plan is simple: place Pierre Toussaint's bones in the Cathedral, urge people to pray to him to intercede on their behalf before God, and, if those prayers are answered in some miraculous fashion, then we'll have our proof that Pierre Toussaint was a saint. O'Connor claimed that it is not necessary for the body to have been preserved intact as a qualification for sainthood. Corpse preservation was at one time believed to be an essential sign of divine intervention.

The Cardinal never mentioned what Toussaint charged for a permanent. Initial reports indicated that the grave exhumation unearthed a portion of a jaw with teeth, which officials believe belonged to Toussaint's wife—there's a joke in there somewhere, but I'll pass because this religious chicanery is too deranged to be funny. How ironic, that the Church, which made death a terror, must sift through a graveyard in search of a saint.

Praying to saints—it seems so crazy now—but there was a time I believed the Catholic teaching that claimed the saints are mediators between the living faithful on earth and God in heaven. I never questioned the rather far-fetched notion that a holy, yet still mortal, person could die, be declared a saint long after his or her death by other mortal men, and suddenly become an advocate for humanity and carry our prayers of intercession to the throne of God, who, of course, could hardly say "no" to one of his saintly creations. Today, it seems silly and childish to think that a finite yet dead human being could carry the wishes of the living to God. "If God is omniscient and omnipresent, then why the need for saintly messengers?" is a question I never thought to ask. There doesn't appear to be any reason, yet we had saints dedicated to every occupation and adversity under the sun.

Teachers prayed to St. Gregory the Great, fishermen to St. Andrew, nurses to St. Catherine, policemen to St. Michael, and pregnant women to St. Gerard, and lawyers to St. Yves. (A glass reliquary containing the decomposed skull of Yves Helory, who died in 1303, is still marched through the streets of Treguier, France each May, followed by a long procession of black-robed lawyers.) And there were saints who specialized in healing every known disease people could contract: St. James cured arthritis, St. Blaise sore throats, St. Lucy eye infections, and St. Giles concentrated on sterilty. We even had saints that handled specific yet common problems: St. Anthony helped find lost articles, St. Joseph assisted women in finding husbands, and St. Barbara would be of help if you got caught in a lightning storm.

Fundamentalist Christians vehemently oppose the Catholic Church's belief that the saints could help in a person's healing. The basis for their objection has nothing to do with the silliness of the concept but rather is based on a principle even more ludicrous than the healing power of the saints. Some fundamentalist

Christians believe that Satan causes illness by means of demon oppression, and he can take away an illness without opposing himself. Listen up, here comes the juicy part. They think that if a Catholic prayed to a saint for healing, Satan would heal the person because it would be to his advantage to decieve the sick person into thinking that the healing was the result of their prayers to the saint. Holy spiritual confusion! You see, the fundamentalist Christian thinks the Catholic Church is under the influence of the devil, and they know that the Bible, which is their God, never mentions anything about praying to saints. The fundamentalist believes that Satan uses the Church teaching about saints to trick people into not finding God and into following unbiblical teachings. Holy spiritual drivel!

As a child, I was encouraged to read the lives of the saints and to follow their holy examples. (In medieval times, people loved reading the gruesome details of the lives of saints who were stoned, stabbed, or dismembered for their sanctity; today, we read the *National Enquirer*.) The false piety of many Catholic adults actually converted the veneration of the saints into something close to the worship of false gods. The saints became a Catholic version of the ancient belief in various gods devoted to specific occupations and human needs. The statues of the saints, some of them proudly riding on the dashboards of our cars, became our modern-day idols. Theologians could state that the statues and pictures of saints only served to remind us of the saint—the way that a photo of your loved one in your wallet does—and that we should not worship the statue. But we did worship the statue.

It is odd to think that I was taught by the nuns to trust in a dead human being rather than go directly to God. Why did we bow down before the images of the saints, and why did we worship them rather than imitate them? Because spirituality had degenerated into superstition, and God became not a spirit within us but a far-off, distant person who was so inaccessible that religion created a saintly messsenger to whisper our prayer into His ear.

I learned as a child to see the saints as perfect and myself as imperfect. Thus the seeds of guilt were sown, along with a belief that I needed some outside help in reaching God, that I needed the Church, without which I'd be lost for eternity.

A group of fundamentalist Christians from Texas believes that the city of San Francisco needs their help in rescuing most of its citizens from the eternal fires of hell. From "Ryan's Believe It or Not" comes this actual newspaper headline: Halloween Holy War in Bay Area. This halloween story is a real treat. It stars a televangelist from Texas, who often preaches in military fatigues and passes out dog tags to his "prayer warriors." Well, this major loon brought ten thousand of his Christian followers to San Francisco on Halloween night for a massive prayer meeting aimed at saving the city from the devil.

The meeting, held in the Civic Auditorium, lasted three days, during which roving bands of prayer warriors infiltrated city trouble spots. Some Christians prayed at pagan Halloween rituals, some at gay events, while others climbed a hill to pray for the salvation of the whole city. They hoped to free San Francisco from the spirit of perversion, including homosexuality and heterosexual couples living together outside of marriage; they hoped to chase New Age thinking out of Marin County, an upscale, wealthy area north of the city; and they also hoped to rid the spirit of greed that is choking the San Jose area, which is the heart of the high-tech industry and is located about forty-five miles south of San Francisco. The invading Christian prayer army considered the beautiful City by the Bay as a hotbed of blatantly open Sodomites responsible for last year's tragic earthquake. San Francisco witches gathered around the auditorium and tried to seal off the Christian's evil energy with ceremonial salts, powders, and curses. The results of this spiritual conflict are not in yet. I'd say both sides are losers.

Far from the lunacy of San Francisco, there is a much more deadly religious war being fought.

In northern India, not far from the Nepal border and about halfway between New Delhi and Calcutta, there lies the ancient city of Ayodhya. Ayodhya is the principle city in one of India's most populous states, Uttar Pradesh. Ayodhya is a Hindu pilgrimage center and also the epicenter of a controversy over a dilapidated Muslim mosque that is pushing India to the brink of a religious war. Religious riots between Hindus and Muslims have spread across India during the last ten days and at least 210 people have been killed. The source of the trouble can be traced back to Ayodhya and the year 1528.

Radical Hindus contend that the Ayodhya mosque stands on the ruins of a Hindu temple that marked the birthplace of Rama, a major Hindu deity. The mosque was built in 1528 by the Muslim Emperor Babur, who, the Hindus claim, first destroyed the Hindu temple. Muslims deny there ever was a Hindu temple on the site.

On the day before Halloween, more than ten thousand militant Hindu pilgrims, some of whom had walked as far as one hundred miles to reach Ayodhya, stormed the historic mosque determined to destroy it. Knowing in advance that the mosque would be attacked, authorities placed barricades outside the main gate of the mosque. At first, the local police, who are overwhelmingly Hindu, did little to stop the onrushing mob. Several thousand chanting, wild-eyed pilgrims easily managed to break through the barricades and the main gate of the mosque. One elderly pilgrim lost half his face when he was hit directly by a tear gas grenade. The throng of bleeding, choking, and shrieking pilgrims tore through the cloud of tear gas and into the shrine, where they began tearing away at the mosque, brick by brick. They chanted, "Lord, Lord Rama! Long live Rama!" The crowd was led by naked Hindu holy men, known as "sadhus," their bodies smeared with sacred ashes. Somebody should point out to George Bush that that's naked aggression.

The rioters had worked themselves into a frenzy, and with their bare hands managed to rip out wall bricks and wrought-iron window gratings. Eventually, civilian officials and government troops arrived at the scene, which prompted the local police to finally take action and the mosque was cleared. Five people were killed in the invasion, which sparked religious violence throughout neighboring Uttar Pradesh districts, as well as other Indian states, killing an additional thirty people. In Bangladesh, an Islamic nation, Muslim mobs began attacking Hindu temples and homes as a response to the anti-Muslim violence in India.

Yesterday a deployment of extra government paramilitary troops around the dusty town forced Hindu groups to postpone a new attempt to storm the mosque. More blood promises to be spilled because the Hindus are determined to destroy the temple and build a new temple in honor of Rama, and the Muslims vow to defend the mosque no matter what the costs. Fundamentalist Hindu leader Ashok Singhal said, "There is no power on earth which can stop us from building the temple. There is no place for Islam in our nation." One Hindu businessman who took part in the riot said, "We'll destroy this mosque and 3,000 more like it if we must to protect our Hindu nation."

India is constitutionally a secular state and there is no state religion; Hindus make up 82 percent of India's 880 million people, while Muslims account for 12 percent of the population and the balance are Sikhs, Christians, and Buddhists. Tolerance of all religion is a part of India's constitution, a part that is ignored by religious believers of all flavors.

Oh, Kate, my dear, I won't bore you with the political ramifications of the Hindu-Muslim violence that has killed at least 900 people in the last year, except to say it is sure to topple Prime Minister Vishwanath P. Singh's eleven-month-old government. Sing, a Hindu, opposes the plan to destroy the mosque and build a temple, saying it threatens the existence of India as a secular society. Once again, a voice of moderation will be silenced by the screams of extremists, and religious tolerance will be shattered by religious bigotry. God dammit, will the world never tire of playing the "My God's better than your God" game!

Politics aside, I would like to fill in a few details that you can't get from the inept press coverage of this story, which more resembles sports reporting than news gathering, giving us only the daily death score and not much more. "Hindus 9, Muslims 3, highlights at eleven." The Hindu-Muslim story may destroy a nation and it gets about the same attention in the press as Eddie Fisher's claim that his former wife, Elizabeth Taylor, is still hooked on drugs. You won't read about Rama in the papers nor will you read why the Hindus get so worked up over him. But, I'll tell you.

First, Rama has nothing to do with the Ramada Inn; he stays at Best Western Inns, preferring their free shampoo. When you were little, we once stayed at a Ramada Inn. I can't remember where we were going, or what the trip was about; but, I'll never forget the way you pronounced—or, more accurately, mispronounced—Ramada as we pulled into the parking lot. I guess you were just learning to read, and you recognized the sign from having stayed at a Ramada Inn on a previous occasion. You said, "Oh dad, this is great. I like the Rama Da Motels." I thought it was funny, because here you are, this little pip-squeak, barely able to read, and you knew the Ramada Inn was a lot classier than Motel 6, even though you mispronounced the name by stressing the Rama portion of the word. Your pronunciation, I might add, had a much more musical quality to it: Rama Da, Rama Da.

I've been calling them Rama Da Inns ever since, always thinking of you. It is funny how little things stick in your head. I can't tell you how many times my saying Rama Da Inn unleashed a floodgate of warm memories of my time with you and how much sadness our separation has caused me. As I sit here now, I can't help but think that I really never dealt with the pain of being separated from you. Frequently, I am ashamed to say, I think I tried to forget about you, tried to act as if you really didn't exist. You see, if I allow myself to dwell on our separation, I become so angry and so sad I feel like I could . . . I don't know, blow up, give up, or strangle your mother. I once harbored thoughts of kidnapping you. But being mad at your mother, or stealing you away from her was not really in your best interest.

So, I guess my way of dealing with the loss of you in my everyday life, the loss of seeing you grow, was to retreat from you. Sure, living three thousand miles away was an easy excuse for only seeing you once or twice a year for a string of many years, but, in all honesty, I could have called and written far more often than I did. I am sorry.

Hey—I was supposed to be telling you about Rama.

Actually, I'm not sure I'm up to the task. Understanding the Hindu pantheon of Gods is complicated and difficult, especially for westerners. OK, I'll give it a shot.

The Rama story begins with Vishnu, who is a Hindu God and is the center of worship in the Vishnuite sect of Hinduism. (Stop yawning, it gets worse.) In the Hindu version of the trinity, called the trimurti, Brahma creates, Vishnu protects, and Shiva destroys. In the *Vedas,* an ancient Indian collection of hymns, rituals, regulations for religious sacrifices, and philosophical essays whose five parts (the Samhitas, the Brahmanas, the Aranyakas, the Upanishads, and the Sutras) form the Hindu scriptures (Vedas is a Sanskrit word meaning knowledge), Vishnu was initially a relatively unimportant sun god, but his importance increased to the point where he is said to have had many incarnations, among them Buddha, Krishna, and Rama.

While Buddha remains an avatar in the eyes of Hindus, spreading enlightenment to all creatures, and his teachings have been assimilated into Hinduism, and Buddhism's two main branches, Hinayana Buddhism and Mahayana Buddhism, Buddha for the most part disappeared from India and became the dominate faith in China and other eastern nations. Krishna and Rama are the last two alleged incarnations of Vishnu, and their followers constitute a considerable portion of the Hindu people.

Rama is described simply as the best of men, a dutiful son, loving husband, and possessor of every virtue—sounds like my cousin Jim. But Rama succeeded in apparently superhuman undertakings and quickly became regarded as more than human—unlike my cousin Jim, who wound up doing time for embezzling funds from his firm. Rama performed miraculous tasks for humans, especially in the area of destroying demons. Perhaps the Christians from Texas should have asked Rama for his help in their war against Satan in San Francisco.

Kate, the point is that Rama's fame and popularity as an incarnation of Vishnu has continued uninterrupted from the tenth century. Rama is to the Hindus what Jesus is to the Christians. The Hindus are outraged that on the spot where Rama was born sits an Islamic mosque, and as long as their faith in Rama lasts, that mosque cannot.

The recent history of India provides further proof that when religious certainty takes control of the mind, humanity moves out. In 1984, Indira Gandhi, the Prime Minister of India, was assassinated. Mrs. Gandhi, who was not related to Mahatma Gandhi, was brutally gunned down by her Sikh bodyguards. The Sikh religion is a blend of Islam and Hinduism. It considers its true followers to be "warrior saints," an unlikely combination that accounts for the religion's bloody history.

I remember watching the news coverage of the assassination and being appalled by the sight of Sikhs around the world joyously celebrating the murder, despite the fact Mrs. Gandhi's murder ignited widespread violence in New Delhi that left more than twelve hundred dead. Kate, I think it is far worse for a mind to be possessed by God and religious certainty than possessed by devils. For instance, the demon of depression, can be exorcised by a few shots of Thorazine, but God possession seems incurable.

Political pundits and social sophisticates push the theory that the trouble in India isn't really a religious problem, but a socioeconomic-political-historical problem of which religion is just a superficial factor used to justify the various positions, just as it is in Ireland, Palestine, and Lebanon.

Bullshit!

If the people in India didn't have a handy religious rationalization to justify their resort to violence, they would be forced to examine the putative real causes of their discomfort. Religion in India divides men and diverts them from the task of advancing civilization. Since religious beliefs are not founded upon logic and reason, and are not modified in the light of facts, reasoned dialogue and rational arguments tend to be impossible in religious disputes, and force is often the only way in which differences are settled. Of course, one act of religious violence begets retaliatory violence, which continues until one side manages to extinguish the other. The real problem in India is an overabundance of religion and religiosity, which divides rather than unifies and blinds people to the nation's real economic and social problems. India is a nation in the grips of human despair, a nation in which half of the population earns less than $30 a month, a nation in which roughly 60 percent of the population is illiterate, a nation in which acute social tensions and religious and political violence threaten its very existence. India is a land of angry, quarrelling, inward-looking, backward-looking people who lack a common vision and face a grim future of almost insurmountable economic, social, religious, and political problems.

Indira Gandhi was succeeded by her son, Rajiv Gandhi. Rajiv Gandhi, who is a political moderate, was unable to unify the various religious factions within his country and was forced out of office. He is now planning on giving it another shot and is going to run for the office of Prime Minister in next year's elections, and many fear his campaign and life will end in a violent pool of blood. If he is also gunned down or blown up by religious fanaticism, I think the future of India will be in grave jeopardy, and the nation will be rendered impotent to fight against her real enemy—ignorance.

Why couldn't the Hindus build a temple in honor of Rama around the corner from the mosque? I guess that is about as irrational a question as, why do people still believe in God? In the name of religion—or more precisely, in the name of God, who is in reality only an undefined concept—men and women are ready to kill, ready to hate. Eventually, for the survival of the planet, the dogmas of religion are destined to be refuted, exploded, and forgotten.

Just in case, dear daughter, you get the notion the lunacy at the mosque is a problem confined to a remote, dusty corner of India, I suppose I better tell you about a similar incident that happened in Israel just last month. On October 8, nineteen Arabs were killed by Israeli police in a violent clash at a holy site.

I didn't bother writing to you about this at the time. I felt I was spending too much time dwelling on the disturbing events in the news. I was getting myself more and more depressed. Also, the incident in Israel was more personal. About ten years ago, I visited Israel. I spent two weeks touring the entire Middle East region, much of it spent within the old walled-city of Jerusalem. I saw the shrines and the soldiers. I heard the hosannas and the gunfire. I stood then where the blood flowed last month. I know what the place looks like, feels like, and sounds like. It is like no other place on earth.

The Old City is completely enclosed by a large, stone wall. The city is divided into four quarters: the Muslim Quarter, the Christian Quarter, the Armenian Quarter, and the Jewish Quarter. Entrance to the city is gained through one of the five gates: the Jaffa Gate, the Zion Gate, the Damascus Gate, Herod's Gate, and St. Stephen's Gate. The Old City of Jerusalem is a place where three monotheistic faiths converge, and conflict.

In the ancient Hebrew tongue, the city's name was Yerusholayim, which means "the city of peace." How ironic that in a city named for peace, peace has remained an unattainable dream. Three great religions and their dozens of antagonistic sects, branches, and factions exist within yards of one another, yet they do not speak, and instead spend their time in an unending squabble for every square inch of the city.

The trouble last month took place in an area that sits atop a thirty-five acre plateau in the south eastern portion of the city. The Jews call the plateau area Temple Mount; to the Arabs, it is known as Haram al-Shariff (the Noble Sanctuary). I'm sure you have seen photos of Jews praying at the Western Wall, which is commonly called "The Wailing Wall." This spot is the holiest site in Judaism. It is all that remains of a retaining wall from the western side of The Second Temple, built by King Herod, which stood atop the plateau until it was demolished by the Romans in 70 A.D. The first Jewish temple had been built on the exact spot in the tenth century before Christ by King Solomon. According to tradition, the plateau is where Abraham brought Isaac to be sacrificed, which is why Solomon chose the site to build the first temple. The Temple was later systematically destroyed by the Babylonians. The area around that wall has been the site of nationalist and religious struggle for more than 2000 years.

After the Second Temple was destroyed, it would take nearly two thousand years before the Jews would regain control of the plateau. In the meantime, in the seventh century, Muslim rulers built the Mosque of Omar, which is commonly known as the Dome of the Rock. It is the most beautiful building in the Old City. The striking, gold-domed mosque enshrines a rock jutting out of the ground. Tradition claims that the prophet Mohammed left earth and traveled to heaven on a white horse from this rock. Don't giggle; people are dying over their belief in this stuff. In the eighth century, business must have been good, so the Muslims expanded and built another shrine on the plateau, just a few hundred yards from the Dome of the Rock. It is called Al Aksa Mosque. It was in and around this mosque that the rioting took place last month. I should also point out that these two mosques were briefly conquered by the Crusaders in the eleventh century, but the Muslims regained control of them in the twelfth century.

Down through the centuries, the Muslim rulers generally allowed Jews access to the wall, so that they could pray. But things changed in 1948, when the State of Israel was created. After the fighting between the Arabs and Jews that preceded the founding of Israel had stopped, the borderline for Israel was drawn through the center of Jerusalem, leaving the Old City under Jordanian control, and Jordan barred the Jews from the site. This pissed the Jews off. Tensions mounted and erupted into the Six Day War in 1967. The Israeli Army captured East Jerusalem, and with it the Old City. After the war, dozens of buildings were leveled to clear the way for a large plaza in front of the Western Wall. Above the plaza and the wall, standing tall on the plateau, are the two mosques proudly overlooking the Old City. At the prescribed times of the day, you can clearly hear the voice of muezzin calling from the minarets beckoning the faithful to prayer.

The Israeli Government decided that the plateau should remain under the sovereignty of the Muslim Waqf, or religious endowment. The Christian holy sites also remained under Christian control. It all seemed fair. The secular Israelis knew that the consequences of taking the mosques away from the Muslims would be disastrous. The religious Jews, for the most part, believed that a third Temple must be built on the plateau, but not before the Messiah arrives, and seeing as he isn't here now, leave the mosques alone, we'll knock 'em down later.

So, since 1967 there has been an uneasy truce around the plateau area, with tensions occasionally erupting into noisy demonstrations. But now the jittery truce is about to become a powder keg. Palestinians consider the mosques essential to their national identity. The mosques on the plateau are Islam's holiest shrines outside of Mecca and Medina in Saudi Arabia. Right-wing Israelis want to reassert Jewish control over the plateau, and radical Jews want to throw the Palestinians out and rebuild the Temple. They agitate the Muslim authorities by sporadically trying to conduct Jewish prayer services in the mosque compound, a practice the Muslims strictly forbid. In 1982, a Jewish gunman opened fire on the mosque, killing one person, and in 1985, police thwarted plans by a Jewish mob to blow up the mosques.

The Palestinians have charged that the plans of a Jewish group known as Temple Mount Faithful to lay a cornerstone for a new temple sparked the violence last month that wounded more than a hundred Arabs and killed nineteen. According to the Jews, thousands of Arabs hurled rocks and bottles at Jews praying at the wall below. The plaza in front of the wall was crowded with Jews celebrating Birkat ha-Cohenian, a day during the week-long Succoth festival when Jews offer special blessings at the Western Wall. The bottles and rocks came down like rain from the plateau, where angry Arabs chanted, "Kill the Jews." About twenty Jews were hospitalized. After the clash, the army closed the Muslims Quarter and arrested about one hundred Palestinians.

The deaths immediately ignited violent protests throughout the West Bank and Gaza strip and set off brief demonstrations in Israeli Arab towns and villages in Galilee. In all, two more Arab men were shot dead, and more than eighty Arabs were injured. Iraq's ruling party threatened to retaliate for the Jerusalem killings.

The press coverage did little more than report: (A) The Arabs blamed the Jews for inciting the riot and also accused the Israeli police of overreacting and using excessive force; and (B) the Jews claimed the Arab attack was unprovoked and was planned in advance by members of the PLO. Television news gave us lots of pictures of rocks being thrown, guns being fired, bodies laying lifeless in pools of blood, women and children screaming in agony, and ambulances racing through narrow streets. It is no wonder the American public can only sit, stare, and wonder what the hell is happening.

The problem is far deeper than who threw the first rock, or even why the rock was thrown. The problem is the Jewish and Muslim concept of God is a lilliputian concept that no one wants to examine. And so the killings will continue to continue. There is no God to stop it.

People are being killed in India and Israel because two monotheistic faiths can't pray at the same spot and neither faith is able to simply go down the block and say their prayers. Why the hell can't Dan Rather say that on the "CBS Evening News"? Imagine if he could: "Good Evening. Today nineteen Arabs were killed for no good reason, and the violence occurred at the very place the dead had believed the founder of their religion had taken off for heaven on a white horse more than twelve centuries ago." That's what really happened on October 8.

Lunacy, lunacy, all around us, nothing but lunacy. But, on the bright side, the New York Giants are undefeated so far this season, their record an impressive 7-0.

Doesn't anyone see the madness of religion? Doesn't anyone see how on balance it has caused more suffering and pain than it has given solace and relief? I really cannot understand how the world can continue to pretend there is a God—or, at least, that there is a God who gives a flying—make that—who cares about us pitiful humans.

I'm going to start wearing one of those living-will dog tags instructing any passerby that if I show any signs of wanting to go to church, they have my permission to pull the plug.

This really has been a day of sadness for me. And a day of nostalgia.

I remembered when you were a kid, maybe three or four years old, and how I escorted you up and down the block so you could go from door to door saying, "Trick or Treat!" You were so cute. And so shy. Only the lure of the anticipated candy giveaway gave you the courage to knock on a door. With your bounty in the bag, you turned and excitedly skipped back to the sidewalk where I was waiting for you. It was a bitter cold day. Too cold for the costume you wanted to wear; I think you wanted to dress as a cat. Anyway, the frigid air forced me to improvise. I bundled you up in your winter coat, cut a hole in a white sheet, slipped it over your head and you went trick or treating as a ghost. We had a fun time together.

I suppose you don't remember those days. The days when I lived with you. Back then, I changed your diapers. I bathed you. I dressed you. I fed you. I played with you. I read to you. I tucked you in at night.

I loved you. I still do.

Listen, kiddo, it's time for me to hit the sack. I know it's a little early, but I managed to slowly sip nearly a half a bottle of port while writing this letter, so, at this point, bed is my only option.

Good night, my love.

Friday, November 2—6:30 A.M.

Hi. Bit of a hangover this morning. I really don't drink that much, but last night I overdid it; this morning I'm paying the price.

Today is All Souls' Day. And you thought I had a lot to say on All Saints' Day!

Don't worry—I'm not going to write a word about the meaning and tradition of this day.

I just wanted to say I love you.

And share a handful of doodlings from my notebook.

*   *   *

Myths are images that are not facts but reflections of an elementary idea of God.

*

The soul—or the concept of the soul—is governed by geography. Had I been born in China, I would never have acquired the desire to save the souls of lost and doomed Americans.

*

Man shaped the putty of his feeling into an idol named God.

*

Time: we always seem to be running out of it, never have enough of it to do the things we want to do. I wonder how many hours I've spent, say just in the last five years, reading newspapers.

*

Imagine all the fasts and self-torture the "saints" down through the ages have endured just to please their God. What does this say about their God, that He/ She would be pleased by their suffering?

*

I'm still confused about mysticism.

*

The Old Testament reflects the wisdom and ignorance, the reason and prejudice of the times in which they were written. There is some good stuff in it, but there is a lot of crap. Some of it is wise, some of it is foolish; some of it is gentle, some of it is cruel. Hey, sounds like it's a book!

*

The pillars of religions are: Ignorance, Indoctrination, and Inadequacy.

*

God is love. Love is blind. Therefore, Ray Charles is God.

*

In a world where the sacred and the secular are waging a fierce battle for our minds and hearts, how do we know what to believe? Is atheism more truthful than theism? I don't know, but I think, for me at least, it's more honest.

*

Children, after meeting kids of dissimilar faiths, must draw one of three conclusions:
    1. All religions are invalid. (Rebel)
    2. Certain religions are valid for certain people. (Compromise)
    3. All religions are invalid except mine. (Egocentric)
    Or, they don't have to reach any conclusion, which only means they didn't think about it.

*

I wonder why historians are so civil to Christianity?

*

From the movie *Postcards From the Edge* comes this memorable line: "The problem with instant gratification is that it takes too long." That observation encapsulates the essence of life in America in 1990.

*

Americans don't have the patience for mysticism.

*

Any professional athlete currently making less than a million dollars a year must view himself as a hopeless mediocrity. That says a lot about our society. And athletes are underpaid compared to movie stars.

*

We are about to go to war to defend an Arab culture that doesn't fit into the twentieth century, and soon it will be the twenty-first century.

*

Self-exploration involves exploring everything.

*

Happiness is difficult to repeat because of the memory of happiness.

*

Life is a battlefield on which individuals, ignorant of the extent of the whole war, fight their own private battles.

*

Every life has a long list of remembered losses.

*   *   *

That's it from my notebook. I do have one short historical footnote to add to my All Saints' Day comments. About 235 years ago, on November 1, 1755, in Lisbon, Portugal, the churches were filled with All Saints' Day worshippers when the earth around the Bairro Alto section of old Lisbon began moving. The earthquake caused the massive stone walls of the churches to crumble, and fires blazed up all over the city from fallen candles. Many of those who survived the quake sought refuge along the banks of the Tagus River and were engulfed by a tsunami that swept over the low-lying, waterfront district of Baixa and far into the heart of old Lisbon. By the end of All Saints' Day, more than 30,000 people were dead, and an estimated 10,000 buildings were reduced to rubble. A lot of saints came marching into heaven on that day. Today, on the hilltop Bairro Alto, a 600-year-old Carmelite church's Gothic skeleton serves as a ghostly memorial to the city's most tragic day.

Well, this tired old soul is going to try to have a nice All Souls' Day . . . catcha later.

Saturday, November 3—7:20 A.M.

Good morning. I feel like I have to do a short follow-up to my letter of Thursday. I read in the papers this morning that militant Hindus tried again yesterday to storm the mosque in Ayodhya. The mob numbered between 5,000 and 10,000.

After initial hesitation, this time the policeman opened fire on the militants with rubber bullets and then with automatic weapons. The mob was driven back and never made it into the mosque. Official accounts list 12 dead in the attack. According to other sources, the death toll varied from 10 to 100 people. The violence also spread across the country, killing dozens more people. India's western state of Gujarat was the scene of one grisly act of brutality. Seven Muslims were tied, beaten, stabbed, and then thrown into a burning house by a Hindu mob. The Indian army has been deployed to several areas of the country, and strict curfews have been imposed in the most troubled districts.

This story is getting very little coverage. The world's attention is still riveted on Iraq. It seems a military showdown with Saddam Hussein is inevitable. The nation's attention is split between the Middle East, the just concluded budget negotiations, and next Tuesday's elections. Hindus and Muslims killing each other in India has no press appeal.

When, dear Kate, is the world going to wake up and reject all it's so-called saviors—Lao-Tse, Buddha, Krishna, Rama, Christ, Mohammed, and all the rest? When will we begin to take responsibility for the chaos that threatens the world? When are we going to open our eyes and see the cruelty that is everywhere?

I do not know. But I'm sure it will not be soon. Changes in the fundamental ways in which humanity thinks and acts move at a glacial pace. I remember hearing a funny story back in 1972 that demonstrates how reluctant we are to drop old beliefs, behaviors, and myths. In November of 1972, the jet age landed in Katmandu, Nepal. The government bought itself a Boeing 707. In the inaugural ceremony, goats were slaughtered and their blood smeared around the cockpit to ward off evil spirits. As Arthur Schopenhauer said, "Every man takes the limits of his own field of vision for the limits of the world."

And so it goes. Man's cruelty will stay its destructive course, uninfluenced by Jesus' claim that the peacemakers shall inherit the kingdom of heaven. The existence of God has not stopped man from becoming the most remorseless killer who ever stalked the earth. For many, God is little more than a symbol to whom they transfer the burden of their problems in order to avoid solving them themselves.

Well, I'm not going to dwell on this stuff now. I'm hoping to have a nice day. I'm taking a drive up to Santa Barbara for the weekend. I hope to be able to catch C-Span's coverage of a Jesse Helms rally in North Carolina tonight on TV at a friend's house. That should be worth a laugh or two.

This time last week, I was getting ready to spend the day with you. I miss you. Still no word on the NBC job. My agent says that the vice-president was very impressed with me; in fact, the agent said that he knows from a "source" inside NBC that I am on the top of the VP's short list of candidates. However, my agent claims there is big turmoil inside NBC daytime, and some management people at the network would like to see the low-rated soap cancelled and replaced with a far less expensive game show. We shall see.

That's it for now.

Sunday, November 4—11:05 P.M.

Back in Hollywood. Had a wonderful time in Santa Barbara. But I really don't want to talk about my weekend. I want to talk about Jesse Helms, or more specifically, coverage of the neanderthal senator from North Carolina's political rally on C-Span that I watched last night.

I'm ready to move to Paris. I'll decide Election Day.

Before I tell you about the Helms's rally, let me first say a few words about Jesse, as a way of introduction. Jesse Helms, who is sixty-seven years old, is a throwback, a leftover from the segregationist South. Jesse Helms is an old-fashioned, "give 'em hell," commie-bashing politician. He is a comic book senator, unsophisticated and very rough around the edges. During the sixties, Helms was a commentator on a North Carolina television station; and he used his electronic bully pulpit to condemn what he perceived to be a growing moral laxity and to attack critics of segregation. During his lengthy senatorial career, he has been the most applauded and the most criticized guardian of a conservative age. His tirades and nettlesome questioning of numerous presidentially appointed diplomats and judges earned him the nickname, "Senator No." Jesse Helms, a Mr. Potatohead look-alike, is a Joe McCarthy without an Un-American Activities Committee. But, unlike the infamous Senator McCarthy, Jesse Helms doesn't say what he really thinks; instead, he feeds racial fears in a muted way. His campaign for a fourth term has drawn national attention because so many are hopeful that Helms's brand of racial politics will finally be retired.

Helms's opponent in the race is Harvey Gantt, a former mayor of Charlotte and a successful architect. Gantt is a moderate Democrat who presented what he called a "noble agenda." Gantt's platform was a mild strain of liberalism highlighting health care, improved education, and increased environmental sensitivities. Harvey Gantt, who is forty-seven years old, is articulate, pleasant, and handsome. And black.

Bingo—an issue Helms knows how to manipulate and exploit, even though race should not be an issue, and actually wasn't until this past week. For most of the campaign, Helms was stuck in Washington, trapped in the middle of the budget impasse that dragged on for months. His continued denunciation of feminists, homosexuality, federal funding of artwork he deemed to be obscene, welfare programs, and diplomats he considered wishy-washy failed to bury the underdog Gantt. In fact, Harvey Gantt had built an 8 percentage point lead over the senator in the polls. Helms's television commercials attacking Gantt as too liberal on abortion and gay rights appealed only to his constituents in North Carolina's more rural areas, but fell on deaf ears in the more moderate cities of the state. Gantt had avoided making race an issue; he rarely used the terms black or Afro-American, and he never referred to Helms as a racist, choosing instead the more euphemistic label of "divisive."

With his back to the wall, Helms played his trump card: exploiting white anxieties. He ran an ad showing Gantt receiving a campaign contribution from Jesse Jackson. Then he unveiled what became known as the "white hands" commercial. It featured a close up of a pair of white hands crumpling up a letter of rejection from a prospective employer. The voice said, "You needed that job, but they had to give it to a minority because of a racial quota. Is that really fair? Gantt says it is." Jesse figures race-baiting is his only way of winning. Never mind that Harvey Gantt does not support a quota system for hiring minorities. The ad put the challenger on the defensive and said to the white voters of North Carolina, "Wake up, white people," which is a forty-year-old white supremacist's motto. Helms is a master at cloaking uncivil, extreme means in apparent civility and common sense. The "white hands" ad stressed one basic concern in order to obfuscate the real issues of the campaign.

Will it work? We will find out in two days. I fear it will, which is why I'm ready to move to Paris.

As promised, here is my review of the rally I watched on C-SPAN last night, which included a lot of praying and flag-waving.

The rally was held in a large school auditorium in Charlotte. The room was packed with Helms supporters waving placards and shouting, "Jesse, Jesse, Jesse." The white walls were decorated with red, white, and blue balloons. The all-white crowd seem to span all age groups. There were plenty of older "church lady" types, accompanied by their white-haired husbands. A few young kids where sitting on their father's shoulders. The frenzied multitude segued from chanting "Jesse" to singing "The Star Spangled Banner," led by a high-school chorus.

First up at the podium was the current mayor of Charlotte, a woman named Sue Myrick. She informed the throng that she would like to begin the festivities with a word of prayer. She introduced a minister who was the pastor of the Bible Baptist Church in Charlotte. Here is the prayer he offered: "Dear Lord, thank you for this wonderful occasion tonight. We want to thank you, dear Lord, most of all tonight, for Yourself, the Lord of Heaven and Earth. And Lord we just worship you, and we praise you, and we thank you dear Lord, and we will forever. But Lord our hearts are saddened tonight because of the break up of the family in America, the terrible moral decline, the huge staggering debt that is upon us and will be upon our grandchildren and great-grandchildren, for the obscenity in our country, for the murder of millions of countless unborn precious little children. And Lord we thank you tonight for this great senator that you've given this state. Thank you dear Lord that he's been able to—he's been willing, dear Lord—to stand alone many times. And dear God how we wish there were ninety-nine more just like him. And we know, dear God, that this election is in your hand; we just pray dear Lord that your precious will may be done. Now be with Mr. Helms, dear Lord; give him the strength that he needs in the last few days of this campaign and we will praise you forever in Jesus' name. Amen."

The crowd all said, "Amen," and cheered the prayer. Then the mayor introduced a young student, who led the assembly of God and Jesse believers in "The Pledge of Allegiance." No doubt about it, God wears a Helms button and an American flag pin in His lapel.

Jesse then introduced a string of dignitaries (including the Ambassador to Bahrain, to whom Jesse had admitted that he didn't even know where Bahrain was when Ronald Reagan called him to ask if the Senator would speak to a man he was considering nominating as Ambassador to the tiny Persian Gulf country), who were seated on the stage, and then the chorus sang another patriotic song. So far, the precedings seemed very similar to a church service.

Then Jesse Helms introduced a young actress named Susan Walden, who stars on the TV show "Danger Bay," which airs on the Disney Channel. Helms claimed the actress was one of the most principled young ladies he ever met. The blonde actress said how there are many people in Hollywood who support the senator. She spoke about the real people, the hard-working backbone of the country who know what's going on and are not easily deluded by the liberal press, the horrors of Marxism, socialism, and communism and about how she feared that our nation was slipping into a strange liberal socialism. Much of her talk was dedicated to bashing the media and the press. She never mentioned any real, tangible issues. Her talk was disjointed and jejune. She ended by saying that not only does North Carolina and the United States need Jesse Helms, but the whole world needs him also. Yea, like it needs a breakout of bubonic plague.

Next up was the Ambassador to Bahrain. I didn't catch his name, and as I was getting up to get a beer I heard him say that he loved his adopted country and the Lord. By the time I got back to the couch, his talk was drawing to a close and he was hoping that God would lead men and women of our land to vote for people of the caliber of Jesse Helms, because with the decline of morality and the rise in drug use, our country is in great peril; but with more people like Jesse Helms in Washington, America can, with the grace of God, once again be a great nation and the land of the free and the home of the brave. He ended with shouts of, "God bless America, and God bless Jesse Helms."

Next up was a former professional football player, the lone black speaker. He claimed that Jesse is a great leader who is not behind the times and that the senator has endured the press's slings and arrows that have insulted his integrity. He said the campaign was not about black and white. He said God wants us to love one another. He claimed a nation without God will cease to be a great nation. The audience frequently interrupted him with shouts of, "Amen, brother." According to the football player, the campaign was not a political battle but a spiritual battle, and God must be our foundation, and race should not divide us.

Next up was the Mayor, who informed the audience that America has turned its back on God during the past thirty years. She asserted that we have become a nation of self-indulgent people and that we must repent, turn from our wicked ways, and return to God on our knees. She quoted the Bible, but never mentioned the Constitution. She said, "We are here to support a man whose whole being is dedicated to helping save us from the evils that are becoming the norm: burning that flag that hundreds of thousands of Americans have bled and died for, removing prayer from American life, unnatural sex that can not propagate the species as God intended, federal funding for such things as murdering the unborn and for filth that some people call art." Jesse Helms and his band of moral troglodytes never tire of trying to pass laws declaring a zygote—a fertilized human egg—

to be a human being, a person with full rights and privileges. The mayor wondered why we are testing God. In a wild somersault of logic, she claimed that the tragedy of divorce has led to the collapse of the underpinnings of society, rampant drug and alcohol abuse, and an alarming increase in violent crimes. She blasted humanism and homosexuality. She decried the removal of prayer from public places. She suggested that Harvey Gantt wants to turn North Carolina into a state where anything goes and wants to multiply the handout programs to aid those who don't want to work, who never have and never will, and, finally, that Harvey Gantt wants to give gays more rights than the rest of us enjoy. She could really sling the mud, and she slung a lot of it at Harvey Gantt, whom she made sound like a total idiot and commie dupe. Her harangue was constantly being interrupted by shouts of, "Glory to God" and "Amen."

Jesus Christ! It was like sitting in on a revivalist tent meeting. This unadulterated mixture of God and politics was shocking.

Finally, Jesse Helms strode to the podium. He said he was going to discard his prepared speech and wanted to speak from his heart. He said he was sorry he couldn't make as many campaign appearances as he wanted to, because he was occupied in that den of iniquity called Congress. He said that Harvey Gantt was incapable of telling the truth about anything. Helms never uttered one word about his policies or programs, preferring to stick with character assassination and accusing Gantt's supporters of being intellectually dishonest. He said Gantt frequently has his facts "ass backwards." At one point he called his opponent "stupid." He claimed the *New York Times,* the *Washington Post,* ABC News, CBS News, and NBC News were all conspiring to help insure that he, Helms, is voted out of office. And the crowd loved every second of his speech.

The evening made me weep for the sorry state of politics in America.

Wednesday, November 7—10:00 A.M.

It worked. Helms's last ditch appeal to racial fears, that is. Jesse won . . . but not by much. He is going back to Washington for six more bruising years. Harvey Gantt needed to capture at least 40 percent of the white votes, and he fell short by a mere five points. The fractious campaign produced a huge voter turnout in white precincts.

Sadly, across America, voters chose to stay home and not exercise their right to vote. Only 36.4 percent of eligible voters bothered to go to the polls, and they returned 96 percent of the incumbents to office. Oddly enough, wherever voters could opt for "none of the above," they did so in large numbers. But the election showed that in American politics, incumbency is a very powerful weapon, because incumbents can raise tons of money. I read that just two incumbent congressmen, one from New York and one from Los Angeles, raised a combined $3,385,606 to finance their re-elections, which was $64,934 more than all 331 congressional challengers combined could raise. Political action committees contributed nineteen times as much money to sitting lawmakers as to their opponents. Money talks, and no incumbent walks.

I was taught that elections were the pulsating heart of our Democracy—but recent national political campaigns prove that is just another myth not grounded in reality. Modern campaigns are vacuous and repugnant spectacles where issues are forced off stage to make room for scandals, mudslinging, and trivia. And it should come as no surprise that voters have become so disgusted that they are opting out of the whole process. In 1990, barely a third of Americans bothered to vote in Congressional elections. Yesterday, the voters fully realized they were presented with very few real choices, and so more than 60 percent of them just stayed home and watched television. Money is the pulsating heart of our Democracy. Somehow, Kate, a nation of free people has given birth to a vast, swollen, bloated bureaucracy that feeds on greed and craves power.

Well, despite Jesse Helms's narrow victory, I guess I won't move to Paris. After all, America is still the best place on the planet to live. Maybe Helms will get the boot in 1996. We can hope.

Sunday, November 11—11:30 A.M.

I've been thinking about the Bible for the past few days. Maybe it was the sight of all those Bible-thumpers at the Helms rally that triggered my thoughts. The people who are always quoting the Bible and holding it up as the one and only effective guide to living seem to be the least bothered by the book's numerous errors, contradictions, inconsistencies, and muddle of myths. I could devote pages to listing just the blatant errors and contradictions in the Bible—but, don't worry, I won't. There are numerous books dedicated to just such an undertaking. What I find curious is that the Bible-believers act as if the book doesn't contain any contradictions, and they seem oblivious to the fact that the book is a hodgepodge of fables, written and re-written by countless hands, masquerading as a unified whole. I remember a time, in my late twenties, when I started the task of reading the Bible from cover to cover because I really wanted to know God's word. I was told it was a handbook for living. I didn't get very far when I was confronted with unexplainable holes in the story, which impelled me to doubt the book's authenticity and believability.

I found nothing "holy" about the Holy Bible. The book seemed to be written by power-hungry priests who presented a divine avenger God and hapless men who were dependent on the priests' powers for salvation. The book's main characters were fratricidal (Cain), drunken (Noah), dishonest (Jacob), and murderous (Joshua and Moses). The creation story told in Genesis amounted to little more than kindergarten cosmology and tells us nothing of what happened at the beginning of time. It seemed strange to me that Satan would take the form of a snake in order to talk to Eve. At the least it is an odd disguise. But the writer used this odd disguise to convey a message. Genesis was written around five hundred years before Christ and long after the beginning of the universe, and, at the time it was written, the Jews were easily led into false beliefs. Just like today, there were many concepts of and ways to God, and some Jews frequently got involved with the religious practices of their pagan neighbors. One pagan group believed God resided in snakes, and many Jews were beginning to accept that belief. The writer, using his powers of imagination, cleverly wove a secondary meaning into the creation story by having the snake represent evil, and by doing so suggested that people who follow strange new teachings wind up in deep trouble. So, the snake was merely a symbol for pagan practices, and the writer was trying to make the point that the Jews need only to listen to their God, Yahweh.

Much of the Bible, I learned later, was stolen from pagan sources and could hardly be considered the revealed "word of God." Some verses are even verbatim quotations from Egyptian scriptures. The story of Adam and Eve can be traced back to Babylonian mythology. Stories of great floods are common to many ancient religious traditions. Biblical law is patterned after Hammurabi's code. History shows us that there were many gospels floating around in the early days of Christianity, and the ones that survived are the ones the priests needed to keep control, and the rest were destroyed by fanatics. The esoteric nature of the writing refutes any literal interpretation of the script; yet, to this day, countless people believe there really was an Adam and Eve.

In the eighteenth chapter of Genesis, the first book of the Bible, I read about Abraham and Sarah. They were an aged couple to whom God had promised a son. In chapter 21, the son is born. Yet, in chapter 20, Abraham is able to pass his wife off as his sister, and he manages do to this because she is very beautiful, and so Sarah is taken into Abimelech's harem. The story doesn't jibe. The Bible clearly suggests Sarah is both old and pregnant, yet she is able to pass for a beautiful, younger woman. Didn't anyone notice her pregnancy? In chapter 25, a similar problem is presented. Isaac and Rebekah already have two full-grown sons, and both parents are now old. Yet, in chapter 26, Isaac, fearing his life, pretends that Rebekah is his sister because she is so beautiful. The chronological framework of many of the stories did not hold up. Was God guilty of sloppy storytelling?

I found the Old Testament to be virtually unreadable and very boring. The Book of Deuteronomy was bogged down in endless dietary taboos. The Bible did, however, contain some humorous incidents, like the time God played peek-a-boo with Moses on Mt. Sinai: "And I will take away mine hand, and thou shalt see my back parts: but my face shall not be seen." But later, in the Book of Exodus, God apparently changed his mind and gave Moses a frontal view: "And there arose not a prophet since in Israel like unto Moses, whom the Lord knew face to face." As I read the Old Testament I found a tiresome, all-too-human God who came close to being a racist who wanted all Gentiles annihilated. I was sickened by the drastic vengeance wreaked by God, who treats Moses spitefully for a minor display of temper and who strikes down thousands of innocent people because some men looked into the Ark of the Covenant. By reading the Bible, I discovered that God also had a sadistic side; he created hell for angels who mounted an insurrection in heaven, which God was powerless to prevent. I could not understand how the God of Love could shower fire and brimstone on Sodom and Gomorrah, cremating innocent women and children, in revenge for a few hardened hearts. God even sadistically turned Lot's wife into a pillar of salt for a look back in horror at the city where her friends and neighbors were perishing in a fiery holocaust.

Silly things aroused God's moral indignation: trimming of hair and beards, adorning the body, eating certain kinds of foods, working on the Sabbath, not circumcising a child—and God got really pissed at homosexuality and prostitution. But God didn't have any problem with such real injustices as slavery, the selling of children, and inequality in the distribution of wealth. I found it odd that poverty made it easier for a person to get into heaven, which sounds more like a political ploy than a spiritual virtue. The God of the Bible didn't seem very refined or dignified; in the Book of Numbers, God promises to "spread dung upon your faces," and in the Book of Ezekiel, Gods orders people to eat barley cakes that are baked "with dung that cometh out of man, in their sight." In the Book of Kings, God promises to punish "him that pisseth against the wall." I was frequently astonished by God's words; in the Book of Deuteronomy, God says, "And thou shalt eat the fruit of thine own body, the flesh of thy sons, and of thy daughters which the Lord thy God hath given thee." Ugh. The Second Book of Kings has a charming story set during the time of a famine in Samaria. According to the Bible a woman boils her son as food for herself and a female friend. The First Book of Kings tells how Solomon used a hit man to get rid of his enemies, including his own brother. Nice guy. The Story of the King of Moab offering his oldest son as a burnt offering during a war with Israel makes repugnant reading. Equally repugnant is the story of King Jehu of Israel, who ordered the widowed Queen Jezebel thrown from a high window by some eunuchs, which I guess didn't take any balls. Athaliah assures her secession to the throne of Judah for six years by killing her grandchildren. In the Second Book of Chronicles, we read that King Asa, a true man of God, decreed that anyone who did not seek the Lord God of Israel should be put to death. The King, I'm sure, is a hero in Pat Robertson's eyes.

I once tried to add up the number of people killed in mass murders ordered or approved by God. I stopped counting when I reached 884,895. That number included 200 Philistine men killed by David to obtain their foreskins with which to purchase Saul's daughter to be his wife, 24,000 Israelites who cohabited with Moabite women and worshipped Baal, and 185,000 Assyrians slain in one night by a single angel. An exact total is impossible, because frequently the Bible doesn't give an exact figure and just says, "All the people of Makkedah," "All the people of Libnah," "All the people of Lachish," "All the people of Gezer," "All the people of Eglon," "All the people of Hebron," "All the inhabitants of Gaza, Askelon, and Ekron," "Every man in Edom," and "All the worshippers of Baal in Samaria and Israel."

It is difficult to read the Bible and not be disturbed by a devious God who orders atrocities and condones injustice and unfairness. The God of Love, I discovered by reading the Bible, was an impulsive, flawed deity, and hardly a candidate for admiration. And Jesus was a superstitious Jewish man who was abysmally ignorant of science and the universe. Jesus knew little about medicine and attributed many ailments from epilepsy to insanity to the possession of the body by spiritual demons, and he spent most of his brief ministry casting out devils and unclean spirits. Using the pagan magic of transference of power, Jesus sometimes used spit or the hem of his garment to heal people.

Enough about the Bible; you get the point, I'm sure.

I wish I could have spoken at the Helms rally. I would have chastised the assembled for trying to turn America into a Christian nation by replacing the Constitution with the Bible. I would have simply quoted from two of our nation's founding fathers: Thomas Jefferson and Thomas Paine. Jefferson said, "God is a being of terrific character . . . cruel, vindictive, capricious, and unjust." Paine said, "Whenever we read the obscene stories, the voluptuous debaucheries, the cruel and tortuous executions, the unrelenting vindictiveness, with which more than half the Bible is filled, it would be more consistent that we called it the word of a demon than the word of God. It is a history of weakness, that has served to corrupt and brutalize mankind; and for my part I sincerely detest it, as I detest everything that is cruel." And no one would have said, "Amen," because the Bible-believers at the Helms rally were convinced it is impossible to find natural grounds for human morals and to establish a nonsuperstitious basis for behavior.

Dear Kate, for what it's worth, I think the Bible was created by man and is nothing but a vain and feeble attempt to impose order onto the chaos that exists in the world and to give meaning to the cosmos. The Bible is hardly holy—in fact, it isn't even good fiction.

Monday, November 12—2:20 P.M.

While walking along Sunset Boulevard this morning, I saw a sweatshirt that really made me laugh. It carried this message:

To Do Is To Be
—Socrates

To Be Is To Do
—Plato

Do Be Do Be Do
—Sinatra

The shirt cleverly summed up 2,500 years of philosophy, and still made you feel like singing!

Tuesday, November 13—11:00 A.M.

I was thinking of going to the movies last night, but I couldn't make up my mind what film to see. Within fifteen minutes of my home, there are four multiplex theaters offering a total of twenty-seven different films!

For a long time now, I've had this nagging sensation of growing indecision. I find it hard to make my mind up when I am confronted with choices. And it seems like I'm always confronted with choices. Take the other day, for example. I had been reading about the importance of increasing fiber in your diet, so I thought perhaps it would be a good idea to try having bran cereal for breakfast. Ok, so I'm at the supermarket, pushing my basket down the cereal aisle. It suddenly hit me: what an incredible variety. I remember as a kid the choices were rather limited: Corn Flakes, Wheaties, Grape-Nuts, Rice Krispies, and maybe a half-dozen others. Today, there are at least two hundred choices of cereal in the average supermarket. (I know you like Golden Grahams.) After a long walk past all the sugar-coated cereal that can't be good for kids, with odd names like Count Chocula, I got to the bran cereals. I was dumfounded by the choices: All-Bran, Rice Bran, Raisin-Bran, Multi-Bran Chex, Cracklin' Oat Bran, Fruitful Bran, Common Sense Bran, Quaker Oat Bran, Shredded Wheat with Oat Bran, 100% Bran, Crunchy Corn Bran, and some others I can't remember. I decided I really didn't want any bran cereal.

Recently, a Soviet chef named Georgi Gorgodze was visiting an American supermarket for the first time. He had this comment: "So much choice. If anything, you people have too many choices, too much food."

Georgi saw what few of us do—choice has become overchoice. Back in 1970, Alvin Toffler, in his book *Future Shock,* wrote, "We are racing toward 'over-choice'—the point at which the advantages of diversity and individualization are cancelled by the complexity of the . . . decision-making process." We are beyond that point now. In 1987, Jeremy Rifkin, in his book *Time Wars,* wrote:

> You can go into a major shopping mall and become totally emotionally exhausted in one hour and you might have been in only one store buying only one item. The reason is there is such a plethora of items to pick from and so much stimuli in front of you that people have a hard time focusing. . . . People are emotionally stressed and don't know it is from the tremendous proliferation of consumer items and the terrific assessments they have to make when they buy a product or service. It's a tremendous emotional burden . . . well beyond the level [of stress] that our parents knew."

If you doubt this, try picking out an aspirin when you have a headache. Do you get plain Bayer aspirin or Excedrin or Tylenol or Ibuprofen? Do you get regular or extra-strength? Do you get capsules or tablets or caplets? What you get is a worse headache!

Want a real headache—go buy a new VCR. There are at least 450 from which to choose. Once you get the VCR home and hooked up to your TV, you can tape shows on any of twenty to fifty different cable channels. As a kid growing up in New York City, we had only six stations from which to chose. Today, if I had a satellite dish, I could pull in over one hundred channels from around the world.

Suppose you want a more healthful diet and you decide to switch from butter to margarine. Among the choices you have are stick margarine, tub margarine, whipped margarine, liquid margarine, diet or reduced-calorie margarine, extra-light margarine, margarine spreads, butter blends, and light butter blends. If that isn't complicated enough, there must be a half-dozen or so brands of margarine offering the above spectrum of choices. To add to the confusion, margarines vary greatly in calories, total fat, and saturated fat. I feel like I have to take a scientist with me when I go food shopping to help me read the labels. Last August, a study published in the *New England Journal of Medicine* suggested that partly hydrogenated margarine contains trans monosaturated fatty acids, which form as the vegetable oils are treated with hydrogen that hardens them into stick margarine or soft margarine. The acids act like saturated fats: they raise blood cholesterol levels. The harder the margarine, the more "trans fatty acids" it contains. What the hell does that mean? It means just buy butter.

I don't think all these choices makes life any easier; in fact, I believe they make it much more difficult. Stress has become a mass phenomenon in America.

Not too long ago, I came across an old photo of my Dad. He was waxing our new car. The year was 1956. The car was a Chevy. The photo was in black and white, but I remember the exact colors of the car: Sierra Gold and Tan. That car made a big impression on me. For years, my dad managed to nurse an old clinker of a Ford from the forties, a black box of car, far beyond the age when it should have been retired. He hadn't held onto the Ford out of love, he simply didn't have the money for a new car. But when the Ford finally died, we set out to get a brand new car. There were only two car dealers near the house: Harrison Chevrolet and Bradshaw Plymouth. We got the Chevy because I liked the way it looked. My brother lobbied hard for us to go to another neighborhood and get a Ford.

Today, if you want to buy a car you must first choose between the domestic models and the imported cars. If you want a foreign car, you must choose between Japan, which offers at least four or five different makes; Germany, which offers at least three different makes, France, which offers at least two different makes; Great Britain, Sweden, and Italy, each of which offers several makes. I saw a magazine recently that reviewed 163 models of new cars and offered repair records on over 300 models of used cars. Once you pick out a model and body style— sedan, coupe, station wagon, convertible, minivan, sport utility, or pick-up—then you have to decide what size engine you want, whether it should be turbo-charged or not, whether to get automatic transmission or a five-speed, whether to get power steering, outside mirrors with defrosters, air conditioning, cruise control, sun-roof, fancy wheel covers, power windows, a service contract, a CD player, power seats, anti-lock brakes, central locking system, or rust-proofing. It almost makes you want to take a bus!

Want to make a phone call? Let's see: should I use AT&T, MCI, Sprint? Who can tell the difference? Try picking an auto insurance company or opening a bank account and you're faced with a dizzying array of options and choices. Tell somebody to buy you a coke, and you'll hear: regular, diet, classic, caffeine-free, or diet caffeine-free? Recent issues of *Consumer Reports* have guided its readers through forty-two different bar and liquid soaps (just the bestsellers), eleven moving-van lines, 538 health-insurance policies, thirty-five shower heads, twenty-four brands of rice, seventeen basement paints, 347 mutual funds, and eight woks. Looking for a magazine to read? There's a newsstand in New York's Pan Am Building that has almost 2,500 magazines for sale. Why do we need thirteen daytime soap operas on the air?

Kate, the world is growing more complex and uncertain at a faster and faster pace, and our decision-making ability can hardly keep up with the demands that are required of us. The more choices we have, the more anxious we become. Maybe I'm not so indecisive, maybe I have just too many choices.

I made one choice lately—the choice to live. I want to simplify my life, and not get caught up in the growing complexity of the world around me. If we let it, life can become exhausting and draining.

Speaking of exhausted and drained—I am, so I choose to end this letter now.

Or maybe I should—never mind.

Wednesday, November 14—3:30 P.M.

I'm a criminal. I broke Public Law 101-547. My crime: failure to pray.

"Failure to pray?" you say. Yes, daughter, that's what I said. Allow me to explain.

Today, the 101st Congress approved House Joint Resolution 673, which resolved: "To designate November 2, 1990, as a national day of prayer for members of American military forces and American citizens stationed or held hostage in the Middle East, and for their families."

I don't exactly know the process the government uses to approve on November 14 a mandate to pray on November 2. The joint resolution was considered and passed in the House on October 24, and three days later, on October the 27, it was considered and passed in the Senate. I guess it takes time to travel down the bureaucratic road from passage to approval.

The joint resolution contained eight "whereas" clauses. Here are four of them (the second, sixth, seventh, and eighth), followed by the actual resolution:

Whereas President Bush, in order to preserve international order and protect American interests and lives in the Middle East, has deployed American military forces to counter Iraqi aggression;

Whereas a strong majority of Americans support the deployment of American military forces by President Bush in the Middle East, and all Americans hope that a just outcome may be reached in the Middle East without war;

Whereas Americans are willing to accept sacrifices resulting from the use of military force, fight armed aggression, defend national interests, and protect the lives and welfare of American citizens; and

Whereas Americans have traditionally recognized that military strength alone is not sufficient, and now should also trust in Providence, and remembering that, according to the Scriptures, "unless the Lord keeps the city, the watchman worketh but in vain": Now, therefore, be it

Resolved by the Senate and the House of Representatives of the United States of America in Congress assembled, That—

(1) it is the sense of the Congress that the President should declare November 2, 1990, a national day of prayer for members of American military forces and American citizens stationed or held hostage in the Middle East, and for their families;

(2) all Americans should pray for President Bush, his advisors, the leaders of American military forces in the Middle East, and the leaders of the other countries which have deployed forces in the Middle East to stop Iraqi aggression, that they retain the wisdom and courage to bring about a just resolution to the Middle East crisis;

(3) all Americans should pray for Iraqi President Hussein, his advisors, and the leaders of the Iraqi military forces, that they will remove their military forces from Kuwait, release all hostages unharmed from their current captivity, resist further acts of aggression against other countries, meet the conditions of applicable United Nations resolutions, and act prudently in the furtherance of peace; and

(4) all Americans should observe such a day in prayer and meditations at churches, in groups, and as individuals.

Approved November 14, 1990.

* * *

Whereas I didn't pray, I have broken the law. Kate, how can the state, in a public law, legislate a "trust in Providence," and quote from the Bible, a religious book of myths and contradictions, to support the notion that its citizens must, in these troubled times, trust in God? How can the state, in a public law, mandate that its citizens go to church and pray? Does any clear-thinking human being believe that any amount of "prayer and meditation" could cause Saddam Hussein to change his ways?

Instead of wasting its time considering and passing worthless pieces of legislature, the Congress should work at resolving the host of problems that can only be solved by hard work and courageous legislative action. Problems are not solved by wishful thinking and trusting in God.

If the crisis in the Middle East should evolve into a war, will anyone look back to November 2 and ask: Why didn't God answer our prayers? No way.

Thursday, November 15—8:05 A.M.

Good morning. A couple of updates. No word yet on the New York soap opera. Although there is a rumor that the head of daytime programming, the guy who interviewed me, is about to get the axe. If so, that is not good news for me.

In case you were wondering, the exhumation process of Pierre Toussaint's remains is moving along nicely. There was a photo in this morning's paper of an archaeologist kneeling in Pierre's grave. Using a tweezer, he had just picked up a tiny metal fragment, believed to be from a cross Toussaint wore. Preliminary tests and physical evidence indicate the bones unearthed are those of a tall black man. What I find fascinating is that the grave site has become a mini-mecca for the curious and the faithful. A steady stream of people come to watch the workers or to pray for miracles. Some ask for bags of dirt from the grave, which they believe to be holy.

Dirt is not holy. Bones are not sacred. Miracles are found in the mundane moments of life, in every unnoticed heartbeat. Yet, we look and long for the extraordinary. The miracle in Toussaint's life was that even though the deck was stacked against him, he never viewed his race or slavery as a handicap or weakness within himself. Instead of moaning and groaning about the cards life dealt him, he went out and helped others in need. He seemed to have nothing, but he gave everything. I find his story inspirational. Pierre Toussaint was a hero and is an excellent role model. He should be admired, but not venerated. Toussaint lived before he died, most of us die before we live. That is the lesson I gleaned from his life. I'm glad the Church has dug up the memory of a life well lived, but I detest turning that life into an icon suitable for worship, and, worse, suitable for sale.

Still no word on what Pierre charged for a haircut.

Speaking of haircuts, I'm getting one today. The guy who cuts my hair is gay. I like him very much. He spends a great deal of his free time at an AIDS hospice. He gives the dying a haircut; it is a matter of dignity. His descriptions of washing and cutting a person's hair while they are laying in bed are poignant. Of course, the Church would never consider this gentle, compassionate man a saint. His lifestyle—god I hate that damn word—condemns him. I think he walks in Toussaint's steps. He cares for those in need—something I don't seem to have the time to do, even though I have all the time in the world.

Be a saint, my love. I'm devil enough for the both of us.

And all God's children said, "Amen!"

Friday, November 16—2:20 P.M.

Finally, after eight weeks, the news has come, and it isn't good. NBC has elected to fire the vice president of daytime programming. Yes, Kate, the guy who wanted to hire me has now joined me in the ranks of the unemployed! I guess my agent was right about the internal turmoil at NBC. There is still a slim ray of hope about the job. If the new VP doesn't cancel "Friends and Lovers," the show will still need a new executive producer, because the person who has the job now intends to retire when her contract expires next month. I might have to go back to New York for an interview with the new VP, but the feeling is that the show soon will be history. "No news" looks like it was "bad news."

Sunday, November 18—10:35 A.M.

The presence of American and other Western forces in the conservative Islamic nation of Saudi Arabia is having a decidedly nonmilitary impact on the fabric of the nation's social life. The influx of so many Westerners is highlighting just how out of tune Saudi Arabia is with the modern world. Arabs are appalled at the sight of so many women soldiers, provocatively dressed in T-shirts that expose far more flesh than they deem appropriate, working closely with males and performing such unfeminine roles as truck drivers and mechanics. The female soldiers stand in stark contrast to their Islamic sisters who are veiled and attired from head to toe in long, black robes that obscure all their femininity.

Edicts from the fourteen-century-old Koran impose strict restrictions on Islamic women. These restrictions spring from interpretations of the Sharia, a set of edicts within the Koran. These codes are interpreted by holy men known as ulemas, who are conservative Islamic scholars. Women in Saudi Arabia are not permitted to mix with men in public or the work place. There are branches of banks that are staffed by women only. Female doctors are permitted only to tend to women or children. Male teachers are prohibited from having female students. Women are prohibited from traveling or leaving the country alone and must be accompanied by male relatives, unless they have written permission from their husbands. An unaccompanied Saudi woman cannot check into a hotel. Women are not permitted to drive cars, and they must be veiled in public. Up until the 1960s, even the doors of education were closed to women, a situation that clearly demonstrates how religious leaders fear knowledge.

These rules are enforced, with varying degrees of strictness, depending on the city, by squads of religious police known as the Committee for Commendation of Virtue and Prevention of Vice. These police patrol the streets in pairs, making sure women cover their bodies and strictly observe prayer times. The Saudi royal family has been pressing for modernization of the country and a relaxation of the severe restrictions on women, but their efforts have met with opposition from the powerful religious establishment.

Last week, the ulemas' worst fear manifested itself: seventy veiled Saudi women openly defied the ban on driving, dismissed their chauffeurs, and drove a convoy of about forty cars, mostly Lincoln Continentals and Mercedes, through the streets of Riyadh. They were stopped and detained by the police and released only after signing a pledge that they wouldn't repeat their action again. The women who participated in the organized protest, many of whom were supported by their husbands, were harassed by religious leaders, who described them as immoral, non-Islamic, and tainted by American secularism. Some of the women were suspended from their jobs as punishment. The women said that religious fundamentalists are controlling their lives.

How odd it is that American men and women, who represent an open, free, and democratic society, are defending a xenophobic country where religious mullahs perpetuate an ancient suppression of women.

How odd it is that American men and women are risking their lives to defend Kuwait, a country that treats foreign workers as slaves who are abused and denied all rights by their rich employers. Less then 10 percent of the Kuwaiti population of three million are permitted to have the rights of citizenship, and many of them routinely humiliate and degrade the foreign servants who cater to their every whim. Over the years, many reports published in the *Kuwait Times* have detailed cases where Kuwaiti servants have been thrown from rooftops, burned, blinded, or battered to death.

Yes, Kate, our forces in the Middle East are protecting a nation that treats women as inferior, and we are rescuing a nation of slave holders. Yes, Saddam must be stopped, no doubt about it, and I guess we must do it because we once treated him as a friend because he was more than happy to slaughter our enemy, the Iranians. What a mess!

Thursday, November 22—9:15 A.M.

Gobble, gobble. While the rest of the nation sits down for a turkey dinner on this Thanksgiving Day, I think I'll have vegetarian Indian food. Alone. Even though my hopes for getting a job at NBC in New York seem slim at best, I do have much for which to be thankful. Most of all, I'm thankful for you. I wish I could be sitting down with you today for a traditional Thanksgiving meal. The Thanksgiving card you sent me is sitting on my desk. I know I'm not a very good father, yet somehow you make me think I am.

Why lie? I don't have a lot to be thankful for and this day only manages to remind me of that fact. I really hate holidays. They only serve to emphasize how I do not really fit in anywhere. I'm tired of not fitting in.

Enough about me. Let's talk about our president, Pastor Bush.

The president of all the people issued a Thanksgiving Day proclamation that at least 10 percent of the population would find extremely offensive. It was, by the way, proclamation number 6229. After the proclamation gave a sugar-coated history of Thanksgiving in colonial times, the President began to sound like a preacher. He wrote:

> The great freedom and prosperity with which we have been blessed is cause for rejoicing—and it is equally a responsibility. Indeed, Scripture tells us that much will be asked of those to whom much has been given. Our "errand in the wilderness," begun more than 350 years ago, is not yet complete. Abroad, we are working toward a new partnership of nations. At home, we seek lasting

solutions to the problems facing our Nation and pray for a society "with liberty and justice for all," the alleviation of want, and the restoration of hope to all our people.

OK, let's pause here for a brief commentary. If the president really believed the bit about scripture saying that "much will be asked of those to whom much has been given," then why is he always fighting to give tax breaks to the rich? Does anyone really think Bush cares about "liberty and justice for all" when his domestic polices, insofar as he has any domestic polices, promote racial prejudice and do little to help ease the economic hardships of the poor? The president goes on to say:

This Thanksgiving, as we enjoy the company of family and friends, let us gratefully turn our hearts to God, the loving source of all Life and Liberty. Let us seek His forgiveness for our shortcomings and transgressions and renew our determination to remain a people worthy of His continued favor and protection. Acknowledging our dependence on the Almighty, obeying His Commandments, and reaching out to help those who do not share fully in this Nation's bounty is the most heartfelt and meaningful answer we can give the timeless appeal of the Psalmist: "O give thanks to the Lord for He is good; for his steadfast love endures forever."

The president then called upon all Americans to gather together and pray today. What drives me crazy is that Mr. Bush says these things as if they were undeniably true. He may fully believe that God is "the loving source of all Life and Liberty," however, many Americans do not subscribe to that view. The source of human liberty is human beings. Humans put people in chains. Humans deny other humans their basic rights.

Take a walk through the streets of Calcutta and see the 400,000 homeless people living in the gutters, washing in brackish water from open pipes, and scavenging for scraps of cloth, metal, and glass which they sell in order to buy food.

Take a walk through Johannesburg and see the young malnourished orphans of apartheid roaming the streets like wild beasts, forced to earn money by subjecting themselves to sexual molestation by pedophiles who gladly give these discarded children a little affection and a meal in order to feed their own sexual appetites.

Take a walk through the ghettos of Detroit, Philadelphia, New York, and countless other American cities and see if you can find any Liberty and Justice.

As we inch closer and closer to war, I do not see any evidence of the Almighty's favor and protection. I do see humans who are brutal, callous, and cruel. Please Mr. President, stop sounding like a preacher and start acting like a man who really cares about the things you claim your God cares about.

I, Christopher Ryan, hereby proclaim that I shall observe this day of Thanksgiving by bringing some canned food to a homeless shelter, after which

I shall partake of some saag paneer and navaratan korma at the Sitar Indian restaurant in North Hollywood.

Sunday, November 25—1:00 P.M.

For the second Sunday in a row, my thoughts have turned to religious practices that seem oddly out of place in the modern world. This time, the story-making headlines doesn't come from the Middle East; it comes from Japan, and it's a doozy.

Last January, Emperor Hirohito of Japan died. He was succeeded by his son Emperor Akihito, who is fifty-six years old. Last week, after nearly a year of official mourning for Hirohito, Akihito formally ascended to the throne during a two-part enthronement ceremony that was accompanied by a nationwide celebration, as well as an intense debate involving the government's participation in a religious ritual and the issue of whether or not Akihito has become a living God.

First, a bit of historical background information. Hirohito ascended to the Chrysanthemum Throne and became a living God in 1928. He was the one hundred twenty-fourth emperor in a dynasty that stretches back to the seventh century. Japan's brutal military aggression during World War II was waged in the name of its monarch. After the war, Emperor Hirohito renounced his status as a living God and he was relegated to a symbol of national unity. Historically, the emperors held little real power, and were primarily figureheads of the state. Following the Shinto tradition, the emperors prayed for bountiful harvests and worshiped their ancestors.

The first part of the ceremony was held on November 12 and was open and public; the second, held ten days later, was secret and solitary. The November 12 ceremony was a formal, state-run affair that was attended by thousands of dignitaries from 158 nations, including Vice President Dan Quayle. Controversy arose over whether or not the government should underwrite an ancient imperial ritual (that has religious overtones), which it did for the first time in history and at a whopping cost of fifteen million dollars. During an age of ultra-nationalism during the nineteenth century, Japan's leaders attempted to have the emperor regarded as the chief Shinto priest. The new state constitution no longer recognizes the priestly functions of the emperor. Yet, the emperor still acts like a priest-king (albeit without political power) and continues to conduct many religious ceremonies each year on the grounds of the Imperial Palace. These Shinto ceremonies disturb many people in Japan, which has become more secular in recent years; it also upsets the Christian and Buddhist population living in the country.

The second part of the enthronement ritual was shrouded in even more controversy, as well as secrecy. This private Shinto rite is known as the daijosai, or great food-offering ceremony. Many Japanese believe that during the daijosai, the emperor is transformed into a living God. The rite dates back to prehistoric times, but was suspended for nearly two thousand years until Japan was reunified in the seventeenth century. The daijosai has its origins in ancient harvest festivals, but the original meanings of the tradition have been lost over the ages.

The ceremony took place in a shrine, consisting of two separate buildings made of pine logs and grass mats, which was built especially for the occasion. The rite begins after a ritual bath. The emperor, wearing flowing layers of white silk robes, which symbolized his purity, solemnly marched into the shrine. He was surrounded by courtiers. He was also accompanied by six Shinto ritualists and two female priests. Once the emperor enters the shrine, he is no longer in public view. He offers rice (the first of the season), millet, and rice wine to the spirit of his mythical ancestor, the sun goddess Amaterasu Omikami and other deities who live in heaven and on earth. He eats some of the food himself and prays for the well-being of Japan and for world peace. Details of what actually happens during the rite are kept secret; but many theories abound. Some believe the emperor, wrapped in cloth, lies down in a special bed and is reborn as a living God. Some think the emperor engages in a simulated act of sexual intercourse with the sun goddess, while others think the Amaterasu just sits on the bed with the emperor. The Imperial Palace says that the bed in one of the buildings is there merely for the sun goddess to rest on, and the emperor never touches it. The actual rubrics of the rite have been orally passed on from generation to generation and are such a guarded secret that no one really knows what happens during most of the ritual.

No foreigners are permitted at the ceremony; however, nearly one thousand Japanese dignitaries, including the prime minister, attended and waited during the three-hour ritual in a separate open room, from which it was not even possible to catch a glimpse of what was happening inside the shrine. More than a third of the Japanese population opposes the government's paying for the daijosai. Christians and Buddhists object to a ceremony of one religious sect being turned into a state function. The socialist and Communist parties insist that the government violated the consitutional ban on state support of religion. But there are some militant nationalists who still worship the Emperor.

Kate, while the world teeters on the brink of war in the Middle East, Japan, which is normally busy buying up real estate in the United States, is working herself up into a lather over whether or not its government should pay for a religious ritual that transforms their emperor into a God. And I used to think these modern times in which we live gradually were becoming free from superstitions that date back to humanity's birth. No way, the past still imprisons the present, and there is no hope for an early release in the future.

Wednesday, November 28—9:15 A.M.

"Good mornin' Mistah Chris. I's hasn't seen your face for a long time now. How's you been?"

"Fine Coop."

"Come on down here, I gots your favorite seat."

I smiled, and said, "You remembered."

"Of course I's remembered. What's you think, I's gone senile or something?"

"Not you, Coop. You don't slow down long enough for anything to rust."

That brief exchange took place about two hours ago. The scene was a little hole-in-the-wall dive called Cooper's. I hadn't been there for—geez, I don't know—two, maybe three, years. Cooper's reflects the simplicity of its owner. From the outside, it looks like a shoe box. A glass shoe box. I'm not good at estimating distances, but I would guess that the small, one-story structure is no more than fifteen feet wide and perhaps forty feet deep. Painted on the front window in a color that resembles a rotting banana is the word Cooper's. The two "o's" are a poor artistic attempt at resembling donuts and are painted in a mousy brown. Just next to the name, is a childlike painting of a steaming cup of coffee. That's it—welcome to Coop's place.

Cooper, known as Coop to the regulars—nobody knows his first name, claims he doesn't have one—is an old black man. He says he stopped counting his birthdays when he hit seventy-five, and that was so long ago he can't exactly remember when it was. Old he may be, but he is far from feeble. Coop is a strapping, healthy looking man. I'd say he is close to six feet tall and weighs about two hundred pounds. Coop's business style and practice wouldn't go over very well at Harvard, but as he himself said in response to a customer who suggested that he update and expand the business: "I's been serving the same thing, in the same way, from the same spot since before the motion pictures came out with the talkies—why the devil should I change now."

And what Cooper has been serving since before the invention of the sound track, which of course is just another of his exaggerations, is two things: coffee and donuts. Make that donut, cause ol' Coop offers only one type of donut, the old fashioned, plain round one with the hole in the middle. "Just like my mama used to make," he boasts. Cooper doesn't offer a choice in coffee either. He doesn't believe in decaffeinated; claims he can't understand why anyone would want to take the caffeine out. Makes perfect sense to me. Customers unfamiliar with his anti-decaf bias are curtly told, "I serves only leaded here. You wants that unleaded stuff you's gonna hafta go to one of them new-fangeled donut places." By "new-fangeled" Coop means "Dunkin Donuts."

So that's it: one kind of donut, one kind of coffee. Coop's philosophy is simple: No frills. And no plates or silverware either. The donuts are placed before you on a thin paper tissue. Ask for a spoon to stir the cream in your coffee, and you'll hear, "That's what the donuts are for." Cooper is a piece of work!

Behind the counter, Coop is king. He has no helpers. The donuts are deep fried and the coffee brewed by him as he simultaneously waits on the customers. The old man has two speeds, fast and faster. And he hasn't lost a step with age. Should a homeless street person enter with an empty cup, Coop rushes over and pours the person a cup of coffee, which they then leave with immediately, fully aware that their benefactor is pressed for space.

Oh, I almost forgot to tell you about the seating. Running the length of the shop is a long counter, in front of which are twelve stools. The stools are the old-fashioned kind that you hardly see anymore: a small round, rotating seat that sits atop a metal spindle. The seat tops are made of red vinyl, most of which are torn and cracked with age.

I was surprised Cooper remembered my seat. About halfway down the counter, one of the stools was broken; so there stood the tarnished metal spindle sans seat. I liked one of the stools to either side of the broken one. Why? Simple: I could use the vacant counter space in front of the dismembered stool to spread out my *New York Times*.

It felt good to be back at Cooper's. The coffee was great. I tried not to think about the lard Coop fries the donuts in. I'm sure cholesterol is a foreign word to him. Why shouldn't it be, I doubt his arteries are clogged. As I sat there, I couldn't help but think how, in a world that is constantly changing, Cooper's steadfastly remains the same. Still no plates. Still no spoons. Still no choice in donuts or coffee. Thank God, there is still Cooper, a warm, caring man who does what he does with a big smile. No frills, no false fronts, no bullshit.

As I sat reading about the sudden change of leadership in England, Coop poured me more coffee and said, "Those politicians play hardball over there in England. I mean I don't gets it. That Thatcher lady done been running that country for a dozen years. She were tough as nails. Hated the commies. They called her 'Iron Lady.' Now that's a great handle. Then all of a sudden, the boys in the back room gets together and figure out she's losing her edge, that she's done outstayed her welcome and was gonna lose the next election, so they pull the rug out from under her and send her packing. I mean, it's crazy. England didn't kick the old broad out, her party did. Don't they have any of that 'We the people' stuff over there?" "It is hard to believe, Coop," was about all I could say to Coop's rather astute analysis of Margaret Thatcher's sudden departure from Number 10 Downing Street, ousted from her Prime Minister's post by a Tory Party rebellion that had more to do with politics than policy. Her successor, who happens to be a high-school dropout, is her political son and young enough, at forty-six, to be her real son. There will be no change in policy, only style; out with the stringent, in with the slick.

Coop than said, "Can ya imagine the Republican Party givin' that two-faced Bush bum the boot because they didn't think he could win in '92? No way man. They would just have to watch him go down in flames." Coop leans toward me and says in a hushed voice, "Just between you and me, I think the Bushman's old lady, that white-haired dame that looks more like his mother, would make a better president than little Georgie. That dude seems bent on starting a god-damned war with those desert rats over oil. Lotta our boys ain't gonna be coming home breathing. Blood for oil doesn't sound too cool to me. Is that Quayle clown still in the National Guard? Maybe we should send him. They ain't got too many white folk over there, ya know." I smiled a bigger smile than I have smiled in a long time. The *New York Times* couldn't have summed it up any better— and didn't.

Cooper's: good coffee, good donuts, and good political analysis—both international and national.

I wish I could have gotten Coop's analysis of the other big story in the news this morning: MTV's refusal to play Madonna's latest video. Why this merits being a hot news story is beyond my powers of reasoning.

Madonna—not long ago the word conjured up images of the mother of Jesus in all her virginal abstemiousness. Now the guileless name stands for the sexual frankness, openness, and diversity that is embodied in the pop singer who seems to love controversy more than music. The blonde star's video for her new song, "Justify My Love," was banned from airing on MTV, which normally loves exposing and exploiting women. But this video has too much hanky-panky even for MTV. The song is from her latest album titled *The Immaculate Collection*.

The video, shot in black and white, portrays the erotic fantasies of the star and a lover during an assignation in a Paris hotel. The video is a carnival of voyeurism, sadomasochism, bisexuality, and leather-and-lace sex. Dressed in a skimpy, near-see-through black bra and high heels, Madonna and her lover roll around in bed as she sings—I suppose it's singing—such memorable lines as, "I don't wanna be your mother, I just wanna be a lover." Isn't that creative! In one sequence of the video, the lover is kneeling at the side of the bed as he lustfully watches Madonna kissing and nuzzling an androgynous-looking female sporting a crew-cut hairdo. In another scene, a topless woman wearing leather pants and suspenders doing a poor job of covering her nipples, which are briefly exposed, gropes a man's crotch. The video sexcapade has it all: transvestites, bondage, and insinuated oral sex. And the video ends with a closing message that is flashed onto the screen as Madonna leaves the hotel laughing: Poor is the man whose pleasures depend on the permission of another.

Kate, I'm a big boy; I've been around. It is not the content of the video that bothers me. What bothers me is Madonna's ability to capture headlines and her ability to pass herself off as some kind of serious artist. She was quoted as saying that the video is "the interior of a human mind. These fantasies and thoughts exist in every person." Fine, I can buy that (with the exception of the word "every," for which I would substitute "many"). But is she telling us anything about those things or just showing them to us. And it is not "us" she is showing them to, it is impressionable young kids who are more than likely not equipped to handle the material. A wishy-washy MTV spokesperson said, "We love Madonna. We have a terrific relationship with her. We respect her work as an artist and think she makes great videos. This one is just not for us."

What crap. Madonna is not an artist, she is a marketing whiz. Within hours of the ban, which must have been anticipated, especially when the video clearly showed a woman's breasts and nipples, Warner Brothers announced it will be releasing "Justify My Love" as a video single for just under ten bucks. Madonna will be laughing all the way to the bank—thanks to the ban and all the press hoopla, the video, which couldn't be shown on TV, is bound to sell like hot cakes in the stores. I'm not sure, but I don't think music videos have ever been offered for sale before—I smell a rat.

I don't find Madonna's showing a couple of girls kissing and couple of guys snuggling offensive, though I do question the need to do so considering the age of most of her fans. I find the movie industry's shameless exaltation of graphic and gratuitous violence far more offensive than any video that frankly deals with sexual themes. If I could give Coop the last word, I would imagine he would say, "If Madonna is an artist, than I am a gourmet cook." Trust me Kate, Cooper's no gourmet cook.

That's it for now daughter. I'll close with my favorite sentence from this morning's newspaper. It came from the mouth of Vice President Dan Quayle, and he spoke the words before a gathering of teachers: "Quite frankly, teachers are the only profession that teach our children. It is a unique profession and, by golly, I hope that when they go into the teaching field that they do have that zeal and they do have that mission and they do believe in teaching our kids." We can only hope.

Tuesday, December 11—7:00 P.M.

During the past few months, the press has reported on some strange religious happenings: there is a painting of a saint in a church in Queens, New York, that weeps; the Virgin Mary has been making daily appearances in a tiny town in Yugoslavia; God has appeared in the form of a cross that is reflected in the bathroom window of a house in Violet, Louisiana; and the Virgin Mary is also making appearances near La Guardia Airport in New York City.

It's true. I mean it is true these stories have been covered in legitimate, respected newspapers, and not merely in the trashy supermarket tabloids that cater to the bizarre and the strange.

St. Irene Chrysovalantou Greek Orthodox Church in the Astoria section of the Borough of Queens in New York City has become a mecca for the faithful and the curious, who wait in long lines to crowd into the small church in hopes of seeing a painting of the church's namesake weep. St. Irene is the patron saint of peace and of the sick. The saint's image was painted on wood in 1919 by a monk from Mt. Athos in Greece and has been proudly displayed in the church since its founding in 1972.

The painting, which was on loan to a Greek Orthodox Church in Chicago, began to shed tears on October 17 following a prayer service for peace in the Persian Gulf. Thousands of people flocked to St. Athanasios and St. John the Baptist Church in Chicago during the next five days before it was returned to New York City. Since its return, people from as far away as Boston, Philadelphia, and Chicago have come to witness the weeping painting. They come by subway and limousines. The crowd swells in the evenings and on weekends, the line stretching down the block. People with serious medical problems come to pray for health. A young girl with a roving eye reported that it was healed. Many of the visitors claim they have seen a miracle. Church leaders are convinced the painting is crying and pleading for peace in the gulf region. There are, of course, skeptics; but their skepticism is greeted with a question: Why would the icon cry from the eyes and not the hands? Church leaders have refused to allow the painting to be removed from the church for independent verification of the tears.

What's going on in this church? Is it just mass religious hysteria? Is there a natural explanation why moisture would form on a wood panel? The press doesn't probe these questions, they just report the alleged facts.

The Virgin Mary has turned the poor, small village of Medjugorje in Yugoslavia into the country's hottest tourist attraction since she began making daily appearances at St. James Church to six young teenagers a decade ago. The Church and government are reluctant to say how much cash has flowed into the area during the last ten years, but the Franciscan priests who run St. James Church report that over a million communion wafers are distributed annually to visitors to the church. Numerous books, brochures, and videotapes help lure pilgrims to the remote mountain village.

But the Vatican is skeptical. They have forbidden parishes to organize pilgrimages to the village, and priests and nuns are not permitted to lead pilgrimages until the Vatican authenticates the apparitions, which could take years. The local bishop has denounced the visions as hallucinations and charged the Franciscans with perpetrating a religious hoax and deliberately squelching information that throws doubt on the apparitions. The Franciscans claim the bishop is telling lies. Yet, the pilgrims continue to pour into Medjugorje. The streets are jammed with tour buses and campers, and the locals do a booming business in religious artifacts, despite the fact that not one verifiable miracle has ever occurred.

While miracles are considered rare occurrences in most places around the world, in Medjugorje, they are regularly scheduled events. Tour guides frequently tell pilgrims that Our Lady will be appearing at a specific time. Two of the original six teenagers to whom the Virgin first appeared (Ivan Dragicevic, now twenty-six years old and Vicka Ivankovic, now twenty-seven years old), say they still receive daily messages from her at 6:40 P.M. (and twice on Mondays and Fridays), and occasionally the Virgin informs them that she will be making a public appearance at a specific time. Word spreads like wildfire throughout the town, and at the appointed hour thousands of Virgin-seekers gather on Apparition Hill, the name that has been given to the steep promontory where two village girls first reported seeing the Virgin Mary as they were tending their sheep. When the Virgin doesn't make public appearances, the pilgrims must settle for the daily public briefings from Ivan or Vicka, in which they relay the substance of the Virgin's message to the crowd assembled in front of Ivan's home. Even when the Virgin does make rare "public appearances," few people actually claim to see her, and most speak of only feeling her presence.

Not only is the Virgin punctual, she is also considerate. According to Dragicevic, she does not want to torture him by making him learn another language, so she speaks Croation during her daily appearances. He says the Virgin appears to him in three dimensions, standing on a cloud. The Virgin tells him of the need for renewal of faith among the followers of her Son. He says the Virgin sometimes touches him.

Is this just another case of religious frenzy being fed by crass commercialism? Do people just see what they want to see and ignore what they don't want to hear? Why doesn't the Virgin Mary pull off a big-time miracle and swoop down on Baghdad and whisk Saddam Hussein off on her cloud while CNN's cameras are rolling?

Now that would be a miracle, one that would convert the planet and insure world peace!

Next stop on our whirlwind tour of religious lunacy is a bathroom in Louisiana. The wallpapered bathroom is in the home of Leo and Loretta Alphonso, who live in a white-shuttered, red-brick home in a crime- and drug-infested neighborhood of the town of Violet. Since the beginning of November, hundreds of pilgrims have lined up in front of the Alphonso's home in hopes of seeing God in the bathroom—and hopefully God will not be using the lavatory.

The Alphonsos are devout Catholics. Before the miracle in the john began, they were offering a nine-day novena to St. Jude, who is the patron saint of hopeless causes. A statue of St. Jude sits near the television (that's fitting, seeing that most TV shows are hopelessly stupid) in the Alphonso living room. (By the way, novenas are public or private devotions that are carried out for nine days in honor of God, a saint, or angels. The Church likes to say that the practice of novenas began with the Apostles who waited for the coming of the Holy Ghost after the Ascension for nine days with the Blessed Mother.) The Alphonsos had just concluded their novena. It was 10:30 at night, and they were about to go to bed when Loretta, who is fifty-seven years old, went into the bathroom and saw a brilliant reflection of crosses in the window. She called Leo in to look at the panorama of crosses. He saw them too. And they have appeared about the same time every night since then. Leo also claims that he has regained part of his eyesight. The sixty-one-year-old pipefitter is blind in his right eye, and he was quickly losing vision in his left eye. He does admit that a doctor had been treating his left eye, and he had been given an injection, but Leo Alphonso is convinced the Lord has intervened on his behalf.

The Alphonsos' pastor has visited their bathroom (I hope he didn't leave the toilet seat in the up position) and said that he didn't find anything that looked miraculous. Still, as word of the apparition spread, people started making their way to the Alphonso home. In groups of four, they are allowed into the bathroom. (Fortunately, Leo and Loretta have a second bathroom.) Some leave convinced miraculous activity is going on, while others leave with doubts and skepticism.

Doesn't it seem odd that God would leave his heavenly throne for one in a bathroom in Louisiana? This is a miracle that needs to be flushed down the toilet, quickly.

The last stop on this supernatural expedition takes us back to Queens, New York, and oddly enough to a neighborhood called Flushing! According to the faithful, the Virgin Mary makes regular appearances in a sprawling park built on top of a landfill.

This story begins in the spring of 1968. On June 5, Senator Robert F. Kennedy was shot in Los Angeles. As he lay dying, a housewife in Bayside, Queens, sat in her car praying for him. When she completed her prayers, Veronica Lueken smelled roses. She associated the smell with St. Teresa, a sixteenth-century mystic and Carmelite nun who is known as the Little Flower and who once said, "After my death, I will let fall a shower of roses from heaven." Shortly after smelling the roses in her car, Lueken claims St. Teresa visited her in her bedroom. The visions continued for two years, and, in addition to St. Teresa, the Virgin Mary began appearing to the Queens housewife. The Virgin told Lueken to hold prayer vigils in her honor outside of St. Robert Bellarmine Church in Bayside, which was Lueken's parish. The Virgin Mary also told Veronica Lueken that she wanted a Basilica built under the name of Our Lady of Roses, Mary Help of Mothers.

The vigils began on June 18, 1970. But they were not well received by the parish priests, who objected to the crowds huddling in the darkness. The neighbors didn't like it either, and the police were frequently summoned to disperse the crowds. In 1975, the Baysiders, a term Lueken and her followers came to be called, began to meet monthly at the park in Flushing that was the site of the 1964 World's Fair. They congregated at a bench commemorating the Vatican pavilion, where Michelangelo's "Pieta" was proudly displayed during the fair. Ever since, the monthly vigils have attracted crowds ranging from a few hundred to ten thousand—depending on the weather. Pilgrims come from all over the world, and the Baysiders have grown into a supercult, and a thorn in the side of the Church.

The Baysiders are not happy with the state of the Catholic Church. They consider Vatican II to have been a serious mistake, and they denounce the changes it instituted, such as: saying the Mass in English, sitting while praying during the Mass instead of kneeling, receiving Communion in the hand, and increasing the role of lay people, especially women, during the liturgy. The Baysiders believe that Satan was present at Vatican II and had excessive influence over it. They believe television, rock music, women's slacks, New York City, and the United Nations are all works of the Devil. They are convinced that millions of children have been kidnapped by Devil worshipers. They think that Pope John Paul I was poisoned and that Pope John Paul II is in danger from evil men working inside the Vatican. The Baysiders also hate commies, think glastnost is a clever deception, and are fully convinced we are living in the final days.

All in all, the Baysiders are not a happy lot.

Despite official condemnation by the Church—or because of it—throngs of pilgrims continue to flock to the vigils. Three years ago, the Bishop of Brooklyn issued a strong statement condemning the movement of Mary worshipers, claiming there is no credibility to the apparitions. But still they come, by the bus loads.

Last week, on the night of December 7, the eve of the Feast of the Immaculate Conception, about 250 people gathered for three hours of prayer, during which time the wind-chill factor dipped to nine degrees below zero. They knelt on the frozen earth and recited seven complete rosaries before a fiberglass Madonna. One woman said she saw forty luminous doves fly over the nearby trees. She also claimed that last year her blue rosary beads turned gold through prayer. Some people say they have been coming for years and have never seen the Virgin, but they still believe—one man said he believed before he ever attended a vigil; he just knew in his heart that the apparitions were authentic. Many of the pilgrims snap photos of the sky during the vigils, trying to capture messages from the Virgin. If the image captured on film amounts to nothing more than a string of lights, than the lights would be interpreted as representing a rosary.

Veronica Lueken lives a sheltered life. She has become a recluse, and her poor health permits her to attend only three or four vigils a year. Lueken claims the Virgin has told her New York is going to be rocked by an earthquake, terrorism will sweep across the United States, and there will be a World War III. And yes, someday Bayside will be more famous than Fatima, which sounds like a case of shrine envy on Lueken's part.

What does this Baysider movement mean? I think it indicates that the Baysiders have lost faith in the Catholic Church and are desperately trying to recapture the faith of their youth. They look around their neighborhoods and the world and hate what they see and so they look for someone to blame, and they found a culprit named Satan. Attending the vigils makes them feel special and protected from the evils that are threatening their lives. They want a heavenly mother who will watch over them and guide them, and their imaginations honor that desire.

These truly are crazy times. Famines in Africa and natural disasters around the globe are killing people at a rate that can not be comprehended. Violence and crime in the streets, and fraud and corruption in business and government are commonplace. War is imminent. Ancient religions enslave women and turn mere mortal men into living Gods. People who have visions of God and his mother receive uncritical press coverage and attract huge followings. But then again, maybe these times aren't crazy, and life on earth today is as it always has been—business as usual.

Thursday, December 13—10:00 A.M.

Some facts and figures from today's newspapers. Madonna's income for 1990 will top thirty-nine million bucks. (In the previous three years, she earned a total of fifty million dollars.) Her "Justify My Love" video, selling at ten bucks a pop, has already sold more than a quarter of a million copies. Draw your own conclusion.

During the past six days, fresh violence between Hindus and Muslims throughout India has resulted in more than two hundred deaths. Twenty-three people were killed yesterday, two of them burned to death. Frenzied mobs are attacking each other with knives, axes, shotguns, spears, rocks, and homemade bombs. The brutality is unbelievable. One report indicated that even an infant child was axed to death during this new wave of violence. Hindu fundamentalists continue to demand that the 400-year-old Muslim mosque in Ayodhya be torn down and replaced with a Hindu temple. The death toll for the past thirteen months now tops 1,400 people.

Christmas is coming—ho, ho, ho.

Friday, December 14—3:00 P.M.

"Friends and Lovers" was canceled. NBC is replacing it with a new game show called "Roll of the Dice." The roll of my life's dice has been coming up snake eyes lately—"Craps, you lose," it seems to be shouting.

Tuesday, December 18—9:10 A.M.

I feel the jingle bell blues setting in. Don't bet on peace on earth for this Christmas.

Just in time for the annual celebration of the birth of Jesus, comes this message from a disciple of the Savior: "We need to re-establish a confederate state of America as a white, Christian republic."

That little bigoted gem came from the mouth of a seventy-year-old former fertilizer salesman named Byron De La Beckwith. Old Byron made the papers today because he was arrested yesterday in connection with the 1963 shooting death of civil rights leader Medgar Evers. Byron doesn't like blacks . . . or Jews, Asians, or any race of people who are not white. Evers, who was the field secretary for the Mississippi branch of the National Association for the Advancement of Colored People, was shot in the back with a high-powered rifle as he stood in the carport of his Jackson home on June 12, 1963.

Shortly after the murder, Beckwith was arrested and charged with the shooting. Beckwith's rifle was found in a thicket across the street from Evers's home; the FBI matched fresh prints from the rifle and its scope with those of Beckwith's. Witnesses also saw Beckwith near the Evers's home just days before the shooting. He was tried twice in 1964, and both all-white juries deadlocked on verdicts. The slaying was a galvanizing event in the civil rights struggles of the early 1960s, drawing national attention to the South and its turbulent race relations. In 1967, Beckwith ran for lieutenant governor and introduced himself at rallies as "the boy they say shot that nigger Medgar Evers," then winked. Still, 34,675 people voted for him. The murder charge was dropped in 1969.

Byron De La Beckwith is a member of a white supremacist church that believes whites are the true Israelites assigned by God to rule over "dusky" races. Beckwith says he'll fight the charges "tooth, nail, and claw." He charged the prosecutors with bowing to pressure from "a handful of Jews, white trash, and several negroes and non-white immigrants." He said, "All this is nonsense and just something to beat the public drum and make the lower forms of life get violent against the country club set."

Hatred, hatred—all around us there is hatred. At this time of year, people like to hide the hatred behind pine trees, wreaths, and colorful decorations. They can hide it, but they can't stop it. Jesus couldn't; nor can those who celebrate his birth by participating in a shopping frenzy.

Bah humbug!

In other news, over the weekend Haiti elected a Roman Catholic priest as it's new President. Preacher-politicians make me nervous. Anyway, I think it will take a lot more than priestly magic to save Haiti. I'm sure he'll be living in exile by next Christmas.

Friday, December 21—8:05 A.M.

Yesterday, the President of the United States met with members of Congress at the White House. During their discussions about the Gulf crisis, Bush said, "If we get into an armed situation, [Saddam is] going to get his ass kicked."

An armed situation—that is the White House whitewash for war—seems inevitable. The reasons for war, as articulated by the administration, are confusing and far from compelling.

Just four shopping days left 'til Christmas.

Joy to the world.

Saturday, December 22—10:40 A.M.

The evil and the armed draw near
The weather smells of their hate
And the houses smell of our fear.

That comes from a long poem penned by W. H. Auden titled, "For the Time Being," which, with its metaphysical musings and theological underpinnings, many consider to be one of the most powerful expressions of the meaning of Christmas.

What is the meaning of Christmas? I'll let you, my sweet, little Kate, answer that question.

CHRISTMAS

by

Kate Ryan

Christmas to me is when you get to see kindness and other characteristics in people you don't normally see. It is when you give out of your heart and not just to receive. I feel it is important to lend a hand to those who are less fortunate. I just think it is unbelievable how one of the richest countries in the world can stand their [sic] and let the poor people rot away. I like the idea that on Christmas we all can help out. You have to admit that even if you don't believe in Jesus, it is the prime reason for the season; in fact, what if God doesn't exist and the Bible was all made up, we still got Christmas from it. So I feel we should celebrate it properly; what is the purpose of going out and getting wasted? We have blown the holiday way out of proportion. Christmas to most people is getting gifts, even to me it is. No one stops to think about poor Jesus who was hung on the cross to save us from our sins. Or even the non-religious side of the holiday; giving of ourselves, sharing, loving, etc. . . . . Things that should be done on a daily basis.

Christmas I think, is the most joyous part of the year because of all the things I just mentioned in the last line; on the other hand, doesn't it make you sad that this time of the year has the most highest suicide rate? I wish the world didn't have to be like that and everyone could live in harmony. Once again, that is why I love Christmas, because when I think of Christmas, I think of peace.

I bet you don't remember writing that, but you did, a couple of years ago. You spent Christmas with me. I recently had bought a computer and was teaching you how to use it. I suggested you write something. You asked what. I suggested something about Christmas, what it meant to you. You ordered me out of the room. "I hate people looking over my shoulder when I'm doing something," was the way you put it as you pointed to the door. In less than fifteen minutes you announced that you were finished and that I should come read what you had written. I was so touched by your feelings and ability to express yourself that I never erased your creation from the computer. To this day, it is still filed under "KRXMAS."

If you asked me to write something about Christmas, I would be at a total loss for words. Because my thoughts on the subject run around my mind like a hamster in a cage, I could never express my feelings as simply and clearly as you did. And I fancy myself a writer, though in reality I'm not much more than a typist.

Why did I just put myself down like that? I think the answer lies in a manger in Bethlehem. We are about to celebrate the birth of, as you put it, "poor Jesus who was hung on the cross to save us from our sins." That is what this season of joy, peace, and happiness is all about: sin—ugly, damnable sin and its insipid cousins guilt, fear, and shame.

"No matter what you do, no matter how hard you try, you can never be good enough to be pleasing in the eyes of God." That repulsive opinion was blazed upon my impressionable young mind by an ordained minister of God the Creator, so it had to be true. I was about seven at the time, and the pastor delivered that toxic message to me and my classmates as we prepared to receive the sacrament of Penance. The subject of the priest's cheery little talk was "original sin." The pastor possessed full, certain knowledge of the unknowable. He walked tall.

His thrust was simple: because Adam and Eve had disobeyed God (even though they were tricked and fooled by the lies of the Devil), they lost God's friendship, the right to heaven, and His original gift to them of divine grace was stripped away from them—and us, also. Everyone born after man's fall in the garden has entered the world without God's original gift of divine grace, which was to have been our birthright. Instead, each of us has inherited a share of the guilt and punishment incurred as a result of Adam and Eve's sin. Each of us, the priest said, is born with a stain on our souls.

Born dirty! The story didn't seem to add up, didn't seem to make sense: why should I be "stained" because of something a couple of people did a very long, long time ago? It seemed like a lot of misery over an apple. But you couldn't question the pastor. He seemed very sure. My parents looked up to him. He was chosen by God to lead us miserable sinners to Heaven: he knew the way. He had the answers; he knew the truth. I was stained; I could never be pleasing to God.

Teaching kids they are dirty and displeasing to their Creator is tantamount to child abuse. The Church has been in the child abuse business for a very long time. During an altar boy training class, Fr. Andrews said,

> If you read the fifth chapter of Paul's Epistle to the Galatians, you will realize that all things considered, the life of a Christian in this world is nothing less than a continuous battle. A Christian's greatest adversary, however, is none other than himself. There is nothing more difficult for him to overcome than his own flesh and his own will, which are, by nature, inclined to all evil. I need to be saved a dozen or more times a day, usually from myself. I am more dangerous to my own self than the rest of the world, for it is up to me and me alone whether or not I condemn my soul to death and exclude it from the Kingdom of God . . . and the same is true for each of you young men.

I am all alone against my evil inclinations and the evil world; it's an endless, almost hopeless battle—I'm doomed. Or so I thought as a kid.

Sr. Saint Dorothy was even more gloomy and morbid than Fr. Andrews. She used to end our morning prayers with a happy little prayer written by Saint Catherine of Genoa: "Straining to leave this life of woe with anguish sharp and deep I cry, I die because I do not die." I'm sure some New Age spiritual practitioner can go on for hours about the high level of spirituality this mystic nun must have achieved, but please—does it make any sense to expose young children to such dark concepts? I say it does far more harm than good.

Thanks to our screwed up culture, kids have enough to worry about, like: is my penis big enough or are my breasts big enough? If not, you are inferior—that is what society is telling our youth. If you are fat or ugly, society says nobody wants you. If your family is poor, that, according to society, is your worth. The message is crystal clear: The way you are is not okay; you better become the way we say you should be. On top of all this cultural pressure and shame, comes the church with its gospel of spiritual inferiority. With the one-two punch delivered by church and culture, it is no wonder kids are so messed up.

Before I was a teenager, I knew I was a failure—in the eyes of the world and in the eyes of heaven.

I hated myself.

Father Andrews and Sr. Saint Dorothy were drawing on a long and cherished religious heritage, which was reinforced every day during the Mass. Just before receiving Holy Communion, which we believed to be the Body of Christ, we prayed a prayer that went something like this: "Let not the partaking of Thy Body, O Lord Jesus Christ, which I, though unworthy, presume to receive, turn to my judgment and condemnation; but through Thy goodness, may it become a safeguard and an effective remedy, both of my soul and body." This sense of unworthiness and fear of condemnation so gripped my imagination, that I became terrified if I accidentally chewed the communion wafer, fearing that Jesus would become mad at me. After we prayed that prayer, the priest would say three times, *Domine, non sum dignus, ut intres sub tectum meum; sed tantum dic verbo, et sanabitur anima mea,* which means: "Lord, I am not worthy that Thou shouldst come under my roof; but only say the word, and my soul will be healed." I really believed I was unworthy; of what and why, I was less certain.

The world is poisoned, and so are each of us. We need an antidote. We need salvation. We need a savior. Christmas celebrates the bringing together of divinity and human flesh, and that combination—Jesus—is that antidote and will save us from ourselves, from the snares of the world, and from eternal damnation. That, dear Kate, is the bottom line of Christianity.

It is also nonsense that was nurtured in the mind of St. Paul, who wrote a major part of the New Testament. According to St. Paul, sin and death entered the world at the beginning of history, and ever since then the world has been in league with the forces of evil. From the moment in which Adam relinquished the domain God had entrusted to him, Satan became the prince and even the god of the times. Man is therefore surrounded and even penetrated by a deceitful world, which is in opposition to the Spirit of God and whose wisdom is naught but folly. Its peace is but a sham and its fashions pass away, as do its desires. The final result is despair, which leads to death. The only escape is Jesus.

By the fourth century the Christian theory of contempt for the world was fully developed. St. Augustine was convinced of the "decrepitude of the world," which leads only to: "bitter worries, disorders, afflictions, fear, mad joys, dissensions, trials, wars, ambushes, rages, enmities, duplicities, flatteries, frauds, theft, pillage, treachery, pride, ambition, envy, homicides, parricides, cruelty, savagery, perversity, lust, rudeness, imprudence, lewdness, debaucheries, adulteries, incests, and so many violations and effronteries against the nature of both sexes that one blushes to name them, sacrileges, heresies, blasphemies, perjuries, oppressions of the innocent, calumnies, deceptions, prevarications, robberies, and many other crimes which do not come to mind but which are nevertheless ever-present in this sad human life." Jesus—that sounds like a plot summary from "General Hospital" or "The Young and the Restless." St. Augustine saw sexual intercourse as a "mass of perdition." Thanks to lust, every child was soiled at the moment of conception. Imagine, we are all damned in the womb.

Kate, to give you an idea how deep the contempt for the world is in the Christian tradition, I'm going to throw some quotations your way. The authors were saints, mystics, monks, nuns, priests, and even a few Protestants.

Man is born for work, for suffering, for fear, and—what is worse—for death.
—Cardinal Lotario di Segni

Miserable life, decrepit life, impure life sullied by humours, exhausted by grief, dried by heat, swollen by meats, mortified by fasts, dissolved by pranks, consumed by sadness, distressed by worries, blunted by security, bloated by riches, cast down by poverty . . .

—Jean de Fecamp

[Earthly existence is an] exterior exile from which we are delivered by death in order that we might enter the interior country.

—Peter Damian (died 1072), Camoldolese hermit

Only that which is detached and separated from all creatures is pure, for all creatures are nought, and thus they are defiled.

—Meister Eckhart (1260–1328), mystic/priest

Lift your heart above the ooze and slime of carnal pleasures—all that the world has to offer cannot appease your desire. You live in a wretched vale of tears where pleasure is mixed with suffering, smiles with tears, joy with sadness, where no heart has ever found total joy, for the world deceives and lies.

—Heinrich Susso (1295–1366), Dominican priest

No sin is as abominable as that of the flesh.

—St. Catherine of Siena (1347–1380), Dominican Tertiary
who was supposedly imprinted with the sacred Stigmata

Our life here below is naught but misery. The whole world is filled with lies. . . . In the midst of pleasures proposed by the demon, there is naught but sorrow, problems, and contradictions.

—St. Teresa of Avila (1515–1582), Carmelite nun/mystic

Every hour of life has its pain. When the sea of life is calm it should be all the more feared, for in the midst of calm lurks the storm. Its quiet and tranquil aspect hides waves higher than mountains. . . . Life is like war . . . because it is so perilous. . . . Men deceive us, fate fools us, animals assail us, and the elements bring death more often than not. In fact, who would ever have guessed the number of invisible things that wage a secret war against us, or divine their number, their ingeniousness, their wiles, or their strength?

—Luis de Leon (1528–1591) Augustinian monk

Alas, man is born on earth for an unjust fate. All other living beings know peace, but man knows neither rest nor respite. He rushes anxiously toward death, year in year out.

—Petrarch (1304–1373), Tuscan poet/philosopher

He who knows himself well, despises himself. The highest and most useful science is the exact knowledge and contempt of the self. Life on earth is truly wretched. Since eating, drinking, sleeping, resting, working are subject to all the needs of [human] nature, life is truly a great misery and a terrible affliction for any pious man who would like to detach himself from earthly things and deliver himself from all sin. . . . Woe to them who do not know their own misery, and even more woe to them who love this perishable life and its misery.

—Thomas a Kempis (1380–1471), Augustinian monk

(Kate—the above quote comes from a popular devotional book titled *The Imitation of Christ*. While its authorship is in question, its popularity isn't. Its success was enormous even before the invention of the printing press. There are as many as two hundred printed editions from the sixteenth century. It was translated into French as many as sixty times in a period of four hundred years. I was given a copy of the book by Fr. Andrews when I first indicated a desire to be a priest. It was from this book that I developed a scorn for earthly life and the affirmation that life is but a sequence of ills and evils. As a teenager, I pondered the quasi-suicidal question the book raises: "How can one love a life filled with so much bitterness and subject to so many evils and calamities? How can one call life that which endangers so much pain and so much death?" Hundreds of thousands of readers have meditated on these words for several hundred years.)

> When He wishes us to know that man is the greatest danger on earth the Savior says: "avoid man as if he were the worst of all evils." . . . Every wild beast has its own special way of doing harm, but man contains within himself all the types of harm possible. And what is more, man is worse than the devil himself.
> —Rudolph of Saxony, fourteenth-century Carthusian monk

The *Spiritual Exercises* of St. Ignatius Loyola, written around 1522 and read by me around 1962, suggests that one should beseech the Blessed Virgin to bestow "knowledge of the world in order that [one] might loathe it and [thus detach one's self from] worldly and vain things." The sixteenth-century Dominican monk and popular writer Louis of Granada suggested we declare war against the senses, the flesh, and the earth. Christians, he wrote, should treat their bodies "roughly and rigorously. Is not dead flesh preserved with salt and myrrh, which are bitter, in order that it not spoil and swell with worms? In like manner the body becomes tainted and filled with vice if it is treated with tenderness and delicacy." He proposes a "holy hatred of self" and the mortification of all passions, which he calls the "sensory appetite," which includes "all natural emotions such as love, hate, joy, sadness, fear, hope, anger and other such feelings." No feminist, Louis of Granada sees the sensory appetite as the Eve within us, "the weakest part of our souls and the most inclined to evil, the one through which the ancient serpent attacks our inner Adam." The message is clear: the drama of the Original Sin is continually reenacted throughout each person's life, which is why each of us needs Christmas Day, each of us needs a Savior to be born for us.

> We are all made of mud, and this mud is not just on the hem of our gown, or on the sole of our boots, or in our shoes. We are full of it, we are nothing but mud and filth both inside and outside.
> —John Calvin (1509–1564), Protestant theologian

> In praising conjugal life, I deny having conceded to nature that there be no sin in it at all. On the contrary, I say that both flesh and blood, having been corrupted by Adam, are conceived and are born in sin . . . and that conjugal duty is never accomplished without sin. But God spares married couples through grace, because the conjugal order is His own creation. He preserves, by His own

means, all the good with which He has blessed marriage, and this even in the midst of sin.

—Martin Luther (1483-1546), Augustinian
priest/hermit-turned-Protestant reformer

Self-knowledge progresses most when one is crushed and abashed by the knowledge of one's own calamity, poverty, nudity and ignominy, for there is no danger that man can go too far in abasing himself.

—John Calvin

* * *

How's that for a merry collection of Christmas thoughts!

You will not hear much discussion about sin during these festive holidays. While Auden's poem expresses concern about barbaric superstitions and a single spark that might ruin everything, it nonetheless celebrates the sacredness of the mundane as he challenges the readers of his oratorio to recognize the miracle of God's entry into all that is routine, ordinary, and earthly. It was written fifty years ago, during World War II, when the evil and the armed drew near, just the way they are today. Hate and fear are still in the air.

While Christians prepare to celebrate the birth of the Prince of Peace, they, along with the rest of the world, hear the drums of war beating. Loudly. Nearly 300,000 American men and women are now in the Middle East preparing to fight what promises to be a deadly war. Not even a shot has been fired, and already seventy-seven Americans have died in various accidents. Just yesterday, twenty-one sailors drowned. They were returning to their ship via a ferry from the port city of Jaffa in Israel, where they were enjoying a day of R&R, when the ferry suddenly capsized and sank.

The chaos of life does not stop for Christmas. Last night, in the suburbs of Detroit, a man and six of his nine children where burned to death in their home during the middle of the night. Investigators believe the Christmas tree fell over, and a light bulb exploded and ignited the blaze. The dead children ranged in age from four to twelve. The mother and three other children escaped. You can count on a couple of stories like this every Christmas season.

I hate Christmas and its frenzied gift-buying, forced family togetherness, social pressures, and its insistence on phony good cheer. For me, Christmas means the old year is dying and a new one is about to be born. It is a witness to the sun's diminishing and return. The winter solstice reminds us that we're mortal creatures and have no control over the great forces that drive and govern us. But we are not weak, cowering victims of fate and chance, we are brave creatures, aware of these limits, joyous in spite of them.

A couple of days ago, I received a Christmas card from a friend whom I have not seen in a number of years. He used to design sets for television shows. He was very good at it; in fact, he won two Emmy Awards. The guy was vibrant, creative, and full of life—that was before he was diagnosed with AIDS. He left Hollywood and has been holding onto life in a peaceful valley near Carmel, California, where his lover and life's companion tenderly cares for him. Tucked into the card was a short brochure titled, "The Solstitial and Equinoctial Seasons," written by Frank R. Zindler. It was a bit too scientific in tone for me; it had illustrations of planets, axle poles, and stuff like that. But once you got past the technical information—like "When all the forces that shaped the early earth had been resolved, they left it spinning on an axis tilted 23.5 degrees from the perpendicular"—there were four short paragraphs that I found very informative and helpful, so I thought I would end this morbid letter by sharing them with you.

> Toward the end of the last Ice Age, people living in the Northern Hemisphere began to notice that at midday in the summer the sun appeared to soar high above the southern horizon. In the winter, it barely rose above the horizon. It was noted also that in the summer the days were longer, whereas nights were longer in the winter. How to account for these facts? Since the ancient watchers of the skies knew nothing of the sphericity of the earth—let alone that it spun on an axis out of plumb with the plane of its orbit—they developed mythological explanations. The sun was a god. After all, it appeared to move across the sky every day. Everyone "knew" that movement was the hallmark of life. The sun was alive—divinely alive.
>
> When the sun was high in the midday sky, the god was healthy and vivifying. When the solar disk sank to its slowest point in the year (when the earth's north axial pole was tilted maximally away from the sun), its feeble rays could scarcely scatter the winter's chill at midday: the god was dying. For a short while, the sun ("sol" in Latin) appeared to stand still ("stitium," in Latin) before "reviving" and starting its journey back north. And so this shortest day of the northern year (often falling on December 25 in the old Julian calender, and on December 21 in our Gregorian calender) was named the winter "solstice." Six months later, on the longest day of the northern year, the sun once again appeared to stand still—now at its highest altitude in the midday sky—and that event was named the summer "solstice."
>
> Midway between the winter and summer solstice, about March 21 and September 23, the length of the day equalled that of the night. These points in the calender were termed the vernal (spring) and autumnal "equinoxes" (from the Latin "aequinoctium," equality between day and night). For the ancients, these dates were occasion for fertility and harvest festivals, respectively.

(OK, Kate, here comes the really good part!)

> Even though the solstices and the equinoxes do not mark the motions of a god traveling across the heavens, they do mark the progress of the space-ship we call earth in its passage through the void. They note the natural pulse of life as it has evolved, sustained, and carried along the same celestial path for time out of mind. As we pass these four milestones on our annual journey about the life-sustaining fusion-fires of the sun—the only star we know that heats the blood of self-conscious beings—we reflect upon our astronomical uniqueness. We appear to be alone, in a universe devoid of plan or purpose. There is no cosmic intelligence that counts how many rides we complete on the merry-go-

round whose axle is the sun. Only we can do the counting. We only have each other. For this reason, it is the custom for many as they mark the passage of the solstices and the equinoxes to pause for celebration: to celebrate and cherish their fellow travelers, to celebrate the wondrous fact that they are part of the human species—the only species known that can understand and appreciate the implausibility of its own existence.

Wow! My gift to myself this Christmas is to cleanse myself of the toxic waste of religion, which covered my being with a crust of ugliness and shame, and to appreciate my own existence and uniqueness. This Christmas, I will not look for a Savior in a manger; I'll look for the child within me.

Monday, December 24—10:00 P.M.

It's Christmas Eve and I think I just heard a mouse stirring. But not much else. The silence seems loud. It feels strange being alone tonight. Inside the darkened womb of my home, there is no Christmas music playing, no tree lights twinkling, no gifts beckoning, no family celebrating, no bells jingling, no children anticipating, no cookies baking, no Santa coming.

There is only stillness and sadness.

For me, it's a silent night, a lonely night.

But I'm not depressed, just empty. No, empty is not right. I'm isolated. Shit, even in Baghdad, the capital of Iraq, there are people celebrating Christmas; in fact, there are gaily decorated Christmas trees in store windows of that militant Muslim country. People in Hindu India, in secular Japan, in atheistic Russia— people all around the globe are getting ready for Christmas.

But I'm not. Is there something wrong with me? Am I missing something? Or is it only that my beliefs only let me see certain things, and also prevent me from seeing other things?

While the rest of the world prepares to commemorate the birth of God in man, I've been sitting alone reading a poem written by Thomas Hardy titled "God's Funeral." In this poem, the God of Christianity is being escorted to his grave followed by a long funeral procession. The mourner's thoughts are overheard by the protagonist of the poem. Most of the bereaved are discussing the history of monotheism from the standpoint of higher criticism of the Bible. Among the funeral swarm, however, the protaganist sees many people who refuse to believe that God has died.

> Some in the background then I saw,
> Sweet women, youths, men, all incredulous,
> Who claimed: "This is a counterfeit of straw,
> This requiem mockery! Still he lives to us!"

I could not buy their faith: and yet
Many I had known: with all I sympathized;
And though struck speechless, I did not forget
That what was mourned for, I, too, long had prized.

Like Hardy, I had prized what I now deny, and I share with the poet his ambiguity. The new scientific view of life holds that an initial energy operating without consciousness or order produced the motions of the stars and the long development of the forms of life found upon our planet. The old theological view claims that an intelligent and omnipotent Being created and ruled the universe. I'm partial to the new view, but acutely conscious always of the old view. Within me there is this dialectic tension. I can hardly be labeled a genuine atheist, because I doubt real atheists are so concerned about what they have rejected. I suppose I am fundamentally religious and essentially possessed by a state of mind in which the old view of life and the new one contest without conclusion.

I wish it were otherwise. Thomas Hardy, who was born in Dorset, England in 1842, sums it up best in a poem titled "The Oxen," which tells of an old Christmas story that recounts how each year the oxen kneel at the hour of Christ's nativity.

Christmas Eve, and twelve of the clock,
    "Now they are all on their knees,"
An elder said as we sat in a flock
    By the embers in hearthside ease.

We pictured the meek and mild creatures where
    They dwelt in their strawy pen,
Nor did it occur to one of us there
    To doubt they were kneeling then.

So fair a fancy few would weave
    In these years! Yet, I feel,
If someone said on Christmas Eve,
    "Come; see the oxen kneel,

"In the lonely barton by yonder coomb
    Our childhood used to know,"
I should go with him in the gloom,
    Hoping it might be so.

Hardy's belief is a disbelief in the truth of Chrisitianity; his emotion is the wish that it was true. Me too. If I should be asked tonight to go to a barn at midnight to see the oxen kneel, I would go "in gloom, hoping it might be so."

Thomas Hardy, remembering the Christmas story of his childhood, cannot help keeping in mind the immense universe of nineteenth-century science, which not only makes such a story seem untrue, but increases one's reason for wishing that it was true.

Merry Christmas, Kate.

Tuesday, December 25—10:45 A.M.

Only a little more than twelve hours to go, and this Christmas will be history.

This morning, I was thinking about one particular Christmas day from my childhood. Christmas was always an exciting and wonderful time in our home. My parents made it a holy time and a magic time. That is, they never let us forget Christmas was a day of profound religious significance, but, at the same time, they entered fully into the Santa Claus way of celebrating the day. They balanced the secular and the sacred. In their wisdom, they knew that the gifts under the tree were more important to us than the baby in the crib in the hearts and minds of young children . . . and Christmas is for young children. As we got older, they tried to focus more and more of our attention away from the tree and onto the crib. For the most part, the first dozen or so Christmas Days of my life have all blended together in one happy, warm memory.

Except for one, which stands tall among all the others.

I was eight years old. Maybe nine. All I wanted for Christmas was a new bike. A big Schwinn two-wheeler. I started a full-court press shortly after Thanksgiving, never letting an opportunity for reminding my parents about my Christmas wish slip by. Well, the big day finally arrived, and I rushed downstairs fully expecting to see my new bike near the tree, fully realizing that it would be too big to be gift wrapped.

It wasn't there.

And, there was no evidence whatsoever that I was getting a bike for Christmas. My heart sunk.

One by one, my parents and brothers and sisters made their way downstairs, and we all gathered around the tree. It was time to pass out the gifts. I was chosen to play Santa, which meant I was in charge of distribution. I would pick out a gift and read the tag out loud. "To Mom, from Chris." "To Matthew from Santa." And so it went, one package at a time. One was barely opened, and the next announced. I performed my role with a smile, but inside my heart was broken from disappointment. There would be no bike this Christmas. When all the gifts had been handed out, and we started to clean up the mess of torn wrapping paper, I held out a faint hope that at the last possible second, the bike would be wheeled into the living room from some secret hiding place.

But there was no last-second surprise.

Most of the family headed for the kitchen, where my father had begun to make a big breakfast of pancakes and eggs. Just as we were about to sit down to eat, my father said, "Chris, do me a favor. Go down to the basement and bring up a folding chair, cause I'm sure Bud from next store will be dropping in any second now." "Sure thing, Dad," I responded. As I got to the bottom of the stairs, I saw it—a bike: a big, shiny Schwinn bicycle with white wall tires. I let out a scream of excitement, and I instantly heard laughter coming from upstairs; they all knew about it!

There will be no last-second surprises this Christmas. Just another day alone. Just another meaningless Christmas.

Wednesday, December 26—9:00 A.M.

On Christmas Eve, while I was quoting Thomas Hardy to you, a man in Queens, New York, was walking up his driveway carrying a load of Christmas presents. On his mind was nothing more, I'm sure, than good will and cheer. Out of the dark, he was approached by two men, one carrying a shotgun. On their minds, robbery. Within seconds, gunshots burst through the silent night, and the man with the gifts was lying on the ground, his stomach torn open by the thug's bullets. He died within hours. The victim was a thirty-one-year-old immigrant from Ethiopia. He was one of nine New Yorkers killed in separate noxious episodes on Christmas Eve and Christmas Day. Among them, a twenty-month-old baby girl in the Bronx was beaten to death by her mother. A sixty-seven-year-old woman died after being punched by her son at a Christmas party. A cab driver was shot during an argument in a Queens restaurant over a fare.

For many, dear Kate, this is not a time of peace and joy, but of hate and fear; for them, noel rhymes easily with hell.

Friday, December 28—1:25 P.M.

Hey, kiddo, during this time of global crisis and conflict, guess what Holy Mother the Church is up to. Give up, you'll never guess—they are making saints! Well, at least debating sainthood for one of its long-dead daughters.

The "holy" lady in question is Queen Isabella I of Spain. Isabella is mostly remembered for sending Christopher Columbus on his voyage in 1492 and opening up the New World for the spread of Catholicism. But the Queen of Spain is also remembered for expelling Jews and Muslims from her country and for her role in the Inquisition, which began during her rule with her husband, Ferdinand II. She forced Jews and Muslims at the point of a sword to convert to Christianity or die. For Jews now living in Spain, she is a symbol of intolerance. In the eyes of Muslims, she is more a demon than a saint.

Supporters of sainthood for Isabella are hoping to obtain it by 1992, in time for the Church's plans to celebrate 500 years of Christianity in the Americas. I see little reason to celebrate; the anniversary should be marked by reflecting on the way Isabella and Columbus exploited the native population and destroyed their way of life.

Well, as with our friend from New York, Pierre Toussaint, the hunt for a miracle has begun. What bullshit!

Sunday, December 30—4:00 P.M.

Why do people hate being alone on Sundays? Most suicides occur on Sundays, and, in addition, they reach a particularly high point at Christmas. Why? The social norms make it a moral responsibility to be with others at these times, and those who cannot fulfill this obligation feel unhappy, so much so that some kill themselves.

Only he or she is free who can be alone on a Sunday during Christmas time. I am not free.

And television doesn't help. Turn on the tube during the Christmas season and you'll see a nauseating series of heartwarming family encounters. Sitcom families will hug each other in complete acceptance and understanding. Unconditional love rules the airwaves. For TV families, life is a Hallmark Card commercial. Too much Christmas-week television viewing can be dangerous to your emotional health. As we watch these wish-fulfillment fantasies, we can't help but notice that our actual lives do not remotely resemble those being portrayed on the tube. In real life, Christmas is usually a big disappointment. Conflicts don't get resolved. Compassion does not abound. Family visits are marred by bickering.

Watching television during Christmas week is bound to make you want to die. Frank Capra's film classic *It's a Wonderful Life* is broadcast twelve times a day, or so it seems. James Stewart plays a small-town banker who is driven to commit suicide on Christmas Eve. Just as he is about to jump off a bridge, a neophyte angel named Clarence appears. The angel shows him what a difference his life has made, and teaches him his value as a human being. The optimistic tale demonstrates the really astounding lengths people will go to nurture us and give us money. Sure, just like in real life. Maybe many of the people who have committed suicide during this past week fully expected Clarence to come along and stop them.

Christmas reminds us that it is not a wonderful life; it's a so-so life at best. For this brief period of time, people attempt to be a little more loving, a little more compassionate, a little more considerate, and a little kinder. Sadly, the effort is superficial and fleeting, a mere pause in the cruelty of daily life. Before the needles fall off the decorated Christmas trees, all will be back to normal, except for those who decided not to continue.

Tuesday, January 1, 1991—10:30 A.M.

Happy New Year, daughter.

The first day of this New Year is darkened by thick clouds of violence and war.

Last night, during the first five hours of the new year, seven people were killed in New York City. Six shot; one stabbed. During the past year, it is estimated that over 22,000 Americans were murdered.

And in the Middle East, Iraq has amassed 530,000 troops in and near occupied Kuwait. Arrayed against them is a multinational force that now totals more than 580,000 soldiers, most of them young American men and women. Imagine —over a million people, armed to the teeth with the most technologically advanced weapons ever manufactured, waiting in that arid hellhole to blow each other to smithereens. I heard on the radio today a story about a company that manufactures rubber linings for use in baby cribs has been awarded a defense department contract to supply the army with 16,000 body bags. Somebody thinks war is coming.

But hey, what the hell, there are a lot of college Bowl games on the tube today.

Oh, I forgot to tell you. The other day, the doorbell rang, and, when I opened the door, there stood a nicely dressed, well-groomed man, perhaps in his early thirties. He sported a big, broad smile, and in a far too cheery and energetic voice he said, "Good morning sir! My name is Bob and I'd like to give you the latest edition of the *Christian Yellow Pages*. Would you like one?" Reading my befuddled look, he left me no time for a response as he almost instantly continued, "It's a business phone book that lists all the Christian businessmen in your area. It's a terrific way of finding out who you can really trust when you need life insurance, or have to have your car fixed, or need a tooth cavity filled. We got it all covered: everything from barbers to bakers, from beauticians to pediatricians!" His broad smile grew even broader when I said, "Sure, I'd love to have one." I took the book, and as he started to turn away he said, "God bless you." I said, "God bless you. Now I know who not to call for insurance, brakes, or cavities." Instantly, he wore the befuddled look, and I the broad smile. Before he could respond, I slammed the door shut.

Christian Yellow Pages—what an ingenious idea. The publishers parlayed religious bigotry into a money-making proposition. The book listed every kind of business and service you would find in a normal "yellow pages," only the proprietors believed that Jesus is Lord. Maybe a mechanic secured from this book would lay hands on your carburetor and pray for a healing before resorting to replacing it with a new one. Bob preyed on people's fears, fears that in most business transactions we are getting swindled; but, if you are dealing with a fellow believer, you will have no need to worry, no need to fear getting ripped off. Sure. I wonder if Jim Bakker is listed under "prison ministries."

Well, kiddo, I gotta go. I have lots of resolutions to make (chuckle, chuckle).

Tuesday, January 1—3:55 P.M.

Maybe I should be making some resolutions. That's what New Year's is all about: a chance to wipe the slate clean, to start over. I realize I had my own fresh start back on July 16—wow, that's almost six months ago. Still, this might be a good time to take stock of life and make some resolutions. I have no particular resolution in mind for myself.

Perhaps I should start by stopping my futile attempts at trying to live up to someone else's fantasy of what I should be doing with my life or someone else's fantasy of how I should be behaving. There's my friend Fred: "Get back into the TV business. Get a new agent. Get a job on one of the New York soaps, and get out of debt." There's my friend Carol: "You should be writing screenplays. I bet you could make a bundle." There's my friend Albert: "Listen, I've got a great connection at Warner Brothers. I'll introduce you. Do lunch.

There's no doubt the two of you will hit it off. He could help you land a job on a sitcom. I think you gotta try something new. Sitcoms would be a natural progression for you." There's my friend Joe: "You must start making financial preparations for Kate's college education. The costs are astronomical and you can't count on her getting a full scholarship." There's my brother: "You are becoming a hermit. You never call anyone in the family. You can't cut yourself off like this." There's my sister: "I think it's California. Why not move back east? It's real here. I think that Hollywood stuff is making you crazy."

Of course, none of these people know me. Nor, for that matter, do I know any of them. Nobody knows anybody anymore. Nobody really talks. We are too frightened to say what we are really thinking, too petrified to admit we have doubts and are confused.

True confession time: I'm afraid to speak my mind. I tend to say what I think people want to hear. A couple of years ago, I was back east during Thanksgiving. My brother invited me to Thanksgiving dinner. I really didn't want to go. I just dreaded that part of the day's ritual that came just before the meal, when we all had to hold hands and say some special Thanksgiving grace—you know, thanking God for all our special blessings. I wanted to say, "Sure, I'd love to come. But, listen, I don't believe in God, I find prayers to be useless, so if you don't mind, I'd like to leave the room while everyone is saying grace before the meal." Of course, I couldn't be that honest.

A friend called a couple of months ago wanting to know whether I was interested in working on an "adult" soap opera for cable television. "Adult" means the soap would feature topless women. (By the way, the caller was a woman. Still is. Her name is Sissy; in Texas, they give girls silly names like Sissy.) So I mumbled something along the lines of: "Well, I might be. I mean as long as it's not just titillation for the sake of titillation. Sissy, you know me, I'd love to explore some really adult themes in an adult way. You know, tackle some topics that might be too controversial for network television." Despite the vagueness of my response, Sissy never pressed me about what kind of "adult themes" I would like to tackle. She just said, "Oh, yes. Definitely, I agree." "Good," I said, "because this has to be every bit as dramatic as the network soaps or it wouldn't fly." "You're right," Sissy concurred, "we need a quality product."

After we hung up, I felt lousy. But I justified myself by saying that I had to respond the way I did because I needed the money, I couldn't pass up any job. Had I the courage to be honest, my response would have sounded like this: "Oh gee, Sissy, I'm sorry. I can't imagine a project like this ever rising above the level of cheap titillation. I have a real problem with exploiting women, and that is what this kind of show will resort to. Let's face it, the name of the game will be 'how many blouses can we remove in a half hour,' not drama. SHOWTIME or HBO isn't interested in exploring mature subjects in a grown-up way. They are only looking for a way to attract more viewers. If they could, they would try to create, franchise, and televise the Woman's World Topless Basketball League. I'm sorry, I'm just not interested. For me, my work has to have some kind of social significance. Sissy, I don't mean to sound like an artistic snob, but I can't just work for a buck on stuff I don't believe in. But listen, thanks for thinking of me."

It really hurts me not to be able to reveal who I really am. It hurts having to hide behind so many stupid masks. I don't think anybody really likes me for who and what I really am, not even me. During my late teens, I pretended I went to church, because I was afraid that if my parents knew that I had stopped attending Mass, they wouldn't like me. It's funny, I didn't even admit that was the real reason back then. I told myself I was engaged in this ecclesiastical charade because I didn't want to upset my parents. There was just enough truth in that to make it sound authentic.

My friend Ron is a genuine intellectual. He lives in his books and for his writing. He was a university professor, who taught psychology and philosophy. We talk about all sorts of interesting stuff. Yet I can't tell him about my more-than-passing interest in football, that I spend most Sundays in a pigskin trance, sitting in a zombielike state in front of the TV for hours upon hours. Ron wouldn't know the difference between a screen pass and a quarterback sneak. I fear if Ron knew of my secret addiction, he would think less of me. Listen, I don't like the fact that I care so much about a bunch of huge, mean, macho, overpaid jocks trying to kill each other. Why, when he asks what I did on Sunday, can't I simply say, "I watched the Giants game, and boy, what a cardiac ending!"? Why am I so fearful?

I've even been in love with women whom I never let see the real me. I hid from them the faults I knew I had, because I feared my imperfections would drive them away. I didn't think I could ever be loved "warts and all."

God, I wish from the deepest chambers of my heart that I could be totally honest for just one day, with just one person. I would be blinded by the purity of it. I'm tired of my overblown concern with appearances, with keeping up the illusion of normalcy. Who is to say what is normal? There is this secret person living inside of me, and I'm scared to reveal his identity. In truth, I am my secrets. I'd love to sit down with my brother and tell him the truth—the truth about me. I'm sick of living a lie. I have this sneaky feeling that most people have lied for so long about so much that they have no idea they are actually living a lie.

Jesus, all around me everyone acts is if they know exactly how they ought to conduct themselves during every situation and during every moment of every god-dammed day. Wouldn't it be nice, if this New Year would see people admitting that they don't have a clue what they should be doing with their lives and admit that they are really curious know how their friends and family are actually getting on in life? I'd love to know how the handicapped do it. Wouldn't it be nice if people could stop hiding behind the roles they are playing, stop hiding their true identity from each other? Wouldn't it be nice if people stopped putting careers ahead of experiencing actual existence, stopped setting goals, and started perceiving reality? If I hear one more idiot ask me my immediate or long-range goals I'll scream! I have friends so obsessed with their goals and careers they have actually become stone-blind to life, can no longer see what is really going on around them. Life has been reduced to the habit of following plans. And the absurd part is that it doesn't really matter what plan we follow or what goal we set, as long as we have a goal and a plan.

We are like ants, scurrying madly in all directions. Did you ever notice how an ant could be marching resolutely down a sidewalk, as if a clear and certain destination were fixed in his little ant mind, and suddenly a kid places a pop stick or a toy in its path, and the ant just changes directions and continues his march, seemingly unperturbed by his sudden change in course? It seems, what is important to the ant is the marching. What is important to us is establishing our goals and executing our plans. We are like ants, and our lives have become habitual. Life has become a trance. If you doubt this daughter, the next time you are eating, stop mid-meal and ask yourself if you are hungry or if you are eating out of habit because it happens to be lunch time. Usually, with me, its the latter.

A thought just whacked me in the side of a head like a blow from the fist of Mohammed Ali: My writing sucks because I'm too damned concerned with what people will think about it. I write a few pages, then meekly show them to friends whose opinions and judgments I trust, and then I anxiously wait to hear what they have to say. I don't write, I wait—shit, I'm no writer, I'm a waiter—and I don't get any tips for the trouble. Oh for sure, my friends give me tips: "Suppose you turn this piece into a detective story. I think if there was a hot-shot detective following the same clues, it would really add to the tension." Or: "I liked your story, but I don't think the general public will be very interested in it. There seems to be something essential missing—I can't put my finger on exactly what it is. Its appeal is just too narrow." Or, "I say throw out the first half." Or, "No doubt about it, this is sensitive writing. It has flights of power and beauty. But Chris, people are looking for sex and action. Deeply contemplative works don't stand a chance." Or: "You're not focused. You're trying to cram too many things into the story. You don't have to tell the reader everything you know. Stick to one or two clearly defined points." Or, the most blunt of all: "There are too many words." The result is that I don't really create; I merely react.

Maybe this year I should write for myself.

Wednesday, January 2—2:00 P.M.

"I do not hope for anything. I do not fear anything. I am free."

That declaration is chiseled into a tombstone in Herakleion, Crete. The tombstone marks the last resting place of the man who made that bold statement: Nikos Kazantzakis. Many consider him to be one of the truly great writers of this century. His best known books are *Zorba the Greek* and *The Last Temptation of Christ*.

Is freedom the essence of not hoping and not fearing? I do not know. It sounds kind of Buddhistic to me: Nirvana, which is freedom from misdirected desires, is reached only after detaching yourself from everything, including hopes and fears. But then again, I know that I am not free, and I also know my heart harbors many hopes and even more fears.

My life is built on hope and fear. Catholic construction!

A couple of days before Christmas, I mentioned to you that my gift to myself was to purge myself of the religious toxicity that resulted from my being suckled on the supernatural. Securing that gift should be my New Year's resolution.

I can say that a God whose existence requires mental gymnastics and anti-intellectual leaps of faith in order to be recognized is not worth seeing or having, but simply stating the obvious does not make the obvious real even to me. This God that I do not see, nor want to see, nor think can ever be seen, still lurks in the shadows. The spotlight of my reason can't illuminate Him/Her for me nor can it clearly show me He/She is not there. Neither does common sense, which tells me that a meaningful human life must be built on human needs and not on blind obedience to divine bidding, help free from the divine deception that was injected into me soon after my birth.

Sweet Kate, I want to take full responsibility for my own life but all I have been taught reenforces a tendency to prefer being instructed how to behave correctly rather than choosing for myself what I know to be correct behavior for me. What I am saying is this: wanting to cleanse myself is a lot easier than actually becoming cleansed. There is no magical, religion-busting soap. Freedom is a burden—and an asset.

The first step in the cleansing process is to scrub away at the stains of guilt and shame. I'm still sporting guilt spots from "The Great Nudie Movie Scandal." I know this sounds silly, feeling guilty for something so trivial from so long ago, but it is true. Imagine, a moment's idle pleasure bringing eternal torture beyond measure. Sounds crazy; yet I still have a hard time believing it's not true. That's how deep the stain is.

The sadly ironic part of the "sin/death/eternal torture" cycle is that it is all based on a fairy tale. Allegory became actuality; fable became fact; an opinion became ceritude.

Reason plus evidence demands that the doctrine of original sin be relegated to the realm of fancy, fiction, and fable. The fable created a paradise in which the tyranny of ignorance prevailed. The fable created a male God who established an androcratic rule, which decreed that woman should be subservient to man and the sexual chattel of her husband, thereby forcing women to endure centuries of being mired in barbarity and oppression. This God created by the fable relishes his role as judge far more than his role as father, and his concept of justice is wedded to vengeance. The fable fostered a neurosis among Christians that forces them to reject any amusement or concession to human nature, since that would place one's salvation in jeopardy.

The fable has caused untold human suffering. From medieval times, straight through the Renaissance and into the seventeenth and eighteenth centuries, life was very difficult. Warfare, plagues, famine, and natural disasters were constantly on attack against a helpless population. In addition to all these external troubles, the Church added a far more vicious menace: an internal awareness that humanity was sinful and inescapably condemned to destruction. Thanks to the fable of original sin, people were bedeviled by a paralyzing, agonizing perception of sin that faith could neither comfort nor assuage; they were expected to live like monks and nuns, denying themselves the simplest pleasures of earthly life in favor of meditating on life's miseries and tragedies, doubting themselves and nurturing their deep-seated guilt and shame. Original sin gave birth to a melancholy outlook that spread like wildfire. St. Hildegard of Bingen, a mystic who died in 1179, wrote, "At the very instant when Adam disobeyed divine order, melancholy coagulated in his blood, just as clarity vanishes when the light goes out, though the still hot oakum produces malodorous smoke. And so it was with Adam, for while his own light was being put out, melancholy curdled his blood, which filled him with sadness and despair."

I bet she wasn't invited to many parties!

Religion for the Western man has become a matter of anxiety and has reduced his life to a continuous battle against his sinful nature. Satan, the Church insisted, was alive and well, living in the hearts of man, who was little more than a sewer of ingratitude and iniquity. Thanks to the fable of original sin, guilt became part of the fabric of life, and denial became a way of life. And so it still goes today. The Catholic Church continues to devalue sexuality, debase marriage, and insist on celibacy for its priests—what garbage!

Does sin exist? I think it does. I sin whenever I fail to love, whenever I resort to lies and deceit, whenever I deny the truth I see. And I do those things almost every day. I need to be aware of my shortcomings; I need to constantly try to improve myself. But there is a tremendous difference between recognizing your failures and striving to overcome them, and the guilt-ridden fear of damnation; the former seeks to perfect humanity, the latter only denies human nature. It is possible, and I think necessary, to discard the doctrine of original sin without denying the reality of individual wrongdoing. We are not born perfect, we all have defects, but it is crazy to tie the imperfections we are all born with to an act of disobedience on the part of a mythical man who lived in an imagined garden long before the birth of recorded history.

We would all be better off if we realized there is right and wrong but no heaven and hell. Paradise, dear Kate, has not been lost; it simply has not yet been created. That is our task, yours, mine, and every living person's.

Sunday, January 6—10:20 A.M.

Good morning, dear daughter. A gloomy, overcast day here in the City of Angels—hopefully that is a sign we might be getting some much needed rain.

Just finished my Sunday morning sojourn with the *New York Times*. I look forward each week to the book review section. But this morning the nonfiction best-seller list slapped me in the face and woke me up to the fact that my hopes of getting a book published are rather dim. Fifty percent of the top ten best-selling nonfiction books are about nothing—nothing more than sugar-coated lives of famous people and a dog and a cat. Let me explain. There is a book about an athlete. There's one about a country-western singer. There is the autobiography of the two-bit actor/politician, Ronald Reagan—a president whose memory was not his strong suit. There is a book by a famous dog, an English springer spaniel who lives in the White House with George and Barbara Bush. And there is a book that features a cat whose owner is a curmudgeon. Five of the ten best-sellers are personality driven tomes that at best can be described as trivial, though the Reagan book could be also characterized as fiction. Of the other five best-sellers, one was written by a well-known network newscaster, who chronicles his life on the road, another explores a high-school football season in a small Texas town, and another is a saccharine-laced collection of inspirational essays.

Last year, I spent a considerable amount of time working on a nonfiction book that was about nothing—the topic was soap operas, the title: *The Soap Behind the Soap.* I was trying to make a buck by capitalizing on the popularity of daytime soap operas. But the more I worked on it, the more nauseous I became— I just couldn't stomach the triviality and superficiality of the soap opera world. If I had persevered, I bet I could have sold it. But one night, I became so disgusted with the project, I burned the damn manuscript in my fireplace. Three months of work went up in smoke within a few minutes. I immediately began work on something more substantial—*GOD: The Unauthorized Biography.* Only kidding. I cleaned out my fireplace, and for the next few months kicked around the idea of working on a book about life in Catholic seminaries during the fifties and sixties.

The seminary book died too, but not at the hands of anger, it was snuffed out by indifference. During the past two years, I have written two novels, three screenplays, and created a television sitcom. I sold none of them. I think it is time I turn in my pen or get a new one.

Of course, my pen is not the problem. My problem is a lack of focus. My mind is like a bee, dancing from one flower to another, searching for the nectar of wisdom. In his *Journals,* French writer Andre Gidé, in examining himself, sums up my problem with my pen:

> Oh, if only my thought could simplify itself! . . . I sit here, sometimes all morning, unable to do anything, tormented by my desire to do everything. The yearning to educate myself is the greatest temptation for me. I have twenty books before me, every one of them begun. You will laugh when I tell you that I cannot read a single one of them simply because I want so much to read them all. I read three lines and think of everything else

My writing is out of focus.

You know something? I like this letter to you better than all my unsold scribblings. I hope it winds up on your best-seller list.

Well, I'm off to see the wizard.

Sunday, January 13—2:45 P.M.

Took a long walk this morning. I woke up restless and agitated, so I decided to skip my usual Sabbath routine of reading papers and watching the Sunday morning network news interview shows. I've read and heard all I can take about the impending war with Iraq.

For the past three days, Congress has been debating whether or not to give Bush the authority to use force in order to drive Iraq out of Kuwait. I watched endless hours of the debates in both the Senate and the House on C-SPAN. Arguments on both sides of the issue were well reasoned and very passionate.

The vote was not supposed to be partisan, but in the end the Senate Republicans (except for two) voted for force, and the Senate Democrats (except for eight) voted for restraint. So the Senate, by the margin of 52-47 (one Senator was ill and did not vote) gave to Bush the authorization he sought. The House gave Bush the power to wage war by a margin of 250-183, with 184 Republicans and 86 Democrats voting to authorize the use of force, and 179 Democrats and 3 Republicans against the resolution (two Representatives did not vote due to illness).

I saw so much of the debate and was so depressed by the outcome, I decided I didn't need to read about what had happened in chambers of Congress or what was about to happen in sands of the desert. Besides, the simple fact is that war is inevitable.

Everyone seems to be in agreement, that President Bush did the right thing in his initial response to the invasion by sending 200,000 troops to the Middle East to defend Saudi Arabia. OK, I'll buy that argument, though not wholeheartedly. The real problem came when Bush, just after the Congressional elections on November 6, doubled the size of our troop deployment to 400,000 men and women, and changed its mission from defending Saudi Arabia to preparing for offensive action against Iraq. Before this move, which was done in secret and without Congressional advice or consent, Saddam Hussein had the burden of sustaining a 500,000-man occupation force in Kuwait over time as international trade sanctions increasingly strained his resources. Time was Hussein's biggest foe. He was isolated and stood alone against the world. After Bush increased the size of our military commitment, time became America's enemy because our force was so large it could not, practically, stay in Saudi Arabia through the rains of winter, the sand storms of spring, and the heat of summer. After nearly six months of waiting in the harsh desert environment, our troops were getting restless.

To complicate matters and move us further down the road to war, Bush intensified the time factor by imposing a deadline. With great political skill, the President seduced the United Nations Security Council into authorizing the use of military force against Iraq if they do not withdraw completely from Kuwait by January 15, 1991. A line in the sand had been drawn, and now a deadline is set. The countdown to conflict has begun.

Nobody seems to want war, but it looks like it is war we will get. Logistics are driving our policy, instead of the other way around. Bush seems convinced his handling of the situation is the only way to resolve the conflict. To oppose him now, as we stand on the brink of war, seems un-American. He is our Commander-in-Chief, and many feel he deserves the country's full support during this crisis. I was in Cooper's the other morning for coffee and donuts, and I overheard a guy say, "I'm sick of hearing those do-gooders say that we got to give the sanctions more time to work. What crap. It hasn't worked so far. It's time to kick some ass."

And count the bodies blown to bits for oil.

It is no wonder I woke up edgy this morning.

Tuesday, January 15—2:00 P.M.

I don't feel quite as isolated today. Along with the rest of the world, I am anxiously awaiting tonight's midnight deadline for Hussein to withdraw his troops from Kuwait. The clock is ticking, and everyone hears it. Only ten hours to go. It doesn't look good.

Yesterday, Iraq's National Assembly endorsed, with fervent enthusiasm, Hussein's refusal to comply with the United Nations resolutions and his stand against "U.S. imperialism, Zionism, and Arab stooges," even if it means war. Members chanted, "With our blood and our souls we are ready to sacrifice for Saddam." One deputy, Muslim clergyman Abulwaham al-Hitti, declared, "We are headed for heaven, and the road to heaven has always been under the shadow of swords. It is either life with dignity or death." Hussein ordered the Iraqi flag be altered by adding the Muslim war cry "Allahu akbar"—"God is great." In the streets of Baghdad, crowds in government-organized demonstrations shouted, "Holy war, Holy war!"

On a TV news report that was documenting the level of fear and anxiety across the country, a frightened little girl in Atlanta said, "If God wants war, than there will be war. If God doesn't want war, than there won't be a war." Everyone is looking to God, hoping for a miracle. Sadly, there will be no Merlin with magical power to stop our march toward war.

Tuesday, January 15—11:00 P.M.

In a national address tonight, President Bush said the impending war in the gulf will not be another Vietnam: "Our troops . . . will not be asked to fight with one hand tied behind their back."

What? I wasn't aware soldiers fought the war in Vietnam with one hand tied behind their backs. But if they did, it should be pointed out that they still managed to drop 4,600,000 tons of bombs on Vietnam (to put that in perspective, the estimated tonnage dropped by the Allied Forces during World War II was 3,000,000); still managed to spray 11,200,000 gallons of Agent Orange; still managed to drop 400,000 tons of napalm; still managed to destroy 25,000,000 acres of farmland; still managed to mutilate 12,000,000 acres of forests; still managed to kill an estimated 1,500,000 Vietnamese. 2,150,000 American troops served in

Vietnam, and 57,900 of them were killed.

If fighting with one hand tied behind their back manages to inflict such damage, I shutter to think what Bush has in mind for Iraq.

Kate, the Vietnam War was over before you were born. You'll probably read about it in history classes, but you probably won't read about Agent Orange. Agent Orange contains dioxin, which is an extremely potent cancer-causing chemical. Agent Orange was used as a technological quick-fix for a guerrilla war fought in jungles; we wanted to take nature's hiding place away from the Vietnamese and force them out into the open. A single Air Force C-123 transport plane could wipe out 350 acres of Vietnam's rain forest in a matter of minutes. Within a week of spraying, huge trees that formed the jungle canopy would wither and die, and a jungle that was alive with bird song and monkey chattering would be silenced. But the trees and animals weren't the only victims. Studies indicate that the South Vietnamese people may be the most dioxin-contaminated people on earth. The terror of Agent Orange still lives. Dioxin is still in people's fat tissue, still in mother's milk. Many people born after the war carry the scars of cruel birth defects resulting from Agent Orange. Liver cancer among adults is abnormally high. It took many years for the food chain to recover from dioxin contamination, but much of the rich terrain has never recovered.

The Vietnamese people weren't the only victims. Thousands of American soldiers have filed claims, alleging that their exposure to Agent Orange has caused cancer, skin disorders, miscarriages, and birth defects. The government says that no causal link has been established. Sure, more lies from Washington.

Our use of Agent Orange was largely ineffective militarily, and it was immoral and probably illegal under international law. Kate, Americans, for the most part, are good people. Our intentions for the most part are honest and honorable. But we are not perfect, and we have made many tragic mistakes in the past. I think it is wise to remember, as we raise angry voices at the atrocities committed by Saddam Hussein, that we once irreversibly poisoned a large population with toxic chemicals and thought it was the right thing to do because we were fighting an ideology we considered evil and immoral.

Wednesday, January 16—3:47 P.M.

The bombs have started to fall on Baghdad. We are now at war.

Dona nobis pacem. (Grant us peace.)

My heart is pounding. Operation Desert Shield has become Operation Desert Storm. I am literally shaking with . . . I'm not sure if it's fear or apprehension, but, whatever it is, I am shaking.

America is at war.

The President claimed we had exhausted all other alternatives, although his televised speech to the nation in which he announced that the liberation of Kuwait had begun, did not convince me of the veracity of that statement.

So much for the kinder, gentler nation Bush promised us.

Thursday, January 17—4:11 P.M.

Missiles, launched by Iraq, are now falling on Israel. The war is just twenty-four hours old.

Madness. I recall once reading that war is the supreme paradigm of irrational conduct. After only twenty-four hours, I agree.

Friday, January 18—5:00 P.M.

During the first forty-eight hours of the war, America has launched 196 "Tomahawk" cruise missiles at Iraq. These unmanned bombs cost about a million dollars a piece. The M-1 tank carries a price tag of 4.4 million dollars. The F-14D fighter jet, which flies at 1,500 miles per hour, costs a whopping 72 million dollars. Since the deployment of troops to Saudi Arabia, the Defense Department has spent 668 million dollars to feed them. In addition, the government has purchased 2.3 million dollars worth of sugar, 1.8 million dollars worth of flour, and 3.4 million dollars worth of coffee for the troops stationed in the Persian Gulf. The soldiers have been provided with 2.2 million tubes of lip balm, worth $300,881; 715,249 cans of foot powder, worth $278,947; 558,588 bottles of sunscreen lotion, worth $834,318; 609,110 bottles of water purification tablets, worth $323,228; and, 31,975 cans of chigger repellent, worth $76,420. A television preacher suggested that one fifty-cent bullet to Saddam's head would be far more cost effective—the Christian solution is cost effective, at least.

Just a few days ago, America was poor, saddled with insurmountable debt and strapped for cash. We could not afford the war on poverty. We could not afford the war on drugs. We could not afford the war on crime. We could not afford the war on illiteracy. We could not afford to provide shelter for the homeless. We could not afford to provide comprehensive education for our children. We could not afford to care for our elderly. Many states could not afford to repair roads and bridges. Large cities across the nation could not afford to repair their crumbling infrastructures. Many cities could not afford to provide adequate police and fire protection for their citizens.

Yet today, we can afford to spend about a billion dollars a day to liberate a country that does not believe in democracy, and to defend another country that is little more than a feudal desert state, which represses women and democracy. When the war is over, and the bodies have been counted and the monuments built, the Emir of Kuwait, despite having scores of wives, will be chasing young European women in Monaco while countless Americans will be mourning the loss of their husbands and wives, sons and daughters, and mothers and fathers.

None of this makes any sense to me. Think about this: during the past ten years, the United States spent 2.7 trillion dollars to sustain its war machine. Yes, trillion! Which looks like this: $2,700,000,000,000.

Sunday, January 20—11:00 A.M.

The war started in the black of a moonless Baghdad night, just a few hours before dawn. Since then the world has lived in what Shakespeare called, "the dead, vast and middle of the night." We do not know when the sun will come up again.

So far, fifteen jets from the Allied Forces have been shot down. Nine of them, American. The fate of their crews is unknown. The relentless bombing of Iraq goes on around the clock. Over seven thousand bombing missions have been flown. It is the most sustained, concentrated bombing in the history of mankind. There is no let up in sight. While watching night footage of Baghdad under attack, the sky lit up like a Christmas tree with bomb blasts and antiaircraft fire, I suddenly saw what George Bush meant by his campaign talk of "a thousand points of light."

During the past few days, nothing that I have seen, heard or read has convinced me that this war was necessary. Will we never discover a creative alternative to bloodletting as a means to resolve our differences? Why do we always resort to bombs and body bags?

But life goes on. Today my beloved New York Giants meet the San Francisco 49ers for the Championship of the National Conference of the NFL, and the Los Angeles Raiders play the Buffalo Bills for the Championship of the American Conference. I'll watch, but with little enthusiasm. Besides, the Giants will lose—they are good, but no match for the mighty 49ers.

Sunday, January 20—8:00 P.M.

Each of today's championship football games was repeatedly interrupted by special news reports. Iraq had launched ten SCUD missiles at two locations in Saudi Arabia. Breathless, nervous reporters wearing gas masks gave live, eyewitness accounts of the shelling. After some initial confusion, it was reported that nine of the ten incoming missiles were destroyed by the Allied Forces' Patriot missile system and the tenth fell harmlessly into the sea. Ironically, debris from a destroyed missile or perhaps an errant patriot missile hit an insurance company building in the city of Riyadh. There were no casualties, and I'm sure claims adjusters, armed with forms in triplicate, will be on the scene shortly. After the reports from the Middle East battlefields, the networks returned us to the gridiron battlefields and stadiums filled with fans waving American flags, with a simple, "Now back to the game." The war is taking on a surrealist quality.

Oh yeah, my Giants beat the 49ers 15-13 on a forty-two-yard field goal with only four seconds left in the game. I celebrated for about two minutes.

Kate, it is difficult for me to shake my addiction to the media's war coverage. Most people have jobs that mercifully provide periods of relief from the war news. As a writer who does his scribbling at home, I have no such escape. But I'm learning a lot of new things. For example, I'm learning about all the highly technological weapons of destruction. I'm learning how attack fighters are equipped with a device that generates high-resolution TV pictures of the ground in darkness in order to enhance their night bombing capabilities. I'm learning how to electronically scramble enemy radar. I'm learning the difference between an F-117A Stealth fighter jet and an F-16 Fighting Falcon, and how a F-14 Tomcat differs from an FA-18 Hornet, and how an A6-Intruder differs from an F-4G Wild Weasel. I'm learning that an F-15 Eagle fighter jet can fly at two and a half times the speed of sound and has a range of 790 miles. I'm learning how the huge E2 Hawkeye early warning aircraft detects enemy targets. I'm learning how satellites circling the earth in outer space can track enemy troop movements. I'm learning how fighter jets are refueled while in flight. I'm learning about laser-guided missile systems on fighter jets.

I'm learning about war strategy. I'm learning about mobile missile launchers. I'm learning tank warfare strategy. I'm learning how to hide a tank in the desert. I'm learning about bomb damage assessment and how we gather post-strike intelligence. I'm learning how to manufacture and deploy chemical weapons. I'm learning how missiles are launched from sea. I'm learning the difference between cluster bombs and gravity bombs. I'm learning the difference between an M16A1 "Bouncing Betty" land mine and a Valsella VS-50 scatter drop land mine. I'm learning how computers, programmed with maps and photos, guide missiles to their targets. I'm learning how to feed, clothe, and house a massive army on the move. I'm learning how pilots eject from an aircraft that has been hit by enemy fire. I'm learning how weather affects war and the machines of war. I'm learning that wars are not won in the air but on the ground.

But, I don't have a clue what the hell I'm going to do with all this knowledge.

Maybe I'll become a military expert and get booked on TV shows to comment on the war.

War today is geared for the Nintendo generation, it has become a real life video game battle. So far, the war has been very clinical. We hear about surgical strikes and see a few seconds of grainy footage of actual bombing hits on faceless buildings. Sometimes the news coverage actually sounds like a sportscast. Today's war news interruptions of the football games sounded a lot like the descriptions of the games themselves. Passes were intercepted, and so were Scud missiles.

During the news report, I heard: "We had two minutes warning before the missile attack." During the football game, I heard: "Time out for the two minute warning." Here are a few lines I heard on television this afternoon, but I'm not sure whether they were spoken during the war coverage or the football game: "The defense's ability to blast between people is killing them . . ." "This battle is being fought in the trenches . . ." "The offence is on the move now." "Everything is going according to plan." "The defence is hanging tough . . ." "Their forces were able to target the attack . . ." "A record for interceptions . . ."

The war coverage is beginning to take an almost routine feeling. During the Giants game this afternoon, CBS newsman Dan Rather broke in during the second quarter. He switched us to a live feed from Dharan in Saudi Arabia, where a reporter wearing a gas mask and breathing heavily said, "The air base here in

Saudi Arabia is again under attack. We are hearing sirens. We assume Scud missiles are heading this way." Dan Rather promised more details at halftime, then switched back to football. "All right, Dan, back at Candlestick Park, it's 3-3," said Pat Summerall, the game's announcer, "You haven't missed a play yet." Thank God.

With only four seconds left in the game, and the Giants trailing by a single point, the teams lined up for the final play of the game. The entire season for both teams came down to one last play, one dramatic kick. Before the kick, the cameras caught fatigued combatants on both sidelines offering last-ditch prayers for victory. The kicker's right foot launched the ball. As the ball climbed through the bracing California twilight, it seemed to be fading left. Both sidelines anxiously looked on as the ball tumbled through the uprights, just inside the left upright, just fair. "Yes!" I shouted, as I raised two clinched fists in the air, "The Giants are going to the Super Bowl!"

Right in the midst of the victor's leaping exultation and the loser's head-lowered despair, suddenly the scene switched from the stadium in San Francisco to CBS News in New York.

Reality returned, abruptly.

"What a game!" claimed Dan Rather, the top gun at CBS News. Then, not missing a beat, he recited the latest war headlines. "Iraqi-fired missiles intercepted by Patriots . . ."

Wow! A game summary and a war summary—all in the same breath. Intercepted passes and picked-off missiles, all in the same convenient, tidy package.

In less than a week, the shock and horror of war had given way to an antiseptic, prime-time television show. With more style than substance, the networks have produced a Middle East mini-series, complete with logos and music. Beyond the slick visuals and hype, the networks offer their viewers little more than self-serving statements from officials of all the governments involved and speculation from retired military leaders (each network has procured the services of an Avis-Rent-a-General to work as on-air consultants; they analyze what the real generals tell the journalists). We see videos of happy pilots and state-of-the-art technology rather than the carnage. Reports are sprinkled with military lingo and sports metaphors.

An anchor thanks his Middle East correspondent for "calling the play-by-play on this thing [a Scud missile attack]." Another anchor asks a government official to comment on what we can expect "now that Desert Storm has kicked off." A soldier, preparing to depart for Saudi Arabia, interviewed by one of the networks complains about pacing the sidelines in the states while his buddies are out on the field. "It's kind of like playing the Super Bowl," the G.I. said, "and our side's winning."

On television, Operation Desert Storm has become a sports game, with journalists covering their winning hometown team. But the reality is much different: people are killing people in a war we will be paying for for generations to come.

Wednesday, January 23—9:20 A.M.

A SCUD Missile hit Tel Aviv last night, injuring over ninety people and causing extensive damage. Three people died of heart attacks during the missile attack. For the first time, television cameras are seeing blood, seeing injured civilians being removed from the rubble of their homes.

The camera sees what language tries to hide.

Military spokesmen report that the United States is successfully "decimating Iraqi troops." Aside from the distorted use of "decimate" (which means "reduce by one-tenth"—orginally Latin for "kill every tenth man" as punishment for mutiny), the use hides the idea that real people are killing real people. When military personnel talk about "collateral damage" in Iraq, what they mean—and are hiding— is innocent people are being killed or hurt, and that nonmilitary buildings and property are being destroyed or damaged. Collateral damage means death and destruction.

Pilots fly "sorties," not bombing missions. (Sortie is derived from the French word "sortir," which means "to go out.") When the pilots site their targets, they say they have "acquired" them. Pilots don't attack a target, they "visit" and "revisit" them. Pilots encounter "triple A," which means anti-aircraft artilery fired by cannons or machine guns from the ground. The planes don't drop bombs, they deliver ordnances. A bomb that misses its target is an "incontinent ordnance." A "surgical strike" is the euphemism used for precision bombing. You don't do surgery with 500-pound bombs. The casing of a bomb dropped from a B-52 gets blown into small pieces, and the shrapnel flies through the air at a very high velocity, like innumerable little knives cutting through the air, potentially slicing people in half. War is more than surgical bombing; it is headless bodies. The military does not even use the word "war." They prefer the more sterilized "theater of operations." One military spokesman claimed we were "throwing a lot of assets at the problem [enemy mobile missile launchers]." Assets are military hardware—i.e. planes, tanks, bombs—and people. When a military offical reports that there is "activity" in a certain section of the desert or a town, he means troops are engaged in combat. The terrors of battle are being masked by language.

Back in Vietnam when Americans burned hamlets, it was called a "village pacification program."

Too bad our diplomatic efforts weren't as creative as our linguistic enterprises.

As if there were not enough trouble in the world, yesterday His Holiness the Pope issued an encyclical in which he exhorted Catholics to go out and spread Christianity, emphasizing the need to evangelize in all parts of the world, including those where Islamic laws forbid proselytizing. "Open the doors to Christ!" the letter said. Aides said the Pope was responding to the rapid growth of Islam.

The 153-page encyclical titled *Redemptoris Missio* (that means "Mission of the Redeemer," although the English version will be titled "The Church's Missionary Mandate") is the result of almost five years work, and it urged Islamic countries to lift those laws that forbid Muslims to convert to another faith. Fat chance.

The papal letter reflects the Pope's fear that Catholicism is lagging behind

Islam in expansion in Asia, Africa, and the Middle East. But more important, I think it reveals the Pope's concern with liberal theological views that suggest Christianity has no special status as a means to salvation. Theologians and scholars in comparative religions have warmed up to the idea that all the world religions, even in their differences, are about equal in their potential to provide spiritual fulfillment for their followers. In the hallowed halls of higher education, inter-religious dialogue is exposing Christian uniqueness as myth, and down in the streets, everyday experience is showing the ordinary Christian the validity of non-Christian religions. Many Christians are waking up to the fact that in the past missionary efforts were linked to colonization or foreign domination, and they are getting queasy about proclaiming Christianity's superiority to other world religions. These trends piss the Pope off—he likes the old, traditional approach: the swashbuckling, heroic missionary priest who heads for exotic, foreign lands armed only with his faith, courage, and ingenuity in order to save souls for Christ.

The Pope's encyclical addresses the tension between evangelization and inter-religious understanding. The clash between recruitment and dialogue is complex. On the one hand, it seems obvious that one important element in achieving world peace is the ability of different religions to relate to one another; but interreligious dialogue and understanding are hardly compatible with St. Matthew's "Great Commission" to "go, therefore, and make disciples of all nations." What Pope John Paul II is saying is that while building bridges between different religions in the hope that they may learn to live together is a noble idea, it nonetheless must take a back seat to the Gospel's call to convert all non-Christians. The Pope, in a throwback to medieval times, believes he represents the one true faith, so it's his way or no way.

The Pope's faith is Christ-centered, not God-centered; and his exclusivist attitude—which opposes the pluralism of the times—suggests that God doesn't really want all humans to be saved and He is willing to condemn all those whose cultural background denies them the possibility of accepting Jesus as Lord and Savior, even though they expressed a sincere spirituality and love of God. The Pope is reversing the direction of the Second Vatican Council, which in 1965 suggested that salvation outside of the Church was possible even though the best way to salvation was through faith in Jesus.

For the Pope, it's full steam ahead—to the past.

More from the religious dribble front: Yesterday, President Bush, defender of the flag and fetus, took a break from his preoccupation with the Persian Gulf War to speak some words of encouragement to an estimated 25,000 pro-life demonstrators gathered in Washington, D.C., to mark the anniversary of *Roe* v. *Wade*. The Commander-in-Chief told the gathering via a phone hookup from the White House "to keep this issue alive and predominate in the halls of Congress, the courts and the minds of the American people."

Sure, the prez would love to divert American minds away from the Gulf War. Bush also said, "I'm pleased that my voice is part of the growing chorus that simply says: 'Choose life.' " But not apparently in the Gulf. One speaker at the rally said, "We are going to impose our morality on America. Save the babies."

The odds are that most of the people at the rally, who claim to have a reverence for life, support President Bush's decision to assemble a massive killing machine in the desert of Saudi Arabia, a Muslim country the Pope hopes will open its doors to Christ by welcoming an invasion of missionary zealots.

What madness!

And the people of God think I'm crazy! As Bush says at the end of every speech on the war, "God bless America."

Thursday, January 24—1:30 P.M.

Soon after awakening this morning, before even getting out of bed, I resolved not to turn on the television to see what was going in the Middle East. People all across the nation claim that the last thing they think about before falling asleep at night and the first thing they think about when they awake in the morning is the war. Me too.

Within ten minutes of brushing my teeth, I did turn the tube on for just a few seconds, just to make sure there wasn't any major development overnight. The news sounded routine, so I quickly turned it off, and it stayed off until just a few moments ago. When . . .

I turned the set on and the station was carrying a live military briefing from Saudi Arabia, which was being given by a Saudi military official. A reporter raised his hand to ask a question. "Sir, as you know, tomorrow is an Islamic holy day. Does that mean the Saudi pilots will be curtailing their activities?" The official responded, "No. Our religion says we should fight and pray at the same time." There was no follow up question like, "How is that possible?"

I turned the television off.

Later in the morning, I sought refuge from the war news and the torments of my own thoughts in a used book store called "Lame Duck Books." I spotted a copy of Julian Green's *Diary 1928-1957*. Born in Paris in 1900 to American parents, Green, a Catholic, became one of the giants of twentieth-century French literature. I opened the book to his January 24, 1932, entry. This is what he wrote fifty-nine years ago today:

Today I found some old negatives in a trunk. Printed a few snapshots. I saw myself again as I was at fifteen. On looking at a photograph taken at the foot of a big oak in our garden, I had the peculiar impression of being on the verge of remembering a thought that had crossed my mind at the very moment when the photograph was taken, and for a few seconds it seemed to me that a ray of light was about to pierce through the obscure depths of memory. I should have attempted to make my mind a blank, and perhaps, among so many others, that minute of my youth would have found its way to me; my efforts made it run away and fall back into oblivion from which it was about to emerge. So much of us goes thus to nothingness, so many hours, so many years. . . . It is an unpleasant and all but sinister sensation to feel oneself drifting slowly toward definitive unconsciousness, and I can only think with horror of the time when everything that I have known and loved will fade from my memory. What remains of my mother? A few letters, five or six photographs, and memories that will be with me till I die. When we die, my sisters and I, she will die once again and for ever.

The entry struck a chord deep within me. I recalled the day last July when I opened that box of memorabilia. "So many hours, so many years" all dissolved into nothingness. I've got to do something to keep myself from feeling myself "drifting slowly toward definitive unconsciousness." I'm stuck in a continual hesitancy, plagued by an incapacity for action. Life, when I'm sitting still, seems false and vain.

I also came across something E. M. Cioran wrote: "When we are in the depths of depression, everything which feeds it, affords it further substance, also raises it to a level where we can no longer follow and thereby renders it too great, excessive: scarcely surprising that we should reach the point of no longer regarding it as our own." I understood those words as well as if I had uttered them myself—in another life.

Saturday, January 26—10:40 A.M.

Had a bad case of writer's block yesterday. Stared at the computer screen for most of the morning. I was hoping to finish a screenplay I've been working on for the past few months. As noon approached, I was about ready to torch the whole project. Not only couldn't I finish it, but I wondered why the hell I ever started it.

Writer's block, at least in my case, manifests itself in desperately blank pages and silent deskbound suffering. Many writers view creativity as a way of easing the tension between inner and outer reality. Not me. The act of writing tends to distort my mind and soul. I fear I cannot create anything original, so my pen is frightened into impotence. It takes every ounce of confidence and strength I can muster to overcome that fear and even try to exploit the tension between what I feel and what I see. I had no such confidence or strength today. So, I sat and suffered.

Eventually, I convinced myself to relax, that my mind was preoccupied with all the war mania that is sweeping across America. Mindless flag waving is back in vogue. Take a break, I thought, go to a movie. And so I did. Two of them, in fact.

With a little hustle, I managed to make it to the theater in time for the first showing of the day of Woody Allen's new movie, *Alice*. The film's title character is a woman in her late thirties. She has been married for fifteen years to a handsome and very successful corporate lawyer. She was a good Catholic girl who as an adult has become lost in the material world of the 1980s. She has a cook, a chauffeur, an exercise trainer who makes house calls, and a nanny for her two cute children. In short, she has everything money can buy. However, she is poor in the intangibles that really matter in life. No one seems to need her, and she has no purpose in life. Her husband doesn't hear anything she says, and she spends her day shopping or in beauty parlors desperately trying to slow down time's march.

In Woody's whimsical tale, Alice seeks help from a crusty, old Chinese herbalist and acupuncturist, who sets her on an herb-induced voyage of self-discovery that leads to an affair with a saxophonist and a trip to India to visit Mother Teresa. Along the way, Alice gradually cuts through the lies and pretenses that have been cushioning her pain and finds in herself the idealistic little girl who once wanted to do good for others. Eventually she realizes that her Catholicism has caused her a persistent sense of guilt that keeps her loyal to her faithless and patronizing husband. Alice's story is that of a woman who takes off her rose-colored glasses and learns to look for answers, not in any prefabricated social or religious framework, but within herself.

The movie was over before three o'clock. I didn't feel like going home. Seeing as I was in a multiplex theater, I checked to see what other film would be starting within the next few minutes. There was just one: *The Godfather Part III.*

Should I or shouldn't I? I felt like Mario Cuomo, I couldn't make up my mind.

I wasn't really in the mood for a gangster movie, but, on the other hand Francis Ford Coppola is an interesting director and even a mafia flick seemed preferable to CNN's war coverage. In less time than it takes a patriot to shoot down a SCUD, I'm sitting once again in a darkened theater, this time with a big bucket of hot-buttered popcorn.

Much to my surprise, this film also had a heavy dosage of Catholicism—though it was ultimately a more hopeful Catholicism than what was presented in *Alice.* In the first two *Godfather* films the Church played an important but mostly ceremonial role. There were lots of weddings, baptisms, and funerals—all rich in visual imagery. But in this film, the Church plays a major role.

The Godfather Part III depicts the Catholic Church at its best and worst.

The aging Godfather and family patriarch Michael Corleone wants to move out of the mob game and turn the family business into a legitimate enterprise. The film opens with the Godfather receiving a special honor from a Bishop after donating millions of dollars to the Church. But the gift had strings, and he would soon curry the Church's favor.

In an effort to take over a major European-based multinational conglomerate, Corleone enlists the help of the Vatican. It is here he meets one of the film's principal villains, a corrupt Cardinal who is the Vatican treasurer. But on the sly, the Cardinal plays a shadowy and suspect role in international finance. The Cardinal proves to be more interested in double crosses than in the cross of his Savior. The institutional Church acts little differently than any powerful mafia family, and the prelate is no more trustworthy than any mob figures the Godfather has had rubbed out over the years.

Sensing the Cardinal's duplicity, Michael Corleone approaches a friendlier power broker inside the Vatican. But this second Cardinal, who by the film's end is elected Pope and then poisoned and murdered by Vatican officials (as some suggest was the case with Pope John Paul I who died in his sleep just one month into his papacy), sincerely cares about Corleone's soul and spiritual well-being. This prelate tells the Godfather that before they talk business, he would like to hear his confession.

At first Corleone declines the offer, saying he didn't mind making donations to the Church in exchange for favors, but to participate in the Church's rituals of salvation while still ordering murders takes more hypocrisy than he has in him. He can confess, he tells the Cardinal, but he cannot repent. However, the Cardinal gently leads the Godfather into confessing his sins.

Michael Corleone begins to confess his long list of sins, everything from adultery to cold-blooded murder, including the assassination of his own brother. As he speaks, slowly something strange yet mystical begins to happen: the power of repentance begins to touch him and Michael breaks down and cries. This tender, extraordinary scene is an eloquent endorsement of Catholic faith.

Despite admiring the work of a master filmmaker, the movie was rather long and lugubrious, and I was glad to leave the theater when it was finally over.

As I drove home, I couldn't help think about how frequently Catholicism pops up in films. Maybe the Church's long history and melodramatic rituals lend it a touch of majesty you don't see in everyday American life. It's also a religion you can't get away from, even those who give it up are still drawn to it. Some people claim there is no such thing as an ex-Catholic. That's true for me. At the core of my existence I am Catholic; but accepting Catholicism for me is an existential lie. This fate leads to a melancholy that I must live through daily.

As I walked up the steps of my home after five hours of cinematic escapism, thoughts of the war entered my mind. As I turned the key to unlock my front door, I wondered whether there were any new developments in the Gulf War. I went straight to the TV, turned it on, and heard the news that there were more SCUD attacks and more innocent civilians killed in Tel Aviv and Riyadh. The line score reads: Tel Aviv—1 dead, 60 wounded; Riyadh—1 dead, 30 wounded. It is a war of numbers, numbing numbers.

In the wake of the pictures of the damage from the latest attacks on Tel Aviv and Riyadh came even more shocking images—images of ecological terrorism.

Iraq released millions of gallons of Kuwati crude oil into the Persian Gulf. Again, numbing numbers. Initial word has it the spill is twelve times larger than 1989 Exxon Valdez accident in Alaska, in which eleven million gallons of oil created an ecological nightmare and killed countless birds and marine life. The spill in the Persian Gulf has produced an oil slick nine miles wide and nearly thirty-five miles long, which is steadly moving South. The oil was released into the Gulf's shallow waters from a terminal ten miles off shore. The terminal is connected to Kuwait's main petroleum refinery at Al Ahmadi. The oil is still flowing from the terminal into the Gulf, and if the flow is not stopped soon, the spill will be the worst in history, easily surpassing the 140 million gallons oil dumped into the Gulf of Mexico in 1979 when the Ixtoc oil well exploded. Numbing numbers.

But numbers carry no emotional weight. Pictures do. The television cameras caught a lone cormorant, fighting to free itself from the sticky goo, tiring and then slowly sinking in a rolling wave of oil, its bill pointed slightly skyward, gasping for air, as it drifted aimlessly, helplessly toward shore. War is cruel for wildlife, too.

The sight of a graceful cormorant awkwardly struggling to escape the oil-slicked waters of the Gulf made me sick.

Next up in the nonstop coverage of the war was a report about how the troops in the desert would be watching tomorrow's Super Bowl—even though the kickoff will be at two in the morning Saudi time. TV's have been set up in tents. The troops will be armed with all kinds snacks for the big game. Of course, they will be holding their gas masks in case Hussein decides to interrupt the telecast with a SCUD attack.

I hadn't been home for twenty minutes, and already I had more than enough reality. It was too late to see a third movie, so I did some channel surfing. Click—up pops "Geraldo" dealing, in it's customary confrontational style, aimed more at provoking than informing, with the topic of bad seed clergy—priests and ministers who raped women and molested young boys.

Click—up pops yet another talk show. This one pitted a fundamentalist Christian against several gay and lesbian activists seeking to have homosexual marriages viewed as legal in the eyes of the law. It was the Bible versus spousal rights. It was a lot of yelling and little listening.

Click—up pops a game show. One of the "celebrity" players is an actress friend of mine. I haven't seen her in years. We worked together on a soap opera in which she played a woman who was hooked on booze and drugs. Her performance was riveting, in part because she was a good actress, and in part because she knew first-hand what she was performing. She cleaned up her real life when she met a rehab counselor, who later became her husband. In a case of art imitating life, I cast him as a drug counselor on the show. It was a two-day part, during which the actress's character attended a group therapy session for chemically dependent patients at a hospital. I remember the actress as being very serious, and it was incongruous to see her jumping up and down in excitement as she and her teammates won the frivolous game.

Click—up pops C-SPAN's coverage of the House of Representatives. A congresswoman from Connecticut is delivering a speech about the terrible state of the nation's economy. She was speaking for just a few seconds when the picture switched from a close-up of her to a wide shot of the empty chamber. The Congresswoman was speaking to about 435 chairs. Government in action.

Click—up pops yet another talk show. This one hosted by an aging, washed-up comedienne whose jokes stopped being funny about three years ago but she keeps on telling them. The guests with whom she was engaged in scintillating conversation were three go-go dancers from New Jersey. One young lady, dressed in a scanty outfit that barely managed to cover her assets, was only nineteen years old. The host failed to ask why these girls chose to dance nude in front of horny men, or if it bothered them in any way. No. She wanted to know how much money they make a night. At least four hundred dollars. She applauded them, laughed with them, and invited them to dance, which they did, much to the delight of the cheering men and smiling women in the audience.

Click—up pops the EWTN, the Eternal Word Television Network, which is run by a chubby, old Catholic nun. There was a girl walking in a lush green field, dressed in peasant clothing, praying the rosary.

Click—another talk show; the topic was post-partum blues. The guest was a woman who was aggitated by her six-week-old baby's constant crying, so she ran over him with her car. Just before a commercial break, the host informed the audience that tomorrow's show would feature women whose husbands had affairs with gay men.

Click—up pops an old war movie.

I turned off the TV.

I was very depressed. I thought that perhaps the notion that I was born-again back on July 16, 1990, was a lie.

Kate, if I still had a gun, I would have shot the television. Not that it would have done any good, but I think I would have felt better. I feel as if I am going to explode, my mind has become a battle ground of conflicting ideas and images. I am waging my own war, under the code name: Operation Mental Storm. Still, I am not giving up. I know that whatever happened last July that made me want to live, made me want to fight on, was not a lie.

For the sake of diversion, I would like to share a few random thoughts from my notebook. Just a few, I promise:

History continues to be a sequence of murders, violence, and injustice. And war.

*

Each of us, each day and every moment, stands perennially and inescapably on the brink of some still-to-be-taken action. This is the root of freedom; this is the terror of freedom.

*

It is impossible to study the Bible and come away with another impression than this: birth is soiled, knowledge is harmful, and death is sacred. Sadly, this belief is what has determined the fate of most of humanity. Imagine if the following unbiblical outlook ruled our lives: birth is joyful, knowledge is wonderful, and death is sorrowful.

*

For many God is little more than a symbol to whom they transfer the burden of their problems in order to avoid solving them themselves.

*

According to the R.C. Church, Jesus was a lust-free Savior. Isn't that special?

*

No wonder I was so depressed for so long: I realized that most of my life was a junk heap that needed to be carted away. I still haven't done it.

*

Peace comes from communication, and communication is not an elimination of difference. It is a recognition of difference, of the right of difference to exist, of interest in finding things different.

*

Each of us yields to habit, each of us erects a framework to support our lives, and for most of us freedom means being able to retain these habits. How bizarre— freedom is the vicious circle of self-chosen limitation. My chair, my stuff, my routine—my cell.

*

When will America become America?

* * *

See? Few were promised, and few were delivered.

Kate, I have to get out of this house. Today, during an early morning walk, I realized that I have been hibernating in my study for nearly a year and a half. I'm sure some old friends may think I'm in a witness protection program. I rarely go out—I have no place to go, no money to spend. Most of my friends are absorbed in their jobs; they seem to have less and less time to talk with me. I feel isolated, detached from the world around me. I haven't earned any substantial money in nearly two years. My savings account has been whittled down to pennies. I am barely scraping by on soap residuals.

I'm worried. Nervous. About the state of the world and the state of my being. I really don't know what to do. The world is at war with itself, and I am at war with myself.

War. It seems like nothing has changed in the last twenty something years. I remember when your mother and I were first married. We had a small apartment in Queens. On one wall, I hung a large poster that pictured an empty grassy field, in the middle of which a rifle with a bayonet on the end of its barrel was planted in the turf, and hanging by its strap, across the butt end of the rifle, was an army helmet that had painted on its side a peace symbol. The poster carried the words: What if they gave a war and nobody came.

The year was 1969.

Back then people my age experienced a time of revolution and social upheaval. Many of my generation fought their parents, fought racial injustice, fought political repression, and fought the use of force in faraway rice fields. Not me. I got caught up in the make-believe world of television. Sure, I supported racial equality and opposed the war in Vietnam, but I wasn't a college radical type. I didn't march for justice, and I didn't attend anti-war demonstrations. I wasn't a young Republican type either; I didn't wear a Nixon button or flag pin in my lapel, and I wasn't consumed with the world of commerce and business.

No revolutions for me. I sat on the sidelines.

Now, years later, I'm in the middle of a personal revolution. This is a time of transformation. I know what I was and where I've been, but I have no idea who I will become or where I will go.

I'm worried. Nervous. And broke.

In the first movie I saw today, Alice, after looking to others for help, finally looked inside herself for answers. She trots off to India, looking for Mother Teresa, but instead finds the real Alice and comes home transformed.

I know something must change, something must give. I cannot go on like this, stuck like an oil-coated cormorant in the polluted waters of my life.

When I try to focus in on alternatives to television and Hollywood, my mind always starts packing for travel. I'm obsessed with the notion of living abroad for a year or so. But the reality of such an undertaking is simple: I cannot afford an extended stay in Europe, plus the war situation makes this a dangerous time to be traveling abroad even if I had the money.

Oh my god—a light bulb just lit up over my head, and it revealed one word: MEXICO.

Yes, yes, yes! Of course, Mexico! What a revelation! It's foreign and close. Shit, I can even drive there. I can try it for a few months and see how things go.

OK, OK, calm down. It's funny, I've been living in Southern California for the past five years, yet I have never been to Mexico. I never even thought about going there. Maybe in my mind the country's rich cultural history was dimmed by the false concept that Mexico is nothing more than a collection of abysmal slums or exotic beaches. But Mexico is a perfect way for me to scratch my itch to travel.

This solution is so simple I never saw it before this instant. I can sublet the townhouse, fully furnished, for a few months; I can sell my BMW and pick up an old VW bug; and I can hit the road. I'll travel light—some old clothes, some paper, and some pens. I'll keep it simple. Damn, Mexico is one of the few places with an economy that is in worse shape than America's. The few bucks I have will go much farther down there.

Imagine: no CNN, no TV, no newspapers, no radio, no computer. I must confess, my computer makes me nervous, I always worry that it will erase everything I've written. I'll take my old, portable typewriter. I'll take a few books that I have been wanting to read, such as *Notes from Underground* by Fyodor Dostoevsky and *Jude the Obscure* by Thomas Hardy.

Of course, dear Kate, I shall continue to write to you, only my letters will no longer contain war dispatches. It is odd to think that my heated war commentary will be read by you at some future time when the passions of this conflict will have died. I suppose in the past, letters from the front written by frightened young soldiers reached their homes long after the battles had been fought and the blood had been shed. In this war, television brings the world to the front, so my letters, like war billets of the past, will reach your home long after the fighting has ceased. I wish I knew what my father thought about World War II and the Korean War.

Anyway, Mexico might be just the medicine the doctor ordered. I need a change of scenery. I need to get outside the walls of this house and my head. I need a time of genuine introspection, a time to settle my mind. In the past forty-eight hours I've wanted to move to Vermont and live in a tiny town, I've wanted go to the city of Riyadh in Saudi Arabia and take pictures of SCUD missile attacks, I've wanted to track down George McGovern and volunteer my services if he makes another run for the presidency, I've wanted to go to Tahiti and live in a grass hut on the beach with a naked, native lady. What, me fickle?

Kate, I'm so crazy that by tomorrow I'll probably throw away this Mexico idea.

NO! I won't throw it away. I'll leave it to chance.

If the Giants lose the Super Bowl tomorrow (and they are the underdogs in the contest), I will stay in Hollywood and earnestly seek a job in television production; but if the Giants win, I head for Mexico. By the way, the Bills are favored to win the game by a touchdown. I don't think the Giants have a chance.

Sunday, January 27—1:19 P.M.

Two hours to kick off, and I don't care. Imagine me, a football fanatic, not caring. But I'll watch anyway. At least innocent civilians don't get killed during gridiron battles.

Sunday, January 27—6:30 P.M.

What a game! Another cardiac finish! The New York Giants squeaked by the Buffalo Bills 20-19 in a magnificently played thriller of a football game. Just as in the NFC Championship, the Super Bowl was decided by a last second field goal attempt. Only this time, Scott Norwood's potential game-winning boot for the Bills missed and the Giants won. For three exciting hours the nation took a vacation from the war. Even the troops got to enjoy a little pigskin diversion from perils of Saddam. During the game, there were live shots from Saudi Arabia of the cheering soldiers enjoying the game.

Mexico, here I come.

Monday, January 28—11:05 A.M.

This morning CNN carried live a speech given by George Bush before the NRB— the National Religious Broadcasters—convention in Washington.

Why do I turn the god damned TV on?

I tuned in just in time to hear Bush say, "God can live without man, but man cannot live without God." I hate it when politicians talk like preachers. Bush endorsed the convention's theme: "Declaring His Glory to All Nations." President Bush spoke of the "eternal teachings of the scripture" which uphold moral values. He claimed his use of force in the Gulf was moral and just, and that "the world (i.e. the nations that comprise the coalition forces) is overwhelmingly on the side of God." The Commander-in-Chief claimed God's love and justice inspires us to oppose tyranny. He claimed the war in the Gulf pits "good versus evil" and "right versus wrong." Bush reiterated his opposition to abortion and his commitment to return voluntary prayer to public schools. He claimed, "America has always been a religious nation" and that "one cannot be America's President without trust in God." Pastor George mentioned the word "God" nine times during his fifteen minute speech. He quoted from Ecclesiastes in the Old Testament and the Gospel of Matthew in the New Testament. Mr. Bush mentioned St. Augustine and St. Thomas Aquinas, a pair of theologians who are the pillars of Catholic pleasure-hating sexual morality. As usual, the President's sermon ended with, "May God bless our great nation. Thank you and God bless you."

George Bush claimed the war in the Gulf was not a religious war, but a "just war." Sure . . . and Madonna is a virgin. The truth, dear daughter, I think comes closer to this: Bush and his team of sycophantic apparatchiks have mindlessly maneuvered America into a war in a region that is incomprehensible to Western minds in general, and especially mysterious and perplexing to the sorry collection of two-bit, dime store, lily-white, wasp politicians who run the White House.

In trying to elevate the war to a higher moral ground, Bush was reaching back in time to a philosophical concept that dates back to the days when armored units were soldiers wearing chain mail, long before high-tech weapons of mass destruction. Back in the fifth century, St. Augustine outlined conditions under which Christians could, with moral authority, fight wars. Over the centuries these conditions were refined by St. Thomas Aquinas and other Christian thinkers.

The accepted conditions—all of which must be met—for war to be considered a "just war" are: The war had to be declared by a "competent authority"—the recognized, legitimate leader of a country (the point here is that generals can't start a war); there must be a "just cause"—such as self-defense, repelling invaders, protecting innocent lives, avenging wrongs, restoring what has been seized unjustly; the good that would be achieved has to clearly outweigh the harm that may be done—a concept known as "proportionality," which states that there must be a proper proportion between the evil that accompanies war and the good that victory will achieve; it has to be the "last resort"—all attempts to resolve it peacefully must have been exhausted; there must be reasonable hope or likelihood of success; and, the intiation of war must be carried out with the right intention—that is, a nation cannot go to war under the cloak of some noble motive when in its heart there exists a selfish hope of national gain (such as oil).

The Augustinian formula can hardly settle the matter; it leaves a few areas of ambiguity. Clearly, the Persian Gulf War does not meet all the conditions for a "just war." At best, three of the conditions for a just war have been met. In fact, Bush's claim that this is a just war has been challenged by many religious leaders and scholars. Of course, many clerics (primarily evangelical or fundamentalist preachers) feel the conditions for a "just war" have been met.

The odd thing about dragging St. Augustine into the "just war" debate is that the fourth century theologian's theorem is drawn from nonscriptural sources. St. Augustine relied heavily on Stoic philosophy, whose roots are well outside the scriptural foundations of Christianity. I find it rather peculiar that none of the Christians, especially Mr. Bush, claiming this is a "just war" ever mention Jesus. Jesus spoke of loving our neighbors and not doing them harm, and even insisted on our loving our enemies.

Mr. President, give me clear, sound, logical, and reasonable grounds for the war and I will respectfully listen, but please stop insulting me by dragging God into the debate and hiding behind a mask of religious righteousness.

Baghdad is a city of 3.8 million people, and the allied military leaders are constantly claiming that we are not targeting civilians, that we are not trying to annihilate the city. Don't ask me to believe, after weeks of what has been described as the most intense bombing in human history, that any question of morality survives. I just cannot buy it.

We Americans like to think we are—and always have been—the most moral people on earth. But do our actions support such a claim of moral superiority? Early American settlers wiped out colonies of Indians, killing perhaps as many as 16 million native Americans. We have enslaved millions of black Americans, granting them freedom only when we had no other choice. We took Texas and California from Mexico. During the Vietnam War, we killed innumerable women and children. We have supported such evil dictators as Pol Pot, Samosa, "Baby Doc" Duvalier, Marcos, and, of course, Saddam Hussein. On August 6, 1945, America set the world record for killing when it dropped the atomic bomb on Japan, which killed hundreds of thousands of innocent women and children. I suppose a strong case could be mounted in defense of our dropping the atomic bomb on Hiroshima, but there is no justification for the gratuitous bombing of Nagasaki, which is nothing short of the most heinous war crimes in history.

Please do not misunderstand me—I love this country. Americans, however, do not like facing reality; we seem intent on proving that life is not tragic. We have a collective "sitcom" mentality, which asserts that all our problems will be neatly resolved by the third act, and everybody will live happily ever after. It's just not true. We are a moral people, yet morality does not belong exclusively to us, and we are capable of performing acts whose morality can certainly be questioned. I simply question the morality of our military involvement in the Persian Gulf.

There is one other factor that people ignore when they use St. Augustine's formula for a just war. St. Augustine did not take into account the possible use of chemical, nuclear, and biological weapons and other modern, conventional instruments of mass destruction. The good Saint could never have imagined the destructive power of one 2,000-pound bomb dropped from an airplane on a population center, let alone the effects of the use of fuel-air and cluster bombs, "bouncing Betty" artillery shells, and tomahawk missiles have on the combatants themselves. We have entered the age where no war can be "won." Both the victors and the defeated are losers, because the destruction on both sides will be reciprocal and complete. In light of the high-tech arsenals available to contemporary military planners, I do not think a "just war" is any longer possible.

The more bombs we drop, the more SCUDs Iraq launches and the more oil they pour into the Gulf. Escalating savagery begets further savagery in response. Each side steps back from the fray and points with outrage at the cruelty of the other. Moderation and judgment quickly give way to frenzy and impatience. In a world where might is right, there is little room for love.

Hiding behind the Bible and his faith in God, George Bush is shamelessly cloaking national machismo and selfish intentions in the mantle of a just cause. Of course, if I expressed that opinion in public, or even in the homes of some family members, I would be resoundly booed. But please don't forget Kate, that a thriving democracy depends on continual informed debate. Protest acquaints us with viewpoints contrary to the prevailing opinion, prompting us to examine the strengths and weaknesses of national policy. Free speech and open debate cannot be curtailed or limited during a war. It is not my intention to insult our troops or give comfort to Saddam Hussein, but the right to protest is meaningless if it can be exercised only when no significant national interest is at stake.

Enough about war, religion, and politics. I must start planning for Mexico, and the rest of my life. One quick last item for now: I mentioned to you that last Friday I happened to catch a talk show hosted by a female comedienne that featured women who danced nude in bars. Well, today after the Bush bullshit, I happened to catch another talk show hosted by a different woman, and her guests were four zaftig ladies, each dressed in her "work" clothes: one danced nude at bachelor parties, one was a hot oil wrestler, one performed at a sex club, and I didn't hear what the last lady did for a living but she was wearing a leather neck-choker and a black bra and panties. This was a nationally syndicated talk show and a leading alternative to watching military briefings from Saudi Arabia or the Pentagon.

God bless America.

Thursday, January 31—11:30 A.M.

It has been more than seventy-two hours since I've reported to you about the war. I just heard that an American fighter jet was shot down and that the Iraqis have captured an American female soldier. Also, Iraq has launched another SCUD missile attack on Israel.

The war grinds on, and yesterday the heat was turned up a notch.

Eleven United States Marines were killed yesterday in the war's first sustained ground combat. Under the cover of darkness, the Iraqi army crossed the Kuwaiti border into Saudi Arabia and attacked the small, abandoned seaside town of Khafji. The battle was described as hellacious. American military commanders claimed the enemy assault was not considered a full-fledged offensive, but was called a minor "probing operation." I'm sure the families of the dead Marines will appreciate the difference between a full-fledged assault and a probing action.

One soldier offered this comment on the fighting: "It felt good. We kicked their asses." Before the coalition forces regained control of the town, an American soldier said, "We're going to go up and spank them pretty hard, so they probably ought to call 911 right now. I expect we're going to expel them rather violently." It is estimated that hundreds of Iraqi troops were killed.

And when the war is over, it will beget other wars in the region. We will succeed in forcing Iraq to leave Kuwait and the Emir will be returned to his throne. But the war will not make the Middle East safe from weapons of mass destruction any more than it will rid the world of aggressors. The war will not erase from the Iraqi psyche the conviction that Kuwait is part of Iraq's Basra province, as it had been for centuries under the Abbasis and Ottoman empires until 1922. After the war, Arabs in Iran, Jordon, Syria, and Iraq will hate America more than ever before.

Violence begets violence. Brutality breds brutality.

Arabs will have a right to question why the United States was so patient with violent repression in China, South Africa, and occupied territories of the Soviet Union, but felt a need to rush to war with Iraq. They will have a right to be angry that the United States could wait leisurely for forty-two years to demand justice for the Palestinians, yet could wait only twenty-four hours after the United Nations January 15 pullout deadline passed before launching the largest air strike in history.

This is a very messy situation. There are a lot of tough questions that need to be asked. Yet according to the polls, 80 percent of the country fully supports the President's policy—without the need to question his judgment. Yesterday, I had to go to Burbank to drop off a sample script at a studio, and I drove past a pro-war rally at City Hall. About a hundred or so people gathered together to show they stand behind the president and the U.S. troops. Among the sea of waving flags and homemade signs, I saw one placard that really troubled me. In big, bold red letters, this is what the sign proclaimed:

GO USA GO
NO SLACK FOR IRAQ
NUKE 'EM TIL THEY GLOW

In my mind, the demonstrator was neither a poet nor a patriot.

Patriot. It is a word that is on everyone's mind and lips. It is the name of the surface-to-air missile that American soldiers have been successfully using against SCUD missiles fired by Iraq toward Saudi Arabi and Israel. Everyone talks about the need for patriotism, the need to support our troops in the Gulf. People are putting small flags on the radio antennas of their cars, businesses are hanging flags in their windows, and many private homes are proudly displaying Old Glory. I care about America. I love America. I wouldn't want to live any place else. However, I'm not sure of all this patriotism stuff. It seems to me that patriotism is built on the foundation of national conceit, arrogance, and egotism. It is as if people who happen to be born in one particular area of our planet assume that through the good fortune of their birthplace, they and their fellow inhabitants are better, nobler, grander, and more intelligent than people living in other areas. Patriotism is a superstition that robs humanity of its self-respect and dignity, and it increases arrogance and conceit. Patriotism can be more inhumane and brutal than religion.

But there is hope. I just turned the television on, and President Bush was giving a speech at a prayer breakfast being held at the convention of the National Religious Broadcasters, the same group before whom just a few days ago he gave a speech in which he claimed the war was moral and just. I tuned in just in time to hear Bush say that God answers prayers. No one asked for proof of that claim. I quickly put a blank tape into my VCR and managed to record the last few minutes of his address. As I was inserting the tape into the VCR Bush was saying how churches and synagogues were setting records for attendance, that people were turning to God in prayer.

Here is a transcript of what I caught of the speech:

> . . . are packed. Record attendance at services. In fact, the night the war began, Dr. Graham [Billy Graham, famous Protestant evangelist] was at the White House and he spoke to us then of the importance of turning to God as a people of faith, turning to Him [God] in hope. And then the next morning Dr. Graham went over to Fort Meyer where we had a lovely service, leading our nation in a beautiful prayer service there, with special emphasis on the troops overseas. So I suspect that when Barbara and I were at that prayer service we were doing, only doing, what everyone else in America was doing: praying for peace. You know America is a nation founded under God, and from our very beginnings we have relied upon His [God's] strength and guidance, in war and peace—and this is something we should never forget. I suppose every president has learned that one cannot be president of our country without faith in God, and without knowing with certainty that we are one nation under God. God is our rock and salvation, and we must trust Him and keep faith in Him. And so we ask His blessing upon us, and upon every member [sic] not just of our armed forces, but of our coalition armed forces, with respect to the religious diversity that is represented in these twenty-eight countries stand [sic] up against aggression.

President Bush designated Sunday, February 3, as a national day of prayer. Yep, that's the ticket America: pray, don't dare ask questions. November 2nd's national day of prayer didn't do much good, what makes the president think another day of prayer will bare any fruit?

I am deeply troubled by those religious leaders who insist the war is just. Why doesn't the press ask a few questions about Reverend Billy Graham's presence at the White House? Is he the resident theologian or counselor for the war effort? Does this minister really think that this mystery we call God has had any part in the tribal bloodbaths that stain mankind's history? Do the Reverend and the President really think God cares about this "new world order" George Bush keeps talking about without explaining it?

The press seems to have forgotten how in the sixties the square-jawed evangelist, who once admitted to not having a good enough mind to discern whether or not the Bible was literally God's word, transmitted to humans without any trace of error, was quick to speak out against communism but never uttered a word in support of the civil rights movement. The press seems to have forgotten that Reverend Graham, who was one of tricky Dick Nixon's strongest defenders, even during Watergate, was an ardent supporter of the Vietnam War. At Nixon's 1969 inaugural, during a prayer Graham thanked God that "thou hast permitted Richard Nixon to lead us at this momentous hour of history." Billy Graham is a political climber who has been used by presidents to add a touch of divinity to their political agendas.

The question that begs to be asked is: Is not this minister's attempt to dress the bombing and killing in the robes of a Holy War the same kind of an idea that is soundly denounced when it comes from his Islamic counterparts?

In Baghdad, Saddam seeks God's inspiration on how to defeat "the forces of Satan and his hirelings" (i.e. George Bush and the coalition forces). Having adopted the persona of the twelfth-century Kurdish warrior Saladin, Saddam is trying to speak with the same voice: "Satan will be vanquished," he said three days after the start of the war. Faced with the French Crusaders at the battle of Hittin on July 4, 1187, al-Malik al-Afdal, Saladin's own son, records how his father rallied the Moslem troops with the battle cry: "Satan must not win." Islam now fills the niche in our national subconscious once occupied by Catholics or Communists or Jews.

Bush is wisely asking only for God's protection for the troops he (Bush, not God) has sent into battle, and has not yet demanded victory for the "new world order." Still, he is trying to firmly set the war on a quasi-theological and moral foundation when he announced the other day that the conflict was between "good and evil, right and wrong." Jesus has been left out of the equation because any manifestation of the Christian religion in Saudi Arabia is about as welcome as the image of Satan. Hence, the young American soldiers who might die in defense of the Gulf states were not allowed to celebrate Christmas in public, nor are they permitted to wear crucifixes. The military ban on all outward diplays of the Christian faith is called "sensitivity" to the host country . . . the host country hates Christianity, yet allows Christians to help defeat a fellow Muslim. The Archbishop of Canterbury elected not to visit British Christian soldiers because his presence would be viewed as desecrating holy soil or rather, holy sand. But the Archbishop has assured his flock that they will be fighting a "just war."

The whole thing is crazy. What we really have in the Middle East is a war that has been blessed by the protector of the Prophet Mohammed's shrines, the putative decendent of Saladin, the President of the United States, and the head of the Church of England.

At this stage of the game, oil and Kuwait are no longer the issue. Bush wants to destroy Hussein, and Hussein wants to destroy the American army. Kuwait merely provides them with a battlefield which they will eventually leave, burning, seeded with mines for generations to come. Little wonder, then, God has been called upon to inspire the legions in the desert. God's going to have a hell of time trying to answer all the prayers for protection and victory.

Well, Kate, I haven't been glued to the tube for the past few days. I have been busy investigating all the options before me in regard to my Mexico trip.

More on that later. But first, lunch.

Thursday, January 31—4:05 P.M.

Bless me Father, for I have sinned. I ate two spinach-and-cheese calzones for lunch.

Sometimes sins can be rather delicious.

Maybe I could strike it rich by opening a chain of Calzone Diet Centers. The plan would be simple: eat one calzone a day. On Monday, Wednesday, and Friday you would eat a spinach-and-cheese calazone. On Tuesday, Thursday, and Saturday you would eat a mushroom calzone. On Sunday you would get a reward and eat one spinach-and-cheese calzone and one mushroom calzone. There can be no subsitutes, and you must drink one glass of my secret marinara flavored liquid formula. Of course, the Calzone Diet Center will sell the frozen calzones in convenient microwavable packages. This easy to follow diet—a glass of secret liquid at lunch and a calzone at dinner (except on Sunday when you have a calzone at lunch and dinner)—will guarantee that you will either lose weight or develop a hunger to visit Rome.

I could even star in my own commercials: "This was me before I developed my revolutionary diet. This diet so changed my life that I opened Calzone Diet Centers all across America to help other tub-o's experience the joy of being thin." I'll become so rich that I will buy the New York Giants and get fat, former players to star in my commercials. I'll marry a cheerleader. My team will win another Super Bowl, and at the end of the game players will pour the secret diet formula on my head as I cheer the outcome of the game on the sideline.

I'll sell the Calzone Diet Center for 167 billion dollars to a Japanese conglomerate, which will market the diet in theaters as an alternative to popcorn. Then I'll sell the Giants to an oil baron from Saudi Arabia for 328.5 million dollars. I'll be on the cover of *Fortune* magazine, which will list me as one of the richest men in America. Then the economy will collapse under the burden of insurmountable debt, the market will crash, and we'll have a recession and a depression. Unemployment will spiral to record highs, and banks will fail. I will lose everything. The cheerleader will leave me for the Saudi oil baron. I'll go back to writing to you.

Well, why don't I just save all that time and trouble and just keep writing to you. Although an Egg Roll Diet Center might not be a bad idea. Never mind. Back to my letter.

Now, from the ridiculous madness of war to the madness of my plan to go to Mexico. Actually, I don't have much of a plan. I have been reading about Mexico, and I still think it is a good idea to spend some time there; however, it is a big, confusing country that offers a wide variety of possibilites. There are the mountains and deserts of the northwest, the Baja California Peninsula, the Mexican high plateau, the eastern highlands, the Gulf plains, the southern ranges, the pacific coastal plains, volcanic ranges, and ancient archeological sites. There are six different cultural regions including big cities and small villages. I don't think I want to spend all my time going from one place to another, trying to see all the different sights Mexico has to offer. I would like to spend time in one place—and that's the problem. I don't know where that place should be. I do know that I want to avoid all the beach resort places such as Cancun, Puerto Vallarta, and Acapulco.

The point is my plans are very fuzzy, and I haven't been able to pull them into focus.

Tomorrow I'm driving up to Santa Barbara for the weekend. My friend who lives there has been to Mexico a number of times, and maybe she will be able to offer some helpful advice.

I'll speak to you in a few days.

Sunday, February 3—9:40 P.M.

Just got back from Santa Barbara. Woke up very early today. I tiptoed out of my friend's house, managing not to disturb her. I took a long walk down to the ocean. Stopped for coffee at a small cafe. I was sitting alone, and I guess the waitress figured I was bored or lonely, so she brought over the local Sunday paper and asked if I would like to read it. I didn't really want to, but I said, "Sure. Thanks."

I thumbed my way through the various sections of the paper. Had no interest in the main news section, less interest in the editorial section, even less interest in the sports section (this is basketball and hockey season, and I don't understand either sport), still less interest in the entertainment section, and, of course, absolutely no interest at all in the business section; then I came across the travel section. At first, I wasn't that interested in the travel section either, but just as I was about to place it a top the rest of the pile of papers and push the mound away, I saw this: Oaxaca is Mexico of Imagination.

According to the article, Oaxaca (pronounced wah-HAH-kah) is an older, grander Mexico that has none of the high-rise hotels of the famous oceanfront resorts, or the smog and mayhem of Mexico City. Oaxaca was founded by Cortes around 1530 and is the most colonial city in Mexico, retaining much of its Spanish conquistador and pre-Columbian Indian cultures. The streets are small, and many of the buildings date back to the eigtheenth century and earlier. In the hills just outside the city are some of the finest pre-Columbia ruins in the country. The sites reflect the elaborate cultures of the Zaptoec and Mixtec Indians who thrived before the arrival of the Spanish.

I can't remember all the details of the article, but I instantly knew that this was to be my destination. Oaxaca is in the southern highlands, about a fourteen-hour train ride from Mexico City. Tomorrow I'll track down some information.

Monday, February 4—9:22 A.M.

Gulf War toll after nearly three weeks of fighting: American dead—13 in action, 20 in noncombat accidents; Americans held in Iraq—8; American troops missing in action—29; American planes lost in combat—13; American planes lost in noncombat accidents—13; Allied bombing missions flown—44,000 plus. The other day I mentioned that 11 Marines were killed in a ground battle at Khafji. It turns out that seven of those soldiers were killed by "friendly fire"—that means that they were accidently hit by bombs launched by American pilots.

Kate, despite the gloomy backdrop of the war, I feel alive for the first time in years. I'm excited about my future, at least the next few months of it. More about that later—now, I'm off to the library to read about Mexico and try to dig up some information on Oaxaca.

Monday, February 4—7:35 P.M.

While Americans are dying in combat in the Saudi desert, a piece of Americana is being commemorated by the Mongolian Government. The Mongolian Post Office has just issued a set of stamps that feature the cartoon characters from the Flintstones. Yes, Fred and Barney are depicted riding dinosaurs across the Gobi Dessert.

Tell me life is not absurd!

In a war that features real-life cartoon characters like Bush and Hussein, perhaps the Flintstones could find a way for us to resolve our conflicts without spilling any more blood. I bet Betty and Wilma could straighten out this mess.

Tuesday, February 5—10:00 A.M.

Before going to bed last night, I was paying some bills and trying to balance my checkbook. The little money I have will go further in Mexico than in this country. Rooms in Oaxaca run about ten dollars a night. This morning I read in the paper that President Bush submitted his 1992 budget to Congress. The bottom line of the two-thousand-page budget is a spending package of 1.45 trillion dollars, which proposes to continue borrowing about twenty cents for every eighty cents it takes in and creates a deficit of 281 billion dollars. The budget does not include the cost of the Persian Gulf War, but does allocate 295.2 billion dollars for the military that includes money to develop many exotic new weapons. Mr. Bush's first term will add more than $1,000,000,000,000 to our nation's debt. Uncle Sam takes in about three billion dollars a day and spends nearly four billion.

By these standards, my budget is in pretty good shape. I borrowed about $20,000 last year. So, a month or two in Mexico wouldn't make any difference one way or the other.

I've got a meeting in Burbank this afternoon. There is a sick flick in need of a script doctor. The movie is titled *Hired Gun,* and it needs some fast rewrites before going into production. The job, if I get it, will take two weeks to complete and will give me some cash for Mexico. Yesterday, my research trip to the library unearthed a wealth of information on Oaxaca, which I'll tell you about next time.

Friday, February 8—4:10 P.M.

Tuesday's interview went well. I think I impressed them. But, then again, they still haven't called and offered me the job. They said I would hear something by Monday. I guess I'll have to wait until then.

I've been reading about Mexico. Mexico is made up of thirty-one states and the Federal District, which is the capital of the Mexican Republic. The city of Oaxaca is the capital of the state of Oaxaca. The city lies in the heart of a broad, wishboned shaped valley that is surrounded by densely forested mountains, including the massive Sierra Madre del Sur Mountains. The city was and remains the focus of Indian life, mostly Zapotecs and Mixtecs who live in the valley and nearby mountains. They come to town to buy supplies and to sell their handicrafts. The city is known for its provincial atmosphere and many small plazas and gardens. By all accounts, the city is graced with many fine examples of colonial architecture. Not far from the city there are two significant archeological sites. Oaxaca has been called the homeland of the gods, birthplace of statesmen, and refuge of intellectuals. Mexicans from other states come to Oaxaca to relax and unwind.

Sounds perfect to me. I can't wait to get there.

I'll be leaving in a little while for Santa Barbara, where I'll be keeping my fingers crossed about the job over the weekend.

Monday, February 11—1:55 P.M.

I got it! Hired, that is, on *The Hired Gun.*

They just called. I've got to zip over to Burbank this afternoon and pick up the script. I know the script is lousy, the producer as much as said so himself. He doesn't expect miracles from me. It is just that the backers are a bit apprehensive about it, and he had to assure them that improvements would be made. Anyway, I'm just going to fake enthusiasm and do the best I can. It is better than cutting lawns, and it pays a lot more.

Wednesday, February 13—11:40 A.M.

Today is Ash Wednesday.

An official from the British Prime Minister's office said it was, "extremely regrettable," but added, "this was bound to happen sooner or later." A British military spokesman said, "Obviously something went wrong." What went wrong and was so regrettable was that a bomb shelter packed with civilians, mostly women and children, in Baghdad was hit by two Allied missiles. Initial reports indicate anywhere from 200 to 1,000 people were killed. The first television reports from the area showed the charred bodies of thirty or so women and children lined up on a sidewalk.

Just yesterday President Bush challenged Hussein's claim that the coalition forces were indiscriminately bombing civilians. In the past Bush claimed we were not targeting Saddam Hussein personally, yet we bombed every place Saddam has eaten a falafel sandwich during the last decade. Our purpose, of course, is to non-operationalize (military-speak for "shut down") the industry that feeds the Iraqi war machine, and not to hit Saddam personally. I have no doubt that we are making every effort to avoid dropping bombs on civilians. Unfortunately, in war, as in life, things don't always go according to plan. To date, there have been over 67,000 bombing missions flown by the allied forces. Accidents are bound to happen.

I had a very strange dream last night. I was in the Oval Office with George Bush and the Secretary of Defense, Dick Cheney. The top two men in our war effort were conferring with me about some big issue—perhaps the discussion centered around when to start the ground-assault phase of the war. I didn't actually say anything, and they turned their backs on me and began looking at something, but I couldn't tell what it was. As they talked, I inched forward and managed to catch a glimpse of what they were looking at. On a credenza along the back wall was a small television: they were watching a porno film. I have no idea what this dream means.

This is going to be a crazy day. Indications now are that the bombing of the shelter was not accidental. Military spokesmen are claiming this was a military bunker that has been on their target list for some time, and that it was an active "command and control" facility. They didn't understand why civilians were in the bunker. If it is discovered that the victims were a mixture of military personnel and civilians, than the civilians who were incinerated would be considered "collateral damage."

War is ugly.

So, at times, is religion. Today in Chalma, Mexico, a one-street village nestled in a gorge near the tumbling, turbulent Chalma River about forty miles south of Mexico City, forty-two people looking for a miracle found death when they were caught in a stampede of pilgrims trying to enter a seventeenth-century church to receive ashes in observance of Ash Wednesday. The church houses a golden statue of Christ on a cross known as "El Señor de Chalma" (The Lord of Chalma), which is believed to work miracles. In 1533, the statue first "appeared" in a sacred cave in which the Indians worshipped the god Tezcatlipoca. I'd bet some clever missionary priest sneaked into the cave one night and left the statue. Folklore claims the statue rid the remote region of wild animals and rescued natives from danger. So popular is "El Señor de Chalma," that the village of Chalma has become one of the great religious pilgrimage centers in Mexico. Festivals at the beginning and end of Lent and at Christmas each year draw up to fifteen thousand from all over the country.

But "El Señor," credited with curing the sick and healing the lame, performed no miracles today. As the multitude of miracle-seekers pushed through the narrow street leading to the church, they collided with throngs of pilgrims leaving the church. In the frenzy to get through the doorway, thirteen children and twenty-nine adults (mostly women peasants) were suffocated, trampled, and crushed to death. One woman, whose sister-in-law's nine-year-old daughter was killed, said, "There was an avalanche of people. We were leaving and those that were coming in squashed those going out."

Authorities suggested that the stampede may have been set in motion by street vendors whose carts blocked the way. The vendors sold flowers, candles, and crosses. According to an Associated Press report, the bodies of the humbly dressed victims were covered with shawls and placed in rows on the concrete courtyard of a public school adjacent to the church until a file of young men bearing blue and white, satin-covered coffins threaded their way through the faithful, whose foreheads were marked with a cross of ash in observance of Ash Wednesday, and removed the bodies. Two dozen injured were rushed from the scene via ambulance.

It is estimated that 3,500 people were at the church door when the panicking and pushing began. Only one passageway leads to the church, which straddles a steep cliff above a river and is bounded by other buildings, making it accessible from only one side. Seven years ago, in a similar incident, seven people were also crushed to death. According to a Rueters News Report, a warden at the church said, "Everyone comes here with a lot of faith. What happened, happened. It's the will of the Lord." Some pilgrims called it a miracle in itself that they got out of the church alive. One woman claimed, "We were spared miraculously, because we cried out to the Lord of Chalma to save us."

A few hours after the injured and dead were removed, men set up a fireworks display in the churchyard and more people gathered for an evening celebration. One woman said, "We still have faith."

The coalition forces had fewer casualties during the thirty-seven days of trying to kick Iraq out of Kuwait than the pilgrims in Chalma had trying to get ashes. Don't tell me life isn't absurd. On my way back to Mexico City from Oaxaca, I'm going to try to visit Chalma. They expect another big crowd during Holy Week.

The incident in Chalma reminded me of a similar disaster that occurred in Mecca in the beginning of last July, just a few weeks before Saddam Hussein turned the world's attention to the Middle East. Every year, two million Muslims make a pilgrimage to Mecca. The pilgrimage is called the hajj. During last year's hajj, 1,426 pilgrims died in a stampede in a pedestrian tunnel joining the city of Mecca with a tent camp set up for the pilgrims. There was a power failure, which caused the air conditioning in the 1,500-foot-long, 60-foot-wide tunnel, which runs under part of a mountain, to switch off in the 112 degree heat, setting off the deadly stampede. The tunnel was packed beyond capacity (the tunnel can hold up to 1,000 people and it was estimated that 5,000 people were inside at the time) when some pilgrims stopped in the middle while people outside continued to push their way into the tunnel. Echoing the words of the Church officials in Chalma, King Fahd of Saudi Arabia said, "It was God's will, which is above everything. It was fate."

Isn't it odd that God, in two separate incidents within eight months of each other and on two separate continents, would "will" to have 1,468 people killed after they had traveled large distances to honor Him.

Ash Wednesday marks the beginning of Lent, a period of forty days intended to commemorate Christ's forty days' fast, which began after his baptism in the Jordan River by John the Baptist. As a child, I was taught to look upon baptism as a call to penance; my baptism was supposed to prepare me for all kinds of activity by mortification and prayer. Lent was forty days of self-denial and prayer in preparation for Easter, a day when we celebrated Christ's resurrection from the dead. I refrained from eating candy and ice cream for forty days in order to indulge on gaily colored hard-boiled eggs on Easter Sunday, which was really a bad deal. The old man who ran the candy store near the school must have hated Lent—for forty days his three dozen or so jars of penny candy attracted few customers. Although it was common knowledge that some not-so-good Catholic boys and girls stockpiled candy during the week before Lent.

As Lent approached, my mother would always ask, "Christopher, what are you planning to give up for Lent?" Lent meant giving things up. I always responded, "Broccoli and spinach." Mom would smile and remind me how important it was to give up things that I enjoyed in order to make God happy. I sometimes wondered why God would be happy if I wasn't happy—I mean what did my not being happy have to do with God's being happy? It made no sense, yet we fasted, went to church more frequently, and gave up lots of things we enjoyed. My oldest sister was the "giving up" champ; she gave up candy, ice cream, cake, cookies, peanut butter, and going to the movies. Except for giving up movies, Lent for her amounted to a diet.

But Lent was more than just giving up things we enjoyed; it really was a time of fasting. The Church had set aside certain days as fast days, and certain days as days of abstinence. A fast day was a day on which only one full meal was allowed, and it could be eaten at noontime or in the evening. The one full meal could include meat. Two other meals, both meatless, were permitted, but together they could not equal another full meal. On fast days, eating between meals was forbidden. A day of abstinence was a day on which the consumption of meat was forbidden. We ate a lot of fish on days of abstinence. Father Andrews never tired of reminding us that the Church commands us to fast and to abstain in order that we may control the desires of the flesh, raise our minds more freely to God, and make satisfaction for sin. "We must deny ourselves for the glory of God and the good of our souls" was his favorite way of explaining the restrictions we endured on fast days and days of abstinence.

Well, enough of this ecclesiastical culinary legal mumbo-jumbo. I've got to get to work on the *Hired Gun* script. I spent most of yesterday reading it and jotting down some notes. It is worse than I imagined it would be.

Here is the story in a nutshell—which is where the story belongs, in a nutshell. A sleazebag businessman in his late fifties is married to a much younger woman.

He discovers that she has been having an affair, which shouldn't have come as a great surprise, after all, he met her in a topless bar where she was a go-go dancer. In need of money, the outraged husband decides to increase his insurance policy on his unfaithful wife and then knock her off, thereby getting rid of her and his mountain of debt at the same time. The old "killing two birds with one stone" gambit. He contacts a two-bit thug to do the dirty work, which also includes—gasp—killing the couple's infant daughter.

A funny thing happens on the way to the double murder—the hired gun falls in love with his intended victim, after he beats her up. Most of the movie takes place in the apartment, where the assassinator and the housewife engage in some very wild sex. The movie has a scene in a porno bookstore that features nude dancers viewed from private booths. It also features sadism and brutality. There is not an iota of virtue in any of the characters. All of them appear beyond redemption, and it's difficult to even care about any of them. By the script's end, we are supposed to feel good that the gunman did the right thing and did not kill the woman and child. Of course, it shouldn't matter that he has killed, for a price, six people, and that he went to the apartment fully intending to kill two more people. This is not a nice guy, and nothing really happens in the script to indicate that he will be a nice guy in the future. After all, he did kill his new lover's husband, the guy who hired him to kill her.

How is it that this modern American romance is going to be produced, you may be asking yourself. Well, it seems the woman is going to be played by a hot, voluptuous actress (whom I have never heard of) who stars in a hit television show (which I have never seen). When I asked what else she has done, I was told she appeared in a five-page spread in *Penthouse* magazine, which means we know that she can take off her clothes. But can she act? That's not important—she's a "hot item" who is willing to "bare" all for screen stardom and that alone will draw people into the theater, or so the studio hopes, even though they know the script is a piece of shit.

Which is why they hired me. My job, as a hired pen, is to transform *The Hired Gun* from pernicious rubbish to nontoxic waste. But it pays. That is if it gets done, so I better get started.

Sunday, February 17—10:05 A.M.

Good morning. In churches all across America, people will be asking God to protect our troops. Many Christians support the war and consider it to be just and blessed by God. I wonder how a God of love can bless the pursuit of war. In the Middle East, the birth place of three major religions, armies are once again waging war, each evoking the name of God. Is there one God or three? Is there a Christian God, a Muslim God, and a Jewish God? Or is there one God with three different faces? Bush and Hussein both are convinced their war plans are exactly the same as God's war plans. (Which God? What God?) This conviction, that (some) God is behind them or they are on God's side, if successfully conveyed to the populace, helps both leaders legitimize their call to arms in the eyes of their citizens in a way that cannot be hoped for on purely intrinsic rational, moral grounds. Is God interested in re-establishing a balance of power in the Middle East and the price of oil? These are serious political problems but hardly just causes for war. When will humanity stop involving God in specific political projects?

In the news today there are a couple of nonwar stories that are interesting. One story reports how the Russian masses, wracked by unrest and uncertainty, are seeking solace in mysticism and the occult. All kinds of sorcerers, prophets, exorcists, and faith healers are rushing in to fill the vacuum created by disbelief in religion and communism. Belief in the supranormal is quickly spreading. The other story also revolves around belief. In Philadelphia, a measles epidemic is spreading. Well over a hundred cases have been reported this year. Five unimmunized children have died in the past ten days. Measles, while highly contagious, is not usually serious. City health authorities claim that the unusually high death rate may be caused by two fundamentalist Christian congregation's shunning of medical care, including highly effective immunization and antibiotics for bacterial infections that can result from measles. All five of the children who have died are members of the two churches. During the past few days, teams of doctors from two hospitals made door-to-door checks of about four children children who belong to the two churches. Because of their religious convictions, the vast majority of parents would not allow their children to be examined. They trust in the healing power of prayer and think God is testing their faith. One doctor said he found the people he visited to be "extremely courteous and caring and honest. And with the exception of the fact that they would stay at home and watch their children die of measles, they seemed like wonderful people."

Another day of war and religion. Too bad the world didn't give up both for Lent . . . imagine forty days of peace and sanity.

I have spent the last four days holed up in my study working on the script—what a piece of crap. For the most part, I managed to insulate myself from all forms of war coverage—no papers or radio, and very little TV—and I am now confident that I will be able to finish this task on time, and take the money and run to Mexico. So, dear daughter, this tired old ink-stained rascal had better get back to *Hired Gun*.

Sunday, February 17—8:00 P.M.

According to all the latest news analysis, the ground war is about to begin, perhaps within a few days. Today, during a border skirmish near Kuwait, an American Apache helicopter fired at and destroyed an American tank, killing two soldiers. The families of the slain soldiers will find little comfort in the fact that they were killed by "friendly fire" delivered by "smart bombs" in a "just war." A British military spokesman admitted that a "smart" bomb released by an RAF fighter jet had malfunctioned and strayed off course and hit a civilian area.

Who can predict what will happen when the ground war begins?

Tuesday, February 19—10:10 A.M.

The last thirty-six hours have seen a flurry of diplomatic action initiated by the Soviet Union in a last ditch effort to avoid the deadly ground war that now seems imminent and unavoidable. Iraq's Foreign Minister flew to Moscow and was handed a peace proposal from Mikhail Gorbachev. The Russians claim it is a concrete plan to settle the conflict by political means. That's funny, it was politics that started the war. Anyway, yesterday there was a heightened sense of hope that maybe the peace initiative would bear fruit; however, this morning President Bush made it sound like warmed-over bullshit. The President's finger is on the ground war trigger, and he is about to pull it. And America supports him.

One way or the other, the war will not last much longer. But whenever or however it ends, one thing seems fairly certain: it will not mean peace. People all over America are praying for peace. Many believe an Allied victory—which is a foregone conclusion—will guarantee peace in the Gulf region. They will be sadly disappointed. War never guarantees peace.

Besides, the Middle East isn't the only place where war is being waged. Millions of people were killed during the near decade-long war between Iran and Iraq, but beyond the Persian Gulf region, there were five million people killed in various other armed conflicts during the past ten years. Most of those wars are still raging. Three million people have died in the struggle for control of Cambodia, and that war is still going on; yet it gets virtually no media coverage. They're still fighting in Afghanistan, where at least a million people have lost their lives, and you don't hear much about that either.

The Stockholm International Peace Research Institute, in a preview of its yearbook for 1991, lists, in addition to thirty-seven major wars in which there have been 1,000 or more battle-related deaths, seventy-five lesser armed conflicts (in places such as the Basque country in Spain, Tibet, the Soviet Union, and China) still being fought. Some of these wars are in inaccessible regions, and the world seems to have forgotten them. Nobody even knows the casualty toll in the ongoing wars in Laos, or Liberia, or Mali, or Uganda. In the horn of Africa, which is experiencing a terrible drought, twenty million people are in immediate danger of starving to death, yet little can be done about it because Sudan, Ethiopia, and Somalia are engaged in a deadly war. I didn't read anything about that today.

All these wars seem tragically foolish; yet, of course, our war in the Gulf isn't.

Michael E. Creamer thought it was foolish and wrong. Creamer was a U.S. Army veteran. He served as a combat medic in Vietnam, winning two Purple Hearts and a Bronze Star for his valor during dangerous patrols. Creamer was a patriotic American. On his mantle he had proudly displayed a picture of himself in uniform with George Bush. But Creamer opposed the war. He called his Congressmen urging them to vote "no" on the Congressional vote authorizing the use of force. On January 23, 1991, he drove into the woods near his home in Connecticut. In an article in yesterday's *New York Times,* Tom Brokaw, the NBC News anchorman, described what happened next: "He wrote letters to friends, pinned on his Vietnam medals, put on his Ranger black beret and arranged his driver's license and Ranger identification card at his side. When all was in order, he picked up his shotgun and killed himself." Creamer left a note that said: "I'm sorry. I know many people will be hurt. This war has brought up too many nightmares of the last war. I don't think I could again endure the pain of mass casualties produced by a ground war—and this is the only way out. When survivors of this war come home, please treat them with admiration and respect we Vietnam veterans never received until it was too late."

It is easy to say you support the war; it is not so easy to fight the war. For the soldier, the war doesn't end when the fighting stops.

In Amherst, Massachusetts, yesterday, a man protesting the war walked into the middle of the common carrying a cardboard peace sign. He then doused himself with paint thinner and struck a match. Seconds later, he perished in a plume of smoke. More than a hundred people gathered on the common after the man died. Peace signs were later placed over the charred spots on the ground. One sign said: *Stop this crazy war.* Some saw his protest as the ultimate sacrifice; others were struck by the irony of protesting the killing of war by killing yourself. The man was the third American to chose self-immolation as a form of protest against the war in the Gulf. As evening fell on the quiet, western Massachusetts town, antiwar groups gathered on the common for a candlelight peace vigil, while others lined up around the edge of the common and sang "The Star-Spankled Banner" and "God Bless America," and urged support of President Bush.

But the war, according to the President, will go on according to schedule. Last night, Baghdad endured the heaviest night of bombardment since the war began. To date, after thirty-four days of combat, Allied pilots have flown over 83,000 bombing missions. Yesterday, two Navy ships hit mines in the Gulf. One ship was badly damaged. There were several injured sailors, one seriously. Estimates are that perhaps 20,000 Iraqis have been killed so far; there was no breakdown of that figure into military or civilian casualties.

Kate, during the past six months, I seem to have been very critical of our country. Please do not think my criticism means that I do not love America. I do love it, which is why I criticize it. Sinclair Lewis, who many considered to be among the top two or three writers America has ever produced, once told George Seldes, a world renowned American journalist and author, "Mencken [H. L., the American writer] and I are the two best one-hundred-percent Americans alive. We are accused of running down America, writing about nothing but her faults. We both criticize America, true, but it is because we want perfection. Others who boast they are one-hundred-percent American close their eyes and walk in dirt. We go with open eyes, and we clean out the dirt. If Mencken and I didn't love America so much, we would not criticize what is wrong with her."

Kate, America must reach for the stars, we must aim for perfection, we must be free to discuss what is wrong and try to make it right. I may be very wrong about the war, but the only way to know is to listen to the voices of opposition and not suppress them. I firmly believe that freedom in America has been severely weakened during this war.

Blind patriotism and intolerance has been legitimized and encouraged by our nation's political and religious leaders. TV anchors mouth censored Pentagon reports. Sadly, most Americans did not care that the government has handcuffed journalists and, in fact, has approved of an unprecedented level of official censorship. America has bought the bogus "national security" crap delivered by the Pentagon. The Government has extended the terms of service for military volunteers without their approval. Experimental drugs and vaccines have been used on our troops without their informed consent. Protesters' rights to assemble and distribute literature have been denied in many cities. Dissenters have been accused of being un-American, and they have been blamed for the deaths of U.S. soldiers. I watched Congress for endless hours on C-SPAN and was outraged to hear dissenters referred to as "unshaven," "shaggy haired," "poor excuses for Americans," "wearing tiny, round, wire-rimmed glasses." Congressional members who did not support the war were charged with disloyalty and attacked for "being on the wrong side." Arab-American citizens have been subjected to surveillance and questioning by the FBI simply because of their national origins. Worse, homes and businesses of Arab-Americans have been bombed and looted.

All that sounds very un-American to me. The American flag is not the sole property of those who supported Mr. Bush's Middle East policy.

A person must be free enough to say, "I love American and I don't support the war." If not, we are not a free nation.

Well, I've got a stupid, violent, sexist screenplay to work on, so I better get cracking.

Wednesday, February 20—9:45 A.M.

Hired Gun is fiction. In real life, people don't quickly and easily resort to murder as a solution to problems. Or do they? The national "body count" for 1990 indicates that homicide is very much a part of daily life.

Take a look at these shocking numbers released by the Justice Department:

In 1990, there were 2,245 homicides committed in New York City. Kate, that is more than six people a day murdered in what many think is the greatest city on earth. Last year, Los Angeles reported 983 homicides; Chicago, 850; Detroit, 582; Houston, 568; the city of brotherly love—Philadelphia, 503; Washington, D.C., 472; Dallas, 447; and Baltimore, 305. These figures are overwhelming. There were 143 people murdered in Boston, and 128 people murdered in Phoenix. Violent crime has reached epidemic proportions here in America. Last year, homicide increased by 10 percent from 1989. Nationwide, more than 22,200 people were slain (that's at least sixty people a day!), and at least twenty cities set homicide records. And we are worried about naked aggression in the Middle East.

Across our great land, the reported incidents of forcible rape rose by 9 percent. 3,126 women were raped in New York City; 2,014, in Los Angeles; 1,657, in Detroit; 1,335, in Houston; 1,344, in Dallas; 831, in Memphis; and 704, in Jacksonville, Florida. The Kuwaiti women aren't the only ones victimized by brutal men.

In New York City last year, 147,123 autos were stolen. Another 63,613 cars were stolen in Los Angeles. There were 26,015 homes burglarized in San Antonio, and 24,144 homes were broken into in Philadelphia. There were 37,156 robberies reported in Chicago and 100,280, in New York City. Nationwide, robbery was up by 11 percent; assault, up by 10 percent; and car theft, up by 5 percent.

Violence is a way of life in America. It has been estimated that by the time a kid is eighteen years old, he or she will have witnessed 32,000 deaths on television, and that's without watching the news.

Well, back to the very real *Hired Gun.*

Thursday, February 21—7:11 A.M.

Yesterday, the combination of working on *Hired Gun,* a thoroughly detestable script, and listening to all the predictions about the start of a thoroughly detestable ground war managed to thrust me into the dark abyss of despair. I hate this constant return to hopelessness. This feeling that absolutely nothing matters is driving me crazy. Life has become nothing but ups and downs, highs and lows. The middle ground is a foreign land. Is struggle all there is? It seems so.

Yet, this morning, I awoke to find yesterday's clouds of despair had scattered. My first stirrings were accompanied by the sounds of the theme music from *The Harvest of Life.* I recalled the voiceover, which claimed the harvest of life was a little stardust caught. When I wrote the opening for the show, I recently had come across these two sentences written by Henry David Thoreau:

The true harvest of my daily life is somewhat as intangible and indescribable as the tints of morning or evening. It is a little stardust caught, a segment of the rainbow which I have clutched.

I don't know why those two sentences were on my mind as I opened my eyes this morning. When I incorporated the sentiment expressed by Thoreau in the title and opening of the soap opera I created and produced, I did so because there was something about them that intrigued me. They were poetic and seemed true. Yet this morning I realized that I had never fully understood what old Henry David was saying. I think that the things in each person's life that make him or her feel unique and worthwhile can be felt only in flashes, quick little bolts of knowing and understanding. Yet we seem either to miss these fleeting moments or we don't know how to seize them. This morning I realized that if I don't catch and savor these flashes, I will be living without growth or exhilaration. I caught no stardust yesterday.

Back on July 16, I caught a little stardust, the stardust of life, and I clutched a piece of a rainbow, the rainbow of living. Yes, there will be peaks and valleys, but my difficulties with depression can only be overcome by persistence and patience, by catching little specks of stardust.

However, I must learn to distinguish between flashes of inspiration, and insight from the glitter of a foolish idea. Jesus, I have invested a lot of time and energy pursuing lame-brained schemes that I thought were great ideas. Every book or screenplay I start seems to be an inspired idea; yet most quickly prove to be worthless. Yesterday, I was having some doubts about Mexico. Maybe the questions the trip raised in my mind grew out of a legitimate concern over money, or from a sense that the entire idea was foolish. After thinking about it this morning, I believe my idea to go to Mexico was the stuff of stardust and rainbows. I have no choice but to go.

Back to the real world: CNN just carried a live radio address delivered by Saddam Hussein; it sounds like he is not about to withdraw from Kuwait without a fight. By the way, capitalism is starting to cash in on the war. For awhile now, pro-war T-shirts and buttons and yellow ribbon have been selling very well. But, as the war drags on, commercialization of it has become more creative. Saddam's face now graces toilet paper and a brand of kitty litter called "Saddam's Sand." Sometimes even foolish ideas pay-off.

Speaking of foolish ideas, I've got to get to work on *Hired Gun*.

Friday, February 22—11:50 A.M.

Hours after Saddam's bellicose radio address yesterday, his Foreign Minister arrived in Moscow, and, after a lengthy meeting with Mikhail Gorbachev, it was announced that Iraq agreed to withdraw from Kuwait unconditionally. But the good news wasn't that good, because the agreement outlining the unconditional withdrawal contained a list of eight conditions. Only in diplomatic circles could something unconditional contain conditions.

This morning President Bush announced that the Moscow peace proposal was unacceptable and that Saddam Hussein had until noon tomorrow to unconditionally withdraw or the ground war would commence. Jesus, high noon deadlines! Sounds like something out of an old Ronnie Reagan western. One way or the other, it sounds like Desert Storm is in its last days.

While leaders were talking, young men were dying. In Saudi Arabia yesterday, a United States Army medical helicopter crashed, while attempting a landing in bad weather. Seven American soldiers were killed.

Meanwhile, on the home front yesterday, Vice President Dan Quayle opened his mouth and let fly another of his trademark "say what?" remarks. Asked by *Newsweek* about his role of campaigner for the Californian Republicans, the veep said, "I love California. I grew up in Phoenix." Close enough, Danny Boy. Talk about frightening, Quayle is only a Bush "heartbeat away" from being president of the United States of America.

I just read that the agent for the ten-year-old actor who stars in this year's smash-hit movie *Home Alone* is demanding five million dollars from Fox for the kid to star in the sequel. It is called "star power." *Home Alone* sold over 200 million dollars worth of movie tickets since it was released at Christmas. By the way, the movie is a nostalgic paean to family values via sadism, sentimentality, and violent mayhem. The story is simple: a young boy is left home alone by his hard-pressed, absent-minded family, and the house is broken into by a couple of thugs. Unfazed, the kid uses every toy and gadget at his disposal and booby traps the house against the inept villains who lay siege to it. The movie is a real-life cartoon, far removed from reality, in which the smart, hip, and resourceful child is turned into a human pre-teenage Mutant Ninja Turtle. Thank you Hollywood for yet another mindless, money-making movie.

A New York Met pitcher turned down a contract offer that would have paid him 4.1 million dollars a year for three years. Noting that two other major league baseball players make more than that, the hurler declined to accept the offer. There are thirty-six major leaguers who earn more than three million dollars a year. Six of those make well over four million a year. In America today, a professional baseball player who makes under a million dollars a year has got to consider himself a hopeless mediocrity.

Speaking of hopeless mediocrity, I got to get to work on *Hired Gun.*

Saturday, February 23—2:05 P.M.

High noon has come and gone, and Saddam has not moved. Bush and Hussein are playing a high-stakes game of chicken, and neither is blinking.

Saturday, February 23—6:00 P.M.

The ground war has started.

Dona nobis pacem. "Grant us peace."

But if this century—our century—is any indication, peace is a long way off. The past ninety years have been the bloodiest ninety years in the history of humanity. During that period, humans have intentionally killed more than eighty million— that's 80,000,000—other humans in war. As civilization advances, our ability to kill increases. We now can kill thousands upon thousands by remote control, by the push of a button.

The thought that we are more civilized and more compassionate than the humans of antiquity is just another of our delusions. We spend more money on the military than we do on education and health care combined. We are as avaricious, as brutal, as savage, as ruthless, as hateful, as spiteful, and as feculent (full of shit) as we have ever been. Religion has not helped. We are still in the Dark Ages, the darkest of ages. We still bow down to idols; we still think God can save us.

Humanity's hope lies in humanity.

Dona nobis pacem.

Monday, February 25—3:08 P.M.

The first two days of the ground offensive have gone very well for the coalition forces. Iraqi soldiers have offered very little resistance. In fact, they are giving up in droves. Over twenty thousand of Saddam's grunts have already surrendered—eagerly surrendered. Coalition casualties have been very light. God chose not to answer prayers for protection in the case of four United States Marines and five soldiers from the other coalition armies. The estimates of thousands upon thousands of casualties have mercifully been wrong. Euphoric is the mood; quick and easy are the predictions.

Then, as if to punctuate the maxim that war is unpredictable, a SCUD missile launched by Iraq hit a United States military barracks and mess hall outside of Dhahran, killing twenty-eight U.S. Army soldiers. The SCUD had been intercepted by a Patriot missile, however, a large chunk of the warhead plummeted through the roof of the steel-and-tin building that once was a lumber warehouse. All that was left was a skeleton of steel girders and shredded bits of tin sheeting dangling from the charred bones of the building. Why, why, why . . . was the question on the minds of the dazed soldiers who survived? The odds against a section of a missile that was successfully intercepted happening to fall on the one spot that had a large concentration of Americans are extremely high. Why, with the war just days, maybe even hours, from being over, would God allow this to happen?

Because God—if there is a God—doesn't give a shit about our petty little wars. God is not on our side. God is not on Iraq's side. God is not even on the side of justice. We will win because we have a better army. Saddam Hussein is sadistic, cruel, paranoic, opportunistic, and ruthless; he suffers from a bad case of malignant narcissism. But that is not the reason he is going to get his butt kicked in this war; he will lose because he made countless tactical miscalculations and misjudgments in both the military and political realms. A surrendering Iraqi soldier, who spoke excellent English, was interviewed by a television reporter. He said that he hated Saddam. "Why," asked the reporter, "did you go to Kuwait?" Looking very sincere (and happy to be in the hands of the opposing army), the soldier said that he did not want to go to Kuwait, but if he failed to obey his marching orders then Saddam's henchmen would have harmed his family. "Better I go," he said.

What makes it difficult for me to oppose this war, is that I realize that Hussein is a real threat to the stability of the region, but somehow I am incapable of understanding how violence and killing is a solution to any problem. The French writer Albert Camus, who won the Nobel Prize for Literature in 1957, wrote in his published notebooks: "I am not made for politics because I am incapable of wanting or accepting the death of an adversary." I understand.

I know that Bush is not a bad guy; yet, I do not trust him. I know that Hussein is rotten to the core; yet, I do not hate him.

This war will be over very soon. Over two hundred Americans have been killed. I'm still not sure why. Their deaths will not insure peace in the Persian Gulf region. That will only happen when people learn to look beyond their countries, learn to look beyond their religion, and learn to accept and embrace all people as their brothers and sisters.

We are one. Or we are nothing.

Bombs destroy; people create. It is time to stop destroying and to begin creating. We must outgrow our childish ideas of God. We must stop clinging to a past that never was.

A final thought on the war—actually, a thought on television's intensive coverage of the war. My impression after watching forty-two days of the war on television is that the coverage can best be summned up with a line from *Macbeth*: "It is [was] a tale told by an idiot, full of sound [bits, talking heads] and fury, signifying nothing [but sensationalism and ratings]."

Monday, February 25—9:30 P.M.

Protest. I've done a lot of protesting in these letters, especially when it came to our involvement in the war. I can't help but get the feeling that many people in this country just bought into our military response in the Gulf without really questioning our leaders. We are a trusting nation; in times of crisis, we believe what politicians say and what our journalists report.

Shortly after World War II, the poet Robinson Jeffers wrote in a poem titled "An Ordinary Newscaster":

> We are not an ignoble people, but rather
> generous; but having been tricked
> A step at a time, cajoled, scared, sneaked into war; a
> decent inexpert people betrayed by men
> Whom it thought it could trust: our whole attitude
> Smells of that ditch.

The poem was part of the poet's manuscript for his collection of poems to be published under the title of *The Double Axe,* however the publisher suppressed the poem, along with eleven others, all of which were eventually included in subsequent printings of *The Double Axe* long after Jeffers's death. Jeffers, who lived in a stone house in Carmel, California, was an isolationist who did not think the United States should have gotten involved in World War II (or World War I either). Jeffers believed that Roosevelt was not forced into the war after the invasion of Pearl Harbor, but that FDR was making war "in fact though not in name, long before Pearl Harbor." The poet believed our involvement in the war was a tragic mistake that wasted American lives by needlessly entangling us in a problem that was Europe's to resolve. His publisher requested that he tone down his stinging attacks against Roosevelt. The book, the poet's fourteenth collection of poetry to be published by Random House, contained a disclaimer saying Random House "feels compelled to go on record with its disagreement over some of the political views pronounced in this volume. Acutely aware of the writer's freedom to express his convictions boldly and forthrightly and of the publisher's function to obtain for him the widest possible hearing, whether there is agreement in principle and detail or not, it is of the utmost importance that difference of views should be wide open on both sides. Time alone is the court of last resort in the case of ideas on trial."

The Double Axe was published shortly after the war and in the preface, Jeffers writes, "It seems time that our race began to think as an adult does, rather than like an egocentric baby or insane person." Time is now running out. Quickly. And we average citizens better wake up. In the title poem, Jeffers writes:

> Be sorry for the decent and loyal people of America
> Caught by their own loyalty, fouled, gouged and bled
> To feed the power-hunger of a politician and make trick fortunes
> For swindlers and collaborators.

In Robinson Jeffers's original manuscript, the line "To feed the power-hunger of a politician" read "To feed the vanity of a paralytic," but Random House editor Saxe Cummings asked him to soften the harshness of his criticism of President Roosevelt and the poet complied with the distinguished editor's request.

I do not consider myself an isolationist. I don't know about World War I or World War II, but I truly believe the American people were tricked into supporting the Gulf War by the vanity and power-hunger of a politician. So were the citizens and soldiers of Iraq. It is time we act like adults and stop settling our problems the way children do.

Tuesday, February 26—11:00 A.M.

War provides many opportunities for creative businessmen to make a buck. One Italian businessmen runs a company that manufactures fake military weapons. His company produces life-size jet fighters, tanks, and rocket launchers that are skillfully crafted from rubber, metal, and fiberglass. Armies use these fake weapons as decoys, intended to lure their enemies into wasting attacks and bombs. Phoney light-weight fighter-bombers, whose surfaces can reflect radar signals thereby reducing the risk enemy pilots suspecting the sham, sell for around $30,000. The Iraqi military has used decoys, which they either bought from foreign suppliers or manufactured themselves, and they have proven to be a nuisance for the American military. The Iraqis have been wheeling out fake SCUD launchers to make it more difficult for allied pilots to spot and destroy the real ones.

I guess it is naive on my part to hope someday humanity may use its creativity to find real ways to avoid war rather than waste it on creating fake replicas of armaments in order to sow confusion. I keep forgetting war provides opportunities to make money, while peace is a poor investment.

Tuesday, February 26—7:39 P.M.

The end of the war is in sight—just a day or two away. Iraqi soldiers are giving up at such a rapid rate the coalition forces can hardly count them, let alone move them to a POW camp. Over 30,000 of Saddam's troops are under coalition control. Some Iraqi soldiers are trying to get back to Iraq with their tanks and equipment, but the coalition forces have crossed into Iraq and are blocking Iraqi attempts at retreat. Hussein is trying to end the fighting, but Bush keeps pushing. Apparently there is a difference between withdrawal and retreat.

On the news tonight, a Republican Congressman, who is a staunch supporter of the so-called "pro-life" movement and who spoke out loudly last year against federal funding going to artists whose work he considered pornographic, suggested that we not cease our war effort until we assassinate Saddam Hussein. What I find odd is not his desire to see Saddam dead—that is perfectly understandable— but how a Christian who is opposed to abortion and pornography can suggest the pornographic act of murder. Our government prohibits the targeting of specific individuals, forbids assassinating political leaders in both times of war and in times of peace. This law applies even to creeps like Hussein. Somehow I can't picture Jesus saying, "Let's blow the bastard's brains out." Perhaps the Christian legislator should be praying for the salvation of Saddam's soul, for who more needs to be bathed in the "saving blood of the Lamb" than the blood-thirsty lion from Baghdad. Unless this Christian doesn't really think Saddam's soul can be saved.

Wednesday, February 27—12:17 P.M.

The end of the war was not soon enough for nine British soldiers. They were engaged in a fierce battle deep inside Iraq when their two vehicles were hit by bombs fired by an American jet. Death by "friendly fire" just hours from the war's end. While diplomats struggle for a cease fire, soldiers are still dying even though the war is clearly over and Iraq has been resoundingly routed. The goals of the war have been clearly met, and yet we keep fighting on in a costly effort to keep what little is left of Iraqi's war machine from getting back to Baghdad. What possible threat could these remaining Iraqi tanks and artillery pose?

President Bush is being hailed as the great liberator of Kuwait. If Bush is such a great liberator, why the hell doesn't he go in and liberate Tibet, and put an end to the systematic elimination of the peaceful, religious Tibetans? The brutality of the genocide being carried out by the Chinese Communists in Tibet is more shocking than anything Saddam did in Kuwait. Why isn't Bush morally outraged at the Chinese? Oh, I forgot why—Tibet has no oil and is not strategically important, and Bush thinks it is politically correct to keep open the lines of communication between our great Democracy and the murderous Communist Chinese Government that is hell-bent on depriving its citizens even the most basic civil rights. Besides, with Kuwait behind him, Bush no longer needs to prove he is not a wimp—shit, I wouldn't be surprised if Bush sent the troops to the Middle

East just to prove he wasn't a wimp. Despite the results of the war, Bush is still a moral wimp, far more concerned with his own image and the politics of his own re-election than with honest morality.

Kate, despite my displeasure with Bush, I am truly thankful the war is over and that American casualties were so low.

I have until Friday morning to complete my rewrite of *Hired Gun*. I should not have any problem meeting the deadline. I'll be leaving for Mexico as soon as possible, perhaps by the middle of next week.

Buenos dias.

Wednesday, February 27—6:15 P.M.

After forty-two days and three hours, President Bush has just announced the coalition forces will suspend all offensive military action as of twelve midnight Eastern Standard Time.

The war is over.

Thursday, February 28—8:28 A.M.

I wish I understood all this war stuff. "Understood" is not the right word. I wish I could have rallied around the flag, trusted President Bush. What Iraq did to Kuwait was shameful beyond all words. The stories of atrocities being reported during their occupation, and even during their hasty retreat, are shocking. Women raped, men shot in the head, buildings burned, oil fields set on fire. I'm glad that the community of nations came to the defense of the Kuwaiti citizens who have been under virtual house arrest for seven months.

I'm impressed with the tremendous job the military did under the direction of General Norman Schwarzkopf. No doubt about it, this is one tough guy; yet, I like him—sort of. I mean I still have a basic distrust of career military officers. But beneath Schwarzkopf's rugged, bulky exterior, I think there is a soft-hearted teddy bear hiding. Stormin' Norman is testy, funny, bright, and arrogant. During his briefings, he can be both belligerent and charming, both boastful and contrite, both candid and evasive. But you knew he knew what he was doing and that he genuinely cared about each and every man and woman under his command. You even got the feeling that while he hated Hussein, he respected the Iraqi soldiers and civilians who would lose their lives. While I can't seem to warm up to Bush, I wouldn't mind having a cup of coffee and a chat with Schwarzkopf. Maybe I could learn about fighting for freedom.

Yet I hate violence—all violence. The Gulf affair makes me wonder about humanity's future.

One last war story. It serves to illustrate the brutal indifference of life. Among the victims of Monday's SCUD attack on the Army barracks in Dhahran were three women. One was only twenty years old, another just twenty-two years old, and the third was twenty-three years old. One of the young women came from a small, coal-mining town in western Pennsylvania. Believing that education would be the only way to escape the poverty of the region, she joined the reserves last October in order to get money to go to college. She was sent to Saudi Arabia on February 17, just eight days before the SCUD attack, just eleven days before the war's end. She didn't even have time to unpack. On the day she left for the Persian Gulf, her boyfriend offered her an engagement ring.

To add to the tragic dimensions of this story, it was reported today that the initial reports of the incoming SCUD having been intercepted by a Patriot missile were wrong. No missile was ever fired. At the time of the attack, the Patriot system assigned to defend Dhahran was out of service for repairs. It turns out that the SCUD missile broke apart in flight and was tumbling out of control. Imagine, a highly inaccurate missile malfunctions and breaks apart, and the chunk of falling debris that contained the warhead manages to avoid miles of open, sandy spaces and happens to land on a building crammed with American soldiers, including a recently engaged young woman from a poor town who only wanted to get an education.

Was she a victim of fate or random chaos?

How will her parents ever cope with their loss? Why was her death necessary? War does not solve problems or answer questions; it creates new ones.

Is there any way we—all the people on the planet—can put the companies that manufacture the weapons of war out of business?

It's doubtful. There is too much money involved.

Sunday, March 3—10:37 A.M.

I leave for Mexico in forty-eight hours. My initial plan of sub-leasing my townhouse, trading in my BMW for and old clunker and spending a few months exploring Mexico have been revised and scaled down. I can't afford an extended stay. Here is the new plan. I'm going to fly to Mexico City on Tuesday afternoon. I'll catch a 7:00 P.M. train to Oaxaca. Fourteen and a half hours later, Wednesday morning at 9:30 A.M., I'll arrive in Oaxaca. I have a reservation at a small hotel—twelve dollars a night! I'll return to L.A. on April 4. I decided to leave the car home because I feel, without it, I'll have one less worry. Besides, I'll absorb more of the culture by using public transportation and mixing with the people.

One month in Oaxaca. I can't say that I have clear goals and hopes for the time. I just want to go, and I'm tired of second-guessing myself, so I am going. The trip makes sense to me, and that's all that is important. After all, I'm the only writer of the screenplay of my life.

The last few days have been very hectic. I delivered my revisions for *Hired Gun* on time, thanks to an all-night vigil last Thursday that concluded at 4:30 in the morning. Since then I've been getting things ready for the trip. Mostly doing laundry and exchanging currency. It takes around 2,900 Mexican pesos to equal one American dollar. It will be weird dealing in such huge numbers.

My room, for example, will cost 33,000 pesos a night—sounds expensive, but it comes to about $11.50.

The Persian Gulf still dominates the news, and I can't wait to leave all that behind me. While all around me bask in the patriotic afterglow of the war, I'm still trying to sort out my emotions. That's what this Mexico trip is all about: sorting things out, looking at my life and future from a different perspective.

I hope dissent does not become a sign of disloyalty. One of the casualties of the Gulf War was the dream of a student athlete from Trieste, Italy. Tall and bright, the young man dreamed of coming to America and playing American college basketball while earning a degree. The dream came true. Two years ago, he came to America on a full scholarship from a Catholic university on the East Coast. He was a standout on the court, scoring forty-one points in one game last season, and in the classroom, where he maintained a 3.8 grade-point average. Then the war shattered his dream. His teammates had decided to sew American flag patches on their uniforms to show their support for our troops in the Gulf.

Inspired by a profound religious conviction that all wars are wrong, the Italian player refused to wear an American flag on his uniform. He said, "From a Christian standpoint, I cannot support any war, with no exception for the Persian Gulf War." During a game at Madison Square Garden in New York City, every time the young man touched the ball he was loudly booed. The Catholic school, instead of understanding and supporting his religiously based position, elected to bench him. He started to receive threatening phones calls. On February 13, he withdrew from the university and returned to Italy.

So much for tolerance in a country where yellow ribbons hang like badges of belonging on everything from trees to car grilles to front doors. American flags adorn T-shirts and homes. The war seems to have shot down the American right to dissent from what we hold in common. I applaud the Italian basketball player's courage. By simply sewing a little flag on his uniform, he could have earned his degree and continued playing the sport he loved. Back home living in the unfurnished apartment on the top floor of his mother's house in Trieste, the twenty-one-year-old said, "A man has to listen to his conscience. And I know I did the right thing. I'd do it again if I had to. I'd do it a thousand times." It is sad that in this great country, there is no room for a bright, sensitive young man who wanted to be part of the American dream.

The final boxscore of casualties in the war appeared in the papers today. There were 253 Americans killed; 105 during Operation Desert Shield, the pre-war build up from August to mid-January, and 148 during Operation Desert Storm. Fifteen British soldiers were killed. Forty-four soldiers from Saudi Arabia were killed. Two French soldiers were killed. It is estimated that 100,000 to 120,000 Iraqi soldiers were killed in action. Additionally, it is estimated that 75,000 to 100,000 Iraqi civilians have died since August, perishing from disease, malnutrition, civil war, and, of course, the air war, in which perhaps up to 15,000 civilians were killed by allied bombs.

Allied casualties were light. Incredibly light. The war answered my sixties poster question, "What if they gave a war and nobody came?" The Iraqi army failed to show up for the predicted long and bloody ground war. The ground war took less time to complete than a drive from Boston to San Diego. To use a sports metaphor, the ground war was shorter than a World Series, and the Iraqi army struck out looking—taking a called third strike right down the middle of Baghdad.

And after all the death and destruction, Saddam Hussein is still in power, living comfortably in a posh underground bunker.

Still, President Bush's approval rating has soared above the 90 percent mark. He is the liberator of Kuwait, the president who buried the Vietnam syndrome in the sands of the Persian Gulf. He made America a winner. Bush convinced us he did what he had to do, and it worked. Americans are happy—we tend to see things in terms of winners and losers, black and white. Bush assured us the war was a battle between good and evil, morality versus savagery, and that God was on our side. And, as it turns out, oils well that ends well.

Billy Graham said that the outpouring of prayer led to the short war. Bullshit! The war was short because Saddam's army did not have the heart to fight, and they were chewed up by America's multibillion-dollar military meat grinder, dying not for a reasonable cause, but because Hussein gave them no choice. Prayer had nothing to do with our success. The malnourished, poorly motivated Iraqi troops led into battle by superiors who did not value their lives were no match for the well-fed, heavily armed coalition forces. Even more basic than that, Saddam lost because he had no air force.

I think Voltaire was correct when he reminded us, "It is said that God is always for the big battalions." The war also provided us with ample evidence to validate Bertrand Russell's claim that "War grows out of ordinary human nature."

Now it is time for George Bush the hero to face the two words he dreads the most: domestic policy. May he be just as successful in dealing with America's internal problems as he was with dealing with the bully from Baghdad. Maybe Billy Graham can pray for that.

And it's almost time for me to head for Mexico. No prayers required, although I might offer a short prayer to Ganesha, the elephant-headed Hindu god of barriers, obstacles, and inhibitions, who must be worshipped and pacified before each voyage.

Monday, March 4—3:25 P.M.

I'm already to go. I'm packed and everything is in order. I'm really excited about the trip. I plan to keep writing to you every day, and hopefully the tone of the letter will become more upbeat.

As I look back over this epistle, I can't help but notice how frequently I've gone into great detail telling you about all the sorrows and violence that I see. I seem to have painted a rather bleak picture of life on earth, a life filled with an endless variety of disasters, murders, and wars. I wonder why it is that I am so bothered by so many things that other people are able to ignore. I guess the ability to disassociate one's self from life's sorrows and violence makes it possible for some people to have been guards at such chambers of horrors as Auschwitz, or to have been able to drop bombs on civilians during wars, or to be able to step over a homeless person in the street and go home and kiss their kids, or to be able to shrug off the squalor that exists in the tenements of our inner cities. I guess I cannot switch off the world at will as most people do; nor can I deny my complicity in the pain I see.

Kate, I'm just not capable of turning off the anguish I feel for the suffering all around me and in places I know only through headlines in the papers. There are still days when I celebrate life and all its wonders; yet there are also an equal number of days when I become bitter at the affluent people whose clever arguments justifying their luxuriant lifestyle fails to consider how many people must live in hunger and inequality under the rule of savage dictators as well as under our own benevolent democracy.

This is an age of ethical indifference, where many speak about morality, but few translate their words into actions. For a long time, I felt as if I had to either disdain money or get in bed with the Devil. But responding to the injustice and evil I see in such an either/or fashion is pointless and has led to a self-loathing and passivity of little use to the victims for whom I feel so much anguish. I need to discover moral options that are less absolute. I need money to live, and I also need to help those less fortunate than myself in order to be able to look in the mirror and not feel disgust.

I'm glad the hopelessness that I felt when I began writing to you has begun to recede; yet, I still, for the sake of my own survival, must discover a way to allow hope to ripen without being so easily bruised.

Maybe Mexico will provide the soil for a brighter outlook to nurture. I can't imagine how, but I hope it does.

Monday, March 4—11:20 P.M.

Eight hours ago I wrote to you about my anguish over all the sorrowful and violent episodes that have disturbed me during the course of writing this letter. I just saw something on the local news that really troubled me.

For a second I thought I was watching a news story from South Africa. But no, the barbarity took place right here in Los Angeles. The incident was captured on videotape by someone who happened to pass by the scene. The images recorded made me sick. The grainy, amateur videotape, shot at night, showed an unarmed African-American male face down on the ground. He was surrounded by more than a half dozen policemen, four of whom were repeatedly beating him with their billy clubs. On the section of the tape that aired, Rodney King was struck fifty-six times within eighty-one seconds by four white cops. The beating was savage. The cops mercilessly clubbed King over and over and over again. Mr. King had to be taken to the hospital. The police said Rodney King led them on a high-speed chase through the San Fernando Valley before he stopped his car. Two of Mr. King's passengers did not resist arrest, but, according to the police, Rodney King did. They thought he was under the influence of PCP and considered him very dangerous and claimed the force they used to subdue him was justified and not excessive.

It looked pretty excessive to me. Rodney King was curled up on the ground and hardly moving, yet the relentless pounding and kicking by the cops continued. I squirmed as I watched the tape. I could feel the bones in King's arms and legs breaking, his skull cracking. Rodney King looked helpless and the force used by the police hardly looked managed or controlled.

This is a city deeply divided along racial lines. It increasingly is a city of haves and have nots. The tensions between Mexicans, Koreans, blacks, and whites are real. Racism in L.A. might not be as visible as our smog, but it is more deadly. L.A. is a social time-bomb. The amateur video clearly highlighted the notion that in America there is justice for all—except for African-Americans. We really don't care about crime and violence in the ghetto, as long as it just stays there and doesn't spill over into our nice neighborhoods. We condone injustice.

Almost thirty years after the deadly riots in the Watts section of Los Angeles, poor, unemployed African-Americans still feel they do not count in this city. Blacks feel disposable and their frustrations are mounting. And nobody cares. Three years ago, George Bush presented us with the image of Willie Horton getting out of jail, hinting the black convict could harm whites. Now, the Los Angeles Police Department has given us the image of Rodney King being clubbed so the white population does not have to fear being threatened by blacks.

Tuesday, March 5—1:00 P.M.

The plane is pushing back from the gate—on time. A good sign. I can use a good sign, some indication this trip is not a stupid idea. As the departure date drew closer, the more nervous I became. I worry too much. Anyway, if the "cluster of three's" theory is correct, this should be a safe flight. In the last few months, there have been three major airline crashes. The latest, just two days ago, involving the airline I'm flying, had no survivors. Still, maybe I should have driven.

Yesterday, while browsing in a bookstore, I looked at some guide books on Mexico. One warned that Oaxaca is the drug capitol of Mexico and that violence and corruption have invaded all levels of society. Great. Another book claimed petty crime, long a part of life in the densely populated areas of Mexico, has started to shatter the peaceful tranquility of Oaxaca. (I'm glad I'm not driving.) The tour books were bad signs. Humans love the comfort of good signs and omens, so much so, we even manufacture them.

I'm seated near the rear of the plane. Window seat. They just started playing a safety video. "In the unlikely event of a water landing, your seat bottom cushion can be used as a floatation device." Sure . . . if the plane can't fly (which is the only reason it would be in the water), why should I believe the seat can float?

The plane is about to barrel down the runway. We will soon become an airborne village, more populated and better fed than some of the remote Indian villages I hope to visit in Mexico. At 39,000 feet in the air, we'll have food and drinks, phones and movies.

I would bet most of the people on this plane do not have a clear understanding of how a plane carrying two hundred people and a shitload of stuffed suitcases can get off the ground. Yet, we all got on because we put our trust in a fact that has been proven. We know planes can fly. (We are not afraid of flying; we're afraid of crashing.) Oddly enough, people trust in God even though His existence cannot be proven. The vast majority of people put faith in religious "facts" that are not—and cannot—be supported by evidence. Religion feeds us answers. But answers do not enlighten, questions do. At times I'm sorry I started questioning the beliefs I was given as a child. A decade of questioning hasn't yielded much enlightenment. But I can't stop questioning, can't stop searching for truth. The childhood inquisitiveness of most adults seems to stop at the door of the dogmas of faith, yet before you can have faith, you must have doubt, you must ask tough questions. Mexico is a very religious country. Superstition and the supernatural are as common as pottery and serapes. Will I find answers or faith?

We're next for takeoff. The plane has turned onto the runway and paused. Time to offer a silent prayer. I can't. Where is Billy Graham when I need him? The sudden thrust of power pushed me back into my seat. The roar of the engines is unsettling. "Hail Mary, full of grace. . . ." Take-off anxiety lasts about ninety seconds, and quickly the confidence level rises. If something is going to happen, it's now or during landing. Unless there is a terrorist bomb ticking away in the cargo bin.

Through the brown haze of L.A.'s air, I watch the skyline of downtown disappear. I'm on my way. The doubts of the past few days have given way to anticipation. I can't wait to get to Oaxaca.

A guy I noticed in the terminal giving his wife a tender goodbye kiss is seated behind me. I can hear him putting "the make" on the woman seated next to him. I recall how sweet his wife looked, her eyes tearing up because of his departure. She should only have heard him say just a few seconds ago, "I'm staying at the Majestic and will be in Mexico City for ten days. My hotel is just a few blocks from yours. . . . Let's get together for dinner one night." The woman—soon to be "the other" woman—responds, "I'd love that." Tacos and el sacko, salsa and sex.

Deceitfulness and duplicity in marriage are deadly. I should know. In all these pages, I haven't mentioned anything about the end of your parents' marriage. I'm not sure if I feel like getting into it now. But I did bring it up. Your mother and I were too young and naive to have gotten married. We thought we needed each other. Marriage isn't about need fulfillment. It's about love, it's about sharing and giving. We didn't share much, and we gave each other even less. It quickly dawned on each of us that love was much more than sex. It didn't take long to realize we weren't really suited for each other. But our Catholic backgrounds said, "Tough. You're stuck with each other." We cried out, "We're sorry. We made a mistake." We heard in response, "Too bad. Live with it."

Jesus, what craziness. You could kill somebody, later regret it, go to confession, and all would be forgiven. But, if you marry and later regret it, tough toenails! The choice we had was clear: stay married or go to hell. So, we stay married, and lived in hell. I cheated on your mother a lot. I hate the sound of that expression—"cheated" doesn't always do justice to what is happening when one person in a marriage seeks comfort outside of the marriage. A few years after you were born, I got caught. She sent me packing. Losing my marriage wasn't that painful; losing you was.

Enough about this for now.

On this flight to Mexico City they take only American or Canadian currency if you purchase beer or wine. How many people flying from Los Angeles to Mexico City have Canadian currency? All the announcements are in English and Spanish. Installed in the back of the seat in front of me is a public phone. Airfone. You insert your credit card to release the phone and make a call. Maybe I'll call my friend Steve on his car phone, if nothing else it will be a "fast" conversation.

The man sitting next to me looks like a typical, American businessman. A salesman perhaps. He is in his mid fifties and looks tired. He has graying hair and uses reading glasses. He doesn't have on a wedding ring. He's wearing brown boots beneath his charcoal gray slacks, a navy blue jacket, and a powder blue shirt. No tie. He read the paper for a while. Hasn't said a word to me—the empty seat between us is an unbridged gulf. A few minutes ago, he reached under the seat in front of him and pulled out his briefcase and removed two Bibles. Each black leather-covered Bible had little tabs indicating all the different books of the Bible. The tabs were well worn from constant use. This guy is a serious Bible reader. I don't know why he needs two Bibles; nor can I make out what versions they are. It just hit me—one Bible is in English, the other Spanish, and he must be a minister off to save souls in Mexico. Yes, yes, yes—he is a minister, I'm sure. I'm tempted to talk to him but will not.

Speaking of missionaries to Mexico, I have a cousin who is a missionary priest in Mexico. When I was a teenager, he was my idol. I wanted to follow in his holy footsteps. His name is Padre Vincente. Actually, his real name is Joseph Ryan, but for some reason that escapes me he is known in Mexico as Padre Vincente and not Father Joe. He came to Mexico thirty-one years ago as a young priest. He works in a small village in the mountains outside Guadalajara. During all those years, I've seen him only three times: one wedding (his sister's), and two funerals (his parents'). Last time I saw him he sounded as if English was difficult for him to speak; he kept dropping Spanish words into his conversation. Guadalajara is northeast of Mexico City, and Oaxaca is southeast of the city. Still, I might try to visit Father Joe—er, Padre Vincente—before I go home. I don't know what we would talk about, but I think I would like to see him.

Looking down from 39,000 feet, there is no difference between Mexico and the United States. We'll be landing soon. The pilot announced that visibility in Mexico City is only seven miles thanks to the pollution. Along the approach to Mexico City, the land is barren and dry. Very little color. We are in the final descent. Time to put my notebook away. Buenas tardes.

Tuesday, March 5—3:00 P.M. (Central time)

I've been in Mexico for a little over an hour, and it is abundantly clear from ground level that this is not America.

At customs, the Mexicans employ a random method of determining whose bags get a thorough inspection. Everyone entering the country presses a button that will illuminate a green "pass" light or a red "stop" light. Get a green light and you breeze through without inspection; draw a red light and your bags are examined. I got a green light. Another good sign. The preacher man sitting next to me got a red light . . . ha, ha.

Inside the terminal I was confronted by a swarm of men asking whether I wanted a taxi. Actually, they were pleading. Each had a badge dangling from a chain worn round his neck. A laminated photo ID stating that they were authorized—by who knows whom—to drive tourists from the airport to wherever they wanted to go. I resisted at first, but eventually said "yes" to one.

In English he said, "Where are you going?" "To the train station," I responded. He looked puzzled, so I added, "I'm taking a train to Oaxaca." He shook his head knowingly and said, "Si, si." Tour books warned to have drivers quote a price before you get into a taxi. "How much is the fare?" He responded, "40,000 pesos." My mind drew a blank—how much is that? He saw my confused look and said, "That's about 15 dollars in American money." I said, "I know." He knew I didn't know shit. "Fine," I said.

My Mexican adventure was about to begin.

The cabbie grabbed my bag and we proceeded out of the terminal. We walked past a long line of new, clean taxis. Official-looking yellow taxis with company names printed on the doors. We kept walking. And walking. We walked across a large, sun-baked parking lot. The air was brown and hot. We reached the end of the parking lot and had to step over a low chain fence. The next thing I know, I'm following this guy, who has all my stuff and is walking faster than I can, down a side street of a poor neighborhood that borders the airport.

My anxiety level is rising, quickly. What am I doing following this guy? Am I going to get ripped off as soon as I step off the plane? I have no other choice but to keep following him.

He stops at an old, blue American car—perhaps a Mercury, definitely dirty. He opens the passenger door to the accompaniment of a loud squeak and tosses my bag into the back seat. He motions for me to get into the car. It was like getting into an oven, preheated to about 375 degrees. The seats were torn. The glove compartment door was ripped in half. The dashboard was criss-crossed with cracks. He got in. We opened our windows. He got the thing started, and we took off on a hair-raising twenty-two-minute ride through dreary slums.

I was nervous. And not just about his driving. Who is this guy? Is he really taking me to the train station? In broken English he asked why I would take a train to Oaxaca. He motions that the train is very slow. After completing a death-defying U-turn, he pulls up to a building, which gives no indication it's a train station, and he says, "Here we are, there is the train station." I grab my bag from the back seat, step out of the car, and hand him 50,000 pesos. He smiles, says, "Gracias," and zooms away. I turn and head for the building he claims is the train station.

I entered the building and was horrified by what I saw. There were endless lines of very poor Mexicans carrying their belongings in overstuffed paper bags and sacks. Kids were crying. The station was loud and confusing. Many people had no shoes. Most wore clothing that was worn out, tattered, and dirty. I almost tripped over a teenager who had no legs and was pushing himself along on a small wooden platform, which had very small wheels attached under each corner. The place was chaos.

My only thoughts: What am I doing? Why am I here?

There were a dozen numbered portals leading to narrow platforms between the tracks. Some had hand-written signs indicating a train's departure time and destination. I could not find a line for the train to Oaxaca. My first impulse was to head for the airport as fast as I could. Then I spotted a woman, dressed in jeans and a T-shirt, whose blond hair led me to assume she was an American. I weaved my way through the crowd and before I could say anything to her, I heard her ask a person in line if the line was for the Oaxaca train. The man she asked didn't speak English and gave her a shrug for an answer. I said, "Hi. Are you an American?" "No," she responded, "I'm Canadian." I quickly blurted out, "I'm going to Oaxaca also." She smiled, equally glad as I was not to be alone in her search for the train.

Her blonde hair was cut very short, barely covering her ears. She was in her mid-forties and had a nervous twitch. Before we could exchange another word, two guys interrupted us. One said, "Hey, English-speaking people." They were obviously drunk. They said they had been robbed and beaten up.

I was scared. No, Toto, I don't think we're in Kansas anymore. Where is Auntie Em?

The Canadian woman and I managed to ditch the two drunken Americans and tried to figure out where to go for the train to Oaxaca. I told her I had a ticket, got it via mail in the United States. She said she didn't have a ticket, but assumed that I should be upstairs in the first class terminal. She was looking for the second class, cheap train to Oaxaca that was scheduled to depart a full two hours before my train. She pointed the way to a flight of stairs leading to the main terminal. I wished her good luck and headed in the direction in which she had pointed.

As I got to the top of the stairs my eyes beheld a modern, marble structure that looked like a train station. I had gone from hell to heaven. Large, electronic signs on either end of the terminal clearly identified the trains, destinations, and track numbers. The chaos, confusion, and crowds of the lower terminal were gone. I breathed a sigh of relief.

I have nearly four hours to wait for my train to Oaxaca. But I don't mind. I'll just sit here and watch the passing parade of people. Jesus, all that anxiety because I had entered the local, second-class train area. At 5:00 P.M. there was a train to Oaxaca that costs only ten dollars. It takes eighteen hours. No air conditioning, no food, no frills, no nothing. It is the way the peasants travel, and they carry with them food for the long journey.

At 7:00 P.M. there is another train to Oaxaca. This is the train I'll be taking. It is called *El Oaxaqueno*. I don't know what that means. It takes fourteen and a half hours. The cost is forty dollars for coach and sixty-five for a sleeper. I have a sleeper. I'll arrive in Oaxaca at 9:30 tomorrow morning.

I'm starting to calm down.

When I got out of my taxi, the first thing I noticed was a guy selling magazines. No stand. He just had dozens of magazines spread out on the sidewalk. His selection included Mexican editions of *Playboy* and *Penthouse*. My dad would be pleased to know that I didn't purchase one.

Well, my sweet daughter, I think I'll take a stroll around the station.

Tuesday, March 5—4:20 P.M.

Hello again. I'm just sitting and waiting. And looking. A Mexican man just walked by. He had on a battered and crushed straw hat and sported two days worth of beard stubble. He was carrying and selling large pillows. He had about a dozen, each in a plastic bag. He was dirty and scruffy; the pillows were pretty and fluffy. Odd sight.

A cute, little Mexican girl just skipped by. She had on a pretty white dress, trimmed with lace. Looked like a "first communion" dress. She had a white ribbon in her black hair. The kids downstairs had no shoes, and their clothing consisted of tattered, dirty rags. Already I'm getting the impression that Mexico is a land of startling contrasts, like America. Another little girl in a white dress just walked by. She is holding her father's hand and crying. He looks annoyed. He is lucky.

Many poor people pass through the terminal on their way downstairs. They carry burlap bags stuffed with who-knows-what. A little boy—no more than five years old—just walked up to me and said, "Chiclets?" In his hand were packages of Chiclets chewing gum. He was alone. This was his job. I said, "No thanks," and he turned and walked away. I watched him as he "worked" the station, approaching everyone he could. There are many teenage boys, carrying wooden boxes crammed with rags and polish, offering to shine shoes. If this is any indication, kids join the work force at a very young age in Mexico. Another kid, perhaps eight years old, just approached me with a silent plea to buy Chiclets. He was very dirty and never uttered a word. He just gave me a sad look and waved his packages of gum at me.

I'm getting restless, so I'm going for another walk.

Tuesday, March 5—5:40 P.M.

The train has just pulled into the station. Boarding begins in about twenty minutes.

During my walk, I helped a young couple from England. They were as lost and confused as I was just a few hours ago. They thought they had missed the train to Oaxaca, when in fact they were booked in the coach section of *El Oaxaqueno*. Both of them had just finished medical school and were taking six weeks off to tour Latin America. They were both tall and lanky. He had blonde hair; she, brown. His name was Adrian; hers, Jane. We spoke of television, politics, and the war. They were very articulate. I enjoyed meeting them. They are only spending a few days in Oaxaca, then they are going to Guatemala, Belize, and Peru. They sounded most excited about Guatemala, which they claimed has more Indian culture and is very inexpensive. Maybe I'll go there also.

But first it's time to board the train for Oaxaca. I'm filled with anticipation about this mysterious city—which up until a few weeks ago I never heard of—that has such a strong pull on my imagination.

I don't know what I'm looking for in Oaxaca. I just have a feeling I will find something, something valuable to me.

All aboard.

Tuesday, March 5—7:11 P.M.

The train pulled out of the station right on time, exactly 7:00 P.M. As we rumble out of Mexico City, an eerie, smoky darkness begins to envelop the train. Still, I'm able to see the houses that boarder the tracks, their lights illuminating their inhabitants. Houses? No, make that shacks. In many of the dirt yards between the shacks and the tracks, there are parked hulks of long-abandoned cars. Kids are playing dangerously close to the tracks. We have passed numerous RR crossings whose streets are backed up with traffic caused by our slow moving train. Within ten minutes, the poor houses give way to a more industrial environment. Nameless, faceless warehouses strung together for miles.

My compartment is small, but comfortable and has all that I could want: a toilet, a sink, a chair, and a bed that folds down to cover the entire space. Compared to the shacks I just passed, I'll be spending the night in luxury. The next car forward is the dining car, and I just heard that the ticket includes dinner and breakfast.

The compartment across the narrow aisle from me is occupied by a German girl—perhaps in her early twenties—who has a tiny pearl earring in her nose. She doesn't speak English or Spanish and is traveling alone.

In the next compartment is a young American couple from Seattle, Washington. They are not married and look far too young and innocent to be traveling alone in a foreign country. When they asked me why I was going to Oaxaca, I realized I had no real answer. I sidestepped the issue by mentioning that I was the producer of "Harvest of Life," and they both got very excited, claiming they never missed an episode and couldn't understand why it was canceled.

The dining car will be open in a few minutes. Just in time, I'm hungry.

Tuesday, March 5—11:07 P.M.

Very interesting evening. That's a gross understatement. It was a mind-boggling evening. You would use the word "awesome" to describe my night. It all started when I met a guy named Charlton Houston, pronounced like the street in lower Manhattan not the city in Texas—"house-ton." Charlton Houston is a large hulk of a man, with white hair and a white beard. He's a slow-moving, nonstop story-teller. He walked out on his wife and life in Cleveland ten years ago, when he was forty-seven years old and has been living in Oaxaca ever since.

Charlton had been in Mexico City on business for two days. He was tired and had absolutely no interest in talking with any dumb American tourists. That was his initial reaction to me, a reaction formed before we even exchanged a word of conversation, an opinion based upon a glance. He was sitting alone at a table drinking a rum and Coke when I entered the club car. I only wanted something to eat and wasn't looking for a partner in conversation. In fact, I didn't really feel like talking to anyone. Yet, when I saw him, I felt this urge to talk to him. I paused at his table, pretending to be deciding where to sit. Charlton sensed my wanting to share his table. He resisted saying anything to me, then without being able to hold back the words, he said, "Would you like to join me?" I unhesitatingly answered, "Yes. Thanks."

I sat down, and, before either of us could say anything, a waiter asked whether I would like something to drink. He asked in Spanish. I looked at the waiter, and then at Charlton. A painfully bored look crossed Charlton's face, as he said, "He wants to know if you want anything to drink." "Oh. Yeah sure. A beer." "What kind?" "Gee, I don't know. Do they have any dark beer." Turning to the waiter, Charlton said in Spanish, "He'll have a Negra Modelo." "Si," said the waiter. Charlton turned to me and said, "So, you don't speak any Spanish?" "Not a word," I responded. I felt stupid, and so I asked a stupid question. "Are you an American?" I got a one word answer, "Yes." After an awkward pause, I asked, "Are you on vacation?" "No. I live in Oaxaca." I stopped with the questions and said, "This is my first time in Mexico. My name is Christopher Ryan."

Charlton looked at me in complete disbelief, then exclaimed, "What?" His response confused me. Realizing this, he said, "Excuse me; but, what did you say your name was?" "Christopher Ryan." "I can't believe it." "Can't believe what?" "Your name." "I don't get it. What can't you believe?"

Charlton drew a deep breath. "Six years ago, I was walking around one of the ancient ruins just outside of Oaxaca. A spectacular place called Monte Alban. People inhabited the place some five thousand years before the birth of Christ. Anyway, I was just walking around, lost in thought. It was a blistering hot day. In the distance, I saw a female figure approaching. All I clearly could see was her dress, a long, flowing white garment. Suddenly, there were no ruins, no history—just her. I watched as she got closer and closer. Each delicate, deliberate step made my heart pound faster and faster. Soon I could see she had red hair and a fair complexion." He stopped talking, as if lost in the magic of that moment. He caught me looking at him, obviously wondering where this story was going. The waiter arrived with the beer. I took a sip. "Do you like it?" asked Charlton. "Yes, very much so," I answered.

Another pause. I said, "OK. You're at Monte Alban, and this woman has captured your imagination. What happened?" He smiled and continued, "I'll cut to the chase. We've been together since that day, but here is the crazy part. Her father's name is Christopher Ryan." "Jesus, what a coincidence. What's her name?" "Kate Ryan." Then it was my turn to say, "What?" Charlton gave me a puzzled look and before he could say anything, I said, "What did you say her name was?" "Kate Ryan." "Hold onto your hat," I said, suddenly realizing that I didn't know his name, "my daughter's name is Kate Ryan."

We stared at each other in disbelief for a few seconds. Then he told me his name and his life's story. And I told him my life's story. I have no idea how many beers we had. His Kate Ryan is about a dozen years younger than he is. She was born in Scotland. She teaches English in Oaxaca.

I know this sounds like a contrived plot from a bad soap opera, but it isn't.

It's a bit late to go into any more detail about our conversation. I'm sure I'll be spending a lot of time with Charlton Houston. He has a Chevy Blazer and wants to show me things tourists don't usually get to see. So, more on Charlton and the other Kate tomorrow. I'm meeting him for breakfast at 8:00 A.M. Good night, my love.

Wednesday, March 6—6:30 A.M.

You don't sleep much in a sleeper. The train shakes, rattles, and rolls it's way through the Mexican night. It's like sleeping through an earthquake. Or inside a blender, set on high. And the noise—a cacophony of squeaks and squeals.

I woke up a little after 6:00 A.M., just minutes before first light. My ears hurt. It must be the altitude. We are crossing rugged mountain terrain. The first thing I spotted when I opened the blinds was a giant cactus. The few flat fields we passed were planted with corn or fruit trees. The occasional roads that cross the tracks are little more than dirt paths. We passed two small villages, each consisting of a cluster of a dozen or so huts. In those villages, some men had begun gathering around old, beat-up trucks, the day's work about to begin. The vegetation is rich; the people, poor. Some fruit trees are planted very close to the tracks. We just passed a small, solitary shack, set back only a few yards from the track, and standing outside was a young boy taking a leak. I'm sure none of the homes I've seen this morning have indoor plumbing. Set high atop a hill in the distance beyond the shack was a large, white church. God's home was the best-looking home I've seen so far today.

The train is stopping. We are pulling into the small town of Tomellin. We stopped in front of an old water tank, last used in the days of steam-powered trains. The track-side town and water tank look like a set from an old western movie. Some men are inspecting under the train. An old lady carrying a basket of fruit just walked by, and it looks like she is delivering it to the club car. Must be for breakfast. The train is drawing much attention. A few shoeless, young girls run by—they turn all giggles when they notice I'm watching them. Another old lady walks alongside the train carrying a pail of corn. The people look very poor. It is 7:00 A.M. and we've been stopped here for about fifteen minutes, but the train is now starting to slowly pull out of the station. Beyond the station, there are dozens of bamboo huts; this indeed is a very, very poor town.

The train is huffing and puffing its way up a mountain gorge. Huge granite walls line either side of the tracks. Very rugged terrain.

I'm going to the club car. I need some coffee.

Wednesday, March 6—7:20 A.M.

There are two women sitting together in the otherwise empty club car. On the table between them is a book titled *Nature, Man and Woman*. Neither one of the ladies looked as if they had any interest in men. Breakfast service begins at 7:30 A.M. I can't wait. I need my coffee—I've been up for more than an hour and no java yet.

The train has slowed to a crawl. The mountain is very steep. My ears continue to hurt. During the past few minutes, I spotted a pig the size of a cow, a giant turkey, and a few kids riding burros. The land is now rugged and barren; the people, still destitute.

It's 7:36 A.M. and my coffee has finally arrived. It is not hot. I hate that. Where is my microwave?

That's it for now. Charlton should be here soon. After we eat, I'll return to my compartment and get ready for our arrival in Oaxaca. I'm stoked; I know this is going to be a great trip.

Wednesday, March 6—11:50 A.M.

I'm sitting in a church. In the pew behind me sits a young man praying, slightly aloud. His eyes are closed and he seems to be in a meditative state. His prayers at times sound like a soft song. Near the side door of the church, an old Indian woman, wearing a red and white checkered dress, kneels on the stone floor before a glass case containing a statue of Jesus. The statue depicts Jesus just after he fell to the ground under the weight of the cross he was carrying to Golgotha. Christ was draped in a purple gown and wore a gold crown of thorns. The face of the statue was covered with blood streaming down from the crown. Christ's hair looked real. The woman, her gray hair braided and pulled back into a pony-tail, is praying and constantly making the sign of the cross.

Except for the young man, the old woman, and myself, the church is empty. A dozen or so candles burning in front of the church's many statues indicate others had visited the church during the morning. The church is known simply as the Jesuit Church—Iglesia de la Compania de Jesus, the Church of the Society of Jesus, which is the official name of the Jesuits. The Jesuits followed the Dominican priests into Oaxaca, and this church was built in the middle of the sixteenth century. Just outside the huge wooden doors, a family is selling pretty cotton dresses. They have fastened a rope clothes line from the church to an iron fence about fifty feet away. About twenty-five to thirty dresses are hanging on display. The merchants seem to be drawing a bigger crowd than the Padres Jesuitas.

After passing under the ornate facade of finely carved statues and balustraded columns, the first thing I noticed in the vestibule of the church was a large, cardboard poster taped to the wall. Lacking the solidity and elegance of the church exterior, the sign simply asked, "Es el alcohol un problema en su familia?" The placard encouraged those in whose families alcohol is a problem to attend a meeting of Al-Anon. For many, the solace offered by religion is no match for the relief found in a bottle. Both drugs are dangerous.

In the rear of the church, on the left side, is a large font of water. Holy water—alleged holy water, that is. Above the marble font is this sign: "El aqua de San Ignacia es medicine para el cuerpo y el alma, tome con cuidada y no meta las manos. Gracias." As I was reading the sign, two peasant Indian woman entered the church and filled three jugs with the holy water, one cup at a time. With the help of my Spanish-English dictionary, I figured out the sign claims the water of St. Ignatius (founder of the Jesuit order) is medicine for the body and soul and warns to drink with care and don't touch it with your hands. The priests are still peddling magic. What crap!

Charlton and I spent most of our breakfast still expressing amazement over the coincidence of two guys with isolationist tendencies meeting, talking, and discovering they both love a Kate Ryan. But I get the feeling Charlton sees more than a long-shot coincidence. I think he detects some cosmic meaning to our meeting. I'm uncomfortable with ascribing metaphysical significance to commonplace events. Anyway, the train pulled into Oaxaca about twenty minutes late. We shared a cab to the center of town, where I got out and he continued on to his home, which is just outside the city in a neighborhood called Xochimilco. The distance between my hotel and Charlton's home can be covered in a twenty minute walk, much of it uphill. We—he, me, and Kate—are meeting at a sidewalk cafe across the street from the zocalo tonight at 6:30 P.M. for dinner.

Zocalo. Odd word. I'm not sure of its derivation, but it means main square or plaza, along the lines of a common in New England. In Oaxaca, the zocalo is the center of social life. At the center of the zocalo stands a lovely, large, wooden bandstand. Like the spokes of a wheel, paths led from the white bandstand hub to the four streets that surround the park that covers a full city block. Along the paths are benches and three of the streets across from the zocalo are lined with unassuming buildings and sidewalk cafes that blend with the serene atmosphere of the square. The Government Palace borders the zocalo's south side, and the

Cathedral dominates the north corner. The zocalo's huge shade trees provide a welcome relief from the sun. Near each of the zocalo's corners is a large fountain. The streets that border the zocalo are closed to traffic. Strolling through or sitting in the zocalo you will find middle-class merchants, executives, soldiers, Indians from nearby villages, serape vendors, beggars, university students, and international tourists. The zocalo is Oaxaca.

My hotel is just one block off the zocalo, a perfect location. I'm a bit tired from the trip. Didn't sleep much on the train last night. So today I'm just going to relax and stroll around the area surrounding the zocalo. When I leave the church, I'm going to the Benito Juarez Market, which Charlton promised would "knock my socks off."

That's it for now, my sweet.

Wednesday, March 6—5:05 P.M.

Buenas tardes, señorita. I'm back in my hotel room. Before I tell you anything about my afternoon, I've got to share with you one image that has stuck in my mind all afternoon. The incident happened, just as I was leaving the Jesuit church. As I paused at the top of the church steps, giving my eyes a chance to adjust to the bright sunlight, I noticed as people walked past the church they lower their heads in respect and blessed themselves. A little piety in motion. As I started down the steps, I saw an affluent-looking man in his thirties who blessed himself as he passed the church. However, he had no sooner completed making the sign of the cross and kissing his finger when he spotted a girl in tight pants coming toward him. As she passed him, he paused, turned back, and took an extended view of her rear end. And a nice rear end it was. What was so arresting about the episode was the act of bowing, blessing himself, noticing the girl, turning back, and eyeballing her was done in one continuous movement. Inside of ten seconds, the sacred and the profane had met and mingled.

The Benito Juarez Market is gigantic. It covers an entire city block and is an exciting polychromy of fruits and vegetables. The indoor market is as noisy as it is colorful. Vendors cry out a never-ending chant of items for sale. The narrow aisles are crowded with bustling shoppers in search of textiles, ceramics, leather goods, hides, hats, and myriad forms of handicrafts. The place is also a virtual snack heaven offering a wide variety of local delicacies.

But make no mistake about it, the Benito Juarez Market bears no resemblence to any mall or supermarket in America. It is organized chaos. The place is damp, dusky, dingy, and poorly ventilated. Pungent odors from the butchers stalls, food vendors, and garbage are repulsive. Stray dogs roam the aisles in search of scraps of foods. The floors are concrete and dirty. The merchants are poor and forced to bring their young childern to work with them. I saw one infant, perhaps eighteen months old, with a rope tied around its waist and the other end fastened to a pipe that ran along a wall just inches above the dirty concrete floor. The child virtually laid in filth. The market was both exotic and disheartening.

The market is named after an orphaned Zapotec Indian from an isolated mountain village in the state of Oaxaca who became a Catholic and entered a seminary. Benito Juarez abandonded his priestly ambitions to pursue politics. He became one of the leaders of a liberal reform movement that championed social justice and was dedicated to reducing the political power of the army and the Church. Juarez and his fellow reformers hoped to establish a democratic society operating under a constitution. The Catholic Church opposed the new constitution and attempted to nullify it. Pope Pius IX declared, "We raise our Pontifical voice in apostolic liberty . . . to condemn, reprove, and declare null and void everything the said decrees and everything else that the civil authority has done in scorn of ecclesiastical authority and the Holy See." Mexican bishops threatened to excommunicate anyone who supported the constitution. Civil servants and military personnel were forced to choose between the new law of the land and the Church. The constitution eventually divided Mexico into two hostile camps and led to civil war and foreign intervention.

Preferring politics to magic, the Holy Roman Catholic Church was never satisfied with performing the heavenly magic act of turning bread and wine into the body and blood of Jesus, they hungered for earthly power. The more I learn about Church history, the more agitated I become.

Benito Juarez was a dedicated public servant who served as Govenor of Oaxaca and Chief Justice of the Mexican Supreme Court before eventually becoming the President of the Republic in 1858. Overcoming the protests of the Catholic Church, Juarez enacted laws that nationalized church property, abolished special legal rights enjoyed by the clergy, and separated the Church from the state. During all his years in public office, Benito Juarez lived a simple life. Juarez was a man of amazing integrity and ability, and his life is an inspiration to countless Mexicans. He died on July 18, 1872, during his fourth term as president. Benito Juarez's birthday is a national holiday. I got the feeling that Juarez was Washington, Lincoln, and Kennedy all rolled into one.

I bought a straw hat at the market. Charlton told me I would need one for protection from the sun during our excursions. I wouldn't be caught dead in Los Angeles in the hat I bought. None of the hats I liked fit me. After every hat I tried on, the merchant said, "More grande." Eventually more grande meant most ugly.

Oops—I'm going to be late. I've got to shower and hustle down to the zocalo and meet Charlton Houston and Kate Ryan—geez that sounds weird—for dinner.

Catchya later.

Wednesday, March 6—10:45 P.M.

What a pleasant evening. We had dinner at a place called Gueletao, a sidewalk cafe facing the zocalo. I had no trouble understanding why Charlton fell head-over-heels in love with Kate when he first spotted her on Mounte Alban. She is beautiful, has long red hair, a great figure, a charming smile, and a sexy voice.

And brains, also. Kate has two masters' degrees, one in English Literature, and the other in History. But hidden behind her grace, glamour, and intelligence are the scars of a very difficult life.

Kate Ryan spent the first eighteen years of her life watching her father beat her mother. Her Christopher Ryan was a drunk and could not control his temper when he drank. No one in her family was spared the rath of his drunken rages. But her mother felt it most of all. Kate said, "Still, Mom never stopped praying for him. She fully believed that God would intervene and Dad would change his ways. But the prayers were never answered."

At eighteen, Kate Ryan left home and entered a convent. "Why did you want to become a nun?" I asked. "I'm not sure I can say exactly what was going on in my mind back then. I do know that I was deeply touched by my mother's faith. She may have looked weak and submissive, but she had unmatched strength. If anyone's faith could have moved mountains, it was hers. My decision to become a nun made her very happy. I knew it would. Maybe that's why I did it. Then again, maybe the real reason is I hated men. The only gentle man there was was Jesus. I wanted to be his bride. I wanted a life of peace and quiet. I thought the convent would give me that. But nuns can be petty and cruel, too. Beneath our habits, we were still human."

She paused and took a deep breath, as if still exasperated by the fact that her idealized hopes for an unruffled religious life were never realized.

"You didn't find peace in the convent?" I asked.

"No. I thought the peace would come because we would be living for God and without sin. But, we stumbled into jealousy and anger and a host of other manifestations of human frailty. Yet each of us was dedicated to trying to do better. Eventually, that's what appealed to me . . . our communal life was not about falling down, but about getting up. In time, I realized the convent was not paradise, but it was a place where we were dedicated to helping each other overcome our weaknesses. No, it wasn't the abode of saints I naively thought it would be, but it was a lot better than anything outside our walls. I was glad it was going to be my home for life."

I could tell it had been a long time since Kate Ryan had talked about this stuff. There was a nostalgia and sadness in her voice. As she spoke, I couldn't help wondering what had happened to her. Why did she leave the convent? How did she wind up living in Oaxaca with a divorced, older man from Cleveland?

The answers to those questions could never have been anticipated.

She was in the convent a little over five years and on the verge of professing her final vows when the Ryan family story turned tragic. Late one night, after spending the evening in his favorite pub, Christopher Ryan came home and staggered upstairs to bed. When he reached the second floor, he was greeted by his wife, who was awakened by the racket he was making. She said nothing, but Christopher started a fight with her anyway. He shovered her. She slipped and fell down the flight of stairs.

And died.

Kate's younger brother, Kevin, who was only fourteen at the time, witnessed the entire scene. Christopher Ryan was convicted of manslaugther and sent to prison, where he served twelve years.

Kate left the convent. She could no longer devote her life to a God that could allow her saintly mother to die such a cruel death. She moved back home and took care of Kevin until he graduated high school.

Kate Ryan's story would be lamentable even if the suffering ended there. But it didn't. After Kevin was on his own, she met a man named Craig O'Neil. She feel in love for the first time in her life. She was twenty-eight. She and Craig were married. "The future was ours. We were in love, and everything looked bright and rosy. I was going to college full time and he loved his job as a master stone mason."

But the picture began to fade when Craig lost his job and began drinking. After two happy years, the marriage began to deteriorate. Craig became distant and fractious. The next three years were a difficult struggle for Kate. The struggle and the marriage came to an abrupt halt on the day that Craig punched Kate and gave her a black eye. He stormed out of the house. She went upstairs, packed two suitcases, called a cab, went to the airport, and got on the first plane leaving Scotland. A few hours later, she landed in Madrid. She has never spoken to Craig O'Neil or Christopher Ryan since.

At thirty-three, Kate Ryan was alone and living in a foriegn country. She lived in Spain for four years. In 1984, she moved to Miami, Florida were she worked as an English teacher. After a year of living in the States, Kate decided to take a vacation in Mexico, where her knowledge of Spanish would come in handy. It was on that vacation she met Charlton Houston on a mountain top—and the two of them have been living in the clouds ever since.

Charlton was fascinated by the fact that Kate Ryan and I have spent most of our adult lives struggling to escape the grasp of our Catholic heritage. After four hours of nonstop talk about our lives, theology, and philosophy, we parted company.

Señor Houston is picking me up at 8:30 tomorrow morning and taking me to Monte Alban.

Thursday, March 7—2:10 P.M.

Just outside of Oaxaca, the past is the present. This morning Charlton took me back to the past. We went to Monte Alban. We drove only ten miles west of the city but we traveled nearly 2,700 years into the antiquity.

Today, words became inadequate. The harmony and majesty of the ancient ceremonial center of Monte Alban that sits silently a top a massive mountain watching over the broad valley where the city of Oaxaca is planted left me speechless.

In fact, the drive to the mountain's peak left me emotionally drained. We drove up a steep, winding road. Both sides of the narrow, two-lane highway were lined with small huts, perilously clinging to the mountain side. The huts were home to the poorest Indians in the region. They have no running water or electricity. Their food consists of little more than what can be produced in small vegetable gardens alongside their huts. Children walking along the side of the road looked undernourished, and their clothing, tattered, secondhand rags. Goats, sheep, and chickens roamed the mountainside, sometimes wandering onto the road to Monte Alban, making the drive even more challenging.

Despite the sensational view, it is hard to imagine living your life under such harsh and primitive conditions. Yet these people do, and they look content, almost happy. Still, I felt sad at seeing so many people living with so little and never seeing anything else of the world than what can be seen from their roadside shacks.

Monte Alban is an ancient Zapotec city and is Oaxaca's biggest and most spectacular archaeological site. It was by far the largest urban center in ancient Oaxaca.

The history of Monte Alban stretches back to 600 B.C. The majority of the buildings that remain were built during a span of 400 years from A.D. 350 to A.D. 750. During that period, the Zapotec culture reached its apex, with its population peaking at 25,000 inhabitants living on 2.5 square miles of mountaintop. The crest of the mountain overlooks the junction of three valleys. Mount Alban was a ceremonial center for hundreds of years before the Zapotec Indians converted it into an urban complex.

The top of the hill was leveled to create a gigantic plaza more than 330 yards long. The plaza is surrounded by pyramids, palaces, a ball court, elaborately decorated tombs, and an observatory. Charlton was most fascinated by the observatory. He told me the Zapotec were astute observers of astronomical phenomena, and they noted cyclical movements of the sun, stars, and planets, and they devised a 365-day solar calendar and a 260-day ritual calender. Zapotec glyphs representing dieties are carved into the stone. One god had a wide bird beak, another a curved nose, and there was one deity that appeared to combine the features of a jaguar and a crocodile with scrolled eyebrows.The pyramid platforms once were crowned with temples and residences for the priests and political leaders. The terraced slopes of the adjacent hills were residential areas occupied by the craft specialists, working in obsidian, stone, shell, and ceramics. Tourists are constantly being approached by Indians selling souvenirs they claim are authentic artifacts. One souvenir salesman whom Charlton knew was able to peddle his carved statues in five different languages—we overheard him deliver his pitch in French and German. The view from atop the impressive, massive structures of the Great Plaza are truly spectacular.

Charlton pointed out a platform near the center of the court and told me that it served as an altar. From the center of the platform, there was a stairway leading down to a tunnel that connected the altar to a building that was occupied by the priests. Charlton claimed that because the tunnel served no practical purpose, experts believe it was used by the priests to create the illusion of magically and mysteriously appearing suddenly, out of a cloud of smoke, on the altar before their audience. Another case of religion and showbiz mixing.

For reasons that are not clear, the Zapotecs abandoned Monte Alban around

A.D. 900 and moved down to the valleys. The Zapotec political chiefs settled in the town of Zaachila, and the priests set up shop in Mitla. At the end of the thirteenth century, the Mixtec Indians began moving into the Valley of Oaxaca, and by the next century had gained control over the area and superimposed their culture on the region. Some Mixtec dignitaries are buried in Zapotec tombs at Monte Alban. During the second half of the fifteenth century, the Aztecs marched into the Oaxaca valley and subdued the population. Before the Spanish arrived and conquered the prized valley in the 1520s, there was a period of many battles between combinations of Aztecs, Mixtecs, and Zapotecs.

Monte Alban saw it all.

It is hard to imagine the huge effort involved in building such a magisterial project. The task seems almost impossible considering the limited means at their disposal. Leveling the mountaintop was tough enough, but how did they lug enormous quantities of stone up the mountain without pack animals or wheeled transport? The project took centuries to complete.

I'm glad I bought the straw hat at the Juarez market yesterday. By noon, as our nearly three-hour-long exploration was ending, the heat of the scorching sun had reduced us to sweltering heaps of baked flesh. I have never felt so parched and dehydrated. We forgot to bring water with us. Fortunately, a shaded outdoor refreshment stand near the parking lot served ice cold Corona beer or else we would have perished. As we quickly downed two beers each, we wondered how the hell the Indians built Monte Alban.

Thursday, March 7—4:20 P.M.

Just spotted a headline in the English paper from Mexico City. It reads: WAR IS OVER, SOLDIERS COMING HOME SAYS BUSH.

War? What war? That sounds like ancient history after just three days in Mexico. I don't miss newspapers or television. Los Angeles seems like a distant planet.

Thursday, March 7—5:40 P.M.

This is strange. I'm sitting on a bench in the small plaza across from the zocalo. What's strange? In this plaza, in front of the Cathedral, the army band is giving a concert. It is an odd sight. The soldiers are wearing green fatigue uniforms, black boots with white shoelaces, and combat helmets. Each soldier is standing behind a chintzy music stand. Clothes pins keep the pages of music from blowing in the gentle breeze. They're not bad. It is a forty-piece band. Mostly trombones, tubas, clarinets, and flutes.

On a second listening, they are bad. The conductor's pot-belly is stretching his uniform shirt to the limits; a button is bound to pop before the concert ends. Attendance is swelling. Perhaps two hundred locals and tourists have stopped to listen. From high on the facade of the Cathedral, St. Mark appears to be looking down at the band and thinking, "Who would have imagined?"

Jesus Christ, the army, consisting of four columns of ten soldiers carrying rifles, is marching into the plaza. I have no idea what is going on. The army is standing at attention next to the band, which has just begun playing a tune. It sounds familiar. Wait a second, they are playing "New York, New York"— right here in Oaxaca, Oaxaca under the watchful eyes of St. Mark.

I just overheard one tourist explain to another that every night at 6:00 P.M. there is a flag lowering ceremony in the plaza and a small group of soldiers march the flag through the zocalo to the Government Palace. However, on Thursday nights the ceremony is extended to include a half-hour performance by the Mexican Army band. What a hoot!

As the band finished playing "New York, New York," badly playing I might add (which is why I had difficulty recognizing it), a soldier motioned for everyone to stand. The pigeon who is now sitting on St. Mark's head remains seated. The band must be playing the Mexican National Anthem, because everyone is standing at attention. Almost everyone. Two Indian women with baskets full of bright red roses balanced on their heads stroll past the band and the soldiers. As the soldiers play, a little boy, perhaps three or four years old, dances just a few feet away. He is all smiles as he sways with the music. After the anthem was completed, two citizens were asked to assist in lowering the flag as the soldiers stood at attention, saluting. Six soldiers, one on each corner and two on either side in the middle of the flag, march out of the plaza with the flag. As the band leaves, the plaza is quickly taken over by the vendors and beggars. After a dose of nationalism, life and commerce go on. One Indian woman is selling large, inflatable Mickey Mouse dolls. A man selling a small toy mouse that moves around in circles is drawing a crowd of kids.

I'm off to get something to eat.

Thursday, March 7—6:45 P.M.

My second day in Oaxaca is drawing to a close. The golden sunset is gradually giving way to twilight. I just ate dinner at a sidewalk cafe, a place called Cafe Del Jardir. The bill (La Quenta) came to 14,100 pesos (just under five bucks), including a bottle of Mexican dark beer and the tip.

I'm sitting on a bench in the zocalo facing the elegant, French-styled bandstand. On Thursday nights, the state orchestra transforms the park into a field of music. The free concerts begin at 7:00 P.M. every Thursday evening. Sitting next to me is a teenage Mexican girl reading a novel. She utters every word of the text in a soft, diaphanous voice. Her thoughts are far from the zocalo.

I've walked a lot during these past two days, strolling up and down countless streets. I brought two guide books with me, each loaded with maps and information on all the sights to see, yet I haven't opened either one of them. I just walk and look. I'm in no hurry, feel no urge to systematically see everything while seeing nothing. My plan is unplanned randomness. I'm simply breathing in the ambience.

I haven't thought much about why I am here. But this I know for sure: I feel more alive than I have in years. I feel invigorated. I've traveled far and wide during my life but nowhere have I encountered such intense contrasts as I have in Oaxaca.

The orchestra has just started playing. They are a major improvement over the army band. The music is happy, upbeat, as am I.

A Mexican woman with two small kids just walked past my bench. She bore the signs of life's struggles on her face. She was carrying a magazine called *Vanity,* and on its cover was a photo of a sexy woman. The gap between the reality of her life and the fantasy peddled by the magazine was unbridgeable.

There is so much I don't understand, but, what the hell, I can't continue to torture myself over what I can't figure out.

I was about to take a stroll around the zocalo and watch the people listening to the music when an Indian woman approached me. Balanced on her head was a large straw basket filled with roses. I bought one, handed it to my young benchmate, who was still absorbed in her novel, and, as I arose, I said, "Buenas noches." She smiled and I began my stroll.

I may have said, "Buenas nachos," I'm not sure. Charlton has a previous engagement for tomorrow, so I'm on my own.

Friday, March 8—12:50 P.M.

I'm sitting in the shade of a sidewalk cafe sipping a cold glass of Sidral. Sidral is the brand name of a popular, natural apple juice. It's good.

I walked to the outskirts of town this morning and happened to come across a small church, known simply as "Temple y Convento Carmen Alto," or the Church and Convent of Carmen Alto. The church sits among some large trees inside a stone wall that encircles the half-block-long complex. Along the wall is an immense, ornate archway that contains two ten-foot-high wooden doors. Once inside the wall, the dirt courtyard has a number of small fountains, none of which look like they have worked for years. The grounds were poorly maintained. Still, you could tell the convent courtyard at one time must have been very beautiful.

I entered the church. It was empty. I sat down in one of the back pews to rest for a few minutes. The church was cool, and I was glad to be out of the heat. The temperature must have hit 90 degrees long before noon. There was nothing interesting or distinctive about the church. I don't think I was sitting for more than a minute, and I was ready to leave. Before leaving, though, I decided to walk to the front of the church.

That's when I saw it, off to the side, in the corner—a glass coffin containing a statue of the crucified Christ. Christ was laying under a white sheet, his head resting on a simple, white pillow. Only his head was visible. The realism was striking. Christ's beard and hair were made of real hair—or at least it looked as if the hair was real. His face was covered with streams of painted blood. The sheet covering his body had blood stains from the wounds in his side, hands, and feet. In the corner of the coffin, near the statue's feet, sat a crown of thorns, and three large spikes—silent witnesses to the brutality of the messiah's violent death.

It was a very effective piece of artistic religious propaganda. Without words it dramatically said how much Jesus suffered for our sins, how this gentle Lamb of God was sacrificed for us, so that we may know the joy of heaven. It said: Yes, you must also endure much here on earth, but someday you will be with Me and the Father in Heaven. I was overcome with sadness. Maybe it was the thought of anyone suffering such a torturous death that saddened me; maybe it was the death of my faith that saddened me. I don't know. But I know I was close to getting down on my knees and praying.

I didn't.

I turned and walked away, pausing briefly to look back at the sight of Jesus laying alone in the corner of an old, neglected church. The myth was dying in silence.

Sitting outside the main door of the church was an old, shoeless Indian woman. In front of her was a small wooden stand on top of which were the items she sold: lollipops, Chiclets, peanuts, and marshmallows. Her gray-haired head was slumped over and resting on the edge of the stand; she was sound asleep. I wondered how much could she earn, if she were awake, selling those few simple things. This was sadder than the statue of Jesus.

Just outside of the archway of the stone wall that surrounds the church, sitting in the dirt under the shade of a half-dozen trees were seven or eight Trique Indian women weaving the most beautiful tapestries. They employed an ancient method of weaving known as back-strap weaving. (In back-strap weaving, a loom consisting of several pieces of bamboo is strapped around the weaver's waist and stretched between the weaver and a nearby tree.) Members of the weaver's families, mostly aged grandparents and teenage children, displayed the fruits of the weavers labor along the exterior walls of the convent grounds. The colorful handiwork stood out in stark contrast against the sun-bleached, worn-out stone wall. Lying in the dirt alongside the women were their young children. Just minutes from the crucified savior, I saw one little boy, maybe three or four, naked from the waist down, squatting down taking a dump in the dirt.

Inside the church, I saw a dying myth; outside, living reality. Perhaps I am beginning to see only what is before my eyes. I hope so, because for far too long I looked around me and saw what was not there.

On the walk back to the zocalo, I passed a movie theater that displayed a huge, hand-painted sign proclaiming:

STALLONE
ES
ROCKY V
Muy Pronto!
En Rusia Realizo
Su Mas Grande Pelea . . .
Ahora Enfrenta El Mayor
Reto De Su Vida!

The life-size painting of Sylvester Stallone beating up a Russian boxer vaguely resembled the movie star. Not even in Oaxaca can you avoid the lure of Hollywood. How sad.

Well, Kate, I'm going to order another Sidral and some enchiladas for lunch and then resume my walking tour. Maybe, I'll even go see *Rocky V*—if it's dubbed into Spanish, I'm sure it would improve Sly's performance, plus I wouldn't have to endure the hackneyed dialogue. Only kidding—you couldn't pay me to see a Stallone film, even if it was dubbed into Spanish.

Saturday, March 9—3:30 P.M.

According to Charlton and just about everyone else I've spoken to in Oaxaca, the thing to do on Saturdays is visit the Saturday Market. The market sprawls over a large area on the outskirts of town. I was told it was the largest, most colorful, and vibrant market in Mexico.

Nothing I was told could possibly have prepared me for the sensory overload I experienced today. Kate, the market was overpowering, confusing in disorder, and intimidating in its vastness. Block after block of merchandise and produce. There was a dazzling array of every fruit and vegetable imaginable, all artistically displayed. Tomatoes, apples, and oranges are arranged in carefully created architectural mounds. I saw piles upon piles of fresh and dried chilies, over one hundred different kinds. Indian women walked around wearing garlic as crowns on their heads. I saw the fattest carrots I've ever seen, along with giant heads of lettuce and humongous watermelons. A vegetarian would have an orgasm just walking through this section of the market.

A maze of aisles and stalls filled with everything from dresses, radios, pails, blankets, pots, belts, batteries, serapes, dishes, shoes, plastic combs, saddles, and toilet paper to live wild turkeys, chickens, ducks, and birds. I flinched as I saw one woman yanking out a turkey's feathers, but the turkey didn't seem to mind. Shoppers carry the turkeys away as the big birds flap their wings. Ocassionally, human legs are pecked by irritated turkeys and chickens. I saw a young, pregnant woman in a pretty pink dress walking along with a rooster in each hand, holding them upside down by their feet. Everybody is jostled and bumped and scraped by baskets of fruit and vegetables. Other unusual items for sale in the market: round, white cheese wrapped in banana skins and crisp, ruffled sheets of cooked pig's skin. Yummy. Indian women are seated on the ground next to cylindrical baskets filled with tortillas. There are striking Indian blouses, called huipils, with marked differences according to the village of origin. There are gold earrings, pendants, necklaces of Mexican jade, and tiny seed pearls. Much of the jewlery is copied from the Mixtec treasures found at Monte Alban.

I ran into a Swiss woman who was staying at my hotel; we recognized each other and she said to me, "What a life . . . so far removed from ours." She was as equally overwhelmed by the market as I was.

Shade in this outdoor market is provided by large pieces of canvas stretched from poles. Spaces in the canvas create great splashes of light. Vegetables, fruit, pottery, serapes—color, color everywhere. The colors flash in pools of sunlight. Everything you see in this happy emporium is the gift of nature or has been honestly made by hand.

Lots of odd sights. A Zapotec Indian, a guy in his midtwenties, wearing a Washington Redskins T-shirt. A Mexican woman wearing a CNN News T-shirt. An Indian selling audio cassettes wearing a Stanford University T-shirt. A tiny infant asleep in a cardboard box on the floor next to her merchant mother. I saw a young Indian woman with an infant strapped to her back walking to the market. Balanced on her head was a wicker basket filled to over-flowing with large onions. She was carrying in each of her hands a plate of fruit. I had no idea how this dainty, dark-faced, silent-footed woman managed such a diverse and awkward load. A few minutes after she passed by, I saw a very old Indian woman making her way to the market. She also had a wicker basket of onions balanced on her head and was carrying additional onions in her hands. Within minutes, I saw the young woman's future and the old woman's past.

The market is so overpacked with vendors that it spills out into the surrounding streets, where you can buy goats and coats. Adjacent to the market, under the blazing sun, there is an area reserved for the sale of livestock—lambs, sheep, horses, cows, and pigs. What an odor! The small animals sought relief from the sun under the old trucks that brought them to market. On my way back to the hotel, I saw a guy walking toward the market with three little pigs, each on a leash. I smiled.

Everywhere you looked, you saw kids. The babies come to the market with the parents. From childhood all they know is selling and struggling. Babies are sleeping on the ground just a few feet away from the pigs his or her parents are trying to sell. In the main market older children try to direct customers to their parents' stalls. The entire family comes to market, everyone works. The economic life of the state of Oaxaca hinges on this market, which is the largest Indian market on the continent. Indian merchants travel in rattling buses from all over the state, crammed under roofs sagging with bales of alfalfa and sacks of potatoes and grains.

A street evangelist, preaching in a high-pitched, fast-paced voice, handed me a track in English claiming "Jesus breaks the chains." In the market, even salvation is for sale.

The market is life in the raw, and I sit in my study at home trying to figure out the meaning of life.

Crazy.

As I walked back to the hotel, it became clear to me that it is not a world of thought that we live in, but a world of commerce. All around the globe, everything is geared to the sale.

I have nothing to sell.

Saturday, March 9—11:10 P.M.

I took a walk to the zocalo earlier this evening, and I bumped into Charlton and Kate. They were sitting on a park bench, each reading a book. Charlton had his nose buried in a book titled *The Sacred Mushroom and the Cross* by John M. Allegro. The book seeks to answer the question: Did the Christ figure evolve from a primitive fertility cult? Charlton eagerly explained that the author believes that Jesus Christ was the personification of a fertility cult based on the use of the psychedelic mushroom *amanita muscaria.*

Listen, I'm all for debunking religious myths, but as Charlton was talking, I couldn't help but thinking the author's proposition was rather farfetched. I half-jokingly suggested that perhaps the author was on a psychedelic mushroom trip when he wrote the book. Charlton's body stiffened in resentment to my comment. "The author," he sternly informed me, "is a lecturer in Old Testament and Inter-Testamental Studies at the University of Manchester in England. He is a serious scholar. In fact, he was appointed the first British representative on an international editing team preparing the Dead Sea Scrolls for publication. Look at this," he continued, pointing to the back of the book, "the book has over a hundred pages of notes, many of them in Hebrew and Greek, and includes many mathematical formulas and countless references. Chris, this book is the result of more than fourteen years of painstaking research."

"OK, Charlton, I'm sorry. I had no idea. I never heard of the book or the author. But understand that even though I consider Jesus to be just a man—and am even open to the possibility that he never existed—still, the notion that his life and death can be reduced to the life story of a mushroom is rather startling."

"I understand Chris. This book was published twenty years ago, and I discovered it about ten years ago. Ever since, I've been fascinated by it. I've read it many times, each time getting more from it. The truth is that I was first drawn to the book because I am interested in mushrooms. I have grown them and studied them for years. But my continued fascination with the book has more to do with religious anthropology than mushrooms."

"Well, tell me something about it."

"OK. The core of the thesis is that the early Christians were members of an illegal drug cult that worshipped a mushroom they considered sacred. Moreover, the Bible, especially the New Testament, is an intricately contrived cover story to perpetuate the names and incantations of the cult and that the legend of Jesus is simply that—a legend."

"Wait a second, Charlton. If a theory like that were true, and I don't know how it can be proven, it would upset the entire apple cart of Western philosophy and ethics."

"Exactly. Which is why Allegro's book was passionately attacked, despite that fact that it gives detailed and documented evidence to support its claim. What's at stake is the validity of the Bible, the status of the Church, and the moral foundations of our thought and institutions."

We talked for at least fifteen minutes about the book. Charlton read me a few passages. I don't know what to make of it. It sounds very interesting; but, at the same time, the book's tone is very scientific. Charlton said the book was hard to find, suggesting there was an organized force out to suppress it, but that he had another copy which he would be happy to lend to me. I said I would like to read it. The copy he was reading was heavily underlined and highlighted, and it looked as if Charlton had carefully studied it.

What can a serious-minded, nonscholar ever really know about the beginnings of civilization and religion? Not much, is my guess. Sure, we can become familiar with a wide range of theories and interpretations, but is it possible for—let's say, me—to digest, evaluate, and synthesize all the available information on the genesis of man and faith into a coherent understanding that has a fairly good chance of being accurate? Highly doubtful, is my guess, even for scholars. But if it were possible for me to complete the task of reaching a comprehensive understanding of humanity and its beliefs before I was so old that it wouldn't matter, would it make any difference in my life? I don't know.

I would say that even the most highly informed person living today does not have a clue as to what happened on the planet yesterday. To reach back two, three, or four thousand years ago and examine the remaining bones and scribblings of antiquity and expect to know what happened and why is ludicrous. We take educated guesses and label them "fact." My guess is that life is random chaos governed by blind chance.

Reducing the birth of Christianity to a psychedelic mushroom cult is easier to understand than the "big bang" theory, which suggests that at one time everything in the universe was compressed into an extremely dense, hot sphere about the size of a baseball, perhaps even much smaller, maybe even nothing more than a mere speck of energy. About fifteen million years ago—on a Tuesday afternoon around 2:35—the little ball exploded. The explosion launched massive amounts of radiation and zillions of bits of matter on an expansionary course, which continues today. Just prior to the "big bang," the ball had reached a temperature of trillions of degrees and within a split second after the blast particles combined to form protons and neutrons, which quickly collided with each other releasing bursts of energy in the form of light waves. The newborn universe has been expanding, thinning and cooling ever since the "big bang." The protons and neutrons fused to form atomic nuclei. The infinitely dense matter expanded and evolved into a giant cosmos of brilliant stars and huge clusters of galaxies.

Perhaps the "big bang" scheme of our beginnings is just a technological myth for a technological age. The "big bang" theory has an underlying symmetry and beauty to it, but it offers no insight into where the small ball of matter came from, or if the explosion was the work of God. It only suggests that time and the birth of the universe began with its explosion. And how will it end? The young boy in the Woody Allen movie knew the universe was still expanding and he was so terrified by the prospect that eventually the expansion might end in a cataclysmic explosion, which would destroy all existence, that he was unable to go to school. "Why bother?" he asked.

We are obsessed with expansion, with growth. We talk of economic growth, of growth in our understanding of "self," of growth in our relationships. Progress has come to mean growth. We act as if nothing is ever completed, that growth is somehow perpetual. But everything that grows eventually stops growing and begins to decay. The decay ends in death. It is in fashion these days to deny decay and the inevitability of death. I once had a friendship that I thought would last forever. It seemed to just grow and grow and get better and better. Then, without warning or explanation, something happened. A stupid incident triggered decay and eventual death of the friendship. The belief that the friendship could never end made its end even harder to accept.

Our American society and culture has been growing for two centuries, but now it seems the natural process of decay has begun. The signs are clearly visible to those who want to look: waste, pollution, anxiety, greed, bickering, overcrowding, and economic decline. I do not think anything can stop it. I'm not being pessimistic. I'm just admitting the fact that people, relationships, societies, civilizations, all have a life cycle of birth, growth, maturity, decay, and death. Someday, maybe in ten years, maybe in a hundred years, the America we know will no longer exist. After fifteen million years of growth, perhaps the universe will soon begin some great cosmic decline to universal death. Who knows?

My individual fate in the cycle of life is incomprehensible; the planet's plight in the cycle is terrifying.

But life goes on. There is a reason the universe began. There is a reason I am here. There is a reason I was born. There is a reason America was born. There are reasons why I grew and why America has grown; and there are reasons both of us will die.

Of course, those reasons shall forever remain unknown.

I am a part of the process of my own decay and the decay of my country, and there is little I can do about it. This is unsettling. Still my job, my destiny, is to continue to exist, continue to examine, continue to question, continue to search, and continue to resist the temptation to ask, "Why bother?"

I must bother because I must bother.

I must learn to live in a world in which I am doomed to die. That is my job. Slowly, I think I am beginning to feel at peace with the natural process of growth and decay.

Still, I am afraid.

Jesus, I was in a good mood when I went down to the zocalo this evening. And I still am in a good mood. As I think about Charlton and the millions of others who earnestly pursue answers to life's tough questions, I realize the thirst for knowledge can never be fully quenched. But if we do not continue drinking, we will die. So, all we can do is to keep drinking.

After our discussion of Charlton's book ended, the three of us took leave of the park bench and headed for Guelato's for some drinks. Kate and Charlton each ordered a rum and Coke, and I had a beer. A mariachi band was entertaining the customers, many of whom sang along. The musicians were dressed in the Mexican cowboy, or "charro" outfits featuring boots, sombreros, breeches, and short, bright red jackets decorated with silver studs. The group consisted of several violinists, guitarists, trumpet players, and a lead singer.

Over the loud music, I asked Kate, "What book were you reading?"

The book Kate Ryan was reading was far less controversial than Charlton's simply because it didn't undermine all of Christianity; it simply was a full, frontal attack on the female-hating sexism of the celibate male leaders of the Holy Roman Catholic Church.

The book is titled *Eunuchs for the Kindom of Heaven: Women, Sexuality, and the Catholic Church.* It was written by Uta Ranke-Heinemann. She has a Ph.D. in Catholic theology and holds the chair for the History of Religion at the University of Essen in Germany.

According to Kate, the book should be required reading for all Catholic women. She said the book was already a best-seller in Germany and Italy, but has been attacked by the Church hierarchy in the United States. John Cardinal O'Connor accused the publisher of "Catholic-bashing," even though he only read the dust cover, which says that "Dr. Ranke-Heinemann proves that for most of its twenty centuries the Catholic Church (as the principle voice and institutional focus of worldwide Christendom) has been cruelly manipulating and mutilating the sexuality of believers." It adds that "the Church has denigrated sex, degraded women and championed a perverse ideal of celibacy."

It doesn't surprise me that Cardinal O'Connor doesn't want to read a scholarly, well-researched, richly documented, highly critical book written by a member of the loyal opposition. The dust jacket says, "As a loyal, but doggedly critical Catholic, Ranke-Heinemann demands that the Church acknowledge the enormous casualties of its age-old war against genital pleasure." That line must have gotten a rise out of O'Connor. The Cardinal wants no part of re-examining the detrimental role of religion in shaping the sexual behavior of the Western world; he would prefer to keep the clerical bedroom police force in business.

Kate said the book unearths countless spiteful statements about women, statements uttered or written by early Church fathers, saints, medieval moralists, and popes. The author's focus is on the ways in which the cultural domination of women has been perpetuated by the celibate male leaders of the Catholic Church, who considered a priestly vocation to be purer and more superior than that of marriage. According to Kate, Ms. Ranke-Heinemann really goes after St. Thomas Aquinas and points out his copious observations on sexuality demonstrates that his hatred of sex was really a hatred of women, whom he considered to be an inferior form of man.

Kate said, "Three cheers for Uta's rubbing the church's nose in its sorry history."

Kate claimed that most of the criticisms of the book were aimed at the author's high level of anger; but she said, "Dammit, she has a right to be angry. We all should be mad as hell at the way the Church has abused women. We should all go to our windows and scream, 'We're not going to take it anymore!' These old celibate farts and sexual neurotics who run the Church need to be exposed as the misogynists that they are." I wanted to add, "Atta girl, Uta," but refrained from doing so.

While Kate was talking about the book, Charlton was reading about sacred mushrooms. Just another fun night in the zocalo.

Here is a brief sampling of some of the sorry history the book digs up:

Prior to the year 1139, priests were permitted to marry; but the battle over compulsory celibacy for priests began in the fourth century. At the forefront of the fight against the marriage of priests was Pope Siricus, who believed it was a crime for priests to continue having sexual relations with their wives after their ordination.

St. Francis de Sales, the bishop of Geneva who died in 1622, suggested that the elephant was a good model for married people. He wrote,

He [the elephant] is only a clumsy animal and yet the most dignified one alive on earth and the one with the most understanding. . . . He never changes his mate and tenderly loves the one he has chosen, with whom, however, he mates only every three years, and then only for five days and in so hidden a manner that he is never seen in the act. But he does show himself on the sixth day, on which he immediately goes straight to the river, where he washes his whole body, not returning to the herd before cleansing himself.

What a trunk full of crap.

The early Church fathers believed that children conceived during menstruation were born impaired. St. Jerome, who died in 420, wrote, "When a man has intercourse with his wife at this time, the children born from this union are leprous and hypocephalic; and the corrupted blood cause the plague-ridden bodies of both sexes to be either too small or too large." Archbishop Caesarius of Arles, who died in 542, wrote, "Whoever has relations with his wife during her period will have children that are either leprous or possessed by the Devil."

Berthold of Regensburg, a celebrated preacher who died in 1272, said,

You will have no joy from any children conceived during the menses. For they will either be afflicted by the devil, or lepers, or epileptics, or humpbacked, or blind, or crook-legged, or dumb, or idiots, or they will have heads like a mallet . . . and should you have been away from your wife for four weeks, indeed should you have been away for two years, you should take good care not to desire her. . . . You are, after all, upright people, and you see that a stinking Jew avoids this time with great diligence.

Ms. Ranke-Heinemann points out that even, "The idea of a menstruating woman's receiving Holy Communion was consistently frowned upon all the way into the

Middle Ages."

St. John Chrysostom, who died in 407, wrote, "In keeping with God's will man and woman dwelt in Paradise like angels, enflamed by no sensual lustfulness. . . . There was no desire for intercourse, there was neither conception nor birth nor any sort of corruption." I wonder why God created such a big planet if He only planned to populate it with two people? As we all know, the Fall of Adam and Eve ended Paradise. St. John Chrysostom wrote:

> Along with that happy life our first parents simultaneously lost too the ornament of virginity. . . . After they had laid aside this royal garment and forfeited the heavenly jewel, receiving in exchange the destruction of death, the curse, the pains, and a laborious life, in the wake of all this came marriage, that mortal and slavish garment.

The message is clear: marriage comes from disobedience, virginity equals mortality, and marriage equals death.

The Fourth Synod of Orleans in 541 stated, "Priests and deacons are not permitted to share the same bed and the same room with their wives, lest they fall under suspicion of carnal relations." The Synod of Clermont in 535 stated, "Anyone who is ordained a priest or deacon may not continue to have conjugal relations. He becomes a brother to his erstwhile wife." The Synod of Tours in 567 stated, "The bishop may look upon his wife only as his sister. Wherever he stays, he must always be surrounded by clerics, and his and his wife's dwelling must be separated from one another, so that the clerics in his service never come in contact with the women serving the bishop's wife." St. Ambrose said that priests who continued having children after ordination "pray for others with unclean minds as well as unclean bodies." In 1054, Cardinal Humbert denounced the Eastern Church for not insisting on celibacy for its priests; he said, "Young husbands, just now exhausted from carnal lust, serve at the altar. And immediately afterward they again embrace their wives with hands that have been hallowed by the immaculate Body of Christ. This is not the mark of a true faith, but an invention of Satan."

Another hummer from St. John Chrysostom:

> There are in the world a great many situations that weaken the conscientiousness of the soul. First and foremost of these is dealing with women. In his concern for the male sex, the superior may not forget the females, who need greater care precisely because of their ready inclination to sin. In this situation the evil enemy can find many ways to creep in secretly. For the eye of woman touches and disturbs the soul, and not only the eye of the unbridled woman, but that of the decent one as well.

Holy hallucinogenic mushroom munchers! What craziness!

Kate Ryan was right—Uta Ranke-Heinemann has every right to be angry. Just skimming through this dazzling book made me angry. *Eunuchs for the*

Kingdom of Heaven is crammed with countless other gems that support the author's thesis. My idea of heaven would be seeing Cardinal O'Connor forced to respond to every page of this book on national television.

Sunday, March 10—7:00 P.M.

Today being Sunday, I thought it might be the perfect day to visit some of Oaxaca's more famous churches. Churches are among Oaxaca's main tourist attractions, as many of them provide visitors with exceptional displays of fine colonial architecture. If my addition is correct, I've spotted eleven churches, all within five or six blocks of the zocalo. The three most distinguished churches, all of which I visited today, are: Santo Domingo, Iglesia de la Virgen de la Solidad, and the Cathedral.

My first stop was Santo Domingo. As I approached the massive church, I was struck by the peaceful tranquility of the vast and handsome plaza that stretches out from the church steps. The plaza, surrounded by flower beds, had a refined air to it. Tourists and locals were leisurely strolling across its broad space, going to and coming from the church. The sound of cameras clicking filled the air. The rose and gray-green colored building, with its two tall towers and its simple balance, combining the vertical lines of its sober baroque facade with the horizontal profile of the stately Renaissance-style structure, turned everyone into a photographer, determined to capture the magnificent image. The radiant facade features carved garlands, molded cornices, sunken columns, and statues of Dominican saints in their niches. Yet this profusion of creativity did little to prepare me for the splendor of the church's exuberant interior.

The dazzling abundance of late seventeeth-century plasterwork is overwhelming. Overwhelming sounds trite—but I literally had to sit down, my senses being unable to take in the torrent of images that confronted me. I reached into my satchel to take out my notebook so I could jot down my impressions. Within seconds, I placed the notebook back in the satchel, frustrated by the fact that I could not find the words to adequately depict the scene. It was as if the church was terrified of empty space; all the walls were covered with gilded stucco reliefs, fresco paintings, or sculptures. And the domed ceiling—wow! Lavish, gold-tinted ornamental designs surrounded more than three dozen huge paintings of saints and angels. The fanciful design of the revolving arabesques is a marvel to behold, and likely to give you a pain in the neck from looking heavenward for so long. High atop the walls, where the dome begins, there are statues of eight cardinals, in white tunics with red capes and birettas. At the base of the central dome are statues of Popes Inocencio V, Pio V, Benedicto XIII, and Benedicto XI, along with statues of St. Anthony and St. Augustine. The floor plan is in the shape of a Latin cross, with large chapels to the left and right of the main altar. The altarpiece behind the main altar features six golden columns, each divided into three separate levels; between the columns are three levels of paintings and statues, five on each level, except for the center of the first level, which has a giant tabernacle. High atop the baroque altarpiece is a painting of the Virgin Mary. The two large side chapels are equally splendid in ornamental richness. On each side of the nave, there are six small chapels facing each other. Despite the plethora of images, a perfect symmetry prevails, a happy harmony and union of architecture and decoration.

Yet the church seems out of place in such an impoverished area. Most Indians live in squalor, depending on begging and a barter system to exist. I found myself trying to imagine what Oaxaca was like in 1572, the year construction of the church began—I couldn't.

Most of the statues of Christ that I have seen in the churches of Mexico depict him as a tortured, bleeding, suffering Savior. And for good reason: suffering is something the natives can identify with, something they can understand. There is a plaque on the wall of the church which commemorates Pope John Paul II's visit to Santo Domingo on January 29, 1979. During his visit, the Pope prayed for the sick and suffering of Oaxaca. The church was crammed with the ill and infirmed, many wheeled into the church on crude, wooden stretchers equipped with bicycle wheels. The Pope, in a postvisit letter to the church leaders said, "I depend on the prayer of the sick very much, with the suffering brothers mediating before God. They are so close to Christ our Lord. And I approach them conscious of Christ living in the sick. We must bow our heads before our weak and defenseless brothers and sisters, not provided with what we have and enjoy every day. Beloved suffering brothers and sisters, we are in debt to you. The Pope is in debt to you! Pray for us!"

Sure, and don't forget to share what little you have with those of us who have so much, after all, it takes money to keep this palace of the gods open. I'm sure the Pope lifted some spirits, but his visit did little to lift them out of their poverty and suffering—prayers are cheap, a helping hand requires true richness of spirit. The Pope can take his papal blessing and shove it up his papal ass, the poor need to be released from the bondage of religious superstitions and magic. God, churches piss me off!

As I left the sumptuousness of the church, I was confronted with an image that stood in stark contrast to the opulence I had just witnessed. An old Indian women with a basket full of candies and gum stood in front of the open church door, making the sign of the cross over herself about a half dozen times. Then she turned, descended the steps and took her place at the foot of the stone steps and waited to sell her basket of sweets to those leaving the church after Mass. I couldn't help but think that she felt unworthy to enter the church. On the bottom step sat a male beggar, his age impossible to tell. He held a dirty straw hat in his lap. He was shoeless. His left foot was swollen to at least two to three times its normal size. The foot was discolored and covered with festering sores. Tough to look at. Tough to pass by. Yet, everyone did, as if he were invisible; and this after they had received the body and blood of Christ. They did not see Jesus in him. He sat through the divine liturgy, the hymns of worship floating out the open door washing over him. Each of us had marveled at the man-made artistic beauty of a temple built for God, yet none of us saw the suffering of this poor God-made man; the compassionate, loving spirit of Jesus was nowhere to be seen. I dropped a ten thousand peso bill (about three bucks) into his straw hat, took a deep breath, and headed for the Church of the Virgin of Solitude.

Iglesia de la Virgen de la Solitude is also a huge church, but it doesn't come close to matching the magnificence of Santo Domingo. This church is dedicated to the patroness of the City, the Virgin of Solitude, and it has a much more working-class feel to it than Santo Domingo. The church was built between 1682 and 1690, as a sanctuary for the Virgin of Solitude and is located on the spot where the "miraculous" image of the Virgin first appeared in 1620. Here's her story. A muleteer was taking his herd of mules to Oaxaca, and along the way he discovered he had one more mule than when he began his journey, which puzzled him. When he arrived at the spot of the present church, the mysterious, extra mule dropped dead. The man looked inside the pack that was strapped to the dead mule and found a beautiful statue of the Virgin, clothed in gold-embroidered black velvet. The mule and its cargo could not be explained, so it was considered a miracle, and the church was built to house the statue of the Virgin. The statue is enclosed in a gilded glass case behind the main altar, surrounded by an awesome array of chandeliers and lunging angels. Many old Indian women were on their knees before the statue. Adjoining the church is a bi-level, bird-filled plaza that is cluttered with souvenir stands selling all kinds of food and snacks. The shaded plaza has many tables and benches, and the atmosphere is festive and lacks the refined air of the plaza at Santo Domingo. In mid-December, there is an annual fiesta honoring the Virgin of Solitude. Oaxaquenos from all over come to join the religious processions and ceremonies, which include fireworks, floats, bands, and dancers. The celebrants march through the city until sunrise.

Fiestas are an important part of Mexican life. Throughout the year, somewhere in Mexico, villages and cities are celebrating something or paying homage to a saint, a hero, or a tradition, with explosions of color, costumes, music, masks, processions, dances, and fireworks. Many of the fiestas are local affairs, but some, like the Day of Three Kings, the Day of the Dead, and the Fiesta of the Virgin of Guadalupe, are celebrated nationwide. Fiestas are strange mixtures of symbolism and religious observance, of history and local folklore, of piety and commerce, of praying and partying, of fireworks and alcohol. Many of the fiestas have a connection with the Indian past, dancing music, and pageantry that had been an important part of pre-Columbian Indian ceremonies. The early missionaries may have banned the Indian idols, but they allowed their idolatry to continue and to be expressed in gaily staged pageants.

A fiesta, no matter what it is celebrating, is a time of release, a time for noise, recklessness, and gaiety. Fiestas allow a complete change in the silence and solitude that marks most Mexican's lives. During fiestas, all social and economic barriers are let down, and the people go from one extreme to another. The humble Indian goes from being silent, stoic, and obsequious to being loud, wild, and boastful. Fiestas are a time to leave troubles behind and provide an opportunity for unrestrained laughter. Fiestas are periodic alternatives to misery.

Octavio Paz, Mexico's foremost writer and winner of the 1990 Nobel Prize for Literature, writes:

> This is the night when friends who have not exchanged more than the prescribed courtesies for months, get drunk together, trade confidences, weep over the same troubles, discover they are brothers, and sometimes, to prove it, kill each other. The night is full of songs and loud cries. The lover wakes up his sweetheart with an orchestra. There are jokes and conversations from balcony to balcony, sidewalk to sidewalk. Nobody talks quietly. Hats fly in the air. Laughter and curses ring like silver pesos. . . . The Mexican does not seek amusement; he seeks to escape from himself, to leap over the wall of solitude that confines him during the rest of the year. All are possessed by violence and frenzy. Their souls explode. . . . This fiesta, shot through with lightning and delirium, is the brilliant reverse to our silence and apathy, our reticence and gloom.

Mexico has become a fiesta for me; a time to escape the solitude that has entrapped me, a time to let go of the torments of my past, a time to celebrate my life—to celebrate all life. I wonder where I can get some firecrackers!

I took a short break from my church tour and ate an ear of corn, a quesadilla, and drank a cold Sidral in the plaza and then headed for the cathedral.

The cathedral is located just across the street from the north side of the zocalo. The tree-lined square in front of the cathedral is always crowded with strolling tourists and locals, along with an assortment of vendors selling handicrafts, balloons, and cheap souvenirs. Despite its massive proportions, the cathedral still has a squat appearance. Construction on the cathedral began in 1544, and took over two hundred years to complete. The pale green stone facade rises in three harmonious sections and is adorned with capricious ornamental forms in sculptures and reliefs. The central section has a high relief of the Virgin of the Assumption, to whom the church is dedicated. The interior of the Cathedral was rather ho-hum and a disappointment after seeing the other two churches. The spacious, dark cathedral has five naves. The cathedral does feature two large, impressive paintings, one of St. Christopher (!) and one titled "The Seven Archangels in Glory."

All in all, it was an interesting day; but, to be honest, I enjoy my excursions into the countryside with Charlton much more than spending a day in churches.

Monday, March 11—5:10 P.M.

I met a genuine artist today, an artist who literally created a new art form and who is also a shaman and claims to be a prophet. Charlton really knows his way around and knows some very interesting people. Today we drove to the villages of Arrazola and Xoxocotlan, which are located at the base of Monte Alban. The villages have become famous thanks to the talents of their woodcarvers, who create fanciful, bewitching, brightly painted, wildly vivid animals. These isolated, peasant communities have given birth to a dream world of psychedelic cats, acrobatic armadillos, leaping dogs, dancing chickens, flying cows, flute-playing ducks, blue bulls with zebra-stripped horns, and an assortment of polka-dotted reindeers, polar bears, rabbits, and giraffes, some with fuchsia ears, and all in poses that are both playful and fantastic.

Charlton told me that the velvet-green Valley of Oaxaca, with its rich and complicated variety of Indian cultures, nurtures an exhaustive diversity of crafts, some of whose origins date back more than a thousand years. There are whole towns dedicated to pottery, weaving, jewelry, and puppet making. As we drove through Xoxocotlan, which is the valley's municipal headquarters, on our way to Arrazola, the dirt streets, ox-drawn carts, and the straw and bamboo huts that provide minimal shelter for the peasants who live in them gave no hint that I was about to enter a world inhabited by artisans with incredibly fertile imaginations. By day's end, I wondered how so much creativity could emerge from a land enslaved in so much poverty.

The artist we visited lives in Arrazola, in a sprawling compound of brick homes and wooden studios tucked behind a tall wall that dwarfs the surrounding adobe huts of his neighbors. His name is Manuel Jimenez. He is a woodcarver. But not just any woodcarver, Manuel is a celebrated master woodcarver and the father of an art form that has enchanted folk art collectors from all around the world with its exuberance of shapes and color. Using only the crudest of tools, his creations sell for four times more than that of his most expensive competitors. His works are on permanent display in many museums. The artist is also a curandero (or healer), a staunch Catholic, and a Zapotec Indian. At seventy-one Manuel Jimenez has more vibrancy than most men fifty years his junior.

Fame and fortune were not always part of Manuel Jimenez's life. His father was a peasant farmer, who frequently beat the young Manuel. He had no formal education and was forced to watch over the family's grazing sheep and goats, which became subjects for his clay models. As an adult, Jimenez worked as a canecutter, mason, band leader, and barber. He also carved masks, which he sold to tourists at Monte Alban. Manuel became an alcoholic, and two of his brothers died as the result of excessive drinking. For most of his first thirty-five years of life, Jimenez was among the poorest people in a very poor village. Arrazola was a former sugar hacienda that had yet to fully recover from a century of serfdom.

How did Manuel Jimenez escape poverty? He credits God. Thirty five years ago, Jimenez was depressed and frustrated by his poverty. Looking for solace and inspiration, he went up to Monte Alban and climbed the ruins of the temples. And sat. God spoke to him, telling Manuel to earn a living with his hands, by carving. Because of his love for animals, they became his subjects. At first he carved primitive animals and sculptures of saints. He remained a farmer, and the oxen and sheep became his models. Manuel quickly discovered his ability to look beyond reality and into realms of imagination. After experimenting with dozens of different types of wood, he began using wood from the trunks of copol, which is carved while it is still green, soft, and easy to handle. The gummy resin in the wood dries and hardens into a sturdy finished product.

Soon his work began appearing in shops in Oaxaca, and folk art collectors were attracted by his striking originality and his use of bright colors. His success bred imitators. It seemed everyone in Arrazola began woodcarving, following Manuel's bold example. The success of Jimenez and Arrazola's two hundred other carvers, including a dozen with far-flung reputations really began to soar in 1986, and gradually brought a new level of prosperity to the village. Some of the artisans now own cars, the church has been remodeled, and the schools now have plenty of supplies. Still, the streets remain unpaved gulleys, ox carts and flocks of sheep are the only cause of traffic delays, and phone service has yet to intrude on the villagers' solitude.

Jimenez spoke very little English, and his rapid-fire speech proved difficult for Charlton to translate, or at least keep up with. He was a very proud man, happy to show me several scrapbooks filled with newspaper articles attesting to his fame. I didn't need to see a scrapbook to realize the level of success he had achieved; a casual look around the room revealed high quality furniture, expensive pieces of art work, a giant screen TV, and a VCR (on which he had his son play a documentary based on his life and art) amply demonstrated the wealth that his carvings had generated. He sat on his couch as if it were a throne, because he knew he truly was the king of woodcarvers. He escorted me into a room in which he had displayed recently commissioned pieces, mostly of a religious nature.

The most interesting part of the visit came when he led us on a walk around the grounds of his property. The walk concluded at his private workshop. It was a simple room that held none of the trappings of his fame. The white-washed walls were barren. Half the floor was covered with a pile of logs. The furniture consisted of a simple wooden table covered with jars of paint and paint brushes, and a very small wooden stool, upon which he sat for endless hours while his imagination guided his whimsical creations. Haphazardly sitting on the floor were three pieces in various stages of progress. It was a scene of utter simplicity.

In the community of Arrazola, Manuel Jimenez is respected not only for his artistic talents but also for his spirituality, which is an unusual blend of ancient Indian beliefs and Catholicism. Like many of the Indians, the beliefs and divinities of Manuel's ancestors are still alive, scarcely obscured under a veneer of Christianity. Charlton told me that Jimenez conducted regular healing services and that he was frequently called upon to offer his spiritual insight.

As a curandero, Manuel Jimenez performs ritualistic healing services. Witchcraft is a very touchy subject in Mexico, and most Mexicans claim not to believe in it. But they do, despite the fact that they speak of witchcraft as a superstition found only in uncivilized Indians. In truth, witchcraft has been a real part of daily life in Mexico since ancient times, and fear of witchcraft is still widespread, and the demand for cures for bewitchment is great. Curanderos are not witches, and one of their primary functions is to perform cleansing rites that remove afflictions sent by witches by passing eggs, pepper tree branches, lime, and other substances over the body of a person who has been cursed by a witch. Curanderos also treat evil air and ghost fright, and they are paid modest fees for their services.

Witches played an important role in Aztec society. They were usually men, who became witches by virtue of their birth—that is born under the sign of rain and destined by the gods to be a witch. Witches had celebrity status in Aztec society. Kings sought their council, and they were revered for their ability to predict the future and to stop such catastrophes as drought and sickness. An Aztec witch could also cause sickness by sucking blood from his victim, after which the witch would seize his victim's soul or insert worms into his body.

How is it that Jimenez can be both a curandero and a Catholic? On the surface, it seems the two are contradictory. But on close examination we can see they are harmonious. When the Spanish arrived in New Spain, despite their Catholicism, they brought with them thier own sophisticated brand of witchcraft. In the Spanish tradition, witches were made, not born, by making a pact with the Devil. The benefit of that allegiance for the witch was a life of carnal pleasure. Spanish witches were usually women, which is to be expected in light of the Catholic view that women were sinks of iniquity. European witches were devoted to black magic and sexual orgies, and healing wasn't on their agenda.

Furthermore, Catholicism viewed the individual as evil and condemned the world. The Indians had no need to be cleansed of Original Sin. Sin for them was tied to the idea of health and sickness in the individual, the society, and the universe. Catholicism stressed the need for personal salvation, while the Indians conceived of personal salvation only as a part of the salvation of society and the universe.

The Spanish priests bridged this gap by teaching the Indians that the world was divided into forces of good, led by God, and the forces of evil, headed by Satan. The priests claimed pagan deities were really demons working for the Devil, and witches were their allies and enemies of Christianity. Witchcraft came close to the Catholic concept of sin, and so the priests exploited it and actually encouraged it by stigmatizing the practice. The priests insisted that babies who were not baptized were witches. The Indians were puzzled by the priests efforts to eliminate evil. The Inquisition in New Spain was instituted to combat witchcraft, superstitious healing, and idolatry. Witches tried to dupe the inquisitors by claiming they prayed to St. Anthony or the Virgin for a cure. The priests introduced their own form of faith healing by introducing the power of relics, bones, and the garments of famous saints. Instead of rubbing unbroken eggs over the bodies of the sick, Indians learned how to rub relics over a patient's body in order to draw out the disease or curse.

Witchcraft is still a serious business among the Indians of modern Mexico. The Zapotec Indians of Mitla believe witches can take the form of cats, dogs, vultures, and burros. They believe witches suck the blood out of sleeping infants, and, to insure protection for the child, parents, before going to bed, tie to the infant's belt a small bag containing mustard seeds, rosemary, a pin, and a picture of a saint. Beliefs and practices vary widely from community to community. For instance, some Indians believe witches or pagan deities can steal a man's soul by capturing his favorite animal, some believe the power to cure comes from rain dwarfs, some believe childhood illnesses are caused by an evil eye (that is looking at a baby with admiration or envy) and that a child's soul can be dislodged from its body by the stare of a stranger or animal, and some believe that evil air emanates from corpses. The various forms of Indian witchcraft have nothing in common with the Satanic witchcraft practiced in the bigger cities, which is a more commercialized enterprise concerned with revenge and pleasure.

In an age of science and rationalism, it is hard to believe that modern Mexico is still supersaturated with superstitious beliefs and practices. Manuel Jimenez represents a blend of ancient Christian and Indian myths that have a powerful hold on the imaginations of many people. Jimenez is a respected pillar of his community, a man equally at home in the world of creativity and spirituality—in fact, each feeds the other.

As Charlton and I spoke about curanderos and witchcraft, I couldn't help but think how for so long I viewed the Christian myths that I was taught as special, and better than the myths of other religions, but how now I was beginning to realize that all religious myths are basically the same and all of them grew out of the fact that ancient man knew so little and feared so much that gods became indispensible. Even today, after centuries of enlightenment, the flame of our intelligence still burns feebly and our hopes still outrun our ability for attainment, and so God is still alive and well in many parts of the world. Jesus didn't say anything unique enough to make the God of Christianity any better than the gods of other faiths; it was the teachings of his followers that gave the Christian God the qualities that made Him superior to the pantheon of gods that inhabited the Greco-Roman world. Catholicism did not upgrade the beliefs of the Indians, it only altered them, perhaps for the worse.

Tuesday, March 12—3:00 P.M.

Charlton picked me up a little before nine this morning. We drove about twenty miles southeast of Oaxaca to the small, tranquil village of Teotitlan del Valle. The name means "land of the gods." Teotitlan is known for its weavers. Over 1,200 weavers make wool serapes and rugs on home looms.

We visited the home of the undisputed master of the weavers, a man named Alberto Vasquez. This short, gentle Zapotec Indian is an artist, pure and simple. His works of handwoven textiles are owned in private collections in Colorado, Texas, and seventeen other states, as well as Canada, Germany, and Spain. One of his tapestries hangs on a wall in the U.S. Embassy in Mexico City. His work is also on display at the Metropolitan Museum of Art in New York City.

A big smile flashed across Alberto's face when Charlton told him I was from Los Angeles. He speaks very little English, but Charlton translated his comments, "He says he really enjoys Los Angeles. He likes the hustle and bustle, and the astounding roads." His work and fame have taken him far from this humble village where he was born nearly fifty years ago, but he always returns.

Teotitlan del Valle is his home and his inspiration.

He seemed very glad to see Charlton and was happy to stop his work and explain the rug-making process to me. And what a long tedious process it is.

Raw wool is purchased from the sheepherders. But before the wool reaches Alberto's loom, all the thorns and blades of grass are removed, then the wool is washed in a stream, combed, carded, washed again, threaded, washed once more, dyed, and washed a fourth time, and then it is finally ready for use. The most interesting part of preparing the wool for weaving is the dying. Vasquez uses a combination of bugs, plants, and rock moss to produce beautiful shades of maroon, blue, tan, green, and brown—the colors of the earth. By experimenting, Alberto discovered that the blood of the cochineal beetle produces a deep red, his favorite color. But manufacturing this red dye is a long process. Cactus is cultivated in his home during the rainy season and then planted outside with the cochineal on them. As the bugs begin to multiply they are put on leaves of palm. The bugs are killed by exposure to the sun and dried for two weeks. The cochineal are ground, mixed with dried lemon and water, and boiled for three hours before the dye is finally ready for use. The master weaver told us that rock moss produces a vivid, living brown; pecan shells yield a soft brown; and peppers deliver a fierce green. Vasquez also uses walnut husks and tree leaves as ingredients for the tints he creates.

Alberto points to himself and says, "I am the color of earth." And the colors he creates are pure and from the earth. Why not use chemical dyes, we asked. "Many do," he responded, "but, unfortunately the false colors fade." He told us that he had a great concern for purity, which caused him to abandon the use of chemical dyes over twenty years ago. During the last century, the weavers of the village began using chemical dyes that could be bought in packages. It relieved the poor weavers of the tedious job of searching for bugs, rocks, and plants, and gave them more time for the actual weaving. Their production increased. When Alberto decided that he wanted to return to the traditional ways of dying the wool, he had to rattle the memories of a few village elders. Gradually, the centuries-old techniques were given a new lease on life.

All the weavers of Teotitlan assure their customers that all the work they do is naturally dyed. Most of it isn't. We asked Alberto if it bothers him that his competitors secretly used chemical dyes. His answer showed his gentleness and compassion: "They are poor. It is hard to be poor."

As we stood talking in the open courtyard of the weaver's unpretentious home, an old man emerged from the shadows of one of the doorless rooms that border the sun-drenched courtyard. The old man was taking slow but steady steps toward us. He wore very thick glasses, perhaps to compensate for cataracts resulting from old age and a lifetime in the sun. Upon seeing the old man, Alberto smiled and instantly broke off our conversation and proudly introduced him to us with these touching words, "My father, my teacher."

In four words, Alberto Vasquez spoke volumes of his love, admiration, and respect for his father. The old man stuck out his hand to shake mine. I was surprised by the strength of his grip. Later, Charlton told me that five years ago he read an article about Alberto in which it was mentioned that his father was ninety-six, which means the old man is now 101! And stronger than I am.

Kate, I keep hearing those words: "My father, my teacher." Alberto's father was very poor, and Alberto grew up in a dirt-floored adobe hut without electricity or running water. Alberto was the only one of five children to survive those primitive conditions. When he was eleven, Alberto left school and began weaving at his father's side. For nearly forty years the two men have been much more than father and son; they have been teacher and student. And now that the student has become the master, there is no doubt who the real master is in Alberto's mind.

We modern Americans are rich and sophisticated. We have the fruits of modern technology at our finger tips. Yet in the home of Alberto Vasquez, I felt poor. I envied his relationship with his father and mother earth. Shit, I don't know what my father did to earn a living. Sure, I know that he worked on Wall Street, but that's all I know about his life's work. I visited his office once when I was about twelve. To this day I have no understanding of the stock market. I don't even own any stocks. I don't have Alberto's understanding of nature either. I could never figure out how to take a sheep's wool and turn it into a rug, and it would never occur to me to squash insects in order to dye the wool I couldn't weave.

The old man and his son know how to love and how to survive on that with which nature has provided them. Despite the externals that say the opposite, they are rich and I am poor.

When Charlton and I got into the Blazer to drive back to Oaxaca, the old man was sitting on a wooden box in front of his son's home at Number 42 Juarez Avenue. As we drove past him, the old man gave us a vigorous good-bye wave, and our trip back in time ended in broad smiles.

Tuesday, March 12—5:05 P.M.

Greetings from the El Zaguan, a little sidewalk cafe on the east side of the zocalo. I'm sipping a cold bottle of Negra Modela. I took a short snooze when I got back from Teotitlan, and I've just been walking around Oaxaca for the past hour or so.

During the walk, I happened to pass a small department store. It looked like something out of the 1950s in Queens. What caught my eye was a display of television sets, all of them tuned to a Mexican soap opera. I went into the store and watched for a few minutes. The soap was so-so. Of course, I hadn't a clue of what they were saying, but nonetheless I was anticipating the camera shots. The camera work was lackluster and the directing predictable; the director could have used a few more reaction shots. A scene featuring a heated exchange between a man and a women ended with the standard zoom to a "bad guy" who entered the room at precisely the wrong moment.

More interesting to me than the show was the sight of a young Mexican woman holding her infant child. Her attention was glued to the soap. I thought of my mother and I doing the same thing at Frankel's Department store forty years ago. Mexico may be very different from America, but when it comes to the real stuff of life it is pretty much the same.

On the way to the zocalo, I stopped at a newsstand and bought a copy of a Mexican soap opera fan magazine. I've been looking at the pictures while drinking my beer. With summer approaching, the magazine contains a five-page spread of sexy soap opera actresses modeling bikinis, plus an additional five pages of male stars wearing very tiny swim suits. One muscular guy was kneeling on the ground squirting himself with a hose. Kate, it's all about marketing: the stars sell their sex appeal and the advertisers sell their sexy apparel. If it weren't for the Spanish, you would think I was reading any one of a half-dozen American magazines that cater to the soap opera addict. Mexico is no more immune from triviality than America is, although it is our chief export.

If I wanna make a buck, I've got to become more trivial. Yea, that's the ticket—trivial pursuit.

Wednesday, March 13—4:00 P.M.

Today, Charlton and I visited two more interesting villages in the valley south of Oaxaca. I find it interesting that each village is known for its expertise in a specific craft. The two villages we toured today specialize in pottery. Our first stop was San Bartolo Coyotepec, which is located about seven miles south of the capitol. Coyotepec means "hill of the coyote," but we didn't see any coyotes. The town is distinguished for its rich production of black clay handicrafts, which are in great demand abroad. We visited the home and shop of Dona Rosa. Dona Rosa, who died a few years ago at the age of eighty, was a simple Zapotec Indian woman whose fame rivaled that of any powerful political or religious leader. She was recognized as a national treasure by one of Mexico's presidents. The walls of her shop are covered with photos of her and visiting dignitaries and celebrities. Her sixty-two-year-old son Nieto carries on the ancient tradition of ancient blackware pottery without using a potter's wheel.

Tourists still flock to the maestras home to observe her son's daily demonstrations of pottery making. Nieto is an outgoing, energetic man, who greets each guest with a big smile and a hearty handshake. He loves speaking about his mother, whom he affectionately refers to as "Mi mama," and for whom he still has great respect and love.

Nieto's tools reflect his simple lifestyle: sticks, pieces of bamboo, remnants of broken old pottery, and pieces of leather. He sits on the stone floor facing a slab of concrete. He does not use a potterer's wheel. Instead, on the concrete rests a small plate, which is placed in an upside-down position. On top of that plate, Nieto places another smaller plate, which he spins once he drops a chunk of clay into it. He spins the plate and shapes the clay at the same time, a feat

I still can't imagine how he accomplishes. Within minutes, the form of a jug begins to take shape. When the jug is completed, he adds a handle and outlines beautiful floral patterns on the jug. The delightful and varied shapes of jugs he creates are more ornamental than utilitarian.

As I watched Nieto work, I thought how all art is really a matter of simplification, and how this simple artist could teach us sophisticated moderns much about life. His education was garnered at the knees of his mother. He generates his living from the things in nature that he finds outside his front door. Most Americans have parasitical jobs that feed off others; we rarely produce anything. Nieto's life seems full. So many people I know have empty lives, which they try to fill with all kinds of things and activities, because they do not realize that what they need is within and around them.

Next up on our tour was the village of Santa Maria Atzompa. The pottery made in Atzompa is the more traditional painted ceramic type. Atzompa is a very, very poor town consisting mostly of bamboo huts and single room concrete shelters. We visited the home of the most renowned potter in the village, a woman named Dolores Porras. Dolores is in her late fifties, and has long black hair with streaks of gray. Her big, broad smile clearly reveals that she has only five front teeth. By Atzompa standards, she is a wealthy woman; by our standards, she lives in unimaginable poverty. She lives in a long, rectangular concrete box of a home. It has three rooms, each with an unprotected window and door opening. The floor is also made of concrete, uncovered by any rugs. Dolores's room is at one end of the building, and contains little more than a bureau, a bed, a radio, and a small black-and-white television. The room at the other end of the house functions as a bedroom for three of her younger children. When I poked my head into the room, a young teenage boy was busy scrubbing the floor. The older, married children live in smaller tin shacks on the property. The middle room of Dolores's home serves as a combination family room and her workshop. The walls are bare except for a few religious pictures. The table is cluttered with works-in-progress. A bookshelf displays completed works. As if in a "what's wrong with this picture" puzzle, I noticed on the floor in one of the corners a blue athletic bag with a *Playboy* bunny logo on it.

The dirt yard is cluttered with toys (there were a number of very young children playing in the dirt and mud); there were several rabbits running around the yard, and I smiled when I noticed a pair of green parrots, a dog, and a donkey drinking water from the same puddle. In the center of the yard was a large oven used to bake the pottery. In one corner of the yard was a three-sided, roofed bamboo hut, in which a few teenage children were painting vases.

Charlton was instrumental in introducing Dolores Porras's work to some of the finest shops in Oaxaca. Her distinctive designs, decorated with her unique painting style, quickly became big sellers. He suggested that she begin to sign her work, in the hope that her name would eventually become a valuable marketing asset. She claimed her work did not need her signature in order to be recognized, because her designs and decorative painting style were clearly her own. The real reason she didn't want to put her signature on her creations was that she did not know how to write. To this day, one of her children holds her hand and helps her put the letters of her first name on all her works of art.

When we arrived, Dolores was working on a large vase, which featured the raised, sculptured figure of a woman. While we were talking to her, she continued to work on the vase and changed the shape and size of the figure's breasts at least three times. While working, she knelt on the floor. She does not use any tools, with the exception of a small toothpick which she uses when she needs to draw a very fine line on the pottery. She does everything by hand, creating intricate details with her fingernails.

The large family functioned as a coherent whole, each contributing something to their little cottage industry. They took great pride in their work and relished being treated as celebrities by their fellow townspeople. As we were about to leave, I purchased a small green vase, gaily decorated with bright yellow sunflowers. I shall treasure it as an inspirational reminder of the time I spent in the presence of a truly remarkable woman.

Wednesday, March 13—11:20 P.M.

Charlton, Kate, and I spent a pleasant evening having drinks at the Cafe Del Jardir and strolling around the zocalo. Some of our conversation dealt with the woodcarvers, weavers, and potters Charlton and I had visited during the past few days. I mentioned to Kate how impressed I was with their creativity and artistic abilities. She managed to put her finger on why the handicrafts of Oaxaca are so appealing to tourists.

Kate the Elder said, "We live in an age in which people measure their lives and activities by tenths of seconds on digital watches. We don't have the time to make things for ourselves, because it takes too much time—just ask any woman who knits how long it takes to knit a simple sweater. Because time is money, handmade objects in this day and age have become a luxury few can justify making. But lack of time doesn't explain why handcrafted objects appeal to us. The real reason is much more complex. Ever since the industrial age began, people have expressed concern over the loss of individuality that mass-produced objects imply. What attracts tourists to the handicrafts is their inherent uniqueness. Anything handmade is a reassuring reflection on the individuality of each human being; it is a gesture of defiance against anonymity and monotony. Against the background of mass-produced objects, things handcrafted take on the luster of art."

I knew that. Jesus, all I did was say how artistic Alberto, Dolores, and Manuel were and I got a lecture on the anthropology of handicrafts. Only kidding, it wasn't a lecture—Kate is just very thoughtful and articulate. What Kate had to say made a lot of sense, without diminishing the true artistic abilities of the those talented people. Each of the artisans I met this week were unique individuals, and everything they created was an original.

When I was a teenager, I made a shoeshine box for my father. Now that

I think about it, it was very much like the ones I saw the boys carrying around the train station in Mexico City. It was the only thing I ever made with my own hands. I wish I had done more.

Thursday, March 14—4:15 P.M.

Took a day off from touring. Spent the greater part of the day in the library—in fact, that is where I am now. It's a small, privately run library offering books in English. It is run by Americans for the benefit of Americans living in Oaxaca, and those just visiting the city.

I wanted to relax and also to learn something about the ancient Indian cultures.

The civilization of ancient Mexico was created by bands of nomadic Asian hunters. The Ice Age had created a land bridge between Siberia and Alaska, across what is known today as the Bering Straits. Somewhere between 30,000 and 40,000 years ago, hunters crossed this land strip in search of mammoths and mastodons. What they found was the Americas. As the Ice Age ended, the melting ice submerged the bridge, along with much of the land, and the hunters, equipped with only the rudiments of culture, were here to stay. Over the millennia, they adapted to a radically new environment. By at least 11,000 years ago, some of the nomads had reached the tip of South America.

Maybe this explains why when I heard a lot of Zapotec and Mixtec spoken during my day at the market last Saturday I was struck by the tonal quality of the language and thought how much it sounded like Chinese, where the meaning of a word is dependent upon the pitch of the voice and the sounds are very lyrical.

The pre-Hispanic era of Mexico is divided into three periods: preclassical, classical, and postclassical. The preclassical period spans the years between 2000 B.C. and 200 B.C. During this period communities were engaged in fishing, hunting, gathering, and very basic agriculture. They slaughtered now-extinct species of mammoth, camels, and wild horses. The big game became extinct around 700 B.C., perhaps as a result of the dramatic shift to a desertlike climate, and the nomads began fishing in lakes and streams and trapping smaller game, such as armadillos, gophers, iguanas, and rabbits. These early Mexicans wandered in bands or family groups, foraging for fruits, seeds, or roots of wild plants. Over time, the bands were incorporated into tribes that grew in numbers, developing distinct languages, and creating more complex cultures. The Olmec culture, with their well-planned ceremonial centers, flourished and exerted a powerful influence over Mesoamerica, an area of land that extended south from the Central Valley of Mexico City into Guatemala, Belize, El Salvador, and Honduras. Olmec art is very distinctive and featured figures with pear-shaped heads, wide noses, baby faces, large lips, drooping mouths, and sometimes jaguar fangs. Toward the end of this period settlement of the Mayan lowlands begins and the foundations of Monte Alban are laid.

The classical period lasted from 200 B.C. to A.D. 900. During this period urbanization and the formation of theocratic ruling castes began; art, ceramics, and writing flourished; deities multiplied; and the calendar was developed. The great cities of Teotihuacan, Monte Alban, Mitla, Palenque, Tajin, Bonampak, Xochicalco, and Uxmal, reached their apex of splendor.

The post-classical period is dated from A.D. 900 to 1521. During this time the theocratic societies became militarized and metallurgy appears. Mesoamerica reached its greatest expansion and had about 25,000,000 inhabitants. The beginning of the end of Mesoamerica came in April of 1519—on Holy Friday, the Day of the True Cross, when Hernan Cortes and his men landed and founded the first Spanish town, Villa Rica de la Vera Cruz (True Cross), known today as Veracruz. On August 13, 1521, after a heroic and bloody battle, the great city of Mexico-Tenochtitlan surrendered to Cortes and the conquest of New Spain was complete. Cortes built Mexico City on the same sight as Tenochtitlan. Three years later, twelve Franciscan friars arrived in Mexico, and the Indians got a new God.

In 1566, Friar Diego de Landa wrote, "It is a marvel to see the freedom with which they know how to count and understand things." All Mesoamerican cultures computed time based on calendars, but the Maya showed themselves to have a particular affinity for calendars. They may have had one of the earliest concepts of zero in the world, a concept that not even the Romans had. And they used a positional system of numbers like the decimal system, only theirs was based on 20, not 10. They computed time millions of years into the past, and even thousands of years into the future. They knew the true length of the solar year before the Europeans. Father de Landa, who became the first bishop of Yucatan, may have marveled at the natives ability to write, but he nonetheless destroyed many of the Maya codices that would have helped us understand their rich civilization.

The Maya had a hierarchy of priests whose duties included prophesy, medicine, education of candidates for the priesthood, and leading religious rituals. The Maya were polytheistic. Two chief gods in their pantheon were Itzamna, benevolent friend of man and inventor of writing, and Ix Chel, the moon goddess who was patroness of healing and pregnancy. There were deities who watched over maize, music, and war. There was even a special goddess of suicides. Fortunately, I don't need her anymore.

In 1579, Friar Diego Duran wrote, "The gods were so honored and revered by the natives that any offense against them was paid for with one's life. They held the gods in more fear and reverence than we show to our God."

The ancients lived in a universe animated by many gods—the sun, moon, rain, wind, earth, and fire being the most important. (The ancient Greeks thought the sun, moon, and planets were each moved by a god, who was actuated by an aesthetic love of regularity.) This universe was perceived to be under the constant threat of annihilation. Living on the eve of destruction, the ancients had much to fear. They thought it was necessary to flatter the gods and perform ceremonies to avoid disaster. To that end, all ancient Mesoamericans practiced human sacrifice to some degree, but the Aztecs were obsessed with it.

Human sacrifice was an indispensable part of the Aztec religion. They sacrificed captives of war and convicted criminals. Victims were dragged up the steps of the pyramid. At the summit, they were placed on a sacrificial stone while four priests held their limbs and a fifth priest plunged an obsidian knife into each chest and tore out a palpitating heart, which was offered to the appropriate god. (Gee, religion can really be fun.)

The Aztecs believed the gods needed nourishment, and, to assure plentiful crops, the rain god and earth goddess had to be appeased or regularly presented with divine food. The sun, it was believed, needed human blood to guarantee its continuance. The Aztecs believed that there had been four previous worlds, or suns, each of which had suffered a cataclysmic end. The current Fifth Sun was doomed to destruction by a great earthquake, but the final destruction could be postponed by human sacrifice. During the rain ritual, children were slain in the hope that their tears would assure plentiful rainfall. During the rite of spring, the priests donned the skins of flayed victims. Because they had so many religious festivals and worshipped more than two hundred deities, the Aztecs needed a great many priests, all of whom practiced celibacy.

Well, enough facts for today. Seriously, my day here at the library helped me better understand the people and the place I've grown to admire.

Friday, March 15—6:30 A.M.

Had a restless night's sleep. It was triggered by some of the stuff I read in the library yesterday. I don't know why, but I couldn't get the notion of religious rituals involving human sacrifice out of my mind. I think it is very, very difficult for a modern mind to fully comprehend the notion of offering human sacrifices to a god. Even though brutality still exists on all levels of modern life, the ancient practices of killing another human to placate a god still seems excessively brutal. It is difficult enough for us to fully understand inner workings of a friend's mind, let alone try to understand the mindset of an entire group of people who lived so long ago and in a culture so vastly different from ours.

To the minds of the first missionaries who came to Mexico, the Indians were bloodthirsty savages whose religious practices were vastly inferior to the sophistication and grace of Christianity. But what did these pious priests know of the early days of Christianity, when Christianity itself was viewed by educated non-Christians as a degenerate and superstitious cult that engaged in debauchery, sexual promiscuity, and the eating of human flesh? Shocking as it may seem, there is evidence that some of the early Christians were guilty of those charges.

I was at a party a few years ago, and I met a young law student who had an unquenchable thirst for truth and justice. His name was John Scinto. John was the brother of the party's host and the only nontelevision person in attendance. Naturally, I wound up spending most of the evening with him. We discussed a topic that was paramount on each of our minds: God.

At the time, I believed God probably existed and was earnestly searching for any shred of proof to support what I hoped was true. Scinto believed that God didn't exist, but he was willing to examine any thoughtful or serious evidence presented in opposition to his supposition. Sounding every bit like a lawyer, John said, "I do not need to disprove God's existence, it is up to the believers to prove it. And nothing that I have heard or read so far about the existence of God has been convincing enough for me to nullify my disbelief. I'm not prosecuting God, so I have no need to call God to the witness stand, but his defenders do."

John Scinto was honest, thoughtful, reasonable, and a straight arrow. He didn't drink, smoke, or do drugs. His interest in law grew from his sense of fairness and had nothing to do with money or power. Despite my disdain for lawyers, I liked him.

Anyway, that night John was excited to find someone with whom he could talk regarding his recent readings about the early days of Christianity.

His voice filled with frustration, John said, "Everything we know about the roots of Christianity comes from Christian sources. Our understanding of the first few centuries of Christianity is based on the writings of such defenders of the faith as Ignatius of Antioch, Clement of Rome, Tertullian, Origen, and Justin Martyr. These guys have been studied for centuries but we never hear what the non-Christians had to say about Jesus and his followers."

Covering my embarrassment at being familiar only with the names Origen and Tertullian, and worse, knowing very little about what they wrote, I asked, "But do we know what non-Christians thought about Christianity?"

Scinto answered, "It is clear that when Christianity gained control of the Roman Empire it suppressed the writings of its critics. Suppressed? Hell, they burned them! Still, the number of fragments that survived is considerable, and they offer a shocking portrait of Christianity."

"Well tell me what was so shocking in the non-Christian's depiction of Christianity."

"Sure. But first let me also say that recently new documents have been discovered in Egypt that were written by Christians who were considered heretics and these discoveries give new insight into early Christianity."

"You're referring to the Gnostic manuscripts discovered at Nag Hammadi?"

"Yes. And there are other less famous manuscripts that have been unearthed lately. The point is, the combination of writings from non-Christians and Christians who were not part of the mainstream of Christianity help us see that Christianity as we know it today did not develop from a single idea, but from an attempt to answer the criticisms of its detractors."

"The point is we forget that Christianity wasn't delivered engraved in stone."

"That's for sure, Chris. It evolved over centuries. But during the first hundred years or so, it is important to know that Christianity was viewed by non-Christians as a strange splinter group, a tiny, odd sect that flourished in the lowest strata of society. One writer claimed that Christianity was just a political club. There are history books written twenty to thirty years after Jesus that never even mention Christianity. The first mention of Christianity by a Roman writer came in the beginning of the second century. Christianity was merely considered a superstition by thoughtful observers."

"John, couldn't calling a religion 'odd' or a 'sect' or a 'superstition' simply reflect prejudice or slander on the part of the observer?"

"Definitely, that could be a factor. But it also tells us something about Christianity and the society from which it grew. Besides, many of the derogatory comments were made by statesmen, physicians, philosophers, and historians who not only had contact with Christianity, but also were more than likely above petty prejudices."

"Come on, tell me the shocking stuff."

"All you television guys only love the juicy, scandalous stories. Recently a second-century papyrus from Cologne was discovered. It was a Greek romance written by someone named Lollianus. He describes a Christian rite of initiation that includes murder and sexual intercourse."

"Great. The two key ingredients of high ratings."

"Hold on, Chris, you haven't heard anything yet. The victim was a young boy who has his heart ripped out. The heart is then roasted on a fire, cut into halves, seasoned with barley, drenched in oil, and then distributed for consumption by the congregation."

"What? Come on John, that's hard to believe."

"That's what was written. But there is more. In the third century, a Roman lawyer and writer named Minucius Felix, who was a Christian, gave a lurid account of a ceremony that included covering an infant with flour. I should say burying a child under a mound of flour, at which point the mound would be repeatedly struck with sharp objects. The child would be killed by wounds that remain unseen and concealed. The infant's body parts would then be eaten. Afterwards, the lights would be doused and a love feast, sometimes involving incest, would begin in the shameless dark."

"Did these rituals actually happen or were they the product of a writer's vivid imagination?"

"I don't know Chris. I'm sure that as tales regarding the secret practices of the Christians spread, they could easily have been magnified. But it seems scholars are unwilling to rule out the possibility that there was some basis for these wild stories. Furthermore, a number of Christian writers mention bizarre rites practiced by some libertine Christian groups, such as the Eucharist being celebrated in the nude. In the third century, Clement of Alexandria wrote about a Gnostic sect known as the Carpocratians whose members had intercourse whenever they want and with anyone they wanted. In the second century, Justin Martyr told of stories he heard of Christians partaking of human flesh."

"This is amazing."

"Wait, it gets worse. Epiphanius of Cyprus, a fourth-century Christian author, wrote about a Christian group called the Phibionites."

"What did they do, tell lies?"

"Very funny. But the Phibionites weren't. Their rituals included wife swapping, covering themselves with semen, drinking female menstruation blood—incidently, calling it the blood of Christ—and eating unborn children."

"Shit, they don't even do those things on 'Days of Our Lives,' " I said, referring to the show Scinto's brother directed.

Our conversation lasted into the wee hours of the morning. It was stimulating. I realized how little I knew about my own religion. John gave me a list of authors to check out if I wanted to read about early Christianity in depth. The kid was a walking encyclopedia. Knowing that I lacked the patience to wade through the scholarly tomes he mentioned, I never bothered. Besides, the books are difficult to find. I did read one interesting book that wasn't on his list that confirmed everything John Scinto told me. It's titled *The Christians as the Romans Saw Them,* by Robert L. Wilken, which you could check out if you're interested.

Speaking of checking out, I've got to get going. Charlton will be picking me up in an hour.

Friday, March 15—1:20 P.M.

This morning, Charlton and I visited a former Dominican church and convent in Cuilapan, a small village located about seven miles southwest of Oaxaca. Over a period of fifty years during the sixteenth century, the Dominicans built a massive monastery and began construction on an enormous church in that remote Mixtec countryside. Before the conquest, Cuilapan was a Mixtec center with a population of over 13,000 people. Shortly after the conquest, Cortes ordered Mixtecs from other areas to be brought to Cuilapan, and the population soared to an estimated 70,000.

The Mixtecs peacefully submitted to Spanish rule, and, having no other choice, they converted to Christianity en masse. So the Dominicans needed a huge church in order to accommodate thousands of worshippers at a time. But, sadly, most of the Mixtecs died during a series of epidemics. In fact, the epidemics killed so many that there were not enough Mixtecs left to support the church, whose roof was never completed. The silent remains of the unfinished church still show the bases of the powerful Gothic-style ribs for what was to be the dome, in a colossal display of lines carved in stone.

The church and convent grounds include a large open-air chapel consisting of three naves and marching ranks of pillars and open arches. The arches frame spectacular views of the valley and the mountains. On the interior walls of the cloistered convent, there still remained fragments of frescoes. The convent had a large refectory and a kitchen with a huge hearth. The second floor consisted of numerous small rooms. Each room had a windowed alcove with a stone bench. I sat for about ten minutes looking out the window at the lush valley and rugged mountain, trying to imagine what it would have been like to have occupied one of these cells and devoted my life to contemplating God.

In the sacristy of a small, present-day church on the monastery grounds there is a large fresco of the crucified Christ. To the right of the foot of the cross are two women, and to the left is St. James, who is the patron saint of Cuilapan. St. James is kneeling down and is portrayed with a sword thrust through his chest and an ax blade impaled in his head. The sword and the ax are symbols of his martyrdom. St. James is pointing to a scroll inscribed: *Credo In Unum Deum* (I believe in One God). Behind this scene, over the shoulder of St. James, is a detailed painting of the Convento de Cuilapan, with the church's domed roof completed.

Kate, it is hard to believe that this serene valley has been the stage for so much horror, violence, misery, and death. The cross of Christ was a sword through the Mixtec Indian's heart, and the missionaries put an ax to their culture.

Saturday, March 16—1:30 P.M.

The afternoon heat is heavy and soporific. I'm tired. I'm in my room, about to take a nap—afterall, it is siesta time. I initially thought that siestas were a pretty silly idea. How can everything just shut down for a couple of hours in the middle of the afternoon? Now I think it's a smart idea. It makes a lot of sense to escape the scorching heat of the afternoon.

I went to Mass this morning. I was taking an early morning walk and came upon Iglesia de San Felipe Neri (St. Philip Neri Church). People were arriving for Mass. The exterior of the eighteenth-century church is captivating and gives the impression of a stone altarpiece. There is a yellow stone carving of St. Philip Neri in a magnificient molded frame, which stands out against the green stone of the church.

Inside the church, there are nine striking alarpieces. This is a functioning parish, and lack of money and attention have caused a serious depreciation in the church's splendor. Still, within the decaying hulk of this large church, you could clearly see signs of its former majestic beauty. The large religious paintings along the side walls were faded, cracked, and bubbling.

Nineteen people were in attendance for the early morning Mass. There was also an organist, a choir of two women, and a man. The altar boy, a chunky teenager, wore a white T-shirt. (Sr. Saint Dorothy would not have approved of his sloppy genuflecting.) Attending a Mass felt familiar yet strange. Spanish is close to Latin, so I was able to follow what was going on. I felt a twinge of nostalgia, but no magic. It was just an empty ritual.

Novelist Milan Kundera, in his book *The Unbearable Lightness of Being*, wrote, "In the sunset of dissolution, everything is illuminated by the aura of nostalgia."

The people in attendance believed. They are good people, and I don't critize their belief.

I just don't share it.

Now for my siesta.

Saturday, March 16—11:00 P.M.

I went down to the zocalo this evening for something to eat. I spotted Charlton and Kate sitting at a cafe with a very distinguished looking older gentleman. His name is Joe Barnsworth, and he is a retired professor of anthropology who spends half the year living in Oaxaca. He taught at the University of California at Berkeley. Charlton and Kate had other plans for the evening, so they quickly split, leaving Joe and me alone.

Joe specialized in the study the Indian culture in the state of Chiapas, which is near Guatemala. Our conversation was more like a private lecture in the anthropology of religion. Joe sensed I was hungry for information, and he was happy to share his knowledge. I told him that my search for the meaning of life had led me into a state of severe depression. He understood.

"For as long as man has been on earth," he said, "he has wondered about who he is, where he came from, why he acts the way he does, and where he goes after death. All of human history basically results from our efforts to answer these basic questions. Because of the limits of knowledge and technology for most of our life, we have been unable to gather enough data concerning our existence to satisfactorily answer those questions. So we relied on myth and folklore for comfort. I became an anthropologist so I could reach a realistic and unbiased understanding of human diversity."

"Have you?" I asked.

"That's a tough question. I'm a human being, and like all humans, I carry around many biases that make objectivity very difficult. Unlike, say a biologist, or other scientists, the anthropologist must suspend his own norms, his judgments, his mental, moral, and aesthetic habits to penetrate the viewpoint of other cultures and assimilate their way of perceiving the world. The anthropologist must enter the mind of the object of his study while maintaining his distance and objectivity as a scientist."

"I'm not sure I follow you."

"Well, for a long time, European anthropologists failed to recognize the common humanity they shared with people everywhere. The societies they studied that didn't share their fundamental cultural values were regarded as savage or barbarian. It really wasn't until a hundred years or so ago that anthropologists began to consider the odd behavior they encountered in remote regions to be relevant to an understanding of themselves. Of course, this awareness of human diversity cast many doubts on the traditional biblical mythology that was the underpinning of their so called 'superior' society. If an anthropologist pursues his study in a subjective or haphazard fashion he could be classified as a poet or philosopher. My chief concern is the objective and systematic study of mankind."

As Professor Barnsworth spoke, I jotted down numerous notes. He was a living encyclopedia, spitting out a barrage of facts, constantly punctuating his thoughts with references to the works of other anthropologists, saying things like, "You should read Clifford Geertz's paper on 'The Nature of Symbolic Behavior'; it's published by the University of Chicago." He frequently quoted others. "Bronislaw

Malinowski said, 'Man resorts to magic only where chance and circumstances are not fully controlled by knowledge.' He hit the nail on the head."

Some of his statements surprised me; such as, "There are no false religions; they all serve a social function," and "Religion is a function of society, not a cause of society," and "Religion is the most powerful force of social control," and "All religions fulfill numerous social and psychological needs. Some of these needs, such as the need to confront and explain death, appear universal. Malinowski has gone so far as to say that, 'there are no peoples, however primitive, without religion and magic,' " and finally, "Religion only emphasizes and preserves those values accepted by the majority of a group at a given time." He said that the common component of the mythology of all cultures is the legend that explains the appearance of man on earth. Citing an example, he said, "The Nez Perce Indians of the American northwest believed that mankind is the creation of Coyote, one of the animal people that inhabited the earth before man."

Barnsworth claimed religions utilize part of the neuro system of humans to conceive of religion in homeopathic and contact ritual expressions; such as, blessings, laying on of hands, kissing bishop's rings, and sprinkling holy water. He said moral religions are associated with complex societies and have priesthoods. High-density populations present more complex problems in dealing with resources, and moral religions provide rules to help regulate interpersonal behavior. He said, "Early cities faced urban problems strikingly similar to ours. Dense populations, class systems, and a strong centralized government created internal stress." Dr. Barnsworth explained how low-energy, low-population societies do not have the need for complex moral religious structures because there are coordinate controls such as gossip and witchcraft that are able to maintain order. In societies where there are few proven techniques for dealing with everyday crises, especially illness, a belief in witchcraft is not foolish, it is indispensible. Witchcraft provides an explanation, and often serves a function of social control. In modern society, people who are involved in witchcraft are usually nonachievers, and witchcraft makes them feel special and reduces their stress and in turn they become less of a threat to society. He said, "Society to a great extent determines an individual's personality. Personality is formed through enculturation, the assimilation of a group's ways of thinking and acting. Every society operates according to a series of norms and ideals. Those who conform to these norms are rewarded; those who deviate are punished. The result is a group personality within which there is considerable variation."

Barnsworth also stressed the difference between religion and science. He said, "Both try to explain the universe. The religious explanation is dogmatized, which means it is static and no longer revised. It is fixed for all time, and sanctioned by the supernatural. The scientific explanation is based on a changing data base. It must test a new hypothesis against the existing data base. Science is in a constant state of flux, ever ready to adapt to new information and understanding."

It went on like that for hours. Rapid-fire, engrossing conversation. I feel as if I only absorbed a fraction of what he said. He left me with much to think about. We agreed to meet for a few beers late Tuesday afternoon.

Sunday, March 17—4:05 P.M.

If it's Sunday, it must be Tlacolula. Tlacolula is about twenty miles southeast of Oaxaca, an easy drive along the Pan American Highway. The town is famous for its Sunday market, which is held in a walled plaza behind a church and is so congested that it spills over into the streets. This market differs from the others I've seen because it is intensely Indian, run by and for Indians. This fascinating market is ablaze with colorful scenes. Indian families come down from the mountains every Sunday to pick up their weekly supplies and to enjoy the day with friends. Many of the Indians take the food they purchased to the church courtyard, where they sit under the shade of fiercely pink bougainvillea trees and eat a picnic lunch. Kate and Charlton purchased some meat and grilled it on one of the many open barbecue pits that sit in the center of a wide aisle bordered on each side by about twenty butcher shops. The smoke rising from the pits dances in the sunlight that peeks in through the loosely hung canvas roof.

Before heading back to Oaxaca, we visited a sixteenth-century church. The church had an excellent collection of colonial art. There were also exquisite plasterwork, high-relief sculptures, and painted religious figures. Amongst all this art were hung mirrors in gilded frames. Charlton said the mirrors symbolized the purity of the soul, and also reflected the Indian belief that mirrors reflect evil.

Mexico's strong background in witchcraft is visible everywhere you travel. However terrible the Inquisition was, it failed to destroy traditional Indian beliefs, many of which are still practiced today, blended with Catholicism. Doctors are tolerated, but at best they treat only the symptoms of an illness, not its cause— that is left to the native healers called curanderos, or shamans. Indians wear rosaries and smoke cigarettes, because they believe doing those things will ward off witches. In truth, the Mexicans were never really Christianized; what happened was that Catholicism was Mexicanized. The wife of the Spanish Ambassador to Mexico in the early 1840s wrote:

> The statues of the divinities frequently did no more than change their names from those of the heathen gods to those of the Christian saints. . . . The poor Indian still bows before visible representations of saints and virgins as he did in former days before monstrous shapes. . . . He kneels before the bleeding Savior who died for him, before the Virgin who intercedes for him; but he believes there are many Virgins, of various gifts and possessing various degrees of miraculous power and different degrees of wealth.

D. H. Lawrence, who spent the winter of 1924 in Oaxaca, best summed up how the Spanish may have dismantled the outward appearances of the Indian religion, but did little to eradicate their inward beliefs, when he wrote: "And to me the men in Mexico are like trees, forests that the white men felled in their coming. But the roots of the trees are deep and alive and forever sending up new shoots."

Mexico is a strange yet wonderful place, and each day offers me more insight into its culture and, strangely enough, into myself. The Catholicism I always thought was so special and unique is really just another imperfect method of dealing with the harsh realities of life, just another man-made opium to quiet our fears.

Monday, March 18—3:20 P.M.

Today we visited the second-most-famous ruins in the Oaxaca Valley. The ruins sit alongside the small, dusty town of Mitla, which consists of little more than a few metzcal shops and craft shops featuring woven goods. While the ruins at Monte Alban are monumental in scale and design, those at Mitla reflect a simplicity that delights in the delicate rather than the grandiose. The ruins at Mitla are like finely crafted jewels, consisting of a series of patios with small palaces and temples in the center surrounded by rectangular rooms. Entrance to the patios is gained by steps on the only open side. The inside and outside walls of the temples are decorated in dazzling mosaics of geometrical patterns, called frets, composed of thousands of pieces of small stone, masterfully cut and fitted together with a precision requiring no mortar. Each stone is perfectly cut on all sides to exactly fit the neighboring stones. Variations of the elaborate and endless patterns are repeated, combined, and contrasted like a Bach fugue. Charlton said that one of the buildings, known as the Temple of Columns, used over 100,000 cut stones. The incredible intricacy of the stone mosaics suggests that the people who lived in the Oaxaca Valley before the arrival of the Spanish were craftsmen as skilled as any the world has ever known.

Towering above the ruins and the town, which is about twenty-nine miles southwest of the capital, is a sixteenth-century church that was built on top of one of the ancient patios. The church was partly constructed with stones and other materials from the ruins. The name Mitla comes from the Nahuait word *mictlan,* meaning "place of the dead," and the town was so named because it contained the burial grounds of important persons and also because it was thought of as a place where the souls of the dead came to rest. Archaeological sites in the area provide proof of human presence in the area dating back to several thousand years before Christ, but the palaces, temples, and patios that comprise the Mitla ruins are relatively new, dating back only to about the year 1400.

I noticed some people hugging a column. I pointed it out to Charlton and he explained that the column was known as "The Column of Life," and visitors embrace the column because it is believed that the distance between their finger tips indicates how many more years they will live. I hugged the column while Charlton measured the distance between my fingertips. Smiling, he said, "Perhaps you might want to consider visiting the church." "Why?" I asked. "Because according to my calculations, your time is just about up," he replied. We laughed and headed back to Oaxaca.

Tuesday, March 19—9:50 P.M.

I met Dr. Barnsworth this afternoon around 4:30. He took me to a barrio bar on the outskirts of town. We sat in an open-air patio next to a shed that functioned as a kitchen. Part of the patio was covered by a corrugated tin roof. The patio had a cement floor and was enclosed by white walls. There were no windows. There were a dozen or so tin-top tables, encircled by old plastic chairs. No tourists here. This was a male bar. On paydays the place is packed with guys drinking Presidente Brandy. As we talked, Joe feasted on roasted iguana and chapulineas (grasshoppers); I passed.

The grasshoppers launched the professor into a discourse on how people in ancient times—as well as the Aztecs—trapped insects and grasshoppers. They would stand at the top of a hill and beat the grass with sticks. The bugs and grasshoppers would hop and fly down the hill. At the bottom of the hill, the hunters had dug a ditch, where the grasshoppers would eventually wind up. The ditch, which was lined with coals, was then set on fire. When the fire had burned out, they would sift through the coals and eat dinner. After a rainy season, giant ants were collected and roasted. The point of his story was that survival depends on knowledge of the environment. As usual, he had a source for me to check, if I wanted to read more. "Read Michael J. Harner's paper 'Population Pressure and the Social Evolution of Agriculturalists.' I think it can be found in the *Southwestern Journal of Anthropology*. It was published in 1970, I believe." He then said we are a purchase society and have forgotten how to gather. We have lost the cultural tradition of finding food for ourselves. Our survival depends on international trade; we have integrated larger numbers of cultural regions.

Quickly, the conversation turned to religion. Professor Joe said, "Man has always been acutely conscious of his insufficiency. No matter how far he progressed technically, nature was always greater than he. The earthquake in San Francisco last year reminded me that it still is. Down through the centuries, the winds blew away man's shelter, the sun parched his crops, wild beasts preyed on his animals. Mankind has always been on the defensive in a losing battle. Out of this sense of dependency and frustration, religion was born. The death and resurrection story of Jesus follows the traditional pattern of fertility mythology, as has long been recognized. The hero is miraculously born, dies violently, returns to the underworld, and is then reawakened to new life."

This calm, bright man was also eloquent.

We also talked about the Aztec religion and Catholicism. Joe said the Aztec empire was a complex society. Politically, their governing system was a hierarchy, ruled by priests with graded ranks, which included nobles, merchants, farmers, and slaves. Each individual had a clearly defined role to play within the civil and spiritual social structure. Church and state were interwoven, and no distinction was made between the laws of the state and the laws of the church. They had an elaborate court system. Lying under oath was punishable by death. Justice was swift and brutal: adulterers were burned, thieves stoned, and homosexuals hanged. Their ceremonial religion had many similarities with Catholicism. They had a hierarchy of deities which they found very compatible to the patron saints of Catholicism. Aztec religious beliefs even included a rite of confession, which was a ritual each person engaged in only once in their life, usually in old age. Catholicism spread quickly because conversion was a matter of substitution, the structure remained pretty much the same. I said, "Similarity plus force equals easy conversion." Joe smiled.

I talked a bit about my struggles during the past year. Joe listened patiently. Finally I asked, "Any advice?"

"What do I look like, Dear Abby?"

"No. You're too tall and probably better looking."

"Thanks."

"Well?"

"Well what?"

"Do you have any advice?"

"I don't know Chris. On a purely professional level I could say we each create roads to our goals and rules to achieve them. We each internalize our cultural system with respect to those goals and our means of achieving them. These roads and rules have been termed our 'mazeway.' Yours is in disorder. In hunting for order and meaning in the universe, you thought too much. You became disenchanted with childhood explanations. On a personal level, I would suggest you shouldn't take life so seriously. This is a plastic world, a cheap world. The cultural system is ambivalent and may not be sufficient for you. The cultural system in America is changing, but maybe not fast enough for you. You've got to get outside yourself—view yourself as a cultural animal, a cultural creature. Cultural considerations are valid to the point that they work, but at the point where they don't work for practical purposes, they become nonsense. You need to reorganize and choose alternative behavior. Guilt is a social conscience. We all live in the shadow of fears. We crave yet dread autonomy. We don't want to live under the burden of fear and guilt. Autonomy means making decisions. I don't think you like making decisions; you probably fear failing. Choosing means weighing alternatives. Religion helps us avoid making decisions and choices. You grew up in a church that lifted the burden of making fateful decisions from the individual. The church told you what you needed to do. I think that suicide is often triggered by an inability to stand alone and make tough decisions, decisions that will dramatically affect your life. It sounds like you've done a lot of drifting, which is a less drastic way of avoiding decisions. You've drifted from one religious experience to another, like a hitchhiker who didn't care where he was going. You're impulsive. This trip was a response to something you felt at one moment. You allow yourself to be governed by caprice. Read Camus's novel *The Stranger,* and you'll see where chance will take you. I applaud you for having the courage to attack the convictions you believed for so long. That's a very healthy sign. Nietzsche said, 'A very popular error: having the courage of one's convictions; rather it is a matter of having the courage for an attack on one's convictions.' But you need to go beyond that now. Open your eyes and make a choice. But don't treat your conclusions and decisions as authoritative, and retain the ability to admit that you may have made a mistake, even in matters that are of the greatest importance. Guilt can be destructive, and as soon as you liberate yourself from its chains you'll be on the way to becoming autonomous—a free, independent man who sets his own goals and reaches them. Discover what makes you happy, and go for it. Does this make any sense?"

I could only muster a soft, "Yes."

Wow—imagine, finding truth in a seedy barrio bar.

Wednesday, March 20—1:15 P.M.

All of the excursions that Charlton and I have taken during the past couple of weeks have been to the east, west, or south of Oaxaca. Today we drove north to the town of Etla. Wednesday is market day in Etla. The market, which caters to all the small towns in the valley, is the best-organized and best-stocked market we have visited. The array of vegetables and fruits was stunning. The town itself was handsome and very clean. Our outing was pleasant but short, because Charlton had to get back to Oaxaca to make some business calls.

Later this afternoon, I'm going to meet with Joe Barnsworth for a few beers at a barrio bar. I'm looking forward to another stimulating conversation. That's it for now—it's siesta time.

Wednesday, March 20—9:05 P.M.

I'm feeling a little sad at the prospect of leaving Oaxaca on Friday. I've really grown fond of this place. I'm constantly amazed by the Indians. They are not remnants of a great classic civilization—they *are* classic. Without knowledge of how great their inheritance is, they instinctively reflect it in everything they do. Their story, which began so long ago, and so mysteriously, is not a closed book, but a part of today.

The high cultures of Middle America began in Oaxaca, eventually touching Peru in the south and the Ohio and Mississippi Valleys in the north. It is a country still living in a medieval system of production and exchange. The machine is almost totally absent. Each family is an entity in itself, working silently and busily, producing everything needed for life, in home, yard, and field. Each handicraft is a village specialty, a collection of homes turning out local products, a system that has been a part of human history for thousands of years. A farmer driving his oxen home at sunset, a potter shaping clay, a woman at a spinning wheel, or a child weaving a basket: this natural and relaxed picture makes me envious, for the instinctive personal satisfaction of making things with our own hands has vanished with the machine age in which we live. The economic life of Oaxaca hinges on the various local markets, which are more essential than the Government Palace.

Oaxaca lies cupped within muted-colored mountains mellowed by age in a valley not hemmed in, but so balanced it's like a gateway to the promised land. Along the horizons, the long majestic ridge of Mount Alban, the double crest of San Felipe, and the Sierra Madre del Sur change with the hours from purple to sapphire to cloudy blue. These mountains provide more than spectacular scenery, they create the climates that make it possible to grow everything from papayas to apples, while their underground harvest yields gold, silver, iron, lead, coal, and oil. There is hardly a climate, a mineral, or a plant that isn't found somewhere in its 36,000-square-mile state.

When the sun slips behind Mount Alban in the evening, and its ruby fire outlines the great plaza and its pyramids, a golden glow descends on the city. In the streets, dim and feeble electric bulbs shine inside open doors, while the aroma of burning charcoal and crushed chilies waft onto the cobbled streets. The houses are painted in a pastel wash of pink, saffron, apple green, blue, and lavender, gently reflecting the brilliant blossoms of bougainvillea, jasmine, and magnolia trees. Churches tower over one-storied houses, while the Indian laurels and Australian pine preside majestically over churchyard and plaza. Downtown, the two-story public buildings are constructed from a local stone of pale green sage with gates of exquisite iron tracery. The architectural style is peculiar to Oaxaca: a combination of Spanish colonial and the Indian tradition of monumental architecture—of simple masses decorated with stone carving and painted surfaces.

Though Oaxaquenos work from dawn to dusk, they always make time to listen to music, and on Sunday nights they converge on the zocalo to listen to the band or stroll under the dense Indian laurels in their Sunday best. Highland women wear preconquest finery—two layers of cloth decorated and woven in the style of their region or town. One length, *falda,* is folded around the hips and held at the waist by a crimson or magenta belt. The other length, the *huipal,* is decorated with woven or embroided colors on homespun white, reflecting the souls of the artists. In contrast, middle-class matrons strolling through the zocalo wear high heals and stockings and are stylish in the American and European sense, but gaudy with many adornments, such as ribbons, frills, and jewels that reflect their husbands wealth.

Within the portals of the zocalo, tourists sit with straw sun hats, cameras, and the standard shoulder bags discussing in loud voices the benefits of first- and second-class buses, complaining about the lack of punctuality and regimentation they have been used to, especially service in restaurants. They try bribery in the form of large tips, believing that tomorrow morning their hot cakes and maple syrup will be served promptly. Their effort is wasted. The waitress pockets the tip and smiles and doggedly holds onto her ancient philosophy of time. Time ticks at a slow speed in Oaxaca. In Oaxaca, time is a conception, an attitude, a way of life, as it has been for thousands of years. The pulse of time is the rhythm of labor and rest, of planting and reaping, of prayer and fiesta—a vast, boundless ocean containing past, present, and future. The Indian is surrounded in the present by an amassed fortune of past experiences, which also teaches him to have faith in the future as part of today.

Indian time contains the essence of the old religion, a time-shared human mortality. According to the old calendar, every fifty-two years the world faced the possibility of universal death. This terrifying conception of time and mortality was such a powerful driving force, that each individual was impelled to live a good life and keep the gods happy through prayer and sacrifice, because not only his life, but the life of his descendants depended on him. (The devout Catholic Indians of today pledge their time and money in caring for the plethora of statues in the churches. They work in four to six weekly shifts, and during that time clean and dust the images and buy flowers and candles.) The ancient Indians were familiar with the movements of the moon, the planets, and the circuit of the constellations around the North Star. The solar year was divided into quarters, which began on March 16. At the end of every fifty-two years, they would gather on the night before March 16 on the main plaza of Mount Alban in an agony of suspense. Will the sun rise or will all life cease? Every pilgrim suffered a personal death. In a token of sacrifice, he draws blood from behind his ears and under his tongue, and puts drops of blood on a bundle of grass to offer the gods. (To this day, small tins containing bloodied blades of grass are left in churches throughout Oaxaca in the middle of March.) At dawn, the great sun leaps the mountain barriers, and the people exalt in the kindness of the gods. Pandemonium breaks out as the music begins and the people dance.

One would think that four centuries of turmoil, oppression, revolution, and religious troubles should have ruined the ancient culture. But its roots are deep and from them have sprung today's Oaxaquenos, who have remembered how to be happy and cherish their chosen way and their liberty. They have taught me much. Mexico was born out of a meeting of the Old World and the New World; in Oaxaca, the past that predates that meeting is still alive and is bound to survive.

Yes, Kate, I am really going to miss Oaxaca. Mount Alban creates a stillness in the heart when one sees its patient pyramids against the golden curtain of sunset.

Thursday, March 21—7:05 A.M.

My last full day in Oaxaca. While sipping coffee at a little sidewalk cafe, I spotted a woman I've seen many times during my visit, and I realized I hadn't told you her story.

She is a very short, old Indian woman, bent over and frail, who goes from one sidewalk cafe to the next, begging. She has the saddest look I've ever seen, almost impossible to resist. As you sit enjoying your food and drink, you can't help but catch a glimpse of her approaching your table. She takes very tiny steps, walking in an almost slow-motion pace. It seems to take forever for her to arrive at your table. During her entire approach she fixes her sad eyes on your face. She never says a word, just holds out her upturned, dainty, yet coarse, hand. One day I was sitting with a retired American Air Force pilot who lives in Oaxaca, and she approached our table. I said, "She is really hard to ignore." He responded,

"Her! She is known as 'Queen of the Beggars.' She organizes all the women beggars who work the zocalo area. I see her once or twice a week on line at the bank, always with a big smile and bigger deposit." I guess nothing is as it looks to be.

Thursday, March 21—10:50 P.M.

I spent my last night in Oaxaca with Joe Barnsworth. We had dinner together— at a Chinese restaurant—and afterward Joe invited me up to his apartment. He wanted to show me some of his photos from his work in Chiapas. He's a damn good photographer. Joe had a story for almost all the photos, and some of them were rather funny. For instance, about twenty years ago, Joe visited Borneo. Borneo is the third largest island in the world, trailing only Greenland and New Guinea; it is located in the South China Sea. Joe was visiting a friend who studied the Dyks, an exotic tribe of former headhunters who lived deep in the jungle, far from civilization. There were few roads, no phones, no running water, but plenty of orangutans and crocodiles. The Dyks live in vast, elevated long houses. They hunt with blowpipes and cover their bodies with intricate tattoos. Joe had photos of half-naked men and women sitting inside a 300-foot-long room, weaving rattan baskets. The photos were interesting in and of themselves, but Joe told me a humorous anecdote about the Dyks, which will help me forever recall the photos. He said, "Protestant and Catholic missionaries hit the shores of Borneo filled with a passion for saving the Dyks' souls. But before they could win them over to Christ, they had to get them to stop headhunting. But the Dyks resisted because they were puzzled by one set of holy men who married but wouldn't touch alcohol and another set of holy men who would drink alcohol but wouldn't marry."

At one point, our conversation drifted into a discussion of Christian fundamentalism that seems to be sweeping across America. Many Americans are abandoning the wishy-washy traditional, liberal churches that condone ordaining homosexual priests, marriages between homosexuals, sex outside of the sacred bonds of matrimony, and the abandonment of traditional family values, for fundamentalist churches that know God's will and preach the undefiled Gospel truth. Joe said, "The Great Commission involves nothing less than subduing the entire earth for the Lord, teaching it the fundamentalist gospel, and getting it ready to be raptured into heaven. To attain these goals the commissioned officers of God's army have built the religious equivalent of schools. The goal is to get children before their minds are capable of critical thinkng, fill their heads with disinformation, and turn them into tithing, obedient, and unquestioning pawns to be used in the war against worldly wisdom. They are creating a generation of intellectual and emotional cripples. The sad truth is that for every seeker of truth, there are hundreds striving to suppress truth, to undo it, and to prevent its rediscovery. At Jerry Falwell's Liberty University, an anthropology course is offered that amounts to nothing more than a course in how-to-convert-the-savages, and the Commonwealth of Virginia helps subsidize this crap." He added that the Amish do not allow their children to be educated past the eighth grade and that fundamentalists of all stripes prevent their children from learning anything of importance in the area of biology and geology. He summed up the whole situation in one line: "The religious have put their eggs in the deception and disinformation basket."

Joe Barnsworth peppered the conversation with numerous gems of simplicity and clarity, such as:

On truth and tradition: "In the absence of an objective and discernable truth, we are faced with the choice between accepting the authority of tradition, and chaos."

On the Gulf War: "We'll always rally round the flag, no matter what cliff it's heading for."

On movies: "The blockbuster mentality that pervades the movie industry discourages thoughtful complex films in favor of infantile spectacles that appeal to the lowest common denominator."

On hate: "Hate must be learned before it's felt."

On belief: "Belief begins where knowledge and proof end."

On fanaticism: "The basic problem with fanaticism of any flavor is that it doesn't know when to stop—especially when to stop talking and to start listening."

On the Reagan-Bush legacy: "And what a time it was: civil rights slashed, racial hatred intensified, freedom of speech limited, privacy rights diminished, abortion rights abolished, individual rights trampled, equal rights for women reversed, Bill of Rights shredded, and the Constitution rewritten."

On bibliolarty: "Wherever the worship of Holy Scriptures has prevailed, bigotry and cruelty have accompanied it."

On the Spanish conquest of the New World: "The coming of the 'true God' to the New World marked the beginning of violence, misery, and suffering, and launched the greatest genocide in human history. It is estimated that 90 percent of the native population of the Americas died in the first century after the conquest . . . as many as fifty million people. Native Americans were exploited and plundered as the landscape of the New World was studded with churches honoring the European God."

On race and religion: "It is a fact that the racial features of the gods and goddesses that people have invented (ignoring, of course, the deities modelled after animals) almost always have coincided with those of their creators. The African gods are black, often with their race-defining features being exaggerated. The deities of the Asians look Oriental. It comes as no surprise that the gods of the Caucasoids are depicted as white: Jesus, Thor, Zeus, Mithra—none of them could be confused with a resident of the Congo or Rangoon. In keeping with the notion that each religion is responsible for enhancing the social cohesion of a particular group of people, it is not surprising to learn that every religion considered its own little group to be 'God's chosen people.' " And, "Once the religious shamans had gotten the warriors into a trance, they could be sent off to war as anxiety free machines that could be counted on to do their utmost to wipe out the genetic competition."

*   *   *

What a night! The evening reminded me of a line written by Amanda Vail, "We talked about life. There was nothing else to talk about."

Not surprisingly, the subject of philosophy came up. I told Joe how I spent endless hours reading philosophy, hoping I would find some clue to the meaning of life, but that I found most of the books difficult to read, especially the works of Hegel. He let out a mighty laugh at the mention of Hegel. "You sound like Somerset Maugham," he said as he got up and walked toward a book case. "He had an intense interest in philosophy, read everything he could get his hands on," he said as he removed a book from the shelf. "In his book *The Summing Up*, Maugham discussed his interest in philosophy. Let me just read a few lines that I know you will enjoy. 'Life also is a school of philosophy, but it is like one of those modern kindergartens in which children are left to their own devices and work only on the subjects that arouse their interest.' He goes on to write, 'I have read pretty well all the most important works of the great classical philosophers. Though there is in them a great deal that I did not understand, and perhaps I did not even understand as much as I thought, I have read them with passionate interest. The only one who has consistently bored me is Hegel . . . I found him terribly long-winded and I could never reconcile myself to the jugglery with which it seemed to me he proved whatever he had a mind to.' Chris, I would say your trouble with Hegel finds you in some rather good company."

As the evening drew to a close, the conversation touched upon Joe's comments the other night regarding my need to make decisions.

"Joe, I guess for a long time now, I've had serious doubts about the existence of God. Yet I went along with Pascal's Wager, figuring it was smart not to bet against God's existence. I remember during my fundamentalist Christian days arguing with my nonbelieving coworkers that even if we cannot know for sure whether God exists, it's wise to gamble on God. I would say to my friends that I decided to live my life as an observant Christian, and when the lights go out, if it turns out there is nothing out there after death—no God, no heaven, only decay and worms—then I haven't really lost anything. I will have gotten through life in a pleasant fashion and died in peace, taking comfort in a well-lived, morally ethical life. But, if you live your life as if God did not exist, and at your death you come to find out that God, heaven, and hell are realities, then you are in a shitload of trouble. So bet on God: you may not win anything, but you won't end up spending eternity in hell."

"Chris, that ploy always works, because people do not think it through. Blaise Pascal came honestly to the logical fallacy that bears his name, but the religionists routinely use it for dishonest purposes. Pascal fell into the trap of the fallacy of the excluded middle. The problem is the argument ignores the fact that there is a middle ground between the Roman Catholic God imagined by Pascal, and the no-spooks-at-all position taken by atheists. Let me explain. For example, there may be a god and she's Chinese and highly resentful of people who masculinize the deity. In this case Pascal would be in more trouble after death than the atheist.

We may find out that there are two gods, one goddess, one celestial eunuch, and an advisory committee of quasi-omnipotent animals. It is easy to imagine theological situations in which both Christians and atheists would find themselves equally in trouble after death, or in no trouble at all, if reality turns out to involve a chorus of divine experimenters who, lacking complete omniscience, have created a human comedy for their amusement and are simply watching to see how it comes out. Chris, considering the thousands of gods, goddesses, and combinations thereof who have been worshipped by humans in their known history, and considering the fact that no convincing evidence exists for any one of them, including Jesus, it is obvious that a person betting on Jesus has even less chance of winning than I have of winning the California and New York State lottery on the same day. Besides, believing in Jesus isn't as easy as it sounds. Every Christian sect has its own rules as to just how and what to believe, and the rules are often mutually exclusive, a fact that even the so-called 'savage' Dyks saw. The intelligent gambler knows there isn't a trump card in the whole deck. By considering the middle ground ignored by Pascal and his successors, the atheist concludes that it is foolish to waste life preparing for death. *Carpe diem,* my friend."

Friday, March 22—3:00 P.M.

The forty-five-minute Mexicana Airlines flight touched down in Mexico City at 12:30 P.M. As I walked through the terminal, I spotted the taxi driver who took me for a ride when I landed here seventeen days ago. He was about to snare another unsuspecting American. I smiled a knowing smile. Armed with information from Charlton, I walked past all the "free lance" cabbies and went to the official airport taxi booth, where I told the clerk my destination and he then quoted me a flat fee. The system is simple and hassle-free: you paid the clerk, not the driver, the fare, and he gave you a ticket, which in turn you surrender to the driver of a new, clean taxi lined up in front of the terminal. The fare to the hotel, which was not far from the bus terminal, was only 20,000 pesos, half of what I paid for the ride in the run-down, dirty old cab that began my Mexican odyssey back on March 5.

I felt like a seasoned traveler—calm, confident, and in control. What a contrast to the nervous anxiety I experienced on my first day in Mexico. While I was looking forward to exploring Mexico City, I felt a twinge of homesickness for Oaxaca. In Oaxaca, I had a favorite bakery, a favorite restaurant, a favorite sidewalk cafe. I knew my way around Oaxaca; Mexico City is a mystery, and the unknown is always uncomfortable.

Mexico City is a large, sprawling, overcrowded metropolis that makes you feel like a confused stranger. Oaxaca, on the other hand, is a small, contained provincial town that makes you feel at ease and at home. In Mexico City, I'll have to take the subway and buses to all the places I want to visit; in Oaxaca, I just took a leisurely walk.

But it wasn't just the extreme physical differences between the two cities that made me miss Oaxaca. During my two weeks in the southern state, I made a number of friends. Before boarding the flight here, Charlton and I gave each other a big hug. We were each fighting to hold back tears. We promised to write to each other. Somehow I doubt any friendships will form here in Mexico City. I'll just be a nameless face in the crowd. But who knows?

Besides giving me the tip about the taxi, Charlton gave me a lead on where to stay in Mexico City. As he put it, "There is really only one place for you to stay, the Hotel De Cortes." He had that right.

Located near the old "Quemadero," or place of public burnings of the Inquisition, the Hotel de Cortes was once the Hospice of San Nicolas Tolentino of the Hermits of St. Augustine. The splendid Mexican baroque building dates back to the end of the eighteen century. The building served as a shelter, refuge, and hospice for passing or aging friars of the Augustinian order. Priests arriving in Mexico would lodge here before moving on to their missionary work in the provinces. The building also served as a retreat house for the order when the monks returned to the capital to rest. Many of the friars came here to recuperate from illnesses, or, in the case of the aging priests, to spend the last days of their lives.

The stone building sits across from Alameda Park, which is filled with fountains and nineteenth-century French sculpture. The park contains two monuments, one honoring Juarez, and the other Beethoven. The park covers about four square blocks, and the many paths that criss-cross the park are lined with trees so lush that the sun can hardly shine through them. The Plaza del Quemadero, where heretics were burned at the stake during the Inquisition, is in the western half of the park. In 1592, the Viceroy Luis de Velasco ordered an "alameda" to be laid out and planted with poplars ("alameda" comes from the Spanish "alamo," or poplar). It has been relandscaped many times over the centuries, and it has always been a social hub of city life and important recreation center for the city's inhabitants, despite its unsavory association with the Inquisition. Today the park throbs with color, life, music, and food. Vendors roll their carts along the paths, selling corn-on-the-cob, hot dogs, cotton candy, jewelry, and balloons. Families and couples relax in the shade on the park benches, enjoy the free concerts, or just take a stroll.

In recent years, the old hospice has been completely renovated. It has only twenty-seven rooms, the walls of which are a burnt orange color. There is a quiet, peaceful courtyard with tables from the restaurant surrounding a large fountain that is garlanded with colorful flowers. The courtyard has numerous trees and bougainvella, and the air is filled with the sweet songs of the many birds that inhabit the trees. The calm, melon-colored exterior walls that face the courtyard and the stone archways of the second-floor balcony with its overhanging ivy adds to the contemplative charm of the courtyard. Although the building is wedged between two busy thoroughfares—Avenida Hidalgo and Paseo Reforma—the massive thick walls of the old hospice manage to shut out the noise.

The exterior street walls of the two-story hotel hardly foretell its inner grace and charm. The stone walls of the squat, drab building are blackened by age and smog. It looks more like a fortress or prison than a hotel. In a niche in an arched gateway in the center of the building's baroque facade stands a stone statue of Santo Tomas de Villanueva, the patron saint of the needy, who is bestowing his blessings on those who enter the building. Below the saint's feet are the words "Hotel de Cortes," and above the archway that covers his head stands a cross.

I feel a bit like a tired, homesick missionary but I'm sure I'll feel rested and at home here in no time at all.

Friday, March 22—11:05 P.M.

Late this afternoon, I walked across Alameda Park. At the other end of the park, I came across the most majestic building I've seen in Mexico: Palacio de Belle Artes, the Palace of Fine Arts. It is the home of the National Theater, National Symphony, and the Ballet Folklorico, and it is the center for the most important cultural events in Mexico.

The gleaming white Palace of Fine Arts is made almost entirely of Carrara marble. The weight of this heavy marble building has caused it to sink more than thirteen feet into the ground, in spite of an attempt to lighten it by removing part of the facing of the dome. The exterior design has elements of Art Nouveau, and the interior is fashioned with Art Deco forms; the contrast between the two is striking. Both the exterior and interior designs use ornamental figures of pre-Hispanic tradition, such as masks of warriors, tigers, eagles, Maya deities, and serpents for the decoration of the building. The first floor of the building features a truly spectacular theater that includes an enormous Tiffany stained glass curtain, which is dramatically illuminated. The crystal curtain depicts two volcanoes and recreates dawn and dusk through a skillful play of lights before the Sunday performances of the ballet. The second and third floors house paintings by such famous Mexican artists as Diego Rivera and Rufino Tamayo.

I was about to leave the building when I noticed some people lining up at the box office. Despite all the signs being in Spanish, I somehow figured out that the National Symphony was performing that evening, and there where good seats still available for only three dollars—a bargain I could not resist.

The orchestra was performing a selection from the Russian composer Sergei Prokofiev's Symphony No. 1, "Classical." They performed the third movement of the symphony, a piece titled "Suite from Lieutenant Kije, Opus 60." I can't profess any familiarity with the composer or his symphony. I was nonetheless enjoying the performance when I suddenly broke out into a smile. The fourth section of the suite is named "Troika," and I had heard that section of the music before. Woody Allen used the music at the conclusion of his film *Love and Death,* one of my favorite Woody Allen movies.

In the film, Woody portrays a cowardly, neurotic (what else!) Russian during the last days of the Czar, and he accidentally becomes a revolutionary hero who is nonetheless put to death before a firing squad for assassinating Napoleon, a crime for which he was innocent. Prior to the execution, Woody is alone in a dungeon, where, after having a last meal consisting of French pastry, he has a funny conversation with an angel, who appears as a shadow on the wall, in which the angel promises that God will spare him. Armed with the belief he will be spared at the last minute, he encourages the soldiers about to kill him to move closer so they don't miss. Next Woody appears with an angel wearing a white sheet and holding a sickle. They are in a field near his wife's home. He tells her he is dead. She asks what it is like. Woody responds, "Do you know the chicken at Tretsky's restaurant . . . it's worse."

Then Woody, addressing the audience says, "The question is, have I learned anything about life? Only that human beings are divided into mind and body. The mind embraces all the nobler aspirations, like poetry and philosophy. But the body has all the fun. The important thing, I think, is not to be bitter. You know, if it turns out that there is a God, I don't think that He is evil. I think that the worse thing you can say about Him is that basically He is an underachiever. After all, you know there are worse things than death. I mean, if you've ever spent an evening with an insurance salesmen, you know exactly what I mean. The key here, I think, is to not think of death as an end, but think of it more as a very effective way to cut down on your expenses. Regarding love, you know, what can you say? It's not the quantity of your sexual relations that count, it's the quality; on the other hand, if the quantity drops below once every eight months, I would definitely look into it. Well, that's it from me folks. Good bye."

Woody then dances off with the angel, underscored by Prokofiev's bright, upbeat, whimsical music. Sitting in the Palace of Fine Arts during the concert, I smiled thinking about that very funny film. Comics help us put the serious things of life into perspective. Woody Allen cleverly juxtaposes deep philosophical questions with everyday absurdities. For example: "What if everything is an illusion and nothing exists? In that case I definitely overpaid for my carpet." "Not only is there no God, try getting a plumber on the weekend." "The universe is merely a fleeting idea in God's mind—a pretty uncomfortable thought, particularly if you've just made a down payment on a house."

Woody Allen was right, the key is not to be bitter. Kate, I became bitter at religion, mad as hell that I was deceived. But generalized anger toward religion doesn't meet anyone's needs. In America today, for the most part, religion is fairly harmless. Sure, some religious fanatics, both in America and around the world, try to impose their wills and morality on the rest of society, but their efforts will eventually fail. Most of us know, or at least feel, the future of mankind does not lie in the past, it does not lie in ancient religious myths.

Does God exist? I doubt it, but who knows? If there is a God, I'm sure he/she/whatever is nothing like what any of us have imagined or believed. The truth is, God's existence is really not important, because either way, we must live out our lives in the most loving, compassionate way possible. I guess I'm an atheist. I say "guess" only because I find it hard to believe how the world got started without some helping hand. The myths of religion were created to answer the question we all have about how the universe began. Perhaps if I were more scientifically minded, I could comprehend scientific theories, such as the "big bang" theory, that attempt to explain a natural cause for the beginning of everything —but I don't, so what can I do? Drive myself crazy, fret and worry about it? No, of course not. I'm here, and it is now, and what is important is living the best life I can, which means trying to love the best I can—but not the whole world, just the people I interact with—and also trying to make the world a better place—and, the world for me, is where I live, which happens, for the moment, to be Los Angeles. More than this, I cannot do; more than that, I do not have to do.

There is for me another key: to lighten up, to learn to laugh at myself. My downward spiral over unanswerable theological and philosophical questions, which almost led to my taking my own life, was really rather absurd. Listening to Prokofiev's music helped me remember that I once was able to laugh, but somehow I had forgotten, and now I must learn to recapture the healing magic of laughter. If there is a God, I'm sure He is laughing like hell over the comic way we live our lives, and I'm sure He also weeps over the way we destroy each other and the planet. Life is a dramady, each day filled with laughter and tears.

The real reason I came so close to taking my own life really had nothing to do with religion, it had to do with my inability to handle the discoveries I made about the reality of religion. I was like a mutant duck born without wax; this religion stuff didn't easily roll off my back the way it did for so many others who could casually dismiss, like water rolling off a duck's back, what they perceived to be foolish or irrelevant. That's it: I was a teenage mutant duck, but there is a cure—laughter can substitute for the wax I lack.

Funny, I just remembered the cartoon of a rabbit and a duck you sent me when you were six, in which you said, "I am the rabbit, you are the duck." Yep, a mutant duck!

Quack, quack.

Saturday, March 23—7:50 P.M.

After my first full day in Mexico City, I'm still astonished by the city's size and congestion. I guess Mexico City has always been crowded. When the city was know as Tenochtitlan and was the Aztec capital, 300,000 people lived here. When the Spanish arrived, they were overwhelmed by the size of the population of the then island city. Back in those days, few European cities approached populations of 100,000. Today, Mexico City is the largest and most populated city in the world. It is estimated that Mexico City has nearly twenty million inhabitants. The city's skyscrapers are dwarfed by the scope of the city and the size of the mountains that surround the valley in which the city lies. To the east of the city are two colossal volcanoes, Popocatepetl and Iztaccihuatl, which only unveil their snowcapped majesty on clear days, which isn't too often.

Based on my experience in Oaxaca, I figured the best place to start a walking tour of the city was the zocalo, and I was right. The zocalo is about a ten-block walk from the Hotel Cortes. The zocalo in Mexico City has none of the charm of the one in Oaxaca. Here the zocalo, whose official name is Plaza de la Constitucion, is a large, barren, paved plaza. Acres of bare cement create a rather forbidding, exposed feeling. Still, the zocalo is the religious, political, and historical center of Mexico City, and it is intensely alive with crowds of people. Major Aztec ruins are located just off the edge of the zocalo. On the north side of this huge square is an imposing cathedral adjoined by a smaller parish church. On the east side of the zocalo is the nearly block-long National Palace, next to which is Supreme Court. I found out that the word "zocalo" means base. In the center of the Plaza de la Constitucion is an unfinished monument. Work began in 1843 to build a Monument to Independence, but the task was never completed and only the base, or zocalo, was built. The word "zocalo" has come to mean any main square of any city or town in Mexico. Up until the 1960s the zocalo had trees, fountains, wrought iron benches, a gazebo, and even an outdoor market. But it was decided that more wide open space was needed to accommodate the large crowds that gathered for such occasions as the Independence Day celebrations.

The Catedral Metropolitan, or Metropolitan Cathedral, is the largest church in Mexico. Construction on the massive church began in 1573 and took almost 250 years to complete. The church replaced a smaller church (which was built by Cortes from stones of the Aztec ruins) that sat next to the construction site and was eventually demolished. Because the construction was spread out of over two centuries, the original design (which was modeled after the Cathedral in Salamanaca in Spain) was modified a number of times to reflect changing trends in architecture. The result is an interesting hodgepodge of styles: renaissance, baroque, and neoclassical.

Almost as interesting as the size and style of the cathedral is its tilt. The church is actually sinking. Much of the city is built on a dry lake bed, and the loose subsoil beneath the cathedral is unable to support its enormous weight.

The cathedral is in the shape of a cross and contains five naves. The side aisles contain fourteen chapels, each one unique. One chapel contains the famous statue of the "Black Christ" (Cristo Negro), which is also know as the "Lord of the Poison" (El Senor del Veneno). The legend surrounding the statue claims it originally had a light-skinned image and was owned by an Archbishop who kissed the feet of the statue every day. His servant tried to kill the Archbishop by spreading poison on the feet of the crucified Christ. But the statue absorbed the poison, and turned black in the process, thus sparing the Archbishop's life. Another chapel, the Crypt of the Archbishops, contains the remains of Mexico's archbishops. Each of the chapels contain magnificent altarpieces and many splendid paintings. The enormous interior of the cathedral projects an air of solemnity.

Adjoining the cathedral is the parish church known as Sagrario Metropolitano, or Metropolitan Tabernacle. While this church is smaller than the cathedral, it nonetheless is still one of the architectural highlights of colonial Mexico City. Built between 1749 and 1760, the baroque-style church is known for its rich ornamentation and balanced proportions. The Churrigueresque (a baroque style named after the famous Spanish architect Jose Churriguera) facades made of wine-colored tezontle stone feature richly carved pilasters and effervescent yet graceful sculptures. Tezontle stone comes from the volcanic mountains, and because of its deep red color was called "stone of blood" by the Aztecs. The interior is laid out in the shape of a Greek cross and contains a monumental painting of my favorite saint—St. Christopher, who was one of the most revered saints of New Spain.

El Palacio National, or the National Palace, is an impressive building with red awnings and bright brass knobs on the balcony rails. In pre-Conquest times, one of Montezuma's palaces had graced this site. Cortes acquired the house for himself and his son. They eventually sold it to the King of Spain in 1562, who converted it into the Palace of the Viceroys. In 1692 a mob partially destroyed the building. A year later the building was almost completely rebuilt. During the eighteenth century the building underwent many renovations, and in 1927 the third floor was added.

The south gate of the Palace leads to the President's office. The gate is guarded by many machine-gun-carrying soldiers. The center gate opens onto a main arcaded courtyard, which features a replica of the original colonial fountain. The Palace attracts many thousands of visitors each year, the majority of whom come to see the famous Diego Rivera murals that decorate the main staircase. The murals trace the history of Mexico from its Aztec origins through the Revolution of 1910 and into contemporary society.

Within a few blocks of the zocalo are numerous points of interest, including: the site of the first University in the Americas, the Archbishop's Palace (which dates back to the 1550s), the site of the first Printing Press in the Americas, the Old Church and Convent of St. Teresa, the San Carlos Academy of Fine Art, the Museum of Mexico City, the Church and Convent of St. Ines, the exquisite Church of the Most Holy Trinity, and a number of smaller churches and museums.

I left about a dozen days to visit Mexico City, which I thought would be plenty. Yet after just one day, I'm not so sure it is. There is much to see in this vibrant city before my April 4 flight back to the City of Angels.

Sunday, March 24—8:40 P.M.

I hit the streets early this morning. There was a chill in the air and it felt good. The noisy city streets had an eerie stillness to them; the quiet was a welcomed relief. There were just a few yellow and white Volkswagen taxis zipping along, enjoying their freedom from the usual traffic jams. I noticed for the first time how dirty the streets were. Curtailing litter doesn't seem to be a high priority. I spotted one lone street sweeper, a man with a broom and a barrel. He was wearing a Buffalo Bills T-shirt, which reminded me how thankful I was that Buffalo lost to the Giants in the Super Bowl, thereby making this trip possible.

Today is Palm Sunday, the day on which Christians commemorate Christ's entering Jerusalem in triumph. It marked the beginning of the end for Jesus, within a week he would be hanging on a cross. Palm Sunday marks the beginning of Holy Week, a time for reflection on the passion and death of Christ. But the week begins on an upbeat note. In churches throughout the world today, palms will be blessed and distributed, and there will be joyful, palm-waving processions. Mexicans take Holy Week very seriously. It is called Semana Santa, and it is a week of full-blooded piety.

Dawn had not yet fully broken through the darkness of the night when I arrived at the zocalo. In front of the Catedral Metropolitana, about three hundred Indians were vying for the best spaces from which to sell their palms. They were spreading out sheets and plastic tarpaulins on the ground, on which they would display their goods. Everyone, young and old, was busy. Teenage girls and mothers with infants strapped on their backs were weaving palm crosses. I stopped to admire their work. The small, six-inch-long crosses they wove included a tortured figure of Christ. The shoots of palm were held together with strands of red wool. I was impressed by how quickly they could bend, shape, and weave the palm into such delicate and diverse images. Older women created beautiful bouquets of palms with great artistic skill. The men were chipping away at large blocks of ice and filling big tubs with bottles of soda. A number of Indian women were cooking stacks of very small pancakes on crude griddles. Many of the Indians were spreading out colorful noisemakers to help celebrate Christ's entrance into Jerusalem. I got the impression that many of these people had been working through the night. These hard-working Indians would spend the day sitting and kneeling on the hard ground beneath the blazingly hot sun.

Directly in front of the cathedral, men were busy finishing construction of a wooden platform, which was covered by a red rug. When the job was done, they placed chairs and microphones on the platform. Other workers were setting up a sound system. I found out that the festivities and procession would begin at nine o'clock.

I left the zocalo and headed downtown, in search of a cup of coffee. I passed many other churches, and the scene was similar, only on a smaller scale. I returned to the cathedral shortly before nine. The cathedral bells had been ringing continuously from 8:00 A.M. The Indians had been joined by hundreds of tourists and locals. The vendors were busy selling statues, romance novels, political buttons, bracelets, rings, masks, decorative plates, and about two thousand types of meals featuring tortillas. OK, a hundred types. Pigeons were flying overhead, watching the entire scene. Many of the pigeons watched from atop the heads of the statues of the saints on the facade of the cathedral. In all fairness, I could definitely call St. Augustine a birdbrain today.

What a scene! Bells ringing, kids running, pigeons flying, vendors selling, and soon priests blessing—it's a real carnival. I noticed again how the two churches are sinking under their enormous weight (how fitting). They were clearly leaning to the right, an unplanned manifestation of the direction Pope John Paul II is aiming his Church. But, hey, I'm not going to think about Church politics or theology; I'm determined to just enjoy the spectacle. The place is alive with commerce and religion, a mixture that has been around for a very long time.

The service began at 9:15 A.M. and, by Mexican standards, fifteen minutes late is early. I was taught that *mañana* meant "tomorrow." But in Mexico, if you take your clothes to a cleaner and they say it will be ready mañana, they really mean they will be ready sometime in the future, perhaps next week or, if you're lucky, in a few days. Their philosophy is simple: you've got other clothes to wear, and I have other things to do. The word *ahora* means "now," but in truth the Mexicans have no word for "now"—"soon" is as close to "now" as they get.

So at 9:15, the bishop, eleven priests, seven deacons, and twenty-one altar boys made their way to the platform. The bishop, wearing his miter and carrying his staff, looked like a grump. The altar boys wore red cassocks and white surplices. Incense filled the square. The faithful held up their palms, as the bishop walked through the crowd sprinkling holy water on the palms (and the worshippers) as he blessed them. I was standing up front, very close to the platform. Standing next to me was a sweet, young Mexican girl with Downs Syndrome, and she liked the sprinkling of the holy water the best. She yawned frequently during the rest of the ceremony.

After about a half hour of scripture reading, the procession began. The people, energetically waving the palms, followed the bishop and priests into the cathedral. Inside the organ played and the choir sang as we marched around the church. Giant, candled chandeliers, hanging from ninety-foot-long chains were lit. With the morning sunlight streaming through the stained-glass windows and the incense filling the temple, it was a majestic experience. I even waved the palm cross that I had purchased. Chills ran up and down my body as I felt ritualistic religion's emotional power. The power of ritual was never clearer. The ceremony had raised the people above the mundane level of daily life and transported them to a higher, mystical level. Who could not believe? Me, for one.

I didn't last for the entire Mass, which seemed to drone on at an interminable, slow-motion pace. Many of the American tourists, wearing shorts, straw hats, and sun glasses looked oddly out of place in such solemn surroundings. One guy had on an L.A. Rams T-shirt. During the liturgy tour guides were leading small groups of tourists through the cathedral. It was odd, while the bishop delivered his homily, tour guides explained the architecture. As I approached the main doors on my way out, I could hear the songs of commerce mingling with the hymns of praise. Outside, flutes being played underscored the hubbub of business transactions. Tourists, and others indifferent to the goings-on inside the cathedral, strolled peacefully through the sun-drenched zocalo, searching for bargains from the Indian vendors. The first thing I spotted as I exited the cathedral was a little girl sitting on the steps coloring in a Mickey Mouse cartoon book. I walked past a newsstand set up in the shadows of the cathedral selling magazines featuring shirtless, muscular men on the cover, and publications dedicated to horoscopes and soap operas. I smiled, finding the incongruity of all the different activities going on within such a small space. One man was selling lottery tickets promising wealth in this life, "*400 Milliones de Pesos*," while the grumpy bishop was selling salvation and eternal happiness in the next life.

Ya gotta laugh—life is too funny to take seriously.

I happened to pass by the zocalo again around noon. In front of the Sagario Metropolitana, the smaller church directly next door to the Metropolitan Cathedral, a ceremony exactly like the one I had witnessed earlier was about to begin. It drew a slightly larger crowd. Walking around the city during the day I caught bits and pieces of five different processions and liturgies, just to get the full flavor of the day. They all tasted pretty much the same. All featured a simultaneous display of commerce and worship. During the middle of the afternoon, I passed a church, its services now over and its worshippers scattered. Sitting alone in front of the church was an old Indian women struggling to stay awake as she tried to sell her pile of unsold palm crosses. Around 5:30, while strolling through Alameda Park, I passed by the monument to Beethoven. A large crowd had formed in a circle. After struggling for a position to see what had captured their interest, I saw a man holding up a snake. I paused long enough to see him make numerous signs of the cross over himself. At the gazebo in the middle of the park, people were dancing to prerecorded music. The many paths in the park were crowded with mimes, lovers, strollers, sitters, and vendors. In the grass, kids were playing ball and couples were lying on blankets.

I topped off a tiring but pleasant day with dinner at a Chinese restaurant. The food was great; the cook was in his nineties. Smack in the middle of the meal, a raucous commotion erupted. I quickly realized a mouse was running around the place, terrifying many of the women customers. The old cook emerged from the kitchen, wielding a broom. With the energy of a teenager, he chased the mouse around the room until he cornered it. He yelled something in Chinese, and within seconds a young man ran out of the kitchen carrying a pot of boiling water. He proceeded to pour the steaming, hot water on the mouse. All in all, it was not the best of dining experiences.

Before returning to my room I made one more trip to the zocalo. As the sun set on another Palm Sunday at the Catedral Metropolitana in Mexico City— its 223rd?—the vendors gathered up their unsold goods after a long day's work. The last Mass began at 7:00 P.M. There were a lot of leftover palms, worth *dos mil pesos* (sixty cents) this morning, and nothing tonight. Many young children are sitting on the curb, as their parents grind out the closing minutes of the business day. They are dirty and tired. I wonder where they will sleep tonight. Tomorrow it begins again; theirs is a life lived in the streets.

As I left the zocalo, my last image of the day was a sad one. A little boy, gingerly holding his infant sister, was sitting on the curb. The infant began to cry. The boy let her down. The infant crawled along the filthy curbside as she made her way to her mother, who was sitting a few feet away on a tattered, torn piece of cloth, selling bags of peanuts. The baby climbed into the mother's lap, and her crying intensified. The woman looked very irritated, which was more than understandable. Within a minute the child was sucking on her mother's breast, even though she looked too old for that. As the child nursed, the mother sold three bags of peanuts to customers who didn't seem to even notice the infant. The sale completed, the mother yawned. The child finished, and the mother motioned to her son to come over and take the baby. She handed the infant to the boy, who once again returned to the curb to wait in silence for the mother's work day to end.

I stood back and looked at the brightly lit church majestically sitting behind the poor Indian family sitting on the ground. It was a crazy scene, wildly out of balance. It has been this way for centuries in Mexico. It is all madness and fruitless to try to make any sense out of it.

I'm ready to go home—the same, yet different.

Monday, March 25—7:00 APM.

Today I visited Teotihuacan, the City of the Gods. Once the home of one of the most advanced cultures to develop in Mesoamerica, Teotihuacan, with its striking pyramids, is today one of Mexico's most popular tourist attractions. The ruins of this monumental city are more than just a remarkable archeological site; it is also the axis of a major part of Mexican mythology—the meeting place of heaven and earth, of God and man.

The vast complex of ruins lie in a valley about twenty-five miles northeast of Mexico City, but the importance of this Olmec ceremonial center reaches beyond time and space. Teotihuacan (pronounced tay-oh-tee-whah-KHAN) began life as an agricultural community about two hundred years before Christ. It reached the height of its development by A.D. 500 and had become one of the largest cities in the world. Its population had grown to nearly 200,000, and it was a highly urbanized city covering about ten square miles, at the core of which was a ceremonial center occupying about two square miles. One can only marvel at the grandiose scale of man's work during those centuries. The excellence of the architecture, ceramics, sculpture, and murals is extraordinary. Teotihuacan was a religious center and the seat of a powerful theocracy ruled by high priests, who were the cohesive force in an increasingly stratified society. Long before the Spanish arrived, the city was abandoned. The decline began in the eighth century. Experts believe overexploitation of natural resources, cultural upheavals, and a deterioration of the governing system led to a total collapse of the city. When the Aztecs visited the ruined city centuries after its collapse, they called it Teotihuacan, which means place of the Gods, or Place Where Men Became Gods. They believed the giant pyramids were tombs of ancient kings who became gods.

Teotihuacan was a carefully planned city, laid out in a grid pattern. The city was divided into four quadrants, each containing apartments built around enclosed courtyards. A river, which has since dried up, cut across the central axis, and was a natural border line between the north and south of the city. The city contained over seventy-five temples, and over 100 palaces occupied by priests, the largest of which had three hundred rooms, a thirty-eight-acre ceremonial plaza, some 600 pyramids, more than 2,000 residential complexes, and over 600 workshops for obsidian, ceramics, and other crafts.

Teotihuacan's central artery was a mile and a half long, a 131-foot-wide avenue called "Avenue of the Dead." The great Pyramid of the Sun presides over the center of the avenue. At the northern end of the avenue is the Pyramid of the Moon, and at the southern end of the avenue is the Temple of Quetzalcoatl and Tlaloc. These three majestic monuments are the primary points of interest in this religious mecca.

The Pyramid of the Sun dwarfs all other buildings in Teotihuacan. The truncated pyramid, measuring 738 feet across each side of its base, rises in four terraces to a height of 213 feet. To get to the top I had to climb 242 narrow, steep stairs. But the taxing climb was rewarded with a magnificent view of the entire ceremonial center and the surrounding valley. The pyramid was completed around A.D. 100, and back then it was completely painted and crowned with a temple. Unlike those in Egypt, the Mexican pyramids seldom contained tombs. They were built as giant bases for temples, and were filled with sun-dried bricks and rubble. Without the aid of beasts of burden, the ancient people of this valley assembled an estimated 3½ tons of material to build this pyramid.

The Pyramid of the Moon, which was erected around A.D. 300, measures 492 feet across each side of its base, and reaches a height of 138 feet in four stages. The summit actually reaches the same height as the larger Pyramid of the Sun because the Pyramid of the Moon is built on the top of a hill. The Avenue of the Dead ends at a plaza that leads to the Pyramid of the Moon. I did not bother to climb this pyramid, it was just too damn hot—besides, the climb up the Pyramid of the Sun nearly killed me.

At the other end of the Avenue of the Dead is the Temple of Quetzalcoatl and Tlaloc, perhaps the most fascinating building of the complex because it best exemplifies the expressive force of Teotihuacan sculpture. The huge reliefs of the two gods establish a link between the earth and heaven. Tlaloc is represented with enormous goggle eyes and fangs and Quetzalcoatl is depicted as a feathered serpent.

A truly wonderful day was made even more so by my travel companion. Many of the area hotels employ the services of a tour company that transports tourists to the remote ruins. I was picked up by a young Mexican in a Volkswagen van. He had with him one other customer from a nearby hotel, a man named Mustafa. At first we exchanged little more than hellos. But as we left the city, we traveled past one of the poorest areas in Mexico. Mustafa pointed over to the hills on our left and said, "They call this area 'The Lost Cities.' It is inhabited by squatters, who live on the land for free. They have no services: no water, no electricity, no gas, no police. Nothing. Most of them are peasants who come to Mexico City looking for work. But there are no jobs. If they are lucky they find work in a factory and get paid 12,000 pesos ($4.00) a day. Most just rummage through the garbage dumps." I told him that I had heard about this area, but had never seen it. Then I said, "What I find crazy is that just fifteen minutes from here, millions of dollars from around the world were donated to build a monument to superstition and fairy tales while hundreds of thousands live in unimaginable poverty." Mustafa looked at me and said, "Such is the power of myth, the power of the Virgin of Guadalupe."

We were kindred spirits. Mustafa, who is in his early sixties, is a Palestinian who lived in Kuwait for thirty-one years. He was in the oil business; he sold drilling equipment. Even though he was an Arab and a Muslim, in Kuwait he was still considered an outsider. He sold his business about a year ago, because everyone knew Kuwait was headed for bad times. He left the country just three days before the Iraqi invasion. His brother is still in Kuwait. He has not heard from him for months. His sister and mother live in Jordan. Mustafa, who carries a Jordanian passport, moved to Toronto last year. On the trip to and from the ruins, we talked about politics, religion, and philosophy. He was very well read and interested in Western philosophy. He knew the Old Testament inside, out, and backwards, and even gave me a few unorthodox Bible lessons.

But our most interesting conversations centered around the Gulf War. Mustafa believed the United States tricked Hussein into war and made Saudi Arabia buy our old weapons so we could build new ones. He said the United States had material interest in the region, and the war had nothing to do with liberty. One man made all the money from the oil resources of a nation. He said, "The news coverage of the war and the build-up to it was an orchestrated misrepresentation, and one of the biggest farces in history. There were just too many big questions that went unasked and unanswered." The war effort was "all Rambo knocking down the bad guy." He said Saddam is no angel, but Bush made him into a larger-than-life evil villain who had to be toppled.

Mustafa told me a lot about the history of oil in Iraq and Kuwait and about how the British first discovered oil in southern Iraq in the 1880s. Mustafa dug oil wells along the Iraq-Kuwait border and said there is no real border, just sand. He spoke of Turkey's invasion of Cyprus and Israel's invasion of the West Bank. He said, "You can't understand history without understanding philosophy." Mustafa's family lived in Jerusalem for thousands of years. He built a home there, but it was destroyed in 1967. Now the life he built in Kuwait is lost. He no longer has any roots. He feels misplaced. I could see in his eyes how this bright, learned man was sadden by the fact he was a man without a country. He spoke eloquently about America. He asked me if I had read the *Federalist Papers*. I was embarrassed to say I hadn't. He knew all about John Jay, Jefferson, and Hamilton.

But while he liked America, he had no use for George Bush. As we huffed and puffed our way up the steep steps of the Pyramid of the Sun, he said, "They called Bush a wimp, so he drops a million tons of bombs on innocent people to prove he is a brave man. Crazy. Hate one man, kill thousands." Later he said, "Bush is so phony it is catastrophic. In time, the truth will be revealed. Notice how the only person who was not euphoric after the war was over was George Bush—he knows what happened. He destroyed a nation to win a second term. Politics is dirty, it has nothing to do with principles."

Granted, Mustafa's criticism of Bush was strong, but his strongest and most accurate comment had to do with television. He said, "Television is a tool that is frightening. It can make day out of night and night out of day."

Over lunch, he spoke of the poetry of Omar Khayyam, the twelfth-century Persian mathematician and freethinker who introduced irreligion to people who had never heard of higher criticism. I told him a little about myself and my depression. He spoke of the checkerboard of nights and days, about gloom being a useless emotion, about enjoying life while you can. He said, "I'm too old to work, but not too old to climb pyramids. Live each day to the fullest. Live without pockets, you're not taking anything with you at the end."

A wonderful day: magnificent ruins, a magnificent man.

Tuesday, March 26—8:00 A.M.

Good morning. A newspaper headline read: *Mas Golpes al Smog.* I'm not sure what that means, but I assume it has something to do with the high number of people who are collapsing every day due to the air pollution. Mexico City has the world's foulest air, and it is growing worse. Even on sunny days, tall buildings vanish in a pale of haze.

Geography and population are the culprits. Mexico City is snuggled up against the closed end of a horseshoe of mountains. Weather patterns tend to come from the north, which is the open end, trapping the pollutants in the pocket formed by a semicircle of volcano peaks that reach as high as 16,900 feet. The broad Mexico City valley that stretches north is carpeted with a seemingly endless sprawl of urban industries and ramshackle neighborhoods that have pushed the population from five million to roughly nineteen million in the last forty years. The city's three million vehicles and tens of thousands of poorly regulated businesses foul the air with 4.35 million tons of pollutants every year. Besides the emissions from furnaces, incinerators, and open air chemical stockpiles, six hundred tons of fecal dust from sun-dried human and animal waste rises from the vast areas covered by urban squatters, where latrines and sewers are often nonexistent, is released into the atmosphere every day.

The most noxious of the city's slums are those located literally on top of a dozen or so municipal rubbish dumps. Some of the older dumps are now 180 feet deep—that's the height of an eighteen-story building. The series of towns where the dumps are located are called "cinturon de miseria," the "belt of misery." The denizens of the dumps survive by scavenging amid the refuse for anything that can be salvaged and sold. Many of them own sheep and goats, which root for sustenance side by side with their owners. The stoic endurance of the dump dwellers is clearly demonstrated by the fact they have become immune to the horrid stench in which they live.

It is estimated that 30 percent of Mexico City residents have no sewage service, and their solid waste is deposited in open areas. Roughly three hundred tons of fecal matter are deposited on the eastern side of Mexico City every day. Some sewage is released into rivers as a means of disposal. The banks of many rivers look more like a thick, venomous stream of black sludge than a body of water. Everything from chemicals to the bodies of dead dogs and cats are thrown into rivers. Most of the streams and rivers have been turned into malodorous sewers, and these dead bodies of water are used, untreated, for irrigating vegetable farms around Mexico City.

The pollution problem in Mexico City is almost beyond comprehension. During the morning rush hour visibility may drop to less than three city blocks, and daytime instrument landings at the city's Benito Juarez Airport are common. It is estimated that 70,000 Mexico City residents a year die of pollution-related illnesses.

Every morning residents of Ecatepec, a northern Mexico City suburb are greeted by a snowlike residue of fine white powder that covers their streets and houses courtesy of a lingering cloud of wind-borne chemicals from a giant caustic soda plant. It kills the trees and causes respiratory problems for many adults and children of this working-class neighborhood. The air is so foul with sharp industrial odors that it burns a visitor's eyes and throat. A gray-brown blanket of pollution covers the Mexico City valley. The pollution level often exceeds— by as much as four times—the maximum exposure limits set by the World Health Organization. Just breathing the air can cause infectious diseases like salmonella and hepatitis. Doctors who treat large numbers of poor patients claim that cases of bronchitis have doubled during the past year.

And how do the Church and state respond to the crisis? The state informs its citizens that there is no proven link between pollution and medical problems in otherwise healthy adults. Sure. The Church tells its members they are forbidden to use birth control. Great.

The government is making an effort to solve the problem and has passed dozens of strict measures aimed at curbing the pollution. They recently shut down an oil refinery, an act that triggered angry protests from the poor workers who lost their jobs. There are grave doubts that the government has the means and the will to enforce the regulations. The problem is just too big for politicians to solve, as workers far outnumber environmentalists.

The Church says if you don't want kids, don't have sex. Population control equals sex control. The Church's war on contraception has been waged with undiminished, militaristic zeal. Of course the Church's ban on the pill stems from its notion that sex for pleasure alone is sinful, even between a married couple. Every sexual act must be able to lead to reproduction. According to the Church, even when married couples engage in sex for the purpose of procreation, the husband had to use pleasure in a moderate way, just enough to excite himself for the conjugal act. The message is very clear: pleasure is sinful, especially sexual pleasure. Pope John Paul II believes that if a wife is on the pill it will unleash her husband's animalistic sex drive.

Pope John Paul II's answer to the world population growth is marital continence, or the ineffective rhythm method of birth control. The world's population is estimated at 5.4 billion people. It is predicted that number will double by the year 2050. In your lifetime, Kate, our fragile, over-exploited planet will more than likely have to support over ten billion people. The world's population is growing faster than had been predicted, and most of the increase is coming in the poorer, developing nations. Our natural resources are being consumed at an alarming rate. His Holiness the Pontiff of Rome is more concerned with policing bedrooms than with protecting the planet. Contraception is essential to our survival, yet the Church continues to say sex is sinful.

"Pontiff" is a frequently used title for the pope. The word comes from the Latin word *pons,* which means bridge, and the Latin word *facere,* which means to make. The pope is a bridge maker, and the bridge he makes connects earth to heaven. In fact, the pope is the bridge between earth and heaven. The problem is that the pontiff is more concerned with the heavenly side of the bridge, and ignores the earthly side. Why care about earth when you are going to heaven? Why bother creating a paradise on earth when you will enter paradise when you die? The answer to both questions is: no need to bother. And so the Church doesn't.

And the pope is not the only culprit in thwarting efforts to help curb unrestricted population growth. The Vatican has an ally in the White House. President Bush used to think population control was important. Back in 1969, when he was a congressman, George Bush said, "We need to make population and family planning household words." But as president Mr. Bush has bowed to political pressure from the right, has changed his mind, and is threatening to veto a congressional initiative that would grant $20 million to the United Nations Population Fund.

As an ambassador to the United Nations, Bush said, "Success in the population field under U.N. leadership may determine whether we can resolve successfully the other great questions of peace, prosperity, and individual rights that face the world." As president, Bush is less concerned with individual rights and more concerned with appeasing the far right wing of his party that is so repelled by abortion that they want to deny help with contraception to any organization that provides any assistance to abortion. So, under Reagan and Bush, the United States has cut off all support to the U.N. Population Fund, even though that fund was never directly promoting abortion. Bush is more worried about the anti-abortion lobby than he is by the fact that the world population is growing at an alarming rate of a million people every four days. In the next fifty years, the world population could double, from five billion people to ten billion.

If we don't wake up soon, more and more cities will look like Mexico City. I fear I have seen the future in this ancient city, and it is dismal, unless we stop polluting and stop having babies.

Tuesday, March 26—4:15 P.M.

"Rise, Lord, and judge your house." Those six little words carried huge consequences for those judged guilty. The words are carved in stone above the entrance way of the Palacio de la Inquisicion, or the Palace of the Inquisition. The magnificent building from which the Holy Office of the Inquisition operated is at the corner of Brasil and Venezuela Streets. The Holy Office set up shop in New Spain in the year 1571, at this very spot. The original building, which housed the unholy ecclesiastical tribunal, was replaced by the present building in 1732. Its arrival was prompted more by the need for political repression than by the need to suppress heresy. In New Spain, the altar and the throne were joined in a powerful union. The Inquisition's political agenda was to squelch a conspiracy led by Martin Cortes, who wanted to make New Spain an independent state. Political motives aside, the papal judicial institution's essential concern was to maintain the purity of religious orthodoxy. The inquisitors were concerned with public and clerical morality. The great majority of investigations and trials involved such charges as bigamy, prostitution, sodomy, perjury, blasphemy, and the practice of astrology.

In New Spain, those accused by the Inquisition were tried in secret; some were tortured to elicit a confession, the first step toward moral rehabilitation. Many persons were censured publicly, others were fined, ordered to do public penance, or imprisoned. During three colonial centuries, forty-three unrepentent apostates were put to death. One of those was Father Miguel Hidalgo y Costilla, who was the firebrand of Mexico's independence movement. Born in New Spain in 1753, Father Hidalgo was accused by the Inquisition of reading prohibited books, advocating doctrines of the French Revolution, doubting the virgin birth of Mary, and keeping a mistress. My kind of guy. The priest was found guilty of heresy and treason. He was defrocked and turned over to the civil authorities, who ordered his execution on July 30, 1811.

The first "auto da fe" in the colony took place in 1574, when five prisoners were sentenced to public death by burning, and sixty-nine others sentenced to public flogging. The public executions assumed the air of a carnival, and people came from near and far to enjoy the spectacle. The last person to be executed by the Inquisition was Jose Maria Morelos, a revolutionary leader who was shot in 1815 because of his dissident political statements.

I took an early morning walk to the Palacio de la Inquisicion, because I wanted to see a concrete manifestation of a part of Church history that really troubles me. The Palacio symbolically reflects the two faces of the Church. The small jutting tower along the roofline of the building gives it a properly fearsome look, while the entrance way, angled at the corner, is lovely enough to belong to a private residence. After the Holy Office vacated the palace in 1820, it became a commercial building until 1854, when it was acquired by the National Medical School, whose home it was for a hundred years. Ironically, the building that began its life as an institution dedicated to convicting, imprisoning, and killing dissenters is now a museum devoted to the healing history of medicine in Mexico.

When I began this letter way back in July, I could never have predicted the myriad directions it would take, but least of all could I have predicted that I would write so much about the Inquisition. Why did I tell you so much about the Inquisition? I'm not sure, but I suspect that I identified very much with the heretics who were punished for thinking differently than the Church would have liked. This morning I wanted to see where some of them suffered and died because of their disbelief. With this visit to the home of the Inquisition in the Americas, I want to close the book on my preoccupation with the atrocities committed by the Church in the name of God. I do not want to forget nor forgive what the Church has done, but I can no longer allow my outrage and anger to consume me. I will let go without forgetting.

I walked across the street from the Palacio to the Plaza de Santo Domingo. During colonial times this plaza was one of the most important gathering places in the city. On the west side of the plaza is the Portal de los Evangelistas, or the Portal of the Evangelists. The long series of arcades does not give shelter to preachers. They serve as a workplace for a different type of evangelist—scribes. Since the mid-eighteenth century, evangelistas, the traditional and popular name for the public scribes, have worked under the arcades writing letters for those unable to write. As a rule, the scribes are older men who sit at tables cluttered with all sorts of pens, inks, pen-knives, paper, and typewriters. They transcribe the thoughts of the illiterate and poor people who come to have them write everything from love letters to business transactions. Using ancient typewriters, as well as IBM electric typewriters, the scribes pound out applications, which is an essential service for many poor people who hope to navigate the bewildering maze of modern Mexican bureaucracy. The scribes also type term papers for university students. Crouched at their typing tables, which are set up in every available cranny in the arcade, the scribes clatter away at their machines, the noise mingling with the grind of the rubber stamp presses and the clanking beat of the hand-operated printing presses spitting out a variety of low-cost printing jobs, such as business cards, public announcements, invitations, and Christmas greetings.

The arcade became a popular commercial center after the arrival of the Dominicans. During the colonial period, this sixteenth-century arcade would have bustled with street vendors who competed with merchants selling clothes from stalls. The clothes sellers were eventually joined by flocks of barbers, and both operated out of the arcades until the eighteenth century, when the public scribes set up shop. During the past few centuries very little has changed under the shade of these venerable arcades. Maybe I could get a job writing letters in English.

After wandering up and down the arcades for more than an hour, I left the plaza and headed across Venezuela Street to the Templo de Santo Domingo. The baroque exterior of the church with its single bell tower has a facade embellished with carvings of leaves and flowers, and wavy fluting. In niches between the ornate Corinthian columns are statues of St. Augustine and St. Francis. A woman and her young son were seated behind a small table at the foot of the church steps. The table top was covered with religious statues and pamphlets. The woman also sold tiny silver legs and arms that were attached to small pieces of red cloth, which the faithful placed at the foot of a statue inside the church as a way of giving thanks for miraculous recoveries. Nearby were vendors selling boiled ears of corn on a stick and pottery to the faithful and the tourists.

The church interior featured eleven side altars leading up to the grand high altar dedicated to the Passion of Christ and designed in the neoclassic mould. Lifesize angels and saints, along with huge paintings, decorate this elaborate piece, which is flanked by two hugely indulgent side altars. The altars are softly brightened by the light from eight magnificent stained glass windows.

As I walked down the center aisle, I noticed an elderly priest hearing confessions in one of the six confessionals. I slipped into one of the pews to watch the ritual. The senescent priest was dressed in his white Dominican robes. He wore thick glasses and looked very much like an American. As one old, gray-haired lady awaited her turn to confess her sins, the priest was engaged in a lengthy conversation with a penitent on the other side of the confessional. As he spoke, the priest fiddled with his hands. After about five minutes, the priest gave his blessing to the penitent, and I then noticed a young man, perhaps twenty, leaving the confessional. I wondered what they talked about for so long. After he left the confessional, the young man quietly knelt in a pew, with his head bowed in prayer as he silently recited his penance for another five minutes. The old lady who had to wait so long was still talking to the priest when the young man completed his prayers. A woman in her early thirties patiently stands awaiting her turn to confess.

As I sat in the pew, I felt an urge to go to confession. I could hear my mother's voice asking, "Christopher, when was the last time you went to confession?" "Gee, I'm not sure, Mom, but it wasn't that long ago" was my typical response to that frequently asked question. My mom would gently nudge me by saying, "Don't you think it's time you go again?" "I guess so" was my usual faint-hearted response. As a teenager, I viewed confession as a spiritual car wash. After a week's worth of dirtying myself with the soot of sin, I would head for confession on Saturday afternoon and get myself spiritually cleansed. I knew that part of the confessional process included an effort on the penitent's part not to sin again. But just as cars always get dirty after a visit to the car wash, I also would sin again after confession. Cars and sinners always need a washing.

As I sat in the contemplative silence of the vast and ornate Templo de Santo Domingo, I thought how confession is far more powerful than a mere "spiritual car wash." My mind wandered back to the dramatic moment in the film *God-father III*, when Michael Corleone experiences the healing balm of confession when he begins to reveal his real identity to the Cardinal and unwittingly starts to redeem himself from his failures in a world that was hostile to his aspirations for power. Confession is more than a religious ritual of repentance, forgiveness, and salvation. Confession is a human impulse to get to know ourselves, because it offers us a possibility of self-understanding and self-acceptance. Any confession, whether delivered to a priest, a civil authority, a parent, a lover, or a friend, is, at its core, an unconscious urge to recover the lost love of the world outside of ourselves.

The young man who confessed his sins to the priest was seeking the embrace of the community, which the priest represented. Church dogma aside, a penitent does not need the priest to receive God's forgiveness; a Christian can take his or her sins directly to God, acknowledge his or her transgressions, and obtain forgiveness. But confession involves more than divine forgiveness; it also involves restoration to the human community of believers. Which is why it was not enough for the young man to examine his conscience in private, because he needs to confess his sins to the priest to give witness to the fact that he is defining himself according to the community's canons and is confirming the Church's authority.

By means of a public confession, the sinner asks for the community's confirmation of himself. By confessing, the young man said that he accepts the religious norm that identifies him as a sinner. Just as a child woos parental love by admitting his or her naughtiness, the sinner attempts to regain the love of the Church by confessing his or her misdeeds and declaring his or her intention to rejoin the community of believers by admitting himself or herself deserving of punishment. Confession, whether religious or civil, is a way for the outsider to return to the family of man.

My dear Kate, I realized today that this letter has been my attempt at explaining my nature to you. You have been my confessor. It is your confirmation I have been seeking. You are the community I need to exist in. I have been a stranger to you, and I need to be a father.

In *The Confessions of Jean-Jacques Rousseau,* the French writer says, "Far from fearing death, I watched it coming joyfully. But I was reluctant to leave my fellow men before they had learnt my true worth, before they knew how deserving I should have appeared of their love if they had known me better." In the weeks before this letter began, I was not afraid to die. But, I was afraid you would not love me. I didn't fully realize it when I began the letter, but my writing to you was really an attempt at helping you to understand that, if you knew me, you would have loved me.

Does this make any sense? I hope so. In his *Confessions of St. Augustine,* St. Augustine wrote, "When you hear a man confessing, you know that he is not free." I'm not usually in accord with St. Augustine, but I must admit that when I began my confession to you, I was not free. I was imprisoned by guilt, despair, and faulty thinking. You have helped set me free.

And now, we can become family. I can't wait to start.

The urge to go to confession passed as soon as I realized that I had already gone. Near the front of the church, two old women sat together in a pew reciting the rosary. As I was leaving the church, I paused for a few seconds at one of the side altars on the left side in the rear. Above the altar was a statue of Mary, robed in a blue toga, her head draped with a white veil. Under the altar laid a statue of Christ in a glass coffin. I felt worn out from looking at so much lifeless piety, so many vivid images that no longer carry any meaning.

The myth of Christianity is dead, and it's time I buried it.

For a few hours today, within the periphery of a plaza whose life span covers four centuries, I breathed in the religious, civil, and commercial atmosphere of colonial Mexico City. I liked the scribes the best. At least they provide a service the people need at a price they can afford.

After leaving Templo de Santo Domingo, I walked four blocks and stepped into ancient pre-Hispanic Mexico City and the center of the Aztec universe when I visited El Templo Mayor, or the Great Temple, which was the most sacred site of the ancient Aztec empire. When the wandering Aztecs entered the Valley of Mexico during the beginning of the thirteenth century, they had to compete with the Otomi, Chichimec, Toltec, Culhuacan, and Tepanec Indians, all of whom populated the two dozen villages and city-states that studded the shores of the five interconnected lakes that covered much of the valley floor in those days. According to Robert Ryal Miller's well-written book, *Mexico: A History,* the Aztecs got permission to settle at Chapultepec from the Tepanec Indians, who controlled the western shores of Lake Texcoco, in return for military service as mercenaries.

About fifty years after their arrival in the area, the Aztecs suffered a military defeat, and their leader was captured and sacrificed. Remnants of the Aztec tribe were scattered, and many of them were forced into serfdom. After about twenty years of oppression, the Aztecs managed to break away and established themselves on a small, uninhabited island in the marshlands off the western shore of Lake Texcoco. They claimed they had been guided to the islands by a priest of their principal tribal deity, Huitzilopochtli, who instructed them to settle where they would find an eagle with a serpent in its beak perched on a prickly pear cactus growing out of a rock. They named the island Tenochtitlan, and it became the capital of Aztec civilizations until its destruction by the Spanish.

The lake surrounding the island of Tenochtitlan provided the Aztecs with a natural defense against enemy attacks. The Aztecs traded by canoe with all the cities along the shores of the lake. The Aztec creativity managed to overcome their lack of cultivable land; they built chinampas, ingenious artificial islands made by piling mud on rafts that were stabilized with stakes until roots eventually tied them to the lake bottom. They grew several crops a year on these floating gardens. The Aztecs also constructed three stone causeways to connect the city with the mainland. The Aztecs excelled in architecture and engineering. They built schools, palaces, plazas, imposing pyramid temples, and waterways.

By 1520, the Aztec capital had a population of about 360,000, making it one of the three largest cities in the world. The population included some five thousand priests, who were in charge of the temples, sacrifices, and the numerous festivals that celebrated their more than two hundred deities. The priests enjoyed a special status because they were viewed as the earthly representatives of the gods. They were the custodians of writing, astronomy, astrology, and medicine. Priests ran the schools, where they taught their pupils law, government, and religious asceticism. The Aztecs demanded strict sobriety and obedience to law. Lying and theft were punishable by death, homosexuals were hanged, adulterers had their heads crushed, and slanderers had their lips cut off.

Just outside the ruins of Templo Mayor, there is large, outdoor model of the ancient Lake Texcoco, which clearly shows how the Great Temple rose far above the seventy-two other temples that constituted the ceremonial center of the island city of Tenochtitlan. Coming upon the temple with its brightly painted facade, adorned with sculptures of feathered-serpent heads, Cortes was so struck that he wrote that its "size and magnificence no human tongue could describe." And he saw it in all its glory; yet, even the ruins induce a sense of awe at what the Aztecs had created.

There are walkways throughout the ruins that allow a close look at them. Adjacent to the ruins is a modern museum, which houses the numerous extraordinary artifacts found during the excavation of Templo Mayor and also traces the history of the Aztec people. Templo Mayor was destroyed by the Spanish conquistadors, and the ceremonial center remained buried for centuries under colonial-era buildings until it was accidentally discovered by workers digging underground for the power and light company in 1978.

The ditch diggers had hit a huge, oval stone sculpture measuring ten feet across, which weighed over eight tons. The sculpture depicted the tragic story of the moon goddess Coyolxauhqui. According to Aztec legend, she was the daughter of Coaticue, who was the mother of heaven and earth, life and death. One day, while Coaticue was sweeping the temple on Coatepec Hill, she found a ball of down feathers that had fallen from the sky and contained the soul of a human sacrifice. She held the precious feathers to her breast. As a result of touching the feathers, Coaticue miraculously became pregnant. When Coyolxauhqui heard the news of her mother's pregnancy, she became jealous and indignant, and vowed to kill Coaticue because she had dishonored their family. Coyolxauhqui enlisted the help of her four hundred brothers, who were stellar gods known as "the four hundred of the south," and they set out to kill their mother. Just as she was about to be slain, Coaticue gave birth to Huitzilopochtli, who was dressed as a warrior and held a serpent afire in his hand. Huitzilopochtli, who was a god of sun and war, decapitated his sister the moon goddess, and hurled her body down the mountain, her arms and legs tearing apart in the fall. Then he expelled his brothers, the stars, which he scattered over the firmament above the earth. Huitzilopochtli had chased his moon sister and star brothers away just as the sun chases away the night and wipes out the stars.

By the sixteenth century, Huitzilopochtli had risen from an obscure god of a small wandering tribe to a powerful god who reigned over the Aztec empire as the sun reigns over the world. "Thanks to me the sun has risen," he cried through the mouth of his priests.

The sculpture of Coyolxauhqui was found at the bottom of a staircase that led to a shrine that honored Huitzilopochtli. Huitzilopochtli sometimes manifested himself as the Sun God and at other times as the patron of war. He always demanded human hearts and human blood be sacrificed to him and insisted that only continuous warfare and human sacrifice could maintain the sun in the sky. The placement of the Coyolxauhqui sculpture at the base of the temple represented her final resting place after her battle with Huitzilopochtli. What a story! And I thought the virgin birth story of Jesus was far out!

Aztec sacrificial practices had a dual symbolism. The sacrifice of victims at the shrine of Huitzilopochtli and the throwing of the dead victims down the steep steps was a reenactment of the Coyolxauhqui-Huitzilopochtli battle. The Aztecs were called upon to help Huitzilopochtli in his daily struggle against darkness. And since human blood was Huitzilopochtli's nourishment, sacrifices at his shrine were necessary to insure the sun would win the battle against the night and rise each morning.

A state of constant war was essential to insure a continuous flow of the precious human blood required to keep the sun in the sky. War was not merely a political instrument, it was a religious rite, a war of holiness. Fighting was primarily a means of taking prisoners, and warriors did their best to kill as few men as possible. Underscoring the practice of human sacrifice was the fact that the ancient Mexicans had no real confidence in the future and believed their fragile world was perpetually at the mercy of some disaster that could only be avoided by keeping the gods happy. The terrible famines that ravaged central Mexico in 1450 were thought to have been caused by too few victims having been offered, so the gods had grown angry. Human sacrifice was an alchemy by which life was made out of death.

It is believed that human sacrifice reached its most elaborate development with the Aztecs. Women being offered to the goddess of earth, performed a dance that culminated with their heads being chopped off. Children were drowned as an offering to the rain god, Tlaloc. Those offered to the fire gods were anaesthetized by yauhtli (hashish) and then thrown into a pit of raging flames. It is estimated that the number of victims sacrificed to the god Xipa annually exceeded the number of people who died of natural causes in the entire country of Mexico. The annual toll exceeded 20,000 people. Cortes reported finding 136,000 human skulls in the Great Temple. Human blood was offered to the gods to keep them young and vigorous and to ensure their favorable disposition. (And when ritual cannibalism was practiced on certain occasions, it was God's own flesh that the faithful ate in their bloody communion.) But this wholesale slaughter was not a manifestation of the madness of a demented people, but the logical application of a religious faith.

The thought of human sacrifice shocks our modern minds. It is understandable that the Spaniards found this aspect of Mexican civilization to be horrifying and disgusting, and it is easy to see why they considered the native religions as coming straight from hell and viewed the Indian gods as no more than devils that had to be crushed. When I visited the Mexican exhibit at the Metropolitan Museum in New York last September, I was angered by the fact that the Spanish conquerors had destroyed the entire Aztec civilization. I was angered at the barbarity of the Spanish soldiers who had ground the Aztec statues into dust and melted down the exquisite gold figurines to strike coins with the image of the emperor. Yet, I suppose, in light of what they discovered, their actions may be understandable, for who would want to have allowed such intolerable practices to have continued? The trouble was that the entire Aztec civilization was based on bloody customs that the Spanish viewed as Satanic, and it was this incompatibility of worldviews that explains the harshness of the measures taken by the Spanish to crush these demons. In all fairness to the Spanish conquistadors, perhaps I was angered at their barbarity because I don't have a real fondness for their civilization. The Spanish took their Christian and Latin heritage very seriously. They had no reason to safeguard the pagan idols and beliefs of the people they had conquered. Saving monuments was not on their agenda. I have no doubt that Cortes and his soldiers were cruel, greedy, and merciless; however, they were also pious men committed to their faith and convinced of their spiritual superiority. What happened to the Aztec civilization is an example of what happens when people do not have any respect for cultures that differ from their own, and that lack of respect is manifested in a dearth of tolerance.

I'm sure the Spanish did not realize that the Aztecs were renewing a bloody sacrifice, which the gods, at the beginning of the universe, had made in order to feed the movement of the sun with their own blood. The Aztecs believed there were two primordial gods who were the originators of all life. These two supreme gods, Ometecuhtli ("The Lord of Duality") and Omeciuatl ("The Lady of Duality"), lived at the summit of the world, in the thirteenth heaven. They produced all the other gods, from whom all mankind is born. These gods, who were descendants of the supreme Duality, were the creators of earth, and the most important act in this creation was the birth of the sun. Legend has it that the gods gathered in the twilight at Teotihuacan, and one of them threw himself into a huge brazier as a sacrifice. He rose from the blazing coals changed into the sun; but this sun was motionless and required blood to move. So the gods immolated themselves, and the sun, drawing life from death, began its course across the sky. This was the beginning of the cosmic drama in which humanity took on the role of the gods and fed the sun its daily food of blood. The gods had sacrificed themselves for mankind and this same sacrifice was repeated over and over again by the Aztecs. This symbolism, although savagely expressed by the Aztecs, is found in many religions, including Christianity, to which it is also mythologically very similar.

To the Spanish conquistadors, Aztec human sacrifice was clearly the work of the Devil, which was the reason they destroyed the temples. Because of our alleged regard for the sanctity and value of human life, we, too, consider human sacrifice an abomination. Yet the Aztec offering of human life took place under the most reverent circumstances, and those who performed the rites were people not unlike ourselves. We still sacrifice thousands of human lives every year. The Iraqis, the Kurds, the Palestinians, the starving in Africa, the homeless, the victims of AIDS, the mentally ill, welfare recipients, drug addicts are all expendable. But because we don't connect our attitudes toward those whose lives we hold cheap with official worship or culture, we say we don't believe in human sacrifice. If we find the Aztec practice of human sacrifice to be unsettling, perhaps it is because it calls into question our comfortable assumptions about human nature. We still practice human sacrifice, but it is no longer carried out in public rituals; instead, it is practiced through daily covert actions that are motivated by private attitudes and bigotry.

While the Spanish had built their new kingdom from Aztec stones and souls, modern Mexico has torn down blocks of colonial buildings and eliminated potentially priceless real estate to expose its deeper Indian heritage and to provide new insights into Aztec civilization and its mixture of the magnificent and the macabre. This truly has been an exhilarating day of sightseeing.

Wednesday, March 27—5:00 P.M.

Today, I visited the one place in Mexico City that I really wanted to see: the Basilica of the Virgin of Guadalupe. This shrine is the most important place of worship in Mexico, since according to tradition it was here that the Virgin of Guadalupe appeared three or four times to an Indian convert to Christianity named Juan Diego in 1531. The shrine draws visitors from all over the country on regular pilgrimages, many crawling on their knees for the last half mile to the Basilica entrance. Each year on December 12 hundreds of thousands of people gather here from all across Mexico to celebrate the fiesta of the Virgin of Guadalupe and sing a birthday song (las mananitas) to her.

Before the Spanish Conquest, the hill of Tepeyacac upon which the Virgin appeared belonged to the Aztec earth goddess Tonantzin. The site was considered a sacred place by the Indians, who had built a shrine on the top of the hill honoring Tonantzin, who was know as "the mother of gods." In those days, the great lake of Texcoco lapped the base of the hill, and a causeway connected it to the island cities of Tlatelolco and Tenochtitlan. Soon after the Conquest, the Aztec shrine was destroyed by the Spaniards.

Shortly after, in 1531, Juan Diego was walking across the hill on his way to the Franciscan monastery at Tlatelolco, when the dark-haired, brown-skinned Virgin appeared to him. The Virgin, speaking in the Nahuatl language, asked Juan to go to the bishop and request that a church be built in her honor on the hill. But poor Juan had no luck in convincing the bishop that the Virgin Mary had appeared to him, and he had tried several times. Diego was sad because he felt he had let the Virgin down. Then on December 12, the Virgin appeared to him again. Juan explained to the Virgin that he could not convince the bishop. She told Juan to bring the bishop a present of fresh-cut roses that he would find growing on the stony knoll where only cactus could grow. After she vanished, Juan found lovely roses blooming in the rocky soil. He placed the roses inside of his cloak, just as the Virgin had asked him to do, and went once more to plead with the bishop for a shrine. When Juan Diego opened his cloak to present his gift to the bishop, the roses were gone. In their place appeared the image of the Virgin emblazoned onto Juan's cloak. The bishop needed no other proof. He ordered a chapel built and had Juan Diego's miraculous cloak displayed permanently inside.

The Virgin Mary, under the title of the Virgin of Guadalupe, became the patron saint of Mexico. The cult that sprung up around the alleged appearance greatly aided the conversion of the Indians, because the Indians associated the Virgin of Guadalupe with the Aztec earth goddess and mother of humanity. Whether one considers the 1531 appearance a myth or a miracle, it cannot be denied that the Virgin of Guadalupe became an important tradition that inspired many leaders and still forms an essential part of the Mexican psyche. Father Miguel Hidalgo's proclamation of Mexican Independence began with his waving a banner of the Virgin, which became the military standard of the crusade. The Virgin of Guadalupe was—and still is—a powerful symbol to attract and hold Indian supporters.

As I walked to the subway station, I passed the Templo y Hospital de San Hipolito. The church was built in the sixteenth century in memory of Hernan Cortes's soldiers who died on this spot in the most disastrous battle fought by the conquering Spanish Army. The hospital was founded in 1566 to care for the needy, especially the mentally ill. As I walked by the church-hospital complex, I noticed a cat sitting serenely in a small garden surrounded by numerous pigeons who seemed unconcerned about the cat. I also saw a little girl giving a duck a bath in a small, red plastic pail, which the struggling duck kept knocking over. The sidewalk was cluttered with a dozen or so stands selling an assortment of religious statues and pictures. Parked at the curb was a portable dentist's office, from which the squealing sound of the drill was easily heard. The memory of this block's violent, bloody past has been trampled over by the onrush of cats, pigeons, ducks, dentists, little girls, and vendors—all busy with daily life.

The subway left me with a five- or six-block walk to the basilica. Those blocks were lined with parked buses and vendors selling fast food, fruit, ice cream, cold drinks, T-shirts, and statues and pictures of the Virgin of Guadalupe. I felt as if I was approaching a carnival. I was.

Approaching the basilica, there was a pedestrian bridge that helped the pilgrims safely cross a busy, six-lane boulevard. The walkway was cluttered with beggars; there were disheveled, unshaven men, old women with sorrowful and despairing faces, young women with infants, and kids of all ages sitting on the concrete holding up their hands pleading for spare change. For the most part, they were ignored.

As I descended the walkway stairs to the basilica grounds, I spotted a large human circle surrounding a man holding a snake. The man, who had two day's worth of beard stubble and a long straggly moustache, was wearing a yellow shirt, white pants, and white shoes. His appearance had shyster written all over it. He blessed himself a dozen times, as he held the snake up high in his left hand. The crowd watching him all held out clenched fists toward him. On the ground was a bowl of water, to which the man poured some powder that turned the water red. He placed the snake on a piece of cloth, which was on the ground in front of the bowl of red-colored water. He picked up some pamphlets, which he passed out, and seemed to be preaching to the crowd. I had no idea what was going on, but it did seem to be a strange spectacle considering the proximity to the basilica. But then again, all forms of spiritism, demonology, necromancy, witchcraft, shamanism, and black magic coexist quite nicely with Catholicism in Mexico— sometimes right on Church property. After watching the snake man's spiritual sideshow for about five minutes, I decided to move on to the main attraction.

The basilica real estate covers a considerable amount of space. There is a huge plaza featuring a much larger-than-life statue of Pope John Paul II; the Chapel of the Roses, which was built in 1537 and sits on the crest of the hill where Juan Diego asserted he had gathered the roses; the Chapel of the Little Well, an eighteenth-century chapel that houses a well, which supposedly opened under the feet of the Virgin during her appearance; the Old Basilica (built between 1695 and 1709); the New Basilica (built in 1976); and a museum. Additionally, part of the perimeter of the property is sheathed by souvenir shops that sell religious objects ranging from small pictures to lifesize statues of Jesus and the Virgin of Guadalupe. Thanks to the heat, the ice pop salesman was doing the best business of all.

The architectural design of the New Basilica (Nueva Basilica) is distinctly contemporary; in fact, the huge circular building looks more like a basketball arena than a church. The Basilica can seat forty thousand people, each of whom is provided with an unobstructed view of the image on Juan Diego's cloak, which dramatically hangs high on a wall behind the altar. The round building is supposed to represent the crown of the Virgin. The beautiful wooden ceiling, which was a gift from Canada, gently flows downward and out from the high, pointed center of the roof and is supposed to represent Juan Diego's cloak. The numerous, soft, pinpointed ceiling lights, which were a gift from Germany, are supposed to represent roses. The marble floor was a gift from Italy. Despite its beauty, the sweeping, modernistic construction of the building lacks the warmth and mysterious majesty of many of the older churches in Mexico.

My visit happened to coincide with the beginning of a Mass, which was concelebrated by four priests. I would estimate that four or five thousand people were in attendance. The Cleveland Indians don't draw crowds much bigger than that. A young Mexican priest gave a rousing sermon, which I think had something to do with the resurrection.

After the Mass ended, everyone headed to an entrance way behind the altar. Behind the altar, there was a moving walkway, the type you see in many modern airports, which allowed the people to stand as it transported them past Juan Diego's cloak. Actually, you passed under the image of the Virgin, which was encased in a beautiful gold frame that was tilted slightly downward to permit a better view. As the walkway carried the people past the image, many blessed themselves and tossed money into a trough provided for just such spontaneous contributions. Above the framed image hung a dazzling crown. At the opposite end of the walkway there was a gift shop—how convenient! It was possible to exit the Basilica from the gift shop, but I elected to walk back through the church. Much to my surprise, there was another Mass in progress, concelebrated by three different priests and attended by another large throng of believers. I found out that Masses are almost continuously celebrated, kind of like a Mass-o-rama.

The Old Basilica (Antigua Basilica) was on the other side of the plaza. The imposing structure has an Italian Renaissance layout with a huge central dome and two towers. Its facade was the richest that had been constructed until then in New Spain, with a central relief depicting the Virgin's apparitions. Due to severe structural damage during the earthquake of 1985, the Old Basilica is closed. The building has a very large, clearly visible crack in its side, plus numerous smaller cracks all around it. Besides the earthquake damage, the heavy structure is also sinking about two inches per year. The smaller, baroque-style Chapel of the Well (La Capilla del Pocito) was also closed because of earthquake damage. Nature doesn't seem to have much respect for the churches honoring the Virgin Mother of God.

I started to climb the stairs that lead to the Chapel of Roses (Capilla de las Rosas), which is located on the crest of the steep hill behind the Old Basilica. I got about half way up and had to stop. The heat was just too overbearing, and the climb just too steep for my weary bones. As I slowly made my way back down, I was embarrassed by the fact that very old, and very fat ladies were undaunted by the climb. But then again, they were pushed along by faith, when I was really only interested in the magnificent view of Mexico that can probably be seen from the crest. At the bottom of the steps there were about ten photographers with Polaroid cameras seeking customers who would like a photographic memory of the beautiful gardens and their pilgrimage to the shrine honoring the Virgin of Guadalupe.

Untouched and unmoved by my visit to Mexico's most sacred shrine, I headed for the subway and a couple of cold beers, which were guzzled in the shade of the tranquil gardens at the Hotel Cortes.

Hail Modelo, full of hops.

Thursday, March 28—8:45 A.M.

Today is Holy Thursday, a day on which the Church commemorates the Paschal meal eaten by Jesus and the Apostles on the night before his death. The Jewish feast of Pasch celebrated the memory of their deliverance from Egypt. On this day, Christians celebrate their deliverance from sin, their being saved by the blood of the Pascal Lamb, Jesus. It was during this last meal of his life, which we now refer to as the Last Supper, that Jesus, the Church tells us, instituted the sacrament of the Eucharist after he had washed the feet of the Apostles. I was taught this was the first Mass, and that Jesus, the celebrant, gave the Apostles their first Holy Communion. Of course that was a gross exaggeration, as it took centuries for the sacramental system to develop, because it took that long for a theological perspective to emerge that could transform a simple commemorative Jewish meal into the complex concept of transubstantiation.

To signify Christ's institution of the sacrament of the Eucharist, tabernacles in Catholic Churches around the world are emptied. During services tonight, bishops and priests will reenact Jesus' washing of the Apostles' feet by washing the feet of twelve men, trying not to tickle any of them.

From Holy Thursday evening to Easter Sunday morning, God is absent, and there is a symbolic suspension of life as in the ancient days before the beginning of the new fifty-two-year cycle. The church bells are mute, and the people don't genuflect in church, because the host isn't present. On Sunday morning, Jesus rises from the dead, and life begins anew.

I think I O.D.'d on church services on Palm Sunday, so I'm going to skip church today.

Friday, March 29—12:05 P.M.

Happy birthday to me, happy birthday to me. Happy birthday, dear Christopher, happy birthday to me.

What luck. My birthday falls on Good Friday, and I'm alone in a foreign country—a Catholic foreign country, to boot.

This is the most somber day of the liturgical year, a day on which the Church asks the faithful to reflect on the passion and death of Christ. The solemn afternoon service is very long and divided into four parts. The first part consists of readings from scripture. The second part consists of solemn prayers for the Church, the Pope, the priests and laity, civil authorities, those studying to become Catholics, the needs of the faithful, the unity of the Church, the conversion of the Jews, and the conversion of pagans. The third part consists of solemn adoration of the cross. And the fourth part consists of receiving Communion.

Good Friday is a good day to skip church, and I shall.

Sunday, March 31—7:11 A.M.

It is Easter Sunday. It is time for me to rise from the ashes of my dead faith. I'm ready to go home.

Back in July, I was very depressed. I saw everything as black and white. I either lived or died. There were no shades of gray. In that darkness, I decided to kill myself. Blinded by depression, I saw no other choice. Bad time to make a decision! Gradually, as the darkness of depression lifted, I saw there were more options than death. Life is choice; to live is to choose.

When I began this letter, perhaps the world's longest, my old worldview had collapsed. Out of the rubble, during the past nine months, I have rebuilt a new worldview, one in which values are no longer linked to a supreme being. I can now look in the mirror and know who I am.

Kate, I have learned over the course of writing to you how important the way we look at the world is. Nearly five hundred years ago, Christopher Columbus began his voyage across the Atlantic Ocean. He set sail believing the world was round. The farther he sailed, the more convinced he was of the roundness of earth. Many of his crew did not share his worldview, and for them the farther they sailed the more nervous they became—they had to be getting close to the end of the world. Same ship, same ocean—different points of view, different reactions.

Five years ago, I discarded my Catholic faith. Or tried to. But I didn't realize that my childhood faith was an integral part of who I was and was not something that could be easily discarded. Without faith, I was left with a case of divine discontent. Everything around me was unsteady and contradictory. I no longer knew how to look at things. I had uprooted the idea we call "God," and the customs and rituals of my faith, and was left with a confused mass of needs and impulses, ambitions and activities, without any control or guidance of the spirit. There was a void that needed to be filled. But with what?

For a few years I dabbled with the exact opposite of the dogmatic affirmation demanded by Christianity and embraced the dogmatic denial preached by the mystical religions of Hinduism and Buddhism. Even though the Eastern religions insisted on internal experience, they nonetheless proved to be as empty and meaningless as Christianity.

The Christian belief in a life after death has diminished life's value on earth. In the eyes of a Christian, the future is more important than the present. As a Christian, I was told to put my hope in the next life, leaving little reason for me to perfect myself here and now. But all indications are that death is final, and nothing follows it but decay. I no longer stand in awe before the great infinity of death. Only life matters; it is absolute. Death is irrelevant and bears no resemblance to the gruesome comedy that Christianity would like to stage.

If I am wrong, then hell will be populated with a helluva lot of strong, independent, thoughtful people who lived life to the fullest, and heaven will be a boorish place populated by anxious, inhibited, fearful, slavish wimps who have suppressed their best natural impulses in life.

After endless years of reflection and study, I think I've finally exorcized the demons of religion from my soul. I'm free, religion's magic no longer has a pull on me. Not even curiosity can get me to go to church today.

In a few days, I'll be going home. I'm going to start over. I'm going to start to live.

Sunday, March 31—7:40 P.M.

Four hundred ninety-nine years ago today, on March 31, 1492, King Ferdinand and Queen Isabella signed an edict expelling the Jews from Spain. The letter was very explicit: "We have decided to order the departure of all Jews from our kingdoms with instructions that they should never return." The King and Queen claimed the expulsion order was warranted because Jews were undermining the faith of those Jews who had converted to Christianity by trying to get them to return to Judaism. The edict gave Jews a clear choice: convert or get the hell out. The edict warned "that any [Jews] who are found here or return here will incur the death penalty and the confiscation of all their belongings." Ferdinand and Isabella gave the Jews until July 31 to make up their minds. Some did become Catholics, but the vast majority of Jews, perhaps as many as 200,000 people, decided to flee Spain, taking with them only the things they could carry.

Monday, April 1—6:50 A.M.

Happy April Fools' Day! This being a holiday for me, I will be taking the day off from writing to you.

Monday, April 1—8:30 P.M.

This morning I said I was going to abstain from writing to you. April Fools'! I thought this was a good time to jot down some facts about the foolish myth of the Virgin of Guadalupe. Everything I am about to tell you was culled from a small cartoon book titled *The Myth of the Virgin of Guadalupe,* which was written by Ruis, the pen name of the Mexican cartoonist-writer Eduardo del Rio. I found the book in a bookstore catering to English-speaking Mexicans and tourists. Before becoming a cartoonist, Ruis was a Catholic seminarian. Ruis informs the readers of his book on the Virgin that, "The goal of this book is not to eliminate faith, fanaticism, or devotion. Its goal is simply to clarify some hotly debated points about the appearance of the Virgin of Guadalupe. The desire and the need to believe in something unseen is inviolable, and I respect this right." He adds, "Human beings should believe in something. But this belief should lead to material and spiritual improvement. It should not make people submissive and exploitable, as worship of the Virgin of Guadalupe has unfortunately done. A nation of idolators and fanatics is the one that can easily be fooled and exploited." Ruis concludes his introductory remarks with the reminder that, "Deception never freed anyone: Only truth will make us free." To which I can only add, "Amen."

Ruis reminds us that the Spanish clergy had a very sophisticated policy of religious conversion: they substituted new gods for the Indian's old ones, matching gods with similar traits. The Indian god of water and rain was converted into St. John the Baptist, the Indian god of flowers became St. Isidore, Huitzilopochtli became Jesus, and Tonantzin became the Virgin Mary. The Indians felt their gods had changed only name and form. The ruthless Bishop Juan de Zumarraga ordered the execution of hundreds of heretical Indians and destroyed over twenty thousand Indian idols and five hundred temples in his drive to eradicate the old idolatry and to impose a new one called Catholicism. A century after the Conquest, Indians were still going to Tepeyac Hill to visit Tonantzin, pretending they had come to pray to the Spanish Virgin of Guadalupe. It was clearly time for a miracle.

The miracle allegedly took place on December 9, 1531, when the Virgin suddenly appeared to a poor Indian on Tepeyac Hill and left her image on his cloak, and instructions for a temple to be built in her honor. Oddly enough, Catholic historians living and writing at the time of the miracle never mentioned this important event. All of the important chronicles of the times fail to even mention the Virgin. Even Cortes and the many priests who kept journals never mentioned the appearance. How could that be? The first printed mention or the appearance came 117 years after the fact, in a book written by a priest.

Historical evidence shows the chapel built on Tepeyac Hill was originally dedicated to the Spanish Virgin of Guadalupe and that it languished in relative obscurity for over a hundred years. During that time Mexico's two most popular shrines were dedicated to the Virgin of San Juan de los Lagos and to the Virgin of Remedios. Each of these shrines made a lot of money, mostly from the sales of prints, and indulgences sold to the pilgrims who visited them. But the Franciscan church dedicated to the Virgin of Guadalupe was very poor, mostly because it wasn't located in the heart of the capitol. The Indians prayed to the Virgin of Remedios, asking her to intercede on their behalf to end the droughts. They gave up as period droughts persisted. They began to offer their prayers to the Aztec rain god, Tlaloc, because they felt the imported Virgin of Remedios was ineffectual. In 1575, Philip II, the Spanish King, wrote to the fourth viceroy of

Mexico asking why there was a temple honoring the Virgin of Guadalupe in Mexico. The viceroy responded by saying that since 1455, there was a shrine that had an image of Our Lady, which they called Our Lady of Guadalupe because she resembled the Spanish Virgin. The viceroy never mentioned anything about the Virgin appearing to an Indian.

It was assumed that the original image of the Virgin was painted by an Indian. In fact, one priest, in a sermon, actually mentioned the name of the Indian who painted the original image. Some time during the first hundred years of the shrine's life, a myth that the painting was the work of angels was born. In 1883, Archbishop Labastida of Mexico directed a respected Catholic historian named Joaquin Garcia Icazbalceta to investigate the matter thoroughly. He studied the evidence surrounding the appearance for several months. The Franciscans who supported the Virgin offered thirteen arguments as their proof of the validity of the miracle. Icazbalceta rejected all the arguments, finding them filled with holes and contradictions, and in his report to the archbishop he said that he had hoped to find evidence to support the appearance because it would bring great honor to Mary and Mexico, but sadly he concluded that he did not find the story to be true. Icazbalceta wasn't the first historian to refute the appearance. In 1794, the historian Juan Muñoz presented to the Royal Academy of History, his dissertation of the false claim of the appearance of the Virgin of Guadalupe.

The historical record shows that many priests did not believe the Virgin appeared to Juan Diego. The record also shows that the original painting was described as being on crude cloth made from the fiber of the maguery cactus and was the work of several artists, and the image had deteriorated due to fungus and humidity. By 1895, the image was in such bad shape that it had to be secretly switched with a copy that was hanging in a Capuchin convent. The copy, however, had one major difference: in the old image the Virgin wore a crown, but in the new one she didn't. The embarrassed priest called the disappearance of the crown a miracle. The publicity surrounding Icazbalceta's report and the disappearing crown drew more people to the church where the image was displayed. Icazbalceta was attacked for his callous betrayal of the people's faith. But a few priests publicly proclaimed the appearance was a hoax. One bishop said, "The belief that the Mother of Christ appeared on Tepeyac hill is clearly false. The notion of her appearance is false, absolutely false. Is there any glory in imposing false beliefs on poor illiterate Indians and making them donate the pittance they obtain from their labor worshipping an old rag at Tepeyac?"

But nothing happened. The press covered it up. The bishop was declared crazy. After Icazbalceta's death, in order to defuse his charges, the Church hired a new historian, a Jesuit priest, to write a book refuting what Icazbalceta had written. The piece of revisionist history penned at the Church's request offered ten arguments in favor of the appearance. All are false.

What I shared with you so far Kate comes from only the first half of the Ruis book. He then details all sorts of bizarre incidents surrounding the myth that have taken place during the past two hundred years, all of which should clearly debunk the story. For instance, the original legend claimed Juan was on his way to find a priest to administer the last Rites to his dying uncle when the Virgin appeared to him. Well, the sacraments at the time of the appearance were not administered to Indians, because the Vatican did not consider them to have souls. They only began to receive the sacraments in 1540. Ruis points out that it is strange that the colors red, green, and white were used by the angels when they painted the image, long before those colors were chosen for the Mexican flag. The undeniable fact is that the old Aztec temple of "our Mother Tonantzin" was converted to the imported Virgin of Guadalupe in 1520 and it was only in 1648 that the appearance to the Indian Juan Diego was invented, and it wasn't until years later that the cult of the Virgin gathered emotional impetus.

Yet millions continue to believe, continue to flock to the basilica. The Virgin is a powerful symbol that links together family, politics, religion, the colonial past and the independent present, Indians and Mexicans. Anthropologist Eric Ware points out the Virgin, "reflects the salient social relationships of Mexican life, and embodies the emotions which they generate. It provides a cultural idiom through which the tenor and emotions of these relationships can be expressed."

The power of the Virgin has nothing to do with the truth or falsity of the myth, and the myth continues to live because it can unify a country, even if that unification comes at the expense of lies that enslave people to religion.

Tuesday, April 2—5:30 P.M.

After four weeks in Mexico, I woke up this morning tired yet exuberant. Ironically, after a month without the *New York Times* and CBS News, I feel more informed than I did before I left L.A. A writer named Laurens Van Der Post once wrote, "I have traveled so much because travel has enabled me to arrive at unknown places within my clouded self."

I came here to explore Mexico and I discovered myself. During the past month, I've begun to see that the way I feel is dramatically linked to the way I think. For most of my adult life, I thought of myself as worthless, and so I felt worthless. I thought that I was unable to diet, unable to stop smoking, and unable to be happy, and so I felt doomed to being twenty pounds overweight, felt like a slave to tobacco, and felt happiness was beyond my reach. My sin has been one of faulty thinking. Nine months ago, suicide seemed like a very reasonable solution to my problems. It was, in fact, only one of many possible solutions, and by far the least reasonable of all my options.

I have allowed my past to overly influence my present. The detrimental effects of my childhood religious training continued to nag me simply because I let them. In truth, I carried my childhood religious conditioning through my adult life because I never really stopped believing the nonsense with which my parents and the Church had indoctrinated me. Rather than undoing the damage, I became angry at those who deceived me. This was a mistake, one which I can correct.

To think that my past must continue to influence me is a gross overgeneralization and an error in logic. Yes, I was victimized; however, I must no longer remain a victim. My past doesn't have to wield an enormous influence on my life. My past is at worst a handicap. I must deliberately work against the negative influences of my past. The past is the past and has no magical effect on the present.

It's time to grow up and face the fact that for the most part, reality sucks. People are fallible; they frequently can be cruel, indifferent, thoughtless, bigoted, obnoxious, irrational, calculating, mean, irritable, and unkind. And society is no better; it is frequently economically unfair, politically oppressive, violent, sexist, superstitious, and ultraconformist. War, crime, pollution, sexual violence, racial bigotry, and religious fanaticism are all manifestations of our common idiocy and inhumanity. It sounds like I had good reason for being depressed and desperately unhappy. Yet people and society were not the real cause of my depression. I slipped into a deep coma of depression because I believed people and society should act better and viewed it as dreadful that I could not find reasonable solutions to the grim realities of life. I could not tolerate the way things are. I have the power, however, if I diligently work at it, to change myself. I allowed the way others act to influence the way I behaved. I wrongly entertained the notion that there was a perfect solution to life's problems.

This is an irrational world. The trick, dear Kate, is to live rationally in an irrational world. How I'm not sure, but I'm going to start by acknowledging that I am not going to be loved or accepted by everyone. I'm going to strive to do what I really enjoy; I'm going to view the approval of others as desirable but not necessary; I'm going to drop my belief that I must be competent in everything I do; I'm going to stop labeling people as good or bad; I'm going to take responsibility for my actions without damning myself should I make a mistake; I'm going to try to realize that while some misery is caused by external causes, most of the misery I encounter is generated by my own irrational thinking; I am going to become more absorbed in people and things outside myself; I'm going to wake up to the reality that compromise is sometimes appropriate because it is unreasonable to expect perfection at all times and under all circumstances; and I'm going to be quicker at forgiving myself and others.

That little list should keep me busy for a lifetime. As for today, I simply took a walk.

Having seen all the major tourist attractions in Mexico City, I decided to spend my last day in Mexico walking around the dozen or so streets near the zocalo that are closed to vehicles. The streets have been converted into a maze of street vendors selling everything from expensive televisions to cheap cigarette lighters. Items such as toy guns, alarm clocks, Dessert Storm T-shirts, umbrellas, irons, diet pills, ponchos, hair dryers, fans, x-rated videos ("Cruising for Sex" was the title of one video), birds, radios, hats, yo-yo's, shampoo, calculators, bras, boxing gloves, dried fish, nail polish, belts, holy pictures, and panties were spread out on table tops and the sidewalks. I saw a lady with a flat, large tray of donuts, cookies, and pastries balanced on her head, and I hoped she wouldn't sneeze. I spotted one man who walked up and down the streets carrying the only two items he sold: crucifixes and statues of bulls—no comment needed. Each of the vendors struggled to scratch out a living. I, on the other hand, have wasted my time trying to scratch a metaphysical itch. It's time to ignore that damn itch.

In book six of his *Meditations,* Marcus Aurelius wrote, "Shame on the soul, to falter on the road of life while the body still perseveres." I read that in the library in Oaxaca. I have faltered, but I did not fall. And here in Mexico, I have regained my balance. One afternoon when Dr. Barnsworth and I were having a few beers, he said, "Life is a continuous series of adjustments to reality. The more readily a person is able to make those adjustments, the more meaningful his or her own private world." Joe Barnsworth suggested that aphorism applies both to the communal life of great civilizations, and to the personal life of ordinary human beings. But you probably know this already, because you have managed to successfully adjust to the reality of my not living with you. Many people, my dear daughter, simply cannot adjust to the cruel blows life hits them with, such as the death of a loved one, the breakup of a marriage, the loss of a job, a crippling accident. The list of troubles and distresses we must endure is endless.

Kate, the human race is engulfed in a great mystery, and our minds, which feebly deal in metaphors, are capable of only catching glimpses of possible solutions to that mystery: to expect or claim more is ludicrous. Even though I tend to think that life has no meaning or hidden agenda beyond the meaning I give to it, I nonetheless cannot and will not substitute searching for living. I didn't find any answers to the big questions of life here in Mexico, but I did uncover a new way of looking at things.

Everything I want I can have, if I do not deny them to myself. I'm finished with my past and will no longer poke around in its debris. My future is not yet here and can still be shaped by what I do today. In the miracle that is this present moment, I must be honest, open, loving, and kind—to both myself and to those whose lives touch mine. I suppose I knew this before I left for Mexico, but my knowledge was purely on the intellectual plain; now I feel it on an emotional level.

The confusion I have felt during the past few years results from the fact that the knowledge I have acquired from reading so much history and philosophy during that time has changed the way I view the world. I can't erase the knowledge I have gained, yet I couldn't accept the changes this new knowledge demanded. The realization that God was either dead or indifferent was hard to swallow, but it is starting to go down more easily now. There was a period when I was tempted to try to turn the hands of the clock back to a time when religion provided me with assurance and comfort, but I realized the effort was futile. Maybe as I get more and more accustomed to the idea of living without the comfort of a helping hand from the divine, or the assurance of absolutes, the confusion I have felt for so long will start to diminish. It already has; in fact, the process has quickened during my month here in Mexico. Hopefully, I will now be able to start reconstructing the civilization of my life, a civilization the conquistadors of knowledge had left in ruin.

Kate, it is time for me to rebuild a new life out of the rubble of my old life.

I'm ready to go home, ready to relax, ready to lighten up, ready to laugh, ready to love, and ready to live.

Viva Mexico!

Wednesday, April 3—11:00 P.M.

Alfred Hitchcock's masterpiece *Psycho* was on television tonight. I watched it. The car Janet Leigh drove to the motel had Arizona plates dated 1959. I must have been twelve or thirteen when I sneaked into the theater to see her in her bra and panties. I thought about that day as I watched.

There were two memorable lines from the film. During an afternoon hotel room assignation, one of the characaters says, "They also pay who meet in hotel rooms." I thought about the guy I overheard on my flight to Mexico City back on March 5. The hotel he was staying at isn't too far from mine. I wonder if he met that woman, and if he did, would he be paying a price.

The other great line summed up my life for the past few years: "We are all in our own private traps."

I have been a prisoner of my life, locked up in my own story.

It's time for me to escape mine. It's time to go home.

Thursday, April 4—11:50 A.M.

Hello from high above Mexico. As I look down on the wide-open, desolate spaces below, my mind has wandered back to those arid, despairing days of last July when I came so close to taking my own life.

The word "suicide" now sends chills up and down my spine. Yet nine months ago suicide held me in its grip of irresistible logic. Logical not in the old stoic sense, but in an unreal, though still convincing sense. I felt as if I were in a nightmare of unquestionable logic. Everything made sense. It is as if I entered a closed, invulnerable but completely persuasive world where every detail fit and each incident reinforced my decision. I saw omens that reinforced my decision everywhere. Little things people said, phone calls not returned, news headlines, even the weather—all were charged with unusual meanings. Reasonable arguments against taking my life seemed absurd. I was charged with a passion for self-destruction. The temptation to put an end to a life I could no longer tolerate never waned. I don't think I wanted to die; I wanted to escape the confusion that tormented me.

You are the only person I ever told about my plans. I'm grateful I chose to tell you. Thanks for helping me find a way back to myself.

Well, lunch is about to be served. I hope it's not tacos.

Thursday, April 4—5:20 P.M. (Pacific Time)

I'm home. It feels good to be back. The familiar is comforting. The condo is as I left it, no break-ins or disasters. The place doesn't look so confining anymore. Had time to stop at the post office and pick up my mail. It will take most of the night to wade through it.

The trip did me a world of good. It was the right thing for me to do and I'm glad I followed my instincts and went. I could easily have rationalized my way out of going. On the flight back, I was thinking about my month in Mexico and couldn't help but imagine what the trip would have been like had I not met Charlton Houston. Obviously, without that chance encounter, the trip would have been entirely different. In fact, I'm not sure I would have lasted the month. I have the feeling I would have felt very alone and out of place. The language barrier would have been a much greater problem. Thanks to Charlton and Kate, I slipped into a very pleasant routine. They gave me countless tips on everything from restaurants to laundry. Without Charlton, I would have never seen all those remote villages, or have met so many interesting Americans living in Oaxaca.

Everything I saw and experienced hinged on a chance meeting. It hardly can be called fate. I guess it would be nice to think that some mystical forces were operating behind the scenes of our lives busily coordinating circumstances that would lead to beneficial encounters if we cooperate and do the right thing. Can you imagine heavenly beings getting up in the morning, going to some celestial gambling parlor, and checking out the master plan for that day in some earthling's life and then betting on whether or not the poor mortal will follow the plan or deviate from it? "What's the morning line on the Ryan-Houston meeting?" "They're 6 to 5 that Ryan will try to talk to Houston." "OK. I'll lay fifty bucks on Chris Ryan not stopping and talking to Charlton Houston."

Fate is a crazy notion. Take the number of people on the planet and multiply it by the number of choices a person makes in a day and the answer would be the number of betting opportunities in that heavenly gambling casino. Most people are unaware of just how many choices they make in a day, and that most of those choices have the potential of significantly altering their lives. Fate is statistically impossible. Chance is the only reasonable explanation for the direction in which our lives go. Regardless of all our thoughts and plans, the end result of our lives is in the hands of chance. But that is something most people do not want to hear because we like order and stability. We want to believe that if we think clearly, plan effectively, and work diligently, we will be in control of our destiny. Look around, dear daughter, and you will see very little order and stability, only the illusion of it, and governments (law and order) and churches (reward and punishment) are in the business of creating and protecting that illusion.

Well, I think I'll take this chance to unpack and then read my mail. I hope you liked the postcards I sent you.

Friday, April 5—10:40 A.M.

Two days ago, in a hospital near Lake Geneva in Switzerland, a *real* writer died. His name was Graham Greene; he was eighty-six. During his sixty-year career, Mr. Greene wrote twenty-four novels (many of which were adapted into films), numerous short stories and essays, three travel books, five plays, and a two-volume autobiography. His work was translated into twenty-seven languages and sold more than twenty million copies. But it was not the sheer vastness of Graham Greene's writing that made him famous. Greene attracted a large following because he had something to say. Graham Greene was the novelist of the soul, and many of his novels plumbed the inner torments of humanity. He traced the journey of the modern soul as it worked out its salvation or damnation amid the paradoxes and anomalies of twentieth-century existence.

Graham Greene also rocked the political boat. He was critical of American military intervention in Vietnam and in Central America. And he was not afraid to speak out. "I think a writer ought to be a bit of grit in the state machine," he once said. "That applies to a democratic state machine, a socialist state machine, or a Communist state machine." This superb storyteller was also a moralist who had a distaste for American hypocrisy and materialism. Greene, who briefly flirted with Communism, also spoke out loudly against violations of human rights in the Soviet Union.

I only recently became interested in Graham Greene's work, thanks to my Mexican adventure. Before then, I ignored his writing because he was labeled a "Catholic writer." How silly. Yes, Mr. Greene was a convert to Catholicism, but he was not a "Catholic" writer. In fact, one of his novels, *The Power and the Glory,* was condemned by the Vatican in 1951. The novel is set in a remote section of Mexico and tells the story of a haunted, driven, desperate priest. In the book, religion is viewed as a cult that restrains people, and priests are seen as the enemies of the faithful. Oddly enough, years later Pope Paul, during a private audience with Greene, told the writer he read the banned book and liked it. Go figure.

Still, Catholicism altered Greene's life and provided him with the clay of his art.

Graham Greene did not poke his head inside the Catholic Church looking for God. Greene was raised in an Anglican home, but by the time he reached his twenty-first birthday he "believed in nothing." In 1925, Greene became engaged to marry Vivien Dayrell-Browning. She had recently converted to Catholicism, and Greene became curious about her religious preoccupations. He decided it was important to learn about his future wife's faith. He slipped a note asking for instruction in the Catholic faith into an inquiry box in the cathedral in Nottingham. He had no plans of converting to Catholicism, he merely "wanted a better grasp of the nature of her faith." Shortly after leaving the note, he began a series of meetings with Father Trollope, who Greene described as "a fat priest who had once been an actor." At twenty-two, Graham Greene was accepted into the Catholic Church. He described his conversion as "purely intellectual." Father Trollope's arguments persuaded him "that God's existence was a probability."

Despite their dual conversion to Catholicism, Graham and Vivien were separated after having two children.

Greene wrote that it was not until years later, when he first traveled to Mexico, that he found "emotional belief" as opposed to intellectual acceptance of his religion. Mexico had the opposite effect on me: I arrived in Mexico having had intellectually denied Catholicism, and during the course of my visit I was able to disentangle myself emotionally from my former faith. Same country, different reactions. Oddly enough, that is perfectly understandable. In Nazi concentration camps there were believers who lost their faith and atheists who found faith. I can understand both reactions: one person could say, "If such atrocities are possible, then there can be no God," and an another could say, "In the face of such atrocities, only God can preserve the sense of life." People are unpredictable, and the circumstances that push us toward one reaction or another are many.

In a 1976 interview, Greene acknowledged a lingering skepticism. "I don't like many English Catholics. I don't like conventional religious piety. I'm more at home with the Catholicism of Catholic countries. I've always found it difficult to believe in God. I'd suppose I'd now call myself a Catholic atheist." Hmmm, a Catholic atheist, that's interesting, that's me or was me. I've dropped the adjective.

Graham Greene was not a Catholic writer. He was a writer, a writer who was obsessed with the inner war between the spirit and the flesh that wore down many of his characters. He often wrote of men and women haunted by sex and God, haunted by fear and guilt; he wrote of tragic figures in search of salvation.

Graham Greene was a writer, a talented writer. Yet he claimed, "I have no talent; it's just a question of working, of being willing to put in the time." He had talent, and he was willing to put in the time to mine it. Few of us can make the same claim.

"If I were to choose an epigraph for all the novels I have written," he wrote in *A Sort of Life,* which was the first installment of his autobiography, "it would be from Robert Browning's 'Bishop's Apology':

> Our interest's on the dangerous edge of things,
> The honest thief, the tender murderer,
> The superstitious atheist . . .

A writer died two days ago. His journey is over and his absence leaves a void. Graham Greene would have understood the way I feel about my letters to you, Kate. In the second volume of his autobiography, *Ways of Escape,* he wrote, "Writing is a form of therapy; sometimes I wonder how all those who do not write, compose, or paint can manage to escape the madness, the melancholia, the panic fear which is inherent in the human condition."

You, my dear Kate, unknowingly offered me a way of escaping the madness and melancholia that lived for so long inside of me.

Thank you Kate. Goodbye, Graham.

Friday, April 5—5:20 P.M.

Last week, Congress passed Public Law 102-24, a joint resolution, which resolved, "That the President of the United States declare a national day of prayer and thanksgiving to express our gratitude for the heroic efforts of our troops and to offer our thanks to God, the ruler of men and nations, the source of justice, and the author of true peace."

And the delusion continues.

Plans are also being formulated to stage numerous victory parades around the country. These parades will cost taxpayers millions of dollars. The parades will do much more than welcome home the soldiers and celebrate the victory. They will also help keep our eyes from seeing the mountain of domestic troubles that lie before us and will gloss over the many complex and troubling aspects of the war. The parades will close the book on the war, and the message at the end of the book says we won and we are great. Of course that message is an illusion. Saddam Hussein still runs Iraq, Kuwait is burning, and its Emir is in no hurry to transform his feudal nation into a democracy; peace in the Middle East has not been guaranteed, and the recession, which we ignored while fighting the war, still ravages our nation.

Prayers and parades are not what we need. Hosannas and confetti are nothing more than diversions. The soldiers deserve to be welcomed home. But the glory of a parade lasts but a day and then is relegated to the province of memory; a more fitting welcome home would be the long-range benefits of jobs and a thriving economy.

Friday, April 5—11:10 P.M.

I can see it now: next summer there will be a movie that will try to exploit this year's western-flavored, Oscar-winning *Dances with Wolves* and the interest in exorcism, which will be intensified after tonight's broadcast of the ABC News magazine show "20/20." The film will follow the exploits of an itinerate preacher prowling the frontier looking for evidence of demonic activity in the lives of Indians and settlers; it will be called: *Dances with Devils*.

The "holy" Roman Catholic Church teamed up with ABC News tonight and the unholy alliance brought the Devil to primetime television. The priests were looking for publicity; the journalists were looking for high ratings. Sadly, both will get what they were looking for—at the expense of honesty and reason.

Oh, Kate, I thought I left superstition behind in Mexico, yet my return to America was greeted by the hoopla and media buildup for tonight's "20/20," which featured Roman Catholic priests conducting an exorcism. I just finished watching the show, which amounted to little more than authorized child abuse and tabloid journalism joining forces to create vivid television. What crap.

The segment opens with a warning from John Cardinal O'Connor that Satan is among us, his evil spreading. Proof of his absurd assertion was not offered. During a sermon last year in which he warned that the Devil was still at work in the world, O'Connor disclosed that he had recently authorized two exorcisms in his archdiocese. Why can't this bellicose prelate from New York stick to digging up old bones in his search for saints instead of resurrecting Satan?

I think His Eminence is in love with the past. The rite of exorcism has been a solemn ritual in the Catholic Church since Medieval times, and it is the Church's way of confronting the Devil and forcing him or other demons to flee a human body in which they have taken up residence. As humanity moved into the scientific age and discovered natural explanations for illnesses (such as epilepsy), mental illnesses (such as multiple personality disorder and schizophrenia), and abnormal behavior formerly imputed to demonic activity, the rite of exorcism was performed less and less. And because the Catholic Church during the past few decades has accepted psychiatric interpretations of abnormal behavior, exorcism has virtually disappeared in our times. But thanks to guys like Pope John Paul II and John Cardinal O'Connor, exorcism is making a comeback.

I still have the Missal, or prayer book, that I used as a teenager. Earlier today, I was looking over some the material concerned with Holy Week when I came across the following prayer for the unity of the Church: "Almighty and everlasting God, who savest all, and willest that no one should perish, look on the souls that are led astray by the deceit of the devil, that having set aside all heretical evil, the hearts of those who err may repent, and return to the unity of Thy truth." But I wasn't led astray by the deceit of the Devil; I simply followed where reason and logic led.

You see, Kate, when I was growing up, the Devil was real, powerful, and someone to be feared. The nuns told us that the Devil was always prowling about, lurking in the corner of our lives, always trying to trick us and lead us into temptation and sin. I was taught the Devil was a personal being, and not just an impersonal evil force. I fully believed the Devil was real. The co-host of "20/20" began tonight's program by asking, "Is the Devil real?"

But is it possible to give a "yes or no" answer to such a question? Hardly. Because neither a "yes" nor a "no" answer can be proven and substantiated by tangible evidence. The fact is, the question is meaningless. Kate, before my trip to Mexico, I considered questions about the existence of God or the Devil to be unanswerable, but hardly meaningless.

On the day that Charlton and I visited the ruins at Mitla, we were having lunch at a small restaurant when Charlton spotted an old man he knew and asked him to join us. His name was Dr. Barry Frank, and he was indeed very frank. Barry Frank was a respected archeologist, who is now retired and living in San Cristobal de las Casas. Charlton guessed his age to be in the upper seventies. Our conversation drifted onto the topic of the Zapotec Indian's religious practices.

I innocently asked Dr. Frank how his work in archeology affected his personal religious beliefs. "It hasn't. Since the time I was old enough to think for myself, I knew all religion was a crock of shit. My work hasn't changed that belief in the slightest." Charlton asked, "Does that mean you don't believe in the existence of God?" The old man responded, "Sir, I can hardly recall a time when I wasn't an atheist." Charlton suddenly turned into Mike Wallace: "Dr. Frank, I'm curious about something. Why are you an atheist and not an agnostic? I mean isn't an agnostic position more justifiable, considering the indefiniteness of the evidence? I always considered atheism a bit dogmatic because it asserts that there is no God—period."

Wow, what a question! It sounded very reasonable to me, in fact, I sort of considered myself an agnostic who didn't have the balls to call myself an atheist. Barry Frank's answer came out of left field. This crusty, old curmudgeon had given this stuff a lifetime of thought.

Looking at Charlton, he asked, "Do you know what epistemology is?"

Charlton said, "Vaguely."

Dr. Barry Frank continued, "Epistemology is a branch of philosophy concerned with the problem of how we know what we think we know. Now if you studied scientific philosophy and modern epistemology these questions of yours would be easily answered. Consider these two propositions: (1) The moon is made of green cheese; (2) Undetectable gremlins inhabit the rings of Saturn. Now would you gentlemen consider both of these propositions to be false?"

Charlton and I both nodded yes we would.

Dr. Frank, from behind a smug smile, said, "I wouldn't consider both propositions to be false. Only the green cheese proposition is false. The gremlin sentence isn't even a proposition and is therefore meaningless. Being meaningless, it can be neither true nor false. Truth and falsehood can apply only to meaningful sentences. Which brings me to the scientific view of how to tell meaningful propositions from meaningless ones. To be meaningful, a proposition must be such that one can at least imagine a way to test its correctness. Do you follow so far?"

Charlton and I indicated that we did. I don't know about Charlton, but I wasn't so sure.

The aging archaeologist continued, "The green cheese proposition is easily tested. Even before astronauts went to the moon and brought home samples of moon dust, it was easy to imagine what one could do to see if the moon was, in fact, made of cheese. But the gremlin sentence, by contrast, cannot be tested even in the imagination. Undetectable gremlins are forever undetectable and thus unverifiable. The gremlin proposition is meaningless and is neither true nor false. And God sentences are exactly like gremlin sentences. There is no way to even imagine how you could test whether God exists, since God gets no more involved in the working of the universe than do undetectable gremlins. Do you guys want another beer? My treat."

Dr. Frank signaled for the waiter and after the beers were served, he picked up where he left off.

"Listen, this religion stuff causes people to get all hot and bothered and their thoughts and actions are all based on passion not logic. The theist says, 'God exists.' The atheist says, 'God does not exist.' The agnostic says, 'Maybe God does exist, maybe he doesn't. I can't tell.' But all of them are wrong because the question 'Does God exist?' is a meaningless question because all God sentences are neither true nor false. For practical reasons, I can say 'God does not exist,' but the logical reality is much more dramatic: the concept of God is meaningless and it is quite safe to ignore the gods."

Dr. Barry Frank was more refreshing than the beer. I wish to hell he could have been on the set of "20/20" when the co-host asked, "Heaven and hell, do they really exist? Is the Devil real?" Of course the show never answered the questions; the producers were more than happy to just point their cameras at a mentally disturbed young teenager as some crazy priests tried to force the evil spirits out of her body.

The subject—or, rather victim—of the exorcism was a sixteen-year-old girl named Gina. The doctor who treated her in the Miami Children's Hospital psychiatric ward before the exorcism was preformed called the girl "actively psychotic." The priests insisted she was plagued by demonic spirits. The priests were not diagnosed.

The rite of exorcism was performed by Father A—the "A," according to the reporter, stood for anonymous, and not asshole, as I would have assumed. According to Father A, "It [exorcism] is a struggle between two opponents for survival as it were in one respect, in this case, the struggle with evil." According to the Church, the Devil—who also goes by the names Satan, Beelzebub, and Lucifer—is a fallen angel who has lost his identity with God but who didn't lose the powers that he had, so he is capable of possessing the minds of innocent human victims and turning them evil. Sure. Dr. Frank's "crock of shit" remark leaps to mind. The Catholic Church's book of rituals includes a group of ancient prayers called the Rite of Exorcism. When these special prayers are spoken to a possessed person, the Church claims the Devil must leave. You could say that exorcism is an ecclesiastical eviction notice delivered to Satan.

Part I of the report chronicled the events leading up to Gina's exorcism, and Part II showed the actual exorcism, which the report condensed from several hours to under ten minutes. I'm sure if they played the entire event, viewers across America would have fallen asleep after about half an hour, but they held our attention during Part II by showing only Gina's screaming and struggling.

In Part I, the priests indicated that they do an intense screening of those people who are seeking an exorcism. The screening process takes as long as six months, during which time the priests make sure that the candidates for exorcism have no medical or mental problems that they are falsely attributing to diabolical powers. The priests state that signs that indicate a person is possessed are: abnormal strength, levitation, clairvoyance, and the ability to speak in languages they have never studied. Out of fairness, the report presented a Jesuit priest who is also a psychiatrist and who had serious doubts about exorcism. This critic, who wore a suit and tie instead of his Roman collar, observed that people with a background in theology are inclined to interpret inner conflict as a battle between good and evil or God and Satan. People wearing theological glasses see things theologically.

Finally, after setting the table, Part I of the report presented the star of the show: Gina. The overweight young lady said, "I came out with strange voices, things that I had been seeing and stuff. I saw demons and stuff, people who died." The reporter told us that Gina had been suffering for years from violent seizures, during which she would spit, vomit, scream in strange voices, and have visions of demons. She had not attended school for several months. In an attempt to stop the bizarre outbursts, her mother, Felisa, took Gina to a psychic healer because she thought her daughter's problem did not stem from natural causes, but was the result of evil forces. Gina and Felisa thought the spiritist was going to perform some sort of exorcism. Gina did not want to go, but her mother insisted, claiming it would do her good. It didn't. The seizures not only continued, they worsened. Gina then spent two months in the psychiatric ward of Miami's Children's Hospital.

Felisa, a Colombian immigrant, and her daughter both spoke poor English, their native tongue being Spanish. It seemed apparent that they fully believed in the supernatural, which doesn't surprise me in the least. My month in Mexico opened my eyes to the importance of witchcraft and magic in Latin America. A Mexican male encountering difficulties courting a lady might very well resort to carrying a dead hummingbird in his pocket, because it is believed that by doing so a male will be sought after by many women. If a guy is trying to seduce a girl, he might slip a leg of a beetle into her Pepsi, because it will make her a little crazy and very horny. If you don't happen to have a beetle leg handy, powder made from a crushed human skull will have the same effect, but if you put too much in the lady's drink it could cause her to go insane. An abused wife might put jimsonweed in her husband's coffee in order to better control him. I gotta get me some beetle legs!

It would be easy for me to describe Felisa and Gina as nuts, but what they both are is highly superstitious. The war between the superstitions of religion and the proofs of science has been a long struggle and, as evidenced by tonight's show, one the Church still wants to fight. The survival of the various superstitions and metaphysics coupled with undying dogmatism and a literal interpretation of the Bible is still being pitted against the accumulated evidence that insanity is the result of physical disease. In the early stages of civilization it was very natural for man to believe in the powers of the occult and the powers of evil. The troubles and calamities humanity encountered were not attributed to natural physical causes because man was ignorant of the physical laws of the universe; and so he attributed his problems to the wrath of a benevolent supreme being, or more frequently the malice of an evil being. The real causes of many diseases were so intricate and so far beyond mankind's understanding that evil spirits became the easy fall guy in unfathomable mysteries.

The theory that mental illness is caused largely by Satanic influence predates Christianity. The influence of diabolic forces in mental disease is presented in all the Oriental scriptures. The early Fathers of the Church universally accepted the notion and spoke of the power of casting out devils as a leading proof of the divine origin of Christianity. Here is a piece of documented Church history that sounds so absurd as to have been manufactured by a writer from *Mad* magazine. The story involves St. Gregory the Great, who was Pope from September 3, 590, to March 12, 604. Considered to be a broad-minded man, he nonetheless related the story of a nun who had eaten some lettuce without first making a sign of the cross, and as a result she accidentally swallowed the Devil. An exorcism was performed on the nun, and the Devil told the priest officiating at the exorcism, "How am I to blame? I was sitting on the lettuce, and this woman, not having made the sign of the cross, ate me along with it."

OK, back to the Devil and Miss Gina.

The doctor who treated Gina during her two-month stay at the hospital was the Director of Psychiatry for the institution. He said Gina was "actively psychotic, very agitated and was having marked difficulty functioning, even as it relates to basic self-care." She was diagnosed as having recurring psychotic episodes. Being a scientist, the doctor doubted there was such a thing as demonic possession. The treatment Gina received at the hospital had little effect on Gina's condition, so her mother turned to the Church for help.

The psychotherapist the Church used to help evaluate the girl said that her first meeting with Gina "sent chills throughout my body." The therapist believed the family's reports of Gina's levitating and being pulled across the room even though no one was there pulling her. During Father A's meeting with Gina, he was astounded by the knowledge Gina possessed. "She possessed knowledge of things and people that there was no way she should have. She knew where I had been the previous week dealing with another case; she mentioned the persons by name. I found that very astounding and revealing." After reviewing several reports by psychiatrists and reading transcripts of Gina's outburst, the priests decided she was possessed by the Devil.

The two New York priests then asked the local bishop for permission to perform an exorcism. Bishop J. Keith Symons of the Diocese of Palm Beach, Florida, granted permission. According to the bishop, "The Devil really exists. He is powerful and actively at work in the world." The bishop hoped that the broadcast would help "counteract diabolical activities around us."

Once permission had been granted, the priests assembled a team that included additional priests, a psychotherapist, a few nuns, a nurse, a doctor, a Spanish translator, and some hefty women to help restrain Gina should she become violent or start levitating. The two priests met with the team and prepared them for what might happen. Father A advised the team, "At no point in time do you address her or anything that comes from her." The other priest said, "It's [the Devil is] looking for an out and if someone falls victim to that then now we have two people to deal with. It's not a game we are playing; it is something very real to the person involved, it is very real to each of us." The meeting concluded with a prayer to God and Saint Michael the Archangel, imploring their blessing and guidance. Father A said he would be fasting for a number of days before the exorcism. At last, after a lot of meaningless gibberish, the stage was set for the exciting second part of the report . . . after these messages.

After a promo (underscored by a loud instrumental version of the Rolling Stones song "I Can't Get No Satisfaction") for the ABC Saturday Night Movie *Raw Deal*, starring muscleman Arnold Schwarzenegger, the co-host of "20/20" reappeared and said, "We continue now our remarkable coverage of an exorcism performed by a Roman Catholic priest." Remarkable? Please, is it necessary to toot your own horn? To be honest, Part II was rather anticlimatic. And cruel. Gina got a raw deal from life, her mother, her church, and the journalists who exploited her suffering.

Gina's ordeal began with a Mass. She showed up at the convent where the exorcism was to take place, thinking that she and her mother where simply going to Mass. Gina was unaware of the real reason she was there. A priest explained that secrecy insures that the demons could not prepare for their surprise encounter with the exorcist. Father A gave Gina a glass of holy water, hoping to provoke a response from the Devil. No response was forthcoming. Another priest explained that "the Devil plays a great game of deception and will not reveal itself or themselves for a long time." Father A probed Gina's psyche, attempting to identify exactly what demons he was confronting.

Suddenly, during the pre-exorcism questioning, Gina started retching, and a low, husky and unfamiliar voice emerged saying: "Gina said to me I have to go. And I tell you I don't want to go at all. You understand!"

Father A responds, "Do you understand?"

Gina, in the same low voice, says, "No, you understand: I don't want to go."

Then Gina turned violent, started screaming, thrashing about, making ugly faces, yelling in a high-pitched voice a string words that sounded like "sanka dali," "rabaya," "san catali," and "booga, booga." Gina screamed, "Get out of here. Gina! We want Gina." Gina contorted her face and said in a squeaky little voice, "My name is Minga." According to the priest, Gina was no longer present and the evil spirit had manifested itself by speaking.

Suddenly, it ended. Gina calmly explained that ten entities are controlling her. She named two of them: Minga and Zion. She claimed Zion was an African. Father A asked, "Is he an African of this type, of today's age, or an African of a jungle?" Gina responded, "A jungle." Gina described Minga as a very short woman. The priests huddled together and decided to go ahead and perform the exorcism.

It began. Pressing a crucifix into Gina's forehead, Father A read the sacred Roman Catholic Rite of Exorcism. "Holy Lord, You who sent your only Son into this world in order that He may crush this roaring lion, throw your terror, Lord, over the beast who is destroying what belongs to you." The prayers he read have remained virtually unchanged since the Renaissance.

What followed was wave after wave of screaming, scratching, growling, and crying. As the prayer intensified, so did Gina's response. Gina's arms and legs were tied down. Father A confronted the demons by screaming, "Death is your lot impious One, because you are prince of homicides, master of the most evil actions, teacher of heretics, the inventor of all obscenity, go out therefore impious One." Gina was being screamed at. She screamed back, "Sinner! More wars are coming." The exorcist yelled back, "I now exorcise you, most unclean spirit, invading enemy." Gina struggled and yelled. Father A continued praying, "May God have pity on us and bless us." Gina screamed over his prayers, "I don't like you. Somebody help me!" The priest pressed, "You will leave now. Jesus Christ commands you. You must leave now."

The rite of exorcism continued without let up for several excruciating hours. The priest commanded, "Zion leave now. In the name of Jesus Christ I command any other spirits that are present in Gina to speak out now and reveal itself.

Minga has to go now, the Cross compels you." Gina who began appearing more complacent, wiggled her tongue in a lewd fashion at Father A. The priest said, "That spirit of lust must leave Gina. I command you to depart now, to leave our sister alone forever and never to return to her or anyone else on this earth. In the name of the Father, the Son, and the Holy Spirit. Amen. Gina kiss the cross of Christ. Mamma is going to take you home."

After more than six hours, it was over. Gina looked as if she had come out of a trance.

Later that night, Gina said some of the troubling voices returned to haunt her in her bedroom. Father A went there and performed an exorcism on the house.

Within a few days, the priests and the mother decided Gina should be brought back to the Miami Children's Hospital for more conventional treatment. She was confined to the psychiatric unit for two weeks. The doctor claimed that she was still distorting reality but not to the same degree that she did prior to the exorcism. Gina gradually responded to a combination of medication and various psychotherapies. Gina continued to take a strong antipsychotic medication after her release from the hospital.

After two months, while still on medication, Gina said, "I feel much better, thanks to God that he liberated me from evil. I had a lot of bad things happen to me in the beginning, but I'm much better now. I'm very happy now. I feel free."

Gina's only complaint is that Father A pressed the cross a little too hard on her forehead during the exorcism, but believes, "those evil spirits were there, and had to leave that day and I'm very happy now."

And so the report ended. The "20/20" co-host returned and said, "That was extraordinary." She then thanked the Catholic Church for letting them film the exorcism. She added, "The spiritual and the scientific can go together." The male co-host said, "You know that I tend to be skeptical about these things. But here we are dealing with mature, responsible people who have a tradition that goes back a long way and a ritual that the Church has used to advantage. And I think the psychological aspect does have to be cranked in, because belief is part of the mix. Belief on the part of the girl, and on the part of the priests performing the ceremony. As we said, the bottom line is that she is better, for whatever reason."

And that, Dear Kate, was journalism in action. The report hardly proved that the spiritual and the scientific can go together. And nothing was offered to support the claim that the priests were mature, responsible people. And what does the length of a tradition have to do with its merit?

Did the viewers of "20/20" see a deeply troubled girl whose anguish was eased by a ritual that appealed to her faith or something else? The program neither offered definitive proof of demonic possession nor answered any questions. The faithful were encouraged by what they saw, devils getting the boot by Jesus; the skeptical were outraged by what they saw, a girl being abused by medieval practices.

We all watched through glasses of our own choice. I'm taking my glasses off and going to bed.

Saturday, April 6—7:30 A.M.

I woke up starving this morning. So I drove to the "drive thru" window at McDonalds and ordered two "Egg McMuffins." It gets worse. On the way home, I stopped at a Dunkin' Donuts and bought a bag of donuts.

The Devil made me do it.

All that devil stuff from last night still has me exasperated. It is hard to believe, but a recent national poll indicated that 55 percent of those polled believe that Satan exists, and 49 percent believe that people are sometimes possessed by the Devil. No wonder the Catholic Church is going back into the exorcism business.

Assuming for a second that Satan exists, why the hell would this powerful fallen angel bother to occupy the body of a troubled, innocuous sixteen-year-old girl? What a waste of diabolical force.

A priest, who is the chairman of the theology department at the University of Notre Dame, responding to last night's exorcism on "20/20" said, "To sprinkle holy water over serious and complex problems is to trivialize them and ensure that they continue."

Kate, looking for the Devil in people distracts us from the real face of evil, which is plain enough to see in the torments of Kurdish refugees in Iraq, in the malnourished bodies of the famine-ravaged Sudan, in the plight of the homeless in America, and in the hatred of racial prejudice and religious persecution around the globe. The theologian from Notre Dame summed it up best: "The important thing is not whether evil is a persona, but that it exists."

Evil will not be eradicated by strapping disturbed teenagers to chairs and ordering the Devil to leave them. In each of us, there is good and bad, and it is a tragic mistake to blame the evil of this world on a sinister spirit from another world. The problem is us, and we are each responsible for the suffering endured by the victims of evil.

Yesterday, John Tower was killed in plane crash. Back on July 13, I mentioned him in this letter. His nomination for Secretary of Defense by George Bush was shot down in the Senate under a barrage of attacks on his ethics and morality. The former Texas senator seemed to have recovered from the pain of defeat and public embarrassment. He had just written a book and appeared ready to resume life. In fact, he was on his way to a speaking engagement for his book when the plane crashed.

I think I need to go for a long walk and try to work off my big breakfast.

Sunday, April 7—3:00 P.M.

I just finished reading Graham Greene's *Ways of Escape*. Kate, there is a sense of excitement running through my body. An excitement that comes from the happy, unexpected discovery of something wonderful. Graham Greene showed me something new about faith.

In January 1959 the writer went to the Belgian Congo. In his mind was percolating a story about a stranger who turns up in a remote leper colony. Four months after his return from the Congo, Greene began work on the novel *A Burnt-Out Case*. For eighteen months he struggled with a life he created, the life of a character named "Querry," the stranger who visited the leper colony. Graham Greene claimed, "Never had a novel proved more recalcitrant or more depressing."

In *Ways of Escape,* Greene explained the circumstances from which *A Burnt-Out Case* grew. Following the publication of his novel *The Heart of the Matter* (which is at its core a story of a man's conflict with himself, a conflict between passion and faith), the author was besieged by letters from readers, most of whom were women and priests. The main character in *The Heart of the Matter,* a man named Scobie, was a Catholic, and Greene had made his faith real even to unbelievers. So readers wrote to the author seeking spiritual advice. Some wanted Greene to lead crusades. Priests wrote what amounted to letters of confessions. Some priests actually visited the writer and spent hours telling him of their difficulties and desperation. A woman from America even implored Greene to help save her marriage. After the publication of *The Heart of the Matter,* Greene was regarded as a Catholic author, a label to which he neither aspired to nor wanted.

Following the book's publication, Graham Greene wrote,

> I found myself used and exhausted by the victims of religion. The vision of faith as an untroubled sea was lost forever; faith was more like a tempest in which the lucky were engulfed and lost, and the unfortunate survived to be flung battered and bleeding on the shore. A better man could have found a life's work on the margin of that cruel sea, but my own course of life gave me no confidence in any aid I might proffer. I had no apostolic mission, and the cries for spiritual assistance maddened me because of my impotence. What was the Church for but to aid these sufferers? What was the priesthood for? I was like a man without medical knowledge in a village struck with plague. It was in those years, I think, that Querry was born, and Father Thomas too. He [Father Thomas, another character in the novel] had often sat in that chair of mine, and he had worn many faces.

I guess I am one of the unfortunate ones, someone left battered and bleeding by faith. As I read that sentence, I understood something about faith for the first time. Faith either absorbs you, or destroys you. Of course, it does neither to many, because for many their faith is simply a matter of routine, put on and taken off as absent-mindedly as a shirt. That kind of faith is not capable of absorbing or destroying. But that's not the kind of faith Graham Greene was talking about, or the kind of faith I once had.

Following the publication of *A Burnt-Out Case,* many people believed Graham Greene was recanting his faith and abandoning the Church. One such person was the celebrated English novelist Evelyn Waugh. Greene and Waugh exchanged heated letters, in which the two men debated elements of the book. Waugh feared that the conclusions about faith reached by the character "Querry" mirrored those of Greene's. In a letter to Waugh, Greene said he thought "Querry" was a better man than he was and explained his motives for writing the book: "I wanted to give expression to various states or moods of belief and unbelief. The doctor, who I liked best as a realized character, represents a settled and easy atheism; the Father Superior a settled and easy belief (I use easy as a term of praise and not as a term of reproach); Father Thomas an unsettled form of belief and Querry as an unsettled form of disbelief."

This faith stuff is so difficult to put into words, so impossible to comprehend. My disbelief, my lack of faith, is unsettled, and that unsettledness has been the source of my troubles. I don't believe in God, in the Church, or in anything religious, yet I wish I did, I wish I could. What I never realized before today was that unbelief, just like belief, has many shadings. Whenever I looked back at my Catholic days, the picture of me that always emerged was one of a boy or man whose faith was firm and unshakable. That is not true, and that picture was merely a trick of my mind. No matter how strongly I believed in God and the truth of the Church, there was always, way back in the recesses of my mind, a small, silent question mark.

I can remember sleepless nights in the seminary, lying awake wondering why God called me to go to China to save souls. I dashed my doubts knowing full well that if they were entertained my dreams of being a priest would never be realized. But even the effort not to doubt created more doubts: was the priesthood my dream or God's will? The other day I was zipping through the channels looking for something to watch, when I paused briefly at "The 700 Club," which is a Christian version of "A Current Affair" and the "Tonight Show" rolled into one insipid hour. The host was plugging some kind of new conference center and hotel he had built, and viewers were invited to come relax, enjoy Christian fellowship, and learn God's will for their lives. If only it were that easy.

I never had a "settled and easy faith." Yet, I wanted a "settled and easy atheism." What I have, I now fully realize, is an unsettled form of disbelief. I must accept this fact. This condition will change in its own time. I cannot force it, nor can I allow it to drive me crazy. I need to relax, enjoy human fellowship, and discover my dreams for my life. If only it were that easy.

Sunday, April 7—10:40 P.M.

I'm tired. I haven't fully recovered from the hectic pace of my month in Mexico. It took a few days, but I have managed to go through all the mail that arrived while I was away. I also finished unpacking. As I sit here in my study relaxing with a glass of wine, my mind keeps replaying much of my trip and making certain lessons I learned very clear.

Back on July 17 of last year, in a new-found flush for living, I wrote, "I am the author of my own life." I presented you with a metaphor that likened my life to a play of which I was the playwright. Like all metaphors and general statements, there is some truth to what I said, and some fallacies.

The point I was trying to make was that I had to take responsibility for the balance of my life. And I do. More emphatically, I must. But (always the "but's") the reality behind the author metaphor sends a far different message than the one I was trying to convey. I am not the author of my life. I did not write the beginning, nor will I pen the ending. Even the vast middle was scripted without much input from me. The truth is that chance and contingency combine to push our lives into sequences we neither desire nor intend. The belief, which many hold true, that our lives are like narratives that we compose as we go along, with a beginning, middle, and an end, gives birth to the notion that death is frequently unjust. Except in war, death is natural. When a person in the prime of his or her life, with young children, a happy marriage (if there is such a thing), and a successful career, is hit and killed by a bus while crossing a street, we tend to call such a death a tragic act of injustice. We view such a death as an injustice because we believe we are the makers or authors of our lives, and the accidental death robbed the deceased of his or her right to complete their story. This view obfuscates the natural role chance and contingency play in the direction of every human's life. J. M. Barrie wrote: "The life of every man is a diary in which he means to write one story, and writes another."

Yes, Kate, I am going to be the author of the balance of my life's story, but chance and contingency will be my co-authors—they are my silent, unseen collaborators who are ever ready to change the direction and ending of my story. My Mexican adventure provides a great illustration of how that collaboration works. I came up with the Mexican plot line for my story, but chance penned many of the details and twists in the plot, which gave my original idea much of its tone and texture.

Monday, April 8—4:30 P.M.

Batter up. It's opening day for major league baseball. The boys of summer are back and earlier today all the teams were tied for first place. The Yankees played at Detroit. Don Mattingly got a hit his first time up to the plate, stole second, and scored on a subsequent hit. After a half inning we had the lead, but it didn't last. Detroit burst the Yanks' spring bubble of hope by winning the first game of the season by the score of 6-4. The season is only three hours old and we're already in last place. It's going to be another long, losing season—a xerox copy of last year, when we were so inept that we lost a game in which Yankee hurler Andy Hawkins pitched a no-hitter.

It's crazy, but being a baseball fan nowadays means that you're rooting for millionaires. I read that 226 major league baseball players earn more than a million dollars a year. Roger "The Rocket" Clemens, a pitcher for the Boston Red Sox (I hate that team), will earn $5,655,250 in 1995, the last year of a contract he recently signed. Jose Canseco, an outfielder for the Oakland Athletics, will earn $5,800,000 during that same season. Darryl Strawberry, an outfielder traded over the winter from the Mets to the Dodgers, will earn $5,300,000 for the 1995 season.

Kate, if you earned $200,000 a year, which 98 percent of the country would consider a fantastic salary, it would take you twenty-nine years to earn what Jose Canseco is going to earn for a summer job in 1995, and that doesn't include the money he'll make from commercials.

I should have taken more batting practice as a kid. Anyway, I'll be rooting for the Yankees this season. Besides, their top-paid player, Don Mattingly, will only be earning a measly $3,420,000 for the summer.

Still, rooting for the Yankees or any baseball team isn't as bad as being addicted to daytime talk shows on television. Nothing has changed on that scene during my time in Mexico. They are still producing shows around such enlightening themes as: truck driver's mistresses, parents coping with gay children, people addicted to adultery, fathers and sons who share the same woman, women whose husbands are transvestites, men who raped their teenage stepdaughters, people who have had sex-change operations, parents whose children were murderers, parents who sleep with their children's best friend, grown children who resent their widowed or divorced mothers re-marrying a black man, women who were stood up at the altar, straight women with gay husbands, children sold by their parents, teenage AIDS victims who want to marry, and on and on and on.

In America, viewers spend on the average of three to four hours a day in front of the tube. For many, it beats facing reality. Perhaps Congress should pass a joint resolution asking the President to declare a national "buy a couch potato a book" week. For that matter, even a national "take a TV junkie out to the ball park" week would be helpful.

Groucho Marx thought television could be educational. He said, "I find television very educating. Every time somebody turns on the set I go into the other room and read a book."

In a speech delivered in Chicago in the late 1950s, Edward R. Murrow, the dean of broadcast journalism, said, "Our history will be what we make it. And if there are any historians about fifty or a hundred years from now and there should be preserved the kinescopes [a method of filming shows as they were broadcast back in the days before the invention of videotape when many of the shows aired live] for one week of all three networks, they will there find recorded in black and white or perhaps in color evidence of decadence, escapism, and insulation from the realities of the world in which we live." And Murrow was talking about the "golden age" of television when quality was the norm not the exception. One can only imagine what he would have thought of such current television fair as "Roseanne," "Amen," "America's Funniest Home Videos," and the glut of daytime soap operas and talk shows.

I'm sure Edward R. Murrow, whose reporting of World War II and whose documentaries exposing injustice in American life are still benchmarks for judging excellence in broadcast journalism, would have been horrified by television's coverage of the war in the Gulf. Its coverage of the war clearly demonstrates how television has removed words from journalism. The picture is all that counts. But pictures appeal to emotions, they appeal to intuitive logic, not empirical logic. Viewers are responding to the pictures television delivers to their homes, and not to words that put the pictures into context. (And during this war, the pictures released by the networks were controlled and censored by our government, which guaranteed the reporting had the "correct" spin.) Fast-moving events are caught by the camera and instantly transported around the world live via satellite. The television reporter has no time to ponder what is happening, no time to gather facts, no time to put events into historical perspective, no time to carefully choose his or her words. (Reporters do, however, make time for hair, make-up, and wardrobe.) Television, with its reliance on pictures, has created a need for instantaneous commentary.

In Murrow's day, the network news operations were strong, independent divisions within the networks and were immune from the vagaries of the ratings-hungry entertainment divisions. Today, the line between the news and entertainment divisions has virtually disappeared, and the news divisions are expected to turn a profit by attracting and holding as many viewers as possible, even if the ratings and profits come at the expense of journalistic integrity.

Viewer beware.

Monday, April 8—10:20 P.M.

Almost six weeks ago, just one week before I left for Mexico, I wrote this simple sentence: The war is over.

But the war is not over, at least it is not over for the Kurds living in Iraq. The Honorable George Herbert Walker Bush has betrayed them, and now scores of them are dying every day.

Here's the story. One hundred hours into the ground war, we had the Iraqi troops on the ropes. Many people wanted to see us march right into Baghdad and get rid of Hussein. The president elected not to do that, claiming that eliminating Hussein was not part of our United Nations-approved goals. I have no problem with his decision. (Besides, how could I oppose military action and then complain we ended it too quickly.) Mr. Bush, however, publicly asked the Iraqi people to revolt, to rise up and depose their dictator. He promised to destroy Iraqi helicopters, if Hussein used them against the rebels in violation of temporary cease-fire accords. Well, Hussein used the helicopters and fired on the rebels; and Bush, in essence, responds to the Kurds' plea for military assistance by telling them to drop dead.

Before and during the war, Mr. Bush never tired of calling Saddam Hussein the new Hitler. Now, the fighting has stopped, Hussein has started a brutal campaign of genocide against the Kurds, and Bush just looks the other way, not wanting to get dragged into an Iraqi quagmire. The President did not even condemn the slaughter, saying only that he was "troubled" by the human suffering the Kurds were enduring.

The Kurds were forced to flee on foot from the advancing Iraqi troops to either the mountains along the Turkish border to the north or to the mountains along the Iran border to the east. They carried their few possessions on their backs. Cars were left behind because the clogged roads were reduced to a chaotic snarl.

Many of the fleeing peasants were barefooted. Numerous Kurds died on the march, some from artillery fire, some from exposure to the bitter cold mountain air. They arrived at the borders destitute and exhausted. They are suffering from napalm burns, dysentery, frostbite, bullet wounds, and a litany of other ailments. Children shivered uncontrollably and the elderly were overtaken by exhaustion. A distraught mother showed a reporter her nine-month-old daughter's stomach. The infant's distended belly was oozing from an infected petroleum burn from napalm.

At the end of their arduous exodus, instead of finding relief and help, the Kurds are floundering in a contagious and collective fear. The dozens of mountaintop refugee settlements, some holding up to 200,000 people, are overrun with sickness, want, and death. There is nothing to eat. There is no water. Cholera is inevitable. The babies are dying; there is no milk. The people have no clothing, except for what is on their backs. Some children are clad only in thin pajamas and sweaters.

They wonder: "Why did George Bush let this happen?"

At night, the razor-sharp winds, the whirling snows, and the plummeting temperatures make sleeping impossible. There is a desperate need for blankets. Most have no shelter, only the lucky have tents. Sanitation is nonexistent. Medical supplies are paltry. Coughing and diarrhea are maladies shared by most of the refugees. Many have frostbitten toes on the verge of gangrene. Many of the women who were breast-feeding their babies are no longer lactating, the result of malnutrition, dehydration, and stress. The camps echo with the cries of babies. Adults groan from the pain of hunger.

Trucks bringing crucial food and supplies are bogged down in the mud at the bottom of the mountains. Death, especially of the smallest children, comes with a sinister cadence. Every morning, the dead are buried. Fathers carry the bodies of their lifeless infants, followed by friends with small shovels and picks, to the burial sight. The dead can't even be wrapped in blankets, because they are desperately needed to keep the living warm.

An international relief effort has begun airlifting food and supplies, but it is far too little to make a real difference. One plane dropped a large pallet of supplies attached to a parachute. It landed on a tent and crushed to death an entire family. It is estimated that over a million Kurds are on the move. Many of the people are engineers, lawyers, physicians, and teachers—city poeple who are unaccustomed to the harsh vagaries of the mountainous borders. This is a disaster on a monumental scale. There are no reliable figures for the death toll, but it is estimated that several thousand Kurds have already died as a result of their arduous ordeal. And those who have survived are living in hell.

And George Bush does nothing. Actually, he has been fishing in the Florida Keys.

It is clear to me that morality does not guide George Bush's actions. His guiding star is expediency. Mr. Bush has a record of doing nothing when foriegn despots trample on human rights. He was silent when the Chinese dictators crushed the pro-democracy movement in Tiananmen Square. He was silent as Lithuania tried to struggle free of the Soviet Union. Bush cloaks American aims in pieties about moral purpose; in truth, morality takes a back seat to hard-nosed politics. By not interferring with the Soviet Union and China, George Bush helped insure both countries would vote his way in the United Nations during the Gulf War. Bush puts power politics above the concern for the lives and rights of people. President Bush defends his hands-off policy by claiming we can't afford to get involved in a potentially drawn-out civil war in Iraq. The truth is, Bush doesn't want Iraq to fall into the hands of the Kurds and Shiites because of the Shiites ties with Iran. The Arab nations in the area would rather have a weakened Hussein in power, than to have a splintered Iraq. Bush wants Saddam Hussein out, but he also wants Iraq whole for geopolitical purposes, regardless of the cost in human lives. Bush is hoping the Iraqi Army can hold off the rebels and assassinate Hussein. But is it morally right for Bush to turn his back on the Kurds after encouraging them to rebel?

I'm sure that within the next week or two, Bush will succumb to the pressure created by the media coverage of the starving and dying refugees, and he will do the honorable thing and make a sustained effort to ease the pain of these victims of the war.

Kate, this is not America's finest hour. Yes, we won the war; but the plight of the Kurds has tarnished the victory. And the hollow victory, won at the cost of nearly three hundred American lives, does not guarantee peace in the future. The Middle East is still a powder keg that can be ignited at any time.

Meanwhile, right here in America, millions of poor people face their own Kurdish-like nightmare of fear and despair. No one is rushing to the aid of our crack babies and our homeless. While ignoring the plight of our own people, we are systematically destroying our environment. Our schools are graduating pupils who cannot clearly communicate a simple thought. Drug use is rampant and violence is a way of life in most large American cities.

Maybe it is time we rescue America. When it came to kicking Iraq out of Kuwait—no problem; when it comes to solving the problems of our crumbling nation—no can do. But there is no need to worry—Dan Qualye is waiting in the wings to fix everything in 1996.

God Bless America.

Tuesday, April 9—8:20 A.M.

Yesterday, a juicy new biography of former First Lady Nancy Reagan hit the bookstores. The book, titled *Nancy Reagan: The Unauthorized Biography*, was written by the queen of poisonous pens and keyhole journalism, Kitty Kelley. The publisher, Simon and Schuster, printed 600,000 books. The steamy tell-all bio is generating headlines and sales. Before the day was over, the publishers received 160,000 reorders. All across the country, bookstores were swamped with requests for the book. Stores are selling the book at the rate of ten an hour. After the Gulf war, it seems America is ready for some good old-fashioned dirty gossip.

And gossip the book delivers. The Kitty-litter bio claims that Nancy Reagan had adulterous liaisons with Frank ("The Lady is a Tramp") Sinatra in the White House while the President was out of town! The Sinatra affair began when Ronald Reagan was Governor of California. According to the author, Nancy and Ron smoked marijuana while he was governor. These revelations alone have best-seller written all over them. And there is even more. Kitty Kelley writes that Nancy lied about her background, age, and family; abused her children; was a cheapskate when it came to giving gifts to her grandchildren; had her nose fixed and her eyes lifted; and either feuded with or ignored family members. We also get to learn that Mrs. Reagan is a tax chisler, and her godmother was a lesbian.

And what about Bonzo's co-star, the Prez? According to Kelley's steamy exposé, Ronnie was guilty of a "date rape." Forty years ago, the future forty-first president of the United States of America forced himself sexually on a nineteen-year-old Hollywood starlet. Wow! The book also alleges marital infidelity on the part of Ronald Reagan. Back in 1951 Ronnie was in love with an actress (not the "date rape" victim) who turned down his proposal for marriage. Nancy, whose own acting career was going nowhere, wooed Ronnie, who offered to marry her after she told him she was pregnant. But alas, Ronnie continued to see the actress who rejected his marriage proposal during his first year of marriage to Nancy. According to Kitty Kelley, Ronald Reagan was with his secret lover when his daughter Patti was born.

Kelley's book reads more like a trashy novel than a serious biography of an influential public figure. Ms. Kelley also claims that the former president, contrary to his numerous denials, has been secretly dying his hair since 1968—what a scoop! According to the author, Mr. Reagan is a homophobe and a bigot who likes telling ethnic jokes. There is no mention in the book that President Reagan's policies led to the largest national debt and worst foreign trade deficit in American history despite his campaign promises to balance the budget. I'd call that political date rape—we invited him into the Oval Office and he screwed us.

The 603-page book sells for $24.95, and for your money you get such scalding prose as: "The former First Lady could not completely drop her lacquered facade to step out of her masquerade as the little helpmate to the Great Man." Ugh.

Kitty Kelley, who has written research-and-destroy bios on Jackie Onassis, Liz Taylor, and Frank Sinatra, claims that Nancy Reagan played a major role in national and international policy matters. Before the president's first meeting with Gorbachev, the book asserts that Ronald Reagan would not look at a detailed agenda prepared for him by his aides until they had it approved by Nancy. Mrs. Reagan, who single-handedly rejuvenated the designer clothing industry, would also arbitrarily scratch the names of prominent politicians off a daily list of people scheduled to meet with the president, and the appointment would be canceled. The First Lady spent $3,000 a month for computerized astrology spreadsheets that dictated the president's schedule. Behind Mrs. Reagan's back, the staff referred to her as "Mrs. President." The book reports that Nancy Reagan frequently disparaged then Vice President George Bush behind his back as weak and spineless. According to the author, who received an estimated four-million-dollar advance for the book, Nancy Reagan is a domineering, mendacious, deluded, scheming, and adulterous woman who has conducted her life as one long scandalous, snobbish, self-centered sham.

The former president, who frequently snoozed on the job, called the book "patently untrue," and filled with "flagrant and absurd falsehoods." (Sure, Ron, and you didn't know anything about your subordinates defying Congress and illegally trading arms for hostages.) Speaking of absurd falsehoods, Mr. President, do you remember the time you told world leaders that you had seen the concentration camps in Europe during World War II, when in fact you did so only on film in Hollywood, where you spent the war years? I guess that was just an innocent mistake of confusing the reel with the real. Coming to his wife's defense, Mr. Reagan said, "I have an abiding faith that the American people will judge this book for what it really is: sensationalism whose sole purpose is enriching its author and publisher."

Ronnie, Ronnie, Ronnie, please don't talk to me about "abiding faith" in the American people. Americans love sensationalism: they read the *National Enquirer;* they shelled out $54.1 million during the past three weeks to see the movie *Teenage Mutant Ninja Turtles II;* they made Roseanne Barr a star; they elected Dan Quayle to the second highest office in the land; and they bought all of George Bush's Persian Gulf lies. And I have abiding faith that they'll make this stupid book a number one best-seller.

The real question is: Who gives a shit about Nancy Reagan?

Is all this news? Hardly. The real news of the past few days, the plight of the Kurds trying to flee from Iraq and the brutality of Hussein, has been buried beneath an avalanche of articles and television shows discussing *Nancy Reagan: The Unauthorized Biography.* During the past few days, Kitty Kelley, America's doyenne of dirt, has been a guest on the ABC News program "Nightline," on NBC's "Today Show," on "CBS This Morning," on CNN's "Sonya Live," and on the syndicated talk show "Sally Jessy Raphael," to name just the ones I've heard about. All three network evening news shows have covered the story of the book's incredible sales. The book has received front-page coverage in the *New York Times,* the *Washington Post,* and *USA Today.* The executives at Simon and Schuster must be laughing all the way to the bank. Kitty Kelley is also narrating a two-cassette audio version of the book.

What does all this hoopla over a dumb book say about our culture, say about us? The answer is too sad to contemplate.

Another addle-brained book headed for the best-seller list is the autobiography by the aging movie star Mickey Rooney, titled *Life Is Too Short.* The former childhood star (who played a bright, energetic all-American boy in seventeen Andy Hardy films and was the number one box-office attraction prior to World War II) tells of his lifetime, tall task of overcoming being short. He also writes about his friendship with Judy Garland and his eight wives. Best of all, Rooney tells us the time an angel in the guise of a busboy appeared to him in the coffee shop of a Lake Tahoe casino, tapped him on the shoulder and whispered, "Mr. Rooney, Jesus Christ loves you very much." The angelic visitation changed his life, which, at the time, was on the skids. It is, as best as I can tell, the first reported sighting of an angel in a gambling casino, and it has been three halos for Andy ever since.

I wonder how many trees lost their lives for these two books.

Tuesday, April 9—2:30 P.M.

I think I died and went to heaven. (No, I didn't see any angels.) I'm in a state of shock; something miraculous just happened. I still can't believe it. This morning I received a phone call from a friend, a guy named Steve Russell. He's a big-shot at Global Films, the most powerful independent film production company in Hollywood. Steve worked for me back in the early eighties. At the time, he was kind of a glorified clerk, but I thought he had tremendous potential. I took a job on another show, and, a few months later, I took a gamble and hired Steve as a producer, instead of choosing someone with a proven track record. I gave the guy his big break in the business, and he more than made the best of his opportunity. Anyway, Steve has stayed in touch over the years, always saying he was keeping his eyes open for the chance to return the favor and hand me a plum position on a Global Films project. I believed his intentions were honorable, but at the same time, during these past couple of years of financial hardship, I haven't once heard from him.

Until this morning. Here's the scoop. Next Monday Global Films is scheduled to begin production on a feature film. Yesterday, the film's director was tossed into jail by the Beverly Hills cops. (No, Eddie Murphy wasn't the arresting officer.) They had pulled him over for a traffic violation. He acted strangely and began tussling with the cops. After they subdued him, they searched his Benz and discovered a briefcase filled with drugs. Global feels the courts will be directing the director to jail, without passing go, or collecting $200.

The incident has put Global in a real pickle. The film, which has a budget of about four million dollars, is all set to roll. The actors have been cast and signed. The production team has been hired. All the location sites have been secured. Every day that shooting is delayed costs a bundle of money and creates a scheduling nightmare. If the project slips for any length of time, the actors will bow out because of other commitments. Global needs to start shooting soon or cancel the entire project. But replacing the director on such short notice is very tough.

Lucky for me, Steve Russell was in the right place at the right time, and he was able to give me a once-in-a-lifetime chance. He convinced Global Films that I could handle the job, even though I've never directed a feature film.

Wednesday, April 10—10:00 A.M.

Why the hell isn't "Wednesday" spelled "Whensday?" Who knows?

Yesterday's *New York Times* carried a lengthy article of fundamentalist Mormons living in Arizona who still practice polygamy. One fifty-four-year-old man, who has nine wives and twenty children, claimed, "Every writer in the Old Testament, except for Daniel, was a polygamist. The way I see it, if you're going to get a degree in engineering, then you have to learn a little something about engineering. And if you're going to understand the Bible, you have to adopt the lifestyle of those who wrote it." What wacky reasoning! The article didn't mention whether or not the guy sacrificed animals, or if he would kill any of his children if God asked him to sacrifice one of them. One woman claimed that polygamy was ideal for the career woman with children because the wives can help each other care for the children. Another woman says that with all the competition, sex never falls into the trap of becoming boring, and because each wife gets only a limited amount of bedroom time with their husband, things always stay fresh.

I guess for the polygamist, love is a many splendored thing.

The ratings for last week's television shows were released today, and, as I feared, viewers were possessed by last Friday's airing of an exorcism on "20/20." The show had its highest ratings in nine years and was the second-most-watched show of the week. Thirty-seven percent of the people watching television last Friday night at 10:00 P.M. were watching "20/20." An estimated twenty-nine million people tuned in to see Satan turned out of Gina's body. No doubt in my mind we will soon see a motion picture or made-for-TV movie dealing with exorcism. The Devil delivers big audiences.

There is some good news on the religion front. Dateline, The Vatican: Pope John Paul II has halted the canonization process of the saintly sweetheart of the Church's right wing—Queen Isabella I. Thankfully, there will be no sainthood for the Spanish monarch (1479-1504) who expelled the Jews from Spain, fought the Muslims, and presided over the Spanish Inquisition. Backers of the Saint Isabella movement claimed the Queen kicked the Jews out in order to protect them from the violence of the anti-Semitic masses. She herself, they argued, was not anti-Semitic. Sure, and the Pope isn't Polish. The bottom line for JPII was simple: he wanted to avoid protest from Jewish and Muslim leaders—so he nixed sainthood for the Queen. Besides, Isabella's actions flatly contradict the teachings of Vatican II, and she is hardly a fit model for contemporary Catholics to imitate.

Listen, kiddo, when I die don't start some movement to have me canonized. Have me simonized instead.

Kate, my sweet, I think the time is quickly approaching for me to end this letter. This new job is going to monopolize all my time, so this may be one of my last opportunities to tell you what is on my mind.

As I awoke this morning, I began thinking about the rhythm of life, the constant flow of ups and downs, the sublime changes that exist in every moment, and the deadly nature of the petty details that rule my life. I thought also about the nature of memories and happiness. I remembered beginning this letter with a long, wandering discourse on memory, which I hope wasn't an impediment to your reading it.

Like most people living today, I know a little about a lot, and a lot about very little. My head is crammed with a myriad of facts that are disconnected and unsynthesized. Bluntly put—I am broadly uneducated. I know a little about art, the theater, drama, comedy, writing, science, history, philosophy, psychology, theology, literature, journalism, politics, economics, geography, music, medicine, animals, cars, sports, the human body, and human nature. I know a lot about television.

I suppose this letter has become an attempt at knowing myself, even though it began as an endeavor to explain myself. As this lengthy epistle nears its end, it is far too early to know whether or not it has been successful on either count.

A number of years ago I developed a taste for reading the letters, journals, diaries, and memoirs of famous writers and artists such as: André Gide, Albert Camus, H. L. Mencken, Robinson Jeffers, George Santayana, Andre Malraux, Nikos Katzantzakis, S. J. Perelman, E. B. White, Franz Kafka, Theodore Dreiser, Albert Einstein, Gertrude Stein, John Steinbeck, Leo Tolstoy, Denis Diderot, Eugene Delacroix, Vincent van Gogh, Anthony Burgess, Thomas Wolfe, and Henry James. I found in these writings, most of which were never intended for publication, a way to penetrate the minds and thinking of men and women who were dedicated to understanding life and searching for truth. These private and personal musings were uncluttered, unadorned, unpretentious, and unguarded; and they honestly revealed the inner torments, struggles, and doubts of their authors. Their journals and letters lacked the contrivances of fiction and exposed the real stuff of restless, creative minds at work. The writers were not fictional, cardboard characters, but flesh-and-blood players fully engaged in the drama of life. Their genius did not reside in their ability to astonish the readers and admirers of their writing or art, but in their ability to be astounded by what they saw in life.

Perhaps my love for this kind of reading is what prompted my effort at putting my personal and private thoughts down on paper in a letter to you. Who knows? In looking over this nearly year-long series of letters I see that it has become a journal of a mind in the process of transformation and an attempt to integrate the clandestine, stormy, and invisible world within me with the chaotic, confusing, and visible world outside of me. The letter is a human work-in-progress, whose daily writing will soon cease but whose job will end only in death.

Sorry, once again I have gotten off the track, so back to my early morning thoughts, which strangely enough led me down a path to the doorway of Eugene Delacroix.

Eugene Delacroix, who was a nineteenth-century French painter and thinker, once wrote, "Mediocre people have an answer for everything and are astonished at nothing." I'm not sure when or where I read that, but I remember being so impressed by the truth of the statement that I copied it down. Perhaps the artist's insight confounded my notion that I was a mediocre person. After all, I fully realized I hardly had an answer for everything, and I certainly was astonished by many of the things I encountered in life.

A few days ago, I was on my way to Burbank (no this isn't another sidetrack), when I happened to pass a used bookstore. I am at my weakest when passing a bookstore or a Mrs. Fields Cookie Shop, and so it was impossible for me to resist the temptation of stopping. I made an illegal U-turn and parked the car. As I wandered up and down the aisles, a book titled *The Journal of Eugene Delacroix* caught my eye. I bought the book and it sat unread until this morning, when, shortly after getting out of bed, I randomly opened it to an entry the artist had written on the morning of April 28, 1854. Delacroix addressed many of the things that were on my mind as I greeted this day, but in a very unexpected way. He began by saying, "On waking up, my thoughts turn to those moments, so agreeable and so sweet to my memory and my heart, that I spent with my good aunt in the country." Delacroix then discussed how an artist uses his memory to shape his art.

> Reflecting on the freshness of memories, on the color of enchantment that they assume in a distant past, I was wondering at that involuntary work of the spirit which, passing pleasant moments in review, separates from them and suppresses anything that lessens the charm of the time when one was in their midst. I was comparing that kind of idealization, for it is one with the effect of fine works of the imagination. The great artist concentrates interest by suppressing details that are useless or repellent or foolish; his powerful hand disposes and establishes, adds or suppresses, and thus makes its own use of the objects which are its own; he moves about within his domain and there spreads forth a feast for you; in the work of a mediocre artist, one feels that he has not been the master of anything; he exerts no influence upon the borrowed materials that he heaps up. What order should he establish in that work where everything dominates him? All he can do is to invent timidly and copy with servility; now, instead of acting as does the imagination when it suppresses repulsive elements, he gives them an equal and sometimes superior rank through the servile manner with which he copies. And so everything in his work is confusion and insipidity. Even when a certain degree of interest or indeed charm appears, by reason of the personal inspiration he may infuse into his compilation, I compare it to life as it is, and to that mixture of pleasant gleams and of disgusts which compose it. In the same way, in the motley composition of my semi-artist, where the evil chokes the good, we barely feel the current of life offering us its fleeting moments of happiness, so completely are they spoiled by the commonplace troubles that we meet every day.
>
> Can a man say that he has been happy at a given moment in his life which memory causes him to look on as charming? He is so, assuredly, in the memory itself, he notes the happiness that he must have felt; but at the instant of that so-called happiness, did he really feel himself to be happy? He was like a man who possesses a piece of land in which there lies buried a treasure of which he is unaware. Would you call such a man rich? No more than I would call happy the man who is so without imagining that he is, or without knowing the extent of his happiness.

Wow! The painter, using a palette of words, said so much with so few.

Eugene Delacroix knew that memory is deceptive, that it makes the moments it recalls brighter or darker than they were when they were created, and the difference between the created moment and the recalled moment is often great. His well-crafted words revealed to me how so much of my alleged "creative" work in television was little more than servile copying that was mired in a muck of confusion and insipidity. The "motley composition" of my life for much of the past few years sadly sounds like the work of Delacroix's semi-artist, a composition in which the "evil chokes the good, we barely feel the current of life offering us its fleeting moments of happiness, so completely are they spoiled by the commonplace troubles that we meet every day."

I have been like the "man who possesses a piece of land in which there lies a treasure of which he is unaware." My treasure is buried within me—and it is me. I no longer must "invent timidly and copy with servility." I frequently have looked back over my life and lamented that it had not produced one single original idea or piece of work. And how could it have, when for so long I denied my own authenticity and chose instead to be molded by the thoughts and ideas of others and, worst of all, by the unholy ideas of the Holy Roman Catholic Church.

But those days are gone, and perhaps they were not as bad as I imagined them back when this letter began. Those dark hours, I see now, were just part of the current of life, the ebb and flow of my emotions. During the past few years I have endured a long, dark night of my soul. But now the sun is dawning. I think I am better for having known the night.

I no longer need to look to others for answers or directions; I can and will create myself.

Well, my sweet, there is much I need to do, much I want to do. I'm sure I'll have time for a few more letters before the movie starts rolling, but already I know that I will miss spending time writing to you.

What a time it has been!

I feel as if we have been through a war together, and now it is time to triumphantly march home.

Wednesday, April 10—2:15 P.M.

A little while ago, I went out to run few quick errands. When I got back, I found a religious pamphlet that someone left in the grill work of my front screen door. It was a simple piece of paper, folded in half to look like a booklet. On the cover was a drawing of a man standing alone on a sidewalk; he was nervously looking skyward. In the sky, a large hand was sticking out of the clouds, with its index finger pointing at the man on the ground. Along with the drawing were printed the words: Someday YOU will stand before GOD. Inside, the pamphlet said, "Dear friend: Someday you and I must stand before God. Can you think of anything more sobering than that? [Sure—facing a tax audit.] Do not think for a moment you can avoid this appointment." In big, bold letters it makes the five following pronouncements, each supported by quotes from scripture:

NONE ARE RIGHTEOUS
THE UNRIGHTEOUS CANNOT GO TO HEAVEN
YOU CANNOT CREATE YOUR OWN RIGHTEOUSNESS
YOU CAN BE RIGHTEOUS THROUGH JESUS
YOU CAN HAVE CHRIST'S RIGHTEOUSNESS RIGHT NOW

The pamphlet then reminds me that my eternal soul is the one thing I must not lose and warns me not to spend another second apart from Jesus, who loved me enough to die for me, and who is knocking at my heart's door this moment asking to come in. It ends with a plea for me to turn from my sin and receive Jesus as my Savior.

What fucking bullshit! Pardon my sinful language, but this stuff really aggravates me and I believe my anger is righteous. What gives these lunatics the right to litter my doorway with their garbage?

I wonder if the person who left the pamphlet even knows what the word "righteous" means. It means acting in a just, upright manner; doing what is right, virtuous. Another meaning is "morally right," fair, and just. It can also mean morally justifiable—as in what Bush wanted us to think the war was.

Oh, Kate, who among us is righteous all of the time? I know of no one. Still, I know many people who are righteous most of the time and want to be when they fail to be. Most people act in a just, upright manner every day. Most of us do what is right. If that weren't true, then the world would be in far more chaos than it is already. Sure, many cheat and don't do what is right in big and little ways everyday. That's life. The simple truth is that righteousness has nothing to do with God. Doing the right thing is in our best interest—some of us know that and some do not. Some world leaders still think violence is a way of solving problems. The problems we face on earth are not the result of unrighteousness or sin, they are the result of faulty thinking. Besides, a strong case can be made that God is not righteous. From what the distributor of that pamphlet would have told me if I had been home, a lot of people have been doing a lot of suffering for a very long time because some lady a long time ago ate an apple. Sounds pretty unrighteous to me. Read the Old Testament and you'll be introduced to a God who is a highly unpredictable and intensely human character who has a rather mean and violent streak. The Old Testament portrays a God who is a reflection of us.

Anyway, enough time wasted on this silliness. I've got to get to work on the script. Time is running out.

Wednesday, April 10—7:20 P.M.

Worked all afternoon on the script. I love it. Around 5:15 P.M., I realized I was starving, so I ordered a pizza. It came just seconds before six, and before sitting down to eat it I turned on CNN to watch "Larry King Live" while I ate. Larry's guest was televangelist Pat Robertson, the preacher who claimed to have changed the course of a hurricane, and who believed God told him to run for the presidency. This guy makes my blood boil. Why the hell is he booked as a guest and then treated with respect?

Larry King introduced Pat Robertson as "an astute observer of American politics and world affairs." Excuse me, but Pat Robertson's astute observations are skewed toward his biblical interpretations of how world events will unfold.

During the interview, King was discussing with Robertson an upcoming meeting arranged by Secretary of State James Bakker between Israel and her Arab neighbors, when the host said, "Now I know, Pat, that you are a literalist and that you believe in Armageddon. . . ." I got excited, thinking Larry King, by calling Robertson a literalist and saying that he believed in Armageddon, was going to ask the televangelist some tough questions. Fat chance. Larry King just questioned whether or not Pat's belief in Armaggedon led the preacher to be encouraged by the upcoming talks, or did he consider peace conferences in the Middle East to be a pointless waste of time.

Pat Robertson said, "Larry I think that this is a respite and everyone of us who loves peace wants to see peace but I don't think we're going to have a permanent peace in the Middle East. The prophet Zachariah wrote many, many centuries ago that one day the nations of the earth would gather against Jerusalem, and I just think it's a question of time before it happens. But this is a welcome respite, maybe it will last during the rest of this decade. I hope it does, but it's not going to be permanent. And what happened in Iraq was like the preliminary bout; the main event is going to be Israel versus the nations, probably the Arab nations gathered against her." No tough follow-up questions were forthcoming.

During the interview, Pat claimed, "The non-European part of the Soviet Union [i.e., the Muslims living in Russia] is going to break away sooner or later and the threat to Israel, for example, would be a Russian or Soviet Islamic Republic armed with nuclear weapons." That prediction from the prophet drew no response from the interviewer. Robertson also claimed, "The KGB is in power. I think the KGB is running the Soviet Union right now." After that statement, Larry King said, "Let's go to some calls for Pat Robertson."

The first caller was a female from Mississippi. "I am a Charismatic, tongue-talking Christian and was a member, and still am, of 'The 700 Club' [Robertson's daily TV show] but have not sent in contributions for quite awhile." The caller went on to explain that she was disturbed by Pat Robertson's strident anti-Palestinian stance. She felt Robertson favored Israel too strongly, and she detected a lack of love and compassion in his attitude toward Palestinian Arabs. Pat Robertson said he loved Palestinians, but "at the same time, the city of Jerusalem and what we know as the Holy Land was given by God to Abraham, Isaac, Jacob, and ultimately the ones that we know as Jews, and I have to go with the Bible on that one, but that doesn't mean I hate the Arabs: it just means that I wish Jordan would be the Palestinian state and not the West Bank." Robertson also said that the Jews should never give up east Jerusalem because it is their patrimony, and that a Palestinian state close to Israel would be "like a dagger to their [Israel's] throat."

Kate, all the problems in the Middle East today are a result of the ludicrous belief that the creator of the universe gave this speck of desert land known as Israel to a "chosen" people for all time. It defies all reason.

Another caller questioned the televangelist's gay-bashing and asked whether the preacher thought homosexuals were entitled to the same rights as the rest of us. Pat Robertson's response: "Homosexuals have every right that I have. But

I think it's wrong to compare a black man, for example, whose difference from me is a question of skin pigmentation with somebody who has chosen a lifestyle that I consider to be perverse, and in a sense self-destructive. I think one is a choice, deliberately taken, of a type of lifestyle, which in my state of Virginia is still against the law, I might add, and to compare that to a woman, or somebody who has a physical handicap, or somebody who is pigmented differently from the Caucasian races—I do not consider this a legitimate minority."

To that bit of rambling Larry King said, "OK. Berlin, Germany, hello." Instead of going to another phone call, why didn't the host point out that most intelligent people understand that homosexuality is not a simple matter of choice? Or why didn't Larry King object to Pat Robertson's classifying homosexual behavior as perverse? In a 1987 radio interview during his run for the presidency, Robertson claimed that AIDS was the result of homosexuals breaking universal moral laws, and that additional research money to help find a cure for the disease was useless. By classifying homosexuality as sinful, there is no need for Robertson to try to understand homosexuality or to be compassionate to homosexuals. For this "astute observer of American politics," sinners have no rights.

During the half-hour interview, Pat Robertson claimed, "We need a moral and spiritual revival in this country." Yup, that's what we need.

During the closing moments of the interview, Larry King mentioned the "20/20" program on exorcism and asked Pat what he thought of the concept of exorcism. (Anyone who has read any of Pat Robertson's books knew what his answer would be. Robertson has written, "The first thing to be said about suffering is that most of it comes about because of the activities of a powerful supernatural being called Satan, or the devil. He delights in hurting people." And, "Although lust, homosexuality, drunkenness, gluttony, and witchcraft are expressions of sinful flesh, these things can also be expressions of demonic activity in the lives of people." Ugh.)

Believe it or not, here is Pat Robertson's reply:

> Larry, I've been involved in a couple of instances of demons that came out of people. In one instance, there was a girl who was about fifteen, who heard voices telling her to kill her mother, and she was in our prayer room years ago at CBN and I prayed with her—and another minister—and she began to choke and gag and something came out. I saw her about a year or so later, and I said, "How are you and your mother?" and she said, "Oh I love my mother." But she wanted to kill and murder her mother before that happened. And I've seen other instances. So was this real? Yes. Is Satan real? Absolutely. And demon possesion is real. But there are a lot of fakes and a lot of charlatans and a lot of hocus pocus that is not correct. But the truth is there are demon-possessed people in this country and around the world.

Larry King responded with "Let me get in one more quick call for Pat Robertson—Newark, Ohio."

Kate, the world is going insane, and you can tune in and watch the craziness every night on CNN's "Larry King Live."

Imagine the Pat Robertson interview going this way: Larry King says, "Pat, I know you believe the Bible is true . . ." Pat Robertson interrupts with, "I do Larry, every word of it is true." Larry says, "OK, that's my point. Would you then favor the stoning to death of rebellious teenagers?"

There is an awkward pause. Robertson looks puzzled and says, "I don't follow your point, Larry."

King, knowing he is about to set a trap for the preacher, says:

Well Pat, God's way of handling the problem of juvenile delinquency is revealed in verses 18 through 21 of the twenty-first chapter of the Book of Deuteronomy, which clearly states: "If a man has a stubborn and rebellious son, . . . Then shall his father and his mother lay hold of him, and bring him out unto the elders of his city, and unto the gate of his place; Then they shall say unto the elders, 'This our son is stubborn and rebellious, he will not obey our voice; he is a glutton, and a drunkard.' And all the men of his city shall stone him with stones, that he die. So shalt thou put evil away from among you; and all Israel shall hear, and fear." Pat, it sounds to me like the Bible insists that stoning is the answer to the problem of juvenile delinquency, and if you believe every word of the Bible is true, doesn't that mean you must support God's order to stone a rebellious child?

Pat Robertson is clearly rattled by King's clear, logical, and devilish question and manages only to say, "Of course not."

Larry, like a cat after a mouse, wastes no time in moving in for the kill: "Obviously stoning a rebellious child is absurd, but at the same time how is it that Christians can dismiss some God-given commandments while insisting we all follow others?"

Robertson, for once, is left speechless. King, trying his best to hold back a smile, says, "We'll be back with your calls for Pat Robertson after this."

If only. Goodnight, Kate.

Thursday, April 11—7:22 A.M.

What a great day! It's great to be alive! I'm really excited about this offer to direct a film. And, as if that wasn't enough, I woke up to the news that Yankee pitcher Scott Sanderson had a no-hitter going into the ninth inning of yesterday's game with Detroit. The first batter in that last inning hit a fly ball to right, but the wind played tricks with it and the ball managed to elude Yankee outfielder Jesse Barfield and fell in for a hit. Too bad. Anyway the Yanks won the game 4-0, their first win of the season.

It's funny, but for the past few years I didn't like the fact that I liked to follow baseball. I mean, I knew that sports were trivial and had nothing to do with real life and reality. I didn't want to be lumped in with the legions of sports fanatics who live and breathe sports. But this morning I realized that there is nothing wrong with being a Yankee fan. Following a sports team is a harmless diversion, a source of cheap entertainment. A person can't spend all of his or her life thinking about serious things, or studying, or working. We need escapes, we need amusements and distractions from the toil of living. The key is moderation—partake without becoming addicted.

A ninth-inning Yankee rally capped off by a dramatic home run that defeats the Boston Red Sox and gives the New Yorkers a divisional title drives half the population of Boston into depression and mourning. Does this make any sense? Some would argue that without movies and sports life would be joyless. Eric Hoffer, the San Francisco longshoreman-philosopher wrote, "I have always wondered whether it is vital for a society that all its members should have some common subjects in which they are equally interested in and in which they all have some expertise. In Byzantium the common subjects were theology and chariot races. In this country they are machines and sports." If it weren't for baseball, I wouldn't be able to have a conversation with my brother-in-law. Love of baseball allows a Nobel Prize-winning biologist and an unemployed construction worker to sit next to each other in a stadium, where they are both simply known as fans.

I'm babbling. I guess what I'm trying to say is that I'm starting to feel happy about myself. I am accepting who and what I am. I don't have to be perfect to like myself. Immanuel Kant wrote, "Out of timber so crooked as that from which man is made nothing entirely straight can be built." The timber from which my life was constructed was pretty damn crooked. So what, the results are far from bad.

Religion came close to driving me crazy, came close to forcing me to end my life. I'll tell you the one and only true universal message of all the religions of mankind: integrity and honesty should live in the hearts of men and women. Dear Kate, integrity and honesty to self and others are the natural fruits of true love.

After years of contemplating the meaning of life, I haven't learned much—only this: My home is my own heart, and it is there that I must dwell. As for the world, I no longer have the need to set it straight, to change it or any of the people in it. The truth is that in changing myself, I'm doing my part in changing the world. The words of Mohandas K. Gandhi, India's "great soul" who fought a war without violence and freed his country from foreign rule without firing a shot, best expressed the way I feel: "Truth resides in every human heart, and one has to search for it there, and to be guided by the truth as one sees it. But no one has the right to coerce others to act according to his own view of the truth."

I am convinced that magical thinking needs to be exposed as a threat to sanity and that the ability to reason needs to be cultivated. In order to change, we need to question. The ability to question, however, has two enemies: the desire for consistency, and the holding of convictions. I believe that it is vital that the freedom to doubt must not only be guaranteed but also encouraged. Religious intolerance proves that it is easier to give people hell than your heart, and illustrates that hatred is an easy weapon to use, but it takes a strong person not to use it.

I believe that life is a mystery to be lived, not a religious puzzle to be solved. For me, there is only one sacrament: the present moment. The only thing I know for certain is that love knows no division. Love is the language of union; it is forgiving and it is for giving. Thanks to you Kate, I'm starting to love myself and I want to give more of myself to you.

Nine months ago today, I sat down to write you a letter. Not even the light of dawn could penetrate the darkness of my spirit that day. I was at the end of my life, or so I thought. Things are far different today. Now, not even the darkness of night can douse the brightness of my spirit. I am at the beginning of the rest of my life. Maybe it is time to end this letter, time to end the introspection. I've gone back in time, revisited the ports of my life. Soren Kierkegaard wrote, "Only robbers and gypsies say that one must never return where one has once been."

He was right. Maybe this letter—or, more precisely, series of letters—has helped me to reduce a chaos of experience to some sort of order. Through the writing, I've become a little more lovable in my own eyes. Today I can forgive myself, I can look in the mirror and smile. I'm OK. Sure, I've made a lot of mistakes and believed a lot of nonsense, which proves just one thing: I'm human. The past no longer has the power to enslave me. I am free and my future is mine to create. And the future is created now, in this very moment, in every moment. What will be is up to me, and the incalculable effects of random chaos. I'm starting to come to terms with the brutal indifference of nature, and the burning desire to have everything make sense has started to cool. I can admit: hey, it's crazy out there and I'm never going to figure it all out. This, I think, is a sign of recovering mental health. This letter helped me to discover the long road back to myself.

I see now that insanity is little more than getting stuck in one thought and not being able to shake yourself free. As this letter began, the "one thought" in which I was stuck claimed: Life stinks; I want to die. It became my mantra. "Life stinks; I want to die. Life stinks; I want to die. Life stinks; I want to die" reverberated daily throughout my being.

Writing to you, dear Kate, helped me enter into the darkness of despair within the prison of that one life-denying thought. I came out transformed by the experience. Life does not stink; I do not want to die.

I see more clearly that the past is really the present. That is, the past only exists in the present. Me and my past are here now. My past is not some separate moment; it only exists within me, here and now. I am keeping my past alive. Zen Buddhism suggests that there is only the present moment, that the past and the future are only concepts in the mind. Who knows? I'm certainly not capable of such esoteric and abstruse distinctions. But I suppose there is a germ of truth in the "now only" Zen viewpoint, because I realize that by going back into my past and retelling the story, I am creating fiction, because my past, as it was lived, is over, and what I say about it now is merely a product of my present state of mind. My past is not some isolated moment frozen in time; it is alive within me now and, like me, it has changed, having been eroded and altered by the sands of time.

There is only now. Today is all I have and within it my past lives and my future is born. Today is both mother and child.

I must, as Joe Barnsworth reminded me, seize the day. It is all I have.

During the Civil War, Abraham Lincoln wrote, "The dogmas of the quiet past are inadequate to the stormy present. We must think anew, and act anew."

That is my task: New thought, new action! My motto for today and forever is: *Carpe Diem.* From now on, I'm going to live, laugh, and love a helluva lot more.

The melancholy, long, withdrawing roar of retreating faith and collapsing confidence in God has finally subsided. I have come to the conclusion that to invest so much time in relating to the ancient past as it never was and to pretend not to be a modern man, to be carping about the present and yearning for a past that never happened is a fatal endeavor. The God debate "issue" itself is pathological. If you seek help in getting off the endless merry-go-round of circular God debates, you will find an army of professionals with institutional interest in having you continue to suffer from that pathology eager to help convince you to stay on for the ride. I've gotten off the ride before, but I always got back on. Not this time. I'm off and I'm staying off. Not only will I not get back on the ride of religion, I won't even think about it.

Besides, now I've got a job, a great job. I'm going to pour myself into this movie. In a couple of hours, I'll be zipping down the Hollywood Freeway on my way to a 10:30 A.M. meeting, during which I will sign the contract to direct a feature film.

After the meeting, I'm heading for Santa Barbara and a celebration dinner with a friend. I'm going to hang out there for a few days of rest and relaxation. I'll come back Sunday night, and Monday morning the job begins. Job, hell— on Monday morning, the fun begins.

So, this is it—the end of a letter that has taken nine months to write. Nine months—incredible. And the labor pains weren't that bad.

Anna Quindlen, a columnist for the *New York Times,* once wrote: "Sometimes it is time to examine your life. And sometimes it is time to just live it."

I understand. It is time for me to live my life.

Thank you, dear Kate, for a wonderful nine months.

Love,

Dad

P.S. Speaking of endings, a cease-fire formally ending the Persian Gulf War goes into effect later today when the United Nations Security Council President delivers a letter detailing the agreed-to conditions of the cease-fire to Iraq's Ambassador. So, the war is over, except for the Kurds, who continue to die in the mud of exile. Before a gathering of the American Society of Newspaper Editors, Vice President Dan "Only-a-heart-beat-away" Quayle said that the Gulf War was "a stirring victory for the forces of aggression against lawlessness." Of course, ArmagedDan meant to say it was a victory "against" aggression and lawlessness. Say good night, Dan.

PART THREE

He ascended into heaven . . .

April 12, 1991
Santa Barbara, California

Dear Kate,

You do not know me. Your father kept me a secret.

He died yesterday.

Of course, you know the circumstances—the lunacy of a car driven by a drunk driver somehow jumping the center divider on the Hollywood Freeway and plowing head on into your dad's car.

Why? Why? Why?

I don't know. It was his job to question. I just listened.

To him.

I knew about this letter. Your father intended to have me deliver it to you after your twenty-first birthday. I thought it was something I would never have to do. I had no idea that he continued writing to you so long after he decided not to kill himself.

I found the letter this afternoon. I read it. I can't begin to imagine anyone having such a remarkable document written expressly for them. You are lucky.

Of course, he did not anticipate his sudden death, but I know that he would want you to have this letter. I shall see that you do.

What can I possibly say? What could I possibly add to such a tortured yet magnificent letter?

Nothing.

Except some memories, some glimpses of your dad.

But perhaps I'd better tell you just a little about myself.

I'm a lesbian.

And a prostitute.

Your father was my best friend. Oh, damn, does that sound trite! Before your father entered my life, I saw myself as dirty. Do you know what I mean

431

by dirty? It has nothing to do with my "trade," except possibly for instigating it. No, by dirty, I mean that I saw myself as lower than some slimy slug slithering along the highway of life. I was worthless, a wretched sinner—unloving and unlovable. But your father saw only beauty. I'm not talking about looks. I'm talking about inner beauty. In his eyes I was good—worthwhile. Yes, even pure. He liked me—ME, not my body, not my wild imagination, not my ability to give pleasure—ME, my head, my heart, my soul—my totality.

He saw the best in everyone. Paradoxically, Chris was a fount of optimism to one and all, except himself.

Your dad had a wide range of friends. There were artists, actors, writers, professors, priests, and, yes, hookers, heretics, and bums. Even lawyers, though for the most part he thought better of child molesters.

But I think I had a special place in his heart. He mentioned me in this letter to you—I'm the friend who likes Thai and Indian food, and offbeat movies.

We had a five-year-long affair. Affair—what a cheap word, a word that can't possibly explain our relationship.

We never had sex. I mean we never had sexual intercourse. But we did have passion and lust beyond words, as we fulfilled each other's fantasies. In the darkest corners of our lives, we pleased each other. No one ever knew.

I was his refuge; he was mine. Mutual safe harbors in an unsafe world. We were free to be open and honest. We didn't try to make our little paradise last forever. We were happy to experience it every once in a while for just a few hours. No guilt, no strings. Just pleasing each other, for each other. Once in a while, your dad tried to make what we had more permanent. It was the romantic in him. He would have married me, but it would have killed what we had. Fantasy can't be legitimized, can't be ritualized, can't be made to last forever. He knew that. I knew that. But he would have tried.

He was a fool for love. In fact, he was a passionate believer in the supreme importance, the sheer necessity of love. He nonetheless proved himself incapable of permanent relationships.

I hope I'm not making you uncomfortable with this kind of talk. I loved your dad. I will always love your dad.

He had extraordinary passion and sensitivity. When he loved, he loved with intensity. The sight of a homeless person brought tears to his eyes. He hurt when others hurt. I remember once saying to him that he was free to do what he wanted. As usual, he had the annoying habit of turning a casual comment into a god-damned philosophical discourse.

"Freedom? What is freedom? No one is free. We are all in chains as long as any one of us lives in bondage. Fuck. I know of no one who doesn't live in a bondage of some kind or another. America—land of the free—what bullshit. We're all slaves to the American dream."

He spoke to me without deleting any expletives. A few managed to sneak their way into this letter, but throughout he managed to display amazing restraint. Perhaps he thought of you as a ten-year-old.

I don't think he would mind me telling you about us. If but for a second

I thought he would, then I wouldn't tell you.

Your dad was unconforming, without ever seeming erratic or arbitrary. He was endlessly curious, endlessly fascinated by the world, which, sadly I think, he discovered to be relentless in its hostility.

With me he was honest. With you, I know he would want me to be honest.

Your father was a priest—in his heart, in his soul, in his head. If only he had become one in reality, he may have known some peace.

But.

But, I can hear him now: "But at what price—total delusion, the surrender of my mind?"

Kate, he is dead. How long will I hear his voice? How long will I feel his love?

Forever, I hope.

There is much I want to tell you about your father. But now is not the time. Let me take a few days to absorb what has happened, then I'll write my farewell tribute to him, seal up this letter, and let it rest in peace until it's time for delivery to you.

Yours truly,

Zoe Spinner

*   *   *

April 22, 1991
Santa Barbara, California

Dear Kate,

It is over. He is in the ground. Ashes to ashes, dust to dust.

I'm ready to end this last letter. Not true. I'll never be ready to end this letter. What ending would be befitting. No, what I'm ready to do is simply stop the letter, bring it to some kind of forced conclusion.

If heaven is peace, your dad is in heaven.

But way too soon.

It seems an injury that he should leave in midst his broken task which none else can finish, a kind of indignity to so noble a soul that he should depart out of Nature before yet he has been really shown to his peers for what he is. But he, at least, is content.

I don't make it a habit to quote poems or literature, but those few lines come from a poem titled "Thoreau," by Ralph Waldo Emerson, written in tribute to his friend Henry David Thoreau shortly after his death, expresses exactly what I feel. I'd be more passionate than Emerson. Your dad's death was hardly an injury—it was a crime, a sin beyond equal. His task of trying to understand can hardly be finished by somebody else. His vision was unusual, his voice unique, his thirst unquenchable. For sure, he was a noble soul. I'd even say royal. I shudder to think what he could have accomplished. He was on fire to write. He had plans for at least two or three books. I'm not sure he is content in the ground where he was placed. Contentment is for the living. For the dead, there is nothing. We like to think our dead loved ones are content, are happy and peaceful. But I think we like to think that because it makes us feel good. Funeral rituals are for the living's benefit, not the dead's. The finality of death is hard to face. Who can look death in the face and smile? We can only tremble.

Jesus, I'm starting to sound like him—your dad, that is, not Christ.

I'd like to tell you some little things about your father that you might not know. Good things, sweet things.

He was charming, funny, and above all gracious. While his mind was attracted to the more serious aspects of life, there was a time when he nonetheless was ever ready to lapse into a softened mode, to be shamelessly frivolous. He wasn't a hugger by nature, yet he was capable of being very demonstrative, ready, on the slightest excuse, to be moved to tears. He was happy to be silent and could easily go days without saying a word; yet, he could also talk your ears off. He had an openness and sensitivity that seemed beyond measure, or at least way beyond the equal of anyone I have ever met. But beneath all this there was a stubbornness of will that resisted any external influence that might threaten his independence—including pets. He did not like to be told what to do or what to think. But above all, he cared. He cared about everyone he met; he cared about all who suffered and hurt.

Chris was a great talker and he never held back, no hedging around with small talk and cautious civilities, unpacking his mind immediately and laying before you all the contents of his thought that day. I never heard him talk about the weather; he opened a conversation with what was pressing, not with what was obvious. What was so refreshing about talking with Chris was that he seemed more interested in what I had to say, what I was thinking, rather than in simply telling me what was on his mind. God, he was almost annoying with his constant interjection of, "Well, what do you think?"

And he was funny, even when he wasn't in a good mood. I remember calling him once and catching him in a pretty depressed state. He went on and on about what was bothering him. I think he realized that I was getting upset—not at him, but by the fact that he seemed to be suffering—so it was time for him to throw in a joke.

"Zoe, things got so bad yesterday that I called Dial-a-Prayer." Actually thinking that he had, I said, "You did what?" He responded, "I called Dial-a-Prayer. I needed someone to talk to." There was a slight pause, then he delivered the punch line: "They told me to go to hell!"

We laughed. He could make a weeping willow tree smile. Two days later, I got a letter from him that was devoid of humor. In it, he wrote:

The personal fate of the individual is largely at the mercy of impersonal forces over which he has little control, or at the mercy of minor mistakes that prove to have incalculable major consequences. The innocent and guilty alike are struck down by these forces and errors, differing only in the way they react to the blows of fate and chance.

It is as if he knew that for him "the blows of fate and chance" would be fatal. The tone of that letter was darker than midnight. It was consumed with bleak introspection. He wrote:

Am I any different than those around me? Is the contrast between my expectations and my performance less than theirs? Is the gulf between my will and my compulsive nature any broader than theirs? Is the difference between the illusions of my pride and the realities of my self-ignorance any greater than theirs?

I wish he didn't need to explore the inner resonances and paradoxes of his life. Some days he questioned life, other days he celebrated it. He was troubled by the moral difference between living for yourself or for another. He lived with a constant tension between apartness and involvement. I never knew what to expect from Chris. He was capable of being very funny, and very serious. The one thing he was not capable of being was boring.

Your dad had a curiosity about anything foreign, anything different from what he experienced growing up in Queens. In a mischievous way, he played with the forbidden, flirted with the exotic. He once told me about some French writer (I'm not sure which one—he would read anything by Gide, Camus, or Sartre—but perhaps it was Gide, who was his favorite of the trio) who said that flirtation with the exotic or the forbidden was a way of moving from one kind of life to another, an effort to move beyond what has become a stagnant or meaningless existence. Chris thought the exotic and the unknown help a person define themselves not so much in terms of the familiar world of one's family or religion, but by discovering a new self within the experience of what is opposite to one's own nature and background. Maybe that is why he was attracted to me, and why he went to Mexico. Who knows?

It is fitting that I should include a testimony to Thoreau in this my little memorial to your father. You see, your dad had a special fondness for Henry David. A couple of years ago he made a pilgrimage to Concord, Massachusettes, the tiny New England town where Thoreau lived and wrote his most famous book, *Walden*. It seems like a lifetime ago that I received your father's famous "Thoreau" letter. Actually it was only seven years ago that Thoreau invaded your father's thoughts. Here is a little piece of the letter he wrote me in which he describes that invasion:

Thoreau. It's all Henry David's fault—the mess I'm in now, I mean. Zoe, I remember the day as if it were yesterday. The date was May 12, 1984. It was a Saturday afternoon. I had decided to put a new stereo cassette tape deck in my car. The problem was twofold: what kind do I get, and where do I go to have it installed? As you know, kiddo, I know virtually nothing about electronics and usually feel like an idiot when I'm forced to deal with salespeople when buying electronic equipment. I went into a big discount store in an effort to save a few bucks, but the salesman left me so baffled, I left out of frustration. While driving home I spotted a small car-stereo shop. (I mean the shop was small, they put stereos in big cars and small ones.) Out front were a number of high-priced cars. I turned in figuring I'd get no bullshit, just some straight advice and good equipement. Sure enough, the salesman was a gem, and before you know it, I'm sitting in a waiting area reading a magazine while they are installing about $700 worth of stereo equipment. When the job was done, I whipped out my Visa card, and minutes later zipped out of the lot. I hopped onto the freeway and popped into the tape deck my favorite Wynton Marsalis tape. Wow, the sound was fantastic. Then disaster. The fucking machine ATE THE GOD DAMN TAPE!

Like I said earlier, he didn't delete any expletives with me. Anyway, the letter goes on to explain how he made a U-turn and angrily sped back to the shop where he bought the stuff. He wrote:

I was so mad I came close to hyperventilating. I thought I would explode from anger. I spent all that time and energy trying to make sure I got good equipment. I opted to spend a few extra bucks to insure that I have no problems and the thing can't play one cut from a tape without turning into a fucking tapeworm. What should have been a simple chore turned into another anxiety horror show. Why do I bother?

Your dad could really get upset. Not with people. But with himself and silly little things beyond his control. His quick temper and impatience were his major faults. Anyway, the letter goes on and tells how the sales guy was all apologies, and they put in a new tape deck without giving your father any trouble. OK, back to the letter and the Thoreau part of it:

As I headed home for the second time, I started to calm down and managed to subdue my fear that the replacement deck would also eat my tapes. I managed to chill out to the point where I could tell myself a silly "tapeworm" joke. There was no explanation for the trouble. Just another of life's little mysteries. Anyway, I got home, parked the car, and was walking toward the apartment when I heard the words: "SIMPLIFY, SIMPLIFY."

Zoe, it was out of the "Twilight Zone." The words came from inside me and from far above me at the same time. They were clear. Crystal clear. Not loud, but firm, sure-footed. Nothing else, just those two words. I literally stopped in my tracks. I looked around. There was no one in sight. Of course, I knew there wouldn't be. These words weren't spoken by a human. I mean they sounded like they were, but somehow they were more majestic, more mystical than mere words issuing forth from the mouth of a flesh-and-blood human being. This is going to sound cuckoo, but it sounded like they were spoken by Mr. Big Himself—GOD, the Almighty Creator of Heaven and Earth. Obviously, I told no one. Can you imagine me calling up Steve or Zack and saying, "Hey, guess what? God just spoke to me." I mean, I knew it wasn't God talking to me. It was some kind of coded message from someplace, I don't know where—maybe my from subconsciousness or the astral plane. But what did it mean? What was the code?

The letter goes on to explain what the coded message from who-knows-where meant. A few days later, your dad was engaging in one of his favorite pastimes: browsing in a used bookstore. He came across a copy of *Walden*. He had never read it before. He was thumbing through it when the words he heard on May 12, 1984, jumped off the page.

He described that moment in the bookstore this way:

There they were, lit up like a fucking neon sign: SIMPLIFY, SIMPLIFY. I bought the book and quickly scurried home, tape deck blasting all the way. I got home, locked myself up in my study and devoured it. I had never read anything so remarkable in my life. I was ready to move to the wilderness, ready to find my own Walden Pond.

Your dad was nothing, if not impulsive. He was on his way to Walden Pond. Maybe not literally, but figuratively his search for Walden Pond began that very day. But he never found it. His task goes uncompleted. Sadly, he never really became at ease with being at odds with himself and the world around him. When he first mentioned to me his thoughts about suicide, he said, "I fear that I shall be forever unsatisfied and incomplete."

So Kate, it was Thoreau who sparked your dad's search for meaning. I can remember his excitement when he told me how he could "taste the way he wrote, the way he shaped his sentences. I could feel his life, the way it moved against the grain of the people of Concord but with the beat of nature. For the first time in my life, I want to read, and, as crazy as this sounds, I want to write." He started keeping a journal and taking long solitary walks in the woods. Before Thoreau, you dad was never much of a reader. Television was his life. He watched every movie released. But he never read. Claimed he didn't enjoy novels. Images facinated him, not words. But that all changed. Suddenly, he had a passion for books.

He learned about writing by reading. But the task was not easy for him. He was easily frustrated by his inability to spell even the simplest of words. He cursed every time he had to interrupt his train of thought to look up a word in the dictionary to see how it was spelled. I wish I had a buck for every time I heard: "How the fuck do they expect you to a find a word if you can't spell it?" Your dad worked hard at learning the rules of grammar. He must have had a dozen college English textbooks in his study. He tried his best, but he was a hopeless case. Fortunately, he had an old friend—I think his name was "Ace"—who once was an editor at a small publishing company, and he graciously read and corrected everything your dad submitted to a publisher—not that it helped.

(He claimed he could wallpaper his study with rejection letters.)

Spelling and the rules and regulations of writing were not Christopher Ryan's primary concern. For him, writing was exploration, a way of finding out exactly what he thought. His writing was the result of an impulse to analyze and an impulse to synthesize. He once told me, "The artist finds in himself the subject of his work. Art rests on introspection. I write, not to cure myself, but to find out about myself." I believe his long letter to you is his artistic look at himself and the crazy world he lived in.

Sadly for him, introspection meant fishing in some very troubled waters. I believe his relentless self-examination was in itself a disease, or even some kind of curse. He was like a sumo wrestler struggling with the heavy weight of his own conscious. He told me how he pursued me during our early days together, but not without great inner conflict. In one of his notoriously long letters to me, he put it this way:

> I was divided within myself. I both acted and also watched and judged. The two of us—the doer and the observer—moved forward together. While enjoying your company, I observed and analyzed the experience at the same time. I was simultaneously involved and detached. There was always this crazy Platonic dialogue going on inside me, with the interlocutors being two aspects of me— the pleasure seeker and the moralist. For a long time, I enjoyed and condemned our time together.

Oh, Kate, I don't know whether I'm helping you or not by telling you all this stuff. Maybe I'd better stop.

There is one thing your Dad and I used to talk about that I would like to share with you. It has to do with chance.

Any life can go in an infinite number of directions. But why does any particular life—yours, mine, your mailman's—go in the direction it went? As Chris once asked, "Why does anyone become a dentist?" For sure, genes and chance play vital roles in every life, but, according to your dad, each life is shaped by a relatively small number—three or four at the most—of people outside your immediate family who will have a profound impact upon your life. In other words, in your life, Kate, there will be three or four people who will have a life-changing effect on your life. They can be a teacher, a friend, a spouse, or just somebody you meet on the way to an airport.

Five years ago, just a few days before Christmas, my brother died. A brain tumor. It was sudden, totally unexpected. I was in shock. We were each other's family. I was three years older than him, and, for as long as I remember, I was his guardian angel. Even after he became a big-shot lawyer, he still called me "Ohee" (as a baby he pronounced my name as if it had no "Z" and it stuck) and called me once a week. After getting the news, I threw some stuff into a suitcase and headed for the airport to catch a flight to Newark, New Jersey.

Right around the corner from where I lived back then in Hollywood, there was a bus stop at a hotel where I could catch an express bus to LAX. As I stood waiting for the bus, a car driven by a women pulled up. A guy in the car leaned over, gave her a hug, got out, and stood on the line for the bus. Nothing unusual; I noticed it, without noticing it. Minutes later the bus arrived. I got on and sat in the last remaining unoccupied window seat. Seconds later, the man from the car sat down next to me. I was so distraught and consumed with thoughts about my brother, that I never even acknowledged his presence. He never said anything to me. The thirty- or forty-minute trip to the airport passed in silence; me buried in my thoughts, he in a book.

The bus driver announced our arrival at the United terminal, and we both stood up. I was struggling with my bags, and he said, "Can I help you with those?" "Thanks," I said without paying any attention to him. Once off the bus, he handed me my bags. I once again only said, "Thanks." He smiled, and in a quaint, gentlemanly fashion bowed his head. That was it, nothing else was said, though I had a fleeting thought or impression that he was sweet, gentle. We turned and walked toward the terminal. He headed directly for the gate. I had to pick my ticket up at the main counter.

Less than fifteen minutes later, I arrived at gate D7, just in time to hear an announcement that the plane was being refueled and the boarding process was going to begin in ten minutes. I took a sigh of relief, glad that everything seemed to be working out. I plopped myself down in an empty chair in the waiting area, which was crowded with happy holiday travelers. I was physically and emotionally drained. I was on automatic pilot, not sure of how I managed to get to the seat on which I was sitting. It was then that I caught a glimpse of him again. I thought to myself, "What a coincidence, that nice guy is going to Jersey also." But that was it, I immediately dismissed him from my mind. I don't think he even saw me.

I had seat 23A. He had seat 23B.

He was your dad.

We exchanged smiles. I'd learn later, he was forcing his too. He once again helped me with my luggage, stuffing them in the overhead compartment. During the first two hours of the five-and-a-half-hour flight, we never said a word to each other.

The cabin crew had just served dinner. But I couldn't eat. I just pushed whatever it was around the dish for a few minutes, and then put down my fork. At the most, I had maybe two or three bites. Christopher sensed something was wrong.

"Are you all right?"

"Yes."

"Are you sure?"

I shook my head yes. He didn't buy it.

"It's OK, you can tell me. What's wrong?"

"Really, there is nothing wrong."

For the first time, I looked directly into his eyes as I said those words. I saw compassion. I saw sincerity. Our eyes were locked in on each other's for just a few brief seconds, but it seemed so much longer. It seemed as if we told each other everything we had to say in just a look, in just a few seconds. I saw his concern. He saw my pain.

"My brother died."

He put his arm around me. He held me tightly. I cried. He never said a word. Nor did I.

Perhaps fifteen minutes or more went by. I felt comforted in his arms. I guess then it must have hit me: who is this guy, this total stranger whose harbor I have sailed into?

I took a deep breath and sat straight up. His arm slowly slipped back to his side. We looked at each other for a few seconds. Again no words. Then he broke the silence. "Do you want to talk about it?" I shook my head yes. "My name is Christopher." "I'm Zoe."

For the next three hours, we shared our life stories.

After we deplaned (gee, I can hear Chris now: "Why if we deplane, don't we deauto or debus when we get out of a car or off a bus? Does anyone ever detrain?") he drove me to my parents home in Wayne, New Jersey. Your dad had reserved a rental car. He was going to pick you up in Montclair and then drive you to his sister's house on Long Island. That was his first Christmas with you after he and your mom split up.

During that week, while he was celebrating Chris: nas with you, and I was mourning with my parents, we spoke on the phone nearly everyday. From strangers on a line at a bus stop to best of friends within hours. (Oh yeah, the lady in the car was his secretary.)

Kate, the story illustrates your dad's point. He could point to three people— a distant cousin who gave him his first job in television, a friend who introduced him to the world of Eastern mysticism, and an executive at NBC who taught him the art of soap operas and gave him his own show—who dramatically altered the course of his life. He felt that any life could be judged successful or good (though he hated vague, meaningless terms like those) if the three or four people who manage to have a strong impact on your life are people who have a positive effect on you. Is this making sense? Someone you meet could get you hooked on drugs or literature. As your Dad once said, "The direction of Peter Abelard's life, thinking, and writing all hinged on his introduction to Heloise."

My whole life changed because of your dad. Before him, all the important people in my life outside of my family ultimately hurt me, shoved my life into a direction it should never have taken. Christopher Ryan turned my life around.

Well, I guess I've about run out of things to say, yet I feel there is so much more to say. Your dad's search for understanding exposed him to ideas that left little room for a benevolent God. He slowly shed the Christian faith he found both lovely and terrible, and he never fully recovered from the loss. He would strongly object, but I'd say he died a Christian without a creed.

Like any artist, he aspired to freedom and novelty rather than to order and discipline. Death stole from us the creation within him that longed to be born, the creation of a new faith, a faith that could unite humanity. Death robbed us of his light. Days before his death, I was depressed. We talked about it, and he said, "The unexpected always happens. The very thing you're not prepared for occurs. Therein lies my hope."

Therein lies my despair. I never expected him to die. I'll never get over his death. "Sure you will," says he from beyond the grave. "Never," I shout back.

Perhaps the best way to end this is to tell you what I think your dad would say to you if he had the chance to come back to life in order to whisper one final thought into your ear. Ever the rebel, I know he would whisper two things: "I love you, Kate. Please, stay out of churches."

Love,

Zoe

EPILOGUE

Well, there you have it, the story of Christopher Ryan, my dad.

When the large envelope containing dad's long letter and Zoe's two short ones—which were neatly bound together between bright red, vinyl covers—arrived, I thought I was the victim of some kind of cruel hoax. Even though my mind was crammed with questions that couldn't be answered, I sat down and started to read it. I knew this was from my dad. It sounded like him. I mean I could almost hear his voice reading it to me. When I was little, he read to me every night. I had two or three favorite books that he read to me over and over again. But he always read them differently. I can't explain it, but he managed to just make them sound new and fresh each time. Sometimes he changed the plots to see whether I was paying attention or to just entertain me.

I knew this was from dad, but how? Why?

I read and read and read. I didn't stop to eat. I didn't answer the phone. I just read and read. It took me nearly two days to finish it. I was exhausted.

I told no one about it. I hid it, like some kind of private treasure, in my room. During the next two weeks, I reread the letters countless times. I still told no one. I was sad yet strangely happy to hear from my father. I was very curious about this "Zoe" person. Who was she? Why did my dad love her so much? Somehow, I was more haunted by her two short letters than by dad's nine-month-long opus. Dad and Zoe were still secretly bound together in my closet. Who was she? Who was she? I wished I could know why my dad was so attracted to a lesbian. I don't understand gay people. The thought of guys kissing guys, or girls kissing girls makes me gag. Still, I wanted to know about Zoe.

And there was the mystery of the money. A few days after dad's letter arrived, a plain, white envelope addressed to me came in the mail. Inside was a money order made out to me for $12,750. No note, no return address, no explanation. Just more money than I could imagine ever having. The postmark on the envelope was from Palm Springs, California. No real clue there, because the big envelope that dad's letter came in was postmarked Santa Barbara, California. I got out a map and saw the two cities are far apart. The address on the envelope the money order came in was typed, while the address on the other envelope was hand printed. I guessed it was dad's money, but somehow it all seemed too weird to be real.

About two weeks later, another letter arrived. It was from Zoe Spinner. It was a beautiful and tender letter in which she told me how she found life in a world without my dad impossible to take. Maybe hookers aren't as tough as they are portrayed in movies. Zoe explained how at forty-two her "career" was just about washed up, even though she was in great shape and didn't really look her age. (She claimed she could still fit in her First Communion dress, though she couldn't button it in the back, and it was extremely short.) Without any real means to earn a living, and without the emotional support of the only person who really cared about her, Zoe planned to end her life.

The decision to kill herself was not a difficult one for Zoe. She didn't agonize over it. After two lonely years, she merely woke up one morning, looked herself in the mirror, and, as she put it in her letter, "saw nothing." She had no life, no love, no meaning—no reason to live. It was that simple, that clear. But first she had just one job to do: Send me dad's letters. She thought I was too young to get them, but she had nobody she could count on to see that I got them in a few years, the way my dad would have liked. The important thing, she thought, was that I have them.

She was right.

On April 22, 1991, she bound the letters together, sealed them up in an envelope addressed to me, and tucked them away. She never looked at them again. Until that morning in early May of 1993, when she mailed the package to me.

The mysteries were starting to clear up. It was beginning to make sense.

Zoe's letter even explained the mystery of the money order. It was her life savings. After she mailed dad's letter, she had a flash of inspiration. She didn't need the money, and she thought I could use it for college. Or, as she wrote, to "just blow it on a car if you want." She was still trying to make my dad happy.

Funny, I can hear my dad's voice: "Please, this sounds worse than a plot from a dumb soap opera. I don't buy it for a second."

Zoe tells me in her letter how she was just about to end her life when the phone rang. (Dad's right, this does sound like a soap opera—cut to a close up of the ringing phone sitting next to the bottle of pills.) The caller identified himself as Dennis Gaffney, a name my dad had mentioned to Zoe many times. Turns out that dad mentioned Zoe and their "secret" affair to him. Gaffney, an atheist-turned-Buddhist, vegetarian wacko, knew about their hideaway in Santa Barbara and needed to talk to her about my dad's death, which he learned about long after the fact.

Dennis and my dad were best of friends—and worst of enemies. They met in 1950; my dad was only three years old. Their friendship lasted forty years, and took about forty seconds to destroy. Before I say anymore about them and the death of their friendship, I have to mention what Dennis said about my dad in a letter he wrote Zoe: "Chris was more at home in the empyrean—creation, thought, contemplation—than in the everyday world of ordinary living."

The word "empyrean" sent both Zoe and me scurrying off to our respective dictionaries. It means the highest heaven; for the ancients, it was the sphere of pure light; among the poets, the abode of God. I guess you could call it the celestial vault, a firmament in the sky. In other words, my dad had his head in the clouds; his home was imagination, reflection, and meditation. I don't know much about any of those things (I know boys, music, and malls). I wish he was here to tell me about them. I'm glad my dad was different. One of my friends' fathers is famous golf pro and a first-class jerk. From what I can see, most of my friends' fathers are carbon copies of each other; sure they have different tricks for making a buck, but that is their game. Not Christopher Ryan. His sport was truth; his quest, understanding. I'm not sure he found it; but he died trying.

Dennis told Zoe that his nickname for my dad was "Opher." It seems that one summer dad went "O-for-the-season"—in other words, he never got a hit in any of the neighborhood baseball games during an entire summer. No hits in a ball game is called an "O-for," which, according to Dennis, sounds just like the last five letters in dad's name. Who can understand men?

As I was saying, before I so rudely interrupted myself, dad and Dennis Gaffney were best of friends. Dennis was four years older than my dad. He moved into a house a few doors down the block from my dad's back in 1950. Dennis liked to remind my dad that Mrs. Ryan, my grandmother, asked him to keep his eye out for her son, to be his guardian angel. It was a job Gaffney took very seriously. Back then, my father was a very devout Catholic. Dennis, however, was an atheist, who enjoyed needling my father about how much more fun the bowling alley was on Sunday morning than church. Despite the differences in their religious outlooks and ages, they became close friends. They enjoyed talking about life and sports. Gaffney was a star athlete whose feats on the diamond were frequently noted in the local paper, and he wanted to play ball for the Yankees; my dad was a klutz and a perennial bench-warmer, who went to Yankee games.

After Dennis graduated from high school, he was drafted into the army and was shipped out to Korea after basic training. But while Dennis was in Fort Dix for his basic training, my dad managed to persuade his father to drive him to the base on a number of occasions to visit his friend, the soldier. My dad hated guns and the military even back then, but he loved Dennis, so he visited the army base as often as possible. After Dennis was shipped to Korea, they began exchanging letters, a habit that lasted nearly four decades.

After Dennis was discharged from the army, he returned to college, and, as my dad put it, "became an egghead." Dennis, the scholar, became a full-time student and earned his doctorate. He then became a college professor in Iowa. Even though they spent most of their adulthood living far apart, they continued to write to each other every week. Every year, one of them would spend a week of his vacation visiting the other, even though each grew into vastly different people. Dad was showbiz through and through, living for the moment when he said, "Roll tape"; Dennis, a professor who lived in his books. The one thing they shared was a crazy sense of humor, always trying to top each other's silly puns.

While Dennis was on the ship going to Korea, something happened. He had some kind of a religious experience during which he instantly realized that God existed. Oddly enough, around this time my father began doubting God's existence. Dennis became heavily involved in Eastern mysticism. He followed the teachings of the guru's of the day, became a vegetarian, and increasingly began withdrawing from the world. But the two friends still enjoyed spending endless hours talking about spirituality. Over time Dennis led my father into a New Age mixture of Buddhism and Hinduism. But my dad's new found faith didn't hold, and eventually he retreated into agnosticism. Still, the friendship remained strong.

Until a year before dad began his letter to me. In July 1989, Dennis visited my father in Los Angeles. Dad had been working on a book about spirituality, a book based on his experiences in the seminary. (The book was never finished.) Anyway, at the time, my dad was very excited about the project and asked Dennis to read it, and offer any comments he wanted to make.

Big mistake.

Dennis never mentioned his thoughts on the manuscript during the visit. My father assumed he hadn't read it and would read it back in Iowa. However, when my dad got back from driving Dennis to the airport, he found the manuscript he had given Dennis on his desk, along with a long letter. In the letter, Gaffney informed my dad that he had read the manuscript, but could offer neither a positive nor a negative comment because he found the "writing to be so far afield from my experience of life" that he was at a loss to comment on it. Instead, he left a copy of a poem written by a seventeenth-century Zen master. The poem was filled with the usual Zen double talk, basically saying life is an illusion, everything is a lie, and it's not worth tormenting yourself over this floating, unreal world of grief, anguish, and distress. The poem further suggested that the demons in our mind are self-created, and that good and bad alike should be rolled up into a ball and tossed out.

Dennis also spoke in the letter about an undercurrent of rot running below California, and worse, my dad's townhouse was once the scene of a long-suffering death, which he thought explained, in part, some of the dark imagery that had crept into my dad's mind and writing.

Needless to say, my dad was truly angered by the letter.

Later that night he called Dennis. He wanted to calmly discuss the letter, the way they had always been able to discuss tough issues. But dad lost his patience, and blurted out, "Jesus Christ, Dennis. I simply asked you to read my stuff, like I always have. But no, you couldn't even talk to me about it. Instead you cowardly left me some drivel about dry rot and a haunted house, and a dumb poem written centuries ago by some alleged master telling me life isn't real. Well, if it's not real then why the fuck does it so hurt much?"

Dennis hung up on him.

Four months later, Dennis was back in Los Angeles. He was attending a conference at UCLA, and didn't even inform my dad he was in town. As chance would have it, my dad was walking along Malibu Beach one Sunday afternoon. Suddenly, out of the blue, he sees Dennis walking toward him. The few minutes that it took to close the distance between them seemed like an eternity for my father. As they got almost face to face, neither of them said a word. Dad was waiting to see what Dennis would say. He said nothing. Without pausing, they looked each other in the eye and kept right on walking. Dad was really upset. He told Zoe that Gaffney passed him by as if he didn't even exist.

Zoe told me the episode was the centerpiece of their conversation for a long time. Dad just couldn't understand it. He figured Dennis had reached enlightenment and had become detached from everything in this world, even his best friend. Dad was furious that religion could destroy a friendship.

Oh—there is one more kicker to the story. The letter Gaffney left my father was written on July 11, 1989, exactly one year to the day before Christopher Ryan started his letter to me. The date had real significance for my dad. He and Dennis met on July 11, 1950. They always celebrated their "anniversary," so it was particularly painful for my father to have read Gaffney's letter on their thirty-ninth anniversary. It was the last anniversary they would ever celebrate. Zoe thought it was very significant that dad began his letter to me on that date, though it never once mentioned Dennis Gaffney by name, and only eluded to him once when he wrote about the value of family.

Anyway, when Dennis called Zoe, he was truly upset about my dad's death. Zoe told Dennis how upset Christopher was over the demise of their friendship. They both cried freely during the phone call. Zoe says the phone call saved her life. Dennis called her every day for nearly two weeks. Together, they helped each other through their grief. She read him many parts of the letter dad had written me, which made them both cry frequently.

Dennis told Zoe that just before his last visit with Chris, he had gotten involved with a woman who was even deeper into Eastern mysticism than he was. The two of them literally became hermits. They lived together, but refrained from sex, not because they thought it was dirty, but because they felt it was best to be completely detached from all earthly desires. They had closed the entire world out and tried to live a life of perfect harmony with the creative energy that ruled the universe. Dennis quit his teaching job. They lived on the woman's alimony. Their life amounted to reading, meditating, and fasting. They had no friends. Dennis was sick over losing his friendship with my dad, but felt pressured into following the woman into a life of total renunciation, which became so severe that they even reached the point of refraining from eating vegetables and existed on a diet of fruits and seeds. Dennis saw the light and left the woman after she began talking about becoming a breatharian, a person who exists on air only.

Christopher Ryan was right: religion can really get wacky.

It was after his breakup with the woman that Dennis tried to contact my father and found out he had been killed in an automobile accident. He was devastated.

Well, I guess that about ends the story. Or, as Woody Allen said at the end of *Love and Death,* "That's about it from me folks." Zoe gave me her phone number and said I could call collect if I wanted, but she would understand if I didn't. I did—call, that is. She sounds nice. She told me I could keep the money. Gaffney had inherited a ton of money from a recently departed aunt, and he was sending Zoe a healthy chunk of it. (It's true, dad. This isn't a soap opera!)

I'm not giving my twelve grand to anyone, but I think I'll use some of it next summer and visit Zoe in Santa Barbara.

THE END

P.S. I love you, dad. And don't worry—I'll stay far away from churches.
P.P.S. This book should end here, but it doesn't; there is one last letter.

EPISTOLA POSTSCRIPTA

Christmas Day, 1991
Ship Bottom,
Long Beach Island, New Jersey

Dear Reader,

It is a gray, overcast day. I am alone. The winter winds sharpen the cold. I've been sitting in absolute silence for most of the day. It's time to share a secret with you: none of what you have just read really happened—except for the things involving real people, like that tiresome troika of turkeys: George Bush, Saddam Hussein, and Cardinal O'Connor.

I invented Christopher Ryan.

Who am I? I'm Brian Davidson. I'm a writer.

I finished writing *Dear Kate* last April, just eight months ago.

Truth be told, there isn't a helluva lot of difference between Chris Ryan and myself. He's nicer. Or was. We both wanted to be priests; yet neither of us realized our childhood dream of serving God. We both worked in television, but I just had a low-level administrative job and never even walked onto a sound stage. We're both the same age and we are both divorced. Kate is a younger version of my daughter, Emily. I lost my job four years ago during a big cutback at the network, but unlike Christopher Ryan, I did not have residual checks to help make ends meet. I lost my house and car and was forced to file for bankruptcy. I live in my brother's spartan beach house on the Jersey Shore, where I endure crowds of teenagers in the summer and the sounds of silence in the winter.

Whenever I go to New York or Philadelphia and see the growing number of homeless people living on the streets I say to myself, "There but for the grace of my family go I." George Herbert Walker Bush, who only recently admitted we were in a recession, now says it is nearly over—bullshit! Our callous, misanthropic president is in a state of denial as to what is really happening in our rapidly deteriorating nation. The recession is far from over, and as a nation we have

453

yet to hit rock bottom. I hit rock bottom at Ship Bottom, New Jersey, far from Hollywood and Santa Barbara, and farther still from any hope for recovery.

Like Christopher, I also wanted to end my life. Three years ago, I was about an hour away from actually doing it, ending it, when I received a phone call from my sister. I never got to the point of putting the gun to my head. Somehow during the conversation my determination was deflected, even though I never mentioned my plans. My sister was having problems at home—normal stuff, an inattentive (and perhaps unfaithful) husband (an oceanographer specializing in beach erosion), and two hyperactive small children. Anyway, after a ninety-minute phone call, I began thinking about her life, our growing up together, and her reaction to my demise, and before long I went to bed instead of eternity. During the next few days, things happened—little things—that combined to push the idea of suicide to a back burner.

Around that time, I had been working on a novel tentatively titled, *At Odds with Myself.* The main character was struggling with a bad case of existential angst, trying to overcome the toxic effects of religion and searching for some meaning to life. The book was going nowhere. Actually, it was going around in circles. I was about to abandon the entire project, when, during a walk, the words "dear Kate" popped into my mind. "A letter! The book is a letter," I asserted to myself.

And so my journey with Christopher Ryan began. Along the way, we became friends. We even went to Mexico together—he observed while I recorded his thoughts and took down all the damn notes on modern Mexican society and ancient Aztec ruins.

Through Christopher Ryan, I traveled back to my past and saw how the past acquires its meaning only in relation to the present. Christopher Ryan's nature was formed by my past. I began to live for Christopher Ryan. In fact, I needed him in order to continue my own existence. The grief I felt about life, which caused me to want to end mine, was transferred to Christopher. I gave him life in order not to feel my own. I lived in him, and he became my reason for living. Christopher Ryan absorbed the pain of Brian Davidson and we became as one, each needing the other.

Eight months ago, Chris had found himself. Or at least accepted himself. He was happy. Or as happy as any sane person could be. Then he died, a victim of chance and the random chaos he came to see so clearly. Fiction yielded to reality and I was alone.

Eight months later, I am still lost. But alive. Barely. In his autobiography, *The Words,* Sartre wrote, "What I have just written is false. True. Neither true nor false, like everything one writes about the insane, that is, about men."

When I finished writing *Dear Kate,* I became apprehensive every time I got into a car, thinking that I might meet the same fate as Chris. I don't know whether life imitates art or art imitates life. A few months ago, there was a movie out in which a crazy guy enters a crowded nightclub and starts shooting the place up, killing a number of dancing patrons. Not long afterward, the scene was re-enacted by a truly crazy guy in a real nightclub. Of course, that is hardly proof that life imitates art, but that sort of thing does seem to happened with a degree of regularity. Anyway, who is to say the movie was really art? Besides, the answer to the question of which imitates which probably isn't a matter of either/or.

Luckily, I haven't been involved in any accidents yet. I miss Christopher Ryan. So much has happened around the world since he died. He would have had a field day with the last eight months of headlines. Imagine his reaction to the failed right-wing coup that held Gorbachev prisoner for a few days and eventually led to the end of Communism and the Soviet Union.

Imagine his reaction when the fragile Yugoslav federation was split asunder in June after the western-oriented republics of Croatia and Slovenia declared their independence, a move that angered Serbia, the largest republic in the federation. A bloody civil war first erupted in Slovenia, where the Serb-dominated federal army was attacked and withdrew. The war, spawned by a renewal of ethnic hatreds, soon spread to Croatia, site of age-old enmity between Serbs and Croats. More than 5,000 people, mostly civilians, have been killed, and about a third of Croatia has been sliced off by the federal army and Serbian irregular forces. An estimated 500,000 people have been left homeless. The beautiful, ancient seaside city of Dubrovnik has been virtually destroyed after months of artillery pounding. The once prosperous town of Vukovar on the Danube River in the rural heartland of Croatia is now an uninhabitable ruin, reduced to rubble. The town's Catholic Church has been severely damaged by the Serbs. The Serbs, who are Orthodox Christians, claimed the Croats, who are Roman Catholics, had stationed snipers in the church steeple. Both sides in this bloody, brutal civil war have accused each other of torturing captured soldiers and civilians.

Last week forty-three Croatian civilians, many of them women or elderly people from the village of Vocin, a small farm town eighty miles east of Zagreb, were massacred by Serbian forces. The killing began on Friday, December 13, and continued for at least twelve hours. Serb civilians from the mostly Serbian hill town led Serb soldiers to Croat houses. The victims appear to have been brutalized. Neighbor is pitted against neighbor. Houses were set on fire and people shot at point-blank range. Seventeen of the victims were over sixty years of age, and fifteen victims were women. One victim was killed by an axe. The Serbs claimed the Croats had massacred 120 Serbs in the region, but it was impossible to tell whether the violence in Vocin was an act of spite or of revenge. Where is the Virgin Mary from Medjugorje when you need her?

Imagine Christopher Ryan's reaction to the tidal wave of violence that swept across Haiti after President Jean-Bertrand Aristide, the popular leftist priest who won 67 percent of the vote in Haiti's first democratic election last year, was overthrown by a military coup on September 30 and forced into exile in Venezuela. What makes the situation in Haiti different from Kuwait? Haiti has no oil, so we can let that nation boil. Haiti might not have any oil, but it does have voodoo, which, oddly enough, has enjoyed a renaissance since the election of a Catholic priest as president. Perhaps it is not so odd; after all, voodoo, which was outlawed in 1934, is practiced by about 90 percernt of the Haitian people, 80 percent of whom are also Catholics. Voodoo and Catholicism even share some of the same saints. During Jean-Bertrand Aristide's inaugural ceremony last February, a voodoo priestess draped a ceremonial banner over the new president's shoulders, a gesture that gave legitimacy to the spiritual practice that features devil worship and sticking pins in dolls. Well, if Ronnie Reagan could practice voodoo economics then I guess Aristide could practice voodoo politics.

Imagine Christopher Ryan's reaction to the Congressional confirmation hearings of Judge Clarence Thomas during which we learned more about the Supreme Court nominee's attitude toward women than about his thoughts—if he even had any—on the Constitution. The networks covering the hearings issued a warning that parents might want to have their children leave the room, or else they might hear frank talk about pubic hair on a Coke can, porno movies, and "Long Dong Silver" as the senators probed Anita Hill's charge that Clarence Thomas sexually harassed her when she worked for him at the Office of Equal Opportunity. I can hear Chris now: "There are 756,000 lawyers in America, more than any other country in the world, and Bush claims the intellectual and legal lightweight Clarence Thomas is the best of 'em. The Supreme Court is becoming little more than the legal counsel to the executive branch."

Imagine his reaction to studies revealing that an estimated seventy thousand people have died from disease in Iraq since the end of the war. The one hundred million pounds of explosives dropped on Iraq reduced much of the country's infrastructure to rubble. The massive bombings crippled public health by destroying water purification systems, sewage treatment plants, and health care facilities. A Harvard University study suggested that by the end of next summer 170,000 children under the age of five will die.

Imagine Christopher Ryan's reaction to the British news story, which reported that American troops were shown porno movies before taking off on bombing missions, a fact government censors would not let the American press tell their readers and viewers.

Imagine his reaction to watching David Duke, a former Nazi, and Grand Wizard of the KKK, garner 38 percent of the vote in the Louisiana gubernatorial race (What are gubers? Why do they race?), and after the loss declare himself a candidate for the Republican party nomination for the presidency of the United States.

Imagine his reaction to the William Kennedy Smith rape trial in West Palm Beach, Florida, which a nation watched on CNN in order to see the alleged victim's undies, and the alleged rapist's uncle. Last March 29, in a letter from Mexico, Christopher Ryan wrote: "Good Friday is a good day to skip church, and I shall." And so did Willie Smith, whose Easter weekend with Uncle Teddy and the family turned out to be a weekend when holiness took a holiday.

On the night of the most somber day of the Catholic liturgical year, Willie and the boys went bar hopping. Willie ran into a thirty-year-old woman—a single parent living on a trust fund—who was out for an evening of fun with her girlfriends. She claimed Willie raped her by the swimming pool when she resisted his advances. Willie said she had led him on and went along for the easy sex. The accused rapist was cheered by crowds as he entered and left the courthouse even though his own testimony portrayed him as a thoughtless, insensitive, callous jerk if not a rapist. The trial never uncovered what really happened that Good Friday night. It only concluded that there were some reasonable doubt about Mr. Smith's guilt, so the jury had to let Willie walk.

Imagine Christopher Ryan's reaction to the news that baseball superstar Bobby Bonilla signed a five-year contract with the New York Mets for twenty-nine million dollars, and that basketball superstar Patrick Ewing signed a six-year contract with the New York Knicks for thirty-three million. Wow—these two athletes will make sixty-two million bucks between them during the next half dozen years. For that same money you could employ 1,550 school teachers for one year at a salary of $40,000 each. Or 310 teachers for five years.

Christopher Ryan would have been troubled by a society that regarded two athletes as being of equivalent value to 1,550 teachers. But these athletes are being paid a mere pittance compared to what actor Michael Douglas is going to earn for his next film. Douglas is being paid fifteen million bucks to star in *Basic Instinct,* a psycho-terror drama, which will be released this spring. The film has already stirred up a lot of controversy as homosexual activists tried to disrupt the filming because they claim it cast homosexuality in a bad light. (More than likely, the film will cast humanity in a bad light.) The film features a lesbian woman who is seducing the character portrayed by Douglas. The film opens with a nude woman killing a guy with an ice pick after they finished having sex. (You hardly see ice picks anymore, except in movies.) The film has plenty of nudity (Douglas reportedly bares his tush), graphic sexual encounters, extreme violence, obscenity, and numerous references to masturbation, voyeurism, bondage, and the use of cocaine as a sexual aid. Sounds like a big hit, which is why the producers can pay the writer $3,000,000 for the script and Michael Douglas $15,000,000 to star in it. Imagine getting paid fifteen mil to nibble on Sharon Stone's breasts! Nice work if you can get it—and a lot easier than hitting a Roger Clemens fast ball.

Imagine his reaction to the assortment of natural disasters that occurred during the past eight months, such as the volcano that erupted in June in Mount Unzen, Japan, covering the seaside town of Shimabara with ash, lava, and gas, killing forty-three people and leaving eight thousand others homeless.

Imagine his reaction to Bush's approval rating plummeting to below 50 percent as the economy continued to nose dive. Imagine his reaction to TV preacher Pat Robertson's banal book about world politics landing on the *New York Times* best-seller list for seven weeks. Imagine his reaction to TV preacher Jimmy Swaggart getting caught with yet another prostitute.

It's been a wild and crazy eight months since April. Even Elvis has been spotted in a few dozen locations across the country, but, mercifully, the Blessed Virgin Mary hasn't been seen lately, although a three-foot-tall fiberglass statue of Mary outside of a Catholic Church in Lake Ridge, Virginia, is making news. Parishioners claim the statue occasionally weeps because of the world's sin. The parish priest, who in 1978 was listed in the Guiness Book of World Records for riding a roller coaster for five straight days, claims that Christ-like wounds have appeared on his wrist and feet and they bleed from time to time. It seems the statue of Mary only cries when the priest is around, which might say more about the priest than the Virgin. Actually, the Virgin Mary has been seen lately— in a bedroom in New Mexico. A husband and wife from Las Cruces claim Mary's image has appeared on their bedroom blinds—and every day, hundreds of people line up to catch a glimpse of Mary on the blinds. Talk about blind faith.

I never intended to have Christopher Ryan interact with real life news events. When I began writing the book back in 1989, I had arbitrarily picked July 11, 1991, as the date of his first letter. I took so long to write the first week's worth of letters that I suddenly found myself in the actual week in which the letter was written. After Christopher Ryan discovered a new will to live, it seemed natural to chart his progress against what was turning out to be a tumultuous nine-month period for the world. Chris began reacting to the world in which he was now determined to live in. I began seeing the book as an effort to explore the consciousness of one man in relation to his time and place, and it became a tale of one man's simultaneous journey through his own imaginative world, and through the world of facts. As the book began to take shape, I began to realize that artists have a right to step up and interpret political events that shape our world, which is something many writers and most citizens feel is best left to journalists and professional pundits. I was confronted with the realization that my character's depression and weltschmerz were triggered not only by religious lies but also by political lies. Christopher Ryan had to confront, examine, and respond to the headlines that unsettled him, to discern the truth from the lies.

Christopher Ryan asked the questions I wanted to ask. Christopher Ryan went where I wanted to go. Christopher Ryan said the outrageous things about Bush and the pope that I wanted to say. But in the end, I still had doubts even though I erased those doubts from Ryan's mind. I'm still struggling to become an artist, still trying to write, still trying to sell my stories, even though I freed Ryan from those struggles by giving him the big job of his dreams. I'm still alive, even though I lifted that burden from Christopher Ryan.

Anyway, after three long, sometimes depressing, sometimes exhilarating years of working on *Dear Kate,* I finished it last April. I was proud of my creation, yet saddened by the reality that it would never be published because of its length and subject. The tone and purport of many of the letters indicate a dying howl of pessimism into a black sky in the presence of death, and an anger at religion, at America, and George Bush. *Dear Kate* simply doesn't fit in any publisher's box. The book is odd in a time when political correctness is in.

Once Christopher Ryan was gone, I stopped following the news as closely as I did when I was exploring how a thoughtful, sensitive person responds to the bleak headlines that greet us each morning. Besides, I was busy xeroxing the manuscript and sending it or query letters to publishers and literary agents. And then I waited for the rejection letters to pour in. And pour in they did. As of last week, I received forty-four rejection letters. Most were form responses. There was no need to read a letter that began with, "Dear Author." Or, I guess, a book that began with "Dear Kate."

I slowly realized that *Dear Kate* would never be published because the marketplace is dominated by books written by celebrities or well-known writers. There is no room for new voices. Discomforting and vexatious voices are quieted by the economics of publishing, which demand that books must have wide appeal in order to be successful. Pessimism doesn't sell; readers prefer fantasy to truth. Publishers expect fiction to lift readers to another world, not plumb the depths of this one. In *The Other Voice: Essays on Modern Poetry,* Octavio Paz, the brilliant and original essayist from Mexico, writes that literature and the arts are threatened by "a faceless, soulless and directionless economic process. The market is circular, impersonal, impartial, inflexible. Some will tell me that this is as it should be. Perhaps. But the market, blind and deaf, is not fond of literature or of risk, and it does not know how to choose. It knows all about prices but nothing about values."

There are days when I get very depressed at having spent so much time and energy writing something that will not be read. I must continually remind myself that I really had no choice, I simply did what I had to do. And the work produced a private harvest that was unexpected and beyond value. While writing *Dear Kate,* I slowly transformed myself. No, that's not what happened. Transformation is too dramatic a word. Besides, it is not quite accurate. I grew and I changed. I'm still me, only a bit wiser.

I look at things differently now. I now know that life is a continual struggle, an endless string of problems. Life is a living problem and to exist is to be a problem for oneself. But humans are problem-solving agents. The funny thing is that the better you get at solving problems, the bigger problems you get to solve. We have managed to trick ourselves into thinking that we can become prosperous and comfortable, that we can find security, happiness, contentment, and peace. This is a lie. We are all victims of our weaknesses, all prisoners of our humanity.

A visitor to a monastery once asked an old monk, "What do you do in here every day?" The monk answered, "We fall and get up, fall and get up."

Life is about falling and getting up.

For so long I allowed my lamentations over falling to weaken me to the point where I was no longer able to get up. I regretted so much about my life. I regretted falling into the trap of religion. I regretted falling into the trap of male machismo. I regretted not learning more about history. I regretted being so naive that I trusted politicians, believed journalists, and thought people were basically good. I regretted falling thoughtlessly into marriage. I regretted falling into a career I did not like. I regretted regretting so much of my life.

My mind had become closed to the possibility that I could escape my prison of depression, even though I had the keys. The helplessness I felt after losing my job grew into a sense that I was powerless to change my predicament. It became increasingly more difficult for me to be able to flow with the ambiguities and paradoxes of life. I had rendered the natural flexibility of my brain into an inflexible organ of torment.

I became afraid of the future, unable to see myself functioning in life. The past was a sad portrait, faded pictures of remorse and regret. But somehow,

I kept struggling to get up, determined to finish my book. I had to see what was going to happen to Christopher Ryan. In an odd way, my long look back at my life helped me see that none of my numerous falls were actually fatal, but they easily could have become so if I had chosen not to get up.

I guess I am hoping for the same kind of stroke of good luck that came Christopher's way when he got the unexpected call to direct a feature film. I guess I am looking for a typical "happily ever after" Hollywood ending to my story. I'm not going to get such a call; "happily ever after" endings mostly happen in reel life, not real life. The simple truth is, I have to get up all by myself. And I will.

Ship Bottom is about as far from "happily ever after" and Hollywood as you can get. This tiny oceanside town is virtually deserted for nine months of the year. Yet Hollywood's influence hangs over this island like a huge cloud. In that regard, Ship Bottom is like any other place on the planet because Hollywood's influence is felt all around the world. The movie myth makers from lalaland are today's kings and dictators. They have neither thrones nor armies, yet they can mold the desires and attitudes of multitudes. Hollywood can even sell America to the world, even though the product is somewhat damaged.

America is the largest debtor nation in the world. The recession has caused hundreds of thousands of middle-class Americans to lose their jobs. The number of homeless families living on the streets is on the rise. Our banks are failing. Our cities are dying. The sick can't afford basic health care. During the past ten years, our nation's capital has had a murder rate higher than that of Sri Lanka or Beirut. Not a pretty picture. America is in tough shape. Yet the world loves everything American. America is the final destination of most immigrants. Millions of tourists from around the world visit our nation every year. Many of them come to see Hollywood, the home of the pop culture that the world craves. The Japanese may excel in technology. The Germans may excel in the making of fine automobiles. The Swiss may excel in making fine watches. The French may excel in making fine wines. But America makes the best dreams, which makes Hollywood the capital of the world.

Hollywood movies transform the realities of daily life in America into a myth that in this land of perpetual innocence anything can happen, any dream can be realized, any individual can triumph over the system. Of course this is not quite true. Hollywood has made America a symbol of innocent dreams. The world has an insatiable appetite for Hollywood's "happily ever after" fare because everyone wants to believe we can be kings and queens, to be lords of our own destinies. We want to preserve our sense of innocence and wonderment, to nurture our hope that we can seize possibilities and opportunities to transform ourselves and our world. Sadly, the reality behind the symbol, behind the myth, is not so innocent. Still, the world looks to us as if we actually possess the qualities they hunger for: freedom and wealth. They do not see our talent for the embarrassing: mindless, issueless elections, insipid sitcoms, tasteless soap operas, greedy heads of banks and corporations, the Oscars, "A Current Affair," the tabloids, and the likes of Clarence Thomas, Jimmy Swaggart, Joan Rivers, Jesse Helms, Geraldo Rivera,

Shirley MacLaine, Madonna, Roseanne Barr, Pat Robertson, and Maury Povich.

Where have you gone, Christopher Ryan? A lonely man turns his eyes to you. I thought of you last week and smiled when I overheard a customer in a bookstore ask a clerk, "Can you please help me find the self-help books?" Such a question should not be surprising in a nation where slogans have replaced reflection and living has been reduced to striking a pose, whether conformist or eccentric.

I thought of you last May when Rajiv Gandhi was assassinated. Gandhi was waging a comeback campaign for prime minister. He was making an electioneering stop in the town of Sriperumbudur in the troubled southern state of Tamil Nadu. Ten thousand people turned out to welcome him. Gandhi stepped out of his touring car to greet his supporters. A small woman emerged from the crowd of well-wishers. She handed Rajiv a garland of flowers and bowed before the former prime minister. Strapped to her back was a bomb; she was on a suicide mission. As the woman bent over she manually detonated a sophisticated explosive device. There was a huge blast and a puff of smoke. The explosion ripped through Gandhi's torso and mutilated his face beyond recognition. He died instantly. And so did all hope that the virtually ungovernable country of India might soon know peace. The blast also killed fifteen other people, including a policewoman whose legs were severed and a photographer who was taking pictures for a newspaper. The assassin's head landed a dozen feet away from the slain Gandhi. The carnage defied description. The future of this land of Buddha and Mahatma Gandhi is in grave trouble.

I thought of you last June when Sikh militants attacked two trains in Punjab, India, and killed seventy-four passengers. Will the violence ever end?

I thought of you last summer when I read that the Girl Scouts of America now offer a "stress management" merit badge. The innocence of childhood is being shattered by stress, and we offer badges to those children who learn to cope with it.

I thought about you last fall when I read about the risks involved in silicone breast implant surgery. The feel-good-through-simple-surgery stories can easily turn into nightmares when the implants harden, migrate, rupture, or cause infections, bleeding, and a numbing of the nipples. During the past year alone, 150,000 women paid about five thousand bucks or so to have their bodies cut open and implants put into their chests in order to enhance their self-image. How sad it is that so many women are duped by society and surgeons into thinking there is something wrong with them, that a part of their body is inadequate. Looks can kill.

I thought of you last fall when the news broke about Pee Wee Herman, the children's television character created and portrayed by Paul Ruebens, being arrested by the Sarasota, Florida, vice squad and charged with indecent exposure. Pee Wee was in a triple X adult movie theater when he was busted. The cops spotted Pee Wee with his exposed penis in his left hand, and later arrested him in the lobby. There was no mention of whether or not the police suffered from any eye strain while catching poor Pee Wee; after all, the theater was dark and Pee Wee had his coat on his lap covering his wee wee. Pew Wee was subjected to public disgrace. His police mug shot was plastered on all the front pages of newspapers, and his TV show was yanked from the air.

Pee Wee Herman's arrest for masturbating in a porno theater was the kind of headline grabbing, sensational story that the video and print tabloids love. It had all the right ingredients: a big star, a taboo subject, and a "see how the mighty fall" theme. The story featured a famous person being denigrated for demonstrating normal human behavior that our puritanical society considers perverted.

Pee Wee's plight illustrates just how contradictory are the times in which we live: we applaud and reward pop star (and marketing whiz) Madonna for simulating masturbation on stage before thousands of impressionable young fans and then humiliate and condemn Pee Wee for doing the real thing in the privacy of a darkened, triple-X theater where such activity is an accepted fact of life and a safe alternative to the dangers of casual sex. Moreover, operating a porno theater in Sarasota is not against the law, and society knows that masturbation is going to take place in these legally operated theaters; yet we arrest people for doing what we know people will do in these places. The practice of allowing a theater to operate and then arresting a patron for behavior befitting the environment just doesn't make any sense. Worse, why all the anxiety over masturbation?

I thought of you a few months ago when I spotted this short, sad news item: The widow of Graham Greene, who died in April, is concerned that she's been cut out of his will in favor of the French mistress he lived with during his last years. So Vivien Greene, eighty-five, has put up for sale thirty-four first editions of the novelist's work plus two portraits. A rueful footnote for the author of *The End of the Affair*.

I thought about you in October when I read about Muslim extremists in Cairo who set fire to two Coptic Christian churches in the slum of Imbaba. A bitter sectarian conflict between Christians and Muslims has turned this poverty-stricken, crowded neighborhood of sprawling brick dwellings, narrow alleys, donkey carts, and fetid garbage heaps into a living hell. Shops and houses have been destroyed, and many people have been wounded. Government security forces ring the churches in an effort to keep peace. The trouble started last August on the eve of the Feast of the Virgin Mary. During the feast the Copts displayed portraits of Jesus and Mary and played sermons from cassette recorders (real "ghetto blasters") outside their shops. Some fundamentalist Muslims took exception to the display of piety and smashed the cassette recorders and defaced the portraits. The rampage of violence has continued for months. The impoverished world of Imbaba is being further brutalized by the violence of religious bigotry as human lives are destroyed over symbols of the sacred. Imagine, hatred for the love of God.

I thought of you last month when I saw the movie *Black Robe*. This intriguing and provocative film, directed by Australian Bruce Beresford, is about a seventeenth-century French Jesuit missionary priest who travels to the wilderness of Canada in order to save Indian souls. The movie follows Father Laforgue, his French translator, and a party of Algonquin guides as they make their way up river to the remote and hostile reaches of northern Quebec.

The priest sees the Indians as hedonistic heathen who need to be shown the way to heaven. But the natives fear his "water sorcery" of baptism as a threat to their way of life and faith in dreams, omens, and spirits. The priest can't understand the shamanistic world view of the Indian tribes, and the Indians can't understand the ascetic faith of the French Jesuits. The natives see the priest as odd and have no desire to go to a heaven where there is no smoking or sex. The Indians honestly cannot understand why the priest would make a promise not to have sex. The Indians have no grasp of atonement and sin, and they are far more interested in what happens in a dream than in the reality of the world around them. The young translator is attuned to the ways of the Indians and observes how their communal and caring ways are very Christian, and he abandons his faith, loses his cultural prejudices, and falls in love with an Algonquin woman. The priest remains a rigid soldier of Christ determined to win the Indian's souls. Along the way there is much suffering and blood-spilling, and the priest gets lost in the wilderness, but finds himself.

While Fr. Laforgue slowly gains respect for the Indian's beliefs and their ability to predict the future through dreams, he never loses his sense that the Jesuits "have been sent by our God, who is the God of us all." The journey culminates in the capture and torture of the priest and his party by the Iroquois, the ancient enemies of the Algonquin. The movie contains moments of breathtaking natural beauty, and fierce brutality as it depicts the consequences of a zealot's efforts to impose his idea of morality on unreceptive converts.

I thought of you on November 10, as I watched C-SPAN's live coverage of author Gore Vidal's address before the National Press Club in Washington. Mr. Vidal pointed out that "as the Soviet Union collapses and our economy crashes, the only question Americans are asking themselves is, 'Can William Kennedy Smith shoot straight half-cocked?' " Funny line. Sadly, it is true. The author suggested that the Smith trial and the Clarence Thomas hearings were a sort of calculated diversion from what really matters. He said, "Since the military budget cannot be discussed in any detail ever, the opinion makers and their dispensers prefer to go on about sex, abortion, prayer, the flag—matters of no public urgency or relevancy. But they are emotionally hot issues and irresistible to any government that has a great deal to hide, such as the one that we are currently saddled with."

I thought of you last month when I read that Vice President Dan Quayle and Senator Jesse Helms attended a meeting in Virginia Beach with televangelist Pat Robertson. The trio met in Robertson's new hotel and conference center to discuss how to best mobilize an army of evangelicals to work for the re-election of George Bush. Jewish, Moslem, and Buddhist leaders in Virginia Beach protested the meeting because Pat Robertson's hotel only hires Christians, a practice they consider to be blatantly discriminatory.

I thought of you last week when a network news magazine broadcast an exposé on three flourishing televangelists. Hidden cameras exposed the fraudulent tricks employed during healing services. The show revealed that only a small fraction of money raised by one minister for orphans in Haiti ever reached the impoverished island. Another minister raised over a million dollars to build a spirit-filled church in Auschwitz, yet the Polish pastors building the church received less than fifty grand. Viewers caught glimpses of where the money really went: palatial estates and luxury cars. Praise God for religious loopholes in the tax codes. But most shocking of all the scenes in the show was that of a dumpster in back of a bank in Tulsa, Oklahoma. It seems one TV preacher, using computer mailing lists, sends gifts of holy water from the Jordan River, miracle anointing oil, and miracle prayer cloths made in Taiwan to potential donors, who are asked to send in their prayer requests along with a donation. The letter promises the minister will pray for answers to their prayers. Well, the checks get deposited in the bank account and the prayer requests get deposited in the bank's dumpster. The real miracle is that people send money to these electronic snake oil salesmen.

I thought about you earlier this month when I read about the civil war in Somalia in which a mad frenzy of violence has reduced the seaside capitol city of Mogadishu to ruin. Somalia is in a virtual state of anarchy. Rival tribal factions kill and maim men, women, and children indiscriminately since the ouster of Mohammed Siad Barre, the country's president—or rather dictator, in January. It is estimated that over four thousand people have been killed in a war the world chooses to ignore. Doctors in the ransacked city can no longer handle the mounting casualties. On December 14, a Belgian Red Cross worker died after being shot in the stomach on a Mogadishu street while trying to organize the distribution of food to the city's starving residents. Relief workers are being forced to leave this once sleepy city of sun-drenched, white-washed buildings and tropical foliage that now seems bent on self-genocide. During the cold war, Somalia was wooed with aid and sophisticated military hardware by Moscow and Washington because of its strategic value. But that has all changed with the collapse of Soviet communism, and now Somalia is left to fight its civil war over who is the rightful ruler of the nation with little outside interest. It's no longer in our best interest to be interested in the suffering of these poor people.

I thought of you earlier this month when I read about the release of a documentary film titled *Half the Kingdom*. The film, which was produced in Canada, examines feminism and Judaism. The two seem mutually exclusive. The Orthodox Jewish faith does not permit women to read from or carry the Torah. Yet women uphold these ancient traditions that discriminate against them. The Jewish faith is patriarchal. Orthodox Jewish men might worship women as mothers and wives, but they scarcely acknowledge them as human beings. In fact, during their morning prayers, Jewish men thank God they weren't born female. How odd that a deeply humanistic religion like Judaism historically denies women their humanity. Odder still is why modern Jewish women struggle to transform such an oppressive monolithic faith as Judaism.

I thought of you on December 7 when I spotted a photo of an anguished woman kneeling on the ground over the body of her dead husband, who was killed in Uttar Pradesh, India, during an overnight shooting rampage that resulted in fifty-one deaths.

I thought of you on December 8 when I spotted a photo in the *New York Times* of a five-year-old boy lying in the hot sun outside the Madina Hospital grounds in Mogadishu, Somalia. This beautiful child was wincing in pain. The stump of his amputated right leg was wrapped in a blood-soaked bandage. His leg was blown off when the child was hit by an artillery shell. Another photo showed a thirteen-year-old boy lying on the sand outside of the same hospital. The boy had a deep wound in his head. He could not survive the gunshot wound, so he was given a painkiller and left to die in the sand. Just two of the over 13,000 casualties from the ruined city of Mogadishu. None of the articles I've read packed the emotion of these two photos.

I thought of you on December 13 when I spotted a photo in the *New York Times* of a young teenage boy walking down the street in Zakho, a Kurdish city of 125,000 in northern Iraq. The boy was carrying a rifle that was almost as big as he was. He had a worried, tired look on his face. Life in the city has been reduced to a violence-filled search for food and shelter. The Iraqi government has imposed an economic embargo on the Kurdish towns of northern Iraq and has blocked the delivery of food and fuel. We may have forgotten the war, but for this teenager and all the rest of the Kurdish people the war is far from over.

I thought of you this week when I saw a report on a Romanian orphan who was last seen on a news story in October of 1990 that revealed the shocking story of the deplorable conditions existing in Romanian orphanages. The boy was five and living in a filthy crib. He had a clubfoot and was abandoned by his natural parents and was about to be shipped out to an institute for unsalvagable children. His life was doomed. During the news story, a visiting American doctor made a plea for the boy's life, insisting someone should be willing to adopt a child with a handicap. A man in Toronto was watching the show and heard the doctor's appeal. He instantly decided to do something. Come hell or high water, he was going to Romania to get that child. With his wife's blessing, he did. The couple gave the child a new life; the doctors gave the child a near-normal foot. Four months after the child's arrival in Toronto, he entered a hospital for a complicated, twelve-hour operation that corrected his deformity.

The boy came from an environment where there was very little if any love and now he is full of love. According to the boy's adoptive father, this once-doomed child, now "gulps life down" and "he loves everybody."

Out of an estimated 100,000 orphans in Romania, about 10,000 lucky children have been adopted. I remember watching that report on ABC when it aired last October. I was horrified by the conditions and overwhelmed by sadness. I wanted to do something. I didn't. Fortunately for the little boy with the club foot, a guy watching in Toronto did more than think about doing something. He acted. Watching the boy's story this week, it was clear to me his new father was the real winner. He did something. He made a difference. This story had a real "happily ever after" ending.

I thought of you this week when I read that the homicide rate in many larger cities in the United States (based on the number of homicides per 100,000 residents) has increased in 1991. Our nation's capital leads the way, as its projected homicide rate for 1991 is expected to hit 83.6, which is up from last year's record rate of 77. In St. Louis, about 61 of every 100,000 residents have been killed this year. Detroit's homicide rate is expected to increase to 59.4. Houston's homicide rate is expected to increase to 42.2. And so it goes. At least twenty-three big cities, including Miami, Dallas, Baltimore, Chicago, Cleveland, San Diego, Pittsburgh, San Francisco, and Phoenix will set new records for murder rates. Even medium-size cities, such as Albuquerque, Anchorage, Colorado Springs, Youngstown, Virginia Beach, and Greensboro are setting homicide records. Nationwide, it is estimated that the total number of murders in 1991 will reach 23,700— up 300 from 1990. We are facing a murder plague as violent death is becoming a way of life in our cities. But no doubt the easy availability of guns is not part of the problem!

I thought of you a few days ago when I read a story about sixty young, clean-cut Mormon missionaries assigned to Philadelphia to scour the streets seeking souls for their Savior. The Mormon marauders no longer go door-to-door selling their Messiah. Modern technology has helped increase their odds of success, and cut down the chances of having doors slammed in their faces. The Mormon Church runs ads on TV, offering a free Book of Mormon, which feature a toll-free 800 number. A few weeks after a viewer calls, two young men in black trench coats show up at the door with a free book. It seems many people call the number simply because the book is free, and usually they are impressed by sincerity and demeanor of the missionaries who personally deliver the book. One woman in the story said the pair of young men returned to her home about twenty times, teaching her lessons from the Bible and the Book of Mormon.

The freshly scrubbed, neatly dressed missionaries work the poorest sections of the city. Because Philadelphia has a large community of Vietnamese immigrants, some of the missionaries studied the Vietnamese language during a nine-week course at the Missionary Training Center on the Brigham Young University campus in Provo, Utah. After the training on the mean streets of Philadelphia, the missionaries can ask, "Anh biet gi ve Chua Su Ky To?" "What do you know about Jesus Christ?"

I know he was a jobless itinerate, which is about the only thing these missionary descendants of Joseph Smith and Brigham Young have in common with Jesus.

I thought of you this week as I read that the Mexican government is about to end more than seventy years of hostility toward the Roman Catholic Church. Legislators have nearly completed making drastic constitutional changes that will give legal recognition to religious institutions and allow parochial education for the first time since the Mexican Revolution. Under President Carlos Solinas de Gortari's guidance, church and state are headed for a reconciliation. Under the reforms, the Church ownership of private property will be permitted, but only for future acquisitions. Religious treasures and colonial churches and convents, like those in Oaxaca, will remain under state control as part of the national patrimony. Priests will be allowed to vote and wear their clerical robes in the streets, but they will continue to be barred from running for political office.

I thought of you this week when eleven Soviet republics formally joined together to form a Commonwealth of Independent States. In one bold stroke, the leaders of the republics swept aside seven decades of central dictatorship and buried the Soviet Union. Detracting from the spectacular nature of this historic event was real worry about who would control the nuclear warheads and whether the independent republics could reverse the slide toward economic chaos that threatens the future of each state. Without government price controls, prices for essential goods are expected to skyrocket, making life even more difficult. The future of the Commonwealth is very uncertain at best.

I thought of you yesterday when I read that the "crying icon" of peace from St. Irene's Greek Orthodox Church in Queens, New York, was stolen. Three armed men and a woman forced two priests and four worshippers to lie on the floor as they pried the twenty-by-thirty-inch wooden painting from its glass display case. The icon, painted in Greece in 1919, depicted St. Irene Chrysovalantou, an eighth-century Byzantine noblewoman from Kappadokia who refused to marry a king and instead became a nun. Police said the icon was worth $200,000, but a church official said the jewels adorning the frame were worth $800,000. During the Gulf War, thousands of people made a pilgrimage to the Queens neighborhood of Astoria to see the icon shed tears and to pray for peace. Yesterday, many people wept as they kissed the spot where the weeping icon had been displayed. A 101-year-old Greek Orthodox nun kissed a picture of the icon and said, "St. Nicholas is going to bring St. Irene back." Perhaps—but I bet the bandits will keep the jewels.

I thought of you today when I heard the news that Sikh separatists, armed with AK-47 assault rifles, halted another train in the Punjab region of India and opened fire on the Hindu passengers, killing an estimated fifty-five people. The killers separated the Hindus from the Sikhs and shot them at close range. Some of the victims ran for cover in the mustard and wheat fields, but they were chased and shot. The Sikhs are a 500-year-old sect founded as a compromise between Hinduism and Islam. The Sikhs' secessionist warfare with India has given birth to a vicious cycle of killing, kidnaping, extortion, and police corruption in Punjab. Daily death tolls routinely hit double figures. It is estimated that 5,700 people have been killed this year in the Sikhs' brutal struggle to win an independent homeland, which paradoxically is called Khalistan, or "Land of the Pure."

I should point out that this squabble between the Hindus and Sikhs has nothing to do with struggles between the Hindus and Moslems over the mosque that sits on a hill in Ayodhya. Tensions and passion are still running high over this hill. The sixteenth-century mosque is surrounded by barbed wire and sandbagged bunkers. Muslims are barred from the mosque, which now contains an assortment of idols and pictures of the Hindu god Ram. This city of saffron-robed holy men and shops crammed with devotional items is still on the verge of an explosion of violence as aggressive Hindu nationalism is dedicated to re-placing the mosque with a new temple dedicated to Ram. Religious chauvinism in India is threatening the existence of India's secular-based democracy.

I thought of you today as I watched news reports of the floodwaters in Texas that left hundreds of families homeless on Christmas Day. A week's worth of torrential rain left fifteen Texans dead and two missing as the Colorado River crested at forty-eight feet—thirty-five feet higher than normal. One infant was swept away by a raging creek.

I thought of you today as I watched live coverage of Mikhail Gorbachev's speech in which he formally resigned as president of a Soviet Union that no longer exists. Gorby, whom *Time* magazine dubbed "Man of the Decade," gave his people freedom but could not give them sausage, and so it was time for him to step down and into the pages of history where he will live forever as the bold leader who ended the cold war and introduced *glasnost* and *perestroika*. When Gorbachev was named Communist Party General Secretary in 1985, he was young and ready to make dramatic changes. He threw out the corrupt old guard and brought in a team of decent, honest men. Hundreds of dissidents were set free. The arts bloomed. Religious faith was tolerated. Intellectuals were allowed to criticize the Party leaders. Nuclear arsenals were sharply reduced. Citizens voted for the first time in multi-party elections. Within a few years, Gorbachev transformed what Ronnie Reagan called "the evil empire" into something far less threatening. But despite all of his accomplishments, Gorbachev couldn't prevent the economy from sinking, and as the economy deteriorated Gorbachev's critics multiplied, and his days in office were numbered and hastened by the failed coup attempt in August.

How ironic that Gorbachev leaves office unloved by the people he freed because he moved too slowly on economic reforms, and because of a series of halfhearted measures that worsened shortages of food, fuel, housing, and consumer goods. The day before his resignation speech, a woman died of a heart attack while waiting in a long line to buy milk in the Ural Mountain city of Chelyabinsk. After the speech, Gorbachev signed a document giving up power and turned over the launch codes to the country's 27,000 weapons to the military chief of the new Commonwealth of Independent States. Minutes later, the red hammer-and-sickle flag of communism was lowered from the Kremlin's flagpole for the last time.

As Gorbachev faded from power, problems continued to mount in Georgia, which is the only one of the twelve former Soviet republics that did not join the new Commonwealth. Four days of intense street fighting in the southern Republic's capital city of Tbilisi have killed at least thirty-four people. President Zviad Gamsakhurdia is holed up inside the parliament building as opposition forces lob heavy artillery at it. Opposition forces accuse Gamsakhurdia of stifling democracy by acting in dictatorial fashion. People are dying and buildings are burning throughout the city.

Joy to the world, let the earth receive her King.

Right.

The interesting thing about having my fictional creation interact with real life current events is that I had the opportunity to closely track headline-making events that normally whiz by faster than a speeding bullet and are forgotten in less time than it takes to brew a cup of tea. A few days ago, as I read about Desert Storm in my manuscript, I was struck with the feeling that that monumental massing of military might that gripped the world's attention for weeks, now, just months later, seems like some inconsequential, distant memory. Saddam Hussein has been replaced by sexual harassment as a primary topic of cocktail-hour chatter, and SCUDs now take a back seat to condoms in board room and barroom banter. We live in a land of benign forgetfulness, where no one inquires too closely about anything complicated, such as life.

By closely following the news from around the world, I began to see patterns in the swirl of current events. For instance, last Lent, Christopher Ryan ruminated on how God could have allowed so many pilgrims in Mexico and Saudi Arabia to be killed while honoring him. Or her. Well, it seems the more things change, the more they stay the same. Last week, on Sunday, December 15, in a case of what Yogi Berra would have called "deja vu all over again," a ferry carrying 649 people sank in the Red Sea after it was struck by ten-foot waves (whipped up by forty-mile-per-hour winds) and thrown against a reef. The ferry sank around midnight about six miles off the coast of Safaga, which is 293 miles southeast of Cairo. Only 178 survivors were pulled from the sea. The other 471 people drowned. Many of the passengers, an estimated 300 people, were religious pilgrims from Egypt who were returning from the port city of Jiddah, Saudi Arabia, after visiting Muslim holy places where they were performing umrah, a ritual visit to the holy city of Mecca outside of the regular pilgrimage season. I guess God wasn't up for any more miracles at the Red Sea.

But the Catholic Church is still looking for miraculous solutions to our problems. Recently, a senior member of the Jesuit order, Reverend Giuseppe Pitau, asked the pope to name St. Aloysius Gonzaga, a Jesuit who died of typhus at the age of twenty-three after working among the plague victims when an epidemic hit Rome back in 1591, as the patron saint of people with AIDS. What we need is a cure for AIDS, not a patron saint for the disease's doomed victims. Back in 1987, the archbishop of Genoa, Giuseppe Siri, said that AIDS was a punishment from God. The Catholic Church wants it both ways: they want to give pastoral care to those suffering from AIDS and also teach that homosexuality is morally unacceptable. How crazy! To me, creating saints for the dying to pray to for a cure is morally unacceptable.

Speaking of potential saints, Christopher Ryan would be surprised to see that Pierre Toussaint is still in the news and is the subject of an intense debate among Catholics who disagree about his fitness for sainthood. Cardinal O'Connor insists the Haitian slave was a model of faith, but many African-American Catholics see Toussaint as an example of passive servility. Symbols of piety do not inspire many black Catholics, whose pressing social concerns are better addressed by the spirit of activism embodied by the lives of Martin Luther King, Jr., and Malcolm X.

Many African-Americans view Toussaint as a namby-pamby black slave who was content not to upset the social order of his time and place. As a plantation slave in Haiti, Toussaint chose to live a quiet life as a house servant rather than join the slave revolt that eventually led to Haitian independence. Rather than fight for his freedom, Toussaint, the docile slave, followed his master to America, where he waited patiently for his liberation, which he was granted just before his owner died. Toussaint is no hero in Haiti, although one Haitian claimed his stomach cancer vanished after he and his priest prayed to Toussaint. Many African-American Catholics consider Pierre Toussaint to be an Uncle Tom and a poor role model for modern black Catholics. Still, Cardinal O'Connor continues his search for Toussaint miracles and urges all Catholics to pray for his canonization.

But Christopher wouldn't have been surprised if he had read last week, as I did, that a company in New York will soon be marketing a shampoo named after Toussaint. I'm not making this up. The product is called "St. Toussaint's Miracle Shampoo." Some saints get cities named after them, but poor Pierre will have to settle for shampoo.

After so many centuries of perpetuating so many ludicrous beliefs, the real miracle is that any form of religion still survives. Actually, it is not a miracle. The survival of religion is a testimony to humanity's weakness, insecurity, and ability to engage in wishful thinking.

Enough about the silly side of religion.

Recently, I've become interested in the mystical side of religion. It all began innocently enough when a friend asked if I would like to join him for a visit to a monastery in Vermont during the Thanksgiving weekend. I initially declined his offer saying that a four-day visit to a monastery seemed inappropriate for someone who had strong doubts concerning the existence of a supreme being. My friend assuaged my concerns by saying there would be "no praying, just plenty of rest and time for reflection." Even though I wasn't in the market for rest or reflection, I agreed to tag along, figuring that any religious lunacy I might encounter could be easily mitigated by an overindulgence of Ben & Jerry's Ice Cream. Besides, the Green Mountain State is about as close to heaven on earth as there is.

I went for the scenery. I got a surprise.

To my surprise, I found myself highly susceptible to the lure of monastic mysticism. The simplicity and dedication of the monks impressed me.

While all of the Benedictine monks seemed friendly and accessible, I liked one monk in particular. His name was Brother James. He was in his early seventies. He was lean yet robust. He had wild, bushy gray hair, like an elderly Albert Einstein. As a young man, he served in the navy near the end of World War II and saw a considerable amount of combat action in the Pacific. After the war, he went to college while working the midnight shift three nights a week in his grandfather's bakery in Brooklyn. After graduating from college with honors, he went to work on the now defunct *Journal American* newspaper. He worked on the city desk, covering everything from grisly crimes to deadly fires. By the time he hit thirty, he was one tough cookie, hardened by combat in the Pacific and the streets of New York City.

The first thirty years of this gentle monk's life gave no indication that he would spend his next forty years seeking God in solitude. Shortly after his thirtieth birthday he heard the call. At first he doubted God was leading him into monastic life. During one of our long conversations, Brother James said, "Given my religious antipathy and alienation, a monastic vocation seemed absurd. I had come to distrust the conventional apparatus of piety and grace. I had abandoned religion, along with its comforts, terrors, and absurdities, but its morality lived within me without any emollient of faith. Of course, that was before Vatican II, when the Church was triumphalist in nature and was ruled by rules and obedience. Back then there was too much emphasis on sin and not enough on forgiveness. In my twenties I saw Catholicism as a religion of the head, not of the heart. Slowly, God became an encumbrance and I became a skeptic. Yet when I hit thirty I became hounded by the thought that my life had no meaning."

Monastic life is built on routine. It is a life of rigors, routines, and rituals. The day, which begins in the dark at 3:00 A.M. with vigils, is divided into periods of prayer, work, and reflection. The monks come together for communal prayer four times a day: at vigils, in the middle of the night; lauds, at sunrise; vespers, at sunset; and, compline, at the end of the day, at 8:00 P.M. Guests are expected to join the monks for those prayer services. I skipped vigils. Three in the morning hardly seemed like a good time for prayer, even for monks.

The guest quarters had a small library stuffed with inspirational books, with titles such as: *The Kingdom Within, Faith Under Fire, A Tree Full of Angels, When the Heart Waits, The Coming of the Cosmic Christ, Christ Among Us, Meeting Jesus, Living With Contradiction, The Way of a Pilgrim, The Way of the Heart,* and *Lord Teach Us to Pray.* Many of the books had a Zen flavor, instructing the reader how to become empty or to cope with distractions. The goal of monastic life is to let go of everything, so that you can be filled with God, and thereby experience true happiness. For the monk, prayer becomes a way of life and everything becomes a prayer, including work. Thomas Merton put it best: "Prayer is pure and perfect, according to the authority of St. Anthony, when the contemplative no longer realizes that he is praying or indeed that he exists at all."

As I glanced over a wall of titles, I recalled a line from the writings of the German novelist Thomas Mann: "The ease with which some people let the word God fall from their lips—or even more extraordinarily from their pens—is always a great astonishment to me. A certain modesty, even embarrassment, in the things of religion is clearly more fitting to me and my kind than any posture of bold self-confidence."

But Brother James was different. He didn't exude a bold confidence in his belief in God. His faith was quiet and gentle. In fact, he seemed more interested in horticulture than in spirituality. I first met him while I was taking a walk around the grounds. He sensed my uneasiness and said, "Don't feel you have to talk about God or religious stuff. I'd rather talk about my plans for my garden next spring." Brother James loved flowers, and the monastery gardens were his personal responsibility. The harsh New England winters depressed him. Somehow during our stroll, the subject of Original Sin popped up. In a fit of frankness, I said, "I think Original Sin is a concept invented by the leaders of the Church to keep the faithful under their thumb. Worse, it justifies suffering in the name of guilt by claiming that our salvation depends upon our acceptance of guilt for the death of the innocent Christ." His response surprised me, "Perhaps you are right. As for me, I found it easy to view the concept of Original Sin as an awareness of my natural weakness and propensity to make mistakes. It is not so much about sin or black spots on souls, but about humanity's deepest desires, desires that may be harmful."

On another occasion our conversation drifted into the area of miracles, and I said how there is no proof that miracles have ever happened. Brother James responded, "If there was proof, it would no longer be miraculous. Miracles are simply God's way of letting us know He is in charge." Such a dodge would have normally irritated me, yet coming from this sensitive monk, I was left wondering if he was right. Maybe my being at the monastery was a miracle. Or a mistake.

During one afternoon I spent about an hour sitting alone in the silent empty church. Like the lives of the monks, their church was simple and unadorned. It was a place where they could converse with God, without any distractions. I recalled something Brother James said, something that really made sense: "We are taught to be consumers, yet the accumulation of possessions does not make us happy." As I sat staring at nothing in particular, I wondered whether it was possible for people to live a full and rich life while denying the Almighty and eternity? My experience has led me to the belief that God is an illusion, yet I lack the confidence to trust the truthfulness of my own experience. Why? I wondered as I sat in the silence and heard nothing. As I got up to leave, a smile crossed my face as I thought of a funny line from the lips of Brother James, "Jesus and Mary weren't Christians."

Early in the morning of my last day at the monastery, Brother James and I took one final walk together. It was Sunday, and the anticipation of the Sunday liturgy filled him with glee. We spoke of faith. As we stood quietly looking at barren field at the end of the path we were on, the old monk said, "Faith is not found nor is it a gift. It is forged little by little, in the womb of the spirit, where it grows tangential to reason, shielded from the sunlight of science, and unconcerned with acceptance or applause, until it gives birth into the blinding light of mystical certainty."

The words made sense to me.

Could they be true?

Clearly, Brother James thought so. He believed deeply. When he took his vow of poverty it was not simply a promise not to own things, but a pledge to stop wanting things. During his life as a monk, Brother James freed himself from the pull of possessions and had opened himself to God. This openness is his freedom, and is a consequence of his poverty. Without distractions, in quiet and solitude, he hears the voice of God.

Or what he believes to be the voice of God. An awful lot of people seem to hear the voice of God. Last week I read about a guy who operates a jackhammer for a water company in California who believed God told him to build a life-size statue of Jesus out of toothpicks. And he did. Took him five years and more than 65,000 toothpicks.

As I was leaving the monastery, Brother James gave me a big hug and handed me a book. It was a copy of *Waiting for God,* by Simone Weil. Inside were five twenty-dollar bills and a short note, which read:

Brian,

I enjoyed our talks. I'm glad we had the chance to meet. This weekend is on us. Your check had already been deposited, so here is a cash refund. You need the money more than we do. About this book. I'm not pushing God by giving it to you. Simone Weil was an interesting woman and I simply thought you might enjoy reading about the way her mind struggled with the same issues that interest you. She appealed to writers as diverse as André Gide and T. S. Eliot—I suppose because she could believe something and still write eloquently in defense of what was contradictory to her belief. Camus said she had a "madness for truth." Simone Weil could extract the truth from atheism and any revealed religion. Like her, you truly want truth, and even though you consider yourself an atheist, I believe you are closer to God than most Christians who sit snugly in the their haven of unearned certainty. I've never given this book to anyone else before. I think it was waiting for you. I hope you visit us again, and in the meantime please feel free to write, I'd love to hear how you are doing.

Pax,

Brother James

I haven't written Brother James, but I have read the book he gave me. Simone Weil was a frail, bookish teacher from France who excelled in literature and philosophy. She was born in Paris on February 3, 1909. She was Jewish, but she rejected her Jewish faith and was strongly attracted to Catholicism, although she never joined the Church. Simone Weil was more than a scholar; she was also an activist who spoke out against injustice and sided with the oppressed. To show her solidarity with the workers, she even took a job in a Renault factory. Weil, who loved reading the *Bhagavad Gita,* believed that suffering was a way of achieving unity with God. While Simone Weil once conceived of herself as a Christian outside of Christendom, a more accurate assessment of her spiritual leanings shows that she was equally open to the mystical aspects of Hinduism, Buddhism, and Taoism; but it seems she best expressed herself in the language of Christianity. Some consider her death at thirty-four to have been an act of suicide by starvation. During this intellectual woman's short life she managed to attract a long list of admirers (including Pope Paul VI, Malcolm Muggeridge, and T. S. Eliot) and an equally long list of detractors (including Graham Greene, George Steiner, and Charles de Gaulle) and both camps were quite vociferous in their praise or attacks.

Here are a few brief quotes from the book, which consists of six letters Simone Weil wrote to a priest concerning Catholicism, and ten essays:

A case of contradictories, both of them true. There is a God. There is no God. Where is the problem? I am quite sure that there is a God in the sense that I am sure my love is no illusion. I am quite sure there is no God, in the sense that I am sure there is nothing which resembles what I can conceive when I say that word.

I have the germ of all possible crimes, or nearly all, within me.

Generosity and compassion are inseparable, and both have their model in God, that is to say, in creation and in the Passion.

The supernatural virtue of justice consists of behaving exactly as though there were equality when one is the stronger in an unequal relationship.

The children of God should not have any other country here below but the universe itself, with the totality of all the reasoning creatures it ever has contained, contains, or ever will contain. That is the native city to which we owe our love.

I never wondered whether Jesus was or was not the Incarnation of God; but in fact I was incapable of thinking of him without thinking of him as God.

It is not my business to think about myself. My business is to think about God. It is for God to think about me.

Joy and suffering are two equally precious gifts both of which must be savored to the full, each one in its purity, without trying to mix them. Through joy, the beauty of the world penetrates our soul. Through suffering it penetrates our body. We could no more become friends of God through joy alone than one becomes a ship's captain by studying books on navigation.

He who treats as equals those who are far below him in strength really makes them a gift of the quality of human beings, of which fate had deprived them. As far as it is possible for a creature, he reproduces the original generosity of the Creator with regard to them. This is the most Christian of virtues. It is also the virtue that the Egyptian *Book of the Dead* describes in words as sublime even as those of the Gospel. "I have never caused anyone to weep. I have never spoken with a haughty voice. I have never made anyone afraid. I have never been deaf to the words justice or truth."

Over the infinity of space and time, the infinitely more infinite love of God comes to possess us. He comes at his own time. We have the power to consent to receive him or refuse. If we remain deaf, he comes back again and again like a beggar, but also, like a beggar, one day he stops coming. If we consent, God puts a little seed in us and he goes away again. From that moment God has no more to do; neither have we, except to wait.

Some of her spiritual or inspirational writing is very interesting and intriguing. But much of her thinking is irrational and far from brilliant. For instance, she wrote:

Anyone who believes that God has created in order to be loved, that God cannot create anything that is God, that God cannot be loved by anything that is not God, is faced with a contradiction. That contradiction contains necessity within it. Yet, every contradiction is resolved through the process of becoming. God has created a finite being that says "I" and cannot love God. Through the action of grace the "I" gradually disappears, and God loves himself through the creature which empties itself and becomes nothing. [Then] God goes on creating other creatures and helps them to decreate themselves.

Wow! Besides presenting us with a misanthropic God, Simone Weil has also picked up her pen in defense of Augustine's "just war" doctrine.

Simone Weil's spirituality was shaped by the time and place in which she lived. Most of her life was spent avoiding the Nazi menace. She was a Jewish woman living in a predominately Catholic society during World War II. If she were alive and living today in Ship Bottom, New Jersey, I doubt her thoughts would be consumed by sin, retribution, and penance. (Perhaps they would be preoccupied with the falseness and hypocrisy of contemporary society.) Prayer, processions, pilgrimages, and retreats were the fashion in France at the time, and Simone wore them all gracefully, while denying the authoritarian and dogmatic trends within the Church.

I can see why Brother James liked the book. He saw in it a number of things he could use to reinforce his own beliefs. The rest he ignored or discarded.

I don't think my receiving this book from Brother James qualifies as a miracle, as his letter suggested, but I'm not sure it was a mistake either. The book was interesting, but it certainly contained no ultimate answer. There is none. Looking for God is not the right course for me, however, the notion behind the title *Waiting for God* has some appeal to me. Although Christopher Ryan might be quick to point out that waiting for God amounts to ignoring God. If he could speak, he might say, "Be real Brian. And be honest, too. You know what you need to do: just forget God."

That's the funny part—the fact that I can't forget God makes me think that He might just be real, and waiting for me.

Why can't I forget God?

Is he a permanent part of my memory?

Memory can be very destructive. Most of us must forget we are mortal just so we can go to work. In ancient times, the Greeks saw forgetfulness as a gift of the gods. Christopher Ryan couldn't forget the Inquisition. The trick I guess is in how we use memory. For instance, humanity can't afford to forget the Holocaust; yet it can't afford to constantly recall it either. Maybe the same goes for God, too.

Circles. After three years I'm still going around in circles. Circles of doubt. Circles of confusion. I'm still trying to draw a circle around God. Wait a second: here comes a revelation: You can't draw a circle around something that is not there; nor can you draw a circle around something that is bigger than any circle could ever be.

This God stuff is really crazy. I suppose the only real regret I have in life is that my parents weren't freethinking rationalists who would have spared me the torment of having been infected with this dreadful virus called God. Simone Weil used all her energy and talent to wrestle with God and the fight killed her while she was still in her prime.

I've given some thought to what Brother James said about miracles: "If there was proof, it would no longer be miraculous." That is the catch-22 feature of miracles as well as faith. The essence of faith is a belief in the absence of evidence. The person of faith believes in some higher unseen power, which he or she cannot observe and cannot logically prove. That's the beauty of faith. If God was susceptible to proof, the very proof would be the death of religion because a God open to human logic, to scientific study, to rational understanding would have to be definable, finite, and obedient to scientific law and thus incapable of miracles. God is not a God of Reason. God is a God of faith. No wonder Simone Weil starved herself to death: she was a woman of reason pretending to be a woman of faith, and her hunger for the absolute literally withered her away. Simone Weil was not concerned about the enlightenment of humanity; she was only concerned with pursuing her own slavation. She wrote, "God created us free and intelligent so that we can give up our will and our intelligence." And she did. Simone Weil offered up her reason and her life on the sacrificial altar of her God—and for that Brother James admired her and I pity her.

From talk of God to talk of Giants. The football Giants that is. The Super Bowl Champion New York Giants have just completed a far-from-super season. Actually, their season was a nightmare. They won only eight games, while losing eight others. They lost to the Rams, the Bears, and the Bengals by a combined total of eleven points. One or two key plays in each of those three loses would have made all the difference in the world. A devastating 19-14 loss to the Eagles on December 8 knocked them out of the hunt for a playoff berth. Last year, the Giants found ways to win the close games, usually during the last minute. This year they found ways to lose games in the last minute. The playoffs begin next weekend. The Giants will be watching on TV. There will be no playoffs this season. No miracle finishes. But the good news is that this year's Super Bowl will not be interrupted by SCUD attacks. And maybe Scott Norwood will get a chance to redeem himself and the Buffalo Bills will win it all this year. But I'll put my money on the Washington Redskins.

From football to the follies of politics, I've just read that George W. Bush, that good ol' boy, is headed for Beeville, Texas, after Christmas to spend a few days hunting quail with Alan K. Simpson, the sanctimonious senator from Wyoming. Our commander-in-chief will drink beer, don a camouflage hat, and shoot defenseless birds on a friend's 10,000-acre ranch. America's favorite urban cowboy will also attend a Chamber of Commerce barbecue to show he hasn't lost his common touch and is sensitive to the worries of average Americans. Maybe the prez will even ride a mechanical bull and sing country & western songs at some saloon. Maybe next Christmas Mr. Bush will be getting ready to move out of the White House. But I'll put my money on his re-election, with George and his Quayle running mate winning a close contest.

As usual, the Christmas season has brought a sleighful of showings of the movie *It's a Wonderful Life* on TV. Few people realize this Capra classic was actually a box office flop when it opened on December 20, 1946, at the Globe Theatre in New York. A film about a man who tried to commit suicide was the wrong picture for the wrong year. In 1946, America was the world's hero for its role in World War II. The film, with its dark side, was just too grim to attract big audiences. Soldiers coming home from the war didn't want to hear that life in America was now ugly, confused, and hopelessly dull. George Bailey, played by Jimmy Stewart, during one of the most despairing moments of his life, says, "I wish I'd never been born." George loses all his money, screams at his wife and kids on Christmas Eve, gets drunk at a local bar, cries, and prays, "If you're up there, show me the way." Fortunately, an angel with "the IQ of a rabbit" floats down from heaven to rescue George from his hell of despair.

It's not that simple for most of us.

I guess Christmas is as good a day as any to ask whether it's a wonderful life. My answer? Despite all the horrors of life, I guess it is a wonderful thing after all. That is, if you don't look too closely.

Most people can take just so much reality, and it's not very much. Most people think they are rational, but most are not. Each of us deceives ourselves in our own unique way by falling prey to misconceptions so subtle that we don't even realize how dumb they are. For instance, by writing, I can tell the truth, avoid the truth, or tame the truth. Mostly writing helps me coax the truth up from the cellar of my memory. The truth is often painful. I've suffered a lot during the past three years. The suffering felt like failure, but it was actually a means of growth. E. M. Cioran had it right when he wrote: "To suffer is to generate knowledge." I understand more about the world and nature now, and I've been able to free myself from a lot of things I thought I had to hold onto at all costs. I'm able to admit now that I frequently have been wrong and also to admit I have many weaknesses; in doing so, I've felt the liberation of a pardon.

And so life goes on.

By this time next week some 35 million Christmas tree corpses will be lining the curbs of America waiting to be hauled away with the trash.

And so it goes.

As 1992 approaches, this much is clear to me: all of the progress humanity has made in the fields of science and technology has not made us humans any happier or even more contented. Every improvement in our living conditions soon becomes old hat. Even humanitarian and intellectual progress has not changed our lot. Terrible suffering still strikes countless thousands of us each day and constantly threatens each one of us. Talk of a new world order is laughable. Every plan for a new, morally perfect social order is absurd because we still have the primitive instinct to hate each other to death because of differences of opinion. We need only look at Yugoslavia, Georgia, Somalia, Beirut, China, Turkey, Israel, El Salvador, South Africa, Ireland, Mexico, and even the United States of America to see that understanding and moderation are only distant ideals. We dress up our hopes in religious solemnity, yet we live a life of moral sophistry. There is little cause for optimism. Yet we must remain hopeful, we must continue to search for truth and a way for all of life to live in harmony.

We need to celebrate humanity and to stop stressing divinity. But I'm not sure we can overcome the transcendental temptation. At least I'm not sure I can.

Nietzsche said, "A religious person thinks only of himself," and Thomas Mann believed the masses of people will never find the slightest reason to be good without a belief in God, without religion. Those sentiments are the twin causes of our problems. We humans want to possess the truth, yet it is only in searching for truth that we can expand our abilities to be more human, more thoughtful, more loving.

As we approach the end of this century, many people have rejected the security of religion and also have lost hope of finding the meaning of life through science. For them, both the outer world and the inner world have become impoverished. They are fearful of revealing the core of their thought, which has become nihilistic, destructive, and fundamentally negative. As soon as they see some cause for hope, intellectual evidence confounds it. The weakness of the human condition made Pascal gamble on God. The challenge for us today is to gamble on humanity even though we lack sufficient evidence for placing such a wager.

A few years ago, I looked at life and asked, "Is that all there is?"

I didn't realize that the question would bring me to a crossroads in my life.

To answer the question required a leap into the unknown, which was something that both excited and unnerved me. My old world, a world of certainty and order, had dissolved and I was left standing in a cloud of ambiguity. Suddenly all my answers had turned into questions.

But I wanted answers. I wanted the impossible—certainty beyond belief.

I turned to Socrates for help. No luck. I turned to Descartes. No luck. I turned to Spinoza. Ditto. Kant couldn't help either. Hegel. Hardly. I turned to Leibniz. Zilch. I looked to Locke. Zippo. I turned to Pascal and came up empty with him too.

And so it went, until I finally found myself at God's funeral. But denial soon set in. God couldn't be dead, could He?

My efforts to unravel my anxieties over the existence of God left me exhausted and confused. My mind had become like a set of wind chimes turning in a breeze. I grew weary of the irrational pretending to be rational. During the past few months I've come to realize that in denying ambiguity I was forcing myself to choose between either nihilism or dogmatism. As usual, for me it was all or nothing. For so long I thought the confusion that surrounded me would eventually fade away. But it never does. Every time I think I spot the truth, the truth moves, leaving in its wake more confusion and uncertainty. Maybe the trick is to realize that all is vanity and to enjoy it anyway.

On this Christmas, I've given myself a present: I'm going to accept the uncertainty of life and simply trust myself.

I invented Christopher Ryan. Now I must invent myself. For the past three years I've played with fiction and reality, which is something each one of us does every day. Maybe there is no difference between the two. On this day when Santa Claus and Jesus share the stage, I sit in the theater of my mind watching a different play.

Tomorrow?

Who knows?